Act of Rebellion

Celia Boyd has written *First Fashionings, Social Conditioning in Georgian Children's Fiction* and *Young Ravens*, a novel for children set in the Midlands during the Second World War. She has contributed to *The Cambridge Guide to Children's Books in English*, and has had two articles published in *Signal, Approaches to Children's Books*.

As Celia Mason, working for the West Midlands Probation Services, she wrote *Are You Here for the Beer?* an in-cell, self-help guide for prison inmates, whose criminality stemmed from alcohol abuse. For this she received the Butler Trust Award. She currently writes full time, and is working on the fourth part of A Reason from the Stars series, entitled *Our Uncivil War*.

Author's Note

Writing as one who, since O. Level Biology, has regularly confused the Eustachian and Falopian tubes, Tom Fletcher and I needed physiological guidance from time to time. Doctor Terry Watson has been unstinting in his helpful advice throughout the series, and we have had many interesting discussions on Seventeenth Century Medical Practice.

A chance conversation before the fire in the bar of the Swan at Hay three years ago, encouraged me to press ahead with my writing, knowing that Graficas would support my endeavours. Without Tom and Jane Allwright, there would be no living tangible Tom Fletcher, sturdily trying to make sense of the appalling circumstances of the Civil War. Without their faith in him, he would have been destined to roam through eternity amongst the shades of insubstantial, half -realised characters of fiction.

As ever I am indebted to Margaret Banthorpe and David Crane for their patient reading of the script. Thank you both for your kind encouragement and particularly for insisting that you looked forward to each instalment.

Celia Boyd

Act of Rebellion

The third book in the series "A Reason from the Stars"

Graficas Books

First published in 2009,
by Graficas Books, Cwmbach, Glasbury-on-Wye

Set in Classical Garamond by
Graficas Books

Printed in Great Britain by
Gower Press, Ceredigion

ISBN 978 0 9554834 2 4

Act of Rebellion

September 1642-April 1643

The series, A Reason from the Stars, commissioned by Charles the Second, covers the reluctant involvement of Tom Fletcher, a young doctor of Worcester in the action of the English Civil Wars. The first memoir, First Dry Rattle, culminates in the Battle of Edgehill in October 1642. Tom is befriended after the battle by Lucius Cary, second Viscount Falkland, the King's Secretary of State.

At the beginning of the second book in the series, A Daring Resolution, he returns home to Worcester only to find his assistance is sought by old friends of his parents, who ask him to seek out their only daughter, from whom they have heard nothing since her marriage to a printer of newsbooks. They believe she is living in Lichfield. Tom sets out on this quest with Phoebe, his assistant and Elijah, his apprentice. The action moves from Lichfield to Staffordshire, and thence to Warwickshire and Birmingham, before finally returning to Lichfield, where Tom is present when Prince Rupert destroys the defences of the Cathedral Close, occupied by Parliamentary forces, by means of the first landmine, detonated on English soil.

In this, the third memoir, Act of Rebellion, Tom returns to Worcester, only to find that all is not well with Joan Bailey, his trusted housekeeper.

For Alexander, Andrew and Brigette Boyd

Act of Rebellion
Introduction

Mercurius Aulicus 20th- 26th of August 1643

Thursday 24th

This day in the morning it was advertised that on Tuesday night the distressed rebels had made two sallies, the one upon the Lord General's quarters, the other on Sir Jacob Astleys; But were soon beaten back again (as who could expect otherwise) with the loss of many of their men. And (which is worth your notice) those rebels, which were taken prisoner at both these sallies, were most purely drunk, the faction in the City having (for the Cause as they call it) filled the poor soldiers full of strong drink, as the only means to make them stand, that is, to pour out their own blood in the act of Rebellion.

From Satire III

"*On a huge hill,*
Cragged and steep, Truth stands, and he that will
Reach her, about must, and about must go;
And what the hill's suddenness resists, win so:.........

As streams are, Power is; those blest flowers that dwell
At the rough stream's calm head, thrive and do well,
But having left their roots, and themselves given
To the stream's tyrannous rage, alas are driven
Through mills, and rocks, and woods, and at last, almost
Consum'd in going, in the sea are lost:
So perish souls, which more choose men's unjust
Power from God claimed, than God Himself to trust.

John Donne (1573-1631)

1

Even now across the changing tapestry of years, I can still hear my wife screaming in pain. A gull sweeping up the Severn, the creak of oars in the docks, a rabbit in a snare.... after twenty years I hear such notes or cadences, and am again powerless and paralysed at her bedside. The screaming rent my soul. And I could do nothing to help her.

My homecoming in spring with Abram had presaged such joy. Why in June was all turned to misery and horror? I had longed so fiercely for my home, yearned for its security and comforts, and for the company of the good friends who husbanded my interests. Phoebe, my betrothed, was overjoyed to welcome me back and delighted to meet Abram, the son of Joseph, the noble brown pedlar, who had died in Birmingham from a terrible wasting disease. Roger and his blind father, Adam, whilst very glad to welcome me safe home, had both an air of apprehension about them. Roger kept glancing covertly to the direction in which he feared his mother might appear.

And Joan, the source of this curious foreboding, Adam's good wife and Roger's loving mother. My housekeeper, the heart of my establishment. It was true that whilst she was certainly pleased and relieved to welcome me home yet there was a sensation, a feeling, an unspoken resentment that perhaps I had dallied upon my road, that I could have hastened back earlier, and that I had not cared that she was left for some days without assistance. In vain to tell her of my imprisonment in Lichfield Close with the Earl of Chesterfield, my parole held by Sir John Gell, Elijah's death and my wish to warn my good friend Joseph of Rupert's imminent lesson for Birmingham. And Joan saw Eleanour's plea that I would return to Lichfield for her, as no reason at all for my delay. "Self regarding strumpet!" was perhaps the kindest epithet she could find for the daughter of my parents' old friends. As for poor Abram, it almost seemed as if she blamed me for Elijah's death, and that I had produced the pedlar's son as some sort of substitute.

And then our marriage. Phoebe had told her of our betrothal, when she returned in the second week in March with Peabody. Joan's disapproval was palpable. Phoebe had told me that she had clearly found the news distasteful. In the privacy of the garden we pondered on what we had done to earn her displeasure.

All had seemed to be well for Phoebe at first. Joan had rejoiced in her safe return. "As if I was her beloved daughter," Phoebe confided to me. Peabody had worked his magic, charming Joan into cooking his favourite puddings and pies, but on the day of his departure, when Phoebe had told the company of our nuptial plans, all had changed.

Phoebe had brought a bellarmine full of her own cider for Peabody and a packet of her little cinnamon cakes. As all had gathered to bid him Farewell, she determined that she would no longer postpone what she considered to be glad news.

Roger and his father had been instantly delighted, and Peabody gallantly kissed her hands yet again. But Joan had frowned, folded her arms and shaken her head sadly. Afterwards she had pleaded with Phoebe to think again about what she was doing.

"The disparity in your heights must surely give rise to some disquietude in your awareness of what is fitting," she had said with something akin to bitterness. "And as I understand it, child, your monthly courses have only recently become regular again. Is not that so?"

Phoebe had had to agree. In households such as ours where the women share all the domestic tasks, such private niceties are hard to hide. But as a physician I knew that the irregular onset of menarche in itself is not a circumstance to give rise to alarm. When her parents had been alive and her life in their manor house had been well ordered, she had experienced no difficulties with her courses, nothing that could not be set right with a posset of hot milk and ginger. But homelessness, the death of her mother and her enforced pilgrimage across the Midlands, had caused her usual patterns of life to become disrupted. But with existence again evenly paced in my household, her body's natural processes had resumed.

"And in any event," she said with a trace of the Earl's Great-niece in her tone. "Why must we be subjected to Joan's rule in this as in so much else? What makes her think she has the right to dictate to us?"

We were sitting in the bower at the end of the orchard which afforded us some little privacy. It was Monday 24th of April. The river bank was just below the hedge and ditch which enclosed my property, and a few yards out in the Severn was the long tree covered island which followed the line of the bank. There was a rumour that this spit of land was part of the Knowles estate, but neither Ben nor I had bothered to pursue the claim being content to leave the herons and otters in peace to enjoy their inheritance. Now as I cradled Phoebe in my arms, I had the notion that if I had "a boat that could carry us over", as the old song spoke of, we would be safe from prying eyes and Joan's irrational disapproval.

I had swallowed my pride and been to see Dean Potter yesterday, after Matins. If only he had had the courage to stand out against the Earl of Essex and object with passion last September, when Worcester Cathedral was used as a vast stable for the Parliament horses, instead of forfeiting his responsibility and allowing my father, a layman, to voice the profound repugnance of such a practice felt by all the Worcester citizens, perhaps my father would still be alive, instead of hanged by Essex' murdering lifeguards.

The Dean greeted me courteously enough and poured me a draught of Hippocras into a fine wine glass. Then sat opposite me and said, "I was pleased to see you at divine service today, dear Thomas. But seldom before, this spring. We have tried of late to fulfil our requirements."

"I was lately at Lichfield," I told him, "With Prince Rupert. Fighting to regain the Close and purify the great Cathedral there after it had been defiled by horse dung."

I was happy to see him look something stricken. "Alas, God has called upon us to take strange twisting paths in these troubled times." he said nervously.

"My father did not take them," I said with some asperity. "He was ever true to our great monument to the glory and grace of God that his forefathers built for us."

"Indeed, yes." The Dean had to agree. "Our lives now are so irregular."

I grew tired of indulging in verbal fencing,and despised myself for my hypocrisy. I knew in my heart that God was nowhere. I felt a pang of sympathy for this poor cleric, be he never so highly placed, who must still acknowledge the existence of the deity, at best indifferent, at worst, totally absent.

So like a faithful son of Holy Mother Church, I asked him how his gout did. I gave him our distillation of comfrey root that had cured the Earl of Chesterfield in Lichfield and explained that it was the Earl's great-niece that I wished to wed. Would he marry us in St Helen's? It was decided that the banns should be said immediately and our wedding was arranged for the 14th of May.

But now, as I sat with Phoebe in the garden for a few stolen moments, we seemed to feel something of urgency. We decided to seal our pledge. Betrothals were seen in Worcester as binding and we had plighted our troth before everyone the previous day. In deference to Joan's unease we had gone solitary to our beds last night but now Phoebe too seemed to wish with me that... that we should no longer postpone the delightful experience of carnal union. The garden bower which was home to spiders and earwigs was not the most comfortable of nuptial couches. Phoebe lay across me, supported in my arms and we kissed and fondled, but there was no prospect of any further gratification.

"Will you come to my room tonight then?" I asked her. I had the larger bed.

"Will I!" she promised and so we parted, she to pick iris for the table and I to see if there were patients in the surgery.

And so it happened. On that night in my uncle's great carved bed, we lost our virginity to our mutual satisfaction. How cold these words are! We were simply in heaven. I tried to restrain myself for fear I might injure Phoebe but as far as I could tell, her proportions were no different to those of any other woman. And she would brook no curbing of our passion. We had to be utterly silent, something of a constraint. But our adoration, one for the other, seemed to transcend our earthly life and transport us to some blissful Paradise. I remember her insisting that I stood, clasping her and within her, kissing her mouth for long moments whilst she had her legs, wrapped tightly round my person. Such love making brought her up to my level and enabled her, so she said, to experience deeper penetration. At dawn she would slink back to her own room.

On one such occasion in the three weeks before our marriage, she silently crept out of my room and closed my door softly, only to find Roger standing fully dressed, shielding a candle in his hand, his eyes wide with fear lest she should cry aloud. Mercifully she did not and no-one else learned of Roger's secret nocturnal ventures. Had his mother done so, his life would have been scarce worth a groat.

And so the days passed. Abram was treated well but with some degree of coolness by Joan. Whether it was his slightly exotic colouring or his lively assurance that Allah had sent me to care for him, I know not. In fact his care and patience with blind Adam was exemplary. Adam had been making a new still for our tinctures and simples and although the design was clear in his head, and his skilful fingers could complete the work, it was a matter of great irritation to him continually to lose his tools. To have Abram anticipating his needs and handing him the appropriate hammer or drill was luxury indeed. Adam, also now the weather was warmer, loved growing and planting and this craft also Abram began to learn from him. They became fast friends and Adam, through the simple tactic of begging to know of Abram's religion, began to teach him what was I suppose ethics and philosophy. They talked of every subject under the sun.

Of their three sons Roger was the one who best appreciated his father's great intellectual prowess, and who strove to read to him sometimes to entertain him. But Roger now had many interests in Worcester to engross his talents. He had an excellent head for figures and kept accurate tables of accounts for both households. He had proved a vigorous and effective barber and could shave and trim a beard, a skill which brought in a steady income. Now too he helped Sam in the Fish Street house to tend the horses, and if a foal was to be broken, the methods his father had taught him, when he had had his sight, were still cherished and practised. However he and his brothers had had little interest in ideas. Now Adam had a willing disciple in Abram, who listened and learned and whose eyes were constantly at Adam's service. Roger was happy that his father now had such a willing helpmate.

I had asked how Joan had reacted to the arrival of Samuel and Patience. Roger had discreetly taken them straight to my Fish Street house, with the instruction to Jacky and Gill that "Master Tommy wishes that Master and Mistress Price remain here." Old Gill was delighted with the help and support that Patience was able to supply. The management and cleaning of the Fish Street house which was large by Worcester standards was now far beyond Gill's strength alone. Sam after an initial visit with Roger rode often to the Bailey's smallholding and was delighted with the foals. He and Patience when he took her with him on Mercury, received a more gracious welcome from Betsy than they had done from Joan at my Newport Street house. It seemed her reception of my friends had been cool at best, encrusted with ice at worst. What was the reason for her current frostiness? Roger when I asked him told me she complained of feeling tired.

"But Phoebe assists her in everything in this household." I argued. "And is a marvel in the dispensary. Abram helps Adam all he can and she now does not need to care for old Gill in Fish Street. Patience is even able to help Matt and Jacky in the shop. As a farmer's daughter she is used to the slaughtering. No, there is something more troubling Joan."

Matters came to a head on the day before our wedding. I was in the Dispensary with Phoebe where we were distilling lavender oil for head lice. Joan came in and watched us for a moment, then said commandingly,

"Phoebe, there are sheets to fold in the laundry. Could you do that now, if you please?"

Phoebe's eyes widened at her tone of voice. She knew however that I was concerned as to Joan's troubled state of mind and that I would see this as an opportunity for her to confide her anxieties. She whisked out of the room in an instant.

Joan sat down heavily with a sigh. "I will say straightway what distresses me. If you continue with this marriage, I am afraid that all will not be well with your bride physically."

"How so?" I asked courteously.

"I do not think her …her organs of sexuality can be regular."

I said nothing for a moment, knowing as I did, that all was natural and well with Phoebe. Having been so secret and discreet I would not now compromise her. Instead I said, "I have been informed that she is small but undistorted. It is her leg which is out of true. It is shorter than its fellow and somewhat twisted. But this is all."

"Who has informed you?" said Joan, angrily.

"Phoebe herself," I told her. "Joan," I went on, "I fear you are tired. After the ceremony tomorrow, why not relinquish the reins of the housekeeping here and take a short holiday. In your old home? I know that Betsy would welcome you. With Adam if you...."

She broke in, her face white with anger. "Ah yes. I see it all now. Lady Phoebe Stanhope will supplant me of course. I am now of no further use. I can be cast aside like an old shoe. Fear not, Master Thomas. I and my poor husband will go and beg our bread, and leave you to your fine house and twisted bride!"

I confess I gasped in horror at the poison of her humour. "Joan! How could you think such.... heresy! You know I would never let you and Adam beg your bread. This is your home for as long as you should want it. I do not understand whence your unfriendliness stems. Why do you suddenly dislike us so much?"

She began to weep. She was suddenly choking for breath, sobbing uncontrollably, wiping her eyes with her apron, crouched on the bench where customers sat to wait for medicine. I went over to her and put my arm round her bony shoulders but she shrugged me away.

And then Roger came in. He had heard her raised voice and entered in some alarm. "Mother, dear mother!" he tried to soothe her. He took her in his arms and rocked her back and forth on the bench, until her sobs slowly became sniffs and she let the apron fall from her swollen face.

I turned to go. As I reached the door, she choked out, "I am sorry, Tom." I turned back and said, as kindly as I could, "Dear Joan, please tell Roger what your sadness is and then if we may we will remedy it. I will fetch Adam."

Phoebe waylaid me in the Hall. Sir William Russell had called and was waiting for me in the withdrawing room and had been served a cup of good claret. My heart sank. As the Governor of the local Garrison and the leader of the Committee of Safety he would certainly want me to contribute something... men, supplies or horses. I asked Phoebe if she would take Adam to the Dispensary to his wife and son where perhaps matters would be resolved.

Sir William rose and greeted me most courteously, congratulated me on my imminent marriage and complimented me on the quality of my wine, and then told me how rejoiced he was to see me safely back in my home.

"Knowing as I do of your efforts with Prince Rupert against the dastardly rebels at Lichfield, I am come to ask for your advice. I cannot encourage the young able-bodied citizenry to assemble on Pitchcroft to drill. As we speak Waller could well be approaching our city. He has lately taken Hereford. Sir Richard Cave, a good man for our sovereign, could not rouse the idle cider sots to defend the place. Waller took it in a day. We must be on our guard. We could be over-run by the vermin at any time, and I fear many of our citizens are only luke-warm for our King. Might I prevail on you to assist with these endeavours?"

Sir William was a good man, who paid his troops well, and raised and sold excellent venison. His loyalty to the King was unwavering and steadfast. I was one of these same luke-warm supporters of the Crown. How was I to extricate myself from a commitment that I could not honestly discharge?

At that moment I heard Abram calling for me. He had been assisting Adam to set sticks in the ground to support the young pea shoots, and wanted me to admire the work, now that Adam had been summoned to his wife. I called him in.

"Abram, a question, if you please. If you wanted to get the young fellows of Worcester like yourself to drill for an hour or two, what would you do to persuade them to assemble?"

He did not hesitate. "Give each one a tasty venison patty and a piece of apple tart."

"Would you shoulder your musket then and come out to practise your skill at arms, my good boy?" asked Sir William.

Abram remembered his manners and bowed low.

"Aye, that I would, sir. And after we have drilled and eaten our fill, Tom could teach us all some merry rounds. He knows good songs, and taught me many as we rode back from Lichfield."

"Abram, I am a physician, not a minstrel!" I objected.

"This young roisterer must then be a kinsman of Master Knowles."

I did not dispute his assumption. Abram was clearly starved of companions his own age. I noted his inclinations.

"So, young man, your advice is to make the occasion akin to a merry-making, do you say? Drill but with good cheer? Well, who am I to begrudge my young fellow citizens a taste of my venison?"

I saw my opportunity. "And Sir William, we still have a good supply of last year's apples, a little wrinkled but still marvellous sweet in the lofts. Let me donate them to your cause for the King. I will have several bushels brought to your kitchen door, after my wedding." That was easier than teaching the youth of Worcester to roar out such ballads as "I am a Lusty Beggar," or "The Three Merry Cobblers."

Sir William was looking something doubtful. "Thank you, Master Thomas. I suppose my wife can.... Well, she will have to... Yes, in these terrible times all must make sacrifices." he concluded firmly and stood, as I thought, to take his leave, telling Abram when the next drill would take place. However the real reason for his visit had still to be examined.

"I am charged, Master Thomas.... Master Fletcher I should say... a householder like yourself... so much to lose... The County Commission for the King has now this last month become the Committee of Safety.... And I must request... nay, insist I fear...."

When public men mumble and stammer in private, it means one thing.

"You want money from me," I told him kindly, taking pity on him. "How much?"

His eyes widened at my frankness. "Er... Yes. That is the difficulty. Of course the City Council... I am bound to tell you this... would rather organise the defences without partiality so they say, but Mayor Hacket is for the cause of Parliament, and I mistrust the Council's neutrality, Sir, mistrust it deeply."

I said again "How much?" and he replied quickly "Six pounds a month."

"This month's contribution will be with you today," I promised him.

"Pray God, Waller finds enough to occupy himself in Herefordshire."

"Amen," I said piously.

"Should you, Thomas, my good boy, good man I should say, should you bethink you of any idle wanton youths who lack employment, could you inform me of their whereabouts? We have great need of them in the garrison."

I promised I would think if I knew any hereabouts, and so he took his leave.

Phoebe called Abram and myself into the kitchen where she had set out bread, butter, cheese and onions for us. Raised voices came from the Still Room. We looked at each other, confused and perplexed. Then at last Adam groped his way into the kitchen. He could find his way around the lower floor unaided. Abram helped him to a chair and he asked if he could speak to us for a moment. He declined food but accepted a beaker of small beer.

"I fear my beloved wife is not totally herself. You will know, both of you, that for some women the passing of the age of fruitfulness causes a lowering of the spirits. With poor Joan, this seems unusually severe. Her depressed state causes her to be angry with herself and sadly with anyone else. On her behalf, I am charged to ask your pardon and to say that she will endeavour to behave in a fitting and agreeable manner tomorrow at the ceremony."

I begged him to fetch Joan and Roger to eat and drink. I had to visit the mercers for my new black velvet doublet slashed with white satin. Abram had asked if he could wear his yellow hose at the marriage and we had been delighted that he should do so. Phoebe had last minute alterations to make for her wedding gown.

As we were going to our respective tasks, Joan came wearily into the kitchen. At the sight of Abram there was a flash of distaste distorting her features. It was gone as fast as it appeared and she sat with a sigh and raised her eyebrows, as we stood for a moment. I did not know whether to speak or not. Phoebe came round to her and embraced her, but Joan seemed unable to accept such concern. She sat rigid in her chair for a moment and then kindly but firmly removed Phoebe's encircling arms.

We left her then. I asked Abram to accompany me. As we walked through the town I wondered again if I ought to send him to my school. I could afford to do so, but I confess I had learned far more of use from Ben than I had ever learned, cramped in my school desk. I asked him what he thought he might do with his life and he replied, "Allah has sent me to help Adam."

"Well, we will talk of this again," I told him. I had begun to appreciate his method of thinking. If he wished to follow a course of action, then he decided that that was the path that Allah had ordained for him. Over the years I had noticed that same complacent confidence placed by my fellow-men in the Will of

God. Briefly their doctrine is, "If I want this, then so does the Almighty." A time-saving and pragmatic philosophy.

Our wedding was all that we could have wished. Phoebe had insisted on wearing the same green gown my father had bought for her. Some of the old beldames tut-tutted at her choice of colour. "Green was the fairies' colour." they muttered. "Only bad luck can follow such a choice." But Phoebe, like myself believed that men and women may make their own luck. "The fairies rejoice that I honour them," she told old Gill, as she dressed herself on the nuptial morning in the Fish Street house. We had decided to respect the old custom of sleeping under separate roofs before the wedding day. Patience acted as her maid and Roger was my groomsman whilst Abram was the envy of all youthful male eyes in his yellow hose.

Our numbers were augmented by the Baileys from the Severnside farm. Betsy, even though her child was due in two months had insisted that she and her husband, Simon and fifteen year old James attended. "For how churlish we should be to forego what is a family wedding to all intents and purposes," she said, in her high bubbling London tone, as she heaved herself out of the cart that Walter had pulled from Clevelode. Simon assisted her and all three went forward to greet Joan. But Joan pointedly turned her head away as they came forward. Simon shrugged but James her youngest, her baby, immediately drew attention to their rejection.

"Mother, why are you so unkind to us? We are your sons, your boys, and Betsy is a good woman!"

Joan's face seemed to crumple inwards on itself. She clung to Adam's arm who wished to greet his sons and daughter-in-law but was powerless to do so, without her guidance. He spoke, welcoming them, hoping in his blind state that he was speaking in their right direction, and Roger and I began to talk at once. But James would have none of it. He went to his father and took him in his arms and then as his mother began to weep, he gathered her also into his embrace. By this means, he brought his mother back from some pit of despair, into which she had been gazing.

Simon clapped Roger on the back and drew Betsy to him, "Look at my little London light of love, brother. Alas, she has grown of late monstrous heavy. Doctor Tom, old friend, can you explain this strange circumstance?"

"Alas, Simon!" I told him, "I thought I was the bridegroom! I look to your guidance in these matters!"

So with laughter and good humour, with Abram's yellow hose, gleaming along in front, we went to fetch the bride from Fish Street in procession. I knocked on the great door, thinking how much my parents would have loved to see this day. It was opened by Patience, carrying a nosegay. She stood to one side to let Phoebe step forward to take my arm. So we came to St Helen's, Phoebe, bewitching in her silken green gown, her russet hair shining, pushed into becoming ringlets and I in black velvet, pretending to be handsome, failing lamentably but happy as a pig in clover and doting as an old Pantaloon when I looked upon my beautiful young bride.

After the ceremony we walked back to the Newport Street house, where all the neighbours had gathered to wish us well. A fine side of beef turned on the spit filling the house with its toothsome aroma. Abram and James went into the orchard and ran races through the trees. Both were starved of company of their own age and each was determined to make the most of the other's fellowship.

There were puddings and pies aplenty. Patience had been in the Newport kitchen during the last week, helping Phoebe prepare for her wedding breakfast, and Joan had also assisted, at first reluctantly but when the younger women had asked her help, had freely given it.

Afterwards Abram insisted that I sing "Back and sides go bare." So I complied with what was I hope a good grace. My household were amazed, they told me, at how tuneful my voice was. Why did I not sing aloud more often, they demanded. I launched into "Joan's Ale is New." bowing to Joan to ensure no offence was taken but she seemed pleased to be sung to thus, and began to guide Adam gently through the dance steps.

"If only we had a fiddler!" said Roger. Sam coughed nervously and drew forth just such an instrument from under his cloak in the corner and began to play "Hey Jolly Broom Man."

"Come on Tom! You know this!" Abram cried, and so I sang again and all joined in the rousing chorus. I wondered if I dare sing "Lavender's Blue" with its reference to keeping the bed warm but Simon with a saucy look at Betsy launched into it with great feeling. I confess that I felt great sadness at the absence of my dear father.

Other friends and neighbours came up to me, pressed my hand and told me that they missed him sorely also. Tears sprang to my eyes but he was instantly there admonishing me in my head. "What ails this company, all with their arses in their hands? If you all will remember me, then no more long faces, I beg you." I said it aloud and John Elmbury, one of his dearest friends cried out, "That is Amyas' voice, I swear it."

The time passed delightfully with much good cheer and good victuals and wine, until the guests began to remember their comfortable beds, and I began to long for the physical union we had enjoyed over the last weeks. The Baileys from Clevelode had returned some time earlier, Simon having a care for Betsy's condition. Patience had worked hard scouring pots and pans as they were emptied and she and Sam returned to Fish Street, supporting old Gill. Matt had returned with Jacky but had then sought his father's house, promising to be at work betimes. Joan went quietly to her bed accompanied by Adam, and Abram asked Phoebe if she would teach him how to wash his prized yellow hose. She laughed, agreed and sent him to his bed, as he was suddenly dropping with sleep. Roger turned to us and said slyly, with a lascivious wink, "A public bridal bedding? Or might that be over and above your needs?"

Suddenly we were alone and finally could retire. I thought of all the Knowles bridegrooms and brides who had climbed this great carved staircase over the past hundred and fifty years... I trusted their ghosts did not resent the new owner, a butcher's boy, whose pretty aunt had caught the fancy of rich young Alderman Knowles, over thirty years ago now. If the ghosts were indignant at my possession, they were silent as the grave... the best place for them, when all was said and done.

Our love making for our wedding night and for the nights that followed seemed as natural and easy as we could have wished. On the morning after our wedding my wife lay in my arms, her russet hair tangled across the pillows and said, "Husband, may I ask a favour?"

"You may ask," I replied ungraciously in play, and then told her, "Anything, little wife."

"When do you go to the Malvern Hills to replenish your clean water supplies?"

"One day this week. Friday, if you wish. Will you come with me?"

"Tom I would dearly love to know how Martha fares. Do you remember? She had allowed me to stay in her cottage, when I was trying to walk to Monmouth when you found me."

Then followed a most pleasing interlude whilst I "found" her again. In truth she had reminded me of an event that I had put from my mind. The villagers in the stone cutters hamlet had been terrorised by an evil foreman. Last September a group of tyrannical boys led by his son had stoned my beloved Phoebe, and they had put poor Joseph in the stocks. I remembered the man's name was Dodgeson. He was hated but feared even more. I asked, "So, Martha? What of her? Do you wish to give her money?"

"If she is sore beset, then I would like to give her the choice of coming into Worcester under our protection."

I thought for a moment. "What about Joan?"

Well," said Phoebe thoughtfully, "Joan tells us that she will no longer carry resentment. I should not wish to place anyone so old as Martha under her governance unless I could be certain of Joan's charitable intentions. If poor Abram could see the dark looks that follow him! And yet Joan is as much your dependant as any of us. But I think Patience would be pleased to welcome Martha."

"My dear wife," I told her, "If you wish for a thing, then be assured it as good as done." And so in perfect accord we rose at last to greet the day.

Three days later, in mid-May, we were up betimes (something of a sacrifice for us during that happy season) and with Abram's help had stacked the empty barrels ready to hoist onto our cart. Roger and I hefted them up and Phoebe and I mounted, and I held the reins. Abram to his delight was on Jupiter and Roger rode Sir John, as we had begun to call one of the Welsh cobs, after Sir John Gell. This same patient horse had carried Elijah's coffin from Stafford to Stratford, and I had great affection for him and his stable-mate Mary. Suddenly there was a shout as we were about to set forth, and Sam, mounted on Mercury asked leave to accompany and help us. Mercury was in need of exercise he told us. He had a great wish, also to visit the Malvern Hills of which he had heard so much.

It was the best part of the year. The air was heady with the scent of hawthorn blossom, and swans and their cygnets were floating at ease down the river as we trotted over. As we were bound for the spring below the stone cutters village at the northernmost edge of the Hills we went alongside the Teme for a space and then rode merrily through two little hamlets before striking up into the hills. The path meandered between wooded slopes and Phoebe resolved that she would seek out old Martha whilst we began to fill our barrels. But then we decided that we would all accompany her as it seemed to us to be fitting that Abram should know the place where both Phoebe and I first came upon his father. And I had apprehensions that the villagers whom I had tried to rouse to rebellion might have found excuses to remain subservient.

My fears were well founded. As we strained our way uphill to the wide village green that lay directly below the sheer cliffs, I thought I heard shouting on the breeze. Phoebe looked stricken and afraid and cried out, "Suppose those terrible boys are still up to their rude tricks!" I could not believe that they could have continued their bullying tyranny unchecked by this. Surely the villagers would not have continued to endure their misrule. But I was wrong. As we rounded up onto the Green, there were the hideous youths, screaming obscenities in Martha's garden, intent on bringing their beastliness to her attention. One had his breeches round his knees and was aping the act of generation in a most repulsive manner.

"Oh, Jesu!" Phoebe cried, "And this has no doubt persisted since last Autumn."

I dismounted and as before retrieved the cattle whip from the side of the cart. At these times my fists seemed to have a life of their own. I had to clench them now to keep them at my side. I told Phoebe to stay in the cart and Abram was to guard her. Roger and Sam still mounted, but with their swords drawn, followed me softly to Martha's garden gate.

"Come out, Martha! Come out and cut a caper for us!" one screamed, and another shouted, "Dance for us, Martha, else today we'll hang your dog!" They were so intent on their hellish enterprise that they had no notion of our approach.

I cracked the whip. "Good day to you, gentlemen." I said calmly as they all spun round. "What harm has the old dame who lives here done you?"

Their gobs dropped to their navels. I sensed that Sam and Roger close behind me, were a formidable sight. As I had thought the wretched bull calves had no answer.

"I ask again," I said "She has in some sort done you wrong?" They were struck dumb and then the fattest and the tallest suddenly screamed "Dadda!"

"You call for your father, Sir?" I asked, with my courteous dog fox smile. "Why so, Sir? I ask again, Sir. What offence has the dame who lives here caused you, that you see fit to threaten her so grossly? Why do you need your father?"

There was some sort of commotion at the inn. The stone cutters were streaming out to stand, gazing at the strangers, who had suddenly dropped from the moon. I cracked the whip again, penning the wretched youths in Martha's garden. A large fat man detached himself from the group outside the inn and began to walk over towards us, instructing his fellows to follow him. However they did not obey. Shovels and pick axes have never been a match for drawn swords.

When he realised he was alone, he stopped perhaps some fifteen yards from us and began to shout, "Leave my poor lads alone, you bastards!" Roger softly rode a few steps in his direction. Sir John was a big cob and Roger controlled him well. The sight of the large horse with a rider ready to slice his arm off was too much for Dodgeson. He turned and began to walk swiftly back to the dubious sanctity of the inn. Roger followed behind him, gently trotting. Dodgeson looked behind him uneasily and increased his pace, until he was in fact running. To my delight his workmates jeered and clapped his retreat, although as he reached the inn, their applause abruptly ceased.

He pushed through them shouting, "Why did you not follow me? There are only three of them." In his anger, viciously he punched the man nearest to him. This action was the spark which lit the match of their long held resentments. The man he had hit rounded on him and struck him twice, once on the neck and once in the stomach. Dodgeson was down instantly on his back, his legs and arms kicking wildly, whilst his workmates began to rain violent blows on him. One or two picked up sticks from a heap of firewood and thrashed him soundly, but most had recourse to their fists. Their pent-up fury once unleashed, they were savages intent on slaughter.

Roger cried out to me, "Tom, they're going to kill him!"

I ran across to him and handed up the whip. "Crack it near them." I instructed him, and he galloped the remaining yards across the Green. The villagers were shouting abuse and now the women were running from the cottages, screaming and yelling like screech-owls at noon-day. The eldest boy penned up by Sam in Martha's garden shouted again, "Dadda!".

We had unwittingly provided the little community with the impulse for which it had long been waiting. I ran after Roger and as he cracked the whip near to the edge of the circle of crazed vengeance seekers, I drew a deep breath and roared out, "Stop! Now!" There was something of a lull and as they paused in their frenzy, Roger cried out, "You will all hang, else. I ask you, my masters, is he worth it?"

With a few final kicks and blows they began to leave their tormentor, now lifeless and bleeding on the ground. I have never known a group of villagers better able to melt into nothingness. Finally there were only the officious landlord standing, arms folded, in his doorway and the man whom Dodgeson had hit and who had made free with his fists in return. I remembered them both from my last visit to this village. The man who had retaliated had been the spokesman for others but had also tried to rouse his fellows to their slavish plight. He had stood back from the fray after his initial blows and now sighed and shook his head. "It had to be," he said sadly. "It should never have come to this pass."

I knelt by Dodgeson. He was bleeding copiously from a wound on his right arm that he had raised to protect his face. To little avail. He had a monstrous cut eye and a split lip. From the kicks he had received, I had no doubt that his ribs were certainly badly bruised, possibly broken. The boys outside Martha's cottage were sobbing like the great babes they were.

"Let them out, Sam!" I called. Three of them were gone instantly, roaring down the hill to their homes in Leigh Sinton.. The eldest boy, the brutish swaggerer of fifteen years, shambled over the green to his father, followed by one whom I took to be his younger brother. Both boys, even though they had not been touched were sniffing and sobbing, as if they were still in small clothes.

In the comparative silence a door opened. I heard Phoebe shout

"Martha!" and then my little wife was running to the stooped old woman who had emerged at last from her cottage. She embraced her lovingly and they spoke for a minute, Phoebe pointing to me and the old woman smiled broadly evidently to hear news of our wedding. But at the sight of Dodgeson on the ground, she kindly seemed to insist that she must view his plight.

They came over and Dodgeson groaned aloud. I was beginning to fear that he might not recover, but when the old woman spoke to him, his eyes opened.

"Well, nephew!" said Martha, "The worms have turned, it seems."

"Get her away from me, the old witch! " Dodgeson cried.

"A witch am I? Would that I were! I would bewitch you, my own sister's son, into a more seemly and respectful humour. What ails him?" she asked me.

"I fear he has broken ribs if nothing worse," I told her. "Alas, I cannot take him back to Worcester in the cart. He needs rest. Where does he live?"

The man whom he had attacked answered. "In the bailiff's house on Colonel Lygon's estate, Madresfield way. He was ever a one for worming his way into the gentry's good offices."

"Well," I said, "Devil a gentleman is here to assist him. He would be in worse case if we attempted to take him down to Madresfield."

"I'll take him in," said Martha "Not for him but for my poor sister. Is there a board to carry him on?"

The Landlord who had been content to act as auditor at a play, now roused himself to action. Yes, he had an old door that had been used for just such a purpose when Dodgeson and his sons had set about some poor unfortunate. He and the spokesman bustled themselves to find it.

As he lay on the unforgiving ground I took the chance of examining Dodgeson's wounds. His arm bled steadily and must immediately be treated. His torso was covered in fearful bruises and he would ache infernally for some days to come. He was developing a monstrous black eye and his lower lip exposed his gums and was bleeding. His teeth fortunately still seemed firm in their bed. I had my box with me and asked Phoebe what tincture she thought could most swiftly heal the unsightly fissure.

But Martha knew her craft and replied before Phoebe could begin to think. "For the lip, comfrey should knit that sort of flesh wound. If 'tis slow to heal, then a poultice of coltsfoot crushed in honey. As for the eye, chamomile will soothe the bruising. Have no fear, nephew, I will not bewitch you."

He did not reply. The landlord and the spokesman who told me his name was Jack Dance brought the old door and laid it beside him. Slowly we half lifted, half pushed him onto it, and carried him across the green. Throughout our efforts the two boys wept and snivelled. At last their father roughly shouted at them, "Cease your noise, you brainless brachets. 'Tis me that is hurt, not you."

At last we laid him in Martha's little cottage. I had become aware lately of the damp smells that pervaded the homes of the poor. Whilst in themselves, such vapours do not carry disease... I did not think... yet the damp in the air must prohibit recovery of any chest complaint. But Martha's cottage was snug, smelling pleasantly of healing herbs. Jars neatly labelled stood on shelves which lined the walls.

Dodgeson was clearly apprehensive at the sight of Martha's stock in trade, and passed his uninjured arm over his eyes. She laughed. "He remembers my sister, his grandmother insisting that he drank stewed prunes with sliced ginger and senna to cure his sluggish bowels. And it did. But somewhat too violently, eh, Silas?"

Dodgeson could not forbear shuddering. "I pray you, Master Doctor for such I think you may well be by your box that you carry, preserve me from this beldame! She will feed me poison, else!"

"And if I did, 'twould be no more than you deserve, you rudesby! No, Silas you are safe with me. I am not a one for vengeance. But these two must go their ways." She gestured to the two snivelling youths. "I cannot stomach them in my house not after the cowardly nastiness I have suffered at their hands."

I was suddenly inspired. "I know of a good home for them!"

Roger and Phoebe gazed at me in horror. "No!" I reassured them, "Not with us but Sir William Russell seeks recruits."

So it was arranged. I treated Silas Dodgeson's arm and left his bruises and his facial injuries to the tender mercies of his aunt. I promised to return for Martha in a sennight if she wished to stay for a day or two to make holiday in Worcester with Phoebe. She seemed excessively pleased at the notion of such a jaunt. Dodgeson was forced to accept the inevitable fact that, due to his injuries, he could now in no way care for his boys, and that he must let them accept the hospitality of others. They had no trade and their mother was dead. I was not wholly happy with myself in that I was providing recruits for the King. What of my much vaunted "fierce neutrality"? But I knew of no Parliament quartermaster in the area. I would have sent one to the King and one to his enemies without a qualm of conscience. So long as these two embryo rascals were out of the way of law-abiding citizens, I confess I no longer cared what their future might hold.

Dodgeson gave me some sovereigns that he had in his pocket for their upkeep until they should be accepted into Sir William's garrison and receive payment.

But as we at last began to fill our barrels with the pure cold water flowing from the Malvern rocks, the two boys overcome with fear and distress at the sudden change in their fortunes began to cry again. Abram from his lofty height on Jupiter gazed down on them with an unintentional air of superiority and told them kindly, "Doctor Tom is a good man, and so is Sir William. They will not beat you for all you are a pair of vile maggoty swaggerers."

This could not but depress them further. They continued to snivel and sob as they passed the familiar haunts of their youth and as we reached the track to Worcester I wondered what to say to put them in better heart. Finally I remembered Sir William's great generosity towards his soldiers, and tossed back over my shoulder, the information. "You get excellent good payment in the garrison. Sir William rewards his men well. You'll receive a good wage. "

The sobs continued. They were sitting, wedged between the barrels on the cart-tail. But as we travelled through the first of the villages, their crying dwindled to sniffs and coughs and I became aware of movement behind me. I turned my head and looked straight into the tear-stained grimy face of the younger of the two, who had shuffled his way along the cart to consult me. "How much?" he demanded.

We went first to Newport Street, where Joan could not contain her angry apprehension that I had added two more foundlings to my household.

"No such thing!" I told her airily, "They are bound for Sir William's Garrison. Give them refreshment, please, Joan, and civil wars being what they are, there is a good chance you will never see them again." She compressed her lips and proceeded to find them small beer and chicken pie. Abram so far forgot or overlooked his superior feelings and condescended to join them at the table and when they had eaten their fill, he agreed to walk with us to the Garrison to see them settled. The Recruiting Sergeant who welcomed and admitted them seemed well disposed towards them and promised them that he would recommend that they become drummer boys. Sir William had been saying only that morning that he wished he had two willing lads to train for those positions. Although the disgraceful scene outside Martha's cottage was fresh in my memory, I slowly began to feel some sympathy for the two plump outcasts, who in a day... nay a few hours... had had their usual way of life completely changed. I promised I would return on the morrow to see how they did.

Our day in the hills had given me something of a desire to enjoy the early summer weather away from the constraints of the town. I needed to inspect the farms that I owned. Every quarter a substantial sum of money was brought by an overseer to the house and was locked away. How was this sum derived from two farms in the northern part of Herefordshire? I had promised myself that I would be sure that I knew how all my money was made. I did not want my land to be ploughed and tilled by wretched mud-encrusted scarecrows such as I had seen, working themselves near to death for the worthless gentry, who by process of inheritance claimed to own that same land. I would be responsible and I would care for my servants.

Later that even I told my wife my sentiments as we sat at ease in the small parlour, which faced west. A finger of the setting sun touched her hair as she sat opposite me, sewing diligently. Even now, so many years later, that pleasant memory of my little wife causes my eyes to fill with tears.

I told her of the fears I had that my farms were in profit because of the back breaking labour and dreadful conditions of unknown serfs who worked for me. She thought for a moment.

"In fact, Tom, these men are not serfs. At every quarter day they are free to seek other employment. No, dear husband, it is their wives and women who are the real slaves. Dependent entirely on their menfolk, these poor drabs do not sit with them as equals as I do now. If a man is made to suffer by his betters, his wife will be in even worse case, believe me. If he is beaten, then in many instances she will suffer the same punishment but at his hands, at the hands of one who of all others should cherish her most."

I gazed at her in wonder. "How do you know all this, little wife?"

"When I and my mother lost everything in Tamworth and had to beg our bread, I learnt of the world that exists under the one in which I had been living, in a fool's paradise. The widow who sold fish in Dudley and who so kindly took us in, so my mother could at the very least die in a bed, told me that the day her husband died of a seizure was the happiest day of her life. She showed me the scars across her poor back and I believed her, Tom. She swore she would not marry again to let a man dictate to her and abuse her. When I went into homes to cure children of whooping coughs, the women trembled in fear lest their husbands returned whilst I was there. Of a certainty they would be beaten for allowing a stranger into the home, even though the life of their child was at stake. My dearest husband, you have seen fearful sights. Your poor father, the best of men, dying so shamefully for naught, the terrors of battle where our own countrymen seek to destroy each other. Horrors indeed! But these atrocities are all the work of men. Women must watch and work and suffer, and can do nothing to prevent the folly of the stronger sex holding sway."

"But women in general have not the capacity to comprehend the affairs of state." I argued, admittedly somewhat feebly."

"Oh, do you think so, husband? How do you think Joan can administer a household? That is, in little, what Queen Elizabeth did as a stateswoman. I do not think anyone questioned her "capacity" or "comprehension." Just as," and here she laughed, "neither of us would dare to question Joan's abilities!"

"Come wife!" I told her, laughing, "let's to bed and I promise I will not beat you tonight."

"Nor any night, kind Sir, I trust." And so with laughter and light words we went to our bed and had great pleasure of each other.

By a strange coincidence the next day my rural inheritance was brought more forcibly to my attention. Joan placed a letter before me, which had arrived earlier with the carrier. It had been written early in April but had travelled into Wales to Llandeilo with a load of sheep's hurdles. Now some weeks later it had found my direction. It was from the tenant farmer who farmed my land near Wigmore, a man I did not know, a distant poor cousin of my deceased uncle, Sir Nicholas Knowles. As far as I knew this tenant was an honest diligent man, but my conscience smote me in that I had not met him. His letter contained news upon which I must act. The County of Herefordshire had declared almost entirely for the King, and the High Sheriff of the county, one Fitzwilliam Coningsby, had ordered that all rents of supposed delinquents were to be paid directly to him to administer for the King. Peter Holdsworth, my tenant, wrote a fair hand and his remarks could not but be seen as just.

"As I have no notion of your Politicks, Sir, in this accursed time, I could not chose but acquiesce, though with much fear that you will see fit to force me and my wife and children out of our comfortable home onto the world, though who can gainsay armed Cavaliers? It may be that you have declared for the King. If it be so I pray you with all speed inform Sir Fitzwilliam of your allegiance. All are at odds here. The Lady of Brampton is scurvily reviled by the common sort for her loyalty to Sir Robert, her husband and the cause of Parliament. But to us she has ever been the best of neighbours, but now we must be strange. Her rents also have been filched for her views are well known. She is of the opinion that your income from your farm near Byton, by the side of Lugg will also have been purloined."

And so it proved. But two days later, a tinker brought another letter, from the good tenant of Knowles Mead, near Presteigne. He too had had his carefully harvested rent taken from him by Sir Fitzwilliam's henchmen, but to add more confusion this man told me of Hereford now being held by Parliament, by Sir William Waller "whom all call Conkeror," he told me. Action was required and hastily. I had not declared for the King and indeed in both of the battles in which I had been a spectator, had doctored for Parliament. But no-one could deny that I had been of considerable assistance in Lichfield to both the Earl of Chesterfield and to no less a lord than Prince Rupert himself, the King's own nephew. Phoebe had the locket with the Prince's likeness in it which might serve as proof, should it be needed, although as she herself said, the miniature could have been myself, although, "'Twas not near so handsome," she told me kindly.

I resolved that my best course was to travel to Hereford over Fromes Hill and ask whoever ruled to ask for justice. After I had retrieved my money I would travel to Byton and Wigmore and acquaint myself with my tenants. A week should see my return.

I had visited the young Dodgeson boys and was told by the Recruiting Sergeant that they shaped well. "Perhaps over fond of their bellies, but when they begin to drill with the pike, all their surplus flesh will fall away," he predicted. When I had seen them, they were both munching apple turnovers, possibly made with the fruit donated from my trees. The younger one went so far as to offer to share his sweetmeat with me. This I felt could only be a kind of progress. They seemed subdued but not unhappy. At the sound of a bell, they leapt to their feet and ran to the ground where Sergeants drilled the Garrison troops. But they were not to be put through their paces. The bell was the signal to assemble for dinner in the Hall.

Starvation would not be their fate. I told the Sergeant I would return and take them to see their father when they had leave from Sir William to do so.

As I was strolling back to Newport Street down the High Street, Sir William called my name and asked permission to walk with me.

"Good news, good Master Fletcher. Waller has gone from Hereford and the King's good servant, Sir William Vavasour now holds it for His Majesty."

As it was a Royalist who had deemed my money was forfeit, it was possible Sir William Vavasour would know of the acquisition. (Some would call it "theft.") I told Sir William Russell I rejoiced with him and explained that I was travelling to Hereford on the morrow and would carry his good offices to Sir William Vavasour. But the speed at which Hereford had changed hands must have taken all by surprise.

"What of Sir Coningsby Fitzwilliam ? He was lately Sheriff I think?" I asked politely.

Sir William smiled forgivingly. "Sir Fitzwilliam Coningsby is his name, Tom. Alas, he and other great men for the King are imprisoned in Gloucester. But it will be safe for you now to travel to Hereford. Is it a call for doctoring?"

"No, Sir. I must explain that I am for the King if I am not to lose my rents in the North of the County. They were confiscated as my allegiance was not known." I did not add, "And still is not known!" Best for Sir William to think me a true servant of the King. And perhaps I was.

"So Phoebe, will you accompany me on this jaunt if not to foreign parts at least to the next county?" I asked her later that night, the evening of the 22nd of May. I expected her to reply firmly, "That will I!" but to my surprise, she paused before answering.

"I had best not, husband. My courses are due to begin in two days and you do not need all that fidget and bustle whilst you are on the road. Better by far that I stay here and order my husband's affairs in his absence."

She had not seemed to be at a disadvantage for this cause in Lichfield. Still what did I know of women's matters? I accepted her decision, and noticed that that night after she had pleasured me as was her wont, she withdrew from me and gently placed my arms away from her person. So it was the next night also. I told myself that perhaps she feared I might fear to be soiled by her menstrual flow should it manifest itself earlier than expected. I was and am a doctor, and such explanation came easily to me. I knew too that some sects view such blood as distastefully unclean. I did not, but perhaps my little wife was unsure of my acceptance of every aspect of her being. I resolved when I returned to tell her that my love had no fastidious boundaries.

"But, Tom. Take poor Abram with you. This will be respite for him and while he is gone I will tell Joan what we know of his history and ask her why she so clearly dislikes his presence under the same roof."

Abram was delighted with the news. His only concern was whether Adam would miss his help. When he voiced his anxiety in the kitchen with all present, we were all astounded by the bitterness of the venom in Joan's reply.

"Have no fear, Master Abram!" she cried waspishly, "My husband will be well served by one who has ever been solicitous for his welfare. Myself! So it was before you came here as Master Tom's dependant!"

There was a terrible silence. Then Adam said sternly, "Wife, I trust that you will withdraw what you have said. In fact we are all

Tom's dependants, and in our case that was at our choice and suggestion. Come now, beg Abram's pardon. He is an excellent youth and deserves better at your hands."

"I shall not!" she shouted and rushed from the room. We heard her crying as she ran upstairs to her bedchamber. Abram sat gazing at his feet. Roger who sat next to him, patted him on the shoulder.

"Don't heed her, my good Jack Pudding! She speaks jabberment!."

Abram looked round at us, "But what have I done?"

With one voice we told him, "Nothing!" and could think of nothing further to say.

"I think she wishes James was here, instead of me," he said suddenly. "On the wedding day, she seemed well content to have her three boys about her, after James had bid her be cheerful. And why," he went on, warming to his theme, "does James not live here with his parents? If my parents were alive I would want to live with them. And if James lived here, we could have great sport, him and me."

Roger looked at me with raised eyebrows. "When we came here, she said she understood he would wish to stay at the Chantry for the horses. But Sam has two cob foals to occupy my brother. If he knew my mother yearned for him, her baby, then he could be persuaded I am sure to forego Betsy's thistledown pastry. Well said, Abram."

"Yes, well said, Abram," I echoed, my heart sinking at the notion of two fourteen year olds scampering in and out of doors all day.

"Abram, you are a clever youth," said Adam, "Here was the solution to my poor wife's distress and only you had the breadth of mind to see it. I fear that when she looked on you, she felt only anger and sorrow that her last born had chosen to forsake her so early in his life. Perhaps if I had had my sight, I might have "seen" her misery. No fool like an old fool, but an old blind fool is worse."

We hastened to reassure him. Roger asked if he might ride to Clevelode, the next day, to discuss the problem, with his brothers. It might be that James could be spared, returning with Roger for a visit. I was happy to agree and suggested that as I would also be from home on the morrow, that Phoebe should keep a housewifely eye on matters in both houses. She and Joan between them could treat most of the minor illnesses that came to our door, although my heart went out to our poor patients whom Joan might suspect had attended for attention rather than a cure.

So once again Abram and I took to the road together. We took the two sweet-tempered cobs that Sir John Gell had found for myself and Elijah. The stallion we had named for Sir John and the mare was simply Lady Mary. I knew that Sam was hoping to breed from them, as their temperaments were so docile and affectionate.

And so on good horses, our own mood took on the lightness of holiday humour and we rode on, Abram telling me courteously of my shortcomings as his elder but for all that he assured me, he was well pleased to be under my guidance. When we came to the summit of Fromes Hill and saw the county of Hereford spread before us melting into the blue of the Welsh hills, I vow there were not two more contented travellers in the length and breadth of the Midlands.

2

Abram was the best of travelling companions. He was a seasoned wayfarer in his own right, having visited many parts of the Middle Lands with his father. They had carried their needle-cases and the smaller items of harness to many of the little towns which were within a day's ride of Birmingham, and Abram had tales to tell of cast shoes, fearful hail storms and sudden summer floods. He was able to speak of his memories of his father without weeping though he was sometimes overcome. On those occasions I told him tales of my own father, of the cow that had run back to St John's to her farm causing a great hue and cry. My father had told the farmer that he would not slaughter such a clever beast, and the farmer had asked what was he then to do with her, as she was past breeding. My father had told him, "Harness her to your cart on market day. Be you never so befuddled and benbowsed with liquor at the end of the day, she'll bring you home."

And so after an uneventful ride on equally matched and willing horses, we came to Hereford. We could clearly see the castle and the cathedral as we rode down to Bysters Gate at the north eastern side of the city. But the citizens seemed wary of us... A musketeer stepped onto the track and bade us Halt. "How many follow you?" he asked, somewhat wearily.

"Why, none, Sir!" I told him. "We are from Worcester. I am come to seek justice from your governor. Can you tell me now who is governor of this city?"

He did not answer that question but told me, "We had Waller here. Poor Sir Richard Cave sent to Russell in Worcester to help us against him, but not a jot or tittle of assistance came hither. How answer you that?"

"Why, sir, I cannot answer it. I am merely a surgeon. Sir William Russell was exercised himself continually attempting to encourage the Worcester citizens to turn out to drill to prepare for Waller. I think he had little success. How fared Sir Richard with these

Hereford bulls?" as groups of labourers had gathered.

"Not at all! He even rang the Hereford Common Bell to summon them to build breastworks to defend the city. They cared nothing for their liberty, nothing for their city, nothing for their King." He glared at the poor fellows, who sensing but not totally comprehending his wrath, slowly dispersed. I dismounted but bade Abram stay where he was on Sir John.

"Will you take a pint of wine with us, sir? Is there a tavern where we might sit at our ease?" I asked him courteously. "I was but four weeks ago at Lichfield with Prince Rupert. You might wish to hear of this."

"Rupert?" he said, his eyes suddenly bright with passion. "Aye, that I would, good doctor. Follow me!"

I led Mary, and Abram trotted after until we came to a tavern in a narrow road our guide told us was Cabbage Lane. And there was perhaps a taint of old cabbages on the air. But there was the Cathedral rising up before us at the end of the little street. I stood for a moment with Mary snuffling down my neck to absorb its beauty.

An ostler appeared and offered to tend the horses. "So they ent gallus, master?" he asked.

"Gallus? What's that?" I asked puzzled.

"So they don't kick or bite." he explained.

"No, they are wondrous well conducted, I assure you." I told him. He nodded and took the reins, and we followed our guide into the tavern.

As we seated ourselves, he asked of Abram, "Your brother?"

"I am his guardian. Abram, your courtesy please to....?"

"John Jones." said our melancholy friend. Abram bowed but was told, "No, young master. I am not gentry. Be covered, I pray."

"Well, sir, our policy is to treat all men and womankind alike, as courteously as we may."

"A good notion," said John Jones, "and one that does you and your young rip roaring blade here much credit. I am a tailor's son and a Welshman from Pembroke in this town. I served Sir Richard as a musketeer. And he is escaped to Oxford and as we hear unfairly imprisoned there. Waller, who if you please only stayed three weeks, left neither sight nor sound of a garrison behind him. We wait for the King's commissioner to order us. Tapster, three pints of your best ! None of your belly vengeance, mind you! or I'll remove your liver and toast it on the fire!"

The tapster grinned broadly and set before us three pewter mugs of golden liquor. I confess although I had drunk cider before, this was the most fragrant, delicate brew I had ever tasted. When I told John Jones that my mother whose maiden name was Nerys Jones had also been from Pembroke, his pleasure in my company knew no bounds.

"So, come then, what of Rupert? Will he pardon poor Richard Cave, a good man, beset with more problems than a man should ever have to carry?"

I told him of my friendship with Rupert and even showed him the miniature bearing his likeness, and we ordered another pint of the miraculous nectar. I did not tell him of the fact that I had cured his grievously burnt bum but I did speak of his indebtedness to me in that I had rescued two miners from death in one of the tunnels, dug to assail Lichfield Close from below. After I had told him of my underground escapade and how Lord Digby was all for earthing us up in the tunnel to save the cost of burial, I felt thirsty again and asked for another pint of the wondrous supernaculum.

"Oh, aye, and we are of a height, and can speak eye to eye."

"A letter to him describing Richard Cave's dilemmas would greatly assist the poor man. Would you write such a letter to the Prince, Tomas, bach?" asked my newfound Welsh kinsman.

I suddenly found that I was having difficulty remaining awake. My eyelids sought each other. I looked at Abram. He was smiling gently but was in fact fast asleep on his stool.

"I will gladly write such a letter but I think we must first find lodgings, Master Jones. Do you know of a hostelry?"

He recommended one close by, and I heaved Abram to his feet and arranged to meet John Jones in the morning. As I pushed Abram up the stairs of an old inn near the bridge over the Wye, my father suddenly spoke in my head, "Remember, son Tom, there are only two dangers to fear in the county of Hereford, bulls and cider. You can never predict how they will deport themselves. As for the inhabitants, they are monstrous peaceable folk…. as long as you do not wake them up."

I was laughing at my father's jest, as I fell asleep without even untrussing. In the morning, although I had slept well, I was suffering from a feeling of tenderness and fragility around my brain, and caused consternation when we came down and I asked for hot water with camomile. The landlady complied with my request but told me, "Why, young sir, you wasn't dronk, just something starry-eyed and naught to eat neither. What will you and your brother have to break your fast? There's chitterlings, tripe and bacon. Does that suit?" Abram nodded vigorously, but my stomach on hearing of this dish seemed to acquire a life of its own and made as if to cast up my accounts.

"Could I have simple bread and honey if that does not put you out, mistress." I asked politely, leaning on the door post.

"Why, young sir, 'tis all the same like Tantrom Bolus!", and she bustled away.

"Who is that?" Abram whispered.

"I don't know," I replied, "and as long as he doesn't make me drink cider again, he can be the devil for all I care!" I lurched out the door of the inn, thinking I needed to "whip the cat", as the common sort express it when they are speaking of vomiting, but a few breaths of Hereford, cabbage-scented fresh air, dissuaded my innards from vacating themselves upon the cobbles. I straightened myself, and resumed my habitual air of dignified control. I paid our shot after Abram had made short work of his dish of chitterlings and we went in search of our new friend.

John Jones was lodged in the castle with about twenty musketeers, waiting for word as to who should govern the town. There were another forty or so Royalist troopers quartered hereabouts. He had not wasted time and furnished me with parchment and quill.

"The difficulty was Sir Richard was faced with great Lords aplenty none of whom would decide what was best to do, mind. Though we've heard that Colonel Henry Lingen is now High Sheriff of the County again and has told us to bide here. But Devil of use were any of 'em to poor Sir Richard." He launched himself into his explanation, surrounded by his fellows, who applauded and encouraged him throughout his diatribe.

"So he, with Prince Maurice's sanction as he thought, in the face of Waller bearing down like a savage wolf on the Hereford sheep took command of the surrender for it could be naught else. Waller had two thousand, five hundred armed men. Sir Richard, a good commander who cares for his men, would not have us massacred, see, so he sent us away. If the Hereford fellows had done aught to protect themselves, he might have thought about letting us stay to defend the town, but it was certain sure these calf lollies wasn't vexed at all about having the Parliament men here. And then after eating everything there was in this Castle, the traitors turned about and left… May 18th that was last week, if you please. And we crept back from the Black Mountains where we had hid out. And Waller sent all the great lords hereabouts who couldn't decide what to do, to kick their heels in Gloucester Gaol, where no doubt they'll find it marvellous easy to come to a decision, except there, no-one gives an English fart. But Sir Richard escaped to Oxford at the start of Waller's occupancy and as we hear was arrested for treason."

"Treason?" I asked "How so?"

"I suppose because he did not sacrifice his boys as he used to call us. What point or purpose to send the sixty of us to certain death, see?"

I agreed and began to write.

"Your Royal Highness, Tom Fletcher your surgeon from Lichfield greets you, trusting you are in good health. I am presently in Hereford come to enquire about certain rents, sequestered unjustly. I am enjoined by one John Jones, musketeer in the service of Sir Richard Cave to write on his commander's behalf, and to explain, though Sir Richard was something lacking in birth, money and lands himself, yet he was surrounded by great ones, who could not decide how best to encourage the Hereford citizens to fight for their town, nor how best to defend it from Sir William Waller, who has swept all before him. Sir Richard judged it best not to sacrifice his good loyal troopers, (and Your Highness will I am sure be graciously pleased to accept, sixty musketeers against two thousand and five hundred is not good odds). Sir Richard's troop is all returned as Waller is gone on the 18th of May and the good Hereford citizens scarce noticed Waller's advent nor his departure, so all is as it was, and Henry Lingen is again appointed County Sheriff but there lacks a King's Commissioner here to order all in this city to good effect. Such an one may at this present enter unmolested as did, but yesterday, your grateful and humble servant, who ever holds you in the highest regard, Tom Fletcher. My humble duty to your highness. I add my direction in Worcester, should I ever be required to perform any further services for my Royal Patient." Perhaps that reminder that I had cured his burnt bum was something saucy but I judged that Rupert would not take offence.

I read out my letter to John Jones who drew in his breath.

"That is excellent well scribed, Tommy, bach. You have said all that needed saying. Indeed, I could not have done it better myself."

"You never said truer word than that, John Jones, for you can hardly write at all, see, you poxy pricklouse." said one of his friends, possibly with more truth than courtesy.

"So if I now write to the future Governor whoever he may be, will you present him with my letter when he finally arrives?" I asked them tentatively. They agreed whole-heartedly so I set to and wrote to whoever might hold the high office to ask his tax collectors to forbear from sequestering my money on my farms, as I did not support Parliament. I then added a postscript to the Prince explaining further my presence in Hereford and asking him to mention to the new Governor that my rents had been unfairly purloined.

"So, Abram, shall we find Sir John and Lady Mary? I entreat you, gentlemen, have a care for yourselves. These wars bring grievous times to us all. If God looks on, I pray that he will bless you all!"

I pronounced these sentiments to everyone within hearing, remembering my Welsh mother told me that Welshmen love an orator and a spokesman, and that they were not like the mealy mouthed English who would as soon deal in blows as words. The musketeers thanked me handsomely and John Jones was all for tasting more cider with me and his fellows. I had learned my lesson, however and asked to be directed to a baker's so that we could furnish ourselves with new rolls, to munch as we journeyed. John advised us to leave by Eign Gate and walked with us as we led the horses hither. After about two miles, we were to strike a track north west and find a village called Weobley where we would find good beds and even better food he promised. Then we must go North and pass an old battlefield of the Civil Wars of two hundred years ago.

"I would not advise that you lodge there, though Tom, bach," he told me. "Terrible sounds still come from there. But Wigmore that you seek, is but a short six miles from the killing ground."

I thanked him and told him if I ever sought out my mother's people in Pembroke, I would look for him. He in his turn was determined that he would find me should he come to Worcester. Abram, like a gentleman borne, thanked him for introducing him to cider. John clapped him on the shoulder and made a step for him to mount and told him, he was "a true brother of the Blade". We clattered through the gate, waving and calling Farewell. And off we rode through the fair Herefordshire country whence my orphaned grandmother, Elizabeth Lloyd, had travelled to Worcester to marry my father's father, nearly sixty years before. My grandfather Piers Fletcher, Master Butcher of Worcester, had travelled to Wigmore to take possession of beef cattle, Welsh blacks for slaughter. But his heart, in his turn, had been slain by pretty Liza. The men of my family married for love, not money. "A sprightly lad can always make money," my father had told me. "Spare yourself the Hell of a rich scold!" My mother had been penniless and so was Phoebe, I reflected, and wished she were there with us to enjoy the hawthorn blossom, bridal white in every hedge.

As we rode at first there were glimpses of the Wye through apple orchards and gardens on our left. But then we found our path divided and we took the right fork into a wooded country of hills and lush meadows. We came towards Weobley at about two after noon. The square church tower with its battlements and steeple looked in good repair, but the old castle lay in ruins. As we approached, a team of labourers called off their work of breaking and cleaning its old stones.

The innkeeper of the Salutation seemed delighted to see us. My impression was that few travellers now sought his custom though he was at pains to tell us that Weobley had seen much action and liveliness in centuries past, being one of the settlements that had seen hostility between England and Wales. He had much to say of Owain Glendower, a prince who had striven to free Wales of English tyranny and had largely succeeded.

"For what were the Tudor Kings and Queens if not good Welsh stock?" he asked as we sat under the apple boughs in the May sun, eating his strong cheese and even stronger onions. I had told him of my farm near Wigmore, and of my grandmother, Elizabeth Lloyd and he told me that there were Lloyds "aplenty in these parts. Be you coochin here then, master?" Abram had found some companions and was joining in some races and contests on the village green, and I was loathe to disturb his pleasure by suggesting that we pressed onwards. And indeed the village was so pleasant, the sun so warm, my seat under the trees so well placed that I reflected lazily that we could pass the old battlefield in the morning's light and be at Wigmore by midday. So I agreed that we would "cooch" at his good inn and would take our supper there, at which he left me to prepare beds and a meal of beef and white beans saying he was "at the arse of the moon with his work." And I dozed the afternoon away.

After we had supped the old gaffers crowded the inn to hear of the outside world.

"How does the King?" one asked me.

"Well enough," I told them. "He is drawing his armies to Oxford as I hear. But there are many men, able and clever who are against him and are with the Parliament. One such, Sir William Waller, even now took Hereford, and stayed there for three weeks."

"Well, master, there ain't much to keep 'im there. Hereford folk.... They're all in with the loaves and out with the cakes! They'm all hell and no notion!" said one wise old Weobley grandfather.

"Ah, the men! You'm right there!" cried another, "But the women! Now they'm birds of a different feather. Not the least simony, the wenches! Sharp as scythes, the lot of them!"

"Your young boy chap!" said the first to me, "He'm a reeksy young feller. The both of you from beyond his Knob are you?"

"Grandmother was a Lloyd.... from Wigmore way ", put in the innkeeper.

"But these two are the both beyond mountains Brecon way, ent you, boys?"

It seemed easiest to agree. And I was half Welsh.

In the morning the fine weather held and we set off with a good will. An old labourer hedging showed us where the battlefield was and told us gleefully that when the owner tried to plough it, he found "it had already been sown with skulls aplenty, what kept a-rearin' up."

We rode past as swiftly as we might, given the stony track. Three miles on we crossed a sparkling river that a milkmaid told me was the Lugg, and then came at last to the village of Wigmore. Sir

Nicholas had named the farms for himself when Dame Alice had brought them to him as her jointure. The one near Wigmore was Knowles Croft and the one a few miles upriver he named Knowles Mead. (He was not known for his modesty but was a good generous husband, father and alderman for all that.)

We were advised to turn back two hundred paces and then ascend into the pastures slightly south west of Wigmore and there nestling in the orchards on the side of the hills that flanked the border with Wales was one of my farms. Two young dogs came running out to greet us, barking to warn us that they were fierce enemies, but with tails wagging at the same time to tell us that if we chose to find them a titbit they would be our closest friends. The farmer appeared round the corner of the barn and called them off. He was not disposed to welcome us however.

"Get off my land!", he roared "Or I'll set all the dogs on you!" There was a frenzied barking from one of the outbuildings. It seemed the two who had greeted us were but the pups.

I am not over-fond of dogs but felt it did not accord well with my dignity to be intimidated by a tenant. So I dismounted and came politely towards him, holding out my hand.

"Good day, Master Holdsworth. I am Doctor Thomas Fletcher of Worcester. I have been gifted these lands by my cousin Ben Knowles and have travelled here on receipt of your letter to know how you and your people do in these troubled times."

He looked at me keenly for a moment and then allowed a thin smile to lighten his grim expression. "Well, I'll go to Hanover!" he said. "I'd never have thought my letter would have fetched you hither, Sir. But I suppose you will want to know how your inheritance flourishes, specially after they tax-gatherers for the King have purloined your rents."

"Something of that," I agreed, pleasantly, "But mainly I would wish to know that all is well with my tenants and that all your household are healthy and well treated."

He frowned. "Well treated?" A woman I presumed was his wife came out, with four or five young maids. They curtseyed and I motioned Abram off his mount, to return the courtesy. The farmer said again "Well treated?" and then began to beat a sheet of metal with a stick. The ringing sound brought two men from the nearby orchard where they had been tending the trees and then more fellows appeared, clearly from fields near at hand.

"Come now, boys!" said the farmer. "This is Master Fletcher, who owns the land you plough and sow. He is come to see his property, to see that all is well with his money, no doubt."

"No, Sir." I told him, something rattled. "You mistake me. I have travelled much in the Midlands, as a doctor in these Wars, sometimes against my will, and I have seen that where men labour on the farms of great men, they are often treated little better than slaves. But yeomen and tenant farmers like yourself have a better notion as to the value of the men who grow our food. I have come to ensure that those who are employed here, in my name, are given fair treatment. That is all."

At this point Mistress Holdsworth came forward. "Master Fletcher," she said politely "Will you not enter the house and sit with your brother and take refreshment?"

"Willingly, Mistress," I said bowing low, "I meant no harm, no interference, I assure you. I have come here merely to see if there are wrongs to be righted. I am anxious that those who work for me are contented in their work."

There was a murmuring amongst the men and girls and one of them was pushed forward. "We're well contented, Master," he told me, "in all but one thing and that don't matter much, nohow. We'm happy as pigs in sh…. the midden, here sir, good beds, good vittles, good cider. And the Master don't hold with givin' us a taste o'knave's grease. He ent never raised a hand to none of us. But on the Sabbath, Master," and he turned to Farmer Holdsworth. "We're all glad to go along to St. Michaels in Lingen, Master and Mistress, in the morn like. The walk there is not irksome, leastways not in the summer. But we would like after that to have our own time and not to have to listen to no Book reading all afternoon… The Lord himself rested on the Sabbath and we would like to rest then as we wish. But it don't matter, nohow," he went on, turning back to me, "if you agrees with Master Holdsworth here that we must heed the Good Book, Sabbath afternoon as well as in the morn."

Here was a dilemma for me! My father had never made me attend Church. He had loved Matins and Evensong in the Cathedral and I used to go with him for the love of the words and music and for the love of the building. But there had been no hint of divine will in the manner of his death, nor as far as I could see, in any aspect of the Civil Wars that plagued us.

I sought more time. "What manner of church service is held in Lingen?" I asked. Some of the men sighed and one or two of the girls raised their eyes heavenward to indicate extreme tediousness. Master Holdsworth replied.

"Tis a godly minister who preaches sensible religion, his texts based often on the words of the prophets. There is no Laudian pomposity or meaningless ritual. Sometimes these here young sinners has the benefit of his oration for two hours or more."

"But dear husband," put in Mistress Holdsworth, "when he overpreaches himself, the meal I and my girls have prepared and left to simmer is spoilt. Surely the Almighty does not wish good vittles to be ruined, specially on the Sabbath."

There was a murmur of agreement. I reflected that "meaningless ritual" did contain within itself the preordained prospect of a timely ending. Nunc dimitis are often very welcome words.

"These young men and women do you credit, Master Holdsworth," I said finally, "You are indeed a virtuous steward. By your charitable and worthy example, I would hazard the view that the Sabbath service in the morn serves all here very well, and that there is no further need of religious readings later in the day. You yourself are their yardstick. What is the proverb? Good wine needs no bush. Believe me, Sir, your own godliness is the best lesson these young people can absorb. They need no other."

"And perhaps Master Fletcher," put in the farmer's wife, "two or three of my girls might remain in the kitchen by rote every Sunday so that the meat does not dry up and harden on the spit."

"An excellent notion, Mistress Holdsworth!" I said gratefully. All looked to the farmer.

"Very well," he said reluctantly at last, "Of late I notice I have read myself into a quinsy and also many of the boys seem to be unable to stay awake while I read."

"And that of course is because they have worked for you so well throughout the week. These seem excellent young workers, Farmer Holdsworth, healthy, clever and respectful. A credit to you, on my word."

And at that Mistress Holdsworth insisted that we went in to taste her chicken stew. I asked for small beer or water from the well, although she offered her own cider.

"And sorry I am that I cannot ask you to bide here the night. Every inch is taken up by these maids and men." she explained. "Though they are good labourers all."

I told her that I had to make for Presteigne to Knowles Mead Farm and asked where we might stay. She pondered for a moment. "You would do best to go to Knighton where there is a good inn, and where they will be mortal happy to see travellers. Believe me, Sir, since these Wars began, everyone is afeared to leave home. The good lady of Brampton is much troubled by thefts and marauders. These so called King's Men, tax gatherers who took your rents, claimed they serve Sir Fitzwilliam Coningsby, and run rampant over the country."

"And yet, as I heard but two days ago in Hereford, Sir Fitzwilliam is taken prisoner to Gloucester, Mistress. Perhaps these so called tax gatherers are now independent of any governance."

"At least the wretches left us with our goods intact. I have heard of Parliament men stealing the very pans off the fire," she said in shocked tones

I told her of being mistaken for a thieving trooper in Henley when I was trying to boil water to complete the delivery of a baby. "For as I take it, mistress," and I was thinking aloud, "These Train Band captains started from London with men and weapons but carrying nothing for them to cook their food, so cooking pots to stew a rabbit over a fire now have twice their value."

"Indeed I have heard of many such thefts even around these parts." Then she said one word that I had heard my dear little bride say when provoked and inflamed by the behaviour of us inferior beings. "Men!" she said, and put a world of frustration into the syllable.

"Yes, mistress!" I said humbly, and she was immediately all apologies.

"Oh, dear sir, I did not mean.... Forgive me.... You are a most good-hearted youth, rich young heir as you are, to come here to ensure the men and maids prosper. And I have heard lamentable tales about beatings and starvation, not in these parts, praise be, but around Ludlow. The evil roisterers come hence from time to time to take up such lads as they intend shall fight for the King."

"Do you then support Parliament, mistress? You may speak freely to me." I promised her, "I strive to retain my neutrality. A good man told me after Powick Bridge that when the wars were over, 'twould be a good thing to have as little on my conscience as I could contrive."

"My man does not like Laud's sanctions, and wishes the King would come to his senses, but I know he would never raise his hand against his sovereign."

"I think we are in accord there, mistress," I told her, "and now I must take my young fellow here and find us lodging."

She apologised again for their lack of room, gave me some barley cakes and elderflower wine and curtseyed as we went our way. The farmer walked with us back to the track through his orchards.

"Sorry I am, you heard the rough edge of my tongue, but in these trying times, we cannot be too careful," he told me.

"My dear Master Peter," I said, smiling like a brewer's horse, "Your caution does you credit, indeed it does, good sir! I am most gratified that all is well with you. I pray you, write to me again, should you need me."

He thanked me and directed me to Knighton and we set off, I chewing a barley cake and Abram trying to get me to sing, and laughing inordinately at my efforts as my mouth was grossly full. In Wigmore, some children playing by the road, asked Abram about his horse. One little maid pleaded for a ride, and as her mother looked on and nodded, Abram chivalrously dismounted and placed her on the saddle and led Sir John round the village green, as she shrieked and chortled and gazed down on her fellows like a miniature queen. I bethought me that perhaps her mother might know if there was a swifter way to Knighton over the fields. She pointed out a field path, telling me, "'Twill bring you to Brampton and that's half way house to Knighton as all the world knows."

We rode through a wooded pleasant country, with sparkling streams, hiding in narrow valleys. We passed a small hamlet where dogs barked at our progress and children screamed but no-one challenged us and then we saw rearing up a large imposing castle. We skirted it and found our way past one or two cottages where roses were beginning to scent the air. We found our way easily back onto the more frequented track which I judged was the way from Ludlow to Knighton, and turned to the left. As we did so, we became aware of a confused shouting up ahead. Five horses had been tethered to some apple trees near the track where we emerged.

My instinct ever that of a coward was to bide quiet until all discord had faded, but Abram was made of a braver mettle, and before I could advise caution he had spurred Sir John on to the bend in the road where he paused and beckoned me. Lady Mary sedately picked her way to the corner and we surveyed a shameful scene.

Five troopers on foot were shouting insults to a woman standing with her back to them in the door of a cottage. She was hammering on the door and pleading to be admitted, to escape their ridicule. One of them, younger than the rest, screamed out: "Roundhead bitch!" The woman wore a black cloak with the hood drawn up over her head and as we watched, one of the men picked up a clod of earth and flung it at her back. She collapsed onto the step, and cried out again "Master Paine, Good Mistress Paine! I pray you. Let me enter! For my life!" But the door remained obdurate and the abuse continued.

There was naught for it. We drew our swords and cantered the few yards along the track.

"Well, masters!" I cried out "What is this? I was at Edgehill where many good men died. Are you now commanded to threaten women in these Wars?"

They wheeled round and gaped at us. In that moment I had the sense that this was the second time I had seen men abuse women in the last weeks, not that Dodgeson's boys could be termed men. What had happened to manners and the chivalry of daily life?

I voiced this thought, using the shocked silence our sudden appearance had caused. "Because as Englishmen we would seem to be irrevocably at odds, have we lost that sense of care and tenderness all men should have for womankind?"

One of the older men looked somewhat shamefaced, but another cried out, "Why, sir, who are you that you dare to teach us good conduct?"

I had learnt that when in doubt as to your reception by strangers, lying preserves a whole skin. I began truthfully but lapsed into fantasy. I had Abram's safety to think of.

"Who am I, Sir? I am Prince Rupert's doctor, but lately come from Lichfield where I left that town in the hands of Lord Harry Hastings. And may I tell you, good sirs, both those noble lords would think scorn to abuse a lady of whatever persuasion. Now, sirs, who are you? Are those your horses in the crook of the road above there? I came but lately from Wigmore where a troop of Waller's were lodged whom he has ordered to scour this county of Royalist tax gatherers. I am advised they are coming this way, and so I came across country to avoid the rascals. I would look to your horses."

They needed no second warning, but took to their heels and were running and stumbling up the track. I helped the lady to her feet. She immediately told us, "I live not five hundred yards from here. Could I ask to mount alongside your boy here and we will be safe home in three minutes? Lest they return!"

She was clearly a woman who thought swiftly and directly. As we set off westwards, the cottage door opened, and a man and woman stood there. "I ask your pardon, my lady," called out the man.

"No matter!" she called back, and then so only Abram and I could hear, "You lily-livered knave!"

She directed us off the track and we found ourselves skirting the great walls of the castle we had seen as we had ridden through the fields not ten minutes before. A moment later we were riding up to a gate-house, set between two stout round towers. As we rode through past an astonished porter, she cried out, "Lock all fast, Aston, and drop the portcullis."

Abram craned round to watch the great grid of antiquated metal clash down. I heard it fall with something of a feeling of dread. The last time I had heard that sound, it had presaged the end of my freedom in Lichfield for some days... nay, weeks, for after the first siege, John Gell had kept me mewed up in the Hartshorn Inn, tending his wounded Derbyshire troopers.

We trotted into a courtyard where two boys ran to hold the horses and lead them to the blocks. A stout little man bustled out and began immediately scolding our hostess.

"My lady, what is this? What are you about? Who are these sturdy wayfarers? How comes it you consort with Paynims? How often have I pleaded with you, not to walk about your village? My lady, it is not safe, not safe at all!"

"Silence, Nat!" she snapped. "I do not know who these young men are, but I assure you they were sent by the Almighty to effect my preservation! If I believed in angels, such they would be! This way, gentlemen." And she led us to a long gallery where two young girls were playing hopscotch.

"Dolly! Meg! Ask cook for refreshment! At once please! And what is this on the floor? Chalk marks, by my troth!" She feigned outrage, which the girls took as true annoyance, but which when she turned to us as they scampered out, we could see was a false vexation, for her eyes danced and she laughed gently and indulgently. When she smiled, she was beautiful, no doubt of it.

"Mistress, may we know who you are, and where we are?" I asked.

"Lady Brilliana Harley of Brampton Bryan,"she said simply.

"The lady of Brampton!" I said aloud, remembering Peter Holdsworth's letter and his wife's comment that "the Lady" had been sorely vexed by thieves and marauders.

"I think I am sometimes known as that," she said demurely, "when I am not called a Roundhead bitch."

"That was unpardonable, your Ladyship!" I said, a smooth subtle courtier to the life. "The varlet should be whipped within an inch of his misbegotten life."

"But you then support the cause of His Majesty? You must, I suppose, having come from the Prince in Lichfield."

I looked at Abram. How was I to begin our tragic stories? I decided I must tell the truth and explained that as Essex had hanged my father, I could not in all conscience espouse his cause, but that I had doctored for Parliament at Edgehill and that a dear friend, a Captain for Parliament, Robert Burghill, had saved my life. Of Abram I told her all that I could and that he too had lost a parent in these wars. His mother had died from inhaling smoke when Rupert's men had fired Birmingham, only two days after Ambram's father had died from a fatal chest ailment..

"And I am here in this part of Herefordshire to see after my farms. But as they could not accommodate us at Knowles Croft, we have had to deviate for Knighton to find lodging."

"No need of that, good sir. I insist that you remain here this night. And... Abram... may I call you? For you I have a surprise from that same gallant little town where you lost so much. This way, if you please."

We looked at each other in wonder and bemused as lambs in a

henhouse followed her. I think we would have followed her to perdition, her smile was so infectious, even though she was a grave and serious lady. She led the way along the gallery and into a wide corridor. She turned a corner at the end and opened the door of a solar or retiring room, where several ladies sat sewing. All rose but one at the sight of Lady Brilliana, but she motioned them to be seated and moved to the woman who sat a little apart, who had not moved at our entrance but who gazed out of the window.

It was Mistress Tillam, the wife of the Birmingham surgeon who had been cruelly butchered as he stood at his door, helping another whom the Royalists had wounded. Abram knelt beside her and took her hand. For a moment she could not believe whom she saw and then leapt to her feet and embraced him.

"And Doctor Tom, on my life! I am rejoiced to see you both." She clasped my hands and began to weep. I remembered that on that terrible day she had been distraught when we came to her house and had wept over her husband at first but as the time had passed had seemed to recover and had helped me and the Bryces. We had treated the burns of many citizens. Now she wept as if she would never stop. There seemed naught else to do but hold her in our arms, whilst the other women looked on amazed.

Lady Brilliana stepped away from us. "This is wholesome indeed, Mistress Wright," she said to one of the women who had risen in concern. "This is the flood that will nurture the arid soil of her sorrow. She will be better after this. Or if not better, she will speak more and live more fully with us."

After Jessica Tillam had calmed somewhat and had seated herself, still holding Abram's hand, I asked Lady Brilliana how she had known we knew her.

"When she first came she told of the young doctor from Worcester, and the brown youth from Birmingham who had helped her tend the godly citizens after Rupert's ravages. After his men had murdered her dear husband. I take it you knew him."

"That I did, and an excellent physician, he was, sensible and merciful. And now I remember Mistress Tillam told us that she would return to her family in Herefordshire. Her husband's death was the most grievous sorrow for her. He was a loving spouse and a clever doctor."

She said in an undertone, "Possibly better than this poltroon I must entertain, who cares only for his reputation."

"But, my dear lady," I ventured to say, "Perhaps he is right. If Royalist troops ride out over the country, you should not hazard your life, outside your castle."

She sighed. "How then am I to feed all these dependants, (and good Doctor Tom, there are near a hundred of them), if I cannot collect my rents? Do you know that Lingen has forbidden the fowler from Wigmore to supply us with ducks or geese? I can send one secretly into Knighton to buy from the butcher there but I must have money. The tradespeople will not give their victuals away upon promises. And I can give you a promise, my good young man. No-one... not honest Roundhead nor curled and powdered lackey of the King, can live upon air."

I agreed. "No, indeed, my lady. But tomorrow I must make for my other farm, Knowles Mead, which is I think upon the road to Presteigne. If you will put me on my way, I will see if my tenant there can supply you with any meat or green stuff."

"Green stuff?" she said wonderingly. "Why would we need that?"

And when we sat down to eat, I understood her puzzled air. Lady Brilliana was an old fashioned lady and kept an old fashioned table of bread and meat. It was a well cooked haunch of venison and good bread made in her own kitchens, she told me proudly, but there was not a trace of green vegetable. I remembered Mistress Hall, with her flawless skin, and her clever husband's posset of scurvy grass, and looked across at Dorothy and Meg, her young daughters. As I surmised, their faces were sadly poxed with blemishes and spots. All the other ladies were pale and something marked, not merely by the small pox either.

"Dear Lady Harley, may I speak to you upon a matter that concerns your health and that of all who are immured with you?"

"Certainly!" she graciously agreed.

"If it concerns our health, my lady, then surely I must be consulted on this matter!" exclaimed Doctor Wright, with something of the outraged turkeycock about his jowls.

"Certainly!" I agreed, echoing Lady Brilliana. "My lady, may we visit your good cook?"

As we neared the kitchens, the smell of cabbage, not stale and malodorous but freshly cooked and wholesome assailed our noses.

The cook, a woman, as round as she was wide but with a skin like a smooth rosy apple, was ladling her cooked cabbage into bowls and encouraging the maids to sit and eat.

"I tell you, maids, and I tell you again. This good green dish will keep your faces as fair as any babes." She turned round and stared at all of us whom she had thought safely at table, but now trooping into her kitchen.

"All is well, good Mistress Jones," said Lady Brilliana. "This good young doctor agrees with you, I fancy."

"Indeed I do, Mistress Jones, but why do you not share your good green cabbage with everyone?"

"Alas! I fear I am to blame in that. It is not a dish I like overmuch," said Lady Brilliana meekly, looking up at me with a winsome guilty air.

"My lady, we are what we eat. This cabbage which your maids eat indespite of themselves will not merely keep their skins from ugly disfigurement but will keep the inner parts of the body working smoothly. I will not enlarge on what I mean other than to say when Shakespeare spoke of the bowels of compassion, he knew that 'twas good to keep those organs well exercised. What other green stuff do you cook for your helpers?" I asked Mistress Jones, who looked both proud and embarrassed in turn.

"Why bless you, young sir, cabbage and cale do well for us throughout the winter and I make these maids drink the water it has been cooked in." I nodded remembering altercations with my mother on this very matter which she had always won through the judicious bribe of a sweetmeat to follow. In fact now, I cannot say I loved cabbage water but I would drink it from choice much to Joan's approval and Roger's distaste.

"And then sir soon there will be peas and beans aplenty. Eaten young they be a marvellous tasty dish and can be dried for the winter, good sir, and me and the maids makes a good dinner from pease pudding if there be not much meat. But then, sir there are all the good leaves that we may grow, salad and spinach, a rare tasty leaf and others that grow wild, rocket, sir, and the leaf with the sweet orange flower, that can be eaten raw, if you please sir and come to no harm in fact 'tis my belief, like cabbage, these leaves makes for good regular digestion, sir, as I think you was a-saying. And then if you have good gloves, nettle soup is a wondrous good potage. Well, sir, look at my maids, if you need proof."

They were a healthy rosy group of girls. They giggled as girls do, but their faces were clear and unblemished with skin like the petals of pink roses. None of them was beautiful like my Phoebe, but they were a wondrous credit to the cook's teaching.

Doctor Wright blustered and threatened me. "This is outrageous, sir!" he cried, "You dare to cast doubt on her ladyship's table."

"Why not, if I need education about what we eat? And Mistress Jones has tried to school me but to no avail," said Lady Brilliana, again with her arch, somewhat flirtatious, expression. "Daughters, I will ensure that from henceforth we shall have faces as clear as these good maids."

"And, my lady, I know an excellent concoction that will swiftly ensure that your girls will attain such clear skins." I told her. "Mistress Tillam, I know that you have skills in the distilling room. May we combine our knowledge and brew such a wholesome beverage? 'Tis scurvy grass and watercress combined, Mistress Jones. 'Tis an excellent receipt."

"May we set about it, my lady?" asked Mistress Tillam.

"Indeed, you may and I thank you heartily for your pains. Mistress Jones, may we gather watercress and scurvygrass from your garden?"

And so we all went out into the gardens beside the moat. It was a calm still evening, with a warm sun still lighting the fresh green willows. The cook brought a basket with her, which she and Mistress Tillam soon filled. The leaves were pounded then by a succession of kitchen maids, and the resultant green mess or matter was placed in a glass alembic. Strangely this mundane domestic task made me feel heartsick for my wife. Phoebe had always been skilled at this art and had acquired even more skills than Joan. She had made this cordial from Master Hall's instructions which I had written down for her, and I had helped her. Now as I helped Mistress Tillam I felt strangely melancholy and bereft without my dear little wife and resolved that tomorrow, after we had seen Knowles Mead we should return home.

But such longing was selfish indeed when compared to poor Jessica Tillam's sad state. It seemed her brother who had been a steward in one of the Harley houses had died. Jessica like her brother had been born with the name Harley and Lady Brilliana had told Jessica that she could view Brampton as her home for as long as she wished.

"And I think," she confided in me as we watched fat green drops chasing down into the quintessence, "I can do a great deal of good here, for these beleaguered souls. At the very least I can reform and revise this still room." She began to cry a little again and then laughed. "I had congealed and crystallised myself, Doctor Tom. My grief was set aside and I had become hard uncaring metal. But now deliquium is in process and I know I can work."

In the morning before we went she sought us out and told me, "I fear for her."

"Do you mean Brilliana?" I asked her.

"She is not strong. She could not sleep. Those devils threw a clod of earth at her and her back is bruised and sore."

I was appalled! I remembered that I had seen them do it and I had done nothing. What sort of physician was I who did not even ask to examine her wound?

"Don't upset yourself," she told me, seeing my stricken face. "She would never have permitted you to doctor her. She has lost no blood. She asked me to dress it for her this morning and I put a soothing unguent on it and she tells me she feels better. She told me she was happy I was here as she did not wish to be doctored by a man. Her modesty forbids it. But she is lamentable thin, Doctor Tom. A breath of wind could destroy her. It is as well I am here, I think. You and Abram jerked me from my lethargy. At least I am useful again."

I promised we would return on our way home if I could find a source of food.

"It matters not how much or how little," Lady Brilliana told me. "You can see there are thrifty housewives here aplenty. All or any meat can be salted down and preserved."

Dr Wright set us on our way. We did not now have to travel to Knighton. In fact we would retrace our steps and pass through the village of Lingen. Was that named for the High Sheriff or the Sheriff for the place, I wondered idly. It was a sweet village with the old church of St Michael and all Angels set in pleasant rolling country. The track wound uphill with the River Lugg sparkling far below in a gorge on our left until we came to an old bridge, where the land flattened out somewhat before us. My farm was set in these meadows with the river meandering close by. Abram wondered if there were fish to catch, worth eating. Although we could see shoals of small minnows, I did not know if there were trout or even salmon in these streams.

My farm was easy to recognize, in a stand of trees, with willows dipping into a duckpond. We could hear the children playing before we saw them. Although there were only six, they made the noise of sixty, lying on the grass, beside the farmyard, playing Jacky Five Stones together. So intent and noisy they were that we were upon them before they were aware. Four of them, girls, all screamed in pretended fear and one of the boys, showing some courage, asked what we wanted. He called the fat old dog that was dozing in the sun at the side of the house.

"Hey, Fang! Here, boy!" Alas, Fang was aptly named for he had but one. He staggered to his feet, ambled over to the boy who had called him and bared his tooth at us. But this effort proved rather too strenuous, for he dropped down again at his little master's feet, panting gently, his long pink tongue protruding.

"What will he do now? Lick us to death?" Abram asked politely.

The little girls began to giggle. The boy who had called the dog tried to silence them, looking at us in fear and at his sisters in irritation. We sat on our horses in the sun, and I wondered how best to reassure our miniature guard, that we meant them no harm.

"Are your parents at home?" I asked at last.

"They've gone to Kington to sell our butter. Rare good butter it is an all! Oh and bacon what Mam's been smoking!"

"But you know what, Master?" piped up another, "That bacon was our old Charlie. He had to go, you know."

"Oh dear," I said, more affected than they would know by this information, "I am sorry. Poor old Charlie!"

The younger boy who had not spoken yet, mused thoughtfully, "He was the king of porkers!"

"Is anyone here to look after you?" I asked

They looked at each other and giggled and the eldest, the boy who had called the dog, told us, "Our Harry looks after us on market day." This provoked another fit of giggling. "Your brother?" They nodded. "Where is he then?"

More giggling. Finally one of the girls shouted, "He's with a girl!"

Another held up a penny. "He gives us money, not to tell!"

I judged it politick to ensure that Harry was at the very least informed of our arrival. "Could you tell him that Master Thomas Fletcher is here from Worcester? When do your parents come back?"

"After noon," said the elder boy. "I'd best get Harry." He ran off round the corner of the homestead, and one of the girls assumed the role of hostess.

"That's Ned," she said, nodding after her brother. "And this is Frankie, aint you?" she explained poking her remaining brother.

"It is Francis, not Frankie, Moll" he argued, I sensed to little avail.

"I'm Molly, this is Polly. Molly and Polly, see. We're twins. Then this is Essie and this is baby Susan. What's his name?" she asked, pointing to Abram.

He told her, with a bow and a flourish that set them off again. At that moment Ned reappeared, followed by Harry, who was attempting to brush off straw from his shoulders with one hand, and to adjust his breeches with the other.

"Oh, Harry!" cried his sister, running to him, "What will mother say?" She began to pick off the straws.

"Nowt, if you don't tell her, Moll. You all got a penny, mind!" he reminded his sisters with a guilty look at his guests.

"Master Harry, we interrupt your stable cleaning," I said courteously. "I am Tom Fletcher of Worcester. Your parents are my tenants. Will they be long?"

There was a faint jingle of harness and a cart pulled by a young cob, turned into the farmyard.

"Oh, Jesu!" said Harry, under his breath. "That was parlous close!"

I had the strong impression that Mistress Andrews understood all that had taken place on the instant. After I had introduced ourselves, Harry received an ear-blasting for not inviting us into the farm for food and drink before this, and to a lesser degree Ned too came in for a mild reproof, more in sorrow than in anger for his lack of hospitality. I surmised that she had known of Harry's dalliance and would have liked to have caught him, if not in flagrante delicto, in a state of guilty undress that would have justified her suspicions.

"All the butter, all the bacon, sold in the first half an hour," she remarked in triumph. "Now, children, I will reward you for your good behaviour today. A penny each. But what's this, Hester? You already hold a penny. Whence came this?" and she glared at Harry.

"Mistress, I gave them all a penny for sweetmeats when they should be in town." I said quickly. Abram's eyes widened at the lie but he wisely held his peace. Indeed, Mistress Andrews was a woman who inspired respect and awe, but discretion most of all. Her husband who had said little so far, now shook me warmly by the hand and told me how happy he was to see me.

"A letter now to Sir Henry Lingen will solve all misunderstandings. I understand he is the High Sheriff. This is, of course, Sir, provided that you hold fast to the loyal conviction that the King should rule without let or hindrance and that Parliament is subject to his will." He looked at me speculatively, a nervous smile playing around his lips.

"Certainly!" I said with vigour. Where did my allegiance lie at that moment? It lay with the excellent aroma of stew that Mistress Andrews had already prepared and was heating over the fire in the kitchen. Molly and Polly ran to assist her, Harry took our horses and Ned bowed us into the house.

I thought that it must have always been a farm, as it was one of those dwellings that in the summer seem to have grown out of the ground. Open doors letting in the sun, scents of flowers, the perfume of lavender and herbs, rooms built higgledy-piggledy off other rooms, old polished chairs and tables, uneven floors, small windows with roses now tapping on them outside, as if seeking admittance. I spoke my thought aloud. It was a compliment to the Andrews but the lady saw below my surface meaning.

"Fortunate indeed, the children who grow up in such a happy house," I said thoughtfully.

"Your grandmother, Elizabeth, certainly thought herself fortunate. This was old Joshua Lloyds' place and he was your great-grandfather. My mother used to tell me stories of your grandmother and her sister and how they set all the young men hereabouts by the ears, they were such handsome clever girls. Tall too, like yourself. Mind, they could wind the old man round their fingers. Kate had to go to Worcester with Elizabeth, when your grandfather Pierce Fletcher came a-wooing and would not take No for an answer. And once," she ceased in her task of buttering parsnips, and looked at me, "I saw your father, Amyas. He was brought here by his father to see the old man. Fair like Pierce and well set and a question and then a joke for everything he saw. Why, Master Tom, what have I said? I ask your pardon!" for tears were pouring down my face.

"It is excellent for me to hear tales of my father and his parents," I told her, "It is me who should ask your pardon, as I did not know that there would be anyone here who would know me and mine."

"Joshua Lloyd was my great-grandfather also," she told me, and informed me of a liaison which was something hole in the corner, but after all these years it no longer could cause hurt to anyone, and could now be spoken of freely. "But grieved we were by the news from Master Ben of his uncle Amyas' death. Although Master Ben was a fine young man, it was heart warming for me when this farm and lands are owned again by a Lloyd like yourself, Master Tom."

"And are you then, my cousin?" I asked her.

"Why, bless you, I suppose I am. I was a Lloyd before I married. Third or fourth cousin, maybe, and this brood of ours further off still. But we make our own way. We make our own luck, don't we, Arthur?" she asked her husband. He smiled and whilst we ate, told me something of his own tale, of how his grandfather had been a priest's son, when priests did not have sons, when Mary was Queen. His great grandmother had lived with her child on the edge of starvation for years in the Welsh hills near Ryader, and then they were found and cared for by the errant priest, when Elizabeth ruled that churchmen could marry. "And as well he did find them, for the townsfolk deemed my great-grandmother a witch. She could not learn to live in her husband's house for all that and died there of a wasting fever. My grandfather told me she had not sickened as much as one day, when they lived in the wilds. My grandfather and my father became reeves, working for the lords of Powys. And I brought my scholar's crafts to our marriage, Master Tom. I figure and calculate and we know thereby of an instant if your farm is in profit by the dairy or if we have sustained a loss one year with the pigs. And indeed all has been in profit for my wife is a worker of miracles....."

But suddenly Harry came running into the House.

"Mother, that madman is shooting at the birds again. As Master Fletcher is here, could his trespass on the farm not be addressed? The more he goes unchallenged, the more he will think he has rights over these meadows."

I had not expected Harry to be so eloquent. I must have looked questioningly one from the other for Mistress Andrews told me, "'Tis some jumped up Fly-by-Night farmer who has bought the land on the hillside yonder. He comes down with his men to shoot the birds with cross-bows."

"What birds?" I asked politely.

Husband and wife looked at each other. "The birds in the water meadows, Master Tom. We do not like him doing so. 'Tis not for food but for sport and we deem it profligate," said Master Andrews.

Polly, a pale sweet girl overshadowed by her twin, suddenly burst forth. "It's horrible! I hate that man. It's bad enough to kill things and I know we have to eat but he cannot eat snipe and baby grouse. He just kills them to count them. Mother, why don't you stop him?"

Men were shouting and dogs barking continuously. Mistress Andrews sighed "Well, Master Tom, maybe we should have objected but we did not know and still do not know your views on the matter." The shouts grew even louder, and a flight of frightened geese swooped over the farmyard, cackling in terror.

Realisation was slowly dawning. "Why, who owns the water meadows?"

They looked at me in surprise. "Why certainly, you do, Sir." said Harry, and all nodded. Mistress Andrews explained further. "He thinks because he owns his land and we are mere tenants that he may rule our lives. He calls himself Squire Siddall. A Squire needs a Knight to serve but he is a man of no family. He thinks his money gives him rights over others."

I thought for a moment. Money gave one power to buy goods or labour, but not rights over another man's freedom or property. Master Siddall had no rights over my water meadows nor over the birds that chose to roost there.

"Little Mistress Polly, pray do not weep. Forget this man who deems himself a squire. Today you have gained two true squires from the old books who will do your bidding and right the wrongs of your birds. Come Abram. Good Master and Mistress Andrews, we will return."

We gained the track again and rode perhaps, three hundred yards to a point where the cultivated land of the farmstead ended and the marshlands began. Someone, my great grandfather, perhaps, had built a stout stone wall that followed the lie of the land and to an extent, enclosed and protected the farmhouse from possible flooding. A deep ditch, dry today, followed the line of the wall. The meadows glistened with sheets of water on which hundreds of birds floated. As each arrow sped through the air, they stirred and sometimes flew upwards, unsettled and afraid but then settled again. Seven horses were tethered to a fence across the water. The hunters had moved some way round to the west. They were accompanied by a pack of spaniels which had been trained to retrieve the dead carcasses.

As we trotted along the high dry path on the edge of the wetlands, behind the hunters who were unaware of our approach, we saw the sorriest of sights. The dead birds, mainly wild ducks and geese, were piled into heaps beside the path. Their heads hung limp and slack in death. I felt my stomach churn. Of course I had seen dead birds in the fowler's store in Worcester, their necks wrung, but these poor creatures had been shot needlessly for sport, not for the table.

I pondered how best to challenge Siddall. He was on my land without my permission. He was killing my birds and effectively stealing them. One or two large baskets lay by the path, already full to overflowing with the carcasses. I dismounted and gave Lady Mary's reins to Abram whom I ordered to wait at this point and urged him to remain out of sight in the ditch. I went on alone on foot to defy six or seven armed men. There may have been more stupid reckless youths in the Welsh Marches on that day but I have yet to hear of them.

"Master Siddall!" I called out, "May I speak with you, please, Sir?"

Three men continued to shoot, but two of them lowered their bows and regarded me with a puzzled air.

"That's the Squire, you're questioning, my boy. Best be civil, eh?" One of them, an elderly man warned me, kindly enough, but I did not know how my request was uncivil.

Siddall's continued to aim his bow, another arrow sped through the air and a large goose tried to alight but dropped, fell and died, the bolt protruding from its white breast... He slowly became aware that his companions had ceased to fire and lowered his cross-bow. He drew a pistol from its holster and walked carefully towards us, his bow on his shoulder, and his pistol pointing directly at my heart, although I could swear that organ had dropped swiftly through my person and was now in the region of my knees.

As he took his ponderous steps in my direction, I had a vision of a hundred years hence. I saw Harry Andrews' grandson, a man grown, with a team of farm labourers, intent on draining away this area of my water meadows. Water flowed from this same place, and there I lay, my skull grinning at the indifferent sky, with Master Siddall's bullets, grimly rattling amongst my ribs.

"Good day to you, Master Siddall," I managed to say, "I thought it was only courtesy as I have travelled here from Worcester to welcome you, and your hunters onto my land."

He looked at me angrily. "What? Your land?"

"Yes, certainly," I went on, gaining a little courage, "These water meadows are part of the large parcel of land of Knowles Mead, my farm, behind me here. The house was enlarged by my great-grandfather Joshua Lloyd. My land extends to the base of the hill yonder. I understand you have recently bought property on the hillside there and felt it only gracious to welcome you to these Marcher lands and to my water meadows today."

"The devil you did, you upstart!" he snarled, "Where's your proof that these lakes are yours?"

"My deed is in the farmhouse behind us," I said smoothly, lying in my teeth, "Ben Knowles, my cousin gifted all his lands in Herefordshire to me only last year. You are welcome to end your sport now and accompany me to see it and to take refreshment with your neighbours, Master and Mistress Andrews, my excellent tenants."

"I'll see you hanged first, you bastard!" he shouted. His face had assumed the purple hue of an angry thunder cloud and as a doctor I began to fear for his future health but as he cocked his pistol and took aim, I began to fear even more for mine!

"Squire, have a care here!" said the older man. "Whether 'tis true or not, best not to draw more writs upon yourself!"

"I also own Knowles Croft near Wigmore," I went on, in the hope that by listing my possessions I might impress him and curb his wrath, "and manufactuaries in Staffordshire and North Worcestershire as well as two great houses in Worcester itself. But I am not a squire like yourself. I serve no-one. Pray, which knight do you serve?"

Would I never learn? Having gained some sort of moral ascendancy over him, why did I now insult him so artfully, and lose my advantage? I know at that moment, he was about to pull the trigger.

A shot rang out. But I did not fall into my watery grave. And it was the younger fowler who had not yet spoken who now clutched his arm and swore, dropping his bow. Five horsemen were galloping towards us under the lee of the wall.

"Renegades!" one screamed "Roundhead traitors! Swear to serve your King or die like dogs!"

It was the five troopers I had tricked in Wigmore. For a moment I thought they had come to avenge themselves on me, but as they hurled abuse at Siddall, his fowlers and servants, I realised they still believed my story.

"Leave him!"another yelled, "Waller's bastards! Henry Lingen will hang you all!"

The fowling party was displaying signs of unease. None were disposed to argue their political convictions in the middle of a marsh and the servants began to walk hastily along the raised path. I guessed that there was another path leading across the marsh some distance away to the field where they had left their horses. The servants began to run and the young fellow who had been winged and whose right arm hung uselessly, ran with them, howling with pain as each step jolted his damaged limb.

"Best leave it for today, Squire!" said the older man following the others. Another shot rang out, whistling perilously close to Master Siddall's purple visage. His mouth had dropped open though whether through surprise or outrage it was hard to say.

"Do you wish to fight for the King, Squire?" I asked insolently. He aimed his pistol at me again and fired but luckily he had lost his aim. The bullet dropped harmlessly into the water, and he turned and began to run heavily after his followers. The horsemen were soon amongst them slashing with their swords and at length the hunters had no choice but to turn to their left under the horses' hooves, and make for their mounts through the water on the far side of the wetlands. Two of the horsemen followed but realised the danger quickly enough, and swiftly regained the dry path. We stood and watched the hunters floundering and splashing, amongst the affronted birds, who fluttered round their heads, secure and superior in their natural elements of water and air. At last the hunters, now the hunted, gained the dry ground and ran to their horses. All but Siddall. He was near the further bank but was in water up to his waist and shouting for help, seemingly unable to move forward. With every struggle he seemed to sink deeper.

"Abram!" I shouted, "Bring the horses!" I had caught sight of the causeway two hundred yards away across the marsh. "Well, you will have one recruit if we can save him!" I told the troopers, who were watching Siddall's plight. Two of them were laughing heartlessly but the others seemed concerned to think he could die a watery death.

Abram came up with our horses and I mounted swiftly. "Come on!" I cried to them. "He and his money are more use to you alive! Now is your chance to gather your taxes!"

As we crossed the causeway at a gallop I cried out to Siddall to stand still. There was a pile of brushwood on the bank. Luckily a great stand of willow had lately been pruned, and a long branch still had twigs and leaves at the end. Abram and I pushed it to him, and he caught it easily.

"Try to wrap the twigs round your wrists and arms," I ordered him. But when we tried to pull him out, his screams were terrible to hear. "My feet are caught!" he sobbed, "In wooden planks!"

"Can you go backwards?" I shouted. "See if you can carefully put your feet the way you came."

He seemed to have a little more confidence now the willow trunk united him with the shore, no matter how tentatively. He staggered and put one foot behind him. But the other was still irrevocably caught. He suddenly found an admirable courage. "I could move it with my hands," he announced, took a deep breath and disappeared. We watched in horror as the water churned and bubbled, but then he emerged, with a grin of triumph. "If you pull me now, I'll kick with my feet and...."

A moment later he was staggering up the bank. One ankle was

considerably swollen so flight from the troopers would have been impossible. We left him to their tender mercy as they discussed with him, how much his freedom was worth to the Sheriff and the King.

A good day's hunting for them but for the self-styled Squire his sport became a sad calamity! As the fowl was mine and the baskets lay on my land, I decided that Squire Siddall could rest easier if I as rightful landowner put all to good use. I called in on the Andrews family to bid them Farewell and told her of the piles of fowl that were fresh and could be salted and preserved, if she and her maidservants could collect them. I told her we would take the baskets to the Lady of Brampton who was sore beset to feed her followers, if she had no objection. Like Mistress Holdsworth, she had only praise for the Lady of Brampton and asked me to give her respectful greetings from herself and her husband. I suggested that if perhaps the Lady sent to ask for game from my wetlands, she might be furnished with a modest supply. The Andrews were happy to agree. Then, as we were cousins, she asked leave to kiss and embrace me and Abram also, whom she took to be a relative of Ben's. And so we took our leave.

We each took a brimming pannier and came back to Brampton Bryan not eight hours after we had left it. Again the Lady insisted that we stayed the night. I had hoped she might so ordain it. When she saw the baskets of game, her delight knew no bounds. Next morning she directed us to Leominster, as being the most direct route to Worcester. Mistress Tillam was sad to see us go but seemed happier and more contented with her fate. She and the Lady seemed to have forged a friendship.

The weather had turned and a spiteful wet wind blew in our faces so that we were pleased to be welcomed at the King's Head in Leominster at about four in the afternoon. Next day, the 28th of May we were up betimes and on the road to Bromyard, where we were told there was to be a bear baiting. I allowed Abram to see this hideous sport as his father had always forbidden him to do so and I judged that he was now old enough to make his own choices. However he came to find me after about twenty minutes of the cruel entertainment.

"I understand now why my father did not wish me to see a bear-baiting!" he told me, somewhat pale and thoughtful.

"You understand also perhaps why I never wish to see such an event." I told him. He nodded sagely and we saddled up and trotted up the track through Bromyard Downs.

"Abram, I have not asked you what took place, when the five troopers rode up to you while Siddall was thinking of killing me. What did you say to them?" I asked him.

"I told them, that the bird hunters were Waller's men who wanted you to go and doctor his army." he said simply.

We rode on for some yards.

"Abram," I told him, "Do you know that you saved my life by that quick clever lie?"

"Did I?" he said. We said nothing more until we were trotting over the bridge over the Severn.

Then he spoke. "I would give anything for my father and my mother to be living still, but I am very happy that you have adopted me, Tom."

"Abram," I said, "I too am happy about that, but you are wrong in one small point. I have not adopted you. You have adopted me!" And we were laughing as we rode under the arch of my house on Newport Street.

3

As we dismounted, I was conscious of Joan standing watching us at the kitchen door. I decided that in any event I would be courteous.

"Joan!" I cried, "How do you? Is all well?"

"No, Tom." she said shortly, " I think not. I fear Phoebe is sick."

I stood stock still, unable to move. "She is sick?" I cried. "How? In what way?"

"She began to bleed yesterday somewhat strangely." she told me, "But it may be nothing."

I pushed past her and calling my wife's name rushed into my house. At length I heard her reply faintly. She was still in her bedgown sitting in my aunt's chair. She looked pale and small as she pulled the soft blue velvet around herself.

"Phoebe!" I shouted, "For Jesu's sake! What is the matter?"

"Tom!" she cried "Welcome home!" I kissed her and stroked her chestnut hair. "It is probably naught." she told me "I had thought, dear Tom, that our union might be blessed, as my courses were so late. Then I began to bleed yesterday, so my hopes of a child, scarcely begun, are already over. I think it is the lateness and Joan's anxiety that have made me feel weak and faint."

"Will you go to bed now, sweetheart?" I asked her, preparing to carry her to our room. She smiled at me saucily, but then winced with pain as she attempted to stand.

"I am best left here for now. Tom, have you dined? There are venison collops in a good red wine sauce prepared for you. And the first peas. Joan will serve you, both of you. How does Abram?"

I left her then as she seemed tired and went to find him. He and James and Adam were seated round the kitchen table waiting to eat. Abram was telling them of Lady Brilliana, not eating her cabbage. Adam greeted me with great joy and some relief. It seemed there were rumours, in fact more than rumours, that William Waller wished to pay Worcester a visit, and Sir William Russell was unfortunately gone to Oxford. At that moment Roger came in and laid a paper on the table.

"Armegeddon begins, Sir," he told his father. "Tom, dear friend, how do you? And Abram, how did you like the Hereford cider? Look Tom, Waller threatens to be with us tomorrow. These bills are everywhere."

The paper was a warning that if we allowed Waller free access to our city, he would graciously suffer us to continue our existence unharmed. Any impediment to his access constituted a hindrance to the Great Cause of Parliament and our lives would be forfeit. Roger read it aloud to his father.

"Who distributed these news sheets, then Roger? How came they into the town?" I asked idly. A notion suddenly presented itself. "Oh, sweet Jesu! It's not that caitiff Truscott, I hope."

I peered carefully at the paper. If anything, the printing was not of his high quality. His Dutch grandsire had taught him well, and his print was clear and bold. This was smudged with ink runnels and some letters were impossible to discern.

Adam said sadly, "Was it for this strife, that brave men, like Tyndale, were burned at the stake so we could all read our own English? How heinous that printing should be used to threaten rather than educate."

James scratched his head and said, "I saw men, aye, and women too giving out these papers."

"How looked they?" I asked him.

"Very usual and sober suited. They did not seem ashamed of their task" he told us.

"These Roundheads are excessive cunning at hiding their horns and tails," said Roger, with a wink. "Tom, what of the Dodgeson boys? Should they be left without a guardian in the Garrison?"

"I'll walk up there and see how they are faring after we've dined. They are too young to be at the risk of cannon fire."

Abram announced like a Presbyterian preacher, "Bragging Jacks, who abuse old ladies, should not expect to be treated like gentlemen."

This set us all a-laughing. "Why, Abram, my best pupil" said Adam, "Whence comes this Puritan unforgiving dogma? I hear the Harleys are for Parliament but I do not think Lady Brilliana would have had the time to convert you."

"Has he told you how he saved my life? I tell you this boy is metal to the back!" I clapped his shoulder and proceeded to tell of my stupid foolhardiness in the wetlands. Joan came in from the garden with newly picked peas whilst I was explaining Abram's wit and my imbecility. She asked pleasantly,

"So, Tom, no wild fowl for us? You did not think to bring us any of this Squire's ill-gotten gains?"

"Alas! Joan, I am sorry. Abram, we should have brought a brace of duck for our table at the very least!"

She nodded and smiled and seemed more like her old self.

"We should have brought back some of the cider," said Abram "'Twas a wondrous rascally drink!"

We had a pleasant meal but at the back of my mind I was concerned for my wife. As I went up afterwards to see how she did, Joan followed me into the hall.

"Tom," she began, "this ague of Phoebe's. Shall I prepare a ground ginger potion?"

"An excellent thought," I told her. "You think, do you, it is a menstrual irregularity?"

"She was certainly very late," she told me, disappearing into the kitchen.

Phoebe had put herself back to bed, and was dozing in the late afternoon sunshine that streamed westward into our room. I did not wake her as she looked very peaceful and small, curled up in our great bed, and I was concerned as to what Waller had in store for us. I set off alone for the Garrison. James seemed to be now permanently ensconced with his parents in my house, so Abram was more than happy to devise sporting contests with him and did not seem to want to accompany me. This was healthy and natural but meant that I would lose my companion. I went into the orchard where they were climbing trees and warned them against breaking limbs, both arboreal and human. I noticed that our old wall which separated us from the river bank had been strengthened where it had subsided.

"I'll go then, Abram." I said perhaps with a hint of disappointment. He somersaulted down from the tree he had been exploring, landing upright beside me.

"Shall I come with you, Tom?" he asked politely.

I laughed, sensing his reluctance. "No, no!" I told him, "Stay

Page 62

with James."

I walked out under the arch to Newport Street and swiftly up Merivale. Everywhere, shutters were being hammered into place and housewives were carrying home loaves from the bakers and meat from the butchers. I called in at Fish Street and suggested that we kept back half a bullock and some chickens that Patience had been preparing to sell. An unusual number of customers were demanding meat. Jacky and Gill looked distressed and apprehensive at the notion of yet another invading army. They were both over seventy and should have been enjoying a peaceful old age. I cursed myself that I had not thought more of them, good old servants that they were. I resolved that Matt should take on another younger worker in the slaughter house. Jacky should not have to heft sheep about at his age, and Patience should have more domestic assistance to spare both herself and Gill. Remembering how Essex' quartermasters had purloined all my father's stock the previous September, I suggested that Matt closed and locked the shop as soon as was possible.

As I drew near to the Castle Mound, I began to appreciate Sir William Russell's frustration with the Worcester citizens in that little of the defensive plans had been thoroughly completed. However, where before there had been apathy, there was now frenzied activity. The boys from my school, the King's School, were building up banks of earth behind the walls, "to withstand cannon shot", Matt's younger brother told me. The soldiers from the Garrison were everywhere, and I caught sight of the Dodgeson boys, carrying drinking water to Sir William's men.

"Who is in charge now?" I asked Matt's brother. It was Colonel William Sandys. I had thought he and Sir William Russell were not the best of friends but it seemed that desperate times produce strange bedfellows.

I called to the Dodgeson boys. To my shame I did not know their Christian names. In a crisis such as this, one should surely let bad behaviour however unmannerly slide into the obscurity of the past, and I wished them to think of me as a friend. They came over to me willingly enough, but when I asked them if they would like to come to my house to be safe they protested that they wished to stay with their captain. Both seemed in better shape, thinner, livelier, and certainly more courteous. They were named for two of the disciples in the good book, they told me proudly, "Philip and Bartholomew but our Mam called us Pip and Barty."

Suddenly their eyes stared behind me. I turned. It was Colonel William Sandys. I bowed in true Jack-Hold-My-Staff fashion and wished him "Good even, Colonel"

"Doctor Thomas Fletcher," he announced loudly, lest he feared I had forgotten my name and calling. "May we then count on your good offices on the morrow, when the cannons pound and the musket balls fly?"

"Certainly, you may, dear Colonel." I told him, my heart sinking at the prospect. "I shall be here betimes but I am something concerned for these two young ruffians, Philip and Bartholomew Dodgeson. They are perhaps too young to be in the very thick of the fray."

"Certainly they are," he said, smiling indulgently, "Philip will beat his drum as we advance to the walls and Barty will fill cannikins at the well. Neither will be near the action."

"Certainly they wish to remain here," I said pondering whether there was any other circumstance that would require the answer "Certainly".

There was. "And certainly, they may do so. They are good boys and have shaped well into young soldiers. Are you their guardian, Doctor Fletcher?"

"Not as such," I told him, "But as their father recovers from an accident in a stone quarry, I have undertaken to be in loco parentis."

He left us then, and I told the boys, if they felt afraid or if they were injured, they were to repair to the Newport Street house immediately. They agreed that they would do so, but I noticed that there were other boys, aye and girls and women too, working industriously to secure the old walls and strengthening the new ones.

Later I discussed the obvious improvement of the Dodgeson boys with my wife. She, as ever, had an explanation for their change.

"They are needed, now, Tom. Being useful is what enables the young to mature."

"And I need you, dearest Phoebe!" I told her lustfully.

But after a moment or two it became clear to me that her right side could not sustain physical contact with another. She complained of feeling sore and tender. The discomfort only subsided when she lay still and unmoving. She confided that the flow of blood she was experiencing was unusual, being a thin brown trickle rather than a red flood.

We slept fitfully. Sandys clearly was determined that Waller should not find Worcester an easy victim and there were noises all night. Men were shouting in the streets and the low rumble of guns being pushed into emplacements could be heard. Bastions had been hastily repaired on the walls and fortified, although when I walked abroad in the grey dawn I had the impression that much was for show and would not withstand a serious bombardment. Nonetheless, there was no doubt that the Colonel had tried to make ready for Waller. The guns in the emplacements were at a deceptive angle so that their muzzles did not seem at first to threaten the enemy. I stopped suddenly stock still. "Waller is not my enemy." I told myself sternly. "Was Lady Brilliana my enemy? What a sorry pass we have come to when we are killing each other for upholding different beliefs!"

I stood behind the Cathedral looking towards the southern and eastern side of the city. Pip came to greet me, beating a welcoming cannonade on his drum. He pointed up into the woods. It seemed Waller had encamped on the Green Hill near the road to Evesham. Part of my restlessness the previous night had been dissatisfaction with my lack of real responsibility for the Dodgeson boys. I decided that it was time to insist that they left the ramparts as soon as the action began.

Pip led me to the point where the old walls had been surrounded by a new wall leading to a bastion that they called the Fort Royal. We walked even beyond this to the eastern Sidbury gate which had been well fortified. Pip pointed up the hill, proud I think that he could show me the exact whereabouts of the enemy. As we looked up the winding track that led eventually to Pershore and Evesham, I became aware of the sound of many men encamped amongst the trees. Wisps of smoke arose and there was the smell of cooking. As we peered carefully over the battlements there was the sound of a trumpet's martial blast and a small party of horsemen led by a herald, trotted down from Waller's camp. They came to a halt near the Sidbury Gate below on our left. This herald was better accoutred than Sir Neddy and myself had been when we had held this office for the Earl of Chesterfield in Lichfield. We had been blindfolded and clad in dirty white sheets. Ned had had to reassure me that we were safe. But Sir John Gell had respected our courage and no-one had hurt or threatened us.

Waller's herald wore the traditional red tabard with false sleeves and gold facings. He carried a trumpet which shone in a hesitant ray of the rising sun. He rode a magnificent white charger and trotted forward confidently to address Colonel Sandys who with a group of Captains waited near us on the wall.

"Colonel Sandys!" he began and had clearly been chosen for his loud commanding voice. "Sir William Waller greets you, and asks for free entrance to this city of Worcester. If you accede to this demand, he swears that not one inhabitant, no, not the smallest babe, not the greyest old grandsire... shall suffer distress at his hands nor at the hands of his army, which you should know numbers three thousand men loyal to the cause of King and Parliament. How say you?"

"I say No!" shouted Sandys The men flanking him cheered. "And I say, if you are for King and Parliament, then you have good cause to throw down your arms and depart, for all here are for the King, God save him."

"Then Sir William Waller wishes you to know that the deaths of all here present whom you represent must be laid to your charge, Colonel Sandys, when we must all come to the Great Day of Judgement," the Herald cried.

"Why, you simpleton," Sandys cried "We who defy you in this city will be in better case on that day than your commander and his army, who are traitors all and renegades, who slight the King and the will of Almighty God, enshrined in his person. In any event where is Sir William? I do not hold discourse with commoners. You can tell him from me that he is not at Hereford now. Worcester men-at-arms are men of a different colour!"

There was a flurry of movement behind the Herald. A small handsome man with black curling hair, dark bright eyes and a long nose had dismounted. He seemed in some way familiar. He took a few steps towards the Herald but before he could proclaim himself, Sandys called out,

"Why, Sir William! I did not see you there. So close to our Mother Earth as you are. You clearly wish to be gathered once again into her bosom. Less of a journey for you than most men, my Lord!"

There was a gasp of outrage from the Parliamentarian captains. Waller rapped out a command we could not hear to the Herald who turned his white horse, seemingly to return to his fellows. He shouted his final proclamation.

"You have chosen your destiny, Colonel. Your decision must be on your head."

Before Sandys could reply, there was a sharp crack and the red and gold of the Herald's tabard paled beside the red flood that poured from his thigh. He screamed and the horse reared. Sandys could not have ordered such a shot. Now he demanded angrily of his men, who was responsible.

Even I, sad country bumpkin that I was, knew that such an action was a heinous unpardonable crime. The Herald had come forward in good faith. His person was inviolable. There was clearly an argument taking place around the Colonel. My attention was suddenly caught by a man who had come from the commanders with Waller. He was speaking to him earnestly and looking up at me. On the instant I knew him. It was Robert Burghill, the Parliament Captain whose life I had saved at Powick Bridge.

I did not know whether to be pleased or sorry. Pleased certainly in that Robert, an excellent good friend, had survived the vagaries of civil war but sorry in that I could guess that my talents as a surgeon were about to be demanded by Waller as recompense for such an outrageous act. The Parliamentary Captains were pulling the herald from his magnificent horse which seemed unharmed. They laid the poor man on the ground. I had to advise them.

I shouted over the battlements, "Robert, prop us his leg and stop the flow, if you can." He nodded and waved, kneeling by the innocent victim, for what is a Herald if not a living mouthpiece, a breathing epistle, free of the guilt of those who employ him. But then Robert rose and shrugged. He called out to us all, "He is dead." With those words another relic of English courtesy died also. Waller's party swiftly retreated, leaving the dead Herald where he had fallen. William Sandys ordered Sidbury Gate to be opened and his body carried into our domain to be spared further abuse or indignities.

I looked down at Pip who had dropped his drumsticks, and

stood, white and amazed at this, his first sight of the horror of war. "It will get worse than this," I told him. He said nothing. I led him out of the way of the gunners who were now, pushing the cannons into their final emplacements, and training the great muzzles onto the areas whence they believed Waller's men might advance. We returned the way we had come, and we came to the well where Barty and a few women constantly let down the buckets to replenish tankards and bottles.

"Barty!" he called out to his brother, "We're going with Doctor Tom." For a moment it seemed as if Barty would object, but Pip grabbed his shoulder. "We could be killed, man!" he shouted in his brother's ear. The women, who knew me approved whole-heartedly of this. "Go on, lads." said Evelyn Dent, "Doctor Tom will bring you back when the cannons have done their work. This is no place for you now."

I was about to say it was no place for them either, or me or anyone, but the first burst of cannon fire prevented my words being heard and persuaded Barty that in fact he would prefer to be elsewhere. The Worcester gunners were attempting to prevent the Parliament men from setting up their emplacements too near the weak walls. Indeed if Waller had known how precariously one stone was wedged on another in some places, he could have settled the matter in an hour.

As we moved down the quiet deserted streets I ventured to say, "I don't think Sir William Russell intended that you should have been present where the guns were blazing."

I took them into Joan and explained the situation. To my surprise she nodded approvingly. "Go and find James and Abram, boys," she ordered them and they trooped off to my orchard so that there were now four young boys in their early teens, tearing down the apple blossom and frightening the hens.

The sound of the cannons was somewhat muffled at this end of the town. We listened for a moment. "I shall have to go back to tend the wounded." I told her as I gratefully ate the bread and cheese that she had put before me. "I'll come with you," she told me. And then she said "I don't expect William Sandys' children were there, putting their lives in danger."

I admitted that I had not seen them. "One thing of which we can be certain," she said bitterly "We can always rely on the gentry to put the poor at risk before themselves."

"Do you not see yourself then as gentry?" I asked her politely.

She laughed. "Bless you, no, Tom! But as I'm a Welsh woman like your dear mother, I have no need of aristocratic birth lines. I was born with many distinct advantages, mental and physical"

"You are certainly cleverer than any woman I know, except my wife," I told her, humbly, "And Joan, what a tragedy it is that poor Adam cannot see how excessive comely you are still, putting all the young women of Worcester to shame."

"Why, Tom, what a courtier you are become!" She was clearly pleased with my flattery, and in fact she was a most handsome woman, though something bony rather than slender. I told her that I had seen Robert and she rejoiced that he was unharmed. I excused myself to see how Phoebe did. She was sitting up and thought she might be a little better though there was still this unnatural brown fluid seeping from her.

"I do not know why my shoulder should hurt me though. What is my complaint, Tom? I have never felt quite so weak, not even when we were destitute in Dudley. Joan has no notion what can be wrong with me."

"When did you last have your courses?" I asked her.

"You know Tom, I have completely miscalculated. When you returned home on the 22nd of April, a Saturday, was it not? they were over. With the excitement of marriage and.... married life, I forget to count. I think it is a little over six weeks. Would Joan be affronted if Martha could come and tend me? As she is so much older than all of us, it may be that she will recognize my condition and will cure it."

I told her about the murdered herald and how Pip had swiftly espoused the cause of non-involvement. "But I do not think Waller will have it all his own way this time. When I came away the Worcester gunners were causing the Parliament men to skip and jump nimbly enough. If you are comfortable, little wife, I must return. And I saw Robert Burghill."

She was delighted to hear that he was well and promised to rest comfortably until I returned. I picked up my box and went down to Joan. We filled a small barrel with our pure Malvern water, so that we would not wash impurities into wounds and made sure we had good supplies of Pares Lotion. Then off we set, pausing only to ask Samuel to come with us. I hated walking in the direction of the hellish noise. All my instincts cried out against this ear-mangling, brain-curdling scourge of the senses that my countrymen deemed necessary to indicate to their opponents that they had the upper hand.

As we came near to the southern area of the city, near the Frog Mill and Castle Hill, it became clear that our fellow citizens were in good heart and were giving "William the Conqueror" something of a challenge. He had three thousand men and we were only half that number but to my amazement in spite of the continuous barrage, the walls seemed intact. I crept up the mound of earth the King's Scholars had piled behind the wall near the old Frog Mill and stole covert glances at the scene. Waller's gunners had clearly been picked off by Worcester marksmen. They lay near their great hideous instruments of death, their bodies contorted and broken. To my distress one or two still lived and called for aid.

Someone pulled me down the heaped-up soil as shots whistled through the battlement where I had been observing. It was Samuel. "For God's sake, Tom, have a care, man!"

I realised that I must rid myself of this delusion that a battle was a theatrical display, performed for my benefit. How foolhardy I had been at Hopton Heath, where I had seen the whole action, peeping cravenly round the corner of a solid stone house! And Elijah had been killed while I watched the military drama. Much though I hated my interest, there was some base enjoyment to be gained from it, if I was brutally honest with myself.

Both Sam and Joan gazed at me now wide eyed as if they did not know me. "Forgive me," I mumbled "I wanted to see if there was any sign of Robert. Waller is getting the worst of it. His gunners are being picked off."

"They seem to be carrying the wounded into the Close," said Joan, and led the way from the walls back into its relative calm. There were two fatalities, soldiers who had caught the full force of a cannon ball, but happily other injuries were relatively few and minor. One Worcester man, the potter Master Moore had sustained a fearsome cut across his cheek which had caused his eye to close. He feared that his sight was permanently damaged, but Joan assured him once his swollen cheek subsided as it would do, he would again win wagers with his skill at quoits. Joan was excellent at tyrannising the sick into an optimistic frame of mind. I think they reasoned if they smiled, agreed and ceased to complain, she might depart from them. Mercifully she usually went her ways, leaving them to rejoice therefore on two counts, firstly that they would recover and secondly that she had gone.

A musket ball had grazed a soldier's arm and I began to clean the wound. He gazed over my shoulder stoically determined not to cry aloud with pain. He had come south from Kidderminster he told me to serve Sir William Russell and was very angry that Waller had chosen to attack Worcester when our true Governor was from home.

"Why could he have not waited until our Commander was returned?" he asked me, furiously. I shrugged, and was silent. There was little to be gained by listing the myriad advantages, Waller could exploit by attacking in Russell's absence...

There was a terrible crash, the sound of timbers splintering, plaster crumbling, and a plume of dust rose from one of the houses in the Close. Immediately a terrible screaming began.

Joan stood upright. She had been leaning beside a young boy, delicately extracting splinters from his hand.

"Oh, Christ! That's Master Tomkins' house."

The pall of dust threatened to envelop us but seemed to fall just short of our wounded. The screaming grew louder and three servant girls ran from the house into the Close. One of them simply screamed at the top of her voice, another cried piteously, "Oh Jesu, our house!" The third said nothing but turned back as if she would return for others.

Joan strode over to the girl who screamed and slapped her smartly upon each cheek. As the frightful noise subsided into coughs and sobs, she asked the silent girl, "How many left in there?"

"Luke and George are bringing them out. Here they are!" and she ran to assist two men who were supporting Master Tomkins and his wife. He moaned and cried "The Cathedral! Is it still standing? My precious organ!"

"Is anyone else still in the house?" Joan shouted. They looked at each other and then Mistress Tomkins said, "No, No! This is all. Madge Cook is from home. I warned her there would be nothing in the market but she must needs see for herself."

"Had she time to make up the kitchen fire?" said Joan.

One of the men answered, "No, Mistress. 'Twas to be cold lamb today. I see where you are at. No, mistress, nothing was left burning but the cannon ball fell through the roof on the Master and Mistress' great bed."

"A sad loss, indeed! Still it seems they were not in it!" said Joan and returned to the extraction of the splinters.

I found a bench for Master and Mistress Tomkins and they sat, trembling, watching as I dressed the arm of the man from Kidderminster. When I dismissed him, Master Tomkins spoke. "Young man, can you assure me all is well with my organ?"

By this I had surmised he spoke musically and not corporeally. "Well, Sir," I told him, noting that no more invalids were waiting. "If you will take my arm we can see for ourselves. Your organ is in the Cathedral, I take it. 'Tis but a few steps past College Hall and through the West door."

He grasped my arm and we tottered over the lawn through the door into the Cathedral. Within the great lofty nave, he walked with more confidence, leading me to where the great organ, completely unharmed, towered over one of the aisles.

"All well, I think. You know, I take it, who made this organ?"

"Alas, no," I told him humbly. Some instinct told me I was about to learn.

He sighed impatiently at my ignorance. "This organ was made by the great craftsman, Thomas Dallam. Do you not attend church, young man?" I nodded. "Well, you will have heard me play this glorious instrument. Have you no interest, do you not care about our great cathedral? Do you not know that these Parliament men would tear this and every other down? And with their destruction goes music, painting, even drama. Do you know that Essex used this building for his horses?"

I took a deep breath, "Now, Sir, you speak of something that touches me very nearly. Know you not that my father, Amyas Fletcher, went to appeal to the Earl of Essex last September? My father, a humble butcher, not a great musician like yourself, nor a great scholar like the Dean, but he alone out of all this city of Worcester went to protest about using our Cathedral as a stable. And Essex hanged him. He claimed he was a spy. My father was hung like a criminal in the Meal Cheapen by Essex Lifeguards. His crime? Protesting at the sacrilegious use of this great building as a stable. I did not see either you or Dean Potter or Bishop Prideaux, at my father's death, crying out to Essex that he was a murderer and a traitor and a heretic. So, I pray you, do not ask me if I care about this Cathedral! Because as I live and die by the blessed example of my dear father, I can tell you that I do indeed care! Master Tomkins, I care more than you!"

I turned on my heel and walked away from him. I had gone about ten yards when he called out, "Young man. Er... Master Fletcher. I did not know you were Amyas Fletcher's son."

I paused. He went on, "Forgive me, young man. Now I think of it, I have heard of you. I am proud to say that I think Amyas regarded me as a friend."

I walked slowly back down to him. He went on, "I must ask your pardon. Your father complimented me on each new anthem. He had great discernment. You do right to revere his memory."

I remembered to my shame that this poor old man had just had one of Waller's cannon balls through his roof, ruining his home. Surely I could show patience and pity at his situation. "Come dear Master Tomkins! We are at accord, and I am much to blame," I said humbly, "Allow me to support you back to your wife."

He took my arm and we walked slowly back out of the West Door, past College Hall where Master Moule had tried so patiently to teach me Greek and round again to College Lawn to his wife and household.

Dean Potter appeared and offered them respite in his own house. "If it does not meet a similar fate," he added gloomily. But it seemed to me that Waller was aiming at the Garrison. One or two of Waller's cannon seemed to have gauged the measure of the walls' height and the balls were landing with dismal thuds harmlessly in the Frog Mill field and on the Castle Mound. The one that had penetrated Tomkins' roof was a single lucky shot, (depending on where one's loyalties lay.)

Sir William Sandys came to see how the wounded fared and thanked us fulsomely for our brave efforts. "Let Waller expend himself, as much as he may. Did I hear screaming here? Was a damsel caught in the fire?"

It seems he wished to deceive the Conqueror into thinking his cannon were causing more carnage than they were. He asked the girl who could scream like a soul in Hell to accompany him to the area where Waller's shots were landing. She and others were to howl and moan so that Waller would think he was achieving great carnage.

"Have a care though, that he does not in fact, cause real hurt and blood shed." Joan was regretting her rough treatment of the poor shrieking maid and warned her to stay far off and protected from the arc of the cannons.

"Tom, can we do aught else here?" Joan asked me. Samuel had been of great use, and had learnt how to clean a minor wound and bandage it. I agreed that there was nothing now that we could usefully accomplish, as the wounded had been taken into the Dean's house, together with the Tomkins household. His magnanimity was admirable.

I arranged to return to the Ovens (as the Dean's house was known) in the evening. William Sandys was a cunning commander. He had scarcely used the Worcester culverin in their emplacements, preferring to encourage the marksmen from his musketeers to bring down the Parliament gunners. Now he preserved his cannon balls and match for the morrow, thinking that if Waller made a mass attack on Sidbury Gate, he would have plenty of ammunition. I wondered again why Waller had not aimed his cannon directly at the walls, instead of over them. One or two strategic shots and he and his men would have been everywhere, like maggots on a dead donkey.

Patience had been working in our kitchen, and chickens turned on the spit.

"Dear Mistress Bailey, forgive me, but I thought you might wish to have assistance, so busy as you have been helping the wounded." she said tentatively.

"Thank you, my dear," said Joan simply. "Your man, here, can now treat a bruise or sprain as well as the best doctor in Worcester. And indeed, there was naught too serious, thank the Lord."

I went up to Phoebe who whilst she lay quiet and still, yet now betrayed some anxiety at her condition. "I do hope that Waller will not stay long." she told me, "I would wish that Martha could come to me."

"My sweetheart, I will fetch her to you, the instant I can cross the river," I told her.

"Indeed, I hope you can cross soon. Are Waller's guards preventing it?"

"Waller's men are in St John's and the Worcester musketeers guard the quays and the approach to the bridge. But we must somehow get over in the near future. Joan needs milk and butter from the farm."

I went back down to the kitchen and sat at the table as Patience bustled about preparing our dinner. Sam had returned to Fish Street to bring Gill and Jacky back to eat with us. Matt had gone to the eastern side of the city to help his brother. There were twelve of us round the table finally, and as we sat waiting for Patience to put all the covers on the table, there was suddenly a quiet knock on the door.

Joan was nearest, and pulled it open. But when I saw who stood there, I gasped somewhat in joy, but more from fear. It was Robert Burghill with Ralph, the poacher turned "honest" dragoon and another trooper.

Joan looked at me in fear, but Robert should never be denied my house. I leapt to my feet and pulled them in, looking under the arch and into the courtyard to be certain no-one had seen their approach.

"Dear Tom, I am rejoiced to see that you are still well and prospering." He embraced me, perhaps, as it seemed to me always, somewhat more lovingly than was fitting. Ralph of course knew Roger and his parents. Fortunately all who were in my house had no strong sympathies for the Royalist cause, except perhaps my poor absent little wife, and she was a well born lady through and through, although somewhat unorthodox in her views. But I knew that she would rejoice at Robert's visit, had she been fit enough to greet him.

"How did you get here?" I asked, disengaging myself from Robert's embrace and stepping back in wonder.

"Ralph had seen a way. He had a fancy for river trout and remembered seeing them in the Severn last October. We crept along between the river and the wall."

Roger was bemused at their exploit. "What of the crane house? Did they not see you?"

"There seemed to be no-one there. It was dangerous (and wet) to avoid the sight of the Worcester guns and perilous also, when we came near the troops on the bridge. But no-one saw us. No-one was looking for us when all was said and done. But I have very little time. Sir William Waller begs you to return with me. There is a camp fever that has overtaken some of the foot. Their bowels are loose and noisome, and they pass bloody stools and are suffering terrible cramping pains in their guts. Forgive me, ladies!" he became aware of their presence and that we were about to sit to table. "All that Richard Allen will do for the poor wretches is bleed them. Remembering that you and Ben hated this practice, I told Sir Will that I would come and fetch you before Allen kills more of the poor devils."

"I know this illness," I said slowly, remembering a visit I had paid with Ben to a farm high in the Martley hills, above Great Witley. The farmer had sworn that he had a visitation of the plague for his ploughboy and cow herd had lamentably loose bowels, and were passing blood, but Ben had immediately reassured him. The malady, though weakening, was by no means fatal. I could hear Ben's instructions, "A quart of clean boiled water, allowed to cool, two good pinches of salt and an ounce of sugar, dissolved therein." The silly youths had drunk tainted water from a brook that had looked clean but which, it transpired, had a dead sheep lying in an advanced state of putrefaction in it, some little way upstream.

"Well, rest assured it is not the plague," I told Robert, "I know this disorder, but I had best come with you. It's easily cured but if your surgeon is allowed to bleed the sufferers, he will most likely kill them, as they are weak already."

There were objections raised at my words. Joan and Patience begged me to reconsider and Roger pointed out sagely that I could be viewed as a traitor by my own city.... "Your poor father's fate must surely make you wary." Adam said from the chimney corner. Jacky spoke of the dangers of the river and spring tides and Abram said simply, "What about Phoebe?"

I knew I could not rest to think of these men dying through another surgeon's ignorance. Some deaths I now had to accept as inevitable, but where I could easily save lives... well, I had taken an oath to Hippocrates. And Robert had saved my life more than once.

"What is your water supply?" I asked Robert. He shrugged but Ralph replied simply, "Cider."

"That is good for you, Ralph, a safe pure brewage, but not for the poor men who void their bowels. We must have a supply of clean water, and even that I will boil."

Jacky spoke again, a most unusual occurrence. "Master Tommy, they'll be near the Lady's Well in the Perry Woods. That's good sweet water, so be no varlet's fouled it."

"Well remembered, Jacky. Robert, we will need vessels to collect the water and boil it.... Do you have them?" He looked at Ralph who nodded. "And Joan.... could you give me salt and sugar? I know not why but with constant involuntary purging, the sufferers of this distemper void out of themselves, life sustaining substances."

It was now dark enough to set forth. Patience had gone out to count and lock up the hens. She returned as we were preparing to depart with the news, "There's a poacher's moon." Ralph looked innocently at the ceiling, and then politely outlined his plan, "Shall I then lead the way, followed by the Colonel?"

"The Colonel?" I asked in wonder.

Now it was Robert's turn to be embarrassed. "Sir Will is a generous appreciative commander, Tom."

"No better man ever graced the office of Colonel!" I told him. "So Ralph, shall I follow Colonel Robert?."

"If you please, Doctor Tom, and Progger here will bring up the rear."

I thought better of inquiring how Progger came by his name. He insisted on carrying my box and all the ingredients for the potion that we would have to make in the camp.

It was easier to stay the city side of the protective wall as far as the Crane House. We crept behind it and then skirted the Key, a tavern much beloved of my father. But after this we had to take to the river bank, which was more hazardous. There was but a narrow strip of stony shore between water and wall, and from time to time the river had encroached right up to the wall. We could jump these incursions and Progger handed across his bundles before he undertook the leap. The wall was much higher as we went under the Bishop's Palace, and as high again as we passed under the gardens of the Close. It was lower around the Castle Mound, but now our real perils began. We could hear the Worcester guards talking and laughing amongst themselves and I was conscious that mouths of great culverins were pointing directly at me. I reasoned with myself that no gunner would point his gun almost directly below himself. That would indeed be to "hoist himself with his own petard" but there was no such danger for him with a musket. Ralph seemed to sense when danger loomed and turning, hushed us to halt. The talk above had grown louder and we stood petrified for a few moments, crouched under the wall.

A wave suddenly swept over our feet. The tide that Jacky had warned about. The Severn was not a river with which to be trifled. A memory flashed into my mind as we stood, silently up to our knees in cold water. Sir Nicholas had enjoyed poetry and a friend who had been one of the Earl of Bridgewater's secretaries had sent him a copy of a Masque, performed at Ludlow Castle in 1634. Our very same river, the Severn appeared as a gentle nymph and was saluted as Sabrina Fair. I could remember my father afterwards saying to those gathered to enjoy the piece, "All well and good, Sir Nick, but Sabrina Fair can swiftly become the most treacherous harlot in Worcestershire. A wanton baggage as will drown a man in a trice." His cousin, Lady Alice, asked him to modify his language before the genteel company and my father had seemed downcast and put down. I, a stripling of twelve years had gone over to him and slipped my hand in his and told him, "I will always have a care of the river, Sir, and of harlots, I promise you." He had laughed and stroked my hair and said, "That's my good boy."

What strange tricks memory can play. I stood still as stone, whilst Sabrina Fair lapped round my knees, and it was as if I were back in the great parlour, (now Phoebe's retiring room) looking round at the polite faces of friends and neighbours, come to gratify Sir Nick. But the voices of the Worcester guards above us faded as they trooped away at the end of their watch. Ralph now indicated that we could continue and we stepped quietly back onto the path, water rushing from our boots and hose.

Another hundred yards and the wall snaked eastwards away from us and we ran from bush to tree in the common ground beyond the Frogmill Fields. The ground began to rise and we had to cross the road to Pershore and Worcester. Ralph ran first to a clump of hawthorn and then hissed to us to follow him. We were over the road as fast as weasels through a warren, and now were in the woods that Worcester folk called the Perriwoods, and became aware of a great company of men camped in the glades among the trees. We were challenged from time to time, "Halt! Who is there?"

and Robert answered, "The fruits of virtue." which I later learned was the Waller motto. At last we came to an old farm house which I had thought long abandoned. This it seems was Sir William's quarters.

And in the instant he was there beside us, his eyes sparkling in the moonlight.

"Why good old Colonel Bob!" he cried, "You have returned as swift as lightening. And this is Master Miracle Worker, I take it?"

I bowed "Your servant, Sir William. It does not take a miracle to cure the distemper the Colonel has described, but I must beg you, do not let your surgeon continue to bleed the poor invalids. That is the way to weaken them and hasten their unnecessary death. Can fires be built and water fetched from the well, a little up the slope?"

He blinked. I realised he was something amazed by my briskness. "Forgive me, my Lord, but speed is essential," I told him.

"Yes, yes, of course. They are scattered about, I fear, but I think are all in the same troop. Skirmager's is it not? Bob, can your troopers find the water and I will have the invalids brought to you, Master Doctor."

"Excellent, my Lord," I told him, "Have you a supply of fresh eggs? They will need good wholesome fresh food tomorrow. Had you thought to treat them together?" I peered over his head into the kitchen of the farmhouse where a fire burned cheerfully.

"Yes, As you wish, in here, by all means. Not the plague you say?" He gave swift orders and men rushed to do his bidding.

"No, not the plague, my Lord but a most unpleasant condition caused by drinking foul water, or eating rotten meat. The body naturally purges itself of the infection through the bowels, but because it has lost so much water cannot recover without an influx of clean boiled water with salt and sugar added. Believe me, they will be hungry tomorrow."

The first of them began to arrive. It was a captain. He was borne upon a pallet and was clearly in great pain. When he saw in what company he was, he began to weep. "Alas, my Lord, I have soiled myself like any suckling babe. So many in my troop... The fearsome stench..."

"Don't distress yourself, sir, I pray." I told him, before Sir William could reply, "The uncontrollable voiding of the bowel is the way that Nature rids itself of something poisonous that you have eaten or drunk. In a few moments I shall assist you to drink a wondrous concoction that will restore your strength. But for now, dear Sir, lie quiet and warm."

"Who are you?" he asked, perhaps surprised at my audacity. The Colonel replied. "This is Doctor Tom Fletcher, whom I have fetched from Worcester to help you, Harold. He knows your ague and has the cure."

"Forgive me for my audacity, my Lord," I said to Sir William Waller who stood to one side, gazing at me dumbfounded. "But when men's lives are at stake, courtesy must give way to expediency."

He had no option but to agree. Ralph already had a cauldron of water boiling on the fire. Other men began to arrive, some staggering, refusing assistance, others helped by their fellow soldiers. I bustled about encouraging them to lie quietly in the warm kitchen. Someone had found clean straw which I fashioned into pallets, and invited the sufferers to lie down which they were only too pleased to do.

"Robert and Sir William, I need bowls and tankards fashioned from pottery, so that I am certain they are clean," I instructed them loftily. I began to pour the boiling water into a clean Tickney ware quart jug, added my sugar and salt, stirred it with a clean knife from my box and instructed the Captain who had first arrived to sip it slowly. Two quartermasters arrived, ordered by Sir William to assist me. One immediately understood my requirements and produced some rough blankets.

"We require bowls. These poor invalids may void their stomachs, and pails also, for certain sure they will need to empty their bowels."

I could not believe what I was hearing. Who was this young man who was commanding great men to assist him as if they were so many simpering wet-nurses? Was this imperious voice mine? Sir William and Colonel Robert hurried to do my bidding, sending troopers to such stores as the Quartermasters had gathered. Then, lest perhaps they should be asked to perform tasks too mundane for their high rank, they disappeared into the night.

The Captain, one Harold Skirmager, called to me. He had drunk my potion and spoke of a great easement in his stomach. He thanked me for my cure and told me that he thought he knew how he and his troopers had come by their illness. All the sufferers were now drinking the concoction, some needing to break off to vomit or excrete, but most retaining the precious fluid. I began to pour out more doses of the clean boiled water, salted and sugared and asked the patients to sip again, as slowly as they wished, until their bowels had quietened and they no longer needed to vomit. I started to pour well water into pails and to invite those who seemed now to be recovering to wash themselves. The quartermasters found some old dry sponges, which were useful in this respect. Whilst they seemed to feel that they could not wash their fellows without losing status, I had no such qualms and began to assist those who had the strength to clean their bodies. I had oil of rosemary and lavender in my box and added a few drops to the cleaning water.

At length most of the seventeen men who had suffered from the distemper seemed to be recovering well. I was concerned for one thin young fellow, who continued to retch most pitifully. I got one of the quartermasters to sit with him and encourage him to sip. "You must drink," I instructed him. "Your poor stomach is so dry, it has nothing to digest and churns about aimlessly. Try to keep this liquid down if you can." He vomited once more but at length he seemed to be retaining my potion, though his colour did not improve.

"So," I asked the room at large. "How came this? You have all eaten or drunk from the same pot or cauldron, perhaps at noon today. What has made you all so ill?"

"Sir, 'twas eel pie." An older man announced this and all concurred and groaned at the bilious memory.

"How came you by that?" I was interested in the forensic history of their poisoning.

"We were with the captain, camped near a cherry orchard, southerly of here when two maids came selling pies early this morning, made so they said of fresh Kempsey eels."

"And did you wait long before you ate them?" I asked

It seemed that most of them ate them as their noonday "snap."

"Did any others eat these pies?" I persisted.

"Two others. They are both dead. Surgeon Allen bled all of us, but they still died."

I swore vehemently, "God's death! They probably died because he bled them, poor bastards.It is the quickest way to weaken a sick man."

One or two nodded in agreement. The imperious young man who had inhabited my person suddenly felt fatigued and was ready now to return home but Robert returned with unwelcome news.

"Ralph has been back to the river. It flows now contiguous with the wall under the old mound. I think it may be a spring tide. You will have to remain with us longer than we anticipated Tom."

"I will have to try to return." I told him. "Did I tell you Phoebe and I are married?"

"That is wondrous good news!" said Robert, and I believe he was in earnest. "I am married myself. It is said to be a blessed state of life. But surely she can spare you for a little longer. Sir William wishes to pledge you."

"She is ill, Robert. I cannot leave her for any length of time. Your coming has prevented us from fetching an old woman from over the river who we think might help us."

He led me out into the night. "Listen, I cannot say much but I doubt we will be here after tomorrow. Prince Maurice emulates his elder brother and may be relying on the element of surprise. Our intelligence tells us that he might be heading this way. Sir William will not wish to be caught between Maurice, the devil, and the deep blue sea of the Severn with your fellow citizens hurling hellish chaos at us from your battlements."

I told him I had best stay with my patients most of whom were now sleeping peacefully. I asked for a chair and covered myself with an old blanket, hoping there were not too many fleas nestling happily therein. I dozed fitfully, helping the recovering troopers from time to time to drink more of my potion and to keep themselves clean. As dawn broke they were all better. The pale young man finally succumbed to the health giving qualities of my concoction and to the demands of Morpheus.

I wondered how I could get back behind the walls. Ralph brought the news that the river was still high and that it was raining. Could I swim? Upriver with my box? I thought not. I wondered if I could disguise myself as a.... as a cowherd or a shepherd and cower under the walls right round the city to the north and unseen by the river guards slip into St Clement's Church and out onto Dolday. But Roger had said something about the north door of that church and the northerly facing windows being boarded up with planks. Could I brave it out and ask for admittance at the Foregate or St. Martin's, pretending I had been from town and had not known about the Siege. The Guards would haul me straight to William Sandys or more probably would not open the gates to one solitary wayfarer. Could I sit astride a cannon ball and be shot over the walls? ...My head drooped onto my chest and I slept again.

"Well, now," said a voice, "Rot my vitals! What goes on here? By God's wounds, all asleep. 'Tis like an old tale, I vow. Who are you, Sir?"

I stood up, the blanket falling to the earth floor to face a busy little man with wispy hair and watery blue eyes. His assistant, the fattest soldier I had ever seen, carried a case which he opened to reveal knives, a silver dish such as doctors used to catch the blood of patients whom they had bled and a sheaf of papers.

"I have cured these men of a distemper of loose bowels. I am a doctor from Worcester," I told him.

"What?" he screamed, "How dare you, sir? God's body, you take too much upon you! I am the doctor who cured these men by our lakin! I bled them all yesterday."

Two or three of the troopers, lying behind him, groaned at the memory. He whirled round to accuse them. "Well, and are you not much recovered, you ingrates? One more incision to release the black melancholy and you will be good as new, by God's heart."

The men were flinging off their blankets and feeling for their hose and boots.

"Where are you going?" shrieked the little surgeon.

"Sir William has ordered us to report as soon as we were well enough." One man struggling into his doublet, was polite but determined to escape. "Your pardon, Surgeon Allen but I cannot stay to be bled again. And my heart-felt thanks to you, Sir" he called as he passed me.

"Well, here's a pretty pass, God rot me!" said the surgeon.

"You can be certain of that, Sir, when we are all called to our last account!" I said piously.

"Be silent!" he cried, "What do you know of Galen and Hippocrates? A mere stripling, a quacksalver! Here, where go you, Cornet West?" he cried to the ashen young man, the last of my patients to wake. Though still pale, he was vigorously tying his gaskins.

"Forgive me, Surgeon Allen, but I cannot endure being bled again. To say truth, I think this young man has brought me back from the dead."

Ralph brought in small beer, bread and cheese as a breakfast for me. It was however immediately purloined by the Doctor who commented on how thoughtful Colonel Burghill was. He shared it ostentatiously with his Surgeon's mate, the impassive, corpulent soldier who it seemed was Master Wind. I busied myself tidying the kitchen, emptying pales of water outside where the rain lashed down. A little verse came into my head, "Sing heigh-ho, the Wind and the Rain." At least the rain was outside!

The noisome straw pallets, on which the men had been lying, needed to be burned. I began to pile them up in an outhouse and gradually fed the fire with them, which still blazed cheerfully, God be thanked. As I toiled Ralph returned. He gasped at the effrontery of Surgeon Allen who sat at his ease in my chair, sharing my breakfast with his Mate Wind, who stood like a stone statue save for the rhythmic chewing motions of his jowls. "I'll be back directly, Tom," he murmured and whisked away.

I continued my task. Perhaps ten minutes later Sir William Waller came bustling in closely followed by Robert.

"So where are they? Where are they? Good day Surgeon Allen, you have been assisting Doctor Tom I see. Excellent, excellent. Where are the poor fellows, Sir?"

Ralph answered for me, "Back at their posts, Sir. All are recovered, thanks to Doctor Tom and his miraculous concoction."

"Excellent, excellent!" said Sir William, rubbing his hands, "Surgeon Allen, I do not think we need detain you here. I am sure you have need of rest after the exhausting work you have undertaken during the last twelve hours."

"I am dismissed, am I? After all the charts I have configured for each of those ungrateful musketeers, all the humours I have diagnosed and their appropriate elements and qualities, all the bleeding I have undertaken after I had correctly estimated that almost all were choleric, with an excess of yellow bile, but all to no purpose! Well, well, Sir William, I know who my friends are now! Or rather, God's bodykins, I know who my friends are *not*. Come, Surgeon's Mate, Master Wind."

He turned on his heel and tripped out of the kitchen, followed by his phlegmatic assistant. As he passed me, he muttered in an undertone, "I shall meet you, sir! Never fear! Oh, yes, I shall meet you."

"Doctor Tom.... I may so call you.... How can I apologise? Surgeons are so hard to find. Colonel Bob does not think I will be able to tempt you into this regiment. I take it there is no chance?"

From some unknown source a degree of courtesy manifested itself. "Sir William, I regret deeply, but my wife is ill and we cannot ascertain her illness. I must return back over the walls as soon as may be. Can you assist me in that, as I have assisted you?"

"Oh, Doctor Tom, forgive me but I cannot. Even as we speak the rogues are planning who knows what devilry! I cannot risk another parley. You saw I think what happened to Talbot, who acted as my herald."

"I did indeed, and Sir William Sandys has vowed judgement on whatever criminal it was who fired that shot. The poor corpse lies in the Cathedral and will be given honourable burial. But Sir William, believe me. I have no interest in promoting either viewpoint. For me, your cause is as just as the King's, and perhaps both factions are as much to blame in that they have resorted to weapons rather then words. For my part, I have the misfortune to live in Worcester where my poor father was hanged by Essex."

"I heard of that and I am doubly sorry, Doctor Tom. Wait here and perhaps something might be contrived."

He bustled away. Robert paused just long enough to say,

"This Surgeon Allen.... Sir William's wife's aunt's husband. Given the post to make for a quiet bed and board, I fear. Tom, forgive me!" and he was gone.

I was conscious that there was a movement of men downhill towards the city. I wandered out through the rain and found a viewpoint amongst the trees. The Worcester gunners had had the forethought and shelter to keep their powder and match dry, and their cannons were thundering dismally among their enemies.

During the night, Waller's men had ensconced themselves in some of the houses, below the castle mound, near to the walls. They were milling about like ants preparing to set up emplacements for their cannon which they were moving forward out of the rain. They had, so far, achieved very little in spite of the heavy pounding they had tried to inflict on the southern end of the city yesterday. As I watched, one of the houses they were preparing for their cannon, suffered a direct hit, from the Worcester guns. A cloud of dust rose and the air was filled with the shrieks and moans of the dying Parliament men. No need now for Surgeon Allen to configure their appropriate humours. The fluid that flowed was blood, and sanguinity or cheerfulness was markedly absent. No need now for him to indulge in further blood letting. The Worcester gunners had performed that operation for him. I remembered Ben's advice on these strange notions, in which many doctors believed.

"So the knaves do not embark on a course that will severely maim or kill their patients, let them believe in whatever hocus-pocus they please. They are so enmeshed in their stupidity, it is useless to attempt to disentangle them. One becomes as crazed and tainted as they are, if one argues with such moonshine."

I returned to the deserted farmhouse where I found a broom and cleaned out the wisps of filthy straw from the kitchen, and fed the fire. It was a welcome sight as this day, 30th of May was cold dull and wet. At length I sat in the chair that had been brought for me, wrapped myself in a blanket, and slept fitfully for a while. Hunger and thirst assailed me and the hideous roar of the cannons woke me abruptly from time to time.

At length the sounds from the city changed and there were the confused shouts of many voices. From the position of a watery sun, I judged it was about midday and walked back to the viewpoint I had found, brushing through the waterfalls of raindrops, from the wet undergrowth. However there was nothing to be seen, save the sad still bodies of the Parliament gunners, lying under the southerly walls. The noise seemed to be coming from the eastern side of the city. I moved some way to my right but could still see nothing, although the noise of men, fighting and dying grew louder.

There came a crashing some few yards downhill and two men appeared supporting a third between them. "A surgeon! A surgeon!" they shouted. For a moment I was tempted to pretend I was a tinker, who had happened upon the siege by accident! But the wounded man's pale anxious face caught at my compassion and I bade them bring him to the farmhouse kitchen and lay him on the table. Thank God I had brought my box with me, though I had not looked for this employment.

He had stopped a musket ball in the left shoulder. I had dealt so often with this type of injury, it had become second nature to me. One of the troopers had a bellarmine of clean water, taken from the well Jacky had spoken of. I told him to moisten the poor fellow's lips with it and to form a screen with his person, shielding his eyes from my excavations. The other fellow said he would help me. We had the usual task of cutting away the material round the wound. When he saw me slashing at his buff coat, the patient became angry, but quietened somewhat when I pointed out that the musket ball had already ruined his precious coat. At length we were able to pull away the shreds of encrusted shirt and see the grey mass of the lead ball, caught in his sinews and bone. I knew my instruments were all clean and I brought out the ball without hindrance. But then there was the task of emptying the wound of shreds of cloth and shards of bone. The poor fellow fainted at this moment and I hastened to remove all the debris. Then I cleaned the area with Pares as well as I could and found lint and clean bandages.

"Give him more water. What is his name?"

But before they could tell me, there was a shriek.

"Again you usurp my domain! This time, Sir, I will have satisfaction!"

Surgeon Allen was dancing about in the kitchen doorway. He was effectively preventing a number of men who sought to enter from so doing. They were carrying makeshift pallets upon which wounded musketeers lay, groaning and crying.

Well, I had cast my dice upon the board by helping the wounded shoulder. It had begun to rain again and the men outside craved shelter. "I pray you, Surgeon Allen, give way, I beg you. Let them bring the wounded in," I asked him politely.

"Do not give me orders, you ignorant peascod. They may come in when I have whipped you to a tailor's thread, you bragging milksop!"

One of the men who had carried in the wounded shoulder thought to fight my cause. "Nay Surgeon Allen, we have watched him even now treat this poor fellow. 'Twas as neat as nine new pence the way he extracted the shot!"

But this was too much for the fiery little surgeon. He picked up the callipers and struck my defender across the face, shrieking as he did so, "Silence, churl! Nay, I will make him jump! Come, Sir, outside with you! Let us try your surgery under my sword."

I thought 'twould be best to humour him. When he saw I did not carry a sword, and was not a fighter, he might be persuaded in reason to allay his pugnacious attitudes. With great reluctance I followed him outside. At least the wounded could now be carried to shelter.

"Come now," he cried, "To me, boy! I shall make you jump like a drunken cricket, you poxy villain! Where's my Mate Wind? Done away with, by you no doubt!"

I was now quite deeply concerned for his sanity. The vicious cut he had given my innocent defender had immediately brought forth a chain of bloody drops, across his cheek. Allen was clearly unfit to deal with the wounded. His fears for his Surgeon's Mate were quickly proved groundless, as there stood his impassive helper beside the track up which Waller's men were toiling from Worcester's walls. And now I began to fear in earnest, for Mate Wind carried before him, one of the longest swords I had ever seen. Into what Hell had Burghill brought me, that I was about to be stabbed like a stuck squealing pig, in dismal weather beside a muddy track not three hundred yards from my own city walls?

4

"Come on then, upstart! Come then, base stripling! Let us see the colour of your poxy entrails!" He danced towards me, waving his sword in my face. "Draw, you craven poltroon! Draw, you rascally knave! By God's wounds! I'll make you dance!"

"I have no sword, Surgeon Allen!" I told him yet again. "I am a man of peace. I hold it shame to attack a fellow man. Please let me go!"

"Let you go! After the indignities you have heaped on me today!" He began to cut at me, tearing my doublet, pushing the sword point into my left sleeve and twisting it until it hung in ribbons. Another twist and I felt my shirt sleeve rip from my shoulder. I stood there dumbly, unbelieving that one man could tyrannise over another in so barbaric a manner. Groups of musketeers were climbing back wearily to their camp and behind them, horses urged on by the gunners, were pulling up a piece of ordnance. When the troopers saw his antics, they all gave pause in their ascent and watched open mouthed as he finally cut off my sleeve. He balanced it on his sword's point and ran round the muddy glade, displaying the torn black cloth. "A favour! A favour!" he shouted. "My lady has granted me a favour."

One fellow cried out to me, "Kick him in his cod-piece, Doctor Tom! You're twice his size!" Practical advice but not an action that I could justify with my conscience. One shouted down the hill to others slowly clambering up behind them, "Come on! Mad Jack Surgeon is up to his crazed tricks again!"

Ralph was climbing up the hill, musket on his shoulder and his sword at his side. I instantly saw my salvation.

"Ralph!" I cried, "Pinion this madman, I beg you! He wants to kill me!"

Ralph glanced at my opponent and shouted, "I will fetch Robert!"

"I could be dead, ere you return!" I screamed, but he was already running up the hill, whilst the lunatick continued to dance in front of me, now ripping at my breeches and my organs of generation.

My shirt sleeve hung from my shoulder in dismal tatters. He would come at me and cut and prod so far only at the folds of my clothes for some seconds and then race round the glade, whooping and screaming defiance at me. My torn sleeve was trodden in the mud. Then the strangest event of all occurred. During one of his master's circular demented dances, Mate Wind moved from the sidelines where he had been standing impassively, picked up my muddy sleeve and returned it to me with a bow. A few of the troopers tried to offer me a sword but were prevented by the whirling demented maniac.

But when the madman returned to me for perhaps the fourth time and began to cut at my bare arm, I knew I must act in my own defence.

I felt a hideous cold pain. He had nicked my arm in good earnest. A gasp went up at the sight of the blood, and the auditors drew their swords to come at him. But now I could not help myself. He was after all a puny little man, and as the Lichfield folk would say, mad as Jack Adams' tomcat! I sidestepped, picking up a stout stick that lay on the ground, held it as though to come at his sword arm. He slashed at it, screaming with glee as he cut it in pieces. But I was under his arm and grasping his twig-like limb with both hands. I twisted in opposite directions, a vicious schoolboy's trick! And although he tried to claw my face with his free hand, he screamed in pain and dropped his sword as I had intended. I stood on it, whilst he scrabbled on the floor at my feet, attempting to dislodge me to no avail. He screamed and wailed, scratching at my legs, howling that he would bring me to justice for my unprovoked attack while my blood dripped on to his sparse wisps of hair.

Suddenly Robert was there with Ralph and Progger. They heaved Allen to his feet and bound his wrists behind him.

"Sir William must deal with this distracted lunatick, relation or not! He is seriously prejudicial to our cause." He turned to me. "Tom, he has wounded you. I am more sorry than I can say."

I said nothing. I had not thought I would ever be angry with Robert, but at that moment, I could not trust myself to speak to him. I was in truth much aggrieved. I had had no food since noon the previous day. I had left my poor little sick wife, to care for these renegades. Yesterday before I had been persuaded here along the river, I had worked at my trade for many hours, assisting the wounded in the Close and in the Ovens. I had left my good dinner untasted to help Robert's sick soldiers. He had allowed the madman to steal my breakfast, had given me no thought or help throughout the day, no food or drink had been forthcoming and now my left arm dripped bloody tears, wounded by a demented bullying ignorant sawbones. I decided I would return to the farmhouse, retrieve my box and lurk in the woods until Waller had gone and then try walking home through the Frog Gate.

He continued to apologise whilst I remained silent, as we walked back to the farmhouse. I wished with all my heart I could divorce myself totally from the taint of these cursed wars. Suddenly I turned to Robert and shouted into his face, beside myself with rage.

"I hate, hate, hate this misbegotten destructive conflict! You must do your worst without me! I thank you for helping me in the past but the score now is even! Never ask me to help you again!"

He looked at me with such sorrow that my heart softened. "Well, Robert, well! I will get my box and begone. Fare well and take care of your person for our Saviour's sweet sake! And I tell you what you can tell Sir William. I am no church goer, neither Arminian nor Presbyter and to speak truth I feel God turns a face of mere indifference to us because of these terrible wars. But that Allen! His every word was a blasphemous oath! How answer you that? That a man should claim he cures his fellows, blaspheming with every other word! Why should godly men who are sick and wounded have to listen to his profanity? An oath is one thing when one is in earnest and have need to invoke a higher power but he calls on the Almighty carelessly with his every breath. Answer me that if you can."

"I cannot!" he said sadly. "I cannot answer your charge for I know it to be true. All I can do is plead with Sir William to send the wretch to his home. He will stay there for a while and then return. He has a sickness of the brain that comes and goes like the moon waxing and waning. He will return after some weeks, as sobersided as one could wish, as tedious as a Latin homily, prating about his humours and his elements, and gradually run as mad as May-butter as your old servant used to say."

I could not help but like him and forgive him for his memory of dear old Jacky. I said again, "Well, Robert, I will not quarrel with you." I began to laugh. "And for the love of God, man, can you give me something to eat? Your mad medical moon calf ate my breakfast." I wailed plaintively, and we both laughed together, our difference at an end.

The farmhouse kitchen was again a sick room. Wounded men lay on the earth floor, some groaning and crying out with pain, some biting their lips to try to control their agony. The fortunate ones had lost consciousness. Progger met us.

"Ralph has gone for clean straw, and the Surgeon is locked up at Sir William's command. "Will you help us, Doctor Tom?," Sir William asks."

I looked round at the moaning invalids, and sighed. Again and again and again, my fellow countrymen scourged and persecuted each other and I was asked to patch them up. "First you will have to help me." I told Progger. "This cut in my arm must be cleaned and bandaged before I can examine others."

I told him how to bandage me which he did neatly enough. The wound ached and throbbed and swelled a little all of which I knew to be the usual symptoms. Although my arm felt stiff my fingers retained their dexterity and as each man was placed on a mound of clean straw on the table, I began my work.

The quartermasters came in and asked if they could assist. I told them to wait as I dealt with a sword gash in a man's thigh. A vein had been severed and I had to hope that I could stay the bleeding. I propped up his leg and applied a dressing of comfrey, bandaged it as well as I could, and asked the quartermasters to bring me any remedies that might have been stored by Allen or any other surgeon of Waller's regiment. They told me there was nothing.

So all we had was what I carried in my box. Surgeon's Mate Wind had taken up a majestic stance at my elbow. I asked how Allen would have treated the loss of blood in the matter of the gashed thigh. He did not reply, merely held out his silver bleeding dish and his case of knives. One of the quartermasters remembered Allen's "remedy".

"Oh, aye, in such a case he would take blood from the opposite leg, to balance up matters."

I said nothing. I could not even begin to combat such wilful ignorance. Had he ignored completely William Harvey's conclusions?

Sir William Waller bustled in. I realised he reminded me a little of Shakespeare, whose bust I had studied in Holy Trinity Church in Stratford, whilst his daughter Susannah had prayed. Both Waller and the poet had broad noble brows and strong pointed chins. Now he thanked me profusely for my help as I cut away a blood encrusted sleeve. I smiled politely but was not deceived. Tomorrow he would be on his next campaign and would have forgotten me.

The task before me was sadly familiar. One after the other, again and again, the wounded were laid on the kitchen table before me, and I attempted to mend what other men had broken asunder. I was told that the troops from the Worcester garrison had made a courageous sortie from St Martin's Gate and had swept Waller's men away from the eastern walls. My presence would almost certainly be sought by Sir William Sandys to bind up the Worcester troopers. Ralph came in and told me that the river was still high. Waller was for Tewkesbury I was told before daybreak.

"What of these poor wounded fellows?" I asked.

"We'll pack them into the carts." Ralph told me and the Quartermasters remembered that they had to prepare this means of transportation. They took themselves off leaving me with a prodigious supply of bandages that they called rowlers. They suggested that I used them as much as possible. The jogging movement of the carts would do least harm if the damaged limbs were bandaged as thick as tree trunks.

Robert reappeared with a snapsack in which there was a clean white cloth wrapped around two apple pasties. These he presented to me instructing me to pause in my endeavours to rest and eat. I did not tell him that in all likelihood these were made by Lady Russell from my own apples. This was almost certainly the property of one of the Garrison of Worcester, who now had no need of food. In any event my stomach began to accept that my throat was not cut, and the subterranean rumblings were stilled.

The night dragged on. One or two of the wounded did not survive it and were laid to rest in Perrywoods, but although I did not have much Pares lotion, I managed somehow to effect passable treatment. There was boiled water aplenty and I was able to keep washing my hands and instruments. At length around two in the morning the word came for the men who could no longer walk to be packed into the carts. There was a rumour that Prince Maurice was bound for Worcestershire. Waller did not wish to meet him, after a trouncing at Ripple earlier in the year.

"Sir, Sir, Doctor Tom, I pray you, can you come with us?" It was the slight young man who had claimed I had brought him back from the dead earlier that morning (except this morning was now yesterday) recovered from his poisoning but now with a musket ball removed from his calf.

"I fear not. My wife lies sick in Worcester." He accepted that. I pleaded with all that could hear and understand not to allow any ignorant madman to bleed them and make them even weaker. "Colonel Burghill knows how dangerous blood-letting is. Send for him and he will prevent the practice."

I had not known that Robert was standing behind me. Now he said respectfully, "Yes, Doctor Tom!" and caused mirth by his humility. I laughed also, "See you do so, Sir," I told him, jestingly.

Throughout all my ministrations, Surgeon's Mate Wind stood like a marble statue, clutching his bleeding dish and his case of knives. He seemed to have no other medical skill. I asked him if there were any instruments to be packed and transported. He shook his head holding out the two items he had held all night. I took pity on him and sent him away. The kitchen seemed suddenly a much larger room.

Sir William Waller came in as I had just finished bandaging the last poor fellow who had patiently waited for my attention all night. I sat heavily on my chair and looked up at him, then leapt to my feet, realising that to sit in his presence might be construed as discourteous.

He laughed and pushed me back down again. "No, no, Doctor Tom, and in fact when you sit I find I am less in awe of you, so tall a man as you are. Was your father high and mighty like yourself?"

"My mother always claimed my height came from her forebears. 'Tis said Swedish giants landed on the south west coast of Wales, sir, generations ago. Neither of my parents were out of the ordinary in length and were somewhat bemused by their Gargantuan only child." I told him, and considering it must have been four of the clock in a wet May dawn, I felt that my response was ingenious for the hour and circumstance.

"I am greatly in your debt, Doctor Tom," he said. "What can I do to repay you?"

Now I had to stand up. "End this accursed conflict!" I did not shout but I looked down at him. "That is what must be done to repay me and other innocents who have suffered by these bloody actions. Surely there are men of good will on both sides like yourself who could discuss and discourse until a solution emerges."

He nodded. I was now so far gone in sauciness that I might as well say my whole mind. "Lucius Carey, Viscount Falkland is the best and cleverest of men. I know he would sway the king to negotiate if he could do so."

"If, If, If !" he agreed. "Have you seen the King avoid disputation? He is like one of those slippery eels that poisoned my poor fellows two days ago and whom you cured. I wish you could cure our sovereign of his misguided mental distempers, my boy."

"Forgive me," I mumbled, feeling I had overstepped the mark.

"For nothing!" he said, "I support your desires. But it will not happen, believe me. I tell you, son, our King is as unyielding and contumacious as a stone wall."

I nodded and was silent. I could only be grateful he had not discovered how fragile and easily breached were the stone walls of Worcester!

The wounded were helped and carried out to carts. I assisted with those who were severely disabled and for whose futures I feared. I could do nothing more for them but suddenly I realised that I might be able to afford them easier passage.

"Sir William!" I called out, looking around. He was supervising the packing of pikes onto another cart. "Sir William, there is one thing you can do for me. In order that these fellows may not be jolted to death and my work go for nothing, there are boat builders this side Severn. If you are for Tewkesbury, three or four large wherries should carry your wounded more smoothly. You could hire the boats and boatmen both at Kempsey."

"I will do so, Doctor Tom, and I thank you for the advice. Do you perhaps also know where I might find a good supply of horses?"

I smiled and shook my head. Boats to aid the wounded were

one thing. Horses for healthy whole troopers would be treachery.

"No, I did not think you would be able to help me in that instance." He smiled also, and bade me Farewell again as they began to move southwards.

I stood in the drizzling dawn and heard rather than saw the army of men striking camp and beginning their march to Tewkesbury. I said Farewell to Robert who again craved my forgiveness. I too was sorry for my anger but he was kind enough to say I was entirely justified. He then embraced me... a mark of affection I had been dreading. Ralph said Farewell in his customary manner with a slap on the back and a wink and a shrug and Progger shook my hands. And they went away into the dawn.

I sat for some while as the creaking of the carts and the voices of the troopers faded. They were slipping away south through the woods and fields towards the river. I trusted no more of them would be tempted by the eel pies made in Kempsey. As the light strengthened I pondered my position. I would see if I could gain entry through the Frog More gate. I decided that the empty kitchen with its dying embers and the smell and echoes of twenty five sick men was a melancholy place, solitary now after so much activity. I took up my box and feeling the morning chill around my ragged shirt sleeve, placed a blanket round my shoulders like an old beggar and trudged out.

The woods bore the traces of many men having been recently encamped. The undergrowth was trodden down and the paths had been churned to mud. Robins and thrushes changed their morning hymns to alarm calls at my approach. But the rain had stopped and the May dawn promised heat, as there was a steaminess rising from the ground. I slithered through the trees down to the Frog Mill in the hope that the gate might have been opened when the guards learned of Waller's departure. But it was locked and silent. I slipped round under the walls past St Peter's to Sidbury, where the road from Pershore came down into the town. This gate also was barred and deserted.

I walked up the road a little way. The cobble stones soon gave place to hard earth. The sun began to strike through the trees. As I felt the first vestiges of its warmth, my eyes became heavy and I thought that perhaps I would find a dry hollow to wait for the gates to be opened again. I wrapped myself in the blanket and sat beside the track for all the world like a ragged outcast. This then was a new dish for me to taste. This was how the beggars felt at the town gate as they saw rich young men on fine horses sweep past them. A strange and hard lesson for a well-to-do fellow like myself. I vowed in future to show more compassion for such desperate sad wretches. I drew my knees up under my flea ridden blanket and dozed.

I woke to the jingle of harness and the shouts of men. A troop of about twenty dragoons were picking their way down to the city. The first riders gave me barely a glance, thinking I was a destitute peasant, crouching by the road in the hope of alms. But their commander, a kind and humane governor, trotted towards me, feeling in a bag he wore at his side, no doubt for food or pence.

"God give you good day, Sir William," I said politely. It was William Russell.

"Doctor Tom!" he cried amazed. "In the name of God, what has happened in this town, that you are sleeping like a beggar on the ground outside the walls? Is Waller in there?" He called on his men to halt immediately. "Here is news, by God! Is this some trick? One brought us news to Stoulton where we lay this night that the devil Waller and all his followers had gone before dawn."

"It's no trick," I told him, standing and bowing. "Waller went south to Tewkesbury before dawn, but he had three thousand men with him. I would not follow him, sir, if I were you. He was not pleased with his reception from Sir William Sandys. I was told that your boys committed themselves like heroes, giving them bloody coxcombs aplenty."

"But why are you here and not in your surgery, Doctor Tom?" This was the question I had been dreading. But I was now learning an important lesson in the art of survival in these wars. When in a situation where the true explanation could be misconstrued, the remedy is simple. Lie.

"I strolled out onto the quay but two nights ago after healing our wounded in the Close and was suddenly overpowered and bundled along the river shore to Waller's camp. Some traitor in Worcester must have betrayed my profession to the bastards. They forced me to treat their injuries. Then this morning as they set off, they set me loose."

"The perfidious rogues!" he cried. "They have ravished your raiment, the dogs! Take my horse! I will walk beside. 'Tis but a short step down to the gate, and I will relish stretching my legs."

And so I returned to my city. Sir William shouted for the gates to open for him and in I rode, with his troopers while he walked beside. I felt like a Conqueror seated on the Governor's horse, ready to receive the nosegays thrown by pretty girls and to accept the plaudits and congratulations of my fellow citizens. Sadly, however, there were but two drunkards arguing the toss of a die, and an old dame and her grandson setting out with baskets to gather firewood. Few of my fellow citizens had as yet left their beds, as they were tired out after their exertions of the last two days. I dismounted and thanked Sir William profusely, and drawing my dirty blanket around me shuffled my way home, excessively relieved that he had not enquired about how I had happened to be carrying my box during an evening stroll on the quay!

I walked into my kitchen with something of the conquering hero's imaginary bays still adorning my proud brow. "Waller has gone!" I announced to my household.

"Yes, we know." said Joan shortly. "Jacky came to tell us an hour ago. Tom, you stink like a pole-cat. Best clean yourself ere you attend to those who await you in the surgery. And Phoebe is not improved."

I ran up to see how she did and realised that if anything she had worsened. She seemed to need to keep unnaturally still and seemed to find any movement of her body very painful. She did not even turn to look at me as I entered our bedroom but remained motionless.

"Sweetheart, how do you?" I asked her and took up her right hand in both of mine. She gave a sad little gasp of pain and I laid her hand down carefully upon the coverlet.

"Tom, why does my shoulder hurt me so?" she asked me plaintively.

"My love, tomorrow I will fetch Martha. She may be able to throw light on your sickness. Shall I fetch her today and leave the wounded?"

She shook her head slightly and mouthed the word "No." But having spoken the notion aloud, it plagued me through the day, as I treated the Worcester injured, both in my surgery and in the Ovens. These were mostly sword cuts and injuries sustained from flying metal or debris from damaged buildings. Anyone who had been struck by a canon ball had died within moments. I was taken to look at them as they awaited burial. One small corpse caused me to groan aloud and wipe away my tears. The shoemaker's son had had his leg blown off above the knee and I gazed at his small face which in death had assumed a pinched questioning look. I had no answers for him or for his grieving mother. I wept as I gazed at the sad ruin of what had been a happy child. My only consolation was that I had acted as a responsible guardian and removed Philip and Barty from that dangerous place.

I worked as well as I could all day and the Worcester wounded were fortunate in that there was a plentiful supply of medicines from our dispensary. I know I worked hard… perhaps I even saved lives… but I was assailed by terrible fears for my wife in particular and for our sad country in general. My mood was downcast. Nothing seemed to cheer me. I reflected that I had had little sleep since… last Sunday when Abram and I had returned from our journey. At last I went back home and after ascertaining that Phoebe's condition was no better, sat down heavily at the kitchen table and watched the preparations for supper, whilst attempting to remain awake and be civil.

I reflected that I had done my best to "patch up" both sides. Was I a traitor? But treachery to my medical vow would have been to have done nothing. I had helped my fellows as well as I could. As I ate, I reflected that Joan must have had a most tiresome difficult day, managing the house and the surgery at the same time and then preparing and serving this excellent lamb stew. I thanked her as politely as I could and promised Pip and Barty that I would take them to see their father before the end of the week, if Worcestershire remained at peace.

However it was to be the next day, the 1st June that I had to take to my horse again. That night whenever I moved in my sleep, Phoebe began to scream. The sound would have been terrible to hear from any creature in pain, but from my own wife, it was as if she hardly knew me. She seemed to be in some sphere of pain inhabited by herself alone. She looked at me as if I was a hostile stranger, but when I leapt from my side of the bed and came round to look at her she mouthed the words, "Tom, I am very sorry."

I gently drew back the blankets to look at her body. She lay fixedly on her back, the slight swelling that had been on her right side, now something larger. I touched the place and instantly she cried out in what was clearly the most agonising of pain. The trickle of brown fluid from her continued to stain the old linen bandages with which Joan had supplied her. I gently replaced the covers.

Although I judged it had passed midnight, there were sounds outside the door. I opened it. Abram stood there, his eyes round and tearful, his expression as concerned as it had been for his father.

"Is all well with her?"

I came out to him and closed the door behind me, "I fear not, Abram. Will you come with me tomorrow to fetch Martha?"

He nodded, happy, I think, to have the chance to help. "Shall I get a drink of water for you... and for Phoebe?"

"That would be a kind service." I told him. He brought back two beakers of water and told me, "I heard her cry out. Is it very bad?"

"I fear so." I told him, "Do you know where Joan keeps spare blankets? I must sleep in the chair. My very presence gives her pain."

He went straight to a cupboard and drew out two woollen blankets for me and I tucked myself up as best I could. Phoebe seemed to have fallen asleep again. She clearly had to stay as still as she could in order for the pain to subside.

Next morning I asked everyone to stay around the table after we had broken our fast. I had to admit that Phoebe was ill, very ill and I could not help her. The feeling of defeat and helplessness that this knowledge engendered caused me to despair. I told my household that I would take Pip and Barty to see their father and that Abram would ride with me to fetch Martha as Phoebe seemed to feel that she alone might have some notion of what ailed her. I asked Joan not to be hurt at this, but she merely nodded and said, "She has the experience of an older generation. We must seek out that knowledge." Roger, as downcast as myself, asked leave to accompany us.

Joan came to me privately afterwards and said that she thought the best thing that could be done for Phoebe was to obtain a supply of poppy powder from the apothecary.

"We may well not need it," she said in a rare moment of affection, patting my shoulder, "But suppose Martha can give us no hope, or even if it is needed to halt the pain as part of her treatment, it is surely best for us to be prepared."

I agreed. I had not allowed such strong drugs to be stored in the house, and asked her to administer a dose while we were gone if the pain was clearly unbearable for Phoebe.

"Perhaps a good notion to give her some prior to cleaning her person." Joan said "As fastidious a girl as she is, it has been a fearsome task for us both to attempt it."

"Yes, yes, do you buy it, Joan, and hold it secure. Mind, 'twill be more peaceful for you here today, with three of our young rapscallions absent."

"Ah, God love them. I have grown used to them all. Let us hope you find their father better, and Tom," …she paused, "Abram is a good youth!" This was so much in the old manner of her compassionate character that my spirits lifted somewhat.

The day was overcast but the sun broke through as we trotted along. I took the boys in the cart behind Hector, with Shireen and Apple trotting alongside to give them exercise. Roger rode Sir John and Abram rode Jupiter. I cannot say that we were merry but there was some relief in being once again on the open road. I allowed Pip to take the reins and then while Barty took his turn, suggested Pip rode Shireen for two miles or so if Abram would permit it. He was graciously pleased to do so. So with the boys taking turn about on Shireen or in the cart we came again to the stone-cutters village and what a different picture met our eyes on the Green.

The quarriers were outside the inn peacefully taking their ease and Martha sat in her garden sewing some garment. She rose up in delight when she saw us, but her face fell when she saw that Phoebe was not with us. I explained quickly that we hoped she would return with us to tend her if Silas Dodgeson was recovered. As if in answer to my request, he came from the cottage at that moment, holding a hammer.

"Dadda!" the boys leapt from the cart and came to hug him. He seemed pleased by their affection, dropped his hammer and stroked their hair.

"I was coming to find you tomorrow," he told them. "Sir Roger has a blight of poachers. I'm not coming back to the quarry. Should you like to go home, lads?"

They cheered in answer but Barty, who had become more conscious of the feelings of others, told him, "But Doctor Tom has been marvellous kind to us, Dadda! And Mistress Bailey! And we learnt to be drummer boys in the Garrison. Even Abram let me ride his pony."

Dodgeson was a man for deeds rather than words. He said briefly, "I thank you, Doctor Fletcher and you too, Aunt Martha. I'll be back to finish mending your fence. But best get them home now."

He moved stiffly but with confidence. Martha's remedies had clearly worked their magic. Would they could do the same for my poor little wife!

"Martha, will you return with us? To say truth I am half sick of worry for her."

She asked a few questions but I did not wish to describe Phoebe's symptoms before the Dodgesons. She gathered her belongings together into a canvas bag and we bade her nephew and her great nephews Farewell. Pip gravely shook my hand, in itself a mark of a new and courteous maturity but Barty hugged me and asked me to give his respects to Joan and Phoebe. I was sorry to see them depart, but was pleased to reflect that there would be fewer active young boys eating us out of house and home and disturbing the horses.

I helped Martha up onto the cart, gathered up the reins and we trotted off behind Roger and Abram. Martha clearly relished her jaunt and cheerfully commented on the flowers and plants she recognised as she passed them. She had known Ben, and had been one of his herb gatherers and now asked if I had news of him. I had not but the fault was as much mine as his. I vowed that I would send him a budget of news when I had the time…. when Phoebe was better.

I asked Martha where she had learned her knowledge of the medical properties of plants. She told me of a spinster aunt of the Lygon family who had delighted to teach the mysteries of herbal lore to any young girl who had the will to learn.

"Lady Matilda cherished little respect for the affairs of mankind. She held to the strange notion, Tom, that women had more… breeding and awareness than their menfolk .

She told me that her Mistress' teaching was based on the notion that any illness below the sun could be cured by a plant that might grow near the place where the illness was first noticed. I nodded sagely. There was at least an element of sanity and practical expertise in such a theory, more so than the derisive laughable claims of the mad surgeon based on the humours and the elements.

She asked about our married life. She wondered if Phoebe might already be with child. I explained that we had hoped for that joy, but that she was troubled now by this strange brown leakage of blood and so we had ceased to expect such an outcome.

"Might I ask how long have you had carnal knowledge, one of the other?" she asked.

I stared fixedly ahead. "We entered into handfast in April and were finally married mid-May, so I would say we have been living as man and wife for six weeks now." This then was what it felt to be a patient, and I must, red-faced, answer for myself.

"But Mistress Bailey does not know of our early consummation." I added. "I believe we would prefer that even now she did not know. It could be seen as something premature, by those who adhere to more puritanical beliefs."

Martha said nothing except to repeat thoughtfully the two words, "Six weeks."

I felt that perhaps I should explain that Joan had had grave doubts as to the wisdom of our marriage, because of Phoebe's slight crookedness and my unusual height. But Martha would not allow that to be an issue, and gave me the comfort of her opinion which was that I had done nothing untoward. "Small chance now of anything "untoward" or otherwise!" I told her bitterly. "My slightest movement in the night causes her desperate pain."

Joan was her courteous self when we arrived back in Newport Street. She had obtained the poppy drug from the Apothecary on the High Street, but had not given Phoebe any as yet, as she had been sleeping for most of the day. She had had a little chicken broth at midday, and was now quiet and still, she told us.

"Will you dine first or see your patient, Mistress?" she asked Martha.

"If she rests, then I will sit down with you first, if you please." Martha decided. "I can see that there is one here who would prefer to dine before aught else." For Abram was peering into the cauldron set over the fire, and picking at chicken patties set ready for our meal. Joan slapped his hand and directed him to find Adam and James and bring them to the table.

And so we dined though I confess I could take little pleasure in either our food or concourse, although the first was delectable as ever and the second far ranging. Adam was interested to hear that Pip and Barty were again in their father's charge and hoped that they would not lose the good respectful habits they had learned under my governance.

"Nay rather 'tis Sir William Russell, whose regime in the Garrison has taught them better manners," I argued, but no-one would allow me to shuffle off the credit for their reformation. "They were different boys, today" Martha averred. "I would not have known them. In so short a time, sure, they have now some of the attributes of nature's gentlemen."

"And certainly, we shall always be pleased to see them," Joan declared.

At last the interminable meal drew to a close, and I led Martha up to our bedchamber where Phoebe lay. She gave a cry of joy at the sight of her old friend which changed to a little scream of anguish, as her delight provoked movement.

"I am sorry indeed to see things come to this pass, my poor maid." said Martha, and indeed the constant pain my poor wife endured could now be seen in her lovely face, which was white and colourless except where dark shadows lay under her eyes. "Which side is it that hurts you so?"

"My right, and there is a swelling here." And Phoebe bravely pushed back the coverlet and blankets. Martha turned to me.

"Tom, may I find you in your orchard, or if you have stable tasks, I will find you there?" In other words, this was women's work, doctor or no. Phoebe smiled at me as I came to the bed. "Courage, Tom," she whispered, "All's well, now Martha has come."

I went downstairs. Abram was waiting for me at the bottom of the staircase and we went slowly out into the courtyard and thence to the garden. Adam was taking a nap his sightless face turned to the sun. I remembered Ben speaking of the hopeless state of his eyes. "Curtains have descended. It may be that one day a clever surgeon can cut them back and he will see again. But we have not the skill, Tom."

Poor Adam, doomed to a world without light. The terrible pity of his condition tore at my heart. I said slowly,

"How much we do not know." We walked through the orchard and sat in the bower where Phoebe and I had decided that we would be handfast.

"If any can help her, it is that good old lady," said Abram.

It was June the first. Oppression hung heavily over me. I was beginning to fear that my wife was past hope but when I tried to make myself confront this possibility, all I could yearn for were the happy days of the past. I stared at the river gliding past through a gap in the hedge and wished it could carry me far away, far from these adversities. With a splash and a flurry, four swans lighted upon the sparkling waves.

We sat for some minutes in silence, gazing abstractedly at the water. Then Abram said, "She is here." and Martha was walking slowly towards us.

Abram stood so that she could sit beside me. "You are a good youth." she told him. "Now I have a terrible thirst upon me. Might Mistress Bailey furnish us here with a pitcher of ale? Could you request such a favour, my good boy?"

Abram, pleased I think to be active, sped away through the trees. Martha took my hand. "Tom, dear Tom, I do not have good news. I can do nothing for her."

I stared at her, a sick feeling of heaviness forming in my stomach. Now the dread knowledge that had been in my heart was become daylight reality. I forced myself to ask, "What ails her?"

"There is a babe conceived but its growth destroys her. It is resting in some passage away from the womb, which is empty. As the child grows, it tears her inner parts, and she bleeds inwardly. Believe me, I have seen this before. There is no hope."

"What can I do?"

"Nothing, save to be beside her. We must begin to give her the poppy drug, so that the agony is dulled. I understand she has not eaten for some days."

I shook my head. "She drank a little chicken soup today but nothing of any significance." She went on, "Perhaps you might wish to encourage her to eat, but for my part I can only assure you that it will prolong her fearful pain."

I said almost in wonder, "If I had not laid with her, she would not now be dying." Martha replied, "That is true, but all women take their chance when they marry. I have no doubt she was pleased and proud to marry you, so excellent a young fellow as you are. It is the common lot of women, to seek a husband. The same unfortunate fate could have followed had she married another man. This is a rare condition. It cannot be foretold or prevented."

I had not known that Martha, a poor old herb gatherer as I thought, could speak so eloquently or be so well informed. I stood and went towards the low wall and stared at the river sliding past. That was one way of concluding my torment. The water seemed smooth and calmly welcoming. I collected myself. I must care for my wife whilst she still breathed.

I asked Martha, "Could Ben Knowles help us? Is there some drug that would enable the misplaced babe to move?"

She replied sadly, "No, Tom, there is nothing. Master Knowles could do nothing if he were here. To attempt to cut away the unborn would kill your wife before her time. That will not be long now. If we can gauge the poppy powder correctly there will perhaps be some moments when you and she might speak of your happy times together. Some men and women never find their soul's mate. You will have that joyous memory, even though it has been all too brief."

I cried out, "I do not want a memory!" I sat in the bower again and I fear I wept without control for some minutes. I could not but blame myself. Phoebe would not be dead if I had not married her. I should never have left her to go with Robert. Martha could do nothing but pat my hand and then we heard voices. Abram and Joan were coming through the blossoming trees carrying beakers and a pitcher. Joan stopped in her tracks.

"Why, Tom, whatever is amiss?" she cried out. I could not speak. I motioned to Martha to tell her of the tragic loss that we must face. She explained as best she could the physical misfortune that had overtaken my poor wife.

I do not think we could have foretold Joan's reaction. She listened gravely to Martha's news and then gave a howl of anguish, like an animal in pain. She clenched her fists and came towards me.

"This is your doing, Tom Fletcher. This is the daughter I never had. Do you know now what you have done? You have killed her with your lust!"

"You cannot accuse me of anything that I do not accuse myself, Joan," I cried. But at the sound of our raised voices, Adam awoke and began to cry aloud in panic, afraid of what might be happening. Abram ran to him to reassure him and Martha took Joan's hands and led her to sit.

"Mistress Bailey, Tom is completely guiltless in this matter. This was a love match, entered into freely by both parties. Phoebe was utterly happy with her husband."

Joan sobbed noisily. Abram led Adam towards her, speaking to him as they came, of the horror of Phoebe's illness. As Adam understood her fate, he groaned aloud. For some moments none of us were able to speak as we were completely oppressed by the knowledge of her condition. How could I ever have taken pride in my profession? I was a useless cipher, with no more skill than the wretched madman who had tried to kill me in the woods above the town.

At length Joan raised her head. "I warned you, Tom. I told you that all would not be regular with her. Her crippled condition and her small stature should have cautioned you against carnal union, such disparity as there is between your heights."

"No, Mistress!" said Martha firmly. "Phoebe is usual physically in her organs of regeneration. This condition is one of desperate bad luck. No more, no less. I have seen it twice before and both women were of regular growth and appearance. One of these women had already given birth to two children. Tom is not to blame. You must not scold him with your grief. Poor lad! He has grief and to spare of his own."

We were silent again, and than Abram said quietly, "So Tom what is to be done? This poppy medicine, which Joan bought yesterday. It eased my father's passing."

I thought for a moment, in spite of myself considering the situation from the physician's viewpoint . "To speak truth, I am afraid of morphia or morphine, as it is known. It is after all a poison. One of the eight substances the College of Physicians try to control. When we used it for your father, I had placed myself under the guidance of Doctor Tillam, who said something after the manner of "Kill the pain but not the patient." I think I will make my use of it known to William Russell, so that there can be no question of secret malpractice."

"No indeed!" said Joan with a degree of unpleasantness that surpassed even her lately venomous tongue. "That has taken place already, in your marriage bed!"

"Shame on you, mistress," said Martha, standing. "Come, Tom. I will sit with Phoebe whilst you and Abram seek this Sir William. I applaud your caution."

As we walked along Broad Street, Abram asked me thoughtfully, "What ails her?" and I knew Joan was in his thoughts, not Phoebe. Then he answered himself, "I don't think she likes her young men to marry. She will never like poor Betsy, and she liked you and Phoebe better when you were bachelor and maid."

I glanced at him as he strode along beside me. He was perhaps three inches shorter than myself but he sometimes seemed to me to display an awareness of human behaviour that belied his years. I had not thought of Joan's behaviour as stemming from... what? Jealousy?

Sir William at the sight of me insisted that I sat and took brandy wine with him, whilst Abram was brought an apple cordial. He sat and listened to our conversation. Sir William seemed something bemused by my insistence that he should know I had to use a most lethal drug.

"You are the doctor, Tom... Master Fletcher, I should say. It must be your decision. And may I say how grievous distressed, I am to hear of Lady Phoebe's illness."

"You are right, Sir William, it must be my decision but I am both doctor and husband. The Pharmacopoeia Londinensis lists opium as a dangerous poison. This decision has something of a moral dilemma for me. My poor girl will die in any event but injudicious use of this drug could hasten that event. Perhaps I am wrong to seek your approval but I have more faith in your moral courage than I have in that of certain of our clerics."

"My dear boy, I am flattered by your words. Perhaps you are right to be cautious. He continued, "In times of civil disquiet such as these, it behoves us to be aware of the possibility of what could be seen perhaps as a potential weapon. Is that the basis of your concern?"

I did not think he totally understood. I stood up and walked over to the window that looked over to the river and the Malverns. I could not forbear from weeping again and he followed me with the brandy. I had half a mind to confess the truth of our early morning encounter on the Sidbury Road but decided against it.

"What I think, sir, is that a higher power than myself, a wiser authority such as you, should know that I propose to use this method of dulling my poor wife's fearful pain. I do not want to carry all the responsibility myself. I have no father with whom to discuss this. Master Bailey is I think too near the circumstances, and as you know cannot look upon dearest Phoebe's pain to judge if I deal justly or not."

"I see where you are at. As well to notify and regulate the use of such dangerous tinctures. In the meantime, Tom, I have every faith in you."

I bowed, finished the brandy and took my leave, something shakily. At least I had a moral sanction to use the poppy drug. I confess I was grateful that Abram bore me company so faithfully. As we walked home a little girl fell as she played with her hoop. He raised her up and dried her tears as I stood watching him.

"Alas, Abram!" I said, "We are alike fatherless you and I. How shall we do, do you think? A father's love and guidance is an excellent yardstick in this world."

"We must care for each other," he told me instantly, "And when we are in doubt, we must ask Adam or Sir William. And Allah puts in my mind what I should do"

I almost smiled. "Well I have not heard of Allah for some time. I had thought he might have stayed in Lichfield."

"No indeed!" said Abram, "He is with us always, caring for us and protecting us from Joan."

"I never thought I would need such protection." I said thoughtfully and so we came home again.

And the heavy days of June began. Martha stayed with us, as the Dodgesons had undertaken the care of her dog. She gave such assistance as she could with Phoebe.

The opium removed the pain but also denied her any awareness of her plight and even of where she was. When in error we had not administered sufficient to cause the blessed oblivion which she craved, then the terrible thin screaming would begin.

It was as if she were a damned soul in Hell. One of us was constantly with her and at length though I would never have admitted it to a living soul, I, even I, her loving husband, began to wish that her suffering could cease. She could not speak to us and, I think, did not even know us.

But on the day when she left us, something akin to a miracle occurred. Perhaps we had now gauged the precise dosage needed. As far as I was aware she was sleeping the drugged slumber which gave us all relief. I sat in my chair by the window dozing in the warm evening sun, when suddenly I heard my name.

"Tom, dear Tom."

I leapt up and came to her bedside. Her beautiful face, pale as the sheets, had a faint animation. She took my hand and whispered, "I love you, sweetheart."

"Oh, Phoebe, dearest one I love you."

She then said her three last words, "Tell my uncle." There was the faintest pressure of her hand in mine, and her lovely head, still framed by the chestnut hair, slipped sideways on the pillow and she left me.

I kissed her then and held her, drawing her to me as I could not do during her illness. I told her of all I had hoped for in our life together, and so we sat, I speaking aloud of the future we would never have, while the rigour of death claimed her. My hands on her back slowly felt the warmth of life drain from her, but I could not now let her go, now that I had regained her. And so we sat, until Joan came up to see if all was well. I had expected recriminations but she merely stroked my darling's brow, and wept a little, and spoke of Phoebe's final release from the terrible pain. After a while she left us and I continued to sit with my wife, kissing her cold lips, and telling her of the places we could never go and the children we would never have, as the diamond window patterns of the setting sun slowly faded from the floor.

There was a knock and Abram came in. He of all my household was most recently acquainted with the finality of death, having lost his father at Easter. Now he gently took her from me and laid her down as I had taken him from his dead father.

"Come, Tom." he said almost echoing my own words over poor Joseph in the little house in Birmingham. "Allah has her now. Nothing else can hurt her."

And so I allowed him to lead me downstairs. Everyone was gathered in the kitchen, Patience and Gill weeping softly. Although there was food on the table, no-one could eat and for a while we sat in silence, overcome with our loss. For everyone had loved Phoebe. Joan gazed angrily out of the window at the last rays of light touching the apple trees. Adam sat in his place in the chimney corner, and sometimes a tear coursed down his brown cheek. Roger pushed over a beaker of claret and I confess I relished the lively stimulus of the wine.

Gill at length rose to make her way home back to Fish Street. She took my hand in her old worn fingers and said comfortingly, "She is forever young, now. Her little body will not know the sadness of stooping old age."

I nodded and she kissed my cheek as she had done when I was a child and said lovingly, "Good night, Master Tommy. You did all you could."

I went back to be with my wife and sat beside her through the short midsummer night. Joan brought me a posset of warm milk with brandy and I sipped it slowly, holding my darling's cold hand. But at last my heart accepted that she was mine no longer. Death had her now, and our unborn child. The child to whom we had tried to give life but who had killed her.

As the early sun crept through the streets I went to the Dean's house, to tell him of my loss. As it was the Sabbath, the 18th June he was up betimes, preparing for Matins. One glance at my face and he asked gently, "She is gone then?"

I nodded and he out of respect for my father said immediately that he would arrange the burial in St Helens. I had known of course that that was the final outcome, but the thought of my darling immured in the cold earth was more than I could bear and I ran from the house and sat weeping for awhile near the Cathedral. There Abram found me. Two soldiers from the Garrison had seen and recognised me and loitered near, afraid perhaps that I was run mad and might do myself harm. Abram asked them to tell Sir William of Phoebe's death.... and as the words echoed in my skull, I wept again.

"Come on, Tom. Come back with me now. You must eat." and I allowed him to lead me back to my house of mourning.

After my father's murder at the hands of Essex, the days that followed were confused and distracted, and always in my mind and memory was the terrible dreadful vision of seeing him swinging there above the silent crowd. I had known that I would lose Phoebe so I had not the excuse of the mortal shock and yet... and yet... I could not look upon her clothes lying lifeless in her closet, on her empty place at the table, on the labels written ready in her neat hand for the jars in her still room, without the sensation of a great yawning chasm opening before me.

I stood alone at her graveside, and there before me was the actual hollow of her final resting place. We were alike alone, she and I, having no close family alive to share our griefs. I said my Farewell in my head and sprinkled the handful of soil onto her little coffin. I stood fixed to the spot as the sexton threw in the spadefuls of earth. I was reluctant to lose sight of the last of her. I was aware that Joan hurried the mourners to the house for refreshment and when at last I turned there was Abram standing alone, still as stone behind me.

As we dragged our way back to Newport Street, Sir William joined us. Abram and Roger had lately assisted with the clearance of the houses that had sprung up outside the walls for some years now. Should Waller return, the danger to the inhabitants of these external suburbs was mortal and their walls and outhouses supplied the Parliament men with useful cover. But many of the householders did not appreciate the danger they were in, and the work of the Garrison in clearing the area.

"Homeless or lifeless?" he demanded of us, as we lurched along. "Which do they prefer?"

Abram made some kind of murmur and with his hand under my elbow, steered me past the applewoman's stall on Merrivale.

"But how negligent of your feelings am I!" Sir William suddenly came to himself. "Tom, good boy, I am sorrier than I can say. Childbirth difficulties they tell me. Alas, the poor sweet girl, so common a fate for womankind!"

I nodded dumbly. There was no response. But when we returned to Newport Street, there was suddenly much to do. Simon and Betsy had ridden over the river from Clevelode for poor Phoebe's interment. Betsy had risen to replenish her bowl with Chicken Cullis, a broth she relished well she was telling the company as Abram and I came in to the kitchen with Sir William. But there was a scream and as she stood there, eyes wide, it was clear from the growing pool around her feet that her waters had broken.

Simon carried her upstairs and turned left at the head of the staircase into my room. And so it came about that within sixty hours of my wife's departure, Rachel Phoebe Elizabeth Bailey made her lusty appearance on the same bed, a fortnight before she was officially expected. Once she had got it into her head to arrive, there was no gainsaying her, even had we wished to. It was a regular birth without any complication and within six hours, there she was, a long pretty child, with excellent lungs. Joan had supplied us with boiled water and clean linen and had then returned to the company, and Martha and I worked away in accord with Betsy, and we were all delighted with the outcome.

I sat in my chair in which I had recently spent so many nights and gazed at Betsy suckling her daughter. It came into my head that Phoebe had willed this happy natural birth, on this the saddest of all my days. A strange fancy, but the circumstances seemed somewhat rare and mysterious. Simon came bounding up to greet his daughter and praise his wife, lavishing his honest affection on them both. I went to see if any more Chicken Cullis remained. Betsy had earned it.

I cannot say that my grief was lessened but perhaps Rachel's hungry cries dulled my anguish over the next few days. Joan's frostiness towards Betsy had melted a little and she and Adam made much together of their first grandchild, who was predictable as a town clock. When she was hungry, she cried and when she was tired, she slept. There were moments when she did neither and surveyed her admiring courtiers with a regard which contained an element of superior disbelief. "Is this then what I was led to expect?" her gaze seemed to imply. "Will the fare and the company improve in time, perhaps?"

I found myself staring at her often with fascination. How Phoebe would have loved this miraculous creature. Somehow there was compensation in her presence. After a few days when it was felt Betsy was strong enough to undertake the journey, Simon took his wife and daughter back, and I took Martha to her home high in the Malverns, on Friday the 23rd of June.

Life returned in the next week to its usual round of healing the sick which was my task, cutting and shaving the heads of Worcester's male citizens, Roger's vocation, and Joan as ever, cooked, distilled, advised and scolded. Abram and I attempted to appease and conciliate her bad humour, by being as thoughtful as we could be in domestic matters. Roger had abandoned his attempts at pacifying her and went his wild ways and James pretended not to notice that aught was amiss. Occasionally Adam would object to her cruel jibes. She never berated him, but after he had angrily pointed out to her that her remarks lacked both compassion and substance, she wept a little and was clearly conscience-stricken.

I cannot say, though, that in those dark days there was much agreement or harmony in our household. Without Phoebe's wise inspiration, there was a dearth of amusing conversation. Patience and Samuel were attempting at all times in my Fish Street house to ease the lot of my old servants Gill and Jacky, although dear Jacky was still hale and sturdy. Patience insisted when Simon and his family had gone that we went to the Fish Street house to dine with them. They were particularly proud of a certain system they had obtained from the ironmonger that effortlessly turned the spit, by means of metal weighted jacks at either end of it. In our household, the menial task of spit-turning was performed by Adam. I did not like that he should assume this lowly kitchen-boy's role and frequently had insisted that he should cease his toil when the fire burned too high and hot. I had tried to cure turnspits' burnt and split faces where a cruel cook had caused them to sit turning for too long. I do not think that Joan liked him to perform this servile labour but Adam claimed that it was a means whereby he could contribute to the smooth running of the kitchen, so she allowed him to do so, in that any action that gave him a degree of independence must cause him pleasure.

But from his first coming to Newport Street, Abram had hated to see Adam turn the spit and had frequently come to me in private to complain when he felt that his mentor was abused. I did not like to interfere between husband and wife, but I had to admit that Joan had changed. When I had left my home for Lichfield in February, she had been a gracious affectionate woman. Now there was a distinct alteration in her character, and it was difficult indeed to please her. Occasionally her original persona would appear and all would be well for some minutes, but then the loving old friend of my parents would disappear and the shrewish termagant would again be in the ascendant. Ben had told me that with the ending of the mesnes, when a woman knows that child-bearing is at an end, certain of her sex can become depressed and irritable. I told myself that this condition was merely temporary, although Martha had pursed her lips and shaken her head at certain of Joan's wilder comments. But if Adam was content with his task of spit-turning, I had resolved to let well alone.

But now one day, before the end of June, perhaps a fortnight after my wife's death, we had been summoned to Fish Street to eat a Spring lamb which Patience had cooked by this new mechanical method. She had perfected the art of roasting by this means and in the tin before the fire which caught the fat had set potatoes and parsnips to cook in the meat juices. The delicious aroma set our appetites ablaze and Patience seated us around my parent's old round table where we waited in delightful expectancy. I had had little appetite since Phoebe's passing but even I felt something akin to hunger as we waited to be served.

"Look, Tom!" said Abram in delight, "The wheels that turn the weights are like unto the innards of a clock. Have you seen so neat a contrivance?"

"And if the meat taste as flavoursome as it smells, then Master Adam I fear you must find another calling." I said with an attempt at levity. "I shall to James Pringle tomorrow and we shall no longer need our best of turnspits. What do you say to the role of Philosopher or Tutor again to my young roisterer here? Although I know well you have never ceased to educate him."

But somehow Joan found my words offensive, and stood up from her place at the table. "Why!" she screamed at me, "Do you think we need your charity, Master Fletcher? I have ever ensured that my poor husband was not burnt at his task. How dare you suggest that I have been neglectful?"

The room was in uproar suddenly. Adam shouted at his wife, "Woman, have a care what you say!" and Roger and James were at her side pleading with her to be silent. But she would not be quiet and launched forth at me again.

"Not content with murdering that sweet girl with your carnal desires, you wish to pervert my loving relationship with my dear husband, and all so your infidel here can prosper. Here's for you, Sir!"

Patience had set down a Staffordshire bowl of steaming gravy alongside her blue-dash charger which held slices of the meat. Joan seized the bowl of gravy and threw the contents at me. My doublet was ruined and burning droplets scalded my face and neck. I rose and went quietly from the room, in truth to return back to my surgery to apply balm of St John's Wort to my face. It was not my finest feature, it was certainly not my fortune, like that of the pretty maid in the old rhyme, but to date in spite of all my tribulations it was as yet unscarred, and what was more was the only one I had!

I believe I left behind pandemonium. Joan was certainly crying and screaming as I left the house and Adam was shouting in both anger and terror, the first because he was angry with his wife, and secondly because he could not see what she might do next.

"Well, they can shout their fill now without me," I said to myself, and I began to weep as the enormity of her unjust accusations bit into my soul. I ran through the streets and went into my Newport Street surgery and lavishly anointed my face, and put the jar of ointment into my pocket. In truth, I was weeping excessively by this time, longing for my little wife to comfort and love me. The knowledge that I would never see her again in this world suddenly struck me with all its tragic force and I howled aloud in my grief.

Unseeing and uncaring on the instant, I determined that I would put an end to all my sorrows. I ran through the house and across the courtyard, down the garden and through the orchard and hurled myself into the Severn.

5

For the second time in my short lifespan of twenty years, I had determined to do away with myself. And for the second time, I changed my mind. As I saw the glassy all-embracing bosom of the Severn directly below me, rising to absorb me as I fell, I realised in that instant that I regretted my action.... whole-heartedly

Whatever my second thoughts might be, Sabrina Fair took no account of them. I sank like a stone. With my arms flailing about like a demented windmill, I rushed back into the world of sun and light and felt a soft object touch my head. I grasped at it like a soul in Purgatory. It was a rope. In the same moment from far away in despite of the confused world of rushing waters singing in my ears, I heard my name. "Tom Fletcher! What in God's name are you about?"

I clung to the rope and was gently hauled to the side of a trow. Providentially, it or rather "she" as I was eventually taught to call the "Pride of Bristow", had been floating downriver midstream and had been hidden from me when I jumped by the long island that lay parallel to the garden. A strong net hung from the side of the vessel. I clambered up hand over hand, heaved myself over onto the deck and lay there gasping like a landed pike.

Lofty, my father's good friend, a Severn carrier, was beside me with a flask of something reviving. "Tom! My boy! I did not know you could swim!"

I coughed, spat, swallowed and answered him. "I can't!" I confessed.

"So we saw!"

The trow was edging in under the bank below the crane house and was clearly expected at the Quay. Worcester watermen were standing waiting to catch the heavy ropes, one of which had been my salvation. I gave a final cough and forced myself to leave the friendly wooden fish reeking solidity of the deck. As I did so, my name was called again. "Tom, wait for me! Don't leave me! Tom!

Allah!"

The last word was almost a scream. Something hard and wooden landed on the deck. It was my box of medicines. But Abram who had been carrying it, did not. For the second time in three minutes, a man was overboard. He had missed the deck in his effort to jump aboard through the bank of trees beyond the crane house, and was now in dire peril of being crushed between the bank and the side of the trow. With a desperate speed, the watermen ran to the oars and to Lofty's calls managed to propel the craft away from the bank where Abram was floundering up to his neck in the Severn. Lofty called out "Ship oars" and the vessel ceased its motion.

"Your apprentice?" Lofty asked. Again the stout rope was flung with a deadly accuracy directly before Abram who caught it with desperation.

"Kick out with your legs behind you, son!" Lofty instructed and slowly they drew him into the side where he too climbed the duck net, and with my anxious help fell onto the deck. He had not swallowed quite as much water as myself, but clung to me, gasping, "Tom! Tom! How could you? You must not leave me with her! Tom! Don't leave me!"

"I was coming back from the Key to find you," I told him. It was a lie but it seemed to pacify him.

Lofty stood, legs apart, hands on hips, gazing at us in mock wonder. "Tell me, young Tom, are there any more male water sprites who need our assistance? To speak truth, we'd rather rescue mermaids if it's all the same to you. More interesting prospect above the waist, if you take my meaning!"

"Aye, and below when they take their tails off!" cried out another of the carriers who I remembered from the inn at Holt Heath. There was a great shout of raucous laughter from the crew. The trow was drifting in to the Key at the end of Cooken Street. I remembered that I had not eaten and that no doubt neither had Abram.

"Whither are you bound, friend Lofty?" I asked him.

"Bristow or as they call it there, Bristol. Come with us! If you want a river voyage there is much to see, and 'tis a might more convenient to see it from the deck of the Pride than in the river. We'll put in at Gloucester the day after tomorrow."

"Gentlemen!" I announced, staggering to my feet as the water drained from my clothes. "I am in your debt, and as I remember owe you good cheer from last autumn, when we last met at the inn at Halt Heath. I beg you let us drink about at my expense and let me buy all a meal in the Key Tavern as my dear father would have done."

They were well pleased at this suggestion. "So, Abram, what happened when I left Fish Street?" I asked him.

He raised his eyes heavenward. "It was all complete uproar! Everyone was angry with Joan. Even Adam shouted when he realised the insult she had made you. Patience tried to reason with her, but 'twas all for nought. She kept crying out that you had killed Phoebe. Roger screamed at her this was not true, and Patience told her of a woman in Stratford, she knew, who had died of this kind of irregular childbirth. Sam told her "Only a superstitious fool could blame Tom!" and James wept. He was afraid you would never allow him to ride Jupiter again. Gill asked Joan to leave your parents' house. She told her she defiled it, and Jacky sat over his empty platter and groaned. All in all they did not notice when I slipped away to find you."

"Aye, I can well believe that they would not have noticed," I said, imagining the scene. Abram caught the laughter in my voice and grinned.

"Perhaps we are well rid of them all," he said with satisfaction. "Where are we going on this boat?"

"One hundred yards down river to the Key Tavern," I told him, "But 'tis a singularly awkward and wet means of travelling a very short distance."

There was oak wood to be unloaded from the Wyre Forest that had been bought by Lofty to sell to boat builders and fence makers in Worcester. There was a small crowd of merchants waiting to welcome him but more importantly to buy his cargo. The sight of the coins changing hands reminded me that I had left home without money. We helped to offload the tree trunks. Some had been planed so that they would fit more snugly in the hold, and the smell of the new wood was to me excessively welcome after the rather noisome aromas of the Severn. Lofty insisted thatI wrapped my hands in clean sacking and made rough gauntlets so that "Master Doctor does not rub splinters into the tender arse of his next lady patient!"

he announced to the company.

Abram had worn his yellow hose to celebrate the new spit at Fish Street. They were now in a desperate sad state, stained with weeds and worse. I began to laugh at the sight of him. There was something of the coxcomb about Abram. He loved to be neat and cleanly in his dress. He caught my eye and cried out, "Nay Tom! Have you seen yourself? Striped red and white like a maypole!"

The St John's Wort ointment with which I had anointed my burns had run down my face, and my ruined doublet gaped open. Fortunately, it was padded, which had protected my chest from the boiling gravy. Now the stuffing drenched and steeped in river water hung down before me, and my breeches and hose oozed the noxious Severn.

I suddenly heard my father speak very clearly in my head. The sensation was so strong, I stood still for a moment and halted the unloading. He said again what he had said after my first attempt at suicide four years ago.

"To take your own life dishonours your dead mother who gave you life. Live for her, son Tom."

The complaints behind me compelled me to recommence heaving the wood, but in that instant I knew I must live for Phoebe also, and remember her opinions and rejoice in her intelligence, some of which I had perhaps inherited. And in that same instant, I knew that I must do as she asked me. I must tell her uncle the sad news.

Today was a day when everyone was calling my name. Now Roger came running along the Key having jumped the garden fence.

"Tom! Tom Fletcher! Where are you?"

"Here, young Roger!" I cried, "You can take my turn for a moment, while I draw breath." I leaned against the tavern wall and relished the sight of others heaving away for a moment. He did not accept my invitation but caught me by my sacking covered hand.

"My father sends me to say our whole family is shamed and will return to the Chantry as soon as we can. James has led him and my shrew of a mother to St. Helens to be quiet and to pray. But he says too, dear Tom, can you forgive us?"

"There is nothing to forgive." I told him, "Joan is not herself. Somewhere, someone knows of a herb which will bring her back to us, as cheerful as she was. There is no need for you to leave

Newport Street. I am going to London to find Phoebe's uncle and Sir Neddy and the Derbyshire knights, and I will ask Ben Knowles how we can ease the knowledge Joan can no longer bear children, for I think that is the sadness that oppresses her and all of us through her."

"You must not leave!" he cried in horror, "It is your house, your calling!"

"My calling is to seek out Phoebe's great-uncle, the Earl of Chesterfield, and to tell him the news of my love's piteous death. Her last words to me were to ask me to do this. If he forgives me as I think he will, Joan can say what she wishes hereafter. And I will ask Ben if there was aught I could have done for Phoebe that I did not know. And if he tells me, as Martha did, that her death was lamentable bad fortune, then Joan can accuse me till the Severn runs dry."

I went on, "So stay here, Roger, with your parents and James. Joan can doctor the patients. She is as good at that as any man. I am for London and will go downriver with Lofty at least as far as Gloucester. And Abram shall come with me. So we shall not provoke her further with our presence."

I told Lofty we would return in half an hour to feast the carriers. I invited Roger also and we returned to my house and washed naked as cuckoos at Christmas in the hot sun, hair as well, under the pump with Phoebe's lavender and oatmeal soap, a pleasanter drenching by far than that afforded us by the Severn. My best doublet was ruined and my second best wolsey must suffice. I pushed shirts and small clothes into a bag and gave Abram instructions to do the like. I then rifled my store of money, reasoning that if I took what I thought 'twould cost to reach London, and doubled the amount, that would see us home again. Then I needed a sum to pay the Landlady at the Key. So I took a large sum to cover that forthcoming debt. There had recently been a sizeable increase in the profits from the manufacturies in the north of Worcestershire and South Staffordshire. It seemed unfortunate that my uncle by marriage, Alderman Sir Nicholas Knowles, had had no heirs of his body and that his considerable wealth had come to the poor butcher's boy, his wife's cousin's son.... myself. Unfortunate, but perhaps not so for me, I reflected churlishly as I pocketed the money.

Calling to Abram to follow me, I went back to the Key and found that Samuel had joined Roger. Both of them were gazing at me as if I had just dropped from the Moon.

"Tom!" Sam called out to me, as I cleared the garden wall, "Are you burned at all?"

"Only my face, a trifle. Fortunately as we all know, 'tis not my fortune!" I laughed off the incident. Poor Joan had attracted enough opprobrium if Abram's account of the aftermath was accurate.

"Roger, I tell you, she is fit to be tied. You must have a care lest she attacks a defenceless victim. Dear Tom, our benefactor, that anyone should mount such an assault."

Roger was excessively distressed. "Tom, what can I say?"

"Nothing!" I said shortly, "Where are these excellent good fellows, my father's friends, the waterman?"

"I have sent them to Fish Street, where a spring lamb awaits us all. Patience will have it so, and Gill and Jacky will not rest until they see you are hale and hearty."

The lamb was still excellent good eating. Lofty said quietly to me, "Dear lad, I hear your sorrows still surround you. Forgive us our joking. We did not know."

"My dearest little wife loved a joke," I told him and when we had eaten our fill, I asked to propose a toast. I rose and raised my glass. "To the memory of Lady Phoebe Stanhope, great-niece of the Earl of Chesterfield and beloved wife of humble Tom Fletcher. A jewel among women, who excelled all others both in wit and beauty. Because of her rare intelligence, I vow I will never think of any woman with other than deep respect. I give you her blessed beloved memory!"

I confess that at the conclusion of my little oration, my voice gave out and I wept again. But as all the company were similarly affected, remembering Phoebe, it did not matter. Then the watermen told tales of my father and of how he had striven so hard to ensure that the Severn remained a free and open river, as open as any street or highway in the country and the property of all English and Welsh men and women and not a waterway that men should pay to use. There had been aldermen who had claimed that the river belonged to the King and that they were merely proposing to collect his taxes, and my father had shouted in council, "Then let the King come and collect his tythes, and I'll buy him a tankard of ale and a mutton pie any day of the week!"

I promised that as long as I had Sir William Russell's ear, I would do my best to prevail on him that the river remained our free trade route, (and indeed for aught I knew that was his intention). In spite of the civil war, trows and barges still plied their way, selling the goods from many trades, floating down or rowing up against the current. Now Abram and I would take to our travels again.

"A good plan to sleep aboard tonight," said Lofty, "As we must catch the early morning tide, and the motion of the fine old Pride will become second nature to you."

They made us snug enough on a pile of nets on the deck and my eyes closed at last as the indifferent golden stars swung round the heavens. Strangely the heat of the day died in the night and I was glad of the blankets we had taken from Newport Street. At first light the trow began to strain against her moorings, there was the quiet splash of waves on the bank and Lofty's carriers were there, obedient to the vessel's needs and, loosed again to the river's impulses, she began to float into midstream and gathered speed so that when I turned over to sleep again, shielding my eyes from the sunrise in the east, the Cathedral was behind us on the left bank, and the town of my birth was disappearing and I had begun my quest.

We passed Clevelode but it was too early for Simon and Betsy to be about. A little later as the sun gained in strength we floated up to a mooring place at Severn Stoke. Lofty sent Abram to a nearby farm where the farmer's wife would sell us new baked bread. There was a strange and heady freedom in tearing the fresh loaves, sitting on the deck, leaning against the low side of the vessel, listening to the crew's talk. One of them had had a sweetheart in Upton. He was the hapless target of their wit and was clearly dreading our arrival at that town at midday where Lofty calculated we could buy food and ale.

"We'll send Doctor Tom, to tell the wench you'm pining for her!" Lofty threatened.

"Never speak of that, Lofty!" the poor fellow pleaded. "You don't know her mother! No, I must just bide quiet here on deck and hope they doesn't come down the quay the morn."

He elected to keep watch of the Pride of Bristow whilst all of the crew and myself and Abram went ashore in Upton to a welcoming ale house, where cider was made and sold, much to Abram's delight. When we returned something "wamblety" about the legs, the watchman, Petey, was lucky in that no beguiled young woman had appeared on shore to demand that he honour his promise of marriage. Shortly afterwards, we moved in to the centre of the stream again, and now in full hot sun let the outgoing tide pull us downstream.

The watermen now bethought themselves of a good supper, and ran their nets from the Pride to the path beside the river. Some mallards obligingly flew into the moving trap, which was instantly drawn in so that the poor creatures could be despatched as swiftly and silently as possible.

"Aye, the Severn is a free river yet," said Lofty, "but the banks are owned by landowners and they are monstrous jealous of their wild fowl."

"How will you cook your ducks?" I asked, an innocent abroad.

"Bless you, Tom, there are inns and alehouses aplenty, that ask no questions as to whence these fine creatures came. A landlord will set to with a right good will. That is good belly cheer for himself and his other patrons whom he will charge for our toothsome stew."

The nets were stretched again as two geese had been seen and they were considered to be even better eating than the humble ducks. Robin, one of the older Watermen, had decided that Abram should be taught to fish, and the afternoon passed pleasantly enough with a cry of triumph as each brown trout nibbled the lump of bread that remained from our breakfast, and was hoisted onto the deck, where Robert hammered them once on their pitiful cold heads. They were then salted in a barrel for some days and then hung on a line to dry.

"And they make good eating if the game dries up." Lofty stood, his tree trunk legs apart approving of Abram's progress. "Your Saracen bids fair to make a fisherman, Tom." At last we moored close to a small place called Shuthongar and Petey, was sent with two bags of game over his shoulders to see if Cross Eyed Bet, the owner of an ale-house could oblige us. I understood why Petey was the ambassador sent to treat with the ladies. He was a tall handsome fellow with fair hair falling over his brow, but even he had developed unnatural thick calves like young oak trees, by reason of his trade as a waterman.

The village was a short way from the river. The banks hereabouts had screens of willow and by means of excellent clever rowing, the watermen secreted the Pride of Bristow in the cool green shade. There was a whistle. Petey had returned with the news that Cross-eyed Bet was delighted with the game which she was cooking and cool ale awaited us.

Although the light would hold for some hours yet, it was a relief to leave the river as with the approach of dusk, mists of insects hovered and buzzed above the surface of the water. I had stood on the bridge in Worcester and gazed at the clouds of flies but they were less pleasing to live amongst at eventide. We moved through a herd of inquisitive young heifers, black and white chequered in the evening light and after a mile perhaps, across two fields, there was the alehouse, built into a steep bank at a cross roads with a few small cottages nearby.

Bet was a handsome woman, twenty-five perhaps, with fair curling hair and a clear skin. Perhaps one eye had a very slight tendency to look away from its fellow, but on no account did this defect, detract from her general comeliness. A very deaf old aunt assisted her, and I was interested to see that rather than shout continuously at old Madge, the pair had devised a simple system of hand movements by which Bet could ask her aunt to undertake specific tasks. I complimented her on her tactful employment of her relative, and she told me, having ascertained that I was a physician, that on certain days, she relied completely on Madge as her monthly pains caused her to be bent double in torment. I advised ginger chopped into warm milk, but had observed that marriage and sexual concourse greatly reduced the discomfort. "And," I went on, warming to my theme, "I have noticed that childbirth puts an end completely to all monthly pain and vexation from the courses."

"Childbirth?" she said thoughtfully, looking speculatively over the watermen, her eyes at length coming to rest on a ploughman, seated gloomily in the chimney corner, scowling at the unwelcome visitors. "Marriage?" she went on, "You say that with that holy sacrament, my pains will ease?"

"It is not so much the ceremony in church that brings the relief, rather, dare I say, the exercise of sexual knowledge," I said as quietly and discreetly as I could.

She nodded and thanked me and with something of the bearing of a gill-flirt glided over to the glowering ploughman and with a knowing toss of her head, her hand on her hip, invited his assistance in serving the company. He leapt to his feet, nearly knocking his brains out on the chimney corner, pathetic in his delight of her need of him. He was a sturdy fellow, not as appealing as Petey but well favoured for all that. I reflected that if she insisted that she and her aunt continued to maintain independent charge of the ale-house whilst he still plied his ploughshare, they might do well enough. Certainly they could never be as happy as Phoebe and......

The awareness that I had no wife kept cruelly creeping into my memory in this way and reducing me anew to abject misery. But I had learned an important lesson in the last two days. Abram needed me. I had undertaken to guard and advise him and my grief for Phoebe however powerful and heart-rending must not conflict with this responsibility. I remembered with a shudder his head bobbing above the surface of the river near the bank and the sudden realisation that he could so easily have been crushed. I looked at him now as he laughed and played the age-old stupid game with Petey of trying to force ones opponent's forearm down onto the table, a tankard of cider at his elbow.

Delicious smells filled the alehouse. Bet had a duck stew simmering in a cauldron and was roasting the geese on a spit. She had green peas, "sweet and tender as a virgin's cry for help," as Lofty later described them and an excellent stuffing of clove, sage and onions.

"Mistress Elizabeth, this is a dish fit for a king," I told her courteously. "And that causes me to ask, what news of our conflicts in these parts?"

An old farmer answered me, "Well, master, we'm so small and poor round here they don't bother to tax us for the war, but in the towns 'tis a different story. My brother, now in Tewkesbury, he don't have no interest in these fights, but they take his hard earned pence, will he, nill he."

"What is his trade, if I might know?" I asked with interest.

"Why, bless you, sir, he's a paviour. You should hear him complain about the way an army will wear down his cobblestones, as often after they have passed in a town, all is to do again."

An old wife who had crept in to help Bet and her aunt had news of a battle fought, she thought, in April to the north of Shuthongar, at a village called Ripple. It seemed that Prince Maurice had not given Waller all his own way.

"Trapped they were in a narrow lane. Parson asked me to tend the wounded. Poor lads they were. 'Twas terrible to see them, every mother's son, torn and bleeding like broken toys. We did what we could, me and the other goodwives but 'twas precious little. I hear those poor lads crying out in my head even now."

"Aye and 'tis terrible what these armies will do to our fields and cattle," said a young farmer, "I'd like to ask the King or t'other feller, Waller is it? how he'd feel if his shire stallion was stolen while he was taking a nap at the side of his own field of turnips. One minute there's old Captain grazing quiet like at the bottom near the brook, and next I know with whoops and shouts, the bastards have made off with 'im. 'Tis Waller's men by all accounts. But poor old Captain. It brings tears to my eyes to think of the hard time they'll be giving him. That horse was my best friend as well as part of my living."

"Still, Jake, best keep your head down and lie low. 'Tis better to endure it. The less they notices the likes of us, the safer we are." the older farmer advised. "What for should we be wanting to kill each other? To my mind that's worse than losing your horse, son."

"When was Captain stolen?" I asked.

"I think 'twere early June. Is it still June?" asked poor Jake. That fitted well with Waller's journey south from Worcester, after he had besieged it in the last few days in May. He had been seeking horses when he wished me farewell, but I feared that Captain's fate would not be easy. Pulling a culverin even for a shire would be fearsome hard work.

"Master Lofty!" said Abram suddenly.

"Yes, Master Turkish Knight, my bold Slasher! What is your will?"

"Tom has an excellent voice. Make him sing for us!"

"Abram!" I shouted. "They do not want...."

"Oh, but we do, and now I remember, your father said something of that to me once. Come then, what shall it be?"

There was no remedy. So I sang "Back and sides go bare" and all joined in the chorus so that the rafters rang. Then "Green grow the rushes, oh," and then Bet sang a sweet but saucy song about the puddings her mother had made her. There was no doubt in the minds of the Watermen that the puddings to which she referred were rather temptingly displayed under her bodice laces. The ploughman scowled at us fit to crack his brow. In order to appease him I asked him if he would give us a song. To my surprise he rose and launched into an excellent ballad, called "Who's the fool now?" He had a powerful baritone and finally I sang a duet with him, he outlining the outrageous drunken stories and I singing the chorus, "Thou hast well drunken, man. Who's the fool now?"

Once started, there was no silencing him. Gloucestershire was clearly a great county for songs. Another which brought him much applause was "The Carter's Whistle" and I was somewhat dismayed that the whistle in question was clearly a physical attribute. Abram was a youth of tender years after all. But I could not be a killjoy and Abram sang and beat time with his tankard. After two or three hours more of jollity and mirth, our ploughman launched into "John, come kiss me now," pretending to play a simpering woman, but then at the sight of Bet laughing uncontrollably, he changed the name of John to Bet and advanced upon her with amorous intent. Lofty sensing that perhaps our rustic lover might now appreciate a clear field, after thanking her and deaf Madge for the excellent meal, hustled us all away into the dawn.

As we walked across the grey fields, Lofty asked me if I knew William Sandys whom he judged to be a great innovator. He had caused the Avon to be made navigable from Tewkesbury to Stratford, and had built locks and gates so that the level of water in the river could be constantly raised or lowered. Now great barges, bigger even than the Pride of Bristow, could carry large quantities of coal very cheaply, from the Severn up the Avon to the Vale of Evesham. Before he had altered the lie of the land, it had been carried with great difficulty and expense overland. I told Lofty of my unwilling part in the Siege of Worcester and that I had met Sandys and how he had proved a very resourceful commander in Russell's absence. Lofty's respect however stemmed from his abilities in improving river transport.

"For, Tom, of what use is a clever craftsman, if he has no means of transporting his wares. I tell you, rivers will be more and more the means whereby we carry...."

Suddenly he paused, put out his hand to stop my progress and turned to his crew.

"Listen, boys!" There was the subdued murmur of voices coming from the willows ahead of us where the Pride was moored. As we crept closer it was clear that thieves were aboard. A plank led from the bank to the deck and two wooden crates from the hold were on the grass, though no cart was as yet in evidence to transport their stolen goods

"Abram and Tom! Stay with the cargo! Sit on it!" Lofty hissed.

When the watermen had left their boat, they had hidden the oars and the wide planks by which we could walk from the trow onto the land, in a thicket nearby. Now they crept across the grass and retrieved them, giving Abram and myself an oar each, with which to defend ourselves, should the need arise.

The thieves were in the hold still unaware that they had been discovered. The watermen trooped with astonishing speed and silence onto their beloved boat, and Petey and two others waited to confront the robbers as they came up on deck. But then Lofty changed his strategy. He pushed one of the planks into place over the companion-way with a great bang, stood on it, and immediately cried, "Now, brethren, time for matins! Let us sing together, "Praise God from whom all blessings flow.""

The watermen could scarce sing for laughing and there came shouts and oaths from the hold. The crates on which we were sitting were swiftly recovered and placed on the plank which held fast the thieves in their nautical prison.

"How many, Petey?" Lofty asked.

"Nay, Uncle Luke, I cannot tell," for the banging and the shouting from below was like unto many souls in torment.

"Cast off, then. When they know we're midstream, they'll cease their prattle!".

The Pride had little motion as the tide had long since ebbed and would not flow for another hour or more. The Watermen took to the oars and with Abram and myself seated on the crates, like bishops on our thrones, we moved into midstream, where the oars were shipped and we floated very slowly and peacefully down river, in the growing light. The shouting from below ceased and the thieves began to plead with us, but it seemed to me there was now something of hopelessness and terror in their voices.

"What will you do with them then?" Robert asked Lofty, during a lull in their appeals.

Lofty opened the hatch a crack. "You can swim for it, one by one, or 'tis the harmans, the wooden hose on Tewkesbury Wharf for you. I am known to the Tewkesbury Constables as the Great Prig-Napper," he roared. "Christ, they stink!" he complained, pushing the hatch back into place.

"Please sir, we were only looking for food," a voice shouted from below.

"Whence come you?" Petey asked.

There was a silence. Then a smooth rich voice with more than a hint of the south told us, "We're Captain Francis Fiennes' men. We were bound for Bristol but we were waylaid by sickness. If you have any crusts of your blessed charity, bestow them upon us for we are lamentable hungry. "

Lofty drew me away. "Is there such a commander as this Francis Fines?"

"Aye, the devil there is," I told him. "He's one of Old Subtlety's brood of boys from Broughton Castle. But they were part of Essex Horse. Where are their mounts? Are they dragoons or cavalry?"

"What's the difference?" he asked impatiently.

"A world of difference to the poor miserable brutes they ride. Dragoons tether their horses out of the battle and shoot at the enemy with muskets. The cavalry ride at them hell for leather with their swords drawn and pistols at the ready."

"Would this Francis Fines have a... a quartermaster to order and receive goods?"

"That he would," I told him, "But first things first. What have they done with their horses?"

The trow was creeping very slowly down river. My fear was that three or more horses were tethered upstream and could well starve if they were abandoned.

"Let's have Master Silver Tongued Jack Bragger up on deck," Lofty decided, and shouted out "He who talks with his gob full of goose grease. He may come up." Then he added, winking at Abram's frightened expression, "But if you try any tricks you'll all be leaping at the daisies in Tewkesbury, and the stocks shall contain better men than you."

Two of the Watermen drew their daggers and waited either side of the companionway as the platform was withdrawn enough for the spokesman to emerge. His voice belied his person. His buff coat was stained and dirty, looking as if he had eaten his dinner from it when he had had a dinner to eat, for certainly he was thin as a tailor's yard, with hollow unshaven cheeks. His thick brown hair hung lankly about his long face, and his teeth were yellow and unsightly. He wore a leather broad brimmed hat to which the remnants of a red feather clung. He blinked at the sunrise and seemed awed by the number of us. But he bowed most like a gentleman, doffing his hat and smiling pleasantly.

"Who the devil are you?" asked Lofty.

"Alas, not so well born, I fear, my dear sir, for we are all told that the Prince of Darkness is a gentleman, and I am reduced to a beggar. I am but a poor pedagogue, pressed into these sad conflicts, Holofernes reborn in that I have indeed lost my labour…. seeking for victuals!"

"Hollow what?" asked Lofty.

"Hollow belly," said the poor wraith.

"What is he saying?" Lofty asked me.

"That he is a teacher and he and his fellows are desperate hungry," I told him.

The stranger bowed. "Sir," he said courteously to me, "I see that you are as learned as you are well-favoured."

"And hunger, alas, dims your eyesight!" I countered. "Come Lofty, we have the bread that Abram fashioned into pellets for bait. How many below, Master Holofernes?"

"But two poor young fellows. Brush handle makers, well disposed for apprentices, on my life."

"They had best not try a brush with us, or I'll see their necks as long as my arm!" said Lofty cautiously. "We are ready for 'em!"

The hatch was slowly withdrawn and two young scarecrows, stinking and filthy as the scrapings of a midden, crawled up the steps and lay gasping, their squalor all the more hideous in the rays of the rising sun.Lofty looked at them with imperial disdain.

"Well, Tom, they had best all have a pellet or two of Abram's bait. And a draught of small beer. And when they have digested their bread, they may each have a dried trout, if their bellies can hold it."

He moved away and said musingly, "I will not have men starve on my boat. That sin shall not nestle in my conscience, by Joseph and Mary. You'd best question them when they've had a morsel to eat and drink. But beware of the stench!"

He was right to warn me. All the Watermen gave them a wide berth and Abram, who was punctilious about his person, could not approach them at all. It seemed that Doctor Tom was the only imprudent claybrained simpleton who could make shift to be near them, and even I had to walk away occasionally to breathe fresh air.

"So your story please, Master Holofernes. I see you were once part of Essex' regiment by the sad rags of your orange scarves. Frances Fiennes, you say. Where did you leave him?"

"I shall have to be up betimes to deceive you, good sir, upon my soul. My tale, indeed, like unto a prize porker's…. a twisted question curling away from what ought to be. We sons of Mars were marching to Bristol with young Frank and his good brother Nat, who now commands his own regiment."

"We are from London," said one of his miserable companions.

"Well, have no fear!" I told him kindly. "In these western counties we do not hang or torture strangers, even if they are unfortunate enough to hail from London."

"Well, sir, well, it pleases you to jest at our expense," said Holofernes, "Were our situations reversed, no doubt I too should mock our wretchedness. It was mid-February that our troop rested in a barn near Cirencester. I learned later that Rupert had been thereabouts earlier that month and his men had thrown a dead dog down a well. The peasants there did not tell us the water was unwholesome and that to drink it was to court our ends. Even in my sickness I noticed that the bumpkins did not drink from that well, filling their pails from a nearby spring."

"I know for a fact that Rupert was at Cirencester in early February," I told Lofty in an undertone. "So far their pitcher holds water."

One of the apprentices took up the tale. "So Master Julius here forbade us to drink what they gave us in our sickness, but made me with a terrible thirst on me, to finish the canaries in his flask and crawl to refill it from the safe spring, often and often, and slowly we gained back our strength while the rest with my elder brother, they all died."

"They did not need or deserve such a fate," said the other boy. They were both perhaps sixteen.

"So what happened after that?" I asked.

"Do you know, good young sir, they made us bury our comrades, weak though we were? We were eating from the pigs' troughs. They said that was good enough for us although 'twas Rupert's men who fouled their well. We men of Parliament had done them no wrong but that was all the victuals they would spare us and we still weak and ill from poisoned water." The poor apprentice sobbed as he recounted his tale.

"In war, humanity and compassion are scarce commodities and soldiers coming where the people and land are already poor, are not welcome visitors." I said, prating piously. "So what then? What follows?"

"Alas!" said Master Julius, taking up the tale, "We are the last of Francis Fiennes' troop. After we had buried the rest, we were told we must leave the barn. And in truth it was an unwholesome place having been the deathbed of so many of our companions. But because we were so wretched and foul from the illness, we could not come near anyone to ask for charity. We heard tell of Waller in Worcestershire and a battle with Maurice but when we found the place, all had dispersed. By this as you can see our clothes were stinking rags."

"One moment," I said, "I must know if it please you. Where are your horses?"

"The men from Cirencester led them all away while we lay like to die. They told us we would have to buy them again in Stroud market."

My father spoke in my head. "Son Tom, poverty begets naught but poverty. It is the devil's own task to heave oneself out of the morass of destitution."

I nodded more at his wise remembered words than at the pity of the tale.

"You believe us, sir?" said one of the youths. "After that we scraped and gathered food from where we could, we ate raw turnips and carrots when we found them harvested, and drank from streams. Thank God we have not again been ailing. You and your sailors are the first to show us Christian charity. Please believe us. I swear we speak truth. What have we to gain by lying?"

I told him I did believe him and would help them, but Lofty did not place much reliance on their words. "I will trust them only as far as I can see them," said he. "If smelling were my yardstick, I would be gullible the length of the Severn."

The man called Julius laughed at his words. "May I say, sir, I like your wit, and your young captain here is sharp as a rapier."

"This is our captain," I told him, "Master Luke Loftus. I am merely a passenger. But why if you were seeking food did you see fit to stack the crates on the bank?"

There was an uneasy silence. The schoolmaster removed his hat again and smoothed down the thick fringe that covered his brow. "Well, we could lie and deceive you but as I said, we have nothing to gain by it. Hunger provokes a man to actions that he scorns when his belly is full. Your crates contain metal articles for saddlers. I will be honest. We had thought to hide the crates on the bank and secrete some of the saddlery about our persons and sell it for food."

Lofty stared unblinkingly at the tutor. He nodded slowly. "As you say, hunger bids right and wrong go hang. Wait, there she blows," as the Pride seemed to launch herself downstream with renewed vigour and waves began to break upon the banks. "That's the tide turning. We are for Tewkesbury now to sell those same metal saddler's items. Best stay in the hold, gentlemen, as I do not wish to deter my customers. Your appearance and aroma is somewhat particular and quaint. Doctor Tom will go ashore and buy breeches and hose but there is an alewife in Deerhurst downriver a league or so from Tewkesbury, who thinks I am Perfection Personified." There were raucous shouts from the crew and one cried, "You'll be married and settled if she has her way!"

"And I could do worse, if I might only drain the Severn from my veins. At all events she will boil water for the three of you. Her dead husband was a tailor, and left her last year with a power of shirts, some half sewn. At the very least we can buy the three of you a shirt each. But, lads, go below, for I tell you, my nose will seek its fortune on another fellow's face, if it is like to suffer longer in your unwashed presence, Master Hollow Belly."

There were more barges and trows to be seen in Tewkesbury, as we floated into the basin where the Avon joins with the Severn. The Pride was expected. As at Worcester a group of merchants awaited on the quay, this time anxious to purchase Lofty's store of Black Country ironmongery. When we tied up I asked to be directed to a mercer who sold me rough kersey breeches, devoid of slashings or ornament, but serviceable enough for all that. I bought also three pairs of woollen hose and now all our thieves needed were shirts to be bought in Deerhurst, and boots or shoon, which I decided we would get in Gloucester. I bought a quantity of bread and a ham from a stall in the market. I judged that smoked meat would be easiest on their stomachs. I saw fine pease pudding on sale from a cauldron and, remembering that the Watermen had shown partiality for this dish at Halt Heath, returned to the Pride for two large bowls to purchase a good supply. Lofty had pots and dishes aplenty although he did not allow cooking on his vessel as he rightly had a dread of fire.

In three hours we were done and cast off from the mooring in Tewkesbury. Our thieves were fed again, as little and often would restore their health more smoothly rather than one great indulgence of the belly. We all slept for a short while as Petey steered the Pride smoothly downstream.

So in a few hours we found ourselves in yet another alehouse. Abram clearly thought that a waterman's life consisted of drinking, feasting and carousing. The alewife was overjoyed to see Lofty, but he in fact was more embarrassed than honoured by her many attentions. He was unlike my good friend Peabody, who knew how to please a woman with his smooth compliments. Clearly he feared the loss of his freedom. Even so, I caught him gazing at Mistress Faith as she bustled about, putting pans of water to boil and taking three coarse long linen shirts from a press. She had a quantity of soap that she insisted that I took as it seemed to be the doctor's task to oversee the washing of our thieves

I had strong tincture of lavender in my box with which I destroyed their head lice. Julius was loathe to have his fringe washed and held on to it fiercely as I rubbed and scrubbed. When we were completed and three hideous piles of rags were consigned to the flames, I found that my own head was itching but told myself that lice could not jump. Even so my exertions were considerable. We had not slept for many hours. Most of the Watermen were drowsing over tankards of ale, but Robin who could shave and cut hair undertook to make neat Roundheads of our three savages who were now fresh and sweet smelling dandyprats. I decided to seek solitude in this peaceful village, beside the Severn, set in a green rolling summer landscape.

There was an air of timeless peace about the place. I wandered over close cropped lawns to the church and idly raised the latch of the door and went inside. It was an old Saxon house of prayer, an ancient building when the first William I had come to England. I sat on a bench by the wall and studied brass pictures of previous worshippers set into the floor. The bones of the subjects must lie, I thought, under the floor near me.

"And look, even in death, she could not be parted from her little dog!" Julius had followed me. In truth, he looked like a penitent from the old days, barefoot, dressed only in his coarse white shirt, cropped close, except for his fringe and shaved cleanly, as if he had risen from his grave in his shroud, skeletal and prepared for the harrowing of Hell. He carried his battered leather hat with the remains of the feather

"You know this church?" I asked him.

"This is a quiet village now but eight hundred years ago, it is thought, our ancestors ruled the ancient kingdom of Mercia hence, and there would have been men and women talking and laughing, buying and selling, living and dying, aye and existing without the terrible present impulse to kill each other. All could speak at the moot, as they called their place of Assembly. If you will walk a little way with me, I will show you where a great palace stood. Only the chapel now remains."

We left the church and strolled down the lane. He seemed much recovered. The small quantities of food I had allowed him seemed to have sustained him well. He told me that Faith would have venison stew for us in half an hour.

"So how do you know so much about our ancestors?" I asked. "And these men and women? It seems by your tone that you regret their passing."

"I do, I confess. It grieves me to think how far we have degenerated since King Alfred gave us a code of law. Men call his time the Dark Ages but I believe that these days, our lives now, are the dark ages, when a civil war, savage and cruel beyond any previous one, ravages our lovely land."

"So why have you thrown in your lot with Parliament?" I asked him. "Why do you not like me preserve a fierce neutrality?"

"Perhaps because it is Parliament which ordains the law for all men. How can an accident of birth give one man the right to decide life and death of all others and claim that he has a divine right to do so? Alfred devised laws that would and did outlast him"

"True, but why now have men risen up against the King? For instance Henry the Eighth was far more of a tyrant, I am told."

"Why now? Why, because men can rise up now. They tried under Henry. Have you heard tell of the Pilgrimage of Grace?"

I hated to think of the horror and betrayal of that tragic rebellion and shuddered at the memories. He caught my thought and said, "If the rule of law is in the hands of Parliament, that kind of tyranny cannot be reproduced."

"But the Pilgrims of Grace wished Henry to revert to the old religion. The men of Parliament loathe the notion that we might be brought by the Queen to worship the Pope again."

"Doctor Tom, do you care what a man believes so long as it harms no-one?"

"No, I do not. He can believe in the Man in the Moon for me, so long as I do not have to join him in his orisons. Master Julius, I have long realised that indifference is the other face of the coin of tolerance. We should cherish both to regain peace and harmony, should we not?"

"Indeed we should. Indifference, as you define it, is a blessed state of mind. God save indifference!"

We had strolled towards a strange square chapel which Julius explained was all that remained of the palace of our early Christian forefathers. An old curate emerged from it and started at the sight of Julius, clad only in his long shirt.

"No need for this, dear son, whatever your offence. The Presbyterian vicar hereabouts would rather that you sought peace and forgiveness in your soul. No need today to humiliate the flesh."

"Thank you, dear sir. I am in fact a cleansed sinner and thank you for your absolution." Julius was deceptively humble. "I and my good doctor here must now partake of earthly sustenance, but first we will, if we may, pay our respects to Odda's memory, for a few brief moments, but a pinprick in the great almanac of time that this edifice has stood here. God give you a good day, dear sir."

"Who was Odda?" I asked as we looked about us in the musty

hall which stood sturdily, clearly impervious to the centuries of wind and rain.

"A Saxon Earl who built this place as part of his palace and dedicated it to the soul of his brother. The rest of the edifice has long been dismantled by the worthy inhabitants of this village, but no doubt they deemed Odda's Chapel to be sacrosanct as a place of worship, and likely to carry unpleasant curses if despoiled. Shall we return, good Doctor Tom to good Faith's good venison stew? I vow I am overwhelmed by goodness, but the venison draws me away from further contemplation of virtue. What say you? Shall we go? I thank you for your company and acquaintance."

"Nay, sir, it is I who am in your debt," I told him, "It is meat and drink to me to meet one who thinks as I do. To say truth, I am partial to argument. What matter if the protagonists are not in complete accord, if they can exchange views and learn one from the other? The cut and thrust of debate is all the conflict I savour. And I must confess to you that, although I have visited two marvellous old places of worship this afternoon, I am still convinced that God, if he exists at all, turns his face from us at this time."

"I think as you do" he replied, "But such thoughts, though rational, are best kept close concealed. Come, I hear the venison calling."

That evening we moored once again under the willows of some rich man's estate and Abram and the penitents sat with me on the nets as the watermen prepared for the next tide which would bring us to Gloucester. They were beginning to lose the pinched aspect of the starving but Abram, I could tell by his restive glances one to the other had some questions.

"Master Julius!" finally he said determinedly, "May I ask a question, if you will permit it?"

"Ask away! If I am a schoolmaster, I must suffer the young to demand of me. It is my calling, it would seem."

"February was not snow bound, as I remember, but there was a desperate frostiness in the air and puddles became ice. How did you and these two live in the barn, where you had been abandoned, without perishing from cold?"

"Alas, as each man died we had the use of his clothes, Master Abram. But remember a barn full of straw is not a cold place. Even if the straw is dirty it retains heat. I taught the boys to bed themselves in with it and the warmth from their bodies remains in the straw that surrounds them."

"Yes!" I remembered piles of hay ready for cattle at Knowles Mead Farm. "Hay is warm. I saw heaps of it smoking in a farmyard not long ago. I thought it was the effusions of the sun."

"And in fact, Doctor Tom, whether we think our God is with us or not, I reminded myself constantly that his dear Son whose words we must heed, was born in a stable in the midwinter and did not die of cold."

John shifted uneasily. "But we would have died, Sir, if you had not determined that we should survive. As we gained some strength it was you who insisted that everything was shared and that we did not give way to animal appetites. You always made us eat first and then when our hunger was something sated, then and only then did you take your portion."

"Well, young Jacob here and I were fortunate you suffered the ague that assailed us but mildly. While we were sick almost to death, you cared for us, John. I will not forget that."

"No, sir" John insisted, "We would have died without your knowledge."

"And we would still be in a parlous state without Doctor Tom, here" Julius insisted

I was finding this effulgence of gratitude, tedious in the extreme and asked instead for Julius to tell me of his life as a schoolmaster. Had he taught in a school in London or was he a tutor to a rich man's spoiled stripling? He promised he would tell me of his life in good time and as it was now full dark, we slept with the slight movement of the boat and the whisper of the willow leaves soothing our slumbers.

I woke early next morning as the first rays crept over the deck. Robin was at the wheel and for a few moments we stood in silence watching the river flashing and sparkling before us. Then he said softly, jerking his head towards the sleepers, "Yon feller's been branded, Tom." I did not catch his meaning, but repeated the word stupidly, "Branded?"

"Aye, on the brow. He would not let me cut his hair on the front."

"Why would that happen?" I asked, "Was it an accident?"

He snorted. "'Taint no accident, Tom. 'Tis one of that devil Laud's punishments. Best say naught for now." The other watermen were stirring now and we floated gently on the flood down into Gloucester. Our three "penitents" were able to earn their passage now and assisted us where they could, and there was laughter and good humour as they helped in the hold to make ready the cargo. But then Lofty ordered silence as we approached a house on our left known he told us as the Weir House. The rushing of waters drowned the creaking of the trow's timbers. As we approached a great bridge it became clear that the central widest arch was the only one through which the Pride could pass. A bar was suspended from above which could swiftly be lowered to hinder the progress of any vessel.

"Softly, good boys!" Lofty hissed as we sped silently towards the central arch. And we were through, into the open water, the river curving sharply eastwards towards the town. But we were not unobserved. There was a shouting and a clanking from behind us and the bar was lowered something too late for the purpose.

A great voice bellowed, "Loftus! Master Loftus! Ship your oars!" and a small man on the bridge was addressing us, whose size belied the loud volume of his voice.

"Let's give poxy Dogsbreath what he craves. Ship 'em, good lads!" Lofty ordered in an undertone and then walked towards the stern and yelled "Good day to you Master Hodgeson. How wags the world with you! I look to have the pleasure of pledging you in the Pig, Master Hodgeson, in a short while... Or if you prefer I look to have the pledging of pleasuring you in the Pig, Master Hodgeson!"

"Loftus, you thieving evil bastard, you ran through our toll yet again."

"What toll was that, Master Hodgeson? I know naught of that. I'faith its monstrous early for my poor boys, and they faint for food. We must begone to the Key, Sir. But we are always up betimes, Master Hodgeson, we men of the Severn, are we not?"

He turned and ordered the oarsmen to bring the trow gently into the current and to bring her into her mooring, as the small man with the voice like thunder, shouted, "I'll see you later, Loftus, you ignorant thief."

"Oh, God's bodykins! I'm all of a dudder!" said Lofty aping a frightened wench. "He's like a sundial in the cellar, that varlet, neither use nor ornament, the miserable Jack Sprat."

The Pride was expected. It was Sunday and in despite of the many bells that called to prayer, there was a small crowd waiting to purchase Lofty's cargo. Horses were tethered nearby. To my dismay the last crates which were carried from the hold held matchlocks for muskets, and swords complete, as well as separate blades and hilts, and it was clear that quartermasters were amongst those waiting to purchase weaponry for their troops, as well as gunsmiths and armourers.

"Oh Jesus!" cried Jacob, at my elbow. "There he is! That's him, George Malten, the bastard!"

Lofty overheard him. "Aye I thought this fellow would prove to be your quartermaster. Wait in the hold, boys. No need to show yourselves till 'tis to your advantage." I was not sure they should lurk like renegades. They had not deserted, rather in fact in their sickness they had been deserted, and as they had recovered, had tried to care for their dying fellows. In fact, I reasoned with myself, Malten owed them money, their pay for the months they had been from London, and surely their efforts in burying their friends ought not to go unrewarded.

We had a swift discussion in the gloom of the hold. "Do you want to come with us to London?" I asked. "You could act as our guides."

Even in the half-light I could see the boys' faces alight with joy at such a prospect. "Home!" said Jacob, and a world of longing was in the single word.

"Aye, home but without my brother!" said young John and there was a sob in his voice. "How shall I tell our mother?"

"Who does Malten serve now?" Julius asked curiously.

"Shall I find out? For all I know I could still be on the roll of Basil Fielding. I'll brazen it out. I'll send Abram back to find you if all goes well."

Lofty cunningly did not close with the first offer for his first crate of weaponry but invited the quartermasters to increase the sums they could afford, topping each other's bid. I could see that Malten was becoming uneasy as he saw the supply of matchlocks he had intended to purchase, rising ever out of the range of his bag of coin. At length all had been sold and Malten had bought nothing but a few ill matched hilts and blades, that no-one else needed. One Quartermaster Elsmore, whom I thought I might have seen somewhere before, purchased the lion's share of the matchlocks.

Now was the moment. "Master Malten!" I called sauntering off the trow as all were dispersing. "A word with you, if you please!"

"Who the devil are you?" he asked crossly.

"Thomas Fletcher, Surgeon to Lord Basil Fielding. He is the Earl of Denbigh now after his father's death on the road from Birmingham to Lichfield."

Malten became somewhat more courteous. "Good day to you Surgeon. Now if you please I must hasten back to my commander."

"Ah, sir! You bring me straight to the nub of the matter. Who is your commander? Three lamentable sick troopers whom I found dying in a barn near Cirencester, abandoned by their officers, tell me your commander is Francis Fiennes. Where can I find him? I would have speech with him. My lord Essex is in my debt. I propose to tell him of a barn full of sick London train band troopers left to rot in their own filth. These were the heroes of Turnham Green, deserted it seems, by Frank Fiennes and his officers. What say you to this, Sir?"

Malten looked satisfying stricken. "Did they not have the plague?"

"Abram," I called , "Ask Master Julius and the boys to come up, if they have the strength."

Our three penitents appeared on deck, clean and clad, though thin as tooth-drawers. They stood and surveyed Malten and Julius bowed. "Your servant, Master Malten!" he called.

"No, Sir, they did not have the plague. They had a fearful disorder of the stomach caused by drinking evil water from a well Rupert's men had fouled. Their companions whom they tried to help all died, and these three invalids, sick and weak had to bury their friends and brothers. Now sir, I pray you bring me to Francis Fiennes who should surely need to know how the men who followed him in good faith have so shamefully been treated by his officers. I learn that these men are entitled to their wages from their first departure from London in February to today. There is also the matter of the burial of their fellows and then there are my fees for doctoring them for... some little time. What say you?"

"What say I? I say you are a damned interfering meddler and I

Page 142

cannot delay further." He turned on his heel and was about to stalk away but unfortunately Abram had knelt behind him to adjust and rebuckle his boot. The Quartermaster fell headlong, his bag of money falling on the Key. I immediately picked it up.

"Why, Master Malten, I thank you. This pays for all I think. Boys, here are your wages. Thank good Master Malten for your earnings."

"Thank you, Master Malten," chorused the apprentices, smiling like brewers' horses.

Malten came at me to retrieve his bag but I had already thrown it to Julius who caught it neatly. The Quartermaster raised his drawn sword to attack me, but suddenly the Watermen were round me, smiling pleasantly at Malten and bidding him a Good Day.

"What, Master Malten? Cold steel among friends?" cried Lofty. "Here are your hilts and blades. These poor shorn boys will carry your condolences to the parents of their fellows, left to die from neglect in the cold. Was there aught else you needed?"

Malten bundled his weapons into a canvas bag. There was naught he could do. We were far too many for him. I knew I had made an enemy, and I must take my chance on that. Even so, he and his commander had failed in their duty to their troopers who had left their homes and their city in good faith. As I watched him retreating up the street which I later learned was Westgate, I reflected that I still knew nothing of the whereabouts of Francis Fiennes.

"Abram!" I shouted to him as he stood watching casks of wine brought ashore. "How comes it that you were crouched on the ground behind that man?"

He shrugged. "This buckle was ever stiff. I had not fastened it aright."

"Come, then Doctor Tom!" roared Lofty. "Bold Slasher Abram, have with you. That was a neat wily contrivance, on my life. We're for the New Inn on Northgate Street, where we've broken our fast before."

"What about the penitents? They must be shod. Is there a cobblers near at hand?"

Julius was beside me with the boys. "Tom, we now have the wherewithal to purchase our boots ourselves, thanks to you. Do you go with Lofty and we will follow. A thousand thanks for our 'wages'."

"Nay, 'twas one of Abram's evil tricks. Thank him. And in any event, you are owed your pay. I know John Fiennes. He is a man of many words but much worthiness. His brother Frank is doubtless cast in the same mould. He would not have countenanced your being left in that barn to die. But I think I have not heard the last of Master Malten. I would I knew what commander he answers to now."

John frowned. "Perhaps none. Himself alone."

"What do you mean? He must have a Captain, else why was he waiting on the Key for the Pride, to buy weapons," Julius asked him.

John said slowly, "Let me alone to think through this tangle. I am remembering now something that has evaded me through sickness. When did we last see Captain Frank? Early February. Where has he been since then? Are we still his men? I doubt it. But we are still here in...." he looked round himself something bemused, as the churchbells jangled, "Gloucester? And we were sent here by the Committee of Safety in London, sanctioned by both Houses, that undertook our welfare. What then is our status, Master Julius? What are our rights?"

"Certain sure, a pair of boots for all three of us." Julius had seen the sign of a shoemaker swinging over the cobbles of Westgate. "Let's bespeak footwear, boys, or these good hose will be worn through and all to buy again. Then we will pledge our benefactors in the New Inn."

He hurried them away. I reflected that perhaps we had best make for London from Gloucester, instead of travelling with Lofty and the Pride to Bristol. We could hire horses along the road. I retrieved my box from the Pride, bade Farewell to Petey who had again been left to guard her. In Gloucester as in Upton he went in severe danger of matrimony.

"I must bide quiet here, and not be seen for fear of the parson's mousetrap, Tom!" he explained, cautiously peering over my shoulder. I did not know whether to congratulate or commiserate with him. Certain sure, success with women such as he enjoyed, carried its own penalties. I rejoined Abram and we left the Key to find the New Inn.

Gloucester was a hive of activity. Men and women were in the streets pushing carts full of earth and stone. I learned that this was to mend and strengthen their city walls. A little maid, about six or seven was pushing a great block of stone near as large as herself. I could not see this and not be aware that she would strain muscle and sinew unnaturally, so I undertook to heft the stone whilst Abram walked with her beside her mother, and finally pushed the cart for her. She explained that all citizens were enjoined to assist Colonel Massey in his defence of Gloucester and that her daughter insisted on helping as well as she could and would not be gainsaid. We pushed our way jostled by many other busy citizens similarly employed, along Westgate Street, and then cut a corner past the Cathedral to reach the Northgate opposite St John's Church. Here the goodwife handed over her cart to soldiers whom she explained were members of Massey's Garrison. One was her husband who kissed her soundly but frowned somewhat at our presence. It seemed they were now free to attend Matins in St John's. She invited us to accompany them, and her husband's frown deepened. I declined politely explaining that we had to find companions in the New Inn. His frown disappeared and we bade Farewell to his wife and daughter whilst he in courtesy, walked the few steps back down Northgate Street to where the New Inn stood, welcoming and inviting. He promised to seek us out later in the day as he wished to buy us a cup of wine for helping his womenfolk.

The New Inn proved to be an excellent hostelry, well over two hundred years old. It was clearly the place where plays had been performed, as handsome galleries looked over the courtyard. The watermen were already assembled there basking in the sun with jugs of ale and a smoking platter of gammon from which Lofty was slicing generous shares for all. The landlord Master John Nichol stood over the table, receiving compliments graciously and offering further sustenance liberally.

"And the Lion's share for this valorous cub who knows exactly how to trip up Master Hackum the Quartermaster. To offer the poor fellows naught! I smell close work here and it offends my nose worse than they did, and God knows they stank like the town sewer, save not so sweet, as Amyas used to say." said Lofty, a trace of sadness in his voice as he remembered his old friend, my father.

"John, who has a head on his shoulders in despite of the fleas and lice who were sharing it with him till yesterday, thinks Malten is almost certainly playing fast and loose. We shall try to piece out his villainy, when our penitents find us." I told them.

I was delighted, when I sought accommodation, to find that Master Nichol could house Abram and myself in two bedchambers at the head of a small staircase leading from the courtyard. It was easy to imagine the simpering Juliet leaning enticingly over the balcony to speak sweet pleasantries to her village idiot Romeo, or more to the purpose, Mark Anthony expounding eloquently over the body of Caesar. I disliked sharing a room with Abram. Invariably he managed to secure the longest bed for himself, and whilst I could appreciate that he was growing, he still lacked two inches of two yards. I overtopped him easily.

The penitents had bespoken boots for the morrow, although the cobbler had a returned pair of the style known as buckets, which luckily fitted Jacob, who now displayed them, thrusting his legs out at impossible angles in unstinting admiration of his newly shod feet, and turning them to their best advantage.

"Come on then, John." I instructed, when all were settled with a mug of ale and bread and gammon. "Let Puss-in Boots here go hang. Now explain your doubts of Malten. Your exposition began with concerns as to the whereabouts of Francis Fiennes."

"Yes, indeed. Tell me, Master Julius, in your view did our Captain take to soldiering? Did you have the notion that he would rather be elsewhere?"

Julius snorted. "Did I not? He frequented our Company like a pale shadow, hovering on the edge of matters. Campaigning was not to his taste. Lieutenant Moore now was a man to encourage and sustain us but even he was not proof against the wretched distemper that assailed us all. Alas, he was one of the first to die. The Cornet Henry Fiennes, no older than these two here, disappeared with his kinsman Francis at the onset of sickness and Master Malten slipped away in search of supplies and medicines or so he claimed and that was the last we saw of officers, save James Moore's cold corpse, which we tipped into the pit we dug, in the frozen corner of a windswept Cotswold field."

"Do you think Malten expected any to survive?" John persisted.

"That he didn't! For that we did, we can thank you, John, my boy, who somehow, though sick as a dying dog, found the strength to fetch us clean water daily. Nay, Malten looked at the noisome hellish scene that was in that cursed barn and went his ways."

"As I think, with our wages," John said softly.

"John has a notion about this," I told them, "Come John, tell us."

"A rider came with a packet for Malten. This was at the time when the malady was making itself felt, and Lieutenant Moore was sick to death. We were all ill with a fearful looseness. I do not like to relieve myself before others and was secreted behind a holly tree, to all intents and purposes invisible. The rider was from Colonel Nat Fiennes, I am sure of it. And I have remembered it all now! I had clean forgotten till I began to piece together the happenings at that sad time. He said "Colonel Nat is now in Bristol, Master Malten. Bring any of these poor leavings thither." By that he meant us, my masters. But then he shouted, "But pay and doctor them first, on your life!" And from then on we never saw Frank Fiennes or the Cornet again. Perhaps they went with that horseman to Bristol, as we were thought to be plague-ridden. And Malten told us he would go and buy us medicines and we did not see him again until this morning. Though we were in that God forsaken barn... how long, Master Julius?"

Julius banged his tankard on the table. "Three weeks and more, my boy, in frost, wind and rain. Well, and if I should meet Master Malten again, be sure I have questions for him and they will all be lodged in the toe of my new stamper, which I shall purchase tomorrow."

"Oh, you will meet him again." I said. "He has a score to settle with me. I am a marked man. Abram, keep your eyes open or our very lives are forfeit."

Jacob asked, wide-eyed, "So what was he doing with our money for..." he counted on his fingers, "four months?"

"I can tell you that," said Lofty," Money is a fruitful harlot, boys, and begets itself shamefully. He has been buying and selling weaponry. This is the fourth time... nay, I think it is the fifth... he was waiting for the Pride on the Key. The packet from Nat contained his first investment... your wages. Today did not go to his liking at all, for Waller's men were there, from two or three regiments, with deeper purses than he had allowed himself today. He will be selling to other quartermasters whom he will meet in taverns, between here and Bristol and who will know by word of mouth that he has pokers and whatnot to sell. He'll not bring his rum bung with him, just a portion. Tom, what do you think? Does the thief mean murdering mischief?"

I felt amazed and confused. "So, friends. Here is a humble quartermaster, turned weapons dealer. These wars have given him unlimited opportunity to make money, selling the instruments of death, to kill his countrymen."

"Hold hard there Tom!" said Lofty, "It is not the sword that kills nor the musket but the hands and brain that own it. If you condemn the man that sells the weapon,"(and he did look guilt-ridden), "you condemn the men that fashioned it in the manufactories, and all their poor families. 'Tis but a branch of trade. No for me, this Master Martlet or whatever is his name, is at grievous fault for his neglect and deceit of these poor fellows. If you can capture him and truss him securely, I'll give him free passage with my pig iron to Colonel Nat in Bristol. I am in no doubt that his presence is looked for. "

"Master Lofty, you are a true blooded swashbuckling Trojan!" said Julius, "I and these two young fellows will be ever in your debt… and to Doctor Tom there too. I beg you, be at accord. Now drink about, gentlemen. 'Tis time for the penitents to stand their round."

And so the moment passed, and I was grateful to Julius for his intervention. I wondered again how so clever a scholar, so gifted in the art of diplomacy could be serving as a humble trooper.

I hoped I had not offended Lofty. I remembered Master Brindley's words. "Have as little on your conscience as you can afford when these wars conclude." And for a moment I sat stock still. I was as much to blame as anyone. I had large shares in several of these new manufactories, thanks to Sir Nick's financial resourcefulness. Every month a bag of coin was brought by a cloaked rider to my house where Joan had placed it in the money chest and locked it. I was as guilty as anyone in profiting in this matter of weapons. My father's good friend was not a man with whom I could ever disagree.

"Lofty," I told him humbly, "I did not think about the weapons trade. I am as much at fault as anyone. You are the last man I would ever wish to be at odds with. Forgive me."

"Nay, Tom," he cried, clapping me on the shoulder, "There's

naught to forgive. 'Tis a poor world if good friends cannot put forward differing notions. And to speak truth, the buying and selling of these soldiers' toys does not sort well with that weak feeble creature, my conscience."

After noon, the Watermen had to retire to the Pride as a consignment of iron from the Forest of Dean was to be shipped in the hold and floated down to Bristol. I offered to come and lend my labour but Lofty thought it best if I stayed close out of sight in the New Inn, but to remember that the Pride would cast off about nine of the clock with the tide tomorrow, if I needed him before that. I thanked him heartily for his friendship and assistance. He had happened upon me twice now when I desperately needed help, and would have drowned but three days before, had he not drawn me from Sabrina's embrace.

"You are my good angel, Lofty!" I told him. His companions roared at this description. He embraced me heartily and then enfolded the slender Abram in his bearlike grip.

"Look after Doctor Tom, my Turkish knight," he told him.

"Allah cares for us both!" said Abram, piously.

"Does he so? Well tell Ally there's a stoup of wine in it for him when next we meet!" and alas, they went their ways to the Pride. I felt sad and forlorn as they trooped through the Inn's arch and turned to wave Farewell in the street.

So downcast was I that it was with considerable effort that I forced myself to bespeak a good dinner of roast beef and cabbage followed by a plum pudding for the five of us, although Julius insisted on paying for himself and the boys. Lofty had warned me to be cautious and not to draw attention to myself, so as a light rain fell in the afternoon, ending a week of sunshine, we withdrew to a quiet corner inside where I could keep watch on whoever came in to greet Master Nichol.

I began to ask Julius about his former life, always treading delicately with my questions.

"Tell me, dear sir, was your calling always that of a schoolmaster? Were you by any chance an actor?"

John and Jacob looked at each other and laughed. Julius looked down modestly. "I do not think my acting skills are great, Doctor Tom, but occasionally I was prevailed upon to carry a spear and once undertook Rosencrantz. No, Doctor Tom I am a playwright.

I create the passing illusions of reality and present them to... well... whoever will listen and watch. Can you believe one of my masques was once performed before the King and Queen. He approved but she found it something too classical and slow."

"What was it?" I asked breathlessly. This was excellent news. Of all entertainments my beloved father and myself had loved the theatre.

"It was a profound study of the deliberations of that famous general, Quintus Fabius Cunctator It was too introspective. I marshalled all the arguments for attacking and then demolished them by turn so that his delay for which he was famous, came as a most exciting climax and conclusion. Or so I thought. It was called Procrastination Triumphant. As I say the King found it engaging, but the Queen claimed it was tedious."

"I am sure it was excellent. She is not known for her scholarship," I said politely.

"No, she was right. It was utterly tedious and verbose and the music was not Master Lawes' best effort. Before I left London I read it again and many of my other pieces too. The plays I wrote of which I thought the least, were those which held the auditor's attention until the end."

Jacob nudged John. "Do you remember The Princess Potiphar and the Apprentice? On my soul, I laughed until my ribs burst. Particularly when Perkin surprised her in her...."

I quietened him. Malten was near the door of the inn, speaking to Master Nichol. We shrank back behind the wooden screen that divided us from the rest of the inn. I applied my eye to a knot hole and saw Malten gesture to his head, indicating a close shorn man or men and Nichol shrugged, and then pointed to another little stair, indicating the bedchambers where the penitents had bespoken good tight clean beds. They had been enjoying the prospect of a comfortable sleep for the first time for many months.

When I judged Malten had gone and would not return, we decided to approach Master Nichol and tell him what had befallen. He started when he saw the close shorn penitents. He had thought they had taken themselves out to view the sights of the town. He made as if to send a potboy to recall the quartermaster. I asked him to hear us out which he did patiently. When I had concluded, he nodded and smiled grimly.

"Well, my friends, this Master Malten even now wished to find you three poor starvelings, no doubt to reclaim the money he has purloined, and I'm afraid, unknowingly, I pointed out your bedchamber. So what say you, Doctor Fletcher? Let us arrange a welcome for him. Harry and Dickon shall sit in that room and when he presents himself, when he thinks all are asleep, they shall greet him warmly. What we need, gentleman, is an end to this matter and Malten needs a lesson. Then he can go about his scurvy weapon selling and you can go your ways to London."

Abram spoke for the first time. "He doesn't look at his feet. Tie a rope across the door and trip him up and he will himself present his person at your mercy."

Our jaws dropped. "So young and yet so shrewd!." Julius said, amazed. "And so observant!" I cried, "Abram, you never cease to surprise me!"

"Well, my friends, let us make preparation," said John Nichol, "And let us teach this wretched quartermaster that in future his usuries must not be practised at the expense of honest poor fellows, who have pledged themselves to break the Tyrant's Yoke!"

6

The Quartermaster returned at midnight. Julius and myself had decided that we would not adopt Abram's method of bringing him down but would give him the chance to speak for himself. We decided also that the two apprentices should not be involved in any altercation and they were ensconced with Mistress Nichol who had been moved to compassion and gingerbread at the tale of their sufferings. Although Abram had never in his life starved, he too when he turned his large brown eyes upon her pleadingly, was awarded a sweetmeat. It was, I judged, wholesome for the three of them to receive maternal attention. At sixteen, the apprentices should not have to play the man continually, and John and Jacob were in sore need of parental nurture. As was I, when I considered it.

Malten did not return alone. He had acquired a following of two broad Gloucester citizens, one a blacksmith I surmised by his leather apron and his hammer, whilst the other carried the chisel of a stone mason, holding it before him like a lance. I had seen them approaching. Master Malten held aloft a torch as they came purposefully down the street. I darted from the upstairs window where I had been spying, and sped to warn Julius awaiting them in his bedchamber. But he was flanked by Dickon and Harry who were eager opponents, relishing the exciting prospect of an affray, and one sanctioned by the authority of their master. Dickon had several broken teeth and Harry's nose seemed to have been refashioned once or twice. But to us, they were as comely as the shining armoured champions of King Arthur's table. Certain sure, they were good lads and grinned cheerfully in anticipation.

As Malten moved up the stairs, watched by the good topers of Gloucester who had paused in mid swallow, their tankards in their hands, John Nichol and myself stepped behind the open door of the next room and waited until the three intruders were in Julius' room. Then we slipped silently out and stood in the doorway behind them. But even before Master Malten knew the odds were against him, the stonemason had changed his mind.

"What! Tis Dickon !" he cried out. "Yon's my cousin, master. My mum'ud flay me if I come to buffets with him. He's a rare tidy fighter! Best not meddle with him, master! Here's your coin." And he threw some shillings on the floor before Malten and pushed past us, crying as he went downstairs, "Your pardon, Master Nichol but I ain't taking no part in no quarrel with our Dickon."

"Come back, you oaf!" cried Malten suddenly aware that the tables were turned on him, but all that could be heard was the mason's heavy shoon clomping through the buttery bar and out to the street. There was a confused murmur from the drinkers downstairs but none climbed upwards either to attack us or support us. The blacksmith took up a stance with his back to the wall. When he saw me, overtopping all in the room, and the stout innkeeper, he began to scratch his nose thoughtfully.

"Is it me you want, Master Malten?" Julius asked, the soul of politeness. "That is good for I have been long a-seeking you, dear sir. Several months, sir, if truth be told."

"You are a cursed thief and malefactor. Give me my money that that dastardly doctor stole from me and we will part without recourse to justice, each going his own way."

"Is it me you want, Master Malten?" I repeated Julius' polite question, sweetly tripping forward like a maid, sought out by her suitor for a round dance. "Before we agree to your suggestion, tell us, please, on what terms these poor fellows were recruited into Francis Fiennes' troop? Now, sir, your rate of pay, as I recall Master William Tovey telling me is four shillings a day, so let us assume these poor troopers were promised three shillings to cover....."

But Malten was staring at me. "Do you know William Tovey?" he hissed through his teeth.

"Why, that I do! We served under Basil Fielding at Edgehill. I told you this morning. He is my old comrade-in-arms." I had certainly served under Basil Fielding. I remembered vividly cowering under a bench during the cannonade on which for all I knew or cared young Basil could have been seated over me, pleasuring his doxy whilst the ordnance blasted the skies apart. And certain it was Tovey who paid me for my surgery, after better men than myself had deemed the necessary carnage was satisfactorily completed.

"Were you at Edgehill, Master Malten?" I asked meekly.

"We were too late!" he replied shortly. "Now as to my money...."

"Ah yes!" I said airily. "As to that 'tis all calculated. Four months pay at three shillings a day for a mounted trooper is 280 shillings, is it not? So these three brave fellows, the heroes of Turnham Green are owed 840 shillings. So, Master Tovey tells me these three must look to receive, say, forty two pounds in all for their sufferings and neglect over the last four months. And I am sad to tell you, Master Malten, there was but thirty pounds in all, in the purse you gave us this morning. So I must ask you now for the missing twelve pounds, Eighty shillings each if you will be so kind. And we will say no more as to the cost of the burial of their fellows, nor my doctoring fees."

Malten was a small man. He had put aside his buff coat and was well dressed in dark crimson three pile. Now his face turned the same hue as his doublet, whilst his gob opened and closed like a trout, recently landed. At last he cried out in his high piercing voice, "Be damned to you, Sawbones!" and pushing Master Nichol roughly aside, sped away down the staircase. Dickon and Harry roared with laughter and the blacksmith detached himself from the wall, smiled ruefully, and betook himself off, pounding his hammer into the palm of his hand.

The following morning after a breakfast of fried gammon and eggs, a dish I loved well, with excellent Gloucester sausages in attendance, Julius and I considered how best to travel to London. I was for taking the road to Cirencester across the Cotswolds and then over the Downs to Reading and Windsor, and if Julius had not disagreed, this history would have been short and uneventful, though perhaps that would have been unlikely in a country at war with itself. It is strange that the decision to take one road rather than another can lead to happenings of which one would never dream.

"I take issue with you, Tom, on two counts.... nay perhaps three," Julius announced. "Firstly I know not what are the perceptions of John and Jacob but I do not wish to pass through or near Cirencester again in my life. I am sure it is a fine town, of Roman origins, but for me it was the cloisters of Hell."

John murmured agreement and Jacob said firmly, "My bowels

turn to water at the prospect."

Julius looked at him with an eyebrow raised, "Well, that is a consideration to which I will return though not with pleasure. Secondly, we should have to take whatever spavined, verminous mounts, the wayside inns can supply, and they will charge a King's ransom, believe me. Now if we were to hire nags to ride only to Bath, my cousins who keep a stable there would supply us with good beasts which you and Abram can return on your homeward journey. What do you say, Doctor Tom?"

"Nay, give us the third reason before I cast my vote." I said laughing.

"Jacob has put me in mind of it. I confess my third reason was but an empty proposition to be filled, should you firmly disagree, but now I find it is a heartfelt desire not to be forced to remember the company of Jacob in the instance he describes. I spent two long weeks lying in stinking straw beside his watery bowels in a barn in Cirencester, having to rouse myself from time to time to bury another poor fellow. For pity's sake, dear Doctor Tom, let me not be subjected again to those dire memories."

"We shall make for Bath, Julius, and no barns, bowels or burials, I pledge my word. You and I shall have discourse on every matter under the sun and if we stray into error, young John here shall set us to rights. And Abram and Jacob, be sure, will remind us when 'tis pudding time. Nought but good inns, clean beds and the best dinners Gloucestershire can supply. But I doubt much they will equal the excellent provision we have enjoyed here." And I leapt to my feet and bowed low over the workworn hand of Mistress Nichol, who had courteously entered to clear the board.

It was Monday the 3rd July. I suggested that as the weather had turned a little cooler that we set out later in the day, after the two unshod penitents had bought their boots, and after I had managed to hire horses. This proved more difficult than I had at first envisaged. Colonel Massey had requisitioned all within the city, save for one skittish mare that had recently recovered of a swollen fetlock. I was advised to hire this creature and to ride her to a village called Highnam on the edge of the Forest of Dean, where there was a farm where cobs were bred. It would have been an easy ride if Madam Mare had been less of a hoyden and more of a lady. There was no question of hiring at Highnam. The farmer bred to sell and was pleased to reduce the price in that he was happy his horses were not to be used in the wars. Though I had not Samuel's gift for appraising horseflesh, I could see that these animals were strong and contented and would cover their twenty miles each day without repining.

My purse was lighter by sixty four pounds, as I had to purchase padded saddles as well. I knew that Julius would insist on paying his share, from his wages. As I returned to Gloucester before noon my string of horses attracted many interested looks, so I resorted to that strange mood of bragging and lying which seemed to carry me forward

"For Colonel Massey!" I cried as each poor man carrying heavy loads to the walls gazed on my cobs with envy. I stabled them at the New Inn and bespoke good hay and provender and water for them all so that they would be rested and ready in two hours. I returned the mare to the stable nearby. We were both well pleased to bid each other Farewell although as she was led away, I followed and fed her an apple. She neighed after she had eaten it, and tried lovingly to eat my hair.

I returned to the stable yard and found my companions discussing who should ride each mount, but Abram took me to one side and told me with a knowing look that a young lady wished to speak with me.

"How is that? I know no young ladies hereabouts," I told him. The others heard and my response drew forth derisive calls from the apprentices and offers to see her in my stead. I ignored such insolence and strode into the inn in a dignified and stately manner, but tripped headlong on a rush mat I had not before observed.

"May I help you, Master Doctor?" a voice enquired, and with a rustle of silk, a becoming young maiden knelt beside me as if to assist me to rise. I scrambled to my feet and bowed.

"Did you wish to see me, Mistress?" I asked attempting to recapture my lost gravity.

"I am hoping that you might advise as to my father's illness. It has but recently come upon him, and whilst I doubt that it is mortal, prevents him from writing his great treatise."

"How did you know I am a doctor, mistress, and may I know your name?"

"Sir, everyone in Gloucester knows everything. Even the ghosts gossip. I am Rowena Smith and my father is the philosopher James Smith, younger brother to Bishop Miles." She led the way up Northgate and turned left to the Cathedral. We walked briskly before the south face, where the niches stood empty of their prophets and saints. I was suddenly put in mind of Elijah's devotion to the old religious ways, and missed with an almost physical ache, the poor boy's sturdy independent convictions. I had lost so much. A sob rose in my throat and before I could choke it back, the strangled sound burst forth. My companion turned to gaze at me curiously.

"Are you well, Sir?" she asked courteously.

"Indeed I am, Mistress. Forgive me. A sad memory only."

She seemed to understand and led me on towards an open space before a church which she indicated we should pass alongside. I stepped into the grassy area before it, where a small hillock stood but she gently took my arm and indicated that we must walk along the path alongside the green.

"Bishop Hooper was burnt there," she told me. "An evil crime! The place is sacred to his blessed memory."

Was she speaking of a Catholic or a Protestant? I cursed myself for my lack of interest in Church affairs, but brazened it out. "A terrible event!" I said piously. Surely one could not disagree with such an opinion, and she seemed to find it a satisfactory response and nodded thoughtfully.

We came near to a street of fine town houses. I followed her under the arch of one such residence, meekly aware that this was the dwelling of the gentry. I suddenly laughed at my self imposed humility. My own house in Newport Street in Worcester was the equal of this in every way. My snort of laughter again gave her pause, and in truth what had she in hand but a tumbling, sobbing, sniggering lunatick?

"You are sure you are able to treat my father," she asked with a hint of coolness.

"I shall not know until I examine him," I replied, equally coolly, and she led the way through a warm kitchen, where a great fire blazed and on through a comfortable retiring room to what was clearly a study, built onto the house at the back. This was a high stone building with arched windows set high in the book lined walls. Even though it was July, one of the hottest months of the year, the room was frigid and chilly in the extreme.

A man sat bolt upright in a high chair, his back to us. As we walked round to face him, I saw he was holding a book, only inches from his face. He smiled grimly at his daughter who curtsied directly in front of him. I stood to one side, wondering why he did not turn his head to look at me, but a moment's observation answered the question. He could not move his head without engendering great pain.

"Who's this then you have brought to plague me, with leg of newt and eye of frog?"

"Alas, Sir, I have no such superstitious impedimenta," I told him. "My name is Tom Fletcher, physician of Worcester, and I believe I can cure your condition if you will permit it."

"Well, well, let us see you, Doctor Thomas Fletcher."

"Willingly, Sir," I said stepping into his area of vision, "but it is I who need to see you and in fact would request to do so in a chamber where the amphibians you have mentioned would not be instantly atrophied by an ice-age. My hands are already too cold to touch you and I must do so to ascertain that the muscles of your shoulder are, as I surmise, in a state of suspension."

"Can you relieve this state?" he asked curiously.

"That I can, Sir. But I must examine you first."

He grunted unwillingly, but stood up, placed a paper on the page he had been studying, closed the book and laid it on a great table along with many others. "My Cornucopia must be neglected then, this precious day, it seems," he remarked peevishly. He was a tall stooped scholarly man, who could almost look me in the eye. As he became aware that we were of a height, he smiled, nodded and led the way back into the kitchen.

The relief on moving into the warmth was considerable. I asked the cook for a bowl of warm water not merely to cleanse my hands but also to take the chill from them, and after I had dried them pushed down my patient's doublet and shirt. As I had thought, his muscles had knotted and would loosen themselves if warmth was applied to the area. I kneaded the area a little, and he sighed and exclaimed, "That is better!"

"You must not enter your library again today," I told him. "Sit near a fire. If not here" (for I had caught the cook's fleeting expression of alarm) "then in a withdrawing room and ensure that no draught can penetrate your chair. What is your name, good Sir?" I asked the manservant who had just entered with a bundle of wood for the kitchen fire.

"Tis Michael, Sir," he told me, glancing at his master and giving me a half bow.

"Well, Michael, it falls to you to cure your good master, here. No potions, Sir. Eat and drink what you will. But, and here I come to the nub of the treatment. The knot of frozen muscle near your spine at the top of your back must be melted safely. Michael, can you get large smooth stones about a foot in length, say from the Paviour?"

"We have just such a heap outside to pave the ground outside the jakes," said the resourceful Michael.

"Good! Take two of them now, wash them and place them in the embers of this good lady's fire. Then after about an hour, remove one onto a griddle, wait until it can almost be touched, place it with tongs in a stout leather bag, in which a bushel of oats might be carried and making sure the stone in the bag will not burn, but merely soothe, place it on your master's back. Wrap the bag in a blanket if you are afraid it might be too warm. When that stone is cool, remove it and replace it with the other stone and put the first one back in the embers, and so on until he tells you that he can now easily move his head and neck on his shoulders. You must be diligent, good Michael. Too cool a stone.... 'twill do no good. Too hot, and alas, we shall have a re-enactment of poor Bishop Hooper. There, I have done. Good Day and God bless all here and may he send you a speedy recovery, Sir. Do as I advise and you will feel considerable relief before nightfall."

And I left them. Mistress Rowena, open mouthed, revealing even white teeth, her father chuckling to himself at my audacity, the Cook with her hands on her hips, outraged no doubt at the liberties I had advised should be taken with her fire, and Michael, good lad, instantly repairing to the courtyard for the two smooth stones.

As I walked round Bishop Hooper's place of martyrdom, I heard a rustle of silk behind me.

"Good Sir, your fee." she gasped, waving a purse in my face.

"Did we discuss such a matter? Mistress, I am of that order of physician who asks for payment on results. When I return I will call on you and we will talk of money if you are still so minded."

"When you return," she asked, bewildered I think by my brisk manner.

"Yes, Mistress, my friends stay for me. We leave today for Bath."

"I wish you Godspeed then, Sir," she said politely, and I took my leave. As I turned the corner by the Cathedral, she was still standing, her fair ringlets something dishevelled, looking after me, in a dazed state. I raised my hand in Farewell and went my way.

Master Nichol professed himself sorry we were going after only one night in his comfortable hostelry. He it was who after Abram had told him I was a physician had informed Mistress Smith that I had a reputation that preceded me. She had come to the Inn to enquire for a doctor for her father, their usual physician having been called to Bristol.

"But Abram is a loyal dependent," I said modestly. "How did you know his word was to be trusted.".

He tapped his nose, with a superior air. "As to that, one of William Waller's colonels stayed here and spoke highly of your skills, upriver in Worcester."

"What? Did Robert Burghill lodge with you?"

"Aye, that he did and his man, Ralph. I did not know there were so many marsh hares to be snared in the water meadows. We had that creature jugged in red wine, day after day. I think he must have caught them all, for devil a hare can I buy in the market now."

"He is a rare good hunter." I said tactfully.

"No question!" he said and told me I was welcome back at any time. "Your cousin tells me you are a rare man for a song! When you return I shall call on the crooked back fiddler and we shall have a night of it."

Abram was my cousin now! It always seemed to take so long to explain his being in my company. "Cousin" perhaps prohibited long explanations, so I decided to adopt the relationship.

"He was ever over zealous in his praise of me," I said smiling modestly. "In any event, Master Nichol, I look forward to my return. But I notice that everyone is heartily engaged in repairing the walls. Does the King threaten this great city?"

"Indeed, he does! If he can conquer Gloucester, he has his swift road to Wales and all the iron ore from the Forest. He has not menaced us yet, but be assured 'tis only a matter of time.

Page 160

Meanwhile Colonel Massey makes all sound. Consider. Upriver the King has it all his way. Your fellow Russell is his servant come Hell or high water. Bridgenorth and Shrewsbury have declared for him. Hereford seems not to know its arse from its elbow.... Waller met with precious little defence, but found the place hardly worth the keeping. Well, well, Doctor Tom, all is in the melting-pot. God save and keep us. That is all one can hope."

"Amen to that!" I said. I had not thought that the towns on the Severn and the Wye were of much importance, but on reflection could see that whoever held their bridges could prevent the movement of armies in and out of Wales.

We bade Farewell to Master and Mistress Nichol and made our way to the Eastgate. We had bread and beef and apples to munch as we journeyed and I hoped that we could ride as far as Stroud with the sun westering behind us. I was reminded of the departure of Phoebe and Elijah and myself under the Sidbury gate of Worcester but a few months since, when we had set out for Lichfield with such high hopes. Now they had both been torn from me, often it seemed as a result of my own actions. Elijah had been the best of apprentices, loyal and so apt to learn. We had laughed much together and our time as master and man had been one of jokes and merriment. And Phoebe, my dearest girl, I could not but echo Joan's condemnation. My lust had killed her. And yet, I had to tell myself, I was not a lewd philanderer, eying every woman as grist to my carnal mill, but a sober serious young fellow, not given to flirtations. I liked the look of a pretty woman as well as the next man but was not one for forcing his attentions on innocent maids, and found such men as did, tedious and wearisome. My destiny seemed to be an arid desert of loneliness. My father, it seemed to me had often, since his death, spoken to me in my head, but whilst I strained to hear in my mind my poor wife's spoken wisdom, there was only silence. The three words "Tell my uncle," were all I could hear.

Something akin to a sob escaped from me as we passed below the lea of a hill on our right. I was riding ahead with Julius whilst the boys trotted, talking and laughing behind us. Julius had made useful enquiries as to our route and now told me, "This is Robinswood Hill." I could make no reply and he said no more, but after a few moments he softly asked me, "Will you not give your sorrow voice? There is plainly some desperate grief that from time to time assails you."

I told him directly, "My wife died less than a month ago."

"Ah, Doctor Tom," he said wonderingly, "And you have given so much of your time and substance to us three ne'er-do-wells, when you would have wished to mourn in solitude."

I smiled. "Solitude is impossible. Abram is my charge." I told him, "Unsought but not unwelcome. I must accept that responsibility. In fact, in less than a year, I have lost beloved father, valued apprentice and adored wife, the best of women. In fact, bereft as I was, a week ago my housekeeper attacked me physically, blaming my lust for killing Phoebe. So we left them to resolve themselves, two households, both my youthful responsibility, and as we came away, I nearly lost Abram who was in the Severn, not on it as is more usual. I cannot give way. Once I did, I fear I would never emerge from the dark places of my grief."

"But to those places you must go," he told me, "You, yourself must determine the course of your mourning. When her loss comes upon you in all its grim reality, it is for you to give way to it. Else you will never be able to let her go and live again."

This was a new concept. Kind friends attempt to disperse melancholy, thinking to cheer and console the sufferer, when in fact he or she needs to submit to grief. Certainly I had noticed that after lonely periods when I had been able to weep alone, I felt better able to face the world.

"You are right, Julius," I said wonderingly. "The mind has the means to determine its own recovery. I have observed this ability in Abram. When he lost his father he was for days in turn weeping and then laughing and singing. He bewildered me but he seemed, not less bereaved, but less diminished. He seems to know instinctively what others feel and why. He, of us all in Worcester, had most discernment into the mental pains of my housekeeper whose ill temper often had his well-being as its target. But I think you have sorrows to impart. May I not share them?"

"Look at this steep escarpment that fills our view, that our way informs us we must climb. I think we must rest the cobs and water them first and then lead them and at its summit, if I still have breath in my worthless body, I will tell you all."

So Julius for a few moments took the burden of leadership from

Page 162

me, and we dismounted, watered the horses (and ourselves) and leading them, began the climb. The cobs seemed to enjoy the freedom and the air (and the brown sugar) and needed little encouragement to scramble up the track, relieved of our weight. I was beginning to like the larger mare I had been apportioned, by reason of my height. She was of that pleasant colour that is not brown and not yellow, which I had seen elsewhere, I was sure but recently. Suddenly as we toiled upwards I remembered. Her coat was exactly the shade of Mistress Rowena's hair, so there was a question answered.

"Well done, my Lady Rowena!" I told her as we gained the final ridge of the escarpment.

"What is her name?" asked Jacob scrambling after me, leading his sturdy brown stallion.

"Rowena. What is his?"

"Is it my horse? My horse to keep? I do not want to name him and have him taken from me."

"Well," I told him, "I think that with what I had about me and what Julius has given me from your wages, we should determine that he is your horse."

We mounted again and rode along the track slowly as the other three gained the summit.

"Doctor Tom?" he asked suddenly. "How comes it that but three short days ago, I was a dirty beggar and now I am a clean well set up apprentice boy again with my own horse? Why is the world so topsy-turvy? Is it Fate or Fortune that sent you to us or is it God caring for us?"

"Jacob, I cannot tell. I am pleased to have been able to help you."

He paused for a moment and then decided, "It must be Fortune. John's brother, Moses, was kinder and cleverer than all the rest of us, and yet he died, one of the first. If God had cared, surely he would have let him live?"

"Perhaps you should speak of this with a vicar or a priest." I told him. "I am not fit to guide you in these matters. A man of God would say that the Almighty loved Moses and could not wait to have him in Heaven. What will you call your horse? No, I have it. If not Fortune, then why not Destiny? That is a good strong name for a good strong fellow."

He smiled and leant forward to stroke Destiny's mane. "Yes, a good name!" he agreed.

After a while he dropped back to ask the others how they would name their mounts, and Julius trotted forward to ride beside me.

"You have a good eye for horseflesh, Tom." he said "These nags are excellent."

"Welsh cobs are both good natured and sturdy, and better for our kind of journeying than their more aristocratic Norman cousins," I told him. "My heart bleeds when I think how these noble creatures are so misused by us. How would we live without them? How evil it is that they are forced to run and die in this accursed war? Men can choose their fates but horses cannot."

"You are mainly in the right of it, Tom," he said slowly, "But my conscription into these sad conflicts was at the last a sad inevitable conviction. We spoke of the reason near Odda's chapel. Parliament eventually must act for the common man."

I laughed. "I think also you must add the common woman. My little wife would never accept that men are the superior sex. You were going to tell me your story. Will you do so now? These three behind are well contented with each other's company and I am well disposed to hear you out."

So as we climbed upwards through fine woods with wide vistas of the Severn far below now glimpsed between the trees, Julius told me his history.

He was born he surmised somewhere in the Midlands, and to parents who had not been married. Unusually for such a child, he had known his father but not his mother. "I was "found" early one morning on the table of the kitchen of my father's castle. There was a crude missive in the basket where I lay, indicting or accusing my father of my parentage. The date was the fifteenth of March, so my father who was a scholar as well as a reprobate, christened me Julius, remembering the Ides of March and it seems handed me to a wet-nurse with money for my welfare. I remember when I was five, playing with my brothers, on the floor of the cottage, suddenly being aware of a man standing watching us. He picked me up from the brawling scuffling heap of infants and held me under my arms at arm's length.

"Why, Julius!" my wet-nurse told me he said. "Should you like to come with me, your father, and learn how to be a man?"

She told me I replied, "Aye, that I would, for I have learnt how to be a boy!" and with that he laughed, tucked me under his arm, carried me out of the place I had learned to think of as home, and placed me before him on his great horse. Although he was good to me as far as he could be, given that his wife and his other sons resented my presence, my life was not easy and I scraped and scratched myself into as good an education and upbringing as the circumstances would permit. I was the youngest of his family but by the age of twelve I was well grown, taller than all my elder half brothers, whom I could wrestle to the ground when they provoked me. In truth, I was more like my father in appearance than any of them. Abundant brown curls and a fearless blue eye, and at fifteen, I became aware that the serving wenches would serve me in ways I had not before envisaged. But my step-mother also, a comely woman of thirty two or three began to ask me to hold her silks when she embroidered and wished to take my arm when she walked in the garden. My half brothers observed this and one night, shortly before my twentieth birthday after their mother had been particularly importunate, my father being from home, there was a knock on my chamber door, after all had retired. It was the steward.

"Master Julius, do not hunt with your brothers tomorrow." That was all he said, and he turned and left me. But I guessed what my fate would be. Since the second William, the "hunting accident" has been so often the convenient explanation for high-born murder, in both song and story.

I set out with them, but dropped behind and veered into a thicket. I had not long to wait. Hob the archer sped past along the path I had left, his cross-bow poised at the ready. I returned to the castle, packed my few belongings into a saddle bag and was swiftly galloping along the road to London. I have never been back."

"May I know your full name?" I asked.

"Bastards rarely have "a full name." My father is a Neville, a minor branch of that family, but well to do for all that. I christened myself, when I reached London. Julius I liked, the name my father gave me, so I added Falconer, a sport I loved, and I prospered somewhat as the boys have told you, in the world of the theatre. I arrived in London, days before the King returned from Scotland, ten years ago and found work, transcribing for James Shirley who wrote the first masque I ever read or saw, The Triumph of Peace.

After its performance the following February the Queen honoured me by dancing with me. Then I wrote Triumphans Cunctatus, and she condemned it, rightly. So I began to write plays which the boys must have seen as children. The character of the apprentice, Perkin was popular I think. But I overreached myself, Doctor Tom. I introduced two comic divines and had them discuss endlessly church matters... even, fool and idiot that I was, where should the communion table be placed. Then Perkin with a blast of what seemed to me to be sanity, cries out, "What matter where a table be in church so the worshippers' hearts be true and compassionate?" Alas, my so called blasphemy was brought before William Laud and I spent months in the Fleet, dimly espying my wounded reflection in the pisspot, they kindly allowed me. See here."

I gasped in horror. He had pushed his fringe to one side and there were the red angry letters S and L for seditious libeller. I had heard that the lawyer Prynne had had these letters inscribed on his cheeks. I had not known that a man could also be branded on his brow.

"Laud instructed that the branding should be here," Julius went on bitterly, "So that my brain would ever be reminded of the consequences of speaking against the Church. He was pleased to say that he thought my blasphemy was unintentional and that I could therefore cover the Scars of Laud with my hair. When I cannot sleep, I devise intricate sports for the Devils in Hell to perform upon that evil Man of God."

I was struck dumb by this dreadful hideous disfigurement. I was silent both from pity and embarrassment. When Robin had mentioned "branding" I had thought it would be a small mark. But this was a lifelong stigma that my poor friend would never lose.

He, sensing my inability to respond, continued his tale. "When I was released, all was in turmoil. Bastwick, Prynne and Burton, the doctor, divine and lawyer, Puritan martyrs all, and of the middling sort, had also been liberated. London was aflame against the King. I had no employment, the theatres had been closed. As I was wandering near Old Jewry by the City Wall, a good man remembered me from my theatre days. It was Jacob's father. A schoolmaster from Coleman Street had recently died, and Master Shaw suggested that I presented myself for the post. The work was not hard, for these good boys wished to prepare themselves for their employment. There was but little Latin and Greek, but writing a good hand and calculating a good wage was what was needed, and all were apt students who never deserved the rod. I could not now in all conscience support a monarch who had allowed my disfigurement, and that of other innocent men and so when the call to arms for Essex came again early this year, I and some of the apprentices I had taught felt moved to answer. Though, Doctor Tom, we have not struck a blow for the Parliament since setting out from London and I think it must be God's will now that we never shall, our commander having deserted us, in our hour of direst need."

He had spoken so long and so intently that we had travelled perhaps ten miles, with a brief pause for a drink and some bread. Our way was high along Cotswold ridgeways and now we were beginning to descend towards a bustling town. Smells rose to greet us. "That is the dyes the Stroud weavers use to colour their woollen cloth." Julius explained. "Now this is a town of five river valleys. We must take the path to the right to Nailsworth along a stream that dances to our left."

We dined and slept that night in an inn where a rushing mill-race invaded our slumbers. John confessed to me next morning that he had hardly slept a wink but had read by the light of a candle purchased in Gloucester, some Newsbooks that Master Nichol had given him, about the sight of ghosts at Edgehill battle field. He wished to know if I had seen any. I noticed we were all dismally scratching ourselves. I replied tersely, "Ghosts then, No! Fleas now, Yes!" I went to pay our reckoning and could not help observing to the Landlady,

"Mistress, we leave with more than we came. There is no need for beds to be flea-ridden. Many wholesome herbs such as feverfew will dispel fleas, and a flea bite can fester and suppurate and be a danger to a man's health. Look to your beds, I pray you, Mistress."

She stared at me open mouthed, never before having had her fleas questioned.

We rode through Nailsworth, a busy little place and began to climb again. The track was steep and wooded and soon we left the sound of humanity far below us. At length we found ourselves high on a bare plain. The trees disappeared, and although the soil could sustain crops where poor smallholdings were to be found, as far as the eye could see, the land was one vast meadow dotted with sheep. Although it was not cold... the fourth day of July is rarely cold... there was a constant mournful wind that depressed our spirits.

Even so we seemed to make good progress but there was no doubt that this Cotswold plain was one of the areas of Gloucestershire or Somerset where few people lived and we began to fear that we should not reach Bath before nightfall. I judged that we had ridden about fifteen miles across this high vast plain. We had seen almost no-one. We came to a crossroads which Julius reckoned would be perhaps five miles from Bath. The road to the right he thought would finish at Bristol, but ahead of us was surely the highest point of the dreary wilderness. He had been told it was Lansdowne Hill. We pressed on a little further, the melancholy wind wailing in our ears. Woods lined the sides of the hill but a wide close cropped swathe of grass led upwards, with our central track gleaming white in the twilight. And then Jacob suddenly drew up on Destiny.

"Listen!" he cried.

The rest of us could hear nothing. "What can you hear, jinglebrains?" John asked affectionately.

Jacob looked embarrassed. "I don't know."

His fellow apprentice scoffed at him. "The wind has blown your understanding ahead of us to Bath. Come on! Let's catch up with your wit!"

"Jacob, tell us if you hear the sound again." said Julius, kindly.

We rode on perhaps two hundred yards, and then I too heard it. It was the sound of Edgehill. A large company of men must be gathered together somewhere to our left. Julius who had an enviable knowledge of the geography of our land expressed the view that the next town to the east would be Chippenham. Curiosity, ever my prevailing vice, possessed me.

"Wait for me, here," I shouted, ignoring Abram's anguished shouts of protests. I spurred Rowena under the hollows of the wooded hills and rode about half a mile in the direction of the noise. God knows, I had been excessively fortunate, in that since my return from Lichfield in April I had avoided much contact with warring armies, apart from my brief sojourn with Waller's men outside Worcester. My fortune had always taken a turn so that I had been either too soon or too late for a battle. It seemed that my luck might now be changing.

And yet... and yet... I was ashamed to admit that I found the planning and tactics behind a battle, of great interest. Why a commander should dispose his musketeers in just such a place, why ordnance were placed at such an angle, why the foot were constrained to wait before attacking.... all these and other aspects of warfare intrigued and possessed me, in the same way that an epic play would be sure to hold my attention. I was ashamed of this interest. At the end of a play all the corpses stood up again and bowed to the applause of the groundlings... no such happy conclusion at the end of a battle.

I trotted to the crest of a rise and there before me was a great plain covered in men and horses. I could not see any banners or insignia, but beheld a surging mass of mankind, cooking, talking, eating and drinking. I gazed out over the sea of humanity, wondering if there was any there whom I might recognise, but when those not far from me, noticed me and began to reach for their muskets, I judged that I had seen enough, turned Rowena, and galloped back. I saw Abram and the penitents standing still on the track anxiously gazing in my direction. I waved and in a moment was with them, though I had little to report other than that Jacob had remarkable hearing and that an army of thousands was resting within a mile of our road. We climbed on some little way the sun far down in the west on our right hand, slowly becoming aware that we must spend a night here on the barren hillside. The horses were tired and so were we.

"Masters, young masters!" a voice called to us from the right of the track. It was still light enough in the gathering twilight to see that the old shepherd meant us no harm. We halted hopeful that he might be able to offer us shelter for the night.

"We have two sorely hurt young fellows. Could you take them up the hill to the surgeon? My wife, Nell, is a clever woman but she is not skilled in wounds."

He stood beside a path scarce discernable in the dusk, leading down into a coomb where a few trees nestled protectively round a sheep cot and a duck pond where the ducks still squawked and fought. I looked at Julius who nodded and we followed the old fellow down to his home.

We dismounted. Two horses were tethered to the trees in the

orchard, and I suggested to the boys that they might feed and water our mounts, making sure that they were firmly secured. Where armies are camped, horses are always tempting pickings. Julius and I followed the old man into his home which was poor indeed. One room alone fulfilled all the functions of the many chambers of my house in Newport Street, and yet here were the old shepherd and his wife, at complete accord together, content with their poverty and each other. She had been gently bathing the thigh of one man, who was alert still, in spite of having a musket ball embedded in his femur. The other fellow at first sight seemed to be in worse case. He was unconscious with an injury to his shoulder. Both of them had discarded red body armour lying beside them. They were, I decided, cuirassiers.

"His horse rolled on him, I think," the old man told us. And his armour would perhaps have saved his life, but would not have prevented grievous injury.

"Well, I had best treat them. I am a Doctor." And I placed my box on the rough table, opened it and prepared to ply my trade.

"Mistress, whence comes the water?" I asked her. As I feared it was unboiled, drawn from the well outside. I set her to boiling the contents of the buckets that they had prepared and Julius helped me lay out the poor fellow with the damaged thigh on the table. I gave him a draft of Hollands gin, and explained that I would need to open the wound further in order to withdraw the ball. He gritted his teeth and I applied my speculum which I had kept wrapped in clean linen, and saw that the ball had in fact shattered the bone. The cavity kept filling with blood which I sponged away with the boiled water. I used my callipers to remove the ball. That was the easy part. There were still fragments of cloth and bone which it was hard to discern with the fading light. There was a chance he might not walk again unless I could remove all the debris. Then with rest and care, the bone itself might knit and mend, if he was fortunate.

John, I remembered, had bought candles so that he could read his Newsbooks at night. The old wife produced a pricket into which Jacob placed a candle which he held carefully for me, wide eyed at the sight of the white bone and red blood that lurks within us all. Now I was able to pick out all the fragments, although I warned him roughly not to allow hot grease to fall onto the wound. He gazed at me wide eyed, surprised by my hard tones.

The femur of this poor trooper might mend itself but after I had pushed the skin together and bound the wound very firmly, I knew that the chances of a complete recovery were slight. If he could rest on a bed for some weeks and not put his foot to the floor, he might walk again after a fashion, lurching ever onto his good leg in an awkward manner.

I felt ready to weep with frustration.

"Julius!" I cried aloud. "What in God's name is the reason for all this Hellish slaughter?"

What sort of a madman was I, who could be fascinated by the prospect of war as a drama, a narrative of strategy and yet cry aloud in horror at the results of conflict? My cry had roused the other poor fellow who moaned at the pain from his shoulder. Yet as I examined him I realised he was not in such a bad way as his fellow. Like the times in which we lived, his humerus was "out of joint". Again my Hollands Gin was administered. I spent about quarter of an hour tenderly feeling the area until I sensed that he had been lulled into an easy acceptance of my treatment. Then I re-set the humerus. It went sweetly and smoothly into the socket.

The screams went on for perhaps two minutes. The shepherd and his wife, Abram and the penitents stared at me in horror. Only Julius and the trooper with the damaged thigh had some notion of the pain of bone setting and smiled grimly at the cursing and swearing that I endured. As the pain subsided, I was able to explain to the poor sufferer that I was not a torturer and that his shoulder would be stiff and sore for some days, but that all would almost certainly be good as new. Now for the ribs. Although he complained of pain in that area, it did not lessen or increase as he breathed, which made me think he had not broken his bones. He was sorely bruised, black and blue all round his ribcage. I wrapped him around stiffly so that if there were a fracture, he could not cause damage to his innards by any sudden movement. He was in much better case than the other invalid and could now stand and walk although he needed rest.

We lifted the poor fellow with the broken thigh onto a pile of sheepskins in the corner of the sheep cot. I hoped he would not be eaten by fleas and sent Abram out for groundsel and feverfew. He returned with what he trusted were the herbs I needed, and the news that many fires flickered on the top of Lansdowne Hill.

"That is where we should be," said the trooper with the dislocated shoulder. "With William Waller."

I exclaimed aloud. "So where has he come from? We heard in Gloucester that he was rampaging around Somerset, in the south of that County."

"Of late he has been rampaging around Bath. Yesterday we were on Claverton Down and last night we withdrew to Bath itself. At length the Conqueror placed himself on the top of this monstrous mountain and today he and Hopton, his old friend, drew blood... but only his!" He indicated the invalid with the wounded thigh.

"That then was Hopton's army, I saw due East, towards Chippenham," I said wonderingly.

"They are quartered on a village called Marshfield. And Prince Maurice, the meddlesome bastard is with them," said the shoulder. "Master Doctor, may I say you are a miracle worker! George, how say you? Shall we make shift to climb back to our supper?"

In answer George groaned and I said in anger, "Why would you have him undo my labour? If he attempts to walk in the next week, I swear he will never walk again. And you, Sir! But fifteen short minutes ago you were screaming like a..."

"Like a stuck pig!" Jacob informed him kindly.

"And now I am a whole pig again!" said the trooper gratefully. "What did you do? My arm hung useless from my shoulder."

"'Tis the ancient craft of bone setting. I learnt it from my Master in Worcester who was kind enough to claim that I surpassed him in this skill. He hated doing it so I gained much practice. The trick is to lull the patient into thinking you are going to do nothing and then suddenly act. I suppose it is a kind of treachery but if the patient is tense and expectant, the chance is lost. But indulge me. I don't understand. As we came up Lansdowne Hill there was no residue of battle, no dead horses or men."

"It was a battle that never was. Hopton found Waller so well ensconced that he drew off without a shot. But the fox had covered his retreat with musketeers in the hedges and ditches. We did not see this but thought to help him on his way and two troops of our horse galloped down to snap at his heels, right into an ambush. The whoreson wretch who fired at me, missed but caused my horse to rear and I was toppled."

George who we thought was asleep or unconscious spoke

slowly, "And I, poor fool, veered round to protect this clown as he lay prone and took a ball in the thigh. Then the bastards retreated following Hopton but by then our loyal comrades in arms had scrambled back up the hill. We were the only two poor devils to feel Hopton's pepper today. But 'twill not be so tomorrow. Tomorrow, these Cornishmen will be after Waller's blood."

The shepherd and his wife listened with growing dread. "Are you after saying, Master, there will be a battle here on the morrow?" the old man asked hesitantly

George nodded. "Without a doubt. Hopton seeks a way to Bath and this is his nearest road. Waller has made himself snug and tight up aloft and will be pointing his culverins down the slope towards the wild Cornishmen and Maurice's gentry...and towards us. Martin, you had best go out and look at the line of fire. I tell you, all of you, tomorrow, 'twould be best to move westwards from here some hundred yards or so away from this dwelling and that smooth slope."

Martin had risen and was walking slowly and stiffly to the door. I beckoned to Julius and we followed him into the warm summer night. There was still light enough in the western sky and we could see that the path rose again behind the homestead westward to a copse mainly of ash encased in a thicket of hawthorn. Beyond that the little valley ended in a steep white quarry wall which enclosed and protected it from the west.

"Now that thicket is good," said Martin, "We can all hide out here, tomorrow, horses and all. And the undergrowth and the tree trunks and even the cottage itself give some protection." He led us back past the duck pond and dwelling, east to the point where the path gave onto the steep broad slope, lined with hedges and woodland. We could hear faint shouts and cries from above where the gunners were bringing their gun placements into position. There was the neighing of horses as great teams dragged the hideous iron instruments of death into their stations.

"What of the trajectory?" I asked, hoping to sound knowledgeable.

Martin stared at me. "They do not need to calculate that, Master Doctor. Have you never seen boys roll pigs' bladders down a hill in sport? Our task is to ensure we are not the targets, all of us, the old man and his goodwife, your young charges and all our horses. They only need to aim the muzzle slightly northwestwards and we are all dead meat. My hope is that they will not expend their cannon ball like profligates, but engage man to man as well. Perhaps I should try to walk or ride up the slope to tell them of our presence. But some simpleton might well shoot me and challenge my corpse afterwards. And I cannot leave George. The poor dolt relies on me. Why does not Dowet send a party down for us? Are he and I of so little account?"

I was at a loss as to what to do. In theory we could even now leave the troopers and the old people and climb up the hill and find Robert Burghill. But George was powerless and Martin was very bruised about his waist, and should not over exert himself. I did not want to endanger Abram, and in my view John and Jacob had already endured too much. Then of course, I knew only too well that the instant Robert and Waller realised I was on the top of Lansdowne Hill, I would be forced to ply my trade. I was about to ask Julius what he felt was our best course of action, when he suddenly spoke.

"Martin, how would it be if we pulled undergrowth over this path where it emerges onto the hillside? If we piled it high, no-one running or riding past would guess there was a homestead here."

"Good!" said Martin. "Very good. But that will still be no defence against cannon balls, if they veer off course into this valley. Still, 'tis a good stratagem. Let's be about it now. Can the lads help?"

It seemed that it was decided that we would sit it out. On consideration I felt that it would be churlish to leave the kind old shepherd and his wife to the mercy of the cannon balls. If the cottage was struck, they would be homeless. So under the moon we all except George and the old woman set about cutting and piling brushwood into the gap where the path emerged onto the hill. At length Martin declared himself satisfied. Soldiers do not waste time reflecting. If their way is blocked, they do not pause to ask why, but move on elsewhere.

I went to the horses and brought in what food we had in the saddle bags. Mistress Nichol had given us cheese and apples and Nell had some rye bread and cold rabbit meat, left over from their meal earlier in the day, so we ate well enough. The soldiers as is the way with them had nothing, so we willingly shared our provisions.

We decided to set a watch on the horses and when dawn broke would break a way into the thicket for them, which Martin thought would be the most protected hiding place, both from Parliament Ordnance and Royalist Cornishmen. Julius watched for two hours with John until moonset and then I and Jacob took our turn.

I dozed with my back against a tree whilst Jacob munched an apple. After about twenty minutes he asked, "Tom, are you asleep?"

"No, Jacob, not now!" I replied .

"Can I ask...?"

"Ask what?"

"How may I become a doctor?"

I assumed that the same rules governing apprenticeships applied in London.

"You will need a kind master who will enjoy teaching you and indulgent parents who will be prepared to pay for new indentures, as by this I understand that broom handle making is no longer to your taste," I yawned. "You will also need some measure of Latin still as some books are as yet not translated into English." I scratched my head. "And a good memory so that you can recognise a complaint, without referring constantly to the standard works of medicine. And you will need to discriminate. Some physicians over complicate the issue babbling about humours and astrology. You need to exercise your reason in your brain and compassion in your heart, and if your stomach can contemplate the blood, bone and sinew inside a man's leg without dispelling your last meal, as I have observed but lately that it can, then you are in a fair way to becoming eventually Doctor Jacob Shaw."

He nodded and smiled. "And bone-setting?"

"That is not a talent for every doctor and indeed some men in London as I have heard, who are not doctors, do nothing but set broken bones. It is a strange craft and one I do not like to practise but often in these wars I must. As you heard, you must steel yourself against the foulest language. The compensation is that the momentary anguish swiftly becomes profound gratitude. Why not sleep now for a little, Jacob? Tomorrow promises to become a busy day."

He settled himself down and we dozed into the dawn. Martin woke us with a drink of water. "Yes, Doctor. It is your boiled water from the cauldron," he told me as I took it doubtfully. "Your followers inside insisted that we could not drink straight from the well."

"They have learnt something from me, it seems," I said and drank thirstily. There was now much more noise coming from above and Martin led the two Parliament horses past the cottage, round to the back of the thicket where there was the most cover from the ash trunks and the hawthorn. He began to push into the copse to make a path but I forbade him as his bruises would be aching intolerably. In fact there was a small clearing, at the foot of the ash trees, and the horses as they stamped about made it larger. In a few moments we had all the horses safely out of sight. We made a moveable bed for George, sheepskins lashed to two long saplings. We brought out the pile on which he had been lying, and a bench for old Noah and his goodwife, and set them near the horses. We brought out the little food we had left and water for ourselves and then I remembered my box of medicaments, and ran back into the cottage to retrieve it.

As I came out I heard a familiar sound, the resounding thunder of hooves. Clutching my box I ran to our makeshift hedge and tried to see through the thick screen of twigs and branches, but although I could sense that many horsemen were galloping past, I could see nothing. I ran uphill a little way parallel to the thick hawthorn brake that lined the hill and found that by jumping up on a little knoll I had a restricted view of the wide grassy slope, but was in time to see the last horses streaming past downhill. After them came a motley collection of carts, empty for the most part, but one or two carried the necessary replacements of match and powder for muskets. As far as I could see, the troopers rode with swords drawn and pistols at the ready but I could not be....

A voice said sternly, "Either side could take you for a spy and blow your head off."

Martin, with Abram, beside him, stood below me.

"I thought all were agreed that we would sit it out here. For the old couple who brought us in, wounded as we were, for us two invalids and because this boy and the others are too young to be put in mortal danger after the privations they have suffered. Why do you put all our lives in jeopardy by your careless curiosity and lack of loyalty?"

I climbed down, shamefaced. Martin was a hard man, no

question, but I knew he was right.

His voice softened slightly. "Do you not understand, Doctor Tom, that you are the most valuable member of our party? For Christ's sake, cherish your safety. So many depend on you. Yesterday I thought my arm would wither on my body."

I became the responsible doctor again. "And even now you should be resting. You have bruises black as midnight's arsehole round your waist, and your arm must be so stiff and sore."

He nodded. "So come back and sit, and while away the morning. This young Trojan tells me you have seen action. At Edgehill and Hopton Heath. George and I would like to hear your tales although Julius claims that you are marvellous close about your exploits."

We climbed back into the thicket and old Nell handed me a drink of water and a piece of bread.

"That was a sortie, to give Maurice and Hopton a taste of steel before they are properly drawn up. But by now they'll be ready." George seemed to know Waller's strategies. "He'll send the horse out in large parties to harry the traitors. When they're back, he'll open with the ordnance. But we're safe until we hear them return."

I did not know how my companions would react if they knew that in my travels I had been a guest of Lucius Carey, the King's Secretary of State, nor if they knew how I had served the Royalist Earl of Chesterfield, as surgeon in the Close at Lichfield, nor if they should know of my companionship with Christopher Peabody, second in command to Sir Jacob Astley, Commander of the King's Foot, nor that Prince Rupert himself had bade me count myself as ever his friend. I judged it best to remain silent on these matters. I told them all that I had never struck a blow against a fellow Englishman or Welshman whatever his beliefs, except in self-defence with a mad surgeon outside Worcester. When I told them how my father died, they were amazed that I should have thrown in my lot with Essex' army.

"Tom, you must know, that we enrolled as Essex' men," said Julius, "All Laud did to me was this," and he pulled aside his hair, to the horror of the old people. "But our Lord General killed your innocent father. How can you suffer us?"

I shrugged and smiled. "If you must know, I remain remote from your loyalties. As I told you, Julius, I pride myself on being fiercely neutral. If a man is injured I will try to cure him if I can, whatever his politicks. I am a surgeon, not a soldier."

Martin spoke. "We are with Hesilrige's Horse, part of Waller's Western Association. But I fail to understand you, Tom. Why are you so intent on the progress of battle that you risk your life to watch it?"

"I don't know," I replied miserably. "All I know is I can view a battle as auditors see a play, without strong loyalty, but with great interest and absorption. I am unnatural perhaps."

"Well, as there are no theatres now for anyone, King or Parliament," said Julius, "it may be that the progress of battle fulfils the desire for… what may I say? Entertainment?"

"And yet I hate it with all my heart," I said sadly. As we sat the noise of skirmishing was heard clearly and constantly, rising from the plain. The piercing screams of wounded men and the frenzied neighing of horses imposed themselves on our awareness all morning. Martin, who seemed to know everything there was to know about warfare, remarked languidly, "He'll send parties of horse and dragoons to harry the Royal foot. They'll withdraw and then reform and have at him again."

He was beating out some dents in his red armour, and explained the names of the various pieces that made up his whole suit. I suggested that he wore the placket, back and tassets to protect his tender waist and to remind him to refrain from bending. John, ever obliging, helped him on with these items.

Jacob had asked my permission to examine the contents of my box and had found an old Newsbook. It was a poem of John Taylor, the London waterman. Julius became excited at the find.

"Where did you get this, Tom?" he asked. "I know this man."

I remembered only too well and did not know whether to feel shame at my neglect or relief at having to confront the gift. Poor, murdered Philip Fosdyke. He had given it me when we had discovered we had shared a love of the theatre, on that wild September night, almost a year ago. I had never opened it and now listened as Julius read aloud to us all from The Women's Sharpe Revenge. It was an interesting piece and one idea intrigued me. The writer taking the persona of a woman exclaimed at the injustice they suffered. Young men could behave barbarously and be forgiven whilst maidens whose conduct ever lapsed from the virtuous and pure would be condemned for life. I could not help thinking how Phoebe would have approved of such an argument.

We sat and listened as Julius read the whole Newsbook and then I asked the two cuirassiers to tell us something of their history. They were but lately "come from the Low Country" and were only too pleased to be recruited by Arthur Hesilrige in London in April past, as, like all soldiers, "they had never a penny of money." When we judged it to be noon we ate some stale bread and drank some water, and I began to fear that this would be all our fare on that day.

But in the afternoon matters took a more eventful turn.

There was the thudding of many hooves again and we all turned our faces towards the track up the hill, beyond our makeshift hedge. "That is our lads returning." said Martin. "Waller still has his guns and his foot untried. Well, Tom, well, I will make a spyhole in the hedge to assuage your thirst for warfare. An eye behind a thicket of thorns is not near as visible as a numbskull's head, bobbing up and down in the air. You had best come with me, you whoreson warmonger! We should know what they are doing."

I felt honoured that Martin wished for my companionship, in these matters of warfare and stratagems. He pushed a stick through the brushwood and peered through but bending his body plainly caused him so much discomfort that he ordered me to stoop and see what I could see.

"Look for an anchor on a green ground, falling from the clouds." He instructed me. I saw the insignia almost at once.

"It has the legend "Only in Heaven" under the anchor." I told Martin.

"Aye that's Sir Arthur. His motto is the most pious thing about him. I can't say he is a compassionate man."

"None-the less, the armour he made you wear, probably saved your life yesterday, when your horse rolled on you." I pointed out. The horsemen were riding slowly up the hill and as the ground grew steeper, many dismounted to save their horses.

"Was not Arthur Hesilrige one of the "birds that flew" when the King forced his way into Parliament?" I asked stepping back from the spyhole and straightening my back.

"Aye that he was and as well he did fly. Charles was determined that the five from the Commons would kick the wind. But the House had had enough of tyranny, enough of bishops, enough of taxes. I read of it all in the Low Countries last year in January and thought of returning then, but our commander wished us to stay another twelvemonth. When we came back in Spring, all London was aflame for Parliament. But what have we now? What's this?"

A great roar was coming from the bottom of the hill. Many voices were shouting, and as I strained to hear I caught the word cannon. Martin gave a nervous laugh. "'Tis the Cornishmen. They are coming to fetch Waller's guns, they say." At length the sound became clearly defined as one voice. "Let us fetch those cannon!" This was roared forth again and again. For all I cared they could have them and welcome. All the Parliament horse and dragoons had now disappeared from our view, their departure hastened ever and anon by shots from below. There was great movement and bellowing from the bottom of the hill. A man's name was shouted often. "God for Sir Bevil", it seemed to be. Martin was listening to the confused sounds and now grasped my arm.

"Back, Tom, back! they will send muskets to cover a pike advance. A musketeer could easily break through this and be well protected."

We ran back to the thicket and told the others what Hopton was planning. We were invisible from our makeshift hedge but the cottage was not. Martin crouched in a lilac bush, beside the cottage door, the heads of the flowers brown now, but the thick foliage afforded him some concealment.

Now the noise, many hundreds of men shouting together, grew closer. They clearly advanced in unison, marching as one and shouting their intention as they marched in time "Let us... fetch those... cannon." It was terrifying to hear. There were the shouts of officers who were mounted judging by the frightened whinnying of horses. I peered round a hawthorn brake and could see Martin, straining to see what was happening. Suddenly he dropped down like a stone. Two men were beating their way through our hedge with muskets. They gave a cursory glance at the hidden valley and the little cottage but stationed themselves, their backs to us, their weapons poised and pointing though the undergrowth at the army mounting the hill.

"Why are they hiding?" whispered Abram.

"They are hoping that Waller's men, his horse, will think the pikemen unprotected as they ascend and be tempted down to attack them," George told us equally softly. "But the Conqueror has a trick or two up his sleeve. I would keep your heads down."

Suddenly a fearful explosion blasted our ears, followed almost immediately by another. There was a roar of derision from the ascending pikemen. Obviously the shot had missed them and as Martin had described it, "came down the hill like pigs' bladders rolled by boys."

"That's it!" said George. "They'll readjust their line of fire. Heads down, lads."

He was right. There was a bang such as I never heard before and hope never to hear again. In the instant a huge spout of water shot many feet into the air and descended everywhere in the little dell, drenching us all. The poor ducks were shot up and fell like stones. The sight of her precious water fowl killed like flies was too much for poor Nell. She rushed out of hiding, careless of King, Parliament, Hopton, Waller and the Devil himself. Screaming with rage at the thoughtless and negligent ways of men, she ran to her dying birds, her pets and her livelihood and began tenderly to stroke them and gather them up.

"Keep down!" George hissed from his bed of sheepskins. But the gunners now had the measure of the pike advance. With the next great explosion, there were no howls of derision on the hillside but screams of pain and shouts for assistance. The two King's men, hearing the sound of an outraged female in all the hubbub, turned to gaze at Nell, their clothes and their bandoliers drenched. They stood open-mouthed, their muskets useless now, as she screamed imprecations and curses at men in general and those who went to war, in particular.

One of them seeing a drake still alive but caught in a small chestnut tree, hastened to free the unfortunate creature. Holding its legs together and stroking its back reassuringly, he bowed to Nell and presented it to her gallantly. This strange act of courtesy in a day of barbarism caused her even more distress. Her tears of rage became piteous tears of sorrow, coursing down her brown face. She cradled the drake against her bosom, and sobbed out her thanks.

Martin, seeing that the situation had progressed beyond the simple rules of warfare, stood up, and beckoned us out of hiding. As Noah was the householder we pushed him to the fore, and he went to his old woman and stood beside her, taking her and the rescued drake in his arms. John and Jacob carried George on his sheepskin trannion, and laid him down beside Martin.

The two Kings' men and the rest of us stood facing each other, as the noise of battle faded up the hill. Martin and George were clearly soldiers of Paliament, Martin wearing his red placket and tassets and George with a buff coat folded across him. Julius and the boys were no longer the sparse skeletons they had been when we found them, but they were still unconvincing Brothers of the Blade... if they had ever been. Abram and I had no quarrel with the King, and gazed at the two soldiers until finally I bowed.

"Thomas Fletcher, Doctor of Worcester," I said displaying my box of medicaments.

One of them, the drake rescuer, bowed in response and the other removed his hat. Perhaps they thought the "penitents" were my surgeon's mates. But they could have no doubt as the identity of Martin and George. At last, they looked at each other, shrugged, and turned back to the hedge. As they passed Nell, still weeping as she gathered up her darlings, the drake-rescuer bowed again.

As his companion began to push his way through the hedge, the other stood aside to allow him free progress for an instant, turned back to us and called out, "God save all 'ere."

I called out, "And you, good Sir!"

He raised his hand to me and disappeared.

For a moment we all stood bemused, the sounds of battle echoing from the summit of the hill, and the outraged squawks of the few surviving ducks breaking the silence. Abram came over to me, his eyebrows raised in a questioning manner.

"Tom, were they our enemy?"

I drew him to one side and asked, "Was Prince Rupert our enemy when we dined with him and Gabriel and Mistress Cornelia in Lichfield?" He shook his head.

"Or Peabody?"

He laughed. "Never Peabody! He loved us like his sons!"

I sighed. "I think you are in the right of it there, and he will be grievous sad, when he learns about Phoebe."

About half Nell's ducks had met an untimely end. I found sage leaves and asked Noah's permission to dig up two or three onions, and placed them beside the sad heap of corpses. Then as the culverins had ceased firing and the sounds of battle seemed now to be from the summit of the hill, I made bold to suggest that perhaps poor Nell might consider making us a meal, as the means to do so lay lifeless on the grass. I supported my request with the gift of two sovereigns. Jacob offered to assist her, and she set him to plucking the poor creatures outside the cottage so she would not recognise one from the other when she finally consigned them to the cauldron.

Martin, meanwhile, who was as curious as myself for all he condemned my recklessness, told us he would edge himself up behind the hedge that lined the hillside and see what was taking place. He and George were confident that there was now no danger to us from cannons. Too many King's men had climbed the hill. The gunners would be fighting for their lives.

"Have a care, numbskull!" said George from his pile of sheepskins. "Those two wont be the only musketeers set to second the pikes, and the others wont have wet match, and be outnumbered six to two."

Martin nodded grimly and set off cautiously uphill, to find out who was getting the best of the day. I could not resist taking up my stance on the knoll that afforded a limited view of the hillside. It seemed that the King's horse did not care for whatever had been prepared for them at the top of the hill for small groups of cavalry rode down in panic, only to meet senior officers who ordered them harshly back to the fray. At length I pushed my way some distance through the hedge and at great peril poked my head through, and looked up the hill.

A great pall of smoke hung over the summit. I could see the tight phalanx of Cornish pikemen standing firm but what was wonderful was that they seemed to have been stopped by Waller on the steepest part of the slope, just below a line of earthworks. From my viewpoint they seemed to be almost hanging in the air, one row below another, with the black cloud above them. Hopton's horse rode about them, moving constantly, making occasional attacks at the earthworks where Waller was clearly well ensconced. The great mass of pikes stood still as stone. There was the occasional burst of fire and smoke from within the phalanx, where a Parliament gun had hit home. As I watched they seemed to make ready to charge again over the earthwork, and the cry went up again. The name of a man unknown to me, "Sir Bevil!"

I became aware of someone tugging at my breeches. "Tom, Tom! Come back! They will see you!" I wriggled backwards, to where Abram stood, white-faced and afraid. "Tom, you must not do that. Who can I turn to if you are killed?"

I said cruelly, "You would have to make shift for yourself, my lad." But seeing his stricken expression, I weakened and asked, "How goes the duck stew?"

The cottage door was closed as George had pointed out that the smell of cooking could be a sudden and irresistible temptation to hungry soldiers. Nell was stirring the cauldron over the fire, whilst Jacob was cutting up a cabbage with his dagger. Abram and I carried George back inside the cottage, and I made bold to examine the wound in his thigh. I was pleased that he had retained feeling in his foot, but the skin around the gash was swollen and sore to the touch. That was natural to a degree. I must hope that my Pares Lotion would continue to enable the sufferer to resist infection.

I anointed and bandaged him again with clean linen that I carried with me. He thanked me and told me that he counted himself the most fortunate of men that I had happened upon them. I could have disputed his opinion. No man is fortunate who has a hole the size of a tennis-ball in his thigh, but I gave my dog fox smile and accepted his compliment with as good a grace as I might.

Martin returned. It seems he had found his way uphill by means of an old gully, now empty of water, but quite hidden from the main slope of the hill. He looked at George, shook his head, and said three words.

"The Cornish pikes!"

"Well, what of them?" said Julius. "Well placed ordnance will devastate them in a moment."

"Not these fellows!" said Martin, "And Maurice's swaggerers have put paid to most of Waller's gunners. I tell you, they are standing like rocks where the ground is steep as the side of St Clements church."

It was excessively crowded in the cottage, and we seemed to be constantly in each other's way. I suggested that all should keep their elbows tucked in their sides but at length Noah suggested that those who could sit with ease should sit outside and we would be apportioned a bowl of stew in turn as he and Nell had only three bowls. Julius, John and myself sat on the little bench we fetched from the hiding-place. The sounds of battle still proceeded from the hill-top and as we placed the bench outside the cottage, there was a terrible groan from some thousand throats.

"No doubt a commander has met his end," said George, who had interpreted the battle all day, solely by what he heard. Now he and Martin insisted that I should be one of the first to eat.

"Our battle cry at Breda was "Keep your match dry and cherish the bloody surgeon." A good precept," Martin pronounced, "You are a mad hothead, Tom, but a good surgeon. Without you, George would have bled to death and my right arm would be useless. Eat, man!"

So I took some mouthfuls and was grateful indeed for the tasty hot food. But as I stood up to return the bowl our makeshift hedge was suddenly and fiercely crashed down.

One of the Cornish musketeers who had broken in before stood there, flanked by others, who were pushing down the briars. To my amazement all five men were weeping. The man I knew shouted to me, gulping back his tears.

"Good Master Doctor, you must come at once. It is Sir Bevil. The blow is mortal but he still lives and we need you to ease his pain.

7

I had thought before I began the ascent of Lansdowne Hill that I had crossed the threshold between boyhood and the world of mankind. I had not. And yet I had married and got my wife with child. I had fought for my life with Brigstock when my only weapon had been a chair leg. I had been present at two major battles of these wars. I had seen my father hanging from a gallows. But I was not a man, in that I had not known the depths to which the human spirit will stoop, until I had climbed that hill with the Cornishmen and seen the degradation of the human soul.

The slope was like an old painting of the Harrowing of Hell. The Parliament guns had done terrible damage to the Cornish pikes. Their courageous attack up the hill was described by the musketeers from Bodmin who escorted me. The fact that the pikemen had ploughed on leaving their broken and bleeding comrades–in-arm to die untended, spoke much for their faith in their commander, Sir Bevil Grenville. He had roused them on with praise of their fortitude and memories of their native land for which they felt intense loyalty. Indeed their steadfastness had triumphed. They had three times come to push-of-pike across the Parliament barriers at the top of the hill, but on the third occasion, they told me Sir Bevil had taken a fearful slash across his brains with a halberd. As we came nearer to the hill's crest, the carnage and the fierce action was such that I was relieved I had insisted that Abram had stayed with Julius. Young Jacob had offered to accompany me, but I had told him, roughly, "Holding a candle over a shot thigh is one thing, but you have no notion of the hideous atrocities of battle you could see. Hold off from it for now." As we went I wished I had taken my own advice.

As we came higher up the hill, there was that terrible darkness in daylight that the smoke from the guns causes. Now the casualties were not the pikes but Waller's horse. Where the King's men gathered jeering round a Parliament man, stuck through the guts on a pike, his horse dying beside him, I stopped in my tracks and would go no further, until the Cavaliers left their wretched victim to die with dignity. To pull out the pike hastened his death. I had learnt this from Martha and the other harpies at Edgehill. As my Cornish companions commanded them as Christians to forbear their filthy scorn and to depart, I found myself hardened by battle and had now the courage to withdraw the weapon and speed him on his way. A strange task for a doctor.

On two or three more occasions, I refused to continue unless similar compassion was shown. We came upon a group of whoreson rogues tormenting a screaming pig which they were killing by degrees. Only it was not a pig. It was one of Hesilrige's men so cut about that it was impossible to descry which was his flesh and which his red armour. They continued to slash at his mangled limbs, and still he lived. Again I used my height and a certain authority I was developing in my voice to insist that he was allowed to die. I summoned up my courage, and said witheringly, "Does Prince Maurice know that his followers are base torturers rather than honourable soldiers?" One man who had been standing at the side remote from the shameful action, nodded, drew his dagger and slit the poor wretch's throat. He looked me in the eye questioningly. I thanked him and we proceeded, in spite of the crude outrage of the King's men who had had their sport curtailed.

My guide told me he was called Justin, a name I had never heard. He hurried me round the hill to a hollow away from the battle where wounded Cornishmen had crept to die. A stand of about twelve pikes surrounded the Cornish leader. We were admitted to the inner circle of ground where he lay in the last hours of his life... He had fair curls and a neat thin moustache and beard. His hair at one side was bloodied through from a fearsome gash to the head, so deep in fact that it was a wonder he still lived. Ben had told me that after the initial shock, blows to the head are not as painful as other wounds but his followers were clearly anxious that he should be spared the real horror of his condition. I concurred. No-one could do aught for him. He lay with his brain leaking onto the tussock of grass that was all there was for a pillow. His eyes were closed though often he moaned aloud and muttered some command, throwing his limbs about. I whispered to the man whom I took to be his servant who knelt beside him, one arm around a boy of about thirteen, the other smoothing Sir Bevil's brow.

"You know there is no hope?" He nodded and said brokenly "All we ask is that you ease his passage."

I looked at the others who surrounded him. "You are all of a mind? There must be no reprisals against me if I administer that which will kill his pain. He is dying now from his wound, not my potion." They all nodded dumbly.

I busied myself in preparing a merciful draft of morphine. I emptied my powder into a small cup of Canaries, that the servant held ready for him.

"Sir Bevil," I asked politely, "Would you pledge me in this cup of Canaries.?"

He opened one blue eye.

"Your Highness," he whispered, "This is an honour indeed." The servant held him up so that he could drink. He did so, sighed and seemed to fall asleep. All I could hope was that he would slip away whilst the morphine still held its effect.

I stood up. The servant stood up also and I gasped. For once in my life I had to look up at a man. This fellow was a giant.

"Thank you, sir." he said courteously and I moved out of the circle of defensive pikes. "Why does Sir Bevil call me "Highness"?" I asked Justin, who was now weeping uncontrollably. I patted his shoulder awkwardly. "At least he is out of pain now, Master Justin." I said trying to be of comfort. "Not like the poor bastards we saw on the way here."

He swallowed and recovered himself. "He thought you were Prince Maurice. He thought a Prince had come to his death bed when in very truth, he himself is the Prince among men."

"I am very sorry, dear Sir. Goodness and virtue in this war are hard to find."

And then my name was called.

"Tom! Doctor Tom Fletcher! For God's sake, Tom! Up here, man!"

A figure was standing on the low wall about a hundred yards away on the crest of the hill, calling to me from Waller's encampment. I looked questioningly at Justin who said, quietly "You are known and wanted, it seems. Our thanks for your assistance." All the Cornishmen in the group nodded their thanks and now their loved Sir Bevil slept quietly, they were content to release me.

I picked up my box and raised my hand to them and said, "God go with you, gentlemen," and in truth, though I never saw such poorly dressed soldiers they were gently behaved. I walked over the rough grass trying to make out who it was that still stood and called for me, smelling somewhere the tang of roast mutton. No doubt one of Noah's sheep that had met a premature end.

As I came nearer to the beckoning figure, I saw to my joy that it was Ralph. Martin had told me that Robert Burghill was still serving as Colonel under Waller. No-one in that hollow where the Cornish wounded were gathered seemed to care that I was about to cross from one army to the other.

I clambered over the wall, helped by Ralph's eager grasp.

"Dear Tom, thank God you are come. That bastard Allen is threatening to cut off Colonel Robert's hand. He is mad as a rutting buck! I've left Progger with the Colonel. I must find Waller so that we could get Allen put into close confinement yet again. I believe that it is the sight and smell of blood that pushes his brain into lunacy."

He hurried me towards a rough wall of stones, a further barrier on the road to Bath. To our right a troop of cavalry rode through gaps in the hill defences to join battle with Royalist horse. As I looked around me from the hilltop I could see that King's men were attempting to surround the summit from the woods that covered the sides of the hill, and that pieces of artillery had been pushed up through the Cornish pikes to attempt to dislodge Waller from his eerie. I had a sudden base concern for my own safety. What of Abram, so dependant on me and Julius and the apprentices?

There was no time for my cowardly fears for my worthless future. Ralph led me over the second stone wall which for the moment was out of the line of Royalist fire. A rough shelter, perhaps for a shepherd at lambing time, had been seized for a few wounded men of Parliament. One side which normally stood open to the weather had been walled up with hurdles and stooks of hay. Surgeon's Mate Wind stood guard at the entrance. I looked round fearfully. Where Wind was, mad Dick Allen could not be far away.

Ralph grasped my arm. "Oh, Christ, Tom, he's done it!" Robert Burghill was sitting on a rough chair facing the entrance. He was blindfolded, his ears were stuffed with what seemed to be hunks of leather and his left arm was bound to his side. But to my eternal horror, his right hand was missing. He held up a bleeding stump, severed below the wrist. He moaned continuously. At his feet lay Progger, his throat slit, his blood seeping over the straw which had been roughly laid over the earth floor. He saw us and recognised us, but in the instant of knowledge his eyes lost their focus and he died.

For a moment we could not speak, but gazed at the carnage before us in appalled disbelief... A captain, I did not know, with a bloody cut to his stomach said softly, "Why Waller allows that madman free reign, we cannot tell. The rumour is that else his house is unquiet."

I knew that I must attempt to take control. Drawing my dagger, I ran to Surgeon's Mate Wind and held the blade to his throat. "Where is Waller?" I shouted.

"Alas, sir. I cannot tell," he muttered. "This was too much... 'twas more than Master Allen should have.... He should not have killed..."

"Listen, Wind!" I shouted near his ear, "Hear this! I am your master now. Allen must not come in this barn. Your task is now is to place yourself in this doorway and let no-one in or out but that man," I cried pointing to Ralph, "Or if you see Waller shout to him that he is to come here at once. If Allen returns, you must call me and I will hang him from the nearest tree. Do you understand?"

He nodded dumbly and arranged his round bulk in the doorway so that egress or regress was impossible.

"Now I will be occupied with these poor fellows," I told him. "You know me. I am Doctor Tom."

He nodded gloomily and gazed at the evening landscape that stretched away southwards, gilded by the setting sun.

We laid Progger to one side and put dry straw over the place where his blood had soaked the ground. I drew out the leather from Robert's ears and began to speak softly to him.

"Dear Robert, it is Tom here. God alone knows what that mad dog Surgeon has done but you are alive and with my help and God's blessing will remain so. I am going to prepare you a draught that will help you bear the pain."

He said clearly, "My fingers ache so." He moved the bloody stump that was his arm, as if to restore life to his absent hand. I had Hollands Gin in my box and mixed a small amount of the opium powder with it in a clean vessel I had, and gave it to Robert. I took off my doublet and placed it behind him in his chair, trying to make him more comfortable. I placed a clean wad of bandage over the maimed arm so he would not see the extent of his injury. He seemed to be growing drowsy and I gently undid Allen's blindfold.

He said almost with a sob, "Ah, there you are Tom. God knows how you came here, for indeed you are the answer to our prayers."

"Dear Robert," I begged him. "I must try to dress your arm and it will be painful in the extreme." I could not bear to tell him that he had been hideously maimed but he forestalled me by saying, "That bastard Allen cut off my hand." He moved his gaze away from my eyes to where his hand had been and mercifully fainted or gave way to the Hollands Gin. I know not what.

Well, I counselled myself, the worst that could happen has happened. No need to unwrap my cerra, chisel or mallet. But a tight ligature around the stump was now essential. I had clean catgut such as musicians used for fiddles as this could be tightened to ensure that blood would not trickle through. I was unskilled in this type of surgery having in the past always attempted to save crushed and damaged limbs. My belief was that even if the limb did not work so well, at least if the injury was clean with sinews and bones given free range within the wound, and all foreign matter removed, there was a chance the body would repair itself.

Now, I had recourse to my needle. There was a flap of skin that I could use to cover the bones that protruded awkwardly from Robert's arm. Only the radius had been partly severed by the enemy's sword. Allen had finished the saw cut through the radius and had then cut clean through the ulna. Instead of repairing it, the crazed surgeon had continued the butchery begun on the field of battle.

I had fine Dutch white hemp and threaded my needle. I had a tincture of valerian and violet that Joan used both to cleanse and dull pain. I anointed the area with it where the stitches would go and set to work.

Robert mercifully remained comatose although he moaned from time to time. Ralph stood beside me and gasped in horror at the process I had to adopt. At last he said, "I have seen where the Colonel's hand is. Shall I bury it?"

"No, indeed! I need it to prove that this maiming was

unnecessary!" I said. "Where is it?"

There was a pail standing nearby. He lifted it warily and carried it over to me. As I had thought, a jagged radius and a smooth but cerrated ulna. The enemy had severed only half the radius. The arm could have been saved with skill and hard work.

There was a cackle of laughter from the stooks of hay in the area which would have been open to the elements. The mad Surgeon's grinning face surveyed us from the top of the pile. He disappeared, laughing still, and attempted to enter the hovel. I was afraid that in his crazed state of mind, he could easily affect more slaughter. To do him justice, Wind did attempt to keep out his old master but Allen was a lithe skeletal creature who suddenly burst past his lumpen servant and was there amongst us in the barn.

"So, renegade! What do you here, numbskull? 'Tis the pillory for you, you foul two yard streak of piss, you spawn of the dunghill!"

"Master Allen," I said rationally, "'Tis true we do not like each other, but I would beg you now to depart ere we come to blows. I fear that you are ill, Sir."

There was a murmur of agreement from the wounded.

"Ill, am I? How so, you bull calf's pizzle? Wind, where is my sword? I'll make him dance, the lying poltroon !"

To my amazement Wind came forward and addressed his master.

"Now, Master Allen, Sir William has your sword. Do you recall? There must be no more accidents, said good Sir William!"

"A pox on him! And a pox on you too, Wind, whom I have raised from nothing! Yea! even sharing with you, you ingrate, unto half my kingdom!"

He advanced on Wind who retreated backwards to escape the moonstruck minimus. Even as I watched, I thought how strange that one man who clearly had such confused evil notions, was yet at large to commit such harm.

Wind was clearly distressed by his master's madness. Perhaps there had been kindness towards him in the past on the part of the lunatick surgeon before he became moonstruck.

"Now Master Allen, sir, gently, gently, I pray you! Let us to Sir William and ask that you might return home again!"

"Sir William? I tell you, a pox on that vile scoundrel! I care not for the ignorant buffoon! Let him go and shake his ears..."

"It grieves me much to hear you speak so!" said a loud clear voice behind Wind. Sir William had entered and because of the round bulk of the surgeon's mate had been invisible to us. Now he pushed past him and confronted his deranged relative. He was attended by two sturdy life guards who with an air of habitual practice, came to stand either side of Allen, and proceeded to tie his arms firmly behind him. He screamed and tried to attack them but, alas! they were impervious to his fists.

"You had best take him to my quarters and tether his feet," said Sir William wearily, "Stay with him until I come."

Allen would not leave peacefully. As he was led away he screamed, "It is because of my labour, he will not contract the rotting sickness. I have saved him, you fools!"

At that moment Waller saw the extent of the dismal horror that Robert suffered and gasped. "What's this? My dear Robert, what has befallen you?"

The Captain who had been waiting patiently to have his stomach wound dressed now spoke.

"Sir William, may I relate our tribulations? I have been here since before the Colonel was brought in."

"Nat West, is it not? But here is Doctor Tom. Dear young man, you are come again like the God from the sky in the play to save us all."

"Sir," I told him, "I must examine and dress this man's wound. May I do that as he speaks to you?"

"With a right good will, Doctor Tom." The Commander of the Western Association sat on a pile of hurdles such as shepherds use to contain sheep. I set Ralph to guarding Robert. I rejoiced that I had equipped myself with a good supply of Hollands Gin. I suggested that if Robert woke, Ralph could spoon it between his lips.

To my relief and certainly to Captain West's I did not think that the glancing cut he had taken in his stomach had pierced his liver. I placed him on a trestle and raised his knees pushing my shirt under them to keep them up so that there was less strain on the muscles of the abdomen. Luckily he had twisted as his assailant had pierced his body and somehow deflected the blade sideways. No intestine was protruding and he complained only of soreness where the sword had entered him. The stomach wall was probably penetrated but that could mend. I cleaned the wound as well as I could and bandaged him. Throughout my ministrations he told Sir William of the horror of Surgeon Allen's misguided service. Ralph and Progger had objected when he had announced that Robert must lose his hand and Ralph had run out to find Sir William. Progger had positioned himself in front of Robert who by this had been bound to the surgeon's chair by Wind albeit reluctantly, and blindfolded. Allen had become enraged at Progger's interference with his designs and had turned his wrath on him pushing him down and drawing his saw across the poor trooper's neck. He had then placed Robert's hand on a board and proceeded to saw it off, " in spite of the Colonel's screams of protest. Although all could see that the original cut, whilst clearly edging on bone, had not by any means severed the whole arm." He looked round at the other invalids who nodded in agreement.

"Allen left the Colonel with the stump of his arm exposed in dire pain and distress and losing blood. "This is hungry work!" says Allen. We could all smell roast mutton. Then Ralph returned with Doctor Tom, and I think we all thanked God for a merciful deliverance from a lunatick, Sir William. Doctor Tom gave the Colonel strong waters so he might sleep and stitched and dressed the poor man's arm."

"But look here, Sir." I said and took the severed hand from the pail, wiping away the blood. "You may see that his Royalist enemy only cut a little distance through the radius. The ulna and the rest of the radius are serrated by a saw. I could have saved his arm if I had been here earlier, or if your Surgeon had listened to these two troopers, one alive and one murdered by his hand. You must dismiss him, Sir."

Sir William, of complexion handsome and ruddy, was white as winter snows on the Malverns. He leaned backwards on his trestles as if to put as much distance between himself and Robert's hand as possible. On reflection it was a frightful sight. But I needed to convince him of his Surgeon's madness and stupidity. Waller swallowed.

"Will Robert live?"

"I cannot tell. The loss and amputation of a limb can cause the body so terrible a shock that he may not recover from that. Then there is the risk that it might become gangrenous. I did the best I could but my hope for him is limited."

"Give my poor friend every comfort, and tell him how much I grieve for his loss. What says the prophet? "Lest my right hand lose its cunning." Tom, will you attend here to these poor lads? Will you help us?"

I shrugged. "I had assumed that you would wish me to do so, sir, although nothing can be done for this poor fellow." I indicated Progger "He has died in battle defending his Colonel as surely as if he had had to defend him from the King's Life Guard."

"Yes indeed!" said Waller. "I shall send a burial party for him. Is there aught else you require?

I had already begun the familiar process of the removal of a musket ball from a shoulder. "May Master Wind bring supplies of bandage from the Quartermasters? Perhaps one might be detailed to assist me? Wind seems to know nothing except how to bleed a patient. Poor Ralph is in no state to help me."

Ralph was attempting to arrange the stiff limbs of his friend into a shape appropriate for his coffin. He was weeping, and who could blame him?

Sir William promised to return before two hours had passed, and vowed to make provision for Robert and the rest of the wounded. We had to consider how best to help them from this lonely hilltop. All needed better conditions than this dirty ramshackle hovel.

Bandages and candles were brought as it was now the dark of the moon and one Francis Pike, a Quartermaster, came to help me, which would have been of great use if he could have withstood the sight of blood. He kept staggering backwards, grasping his throat and retching. At length I suggested that he helped those I had already tended to eat and drink and prepared bandages.

"Is there not another surgeon?" I demanded angrily.

"Well, there is Walter Stevenson," Pike replied slowly.

"Well, where the devil is he?" I asked.

The answer came from several invalids at once and was a single word.

"Drunk!" they chorused.

At length I had done all I could do for everyone, and Sir William had still not returned. I told Francis Pike to watch the patients, told

Ralph to join me if he or Robert needed me and went outside into the cool air away from the smell of blood. Then I realised that the sounds of battle had subsided and in fact we had had a blessed silence for some while. There was no one on the hilltop. The silent still corpses that littered a battlefield had been moved. I judged that Waller must have ordered this. The moon was rising and as I peered below me southerly, I could see a dark mass moving over the fields towards Bath. I looked back to the northern side of Lansdowne Hill and could see a row of lights, glowing along one of the earthworks. Waller must have left a body of musketeers to light us to the resting-place he had promised to find.

I walked towards the torches which gave a comforting glow on the northern side of the hill. Perhaps the men who held them would know if Waller had gone with the army. As I approached, however I realised that it was a ruse to deceive the King's men. No-one was there. Instead a row of broken pikes of differing heights had been placed along the rough wall and lengths of lighted match affixed to each, so that Hopton and Maurice would think Waller was still encamped. The flames made a whispering rushing noise occasionally flaring as the breeze increased.

In the fitful moonlight I could see the king's army, resting about 400 yards down the hill. But what of us? Had Waller forgotten us? At least four of the invalids could not walk. How could I get them from the inhospitable hilltop without horses and carts?

There was a movement to my right. I fumbled for my dagger, and peered through the row of torches. Someone else was looking through the pikes about ten yards away. All I could see was his ragged breeches but then, that would have been all he could see of me.

"Who are you?" I called at last.

"The unluckiest lad this side the Tamar. I drew the short straw." came the reply. "Who are you? Kill me if you must but, Christ's wounds, be merciful."

This was an unlikely encounter. "You are safe with me" I called. "I am a doctor! I try not to kill people."

"You're a rare uncommon doctor then." he said, walking towards me, his sword drawn.

I held up my hands. "All I have in my pocket is a dagger for slicing bandages, not my fellows. I am of neither side, not for King nor Parliament." I sat down on the close cropped grass. I had observed that soldiers usually only attack those who seem likely to attack them. He sheathed his sword and sat down beside me.

"I thought I was the unluckiest man on Lansdowne Hill and now you have come to unseat me from my pinnacle," I told him. "Waller has abandoned me with his wounded."

"But where's his army?" he asked.

"Trotted down the hill to Bath," I told him. "There are just a few poor wounded in that byre there from whom I have stolen some of your musket balls, that you would bestow on them."

He smiled and found some hard black bread in his pocket, which he broke into pieces and indicated I should help myself.

"You are looking at a rich man, Doctor," he told me, finding his pipe.

"How so?" I asked munching away. "If you are rich, why do we eat stale rye bread and not a venison pasty?"

"I have earned gold this night for climbing this hill and meeting you, you quacksalver! Christ's wounds, I wish all gold was so easy come by. They wanted to know if the lights were Will o' the wisps. And in faith they are that, with Waller gone! Are you of these parts?"

I told him my name and city and he repaid the knowledge. He was Christian Trewalden, born in a place called St Austell. He had left his wife and daughter to follow Sir Bevil. He built and repaired boats on a river called Fowey.

"But devil a boat shall I find up here, eh, my handsome? I'm for home tomorrow when they gives me the promised gold. And maybe I'll go my ways downalong this 'ere hill, Tom Fletcher, for they'll be thinking the bogeyman has got me.... but Hark 'ee."

There was the noise of a party of men climbing up the south escarpment, making for the shelter where the wounded lay. I took a few steps and in the moonlight saw the small busy figure of Sir William urging on a horse and cart. "He has not forgotten us." turning back, I said aloud to my new friend. "God bring you safe home, good Christian."......but I spoke to the moon and night breeze. The Cornishman had slipped away into the darkness.

I called out, "Sir William, I am here!" and a voice at my elbow said, "Aye I know you are. Who else is up here? You were talking."

"The poor shepherd trying to find his lost sheep," I told him, resorting to my habitual means of survival…. lying.

"I'faith, Tom, you sound as if you have just communed with Our Lord, on the lonely hilltop here!" he said piously.

I laughed. "A good Christian man, 'twas all!" There, I had slightly expiated the sin of my lie! "What's to be done, then Sir?"

"Battle will be joined again hereabouts in a few days, no doubt of it. Robert must get away to rest. Could you take him back to Gloucester with you, as I assume that is where you were bound?"

I was silent. Retrace my steps? "Could we not find a good quiet lodging for him in Bath?" I asked as we returned to the byre.

"Listen, I have spies in Oxford. Rupert will be here before the month is out. The devils want Bristol. They'll be all over Somerset like maggots on a dead dog. I shall deal with Maurice, but Robert cannot help me in the field now. Gloucester is safe and quiet for now. He can recover there and as he does so he can act as my spokesman with Massey. I shall ride to Gloucester to find you. Massey knows his trade, I think. I hear Gloucester is well fortified."

"Well, it is fortified," I said doubtfully. "In fact, Sir William, I was bound for London." The moon had reappeared from behind a bank of thin cloud and we stood outside the tumbledown hovel and debated together, no easy task as I was twelve inches higher than my companion.

"London heaves and bubbles like a cauldron of porridge! What is a country mouse like your good self to do with that seething hotbed of lunatick notions?"

"I was complying with my wife's last wish. As she died she asked me to tell her uncle of her passing."

"Who is her uncle?" he insisted.

"The Earl of Chesterfield," I told him, "I fear he is in the Tower."

He snorted. "That Jack Bragger! Aye that he is ! And do you think you could have sailed unchallenged into that hideous fortress, with your potions and your plasters? If there is one who can discharge your errand, I will write a letter to the Governor desiring that your messenger is granted access to the whoreson Earl."

I thought of Julius. "Well, I am travelling with someone who could take the news. A writer scarred by Laud. And in February abandoned by his Commander, Francis Fiennes at Cirencester."

He snorted again, "Old Subtlety has so many sons, he is hard put to count them all. Young Master Nat will have his work cut out at Bristol. Believe me, the King's army is coming. This is no place for Robert."

His men were helping and carrying the wounded into the cart he had brought for them. Robert was conscious and Ralph was cutting up cold mutton for him and tenderly trying to persuade him to eat.

"You had best move from here, my good friend. There are three horses for you," said Waller, and explained to Ralph that he wished Robert to travel to Gloucester." I have a notion that Hopton will know I am gone from this hill and be up here by morning."

Was there a hint of accusation in his tone? What had he heard me say to the Cornishman? He had earned his name, Night Owl, for his hearing and night vision seemed second to none. I turned to Robert.

"Robert, can you walk down hill, do you think? There is a secret gully that will shield us from the King's men. There are friends in a cottage halfway down the hill.... Parliament friends! I assure you, Sir William. A kind old couple live there and have taken in my companions." He nodded, looking with heartfelt sympathy at Robert's bandaged limb.

"You are a good boy, Doctor Tom, for all you are higher than any man has the right to be." He called to one of the men, helping the wounded, who produced parchment and quill from a pack he carried on his back. A place was made on one of the trestles and a letter dictated to one Sir Isaac Pennington, at the Tower, which was sealed and handed to me. I retrieved my doublet and put the document next to my heart for safekeeping.

But then the Commander bethought him that he had best write to Massey back in Gloucester. "I want him to know that he is still in my eye and that I will be with him in days, not weeks, if all goes well. And Doctor Tom, I will commend you to him. The Gloucester doctors are proud money-grubbing arselickers. He will be delighted with you, my boy. But five minutes and the letter is written."

I went out to the cart and tried to help make the wounded more comfortable. The Captain whose stomach would probably heal as good as new, as long as he rested, called to me saying, "The madman had completed that terrible amputation before we knew what he was about. Forgive me that I did not kill him like a dog."

"In his way, he is as sick as any wounded man," I said suddenly aware of this truth for perhaps the first time. "But to cure distempers of the mind is as yet a closed book to me."

Waller called me back in and gave me the letter for Massey. I promised that Robert would deliver it. He rose unsteadily to his feet and holding his bandaged stump to one side tried to bow formally to his general. I wished him well, Ralph bowed, and we set off down the northern slope, veering into the gully before we could be seen in the light from the row of pikes. The sounds of Sir William's men slowly faded behind us. As we progressed downwards, we became aware of the great body of the King's army above us to our right. From time to time, I had cruelly to heave aside a corpse that had tumbled downwards from the battlefield. Ralph followed us leading the three horses.

It could not be described as a merry meeting when we finally came out into the dell, where the cottage was, but there was considerable relief shown on the part of everyone crowded into Noah's ark, that I was still alive. If I had not been dropping with weariness, I would have been flattered. But sleep was impossible, as there was so much to discuss and arrange, and very little room. Somehow a chair was found for Robert and he seemed to doze. I gave him another draught to kill pain and enable him to sleep. Ralph stretched out beside him.

Abram said nothing but his thankfulness at my return was palpable. He would not leave my side. I had to ensure that Julius remembered how Phoebe died. I gave him the document from Sir William and asked him to give the Earl my loving respect, and then asked Julius to send any replies to the New Inn in Gloucester, should there be the opportunity for him to get letters to me.

I had wished so much to see Ben but a letter must suffice. Scholarly John had a quill and a small well of ink and I wrote to him on the back of the water poet's news sheet as we had no other parchment. I told him of Phoebe's strange pregnancy and her death and asked if I had done all that could have been done. I told him briefly of my travels and told him also that I thought I had cured many more than I had killed. In fact my beloved wife was the only patient I had been accused of killing. I told him of Joan's change of character and wondered if he knew of a cure that would restore her sunny nature.

Then I recommended Jacob Shaw as a likely apprentice, should he need one. "He is curious, clever and has a good memory and is not deterred by the sight of blood."

"But what of your indentures with the broom handle maker? What will your parents think of your changing horses or rather broomsticks in midstream?" I asked, a feeble attempt at a joke. Still it sufficed. Everyone was kind enough to laugh, even Martin.

"Well, John wants to continue in that occupation. But he and Julius want to record our travels."

"We shall write an epic in iambic pentameter," Julius announced, excited by the prospect of writing again. "What think you of the title, "A Gloucestershire Odyssey" Tom? Does it not have the ring of classical significance?"

"An excellent conceit. I am grieved indeed that I shall not be there to marvel at its fulfilment." I said pompously.

At last we subsided into some sort of repose. But during the hours of darkness, Robert's condition gave rise to alarm. His face was grey, though whether with pain or fatigue or the combined effects of both, it was hard to say. I made a sling out of one of his shirts and re-examined the terrible maimed arm. A little blood had seeped through but my stitches and the bandages were intact. He asked me despairingly, "Tom, could you bring me for a few moments into the fresh air? I find the vapours in here somewhat noisome." He was right. The cottage smelt overwhelmingly of sheep and dirty male humanity.

I edged his chair into the doorway so that a draft of cool air blew over his face.

"Ah Tom, that is much better. I can sleep again now I think." He seemed to drift away into oblivion.

I thought it might be better if Julius and the apprentices departed at sunrise and that Robert should rest in Noah's Ark this day, the 6th of July, and we would set out for Gloucester early tomorrow.

So as the sparrows began to chirp, we said Farewell to our three "penitents" and sad I was to see them go. The boys were clever and eager for learning and Julius as good a companion as I had ever had. I would miss our converse. Julius had determined to go cross country to Chippenham, deciding not to seek his connections in Bath, and not wishing to draw attention to themselves with either army. Then they would find the London road, he said confidently. I watched them cross the slope of Lansdowne Hill and strike into the woods well above Marshfield. They were gone with the dawn.

The Royalist army had taken themselves back down the hill again, but a few men were engaged in gathering up discarded weapons and placing them in a cart. They did not seem enthusiastic about their task, moving slowly and deliberately as if they wished to lengthen their labours. I reflected that perhaps they wished to postpone their next drudgery which could well be the digging of graves.

Martin wished to find Sir Arthur Hesilrige but George asked him to stay. His helplessness had given him pause for thought. His wound was healing but it would be slow progress and he would not be able to mount a horse unaided for some weeks. I told Martin of the "lobster" I had seen so disgracefully treated on the battlefield. He nodded his head thoughtfully. "When men who have been feared are found at a disadvantage... Well, Doctor Tom, I swear I am close to despair. To kill and be killed by ones fellow Englishmen.... this is a dreadful fate. But I am a soldier. What other life do I know? What other life does George know?"

I had no solution.

I placed three sovereigns on the table and told Noah that I could not replace Nell's ducks but that there was a present of a horse for him if he would allow us to remain one more day.

"Bless you, Doctor Tom, me and Nell hain't had such to-ings and fro-ings and comings and goings, since old Sparkes's bull got in among the Earl's heifers. It will be powerful dull when you go your ways. The sick gentlemen can stay and welcome."

So I busied myself finding willow wands and fashioning a crutch for George. My workmanship was poor beside Elijah's, and I was sitting outside, whittling away, cutting my fingers, swearing to myself and wondering if there was any chance of a meal when Abram came and found me.

"Tom," he began. "I have been thinking."

My heart sank. "Did it cause much pain?" I asked .

"My father used to make me work for him and I think you should, Tom."

My father spoke in my head as clearly as if he had been standing behind me. "A man must have a calling or the devil in him thrives."

I stared at Abram. "You are right. What calling will you follow?"

"I used to cast the accounts for my father and keep a tally of all we sold, where we sold it and for how much"

"Jesus, Abram. Forgive me. Do you know, I never even knew you could read or write. Mad Dick Allen was right. I do deserve the pillory. But, believe me, my lad, I have noticed that the horses have been well fed and watered and without a word of complaint the three newcomers have been well tended, even this morning. That is already good responsible work. So how could you help me further?"

"I could list what you have in your box and when we come to an apothecary's then I will replenish what you need."

I pushed the crutch to one side, stood up and clapped him on the shoulder.

"Abram, that is an excellent notion. There are three difficulties. Now John has gone we have no quill or ink, we have no paper or parchment, and I have not seen an apothecary on Lansdowne Hill."

"Tom, again you make game of me! You always do that. You have hardly spoken a word to me since you befriended those three soldiers. I meant when we are back in Gloucester or back home. When we are home what do you say? I could be your clerk and do what Phoebe...!"

But as he said her name, as if in contrast to the beloved sound, we were suddenly assailed by a most hideous noise, a great explosion followed by a number of minor cracks. It came from down the hill. Noah hastened out and pushed aside the hedge, and I followed him. The Royalist army had spread themselves out over the low hill where we had rested when we first came to this benighted country, and where Jacob had first heard the great concourse of men. How long ago? But a scant two days. And now there was a column of black smoke rising a little way beyond that same hill. I remembered where I had heard a similar sound. With my face pressed into the ground of the marketplace of Stratford whilst the new town hall collapsed behind me. Phoebe was trying to assist me to rise. Captain Cross' numbskull nephew had wasted our time by constricting his breath in an overtight breastplate. The clever woman had seen what would happen when Brooke's musketeers tapped out their pipes on barrels of gunpowder. She it was who had cleared the hall, by screaming at everyone. Strange that there was no possibility of mistaking this sound for cannons. Cannons roared. Exploding gunpowder boomed and then cracked.

Noah had hastened down the hill and now returned more slowly. He shrugged, saying, "Nay I'm fair flummoxed about that gurt noise." He went into the cottage shaking his head.

I went back to Abram who was standing with his head drooping. I had clearly been lamentably remiss in my treatment of him. It was hard for me with my own feelings of grief and hurt to respond to the needs of another younger orphan, but my conscience was smiting me pitilessly. How could I have neglected him?

"Abram, please forgive me for not thinking enough about you. I will make amends. I swear it. You are all the family I have now. My brother, cousin, what you will. You saved my life in the wetlands. How could I have been so thoughtless?"

He smiled and nodded and then surprised me again. "Tom, did you know that I can read Arabic as well as speak it, and write it a little. And Tom, my father's people are not savages as people say. Many were great doctors, like you. I can tell you of...."

But my name was being called from the hill path. "The Doctor? Is Tom Fletcher there? Doctor Tom?"

"Abram, forgive me. I think I will have to go. Tell Martin and George to stay concealed." I snatched up my box, and pushed through our hedge.

As yesterday, I could see through the foliage a group of Cornishmen standing on the path. As I thrust aside the clinging thorns, there was relief at the sight of me and shouts of "He's here." Justin pushed through and grabbed my arm. "Doctor Tom, will you come for God's sake, boy? Here is a frightful calamity. A group of Parliament men have blown themselves into the next world and have bid fair to take our Commanders with them. Will you come? 'Tis a terrible sight! We hoped we might find you still here. See, we are unarmed."

"I'll come" I told them, "So there are burns you say?"

"Burns the like of which I hope never to see again. Major Sheldon, and he as fair as pink May blossom is burnt as black as the fire back!"

"Have your surgeons no supplies of ointments? I need clean bandages and there is a marvellous good salve, Balm of St John's Wort, that both heals and soothes. Do you have any?"

They looked blankly at each other. "Abram!" I shouted through the hedge.

"Yes,Tom?" he replied, pushing his way through.

"Now is your moment. Comes the hour, comes the man. Can you saddle up Blackbird and ride into Marshfield and see if there is anyone there skilled at distillation? A wise woman perhaps? If so, ask if they have Balm of St John's Wort. If none there can help us, then ride on to the Apothecary whom you were speaking of in Chippenham. Can you do that for me?"

"Willingly, Tom" he shouted, turning back for his horse.

"And tell Martin to move these thorns while you are gone. I have been scratched more raw by this pox ridden hedge than if I had been let loose in a school of pole cats."

"Come then, gentlemen." And we walked briskly to where the smoke hung in the welkin over a rise that I learnt later was known as Tog Hill.

The King's army was spread over the area. Men were resting or standing about talking, no doubt about this latest of tragic accidents. A few curious gazes were turned towards me, but I marched on, flanked by the Cornishmen, like a man with a serious object in life. I was bound to cure, they to kill.

We walked through the army to where the column of black smoke was slowly fading. The air was thick with small flakes of soot. In moments we were filthy but our condition was as nothing compared with the victims of this horror. The Parliament men who had been permitted to smoke on the barrels of gunpowder were so many blackened manikins, wizened and charred, blown together in the remains of the wagon on which they had been sitting. A Major, a little distance from the cart was in like condition but he yet lived. His hair, face and clothes were scorched and shrivelled. He lay on the ground moaning pitifully. Other King's men who had been nearby had fearful burns, on faces, arms and legs. One officer, a captain, seemed unhurt and was attempting to help a portly fellow who was clutching the remains of a large hat. His doublet was burnt beyond recognition but had clearly been thick enough to protect him. His horse lay dying beside him

"That's the commander!" I was told. "That's Sir Ralph."

The Major was clearly the most in need of help but the Captain with Sir Ralph beckoned me over. "You are a physician?" he asked abruptly.

"Thomas Fletcher of Worcester." I replied, conscious that my shirt was torn, my breeches ragged and aware that I smelt of several days of perspiration, other men's blood and possibly even worse.

"This is Sir Ralph Hopton, our Commander. He was speaking to the prisoners, backing away and wafting his hat before his face, as he did not care for the smell of their tobacco, when the wagon exploded. His horse was grievously burned and Sir Ralph cannot move his arm and worse still, he cannot see."

I looked at the wretched horse writhing on the ground.

"Sir, I beg you, draw your pistol and put a bullet into this poor creature's brain. He is beyond help."

Sir Ralph cried out aloud, "No, don't kill me. No need yet."

"Sir Ralph, forgive me. I spoke of your horse, not you, Sir. All may yet be well with you."

His eyes were tightly closed and I drew him some way from the hideous scene and asked him to open them one at a time. I had heard of fearful shocks and sudden bright lights causing temporary blindness, and I judged that it was from this that he was suffering. I asked him to open each eye in turn and although the central iris was somewhat larger than was usual, I could see no lasting damage.

"Is the world dark or light when you open your eyes?"

"Well, it is light but I can see nothing, no details, not your face, young man!"

I laughed. "Then Sir, believe me your temporary condition allows of a great compensation! Over the next few days your sight will return. Your optical nerve has, as it were, demanded respite, after a terrible shock. Do not allow anyone to pour any supposed healing unguents into your eyes. They will recover of their own accord, I assure you."

We could both hear the groans of the Major, and I asked leave to treat him, promising that I would return to examine Sir Ralph's arm. The backs of his hands were sorely burnt where he had been holding his hat. The Captain was attempting to lift the Major, calling him by his first name. He was a Thomas like myself, and was in most pitiful case.

I examined him as he lay on the ground. The features of his face were hideously mangled and his clothes and skin were hopelessly commingled. His breeches had been roughly torn from his person in an attempt to extinguish the fire that I was told had engulfed his person in the moment of the explosion.

"Listen Captain. Forgive me. I do not know your name."

"Richard Atkyns. Can you do anything for him?"

"I can give him a draught that will somewhat numb his fearful pain. He is burnt beyond healing. Burnt like the Parliament men but 'tis his misfortune that he still lives."

"Do you think he will die?"

"I am afraid that I must say I hope so for his sake. His face, his eyes, his hair, and I fear his manhood, all have been scorched irreparably. I will try to get a draught of opium into him and perhaps you could move him on horseback with careful support to a sheltered place of safety."

As I spoke I was shaking one of the powders of oblivion into my strong Hollands Gin, Ben's aqua vitae of choice. I dissolved it with a clean spatula and with Captain Atkyns holding him upright, I poured the liquid between his blackened lips.

After a few moments he ceased to moan and we managed gently to seat him sideways upon a steady horse. "There is a house in Marshfield that we have used as our quarters. Will you come thither to treat him?" the Captain asked me.

"With a right good will," I told him, "But what do you think I can do for him?"

He looked me in the eye. "Is it then so hopeless?"

"I fear so, Sir. But I will come. Here is my helper."

Abram galloped up to the site of the explosion. He had seated behind him a comely matron who carried a large bag. She called out to me.

"Balm of St John's Wort, the young master asked for and I had a good supply about me. Nothing better for a painful burn and no mistake." Abram courteously helped her from the horse.

"This is Mistress Dorothy Burnett, Tom. She will help us, for a few pence."

"Mistress, you are more welcome than I can say but I fear I must show you a most sorry scene," I said politely. "Perhaps we can dress these burns together."

I was concerned lest Abram's stomach would turn at the sight of the dead husks of the Parliament men. But I had forgotten he had been with me in Birmingham when we had treated burns in profusion, and also, (and more to the purpose) I recollected that the poor boy had nothing in his stomach. Captain Atkyns told me he would see me later and set off to Marshfield with troopers surrounding the Major's horse, to ensure he remained steady. I returned to Ralph Hopton.

"Dear Sir," I told him, "When I have dressed the wounds of the victims who were standing nearby, my helper and I will assist you to Marshfield. There is a very steady cob here that will bear you gently and smoothly. This is a strange time for me, Sir. After midnight in the early hours of the morning I was with your erstwhile friend William Waller."

"Nay he is still my friend, God save him. He is well?"

"He is, Sir, but his Colonel, Robert Burghill to whom I owe my life, has tragically lost his right hand."

He sighed. "These wars! I would give a King's ransom never to have begun what we must somehow bring to a conclusion. My major, Major Sheldon, did I hear that he is sorely hurt?"

"I fear he may not live, Sir Ralph. One Captain Atkyns has taken him to Marshfield. May I examine your burnt hands and the side you say you cannot feel?"

It seemed that as with his loss of sight, the paralysis that affected his right side was but the effect of shock to the body's healthy system. Although he complained of numbness, yet it was clear that the blood still coursed through his veins, and no part of his body was without warmth and life. "I am of the opinion that sight and sensation will be restored, without the aid of a physician. Let the body work its own recovery. Now, sir, for your hands if you please."

He sighed as the Balm began its healing effects. "Ah, young man, that is better. Where are you from? Gloucester, you say?"

"No, sir, I am but a Worcester butcher's boy, borne and bred. No doubt that is why I am a good surgeon."

"And yet you speak with an assurance that belies your breeding." he said thoughtfully, as I carefully bandaged his hands.

"When I spoke with no less a lady than Shakespeare's daughter, she told me that the future lay with me and those like me. We of the middling sort who have brains and ambition and good will may not need breeding in the future."

He was silent and then said thoughtfully, "Certainly the King's best advisers are not always those who can trace their bloodline back to the Normans."

"Tell me Sir do you know an assistant to Sir Jacob Astley, one Christopher Peabody.?"

Sir Ralph laughed. "I know him, not well, certainly, but I know him. He is one such as you mention. A clever loyal servant to the King, but without, shall we say, aristocratic airs and graces. How do you know him?"

"We were ensconced with the Earl of Chesterfield in the Close at Lichfield. Is he well?"

"Indeed he is, and faithfully assisting Sir Jacob. He teaches the recruits, I think. They are said to hate him at first acquaintance, but grow to value and love him."

"I wish I could see him again," I said, thoughtfully, "He is one of the best friends I ever had." But it was necessary to be the Doctor again. "Sir Ralph, please sit here and rest. I must help my assistant and this good lady from Marshfield."

Abram was carefully preparing bandages as Mistress Dorothy applied her salve. As she worked she told each casualty, that they would need another application for some days to come. She sold each of them a pot of the salve, which she placed in their pouches so as not to disturb their dressings.

When we had finished, Captain Atkyns who had returned for Sir Ralph, helped me place him on Blackbird and we walked alongside the short distance into Marshfield. We must have seemed a strange little company accompanying the great Royalist commander.... myself, dirty, and no doubt somewhat lacking in fragrant aroma, overtopping everyone, Captain Atkyns, a hard soldier but clearly loyal and compassionate, Abram pin-neat and handsome as ever, and Mistress Dorothy Burnett, round and wholesome as new bread, telling me in an undertone that the shillings she had earned this day would go to her store which she was saving to build another room on her home so that her daughter might marry. Her immediate domestic concerns were in such contrast to the horrors of war, that it was hard to accept we were citizens of the same regime and country. And yet for me that morning she was a veritable heroine and Abram, a hero.

She came in with me to see the Major, in his lodgings. His host was the local rector who avidly supported the King as God's Anointed. The sight of the Major's shocking condition seemed to have assailed his opinions. "Why did this happen?" he clutched at my arm. "He is the King's most faithful servant. What have we done to incur God's wrath?" I shrugged. I had no answer for him

The Major still slept but fitfully. I left another draught for him and explained to Mistress Dorothy what the proportions of opium and gin were. She nodded gravely, understanding that it was necessary to allow the patient to die naturally if possible, although she said wisely that where the boundary lay between painless unconsciousness and oblivion was hard to gauge, and in this case, death was a necessary merciful outcome. I asked her if we could buy food from her or from anyone in the village as we had friends in the cottage on the side of Lansdowne Hill who were desperate hungry. I gave her two guineas and she promised to send us food during the course of the day. She knew Nell and Noah and would collect any trenchers later in the week.

Whenever I hear the story of the Good Samaritan now, he has changed from male to female. In my mind he is no longer a hook-nosed Eastern worthy, but a buxom blue eyed matron from Marshfield in Somerset.

The King's army was preparing to march away. "To Devizes" I heard one fellow tell his friend, "But I doubt that Waller will leave us to our own devices!" As so often happens when a jest is made in a tense predicament, all who heard laughed inordinately and passed on the pleasantry. I went to bid Farewell to Sir Ralph. He was more composed although both he and Captain Atkyns were distressed to leave the Major. Sir Ralph thanked me courteously for my assistance and asked what my charges were. Perhaps I was a fool but I could not bring myself to profit from these circumstances and asked him to give any coin to Mistress Dorothy, who, God bless her, had no such compunction.

I insisted that Abram rode his horse, an excellent cob, whom he had named Blackbird, not for his colour but because he turned his head and seemed to listen when birds sang close to him. I walked beside him back to the slope of Lansdowne Hill.

"You did wondrous well today," I told him, "That good lady was an excellent find."

"I think she felt pity for me," he told me, soulfully. "I told her how cruel you are."

I looked him in the eye and he winked impishly. "Did that Sir

Ralph say that Peabody was with this army? I should like to meet him again."

I heartily agreed. "And so should I. But Peabody either rides alone on Royal missions or he serves Sir Jacob Astley as a master of new officers. He has a rare talent for teaching, it seems."

When we reached our hidden valley, I was relieved that Martin had pulled aside the thorns at last. Both armies had gone and we were safe from reprisals I was overjoyed not to have to struggle through them again. My clothes had taken considerable punishment as had my skin. "And in any event," said Abram, practically, "Dorothy would not be able to bring our food through if she had had to push her way in with our dinner."

George was sitting up, somewhat recovered, and asking Noah about breeds of sheep. It seemed that twenty years ago he had been a farmer's boy in Kent, the youngest of thirteen.

"My parents were good at making children but poor at making money, and poor is what we were. So when I went for a soldier, though they were sad to see my back, they were pleased to see one less open mouth. I like sheep, though."

"Why's that then?" asked Ralph, "One sheep is pretty like another 'cept when they're spring lamb and then they're rare good eating."

"Oh, I grant you that." George's eyes gleamed at the thought of spring lamb, "But mutton now, Roast it long over a slow fire with caper sauce. Now that's a meal fit for a King as long as the evil bastard don't come 'ere to eat it."

"He's gone," I told them, "Gone to Devizes. Or rather his army has. And I have paid a good woman to bring us all a meal here."

This met with general acclaim, apart from Martin that long faced lobster, veteran of Breda, who did not believe that I would see any food or my money again.

"These Somerset yokels will cheat you, soon as look at you, Tom, you clown."

An old anger rose in me. This sweet good woman had left her house to help me for a few pence. I knew she would not fail me. I am ashamed to say I squared up to the grim lobster and his rude notions of good country people, for what were Nell and Noah who had taken him in, but kind folk of that same county. There was immediate consternation from everyone, at the sight of my clenched fists. The old shepherd placed himself between Martin and myself, crying, "Good Masters, be of accord. You have endured much these two days." and Ralph called from beside Robert, "Dear Tom, no need to take pepper in the rose. He meant no harm."

I subsided. Where men are herded together in cramped conditions, tempers flare easily.

Nell spoke which she did rarely. "If 'tis Dorothy you'm talking of, Tom she is pure gold. And to speak truth, lad, Noah and me ain't got nothing more to give you". She was a sweet hospitable woman, but it is difficult to share when you have nothing.

I examined my invalids. Martin's bruises were fading, and he assured me he could take breaths without pain. His reset arm was naturally stiff and sore but the fingers retained their power of movement. George's wound was healing but it was too soon to know if he would regain the use of his leg. But poor Robert! I dressed his stump again and smelt it carefully. There was no trace of putrefaction, and my stitches held. But there was no doubt that Robert himself could not adjust to this cruel maiming. And I could not find words of comfort. I had told him in Worcester that Dick Allen should not be let loose on the sick... or on the healthy for that matter. I could not say piously to Robert that I believed this tragedy to be the will of God, because I did not believe such a thing. God if He existed had no part in it, just as the burnt and broken Royalist Major was not the proof of God's wrath. How poor a notion we must have of the Almighty if we attribute men's ignorant carelessness to Him or hold Him responsible for human madness.

"We will be in Gloucester, Robert, in two days time. You will be pleased to see John Nichol again at the New Inn."

He smiled sadly and said, "Yes, indeed."

A female voice was calling out, "Mistress Nell. Viands for you all" Dorothy and her daughter had come with a feast fit indeed for a King. Three roast chickens, parsnips and peas and beans and afterwards a frumenty pudding and cream and cheese.

"Abram, we shall serve the others first." I directed. This was indeed a sacrifice for him, whose stomach was his first concern. Dorothy had brought wooden platters so we were able to eat like civilised creatures, and she stood for some minutes as we exclaimed over the excellent sight and taste of her food. I noticed that Martin thanked her with unusual courtesy and even smiled in her direction, a rare occurrence. Ralph undertook to feed Robert but the Colonel insisted on attempting to do so with his left hand alone, and made but a pitiable meal. When all were served I had to curb my desire to gulp my meal down like a wolf, I was so hungry. Never were three chickens picked so clean.

Abram insisted that after we had finished that I should sing for our supper. As I had already paid for it, this seemed an unnecessary nicety but as Robert seemed pleased that I should do so, I launched into "Back and sides go bare." in which Martin and Ralph joined. Then the three of us stood together and launched into "We be soldiers three, Lately come from the Low country, With never a penny of money." That was certainly the truth of it for Martin. He and George seemed to be penniless. There had never been any mention of their attempting to pay for their food and lodging. This unworthy thought assailed me, whilst I sang like a pieman, warbling his wares.

Afterwards I walked out with the ladies. It was sunset and I walked down the hill with them, our shadows stretching away to our right. I thanked them for their goodness to the Major though why I had undertaken his care I know not. I promised I would come and see him in the morning.

But there was no need. I had noticed that water from a spring fed the duck pond. Next morning I immersed as much as I could of my person in the clean water, and cleansed myself with some soap from my box. I was reaching for a towel when someone spoke. It was the Rector.

"Our guest, your patient, died this morning. God released him from his earthly torment and has washed away all his sins."

"Alas, sir," I said respectfully, covering myself with my dirty shirt, "There could be no other outcome."

"No, no, indeed !" he said, "But his passing was strange. When he heard that the wounded were to be moved away in carts, as it was thought Waller was returning, he roused himself from his bed all broken and burnt as he was, staggered outside, demanding a litter. When he realised there was but a farmer's cart to transport him, he sighed, cried out to the King, crumbled to the ground and died."

I could think of nothing to say. The plight of those who die for loyalty, religion or simply an opposing idea was terrible indeed. The

Rector bowed and turned to go. "Thank you for coming to tell me." I called after him. He raised his hand in Farewell and went his way.

As we had eaten well yester even, I judged that Robert should have the strength to ride with Ralph close beside him. They would ride two of Waller's horses which left a third sturdy handsome beast that Waller had given me. I judged that if I gave Nell more money to care for George and gave Noah the third horse that might pay our reckoning. I knew that the Lobsters had coins sewn into their clothes as is the way with soldiers, but they were perhaps afraid that their money would turn to dross should it be shown the light of day. Soldiers are superstitious creatures.

I was surprised however by the decision they had come to, when I returned to the cottage and was something ashamed of my previous sour thoughts.

"Well, Doctor Tom," said Martin, as I stooped under the lintel "Here's a strange thing, now. You have quite unmanned us. We find that we are fit for naught but the pastoral life. I have decided to stay with George and help Noah, and here's the oddest thing of all. We find we have some guineas in our coats and can pay for ourselves at last. No more leeching from the Fletcher fortunes." As he spoke he was unpicking his coat seam, and a small pile of coin was growing.

I confess I was relieved, not simply because Noah and his wife were compassionate understanding people who as they had no sons to protect them were particularly vulnerable in these times, but because I had seen how the King's men served any Lobsters whom they caught. They seemed to exact much harsher treatment than men of less noticeable companies. I suggested that they hid their distinctive red armour, in the duck pond perhaps?

Noah was delighted with the horse, a sturdy mare that would carry both him and Nell should they wish to trot to church or market. So overall I judged that the good shepherd's fortunes were improved by our visit rather than depleted. Martin had undertaken to ride into Marshfield to buy more food for the four of them. I was interested that he seemed determined to go there. His eyes had widened at the sight of captivating and capable Mistress Dorothy.

"Well," I told myself, "They must fend for themselves now. We must make Nailsworth before nightfall. Robert cannot sleep in the open."

Nell wept to see Abram go and embraced me lovingly as well. Why she and her husband felt such sorrow at our departure, I cannot tell. We had crowded her home, destroyed her comfort and privacy, and eaten all her food, and yet she wept. Her husband shook his head sadly saying, "We shan't see such life in a month of Sabbaths. And a rare good voice for a song, Doctor Tom."

Robert contrived to mount one handed, using a large log as a block, and at last the four of us were ready. Nell and Noah came out to bid us Godspeed and Martin clapped me on my boot, saying he was ever in my debt. I did not argue with him, merely wished him Good Fortune. And so we trotted down the hill, which we had ascended with such high hopes on the 4th of July. It was now the 7th, yet it felt as if I had passed long years on Lansdowne Hill.

The weather continued warm and pleasant. However, Robert, understandably, was silent and depressed. We passed through a village called Old Sodbury where I was able to buy some food and small beer. We ate as we rode, which Robert found difficult, but he claimed he was not hungry. At length as we journeyed over the top of the Cotswolds, he asked Ralph to ride with Abram and to let me ride alongside him. I willingly did so.

"Tell me, Tom," he asked, "Why are you returning to Gloucester? It seems your errand was to London."

"Sir William wished it, lest you needed urgent medical assistance. He hoped that you might support Massey."

"Did he indeed?" he said despairingly. "Well, let me tell you, Tom, now I wish both Waller and Massey at the devil."

I said nothing. What could I say? There were no words of comfort or hope. The most one could hope for was that he would accept his loss and that his terrible wound would not become poisoned. We rode for a half mile in silence. Then he said, "You were right certainly."

I said with a smile, "An unusual circumstance!"

"No!" he said angrily. "I tell you, you were right! A dangerous lunatick like that should not be set lose on an army. He killed two men at Worcester by bleeding them when they were so weak and enfeebled, that was the very last policy he should have adopted. Do you know who is the real Commander of the Western Association?"

I answered, "Why, it is Waller, is it not?"

"No, it is not!" he said bitterly, "It is Waller's wife!"

He lapsed into silence. I was beginning to be afraid that we might not reach Nailsworth before nightfall, Bur when we came to a point where the land sloped gently downhill, Robert said, "I can canter, I think, if I hold my ruined arm rigidly and unmovingly against my chest. It will make my fingers ache more but since they are somewhere on Lansdowne Hill, I will make shift to forget them."

Cantering ate up the miles satisfactorily. Robert, still a good horseman, was learning to control his mount with his left hand. I remembered how distressed he had been to think that his horse, which had rolled on him at Powick Field, might have had to be destroyed, and reminded him of how he had hoped that Rupert had stolen him, not shot him. "Ah, yes. That was Thunderer! A good old boy!"

After a while he said again, "Had a common trooper murdered his fellow, as Allen killed poor Progger, Waller would have hanged the felon from the nearest tree. Instantly! And yet Allen continues with the regiment and not a word is said ! Waller dreads his wife. Allen is married to an old aunt of hers, and they will do aught to ensure the madman is always in the field, and not at home, as his management is irksome to them."

It was after noon by this time. We all needed to drink and to relieve ourselves but as we had no friendly tree stump, it was more difficult to enable Robert to dismount. He became angry with us, as we tried to help him, saying angrily, "There is nothing amiss with my legs."

I said trying to placate him, "No, indeed, Sir. It is merely a question of balance." Sadly as his feet touched the ground, he stumbled and Ralph caught him. He said nothing. I noticed his hitherto cheerful countenance was beginning to appear strained and thin.

"Are you in pain, Robert?" I asked him as we set off again, "As soon as we find a good inn, and we have eaten well, I will prepare an opium draught for you."

"A final draught from which I shall not wake for preference," he said wrathfully. Then looking at my face, he continued, "Poor Tom. Forgive me. You know why Waller has sent me away?"

"To advise Massey. I had heard him say as much."

"Oh, do you think so? There are two more telling reasons. The first is that when Waller looks at me and my stump of an arm, he is reminded that his dear good lady wife rules the roost and that he is henpecked to the bone in that he must keep that villainous surgeon with him. And the second reason is that if I am absent, he can the more easily ignore the outrage of my fellow officers. Still be assured that Captain West will have a tale to tell. I ask you, Tom, would you put your life at the hazard against the King's dogs when you knew that that deranged scoundrel was all that stood between you and death, should you be wounded?"

"As you know, Robert, I am not a champion of either cause."

He nodded grimly. "So be it. Your opinion is well known to me. A tempting vantage point indeed, sitting on the fence, condemning both factions, from your superior station. But I fear I am a popular man with my fellow officers. To be honest with you Tom, I would not hazard a groat on Waller's victory in the next battle. Also the Cornish stand like age-old cliffs. There's no moving them and Sir Bevil, once they have taken up their position."

"Sir Bevil is dead, I fear, Robert," I told him. Of course he would have left the field before Sir Bevil received his fatal blow from a halberd.

"What do you say, Tom? How so?" He was clearly distressed to hear this news. I told him what I knew and he observed sadly, "There then, another good man gone! Soon there will be none left, but madmen, cripples and toadying time-servers."

By this we were descending through the steep woods that lined the hills that surrounded Nailsworth. Robert seemed to me to be greatly fatigued, and although Ralph and Abram and myself could have ridden on to Stroud, the track thither along the river was not wide and very stony. But on Market Street I found a clean and comfortable inn, where Robert was offered a posset of brandy wine, cream and honey, certainly a strengthening potion He seemed well satisfied with this, but asked to seek his bed afterwards, saying that if he woke as it grew dark he would find us. I hoped that his exertions this day on horseback would cause him to sleep long and deeply.

The landlord had only recently inherited the inn and seemed determined to please any customer who should come to his door. He invited us to try a dish that we had never previously heard of, called a Dutch Pudding. When it was presented to the three of us, it looked like nothing so much as a large cabbage, resting on a platter, but when I cut into it, a host of savoury aromas arose and within the "cabbage" was spiced and tasty sliced beef, which served with mustard we found to be an excellent meal.

Our host told us that before he had become an innkeeper, he had been a weaver of the famous Stroud broadcloth but that he had always wished to be a cook and now that his ambition had been realised, he was the happiest of men. I said politely that if his other offerings were as excellent as his Dutch Pudding, it would be his customers who should be the happiest of men.

In the night Robert had a most fearful nightmare, in which he thought Dick Allen was cutting off his feet. When he woke and saw the pitiful stump of his arm, he told us next day that as far as he was concerned, he was still in the nightmare. He seemed content however to continue to Gloucester and claimed that his sleep had refreshed him a little.

The weather had broken over night and though all crops needed rain, it was certainly hard going up again into the hills. We left Stroud far down in its five valleys with the mill wheels turning and the water gurgling. The strange smells of the weaving followed us some little distance, but then as the rain brought down mist with it, all that we could see were sheep nibbling and all we could hear were sheep coughing.

At last the clouds parted and there was the height of Robinswood Hill again on our right as we approached the city walls. Now to my surprise, at the Eastgate we were challenged by a number of guards. Robert by now was greatly fatigued again and asked me to speak for him. So I squared my shoulders, looked the Captain in the eye, and spoke as briskly as I could.

"This is Colonel Robert Burghill, lately wounded in Waller's service at the Battle of Lansdowne Hill near Bath. Waller has instructed us to report to Colonel Massey. The Colonel here has useful information as to the numbers and troops of both the Southern Association and the Royalist forces. Believe me, Sir, Colonel Massey will be rejoiced to welcome us."

And so without further questioning we were admitted back into the city we had left with such high hopes but a few days before.

8

Four guards were instructed to bring us to Edward Massey's house on Westgate Street. They marched two by two before us clearing the way for our four horses. I thought I recognised one of them. He, it was, whose wife and daughter we had helped carry earth and a boulder to the fortifications. I called a halt, dismounted and walked beside him, leading Rowena, and asked him how he was faring. He looked around to be sure his fellows could not hear, then said in an undertone, "Too many Puritans in this city. Let a man worship how he will, so he does not impose his ideas on me. I tell you, Master, there are too many ideas in this town. A man trips over them at lane end, market place and street corner. Massey listens to all, says naught and does even less, save make us work night and day on the damned walls, devil take 'em. There I have done. You are Doctor Tom, are you not? Are you for the New Inn this night? I will thither and buy you a cup of canaries, Master. I swear you are owed it for your service to my womenfolk. Davy Wainwright does not forget a kindness."

I thanked him for his friendship but by this we had arrived at a great town house on Westgate Street, with large windows of fine mullioned glass. The sergeant assured us our horses would be safe with them. I watched them lead the tired creatures down a narrow lane to a courtyard at the back of the dwelling, so narrow was it, that poor Blackbird's rump was grazed slightly by the rough walls.

But we were for the front door. I had again to announce ourselves to the porter who showed us into a room off the hall, where there were chairs for all, including a large carving chair behind a table. There was a fine painting of the expulsion of Adam and Eve from Paradise. Eve had long hair, the colour of my horse, judiciously arranged over the upper part of her person. We waited patiently in silence for a few moments. Then there was the sound of hurrying footsteps and Edward Massey came in.

What impressed me immediately was his youth. He was clearly only two or three years my senior, dressed like a gallant, long curls

and a hesitant moustache. I could sense immediately that Abram
was impressed by his fashionable appearance. Sir Edward bowed
low and spoke courteously to Robert.

"Welcome back to Gloucester, Colonel Burghill. Forgive me. I
did not know you were accompanied." He went to the door where
a servant waited with two glasses of wine. Sir Edward gave
instructions for more refreshment, handed a glass to Robert,
unaware that he could not receive it in his right hand. When Robert
held up his mangled arm, Sir Edward gasped, closed his eyes tightly
and averted his gaze.

"Dear Colonel, how comes this?"

"A cut from a Cornish blade at Lansdowne Hill, Sir Edward, but
my hand was removed by an over-zealous whoreson sawbones, a
relative of Waller's by marriage. This is Doctor Tom Fletcher, who
found me in dreadful case and to whom for the second time I owe
my life. The first occasion was at Powick Bridge." He stopped and
sighed. "Tom, can you tell Sir Edward the events of Lansdowne
Hill, if he has not heard the full account? I confess that talking
fatigues me more than anything."

"As you wish, Sir." I rose and bowed, the peak of courteous
perfection. "I would assume, Sir, that messengers have brought you
news that the outcome was a Pyrrhic victory for Hopton and an
honourable defeat for Waller."

"Er... something of that," said Sir Edward.

"Perhaps what you will not have heard is that there was a
disastrous explosion the day after the battle, in which Hopton was
injured, one Major Sheldon killed and the Parliament prisoners who
had been allowed to smoke on an ammunition wagon, were burnt
to grotesque cinders."

"How badly was Hopton injured?" asked Sir Edward eagerly

"Temporary blindness and numbness down one side. Burns on
the hands. I believe he was saved by his hat which he was wafting
before his face."

"Ah," said the young Deputy Governor of Gloucester, plainly
disappointed.

A servant entered with tankards of small ale for Ralph, Abram
and myself. It was clear that Sir Edward felt that we common folk
would be unappreciative of fine wine.

"And will you remind me of your name, my fine fellow?" he

asked Ralph.

"Corporal Holtham, Sir," said Ralph disclosing to me for the first time, his rank and surname.

"And may I be permitted to present my adopted younger brother," I said giving Abram a tactful push on to his feet. He bowed as courtly as any Jack-Hold-My-Staff, and I felt that perhaps we could soon make our escape. But it was not to be.

"Colonel," announced the Governor, "How I wish, dear Sir, you had been with me, a short while ago at the end of June."

"How I wish, dear Sir, I had been with you, for then I should probably still have had the usual number of hands." said Robert grimly.

"Er-yes, indeed." said Massey, "Dear Colonel, what can I say? There were... how can I put it? ...doubting Thomases in this town of Gloucester who thought a local older man would have filled my office with more weight of experience. So I determined on a stratagem that would silence them. I took all my horse and dragoons from the Garrison here, and ventured forth with Colonel Stephens to Royalist strongholds in the Cotswolds. May I say, Colonel, with great success initially, particularly at Lower Slaughter, where we took twelve prisoners. It would have been thought that my cavalry, having tasted the heady fruits of success, should have followed me to the mouth of Hell and back. But no such thing! By the time we reached Andoversford, David Walter's men had been reinforced from Sudeley Castle. 'Twould have been a fair fight of equal numbers and I, like a latter day Hector, ploughed forward to assume the sweet crown of victory. But do you know, Colonel, when I looked behind me there was no-one there! The craven recreants were galloping for home. There was nothing for it but for me to follow them. And so it came about that the Royalist curs chased after us, killed four and took twenty seven prisoners, including good Colonel Stephens. So, what do you think of that, Sir? I have still not had a clear explanation as to why they turned tail."

"And Colonel Stephens?" asked Robert. I had a notion that he already knew the answer.

"Taken by the whoreson rogues and imprisoned in Oxford, as we hear."

"Much to be regretted," said Robert. "A fine soldier. Well, Sir

Page 221

Edward," he went on slowly, "May I take it that your men who fled are still here with you in Gloucester?"

"Indeed, they are. I could hardly hang ninety odd men. Is that where you are at?" asked the latter day Hector.

"Certainly not, Sir Edward. And I have to tell you that their loyalty to you is unimpaired in that they have not melted away from Gloucester like hail in June. But you must consider, Sir. A poor cavalry soldier who may have invested in his horse, who has begged from his parents and his grandam, if he has the choice will not put his beast at too much risk. Without his horse he is nothing. Even if Parliament issued him with his mount, that beast's wellbeing is the difference between life and death for the good horseman. When you use a cavalryman, you have two living beings under your control, the man and his horse. If after your attack on the Slaughters, these good fellows knew their horses were tired and their pockets were not deep, then if they are men of good sense and not Bragging Jacks, they know their animals must be fed and rested. They could not hazard all that they owned on a second sortie. Believe me, Sir, their loyalty is not in question. You have valour and to spare. Let your poor troopers teach you discretion."

There was a long silence. Sir Edward stroked his moustache, and still did not speak. I felt apprehensive and realised I was perspiring freely. I took another gulp from the tankard of small beer. The crude noise of my swallowing seemed to echo resoundingly around the room. At last Sir Edward gave a short sharp laugh.

"As I say, Sir, and as you logically demonstrate, I needed you here. I need you here now, Sir. God bless you for your candour and good sense. And welcome back again, Colonel to Gloucester. Will you take more wine? And you are a Doctor, are you? But not the wretch who sawed his... Well, well. You are heartily welcome."

"May I address you, sir?" I asked with unaccustomed humility. This man stood more upon his station in life than ever Rupert did, although I thought they were of an age.

"Certainly, you may, young man," he graciously inclined his moustache.

"My brother, here, and myself will begin tomorrow to buy and collect medicaments so that your Garrison may rest easy that their needs will be met should they be injured in any future combat."

"Very good, very good." said Sir Edward, "We do have doctors but I would hardly describe them as being in a state of preparedness. My spies in Oxford tell me it will be but a matter of time, before we are besieged. I have built up good store of provisions but medicines? No-one has thought of that."

Robert clearly greatly fatigued now stood, and asked leave to depart. Sir Edward was graciously pleased to allow this and asked Robert to dine with him in three hours time. But Robert had to decline.

"Indeed, Sir Edward, I am very conscious of the honour you afford me, but I fear that the fatigue from which I am suffering as well as my total loss of appetite, together with my difficulties at using only my left hand, would make me a poor guest. When I am something recovered, perhaps I may avail myself of your kindness?"

And so with a plethora of empty compliment and bowing like demented lackeys, we took our leave.

John Nichol excitedly invited us to sit and take a cup of canaries, but on seeing Robert's condition, he cried out in horror. His wife came running and on seeing the sad pathetic result of Allen's barbarity, burst into tears. Robert sat and maintained silence, looking downwards, almost shamefaced at his ugly disfigurement. It was agreed that we should stay at the New Inn, as there were rooms for us. Abram and I by good luck were able to stay in the two rooms at the head of the short staircase where we had been before. I asked if I could have a bucket of hot water in the inn yard and proceeded to wash myself thoroughly. I had just asked Dickon who was going into the brewhouse to pour the remains of the water over my head and was wiping soap from my eyes, when a lady's voice behind me said, "Welcome back to Gloucester, Master Doctor!"

It was the golden-haired young lady after whom I had named my horse. I wrapped a clean napkin around my person, and bowed with water streaming down my face.

"Perhaps you might be kind enough to call upon my father, your patient, and assess his progress." she said looking modestly downwards.

"Certainly!" I replied, "but perhaps you will permit me to dress before I venture into the street."

"Certainly!" she said. Was there a hint of sauciness in her tone? "We shall look for you tomorrow."

She turned and lifting her skirts with a whisper of silk to avoid the puddle of my soapy water, she made for the street.

"How is your father?" I called after her.

"Oh, perfectly recovered," she called back over her shoulder.

I had found a clean shirt, but despaired of my breeches. Battlefields are not places where ones clothes fare well, and from a child I had found it difficult to be particular about my garments. I would have to find a mercer on the morrow. I went back into the inn, wondering how Mistress Rowena knew I was back in Gloucester.

I sought out Master Nichol to order an evening meal for the four of us, but he was already seeking me. "One has come from the Deputy Governor asking for you." He indicated a woman and boy who stood nervously in the taproom.

"Master Thomas Fletcher?" she asked hesitantly.

"Yes indeed, if I have not washed him away." I said drying my hair vigorously.

"Master Fletcher, I have permission from Sir Edward to request that you visit my poor husband who is wounded in Babylon."

"I had not thought to travel as far as that," I said pleasantly. "Where is Babylon?"

She smiled. "It is the old Infirmary that the monks built, but there is little of that now. The wounded are housed there in the midst of the families of minor cannons. My poor husband is sore perplexed by the noise and is supposedly treated by a physician but that man does nothing for him to the purpose."

I sighed. "May I see him early tomorrow morning?" It was already almost supper time. We had eaten little during our ride from Nailsworth. I knew that Abram would be chafing at the bit.

She smiled again "If you please, Sir. My son here will come to escort you when the clocks strike nine. And, Sir, we can pay. Have no fear, that you will be unrewarded."

"Let us think of your poor man's leg rather than my payment." I said piously. But I reflected as I went to find Abram, if he was as proficient as he claimed at keeping accounts, perhaps I should employ him to collect a modest sum from relatives of the sick. I had no doubt that most of the medical profession would be more than eager to extract money from their patients.

That evening John Nichol told me there was general unease amongst the Garrison at the inability of the surgeon John Rice to do much except to predict how a wounded man would recover. He was reluctant to treat a patient should his patient's humour be in conflict with the doctor's expectations. Therefore should a depressed miserable man get a cold, the surgeon would see the humours of phlegm and black bile in impossible opposition with the poor sufferer's "elements" and "qualities", and nothing would be done and would continue to be done, whilst the sufferer got worse.

Ben used to call such surgeons, graduates from the University of Hocus Pocus. "If they are not committing active harm, no need to interfere, Tom," he would say. Allen clearly had some vague knowledge of this excrescence of Galen's teaching. But Ben always claimed that logical medicine was the province of the Arabs......

I suddenly remembered that Abram had wanted to talk to me about the great Arabian physicians of whom his father had told him. I looked at him now as he greedily caused Mistress Nichol's roast pork to disappear. Poor Robert in contrast had little appetite and sadly caught my eye as Abram helped himself to more cabbage.

As we pushed aside our empty plates, I asked Abram,

"Come then, Abram, if you please. I do not ask that you sing for your supper but now is an excellent time to speak of the great doctors and scientists about whom you wished to educate me."

"If you don't jest and make out I am a fool, Tom," said my adopted brother cautiously.

"I promise I will not. See we are grave pupils, eager for knowledge, are we not, Robert?"

Robert smiled and said pleasantly, "We are attuned to hear, Abram."

"Well, know then," Abram began, "Your William Harvey was not the first to discover that the blood circulates. A great Damascus doctor called Ibn al-Nafis described how the blood moves through the heart, many years ago."

I remembered Ben telling me about this man. "Abram," I told him humbly, "I am sure you are right but how did you know about him?"

"My father told me. He was a scholar before he gave way to his desire to see strange outlandish places like this country. He found himself here with no money and helped an old pedlar, and learnt that trade, and had his own house and cart, Tom, as you know, and married my mother. But he never forgot the great doctors and scientists of the East, Tom, and told me of them."

John Nichol brought us a syllabub, a dish I loved well, as the scent of lemons reminded me of my mother for some reason I did not understand. Poor Robert was close to exhaustion and after Ralph had helped him to bed, I examined his hand, or rather the vacuity where his hand had been. Although there was pain and soreness around the horrible wound, there was no sign or smell of gangrene. But I feared for Robert in that there seemed no longer any savour of life, no enjoyment, no appreciation of existence. He sat always like a dull child who has been bidden to sit still and silent. Often he seemed to hang his head as if in shame.

He caught my expression of concern and smiled sadly. "Waller was right to dismiss me, Tom. What a death's head am I, at any feast!"

But then Dickon came to tell me Davy Wainwright sought our company. I and Abram left Ralph with the Colonel. Another posset was ordered for him and Ralph undertook to sit with him. His devotion and affection for the Colonel like that of Jonathan in the Bible seemed to surpass "the love of women."

We sat in a quiet nook and Davy offered us what we wished to drink. "But I tell you what, Doctor Tom. This man Nichol gets his wines from Bristol and has a marvellous rare tasty potion from Cadiz that they call Taint in these parts. 'Twill give you an excellent night's sleep and up at sparrow fart, fresh and lithesome as an old maid's marriage bell!" The wine was ordered and proved as excellent as he had foretold. In fact I found myself even more alert and awake at that hour than was usual with me.

"So, what think you of young Massey?" he asked me.

I replied with care. "He is very young." I observed cautiously. "But then so is Rupert."

"But what thought you of his leanings?" he persisted. "Is he out and out for Parliament? Or think you he might be…. luke-warm?"

I and my second glass of Taint considered the question. "I saw no sign that he might be regretting his allegiance. Rather he was persuaded to accept that his cavalry on his Cotswold sortie were perhaps more cautious and careful of their mounts' welfare than he was." And so we passed a pleasant hour, chatting of this and that, a time unTainted by care and sorrows until I realised that

Abram was sitting bolt upright on his stool, smiling like a gracious lord and fast asleep.

Next day, after breakfast the small boy whom I had seen the previous day with his mother came to bring me to his wounded father in Babylon. He led me round the side of the Cathedral where there was a tumbledown accumulation of buildings. One longer than the others was divided into a line of cubicles, some occupied by sick soldiers and others by families. I was annoyed to see that little boys played at football, unchecked down the centre of the hall. At the very least the sick should be preserved from the chaos and noise of family life. I resolved to go and see Edward Massey again, and plead for peace and quiet for his invalids. They had, after all, obtained their wounds in his service during his ill-judged attack on the Cotswolds.

The boy who told me he was Hal to distinguish him from his father who was Harry Armitage, led me now to a bed near a fire. The woman whom I had met previously, rose to greet me and thanked me graciously for attending her wounded husband who also nodded and smiled his thanks. But the poor fellow displayed a courage and cheerfulness not at all in accord with his injury. As he was in his nightshirt examination and diagnosis were easy, but the cure would necessitate patience and time. We were now well into July, today being Monday the 10th. Massey's ill fated attack had been in June. The dislocation of his calf had been shamefully neglected, and the lower part of his left leg was twisted and warped.

"If I try to stand, I feel the bones grate," he told me. This was crepitus. It was to be hoped it was not too late or he would never walk again on two legs. The bone could not be set immediately, but it could be gently pulled over into a natural position so that slow healing could ensue. Such a process was time consuming and could be painful but I judged that there might still be hope. Harry had adopted the most comfortable posture he could, and his leg was swollen and at a most unnatural angle. There was great tenderness over the area of breakage.

"Mistress", I said courteously, "I will begin a process which you and your boy can continue when I have gone, if your husband can bear it. We must very slowly straighten his leg and when we have achieved a natural setting we must tie it to the other so that the process of healing will begin, unimpaired. There is nothing to be gained by allowing your poor husband to remain like this."

I spoke to my patient. "My dear Sir," I began, "I must hurt you, I fear, as your shin bone is broken, and I cannot set it. Indeed your leg is so swollen over time, no bone setter could or should undertake such a method. We must slowly edge your leg back into its natural position so that bones and sinew might knit again and enable you to walk once more, though I can make no promise of complete success. All I can tell you is that if you remain like this for any more time, you will be a cripple for good."

There was feeling in his left foot which was a hopeful sign. I asked him himself to move his leg as close as he could to its uninjured fellow and then began to stroke his shin. Fortunately by a miracle his shattered bone had not pierced his skin. As I stroked with my right hand I grasped his heel gently in my left and moved it an infinitesimal fraction towards the centre. He gasped with the pain but said, "Well, Doctor, I fear that I must suffer somewhat to be whole again."

I continued my stroking, interspersing my soothing movement with the smallest motion to the centre. I explained that I could not set the leg with one attempt as the injury was "unstable". I asked how it had happened as I continued my manipulation and was told that the wooden heel of his fellow trooper's boot had caught his leg as the other man had mounted in fearful haste, throwing his foot carelessly into the patient's shin. His face seemed strained as he told me that in the same instant he had heard the crack of broken bone. They had ridden hell for leather back to Gloucester, where he had had to ask his friend to assist him to dismount. He could not walk and had had to be carried to his house whence Massey had instructed, he should be carried to Babylon with the other wounded troopers where he had lain ever since, solely for the convenience of the Gloucester doctors.

"But surely Massey ordained that you should be seen by a surgeon?"

His wife answered for him. "Indeed he did, but to little avail. The surgeon one George Edwards, called a bone setter who pronounced that as it could not be set in one operation, he had not the time to undertake what you are now doing, Sir. And the surgeon made us pay dearly for arthritical joint medicine, distilled from rosemary such as my mother could have made us for naught."

"Rosemary is a good herb and has done no harm," I conceded, "But it cannot move a bone back into line. Only you and I, mistress, can affect such a measure by this daily manipulation."

By this, I had by painful degrees, brought the calf perhaps an inch back towards its rightful course. But the discomfort was extreme for poor Harry, and I had to balance the eventual benefit of the manipulation with the terrible strain I was causing him. Although the leg was slightly straighter, the bruising was intense.

"We need an unguent to kill the pain," I told her. "Is there a good apothecary in Gloucester?"

"Master Simeon Walsh told Edwards my husband needed an unguent." she told me excitedly. "Master Walsh is the best apothecary in Gloucester. But Edwards would not have it and told him he was the physician and knew best. Master Walsh tried to explain that my poor husband needed a drastic cure such as you propose, and would not benefit from an arthritical potion. But Edwards would not listen."

She instructed Hal to remain with his father and suggested that we visited Master Walsh at once. His shop was near the Westgate, near the river and was neat and clean with a well swept flagged floor, and his pills and potions clearly displayed and labelled and he seemed a cheerful soul, thin with a nose like an eagle's beak, knowledgeable and helpful in all things medicinal.

"I am very glad to meet you, Doctor Tom Fletcher," he announced. "But know, Doctor Tom, that I fear for you. When once the concourse of charlatans and quacksalvers who think they rule the roost here, learn of your sojourn in Gloucester, then dear Sir, your life is not worth a penny piece. I have heard of you from Waller's men who were here in May and whom you cured most efficiently and courageously, I hear, of a surfeit of rotten eels."

"It was the simplest of cures, dear Sir," I told him, "Boiled water with sugar and salt added. Nothing more."

"What?" he affected mock disbelief. "Do you mean to tell me you did not consult your Table of Causes? Nor your Table of Afflictions to the Ascendant? You simply cured your patients by supplying them with what they had expelled from themselves by excessive vomiting? What misbegotten logic was this, Sir? Dear God, if Doctors begin to cure their patients in this efficient manner, then what hope for their overstuffed purses? They will start to number themselves amongst Pharaoh's lean kine, and waste and pine away lacking their usual fat fees. Dear young man, have a care, I beg you. Do you take my meaning?"

"I think so, Sir." I told him. "My master studied under the great Doctor Iqbal of Bologna. I would say I had been trained to study Cause and Effect, and to use the wholesome native medicines of our woods and fields rather than the philosophy of Galen."

Whilst we had been talking he had produced a chair for Mistress Armitage and had found three crystal glasses and had poured muskardine into them, a welcome mid-morning beverage.

"Now then, Doctor Tom and fair Mistress Grace Armitage, I beg that we might drink confusion to the blinkered apostles of Galen, who are killing far more than they are curing." He tossed his wine back in a gulp and then enquired, "So for Master Armitage? How may I help? What is your prognosis, good young man?"

"I fear his shinbone is shattered, but the fracture has been so neglected that I must proceed little by little to bring back the leg from its twisted state. It is painful in the extreme, but with patience and daily manipulation and a long period of healing rest when it has been completely straightened, he might walk again."

I spoke both to Master Walsh and Mistress Armitage. She wept a little on hearing my plan for her husband's treatment, but the apothecary beamed and clapped his hands together. "My dear young man, what a refreshing breath of air you bring with you. Do you have Massey's ear?"

"No," I told him "but my dear wounded friend, Colonel Burghill, advises him and Massey respects him."

"Well," said Master Walsh, "that is one weapon in your armoury. Believe me, dear sir, when the medical warlocks begin to gather and the surgical wolves start to howl, then you will be marked out for sacrifice. But for Master Armitage. Unguent of sage and there is but lately come from Bristol and before that from the Indies, an amazing tincture of Jamaican Dogwood. A few drops before you begin your manipulation will dull the pain and enable him to bear what your treatment necessitates. The unguent spread on the bruising will reduce the aches. I will bring them to Babylon later in the day. Shall we say when the bells of St Mary de Crypt chime six? Then I will leave my shop and repair to his sick bed. Will you meet me there?"

"Indeed I will," I told him, "and am right glad of your good counsel, Sir"

We returned to Babylon and found Harry Armitage fast asleep and Hal, sitting by him, gazing enviously at the boys playing football. But in the instant of our return, there was a sudden silence, and the boys seemed to remember a pressing appointment elsewhere and disappeared, Hal dawdling behind them. For a right royal figure had entered the long hall.

"This is Master Edwards," Grace Armitage whispered.

Manners may make the man, so the proverb teaches us, but clothes do not. Indeed if apparel were the yardstick by which ones fellows should judge one, I would be the most pathetical pauper in the town gutter. My boots were dull and dirty, my hose were torn, my breeches stained with other men's blood and my shirt was a mourning one, in dire need of the good offices of the laundress.

I had never seen so much lace round a male personage. There was lace around his neck in the form of a collar, at his cuffs, drooping over his white hands, and most incredible of all, adorning his boots. He was, for all the world, like the popinjay toadeater, Digby who had wished to wall up Peabody and myself underground when we rescued the two miners, to save the cost of our funerals! That memory did not endear me to this scented stranger at the outset. There had been other followers of Rupert in Lichfield who had dressed like simpering maids or hermaphrodites, but who had demonstrated that they were men for all their finery, when the musket balls and granadoes fell like hail. This was a Roundhead Doctor in a county town, not a perfumed pug-nasty in a pushing school!

He waved a staff in my direction and said imperiously to Mistress Armitage, "Tell this fustilarian to make his way back to Jumblegut Lane, Mistress. The sickbed is no place for low interlopers."

Perhaps my jaw dropped. For a moment I had no words to combat his insolence and Mistress Armitage said pleasantly, "I fear you mistake, Sir. This is no low fellow, but Doctor Thomas Fletcher of Worcester, who rendered our soldiers such service in that place, when they were like to die of poisoned eels."

I managed to bow. "Good day, Sir," I said politely,"I have but lately come from the bloody fight at Lansdowne Hill and need to patronise a mercer."

He looked me up and down. "Yes, perhaps you do," he said with a condescending air. "I prithee then be on you way, my good fellow."

He turned to the patient. "How do you, Master Armitage?"

"Better for Doctor Tom's diagnosis."said poor Harry. "He has given me a morsel of hope. I pray you, Sir, speak to him again with courtesy. He knows a method whereby I might recover my leg."

"Oh, does he so?" said the threepile vision. "And what is that, pray?"

"The gradual manipulation of the leg from its present twisted posture to its natural position, so that the bone might knit safely." I said, and then perhaps I erred for the first time. "That is basic skeletal practice, but takes many patient days."

"Oh, does it so?" he screamed. "By my faith, I have just left my grandam a-groping ducks! How dare you tell me what I should be about?"

And here I made my second mistake and made another enemy in Gloucester, apart from the dishonest Quartermaster.

"Surely this was the advice of the bone setter you employed? There can be no hope for Master Armitage's mobility, unless patience is practised?"

"Patience!" he shouted, "How dare you tell me I lack patience? I am Patience personified!"

"Well, why have you not begun the correct, nay, the only treatment ?" I cried. "If you knew what was needed? Why allow your patient's limb to grow set and stiff? Why did you not begin the treatment when it was still pliable?"

"Silence!" he shrieked. "I will not stay to be questioned by a whippersnapper of a boy! Look to hear more of this outrage, Sir!"

He turned on his heel, which was now I realised, something higher than was usual in a man's boot and stalked out of the hall.

There were other wounded men lying near Harry Armitage. One who sat on his bed with his arm in a sling called out to me. "Alas, good Doctor, I fear you are for the pillory! But have no fear! They do not throw stones in Gloucester, by the Mayor's edict, only eggs!"

"How can I be punished if I have done no wrong?" I asked simply. This caused a shout of laughter! "Join Gloucester Garrison and ask that question! Who said aught about doing wrong?" asked the winged soldier.

"Well," I said simply, "It is to be hoped that my friends will come to my assistance. Massey himself gave orders that I was to look to Master Armitage, so perhaps he may prevent that gentleman from his course of vengeance."

Harry Armitage spoke now, lying on his back with his eyes closed. "George Edwards is a turd in velvet breeches. He is not respected by his fellows of the Worshipful College of Gloucester Physicians, but that is not to say they will welcome you or your practices, Doctor Tom. We welcome you, by God we do. When Ensign Baker brought the news yesterday that you had retuned to the city, my Grace went at once to ask Massey to send you here. Like all men, Massey is not proof against the allure of a pretty face."

I felt strangely flattered both by their faith in me and the fact that my fame had something gone before me. "Well, what of this arm?" I asked the jester who had warned me of the pillory. It was a sword cut that had begun to fester and was causing him much pain. I cleaned it as best I could and then anointed it with Pares Lotion and bandaged it with clean linen which he claimed gave him some ease.

"I shall look at it again this evening. I shall return at six," I promised them and turned to go.

"Do you know what my grandam would have done for me had she still lived?" asked the jesting trooper.

I sat beside him. "I fear you are about to tell me. Enlighten us."

He looked around, unsure whether to confide in me or boast. "She would have bound it up as you have done but she would have placed maggots in it."

"Maggots?" I found that difficult to stomach.

"Aye, for they eat away the rot and leave the healthy flesh."

"Well," I said cautiously "I have great respect for the cures and simples of our grandmothers. Let us see if this lotion gives you ease and if it does not... Well, we shall again consider."

Harry spoke again, leaning back against his makeshift pillow. "Even the maggots disdain the meat they give us here. Were it not for my Grace, Massey would have all but forgotten us."

"Then I am determined." I said with more assurance than I felt. "Massey must make better provision for his wounded soldiers. I had best buy myself new clothes and then I will visit him and tell him of my disquiet at your conditions."

The mercer was horrified at the condition of my clothes but was then delighted that I did not stint myself in rectifying my poverty-stricken appearance. I felt some shameful relief that Abram was not with me as I would have had to buy him whatever was fashionable. But surely even Abram could see the futility of arranging lace round his boots.

I decided that I would buy myself some workaday garments, serviceable and hardwearing, and was fortunate in that the mercer had a pair of kersey breeches by him that would fit me. "They were ordered for some poor fellow who did not return from Massey's excursion." said Master Rawdon grimly. "As he was over tall like yourself, I did not look to sell them so soon, so I am very pleased to see you this day." I bought the funereal breeches and two pairs of hose at thirteen pence the pair, and two shirts at nearly three shillings each. I asked leave to wear my new clothes which I was pleased to pay for there and then, but was also moved for some reason to buy myself breeches and doublet in a more pleasing fabric. I decided against Watchet blue coloured satin and resisted the appeal of scarlet mohair and fixed my mind instead on a very fine woollen cloth, the mercer told me was called cheyney. The colour looked black but he assured me I had chosen a deep blue and invited me to the street to see the cloth by the light of day, as he had not many candles burning in the shop.

"There, Sir!" he said, holding it up to my face. "It is good that you have eschewed black. With your complexion, black causes sallowness. In a man as young as yourself, that is not a hue to be sought after. This naval blue is much more flattering."

"Oh, yes, indeed," said a voice I recognised. I turned and Rowena Smith, with her mane of hair, precisely the colour of my horse, stood there laughing at me. "Oh, Master Rawdon, dark blue is exactly the shade he should wear."

"There, you see, Sir. The prettiest young lady in Gloucester bids you wear blue. Now you cannot gainsay her, I think."

"But he will, Master Rawdon, for he breaks his promises." she said saucily. "He has promised to see my father today but is on the gad buying fine new clothes."

I swallowed my irritation. "At what time shall I attend your father?" I asked finally. "I must find my brother in the New Inn and then see Sir Edward Massey."

"Then bring your brother to supper, I pray you. We shall expect you at five."

I bowed, relieved that at least that I was wearing my new clothes, and she went her way, looking back at me with a shy smile. Indeed, it seemed to me that she was not usually a pert and forward young lady. I had the impression that the mercer was slightly surprised by her flirtatiousness.

He looked at me with raised eyebrows. "Well, Sir, I see you have a way with the ladies."

"No! Indeed not, Sir. Not at all," I protested. I should have told him that I was a sober young widower, but my new persona like my new clothes, seemed intriguing and interesting.

I took my new cloth to the tailor he recommended, who like all tailors measured me, whilst bemoaning his lot with lavish wit, and then took my money with equally lavish greed. I bundled up my old clothes and made for the New Inn.

Abram was looking out for me and ran down the street to greet me but stopped in surprise at the sight of my new clothes.

"Why, Tom! What a courtier you have suddenly become! You look for all the world like Prince Rupert. You washed everywhere yesterday, oxters and hair, and today fine new clothes! What means this?"

"It means that tonight you and I are bid to supper at a great scholar's house, the brother of the Bishop, no less. What say you to that? And Yes, if you lack aught, bespeak it from Master Rawdon, a mercer in Blackfriars."

With admirable restraint, Abram denied himself, though I knew he longed for coloured hose. "No, Tom. You have bought me enough. I want you to set me to work, not to deck me out like a Maypole. I have been walking about looking for the pestle and mortar signs of the apothecaries"

We walked into the Inn to find Robert and Ralph who were sitting in the sun in the courtyard at the back. Ralph was idly watching the servants performing the various tasks that made for the smooth running of the inn, but Robert, coaxed out by his devoted corporal, sat now unheeding the bustle of the tapsters and maids, his head lowered, despondency hovering over him like a grey cloud.

I spoke to him as cheerfully as I could and asked after his "wrist". He smiled sadly.

"No Tom. No decay. But it itches and aches as if my dead hand called to me. Why is that, do you suppose? God have mercy upon me, how could I have walked past limbless beggars all my life, when they sought pence for a crust? I cannot help now but dwell on their terrible plight. What a blinkered life we lead! Like cart-horses in harness whipped on by whoreson politicians!"

Ralph tenderly wiped away his tears and took his good hand and raised it to his lips. "Captain Rob, try to be of better cheer! Here's Doctor Tom, trussed up in new clothes like a Christmas goose. I offered his old suit to a scarecrow but the straw man disdained it! Whence this finery, Tom?"

"Abram and I have been asked to sup this even with a philosopher James Smith, whose learning did not prevent the muscles of his shoulder contracting painfully. I cured him as I think and his daughter bids us to eat with them. If he has any thoughts on our perplexed land I will ask him to meet you, Robert. Does that suit?"

"As you wish, Tom!" Robert, his face sunken and his complexion leaden, was the soul of indifference.

After a brief but savoury and memorable meal of Cheddar cheese with onions, accompanied by small beer for the others and a glass of the excellent Taint for myself, I told Robert about the conditions in Babylon and suggested that he accompanied me to see Massey to ask for better treatment for his wounded soldiers. Robert sighed and stood unwillingly, but I judged that it was better that he should concern himself about the plight of others, rather than remain sunk in his consuming melancholy.

"Come then," he said crossly. "Let us go and teach the gilded upstart his duty."

So we set off for Massey's fine house in Westgate Street, and were shown again into the room with the chairs and the painting, by the servant. We waited for some little while and then were received by a dignified personage whom Robert addressed as Master Pleasance. He apologised for Sir Edward's absence saying gravely that affairs of War were detaining him, and that he was even now with his Captains, but that if we would be pleased to remain here, Sir Edward would wait upon us at his earliest convenience. A door upstairs opened suddenly and there was a burst of woman's laughter, swiftly hushed and the door closed. Robert rose.

"Master Pleasance, (and may I say your courtesy and loyalty is as impressive as your name) we are not deceived. I know better than any man in Gloucester, the disposition and strength of the armies in Somerset. Any conference regarding "affairs of War" should surely include myself. Sir William has ordered my participation. I have lost my hand, not my brain or memory. But have no fear. Sir Edward is as entitled as any man to take his pleasure. If he will send to the New Inn when he again has leisure, I would be indebted to you."

He inclined his head and Master Pleasance bowed, discomforted, and we moved out as dignified as turkey cocks, our wattles a-quiver with repressed indignation.

As we walked back to the New Inn, Robert began to laugh gently.

"There's for the lusty young pup! That will teach him to entertain his doxy during the hours of work."

At nearly five o'clock, Abram and I set out for the Smith household. Robert had told me that he was pleased that we should enjoy ourselves and not feel bound to sit with him at all times. He seemed well content to spend time alone with Ralph. If I had reflected I might have thought that it was strange for a Colonel to be happy with the company of a Corporal, but Ralph seemed to be able to dissipate the gloom that hung over him better than any.

James Smith was clearly delighted to welcome me into his home. "Who is this?" he asked as Abram made his bow. I explained that he was my adopted brother, and that he had chosen to throw in his lot with me after the sack of Birmingham, having tragically lost his parents in that incident.

"Incident? Nay, 'twas an atrocity. To fire on unarmed citizens! You are welcome, young man, and Doctor Fletcher is thrice welcome. Your advice cured my shoulder in one day, though the cook objected to cooking stones in her hearth. So young Abram, whence is your parentage? We are pale puny fellows beside your golden hue."

So Abram began to tell him of his Egyptian forebears and of the great thinkers and philosophers of whom his father had spoken.

The parlour was warm with the afternoon sun of July and for a little while, I fear I fell into a doze, my glass of Mistress Rowena's cherry wine held carefully in my hand. She, it seemed, was busy assisting the cook with the preparation of our meal. Abram talked and Master James questioned and listened until suddenly chimes from the Cathedral bells thrust me into wakefulness.

"Oh, dear God!" I cried. "My patients in Babylon. I was to see them at six and meet with Master Simeon Walsh. I will at the most be half an hour. Can you forgive me and excuse me, Master Smith?"

He laughed. "Off with you, my boy. This young scholar and myself will while the time away."

I arrived panting and puffing in Babylon. The boys were still playing football down the middle of the long hall and Harry Armitage still lay with his eyes closed, as if he had stayed in this posture since I had left earlier in the day. But when I spoke he opened his eyes and smiled. "Have you come to put me on the rack again, Doctor Tom? Go to it, then."

"Let us wait for Master Walsh." The apothecary was hurrying towards us, pausing to send the boys outside to play. He presented me with his tincture and unguent. I anointed Harry's bruises, and placed two drops of the Jamaican dog wood on his tongue. Grace paid for the medicine and I moved the leg a little further back into its natural line, a process which took me some minutes.

Then we looked together at the jester's arm. It seemed calmer and cooler. "Shall I summon the maggots, then?" I asked him.

"Tomorrow!" he said laughing with a degree of relief, I thought.

"Well, so be it. I will see you in the morning," and I took my leave.

I strolled out of the door, humming to myself, relishing the prospect of the evening ahead of me, not least of which was the memory of the fair Rowena, who had no doubt cooked a fine meal and whose pretty face illumined....

I was suddenly grasped from behind and a blindfold was pushed across my eyes. I gave one outraged cry and a great hand was thrust across my mouth. Instinctively I bit it. The rogue gave a roar and beat me twice about the head, stuffing a filthy cloth into my mouth. I realised by this that there were two of them, one behind me. I kicked backwards, following it with a swing of my wooden box of medicaments. I have always been happy to remember that either my boot or my box made contact with the softer parts of the anatomy of the fellow behind, who howled and let go of my hands.

A voice I recognised.... "You arrant fools! Bind him, I tell you! Bring him down!" I was tripped and forced face downwards into grass. Better than flagstones I reflected, but I could smell foul dog excrement, and irrationally began to fear for my new clothes so recently assumed. My box was wrested from my hand. Before they could kick or stamp on my hand, I instinctively drew it under my body. "A surgeon's hands are his most precious tools," Ben spoke in my head.

They wrested them behind me as I lay there and roughly tied them with rope. Blind and dumb, I was kicked to my feet and forcibly marched away from Babylon as I thought. I had a sudden fear that I was to be thrown into the Severn, bound and gagged with no comfortable Lofty to rescue me, but we seemed to be heading for another part of town. As we walked the treacherous physician George Edwards (for it was his voice I knew) cried out constantly "Convicted felon! Thief caught in the act!" He called out these words whenever I heard we neared passers-by. "Thieving maunderer! Gallows fruit!" No hope of anyone recognising me, thus encumbered and trussed like a fowl on the spit.

I had no notion of our direction except that I could hear we stayed in the town. I knew I was in the midst of crowds but what of that when I could see no-one. I sensed that our road rose uphill and then came a slight downhill slope. A door was unlocked and I was thrust down a flight of dank steps. I could tell that they led underground by the smell of damp stone. I had the good sense to stay as upright as I could and to feel my way with my feet. I had the advantage of height on my two assailants and though I hit my head once, they too, I thought were afraid of falling as we descended. The stairs twisted round and at last there seemed to be even ground before my feet.

I sensed George Edwards had remained abovestairs. I could surely now try to bribe his henchmen. I had money in my pockets. But as I gathered myself to offer them a reward, two facts oppressed me. Firstly I could not speak and secondly I had left my money in my old clothes, so my frenzied mumbling was of no use. I vowed never to buy new clothes again.

I was pushed roughly to one side and heard the clatter of keys, and the squeak of a lock. Then I was hurled forward through the door like a sack of turnips. For a shuddering moment of horror, I feared I was being pushed down a well. The falling sensation lasted but two seconds however, and I landed face down and legs spread everywhere, my upper body in a puddle of filthy water. I twisted myself immediately to one side so that I would not drown and lay for some minutes the side of my head immersed, but my nose well clear so that I could breathe.

The key turned in the squeaking wards and I heard the two villains climbing the stairs up to the world of light and freedom.

For a while I could do nothing but lie still. I might have lost consciousness for a while, and yet although I despaired I could not help comparing my situation with that of the previous occasion, when I had been bound and thrown in a cellar. Then my face had been severely grazed by being dragged up the steps to the farmhouse kitchen in the homestead off the Bridleway. Now my cheeks still stung with the blows I had received and no doubt there was a lump on the top of my head from the roof of the twisting stairwell. Apart from these three hard knocks, I was uninjured. And if I could still think and remember my life, perhaps my brain was undamaged? If I could defeat Brigstock with a chair leg I reasoned with myself, then surely my case was not hopeless.

I lay listening. From far away the noise of the town penetrated this cellar from above. Men and women still cried their wares, there was the faint wail of a fiddle, a child or was it children crying. The world continued in spite of Tom Fletcher's unjust incarceration.

There was a rustle on the floor behind me. I had thought I was alone. I tried to cry out. "Who's there?" but all that emerged from my gagged mouth was a confused mumble. Silence. Then the faint noise again.

"Who are you?" I tried to shout, producing a muffled hum. Again the silence, filling the vault. The cellar had a high ceiling. The sounds I was making were producing something of an echo. And the air was not foul.

Who was penned up with me? The rustling came again. Nearer this time to my body sprawled on the ground. And then whatever was making the rustling sound scuttled across my legs.

As a boy playing sports with the others, one of our tests of strength and dexterity had been to get to our feet without using our hands. I was lying on my side. I rocked myself upwards on to my knees and shuffled in what I judged to be the direction of the door. It seemed many yards away, but at last my thigh scraped against rough stone. I realised by inclining my upper body and meeting resistance that I was parallel with a wall. I remembered that the trick of standing without hands was again to rock oneself upwards. I tried and failed, but then some instinct made me force my feet under me into a crouching position. From this somehow using the wall as a guide to lever myself, I hooked my elbow onto a protruding stone and forced myself to stand. I tore my new shirt, and my arm inside it, on.... on some sharp protruberance from the wall.

I knew that the creature that had scurried over my leg had been a rat. Now I was on my feet and in control of my limbs once more, I comforted myself remembering my father's advice as to how to protect myself should I meet a mad or ferocious dog, without a weapon. "Remember, son. You have two good weapons on the end of your legs. Your feet in your boots." At least, now if I felt the rat near me, I could kick it away.

I was standing with my back to the wall. I realised that if I edged along with it at my back, I would come to the door. As I did so, the same sharp object tore my shirt again along my back. I raised my bound arms behind me to find it and felt the knot catch on it. The rope was wet from the water where I had lain, and though the pain around my wrists was cruel in the extreme, when I pulled my upper body away from the wall, I thought I felt a loosening sensation. I judged that a few strands had been pulled away. Could I hook myself on to it again?

I raised my arms behind me and brought them down again. The hook caught again and I strained away from the wall. The hook tore at my inner wrist, and I became afraid that my blood might make the rope even wetter. I swiftly learnt that if I caught the rope between its complete coils, all I could do was pull it very slightly looser but if the hook was pushed into the denseness of the coil and if I moved my hands up and down I could gradually weaken the strand so that eventually my hope was, it would break. But only a few fibres at once could be frayed and broken.

I do not know how long I stood there, my back to the wall, speechless and sightless, continually catching and re-catching the rope on the hook. I realised that I must at one point have caught a completely new coil as surely I must have broken one as I had been striving for so long. The rat came back once and I caught it with a lucky kick. But in that movement I almost overbalanced but was held upright by the hook. I began to fear that if the rat returned and I kicked it violently again, I might pull the hook out of the wall. Then I would again be in a hopeless situation. I could feel or sense on my tied hands that the rope was being frayed into single strands. Perhaps one hearty pull away from the wall would break the rope once and for all.

I tried but the rope held. Wearily I hooked myself again. I continued the punishing movement of my arms up and down for what felt like several hours, and I swear at last I was almost sleeping on my feet.

I finally resolved to rest and by raising my arms higher than the hook, freed them from it. I pulled my aching limbs sideways away from the knot and to my amazement the remaining strand broke and my arms fell to my sides. I felt the rope falling away. Unknowingly I had at last destroyed my fetter. I tore off the blindfold and pulled away the gag.

I do not know how I had schooled myself to endure the utter torture of my plight. I immediately voided up the contents of my stomach. God knows what foul purpose the filthy cloth that had been stuffed in my mouth had previously served. Somehow I had forbidden my brain to dwell on it. The blindfold was a stout wide leather strap, which would be useful for deterring rats. It was of course by now quite dark. I had not noticed that the sounds of the town had faded and all outside was silent, but high on one wall there was a grating. This was the reason for the wholesome air. Through the bars far above me I could see the night sky where a few disinterested stars shone.

I listened again. Nothing. From far away I could make out the friendly sound of a dog barking. At a fox perhaps? I began to explore my prison. I went first to the door. No latch or handle, just an empty key hole. I hammered on the stout unyielding wood for a few moments, crying out for help, but the town was by now abed, and my voice seemed weak and feeble. Would any watchman heed my cries? Or would I be deemed merely a guilty felon, objecting to the justice of my punishment?

I avoided the centre of my prison knowing that a pool of water lay there. But the dungeon was not damp and I realised that the water had been blown onto the earthern floor from the open grating in the last rains, two days ago. It had cushioned my fall a little. Even so I did not wish to share my drink with a rat. I turned my attention to the walls, running my hands over the rough stone surfaces. I found that there were several hooks, embedded in the wall at roughly the same height. Their purpose suddenly presented itself to me. Manacles! I shuddered imagining if the two ruffians had had access to such instruments of torture! In what state would I have been, had I been pinioned to the wall, blinded, aching, motionless and dumb. Remembering the horror of the gag, I retched again but then controlled myself. I had at least achieved my physical freedom within the confines of this hideous place. I continued my careful examination of the walls. The rough stone stretched upwards in an unbroken wall, with only the grating letting in the faintest breach in the black darkness. I wondered if the dungeon had been built alongside a dwelling of any kind. Perhaps it abutted onto the cellar of a house. I began to knock where I could locate a smoother stone in the wall, listening for any change in the echo of the sound. There was none.

I had almost despaired of this activity, when my fellow inmate announced his presence once more. I could not see him but I could hear him and of a sudden he hurtled across the floor to my feet. I kicked out, praising whatever guardian angel had made me buy good boots. There was a squeak and he was silent. Had I killed him? It was somehow vital to know. Already I was regretting my barbarity towards him. He had not hurt me, had not bit me. I placed my palms on the wall where I was standing and slowly moved them downwards, feeling the rugged surfaces and having a care for any snags or rough protrusions. I came to the base of the wall. There was no rat but my fingers moved unhindered inside a hole, into which he had surely disappeared.

I felt around inside the hole, hoping that his lair and wives and family were some distance away. There was a stone hanging proud inside the hole, one end secured in the wall, the rest of it easily grasped. I shook it.

To my delight there was the rattle of masonry and a little shower of what felt like dust and small stones fell around my hands. By this

I was lying on my stomach, my hands inside the hole. I withdrew them quickly, suddenly afraid. If a large piece of stone should damage my hands? What use was a doctor with ruined unseeing hands? Nonetheless I felt a certain triumph. This prison was not impregnable. If I could find the noisome gag I could wrap it round my......

And then I heard it. The most wonderful sound I had ever heard, would ever hear. My own name. "To o....o m! To o...o o m!"

It was so far away, so high above me in another world. But I knew who it was! Abram! Abram looking for me in the middle of the night, in a strange city, perhaps alone in the unfamiliar streets. My name again, fainter this time. "To o o...o o m!"

Somehow I had to let him know where I was. Summoning my strength I shouted with all my might. "Abram!" But my mouth had as yet not recovered from the violation of that abhorrent gag, being dry and sour. I had no spittle. I coughed, swallowed and tried again. "ABRAM!"

This time the sound resounded around the cell and a further cascade of stones fell inside the rat's hole. I shouted again and again, reasoning that if I kept up the noise, he would hear me if he returned along the same route.

Suddenly the lesser darkness of the grating disappeared. I could dimly discern the head and shoulders of my adoptive brother blocking the stars. "Abram" I screamed. "Help me!"

"Tom, are you really in this black hole? I'm going for help. Wait there!"

I laughed to myself aware that I had no other choice. I felt my way round to the door and sat near it, my back against the wall. At least now my friends would know where I was. I strained my ears but could hear nothing. Somehow though, now I knew I would be rescued. Robert and Ralph had seen Abram's worth over the last few days. They would trust his word. I strained my ears, trying to hear if he had found the Watch who might well have keys to this fearful place. I listened but all I could hear was the sound of my own heart beating. It had been such a relief to have been found....

I must have slept. Suddenly there was a bright light and Sir Edward's face peering into mine, Robert beside him. More and more people were pouring down into my subterranean hellhole.

The light of the torches blinded me. I became aware that Sir Edward was wearing a most sumptuous bedgown, but that everyone from the New Inn including John Nichol was fully clothed. The word which I heard that seemed to be on everyone's lips was "Outrage!"

Sir Edward helped me up and there was Abram on my other side. "Thank you, my brother," I said simply.

There was another rich bedgown with a most dignified person inside it. It seemed this was the Mayor. Sir Edward turned on him, as if he would tear him limb from limb.

"My Lord Essex has hung mayors for less than this, Master Wise!" he shouted. The poor Mayor appealed to me, from behind as by this I had fought my way through the throng, determined to mount to the open air.

"Doctor Thomas!" he cried. "Had I aught to do with this? Tell me who was the wretched caitiff who cozened you into the dungeon and I swear he will spend the rest of his life there."

I swayed and stumbled as I came up into the street, my hand on Abram's shoulder "Could we speak of this tomorrow? I fear another doctor arrested me through jealousy, envy. I know not what or why. He waited for me with two ruffians with the keys outside Babylon."

John Nichol who knew everyone and everything, had a word to say. "That will be the fellow the people call the turd in velvet breeches, Your Worship."

Sir Edward stopped abruptly half way up the twisting stairs causing some sort of consternation in those attempting to climb up behind him. "Do you mean Edwards? But he is so... plausible...."

Robert, who was beside me now could not forbear to add his contribution. "Sir Edward," he said sternly as the younger man gained the street. "You will have heard it said with truth, "Handsome is as handsome does." Doctor Tom here cured not one, not two, but a whole troop of my musketeers at Worcester when in great personal danger. His worth and ability has been proved in my experience many times. At Edgehill he was the surgeon who acted for Lord Fielding's regiment and acquitted himself excellent well. He has even now come from Lansdowne Hill where he worked for Waller himself." He was rousing himself up to an almighty fury. "Where was Edwards on those battlefields? Where was this worm in those bloody conflicts? He is rightly termed a turd in velvet! He is not fit to lick Doctor Thomas Fletcher's boots! This man is a jewel, Aesculapius reincarnated, and you stand by and allow a common dandypratt who dresses in cheap finery to abuse him. Look at the state of him! Look at his head and wrists! Tortured and bound like a common felon, instead of acknowledged by you as one of the best physicians in the land!"

I became alarmed lest Robert in his anger should cause his blood to flow too fast and thickly and the healthy scab that was forming around my stitches should give way.

"Come, Robert," I pleaded. "Your testimony is generosity itself. I only hope I deserve it. Let us go back to the New Inn."

It was arranged that I would see both Sir Edward and Master Dennis Wise, his Worship the Mayor, on the morrow, and I was very nobly escorted away from the dungeon in the dead of night. A strange contrast to my arrival some hours earlier at this fearsome gaol in the light of day.

Good Mistress Nichol had bowls of hot water waiting and I was able to wash myself thoroughly. "Hair, as well, again!" I boasted to Abram. It was a blissful comfort to stretch out in my bed in my nightshirt, having been constrained to eat a piece of apple pie and drink a posset of brandy, cream and the juice of an orange.

"There then, Doctor Tom, sleep tight!" said the motherly lovely woman, kissing my cheek as I lay smiling like a tired child. And they left me alone at last.

But in the morning all was not well with me. I had some sort of ague that tightened my chest and caused me to cough painfully. I tried to leave my bed, but the swimming in my head caused me to seek it again almost at once. Abram brought me fruit and water at my request. I contrived to eat and drink a little but at length realised I must get some sort of tincture to lower my fever. I asked Abram to fetch Master Walsh, who kindly shut his shop and came immediately.

It seemed the story of my capture and imprisonment was all over Gloucester. I did not seek for news of the reprobates. It became clear to me that I was too ill to be concerned about anything except my own recovery. Master Walsh on hearing that I had lain with my head in a pool of muddy water for some time, concluded that I had contracted a severe feverish cold. He prescribed a solution of aconite, a dangerous herb which he insisted on administering himself daily, and recommended thyme tea and elderberry wine which Mistress Nichol had in her still room in abundance. Thanks to these prescriptions I lay in bed for some days, sweating like a pig and drunk as a fish. One morning I coughed so violently that I thought I would loose all my vital organs. On hearing me Mistress Nichol brought me up her own remedy. A fierce infusion of ginger and lemon sweetened with molasses from the West Indies, and certainly it seemed to calm my crumbling chest. I experienced what my patients must have often suffered, a sensation of disbelief in that my good health had disappeared and was showing no sign of returning.

Abram came in on many occasions and brought me messages including one from Mistress Rowena. She told him that she hoped with all her heart that I was recovering, but that I was not to fret. She would not offer to cook for me again as I would clearly undergo any suffering to avoid eating her meals. Feeble though I was, I knew that her jesting signified understanding friendship.

Finally one morning about a week after my ordeal, I woke one morning to find that although I felt weak and wamblety, I was no longer ill. I heaved myself out of bed, found a new shirt and a pair of neatly cleaned and darned breeches, and staggered down our little staircase to face the world. There was gammon and eggs, with fresh bread and butter, and I found that I was hungry. Not hungry in the Abram fashion, but somewhat hungry all the same.

After a delicate breakfast, small quantities of everything, I went to sit with Robert, to thank him for his eulogy on my behalf in the dungeon.

"It was no more than the truth." he said, pushing a glass of wine towards me.

"It was not exactly the whole truth," I said cautiously, "If Rupert had been in a like condition to yourself, if he was brought in before me now, bleeding and broken, I would do anything to save his life. I could not help myself. Like you he is a friend. Perhaps not such an affectionate, stalwart or steadfast friend but still a friend."

He sighed heavily. "And who is to say you would be wrong?" He laid his left hand on my arm. "Believe me this "accident" has made me consider, has given me a deeper insight into men's motives. The character of this King, that and the tumult of our beliefs has laid the way open for a multitude of differing incentives. Whilst you were ill, news was brought of Waller's defeat, at a place near Devises. I remembered those two good fellows who had been Hesilrige's men, and rejoiced at their decision to cease soldiering. The lobsters as they were called were horribly slaughtered at Devises. Believe me, dear Tom, the notions that one holds dear, do not seem so pressing or important, when one has only one hand."

I was overcome by his sadness. There were no words of comfort. Despairingly I took his left hand, a gesture he appreciated though I found it too intimate. "So what is Waller doing now?" I asked.

"What was left of his regiment went to London. They are all afeared for Bristol now. I think your friend Rupert might have that town in his eye and then after? Who knows? Here? But there is no doubt that Waller's Western Association is over. The infantry paid a terrible price. I predicted no less, if you recall."

"Where is Waller himself?" I asked.

"Possibly on his way here, to stiffen the Deputy Governor's elegant sinews. I think Massey's courage falters at the prospect of defying the King. Well, we can only wait and see. That Abram now. What a loyal young fellow! And good-looking also."

For some reason that I could not identify I did not want Robert to praise Abram's looks. His admiration of my adoptive brother made me uneasy. I drew back my hand.

"I confess I was never more pleased to see him peering through the grating of the dungeon." I said thankfully, "It seemed no-one here had gone to bed?"

"To bed? I should think not indeed. When at about eight that night Abram came running from Babylon, whither he had gone from the Smiths, when you did not return as expected, then the hue and cry was raised. We scoured the town, crying and shouting, and I have to admit finally I felt that the daylight would bring answers and came back to the New Inn with mine Host and Ralph. But Abram was having none of that and continued his lonely vigil. Then when we knew your whereabouts we roused Massey and he roused the Mayor, Dennis Wise, who roused the Watch, who kept the keys. But one of them had earlier agreed to lend those same keys to a hired ruffian, who claimed he was a servant of George Edwards. This slave had to be found by Massey's life guard and the keys retrieved. As I understand matters, the Mayor has placed the three villains who captured you under arrest. And no, Tom they are kept in better case than they were prepared to condemn you to, my poor boy. The Dungeon is empty. They are in the Garrison, charged with unlawful imprisonment, which even in these uncertain times is still a crime." He smiled grimly. "Do you know the wretch, George Edwards, had the audacity to claim that if he had known what noble friends you had, he would not have meddled with you. In other words, if a man is poor and without high connections, any Jack-in-Office may imprison him. That is the England that I hate, Tom. That is why I took up arms. That is why I do not wish to see Waller again if he comes here, which I think he will. The runnion-ridden, mangy cur fights because his wife, the Finch woman, tells him he should, and he retains mad Dick Allen because it suits her. I do not think Rupert for all his papish heresies would allow that lunatick within one mile of his Cavalry!"

He sat back in his chair, his face enraged and bitter as the force of his emotions possessed him. He was right. Rupert tried to put the safety of his fighting men before all other considerations. How Robert knew this was a mystery. I did not know what I could say to comfort him and finally compromised with, "Well, if Waller comes, no doubt we shall contrive something." I felt considerable apprehension at the thought of such an encounter.

"So, then Robert, what now with these miscreants? What is their fate?"

"That must depend on you."

"On me?" Surely the process of justice in this city did not rest on my word.

"Oh yes. You bring the inditement. Massey delays their judgement, threatening to bring them before Waller when he comes. There is dissension, it seems, between the apothecaries in this town and the physicians. If we are to be brought to a siege, then a proper arrangement for the care of the wounded must be discussed."

I suddenly felt weak and unsure of myself. "Robert, if you will forgive me, I will return to my bed. You have no pain?"

He eyed me rancorously. "I'faith, Tom, I have the finest stump, that ever man was blessed with. My good fortune knows no bounds!"

I escaped and as I climbed the staircase was hailed by Ralph. He was happy to see me again on my legs but very concerned for Robert. He followed me into my chamber, helped me off with my

Page 249

boots and seating himself, voiced his fears. Robert was not eating. "Not enough to keep a sparrow alive, though he is drinking, more than he has ever done whilst I have known him."

"I take it you are not speaking of water?" I asked.

"Indeed I am not. He claims that he needs brandy wine before he can bring himself to leave his bed in the morning, and as the day progresses, he constantly refills his wine glass from a bellarmine that John Nichol must replenish. Master Nichol is alarmed at his consumption. Robert has paid in advance for all of us to retain our rooms here until August, and John is loathe to be at odds with so good a customer, but I know the landlord fears for his guest's health. I know he is drinking spirits to drown the loss of his hand. Can you persuade him to be more temperate?"

"I can try," I said very doubtfully.

Next day which I judged was the eighteenth day of July, I felt recovered enough to visit my patients and was pleased to find Master Amitage and his wife had continued my treatment. It was a painful remedy but a necessary one if he was ever to use his leg again. The poor man groaned when I claimed that we could move the leg another half inch that day but clenched his teeth and allowed me to manipulate it that little distance. The leg was growing considerably straighter, although I was aware that the discomfort was formidable. Still in repose, it was much closer to its fellow and the swelling had gone. The Apothecary had helped them and now he appeared walking down the length of the hall they called Babylon, his black robe flying out behind him. He clasped my hands and told me that he was rejoiced that I was on my feet again. I thanked him, particularly for his use of the aconyte tincture which I was sure had broken my fever.

He nodded saying, "Not a doubt of it! Now, young Doctor Tom, a word to the wise. If it should come to a hearing which John Rice is threatening, you have every apothecary in Gloucester at your back as well as one of the town physicians."

I stared at him. "Why a hearing?"

"George Edwards is claiming that you stole his patients. Have no fear. Mistress Armitage here and her husband will refute the claim, stating that they appealed to you, being lamentably neglected by Edwards. No more than the truth. But it might descend to futile superstitious assertions based not on medicine and good medical practice but on star gazing. Rice and Edwards are the Earl of Stamford's men. Massey is his Deputy."

"Where is the Earl of Stamford then?" I asked, my heart sinking.

"Cudgelling Royalist arses in Devon. Massey acts for him in this as in everything. But his actions are controlled by your Colonel's friend and patron, Waller. So in effect you have nothing to fear. But I beg you, if Rupert storms our walls, if you care anything for Gloucester men, citizens and soldiers, aye and women too, make Massey provide better conditions for the wounded. You will be in the public eye in a day or two. Your sane and clever influence can do much for us. You can save many lives by judicious exposure of the notions of these two fantastical pantaloons, Rice and Edwards. Edwards has already damned himself by his treatment of you, but Rice keeps his state and has his followers. Well, I have done."

"But as I understand it, sir, there is more at stake here, than just a raw young sawbones, myself, standing on the toes of a charlatan in three pile. My offence has been simply to heed the entreaty of Mistress Armitage. Am I right in thinking you have waited for just such an instance as I have provided?"

He chuckled. "So young and innocent in visage, so much perception and understanding of the underhand motives of his elders. But grant me this, young Tom, we are alike in that the currency we value is human lives, not guineas. Are you with me thus far?"

I nodded and thanked him for his advice and walked slowly back to the New Inn. The town seemed of a sudden to be more crowded than ever, and I caught sight of the Tree of Virtue, Waller's device being carried down Southgate. My heart sank. A returning army would mean there would be wounded, unless Waller had disposed of them elsewhere.

I walked in under the arch, wondering idly what good John Nichol had to give us to eat today and where Abram was, when suddenly there was the Conqueror, himself, descending the stairs from Robert's room. I bowed and he addressed me in something of an ill humour.

"Well, Doctor Tom, can you not give Robert some salve, some potion to sweeten his temper? One would think from his surliness and ingratitude that it was I, myself, who had taken an axe and chopped off his hand!"

9

I stared at him, unable to reply. That he should belittle the terrible loss of a hand was incredible. Sure, the man had no imagination or else he would not dare speak so slightingly of Robert's tragedy. "And what else have I heard?" and now he was laughing, "What's this, young Tom? You have been ruffling the fur and feathers of the died-in-the-blood Gloucester physicians, I hear, and I am to judge between you all tomorrow. At least so Sir Edward requests."

I seized my chance. "Perhaps it would be a golden opportunity to bridge the ever growing rift between the apothecaries and the physicians in Gloucester, as elsewhere, and to set up a firm system of care for the sick. Everything is piecemeal in this town, and who suffers, Sir? Your loyal wounded troopers."

"Yes, well, of a truth you are in the right of it there," he said swiftly. He seemed to prefer not to think of misfortune and unpleasant reality. Perhaps that was the philosophy of the successful Commander or even the unsuccessful one if the reports of the recent rout near Devises were to be believed. If he allowed reality to sway his thought, if he concentrated his mind on the terrible detritus of human suffering that was the result of every battle I had seen, then he could never order another conflict.

"Well, have your arguments well polished" he continued. "As I understand it, you are accused of stealing patients from your colleagues. You had best have faith in your basic down-to-earth methods, Doctor Tom, for we shall hear a great deal of the stars in their courses, and much about the planetary timetables and precious little about curing the sick and the lame. You have set yourself at odds with the heavens themselves, or at least with the Gloucester leeches who fear for their livings, and who is to say which is the more terrible? Pray God that He Himself supports you. Tomorrow in Massey's stateroom. At noon, if you please."

Now my heart and mind were in turmoil. What had I started? I had simply responded to Grace Armitage's plea that I try to save her husband's leg. Edwards had neglected totally her husband's twisted and broken limb, and I had been falsely imprisoned for my pains, in the town dungeon. Had I best hire a lawyer to plead my cause? I knocked on Robert's door.

"Well, Tom?" he said sourly, but at the sight of my anxious face, he relented. "Why, son, what ails you?"

"I had thought that I was to have indited Edwards on a charge of false imprisonment but it seems he brings a counter-charge against me of stealing his patients."

"Get whoever applied to you... this woman Armitage, is it not?... to state that she did so independently of any action on your part, and the wretched Edwards has no case to answer. You have advocates enough in this town it seems. Use your native wit, Tom. You will overcome." He took a sip from the glass which stood ever at his elbow. "I shall accompany you."

"Thank you, sir," I said formally, and felt slightly more hopeful.

"Twelve o'clock noon tomorrow is it not? You had best go your ways and elicit this Armitage dame to your cause. Make sure she knows at what hour she must attend and support you. Women are giddy creatures and she is just as likely to attend the day after or at twelve midnight."

"I do not think you would have hazarded such a claim, had my dear Phoebe still been alive to hear you," I said, half sorrowfully, half indignantly.

At that he smiled and there was something of the old Robert in his face, compassionate and humorous. "No, indeed. I would not have dared," he admitted. "There was ever something of the grande dame about her, for all she was such a miniature lady. I know not how you sustain such a loss, so excellent a companion as she was."

"It is a loss indeed," I admitted and returned to the inn-yard. I asked for a glass of taint which I hoped would inspire me to prepare a defence. Here it was that Abram found me, racking my brains.

"May we eat, Tom?" he asked me. "You seem worried. I have been engaged with Master Walsh listing all the apothecaries and also the wise women of the town who could help us both with nursing and distilling in the event of a siege. Shall we have something to eat? The noonday bell has long struck."

"And the clock in your stomach reminds you that there is a void therein. See what good John Nichol can supply."

He was back in an instant with the words "Rabbit pie" joyously announced. "Master Walsh tells me that tomorrow you must decide what punishment that villain Edwards should suffer."

"I do not think it will be quite so simple. He is claiming that I stole his patient."

"But you did not, and Allah protects you, Tom. Remember that. If you have done no wrong then Allah will find a way. He sees everything and is everywhere, in the street, in the ale-house, at our bed and board."

A black gowned man paused at our bench on his way into the inn. "Why, my good young Sir." he said to Abram. "It does my sad old heart good to hear you speak so passionately of the Almighty's presence in our lives. I have come to invite John Nichol's guests to praise God with me and my kinsman the hospitaller at St Bartholomew's near the quay at evening prayer today. The Gloucester citizens are so exercised in their efforts in the defence of their town, that we men of the cloth must ensure that divine service continues to be well attended."

I could tell by his worn gown and the dingy bands around his throat that he needed to swell his coffers rather than his congregation. To my eternal shame, I saw of a sudden a clear route out of my difficulties. What had Waller said? Pray to God that He supports you. Abram courteously replied to the stranger.

"Sir I spoke of Allah, who I worship in the same guise as the Almighty. Like you, we believe in one God, maker of earth and heaven."

"Do you so? May I sit with you and discourse on these matters?" Without waiting for permission the parson sat down and called for small beer. Abram looked at me somewhat apprehensively. He knew I was not one for prelates and preachers, but I smiled encouragingly. Here was literally the answer to my prayers.

"Yes, Sir. Pray be seated." I said courteously after the event had taken place. "This is my adoptive brother. He is a Musselman, but I assure you the followers of Mohammed have beliefs similar to that of any Christian except perhaps he puts me to shame with his piety and devotion."

Abram was in his element now. "For, know you, Sir that we hold Jesus Christ to be a great prophet in our religion." It was clear our new friend knew nothing of this. His eyes bulged slightly and he repeated the words, "A great prophet, indeed?"

"Yes, Sir and we are all designated Children of the Book, both Mohammedans and Christians. You knew that perhaps?"

"Er. Yes I believe so." The poor man had clearly wished to convert backsliders into devout church goers. The boot was on the other foot. Abram was not going to let him escape without some tenets of comparative theology. But here was my chance.

"Sir, would you have leisure to attend a hearing tomorrow, to read two verses from the Gospel of St Matthew? It will be a gathering of citizens, godly and pious, no Romish idolaters, crazed with ritual, I assure you, but sober and upright Puritan worshippers, such as one may find in Gloucester. I would begin my defence with a reading from the Gospel. Will you do it for me? Do you have your bible with you?"

"Er- yes, I do." He felt about in his poke, removed two collops which he placed reverently on the table where we sat, and then found a tattered old volume, which he passed to me. My memory was poor but for some reason, I had always liked the tale of the practical centurion who so unemotionally asked Jesus to cure his servant. My father had always said the centurion put him in mind of Sir William Russell. I knew there was another miracle in the same chapter of St Matthew. I found it after turning the well worn dirty pages. I explained when and where I wished him to attend and apologised for my absence at Evensong due to my recent illness.

"All I require is that you read aloud these two verses, 2 and 3 in Chapter 8 tomorrow morning? If I may say you are the chaplain of myself and Colonel Burghill, well, perhaps we might contribute to the future wellbeing of... Saint Bartholomew? And for you now. Shall we say a guinea a verse?"

"I could read more if you wished and discourse at length on the Gospel's holy words, sir." His eyes gleamed at the prospect of sermonising to the leading citizens of Gloucester.

"No, sir. I thank you but I want nothing "at length" The two verses are all that is required. Read them with due severity and grandeur and do justice to our Saviour's powers as a divine healer, I beg you." I returned him his ragged book, and as our rabbit pie and cabbage was now laid on the table, offered to share with him. He accepted with alacrity and I vow, competed well with Abram.

The one had the appetite of youth, the other was lamentable hungry. Both had finished before I was half way through my food.

"May I know your name?" I asked

He drew himself up. "It is Absalom Hooker, a very remote descendant of the mighty philosopher and divine."

"And have you lived long in Gloucester?" I continued my catechism.

"Alas, no. I am but lately come from the Forest, knowing that this town is godly and upright, and that its citizens walk in the way of righteousness."

This sorted better and better with my design. This man would not be known to the Gloucester physicians who wished me ill. To have a man of God supporting me could not but benefit my cause.

"You say you are come from the Forest, sir?" I pursued my enquiries.

"From Coleford, Sir, where a battle was fought in March with Welshmen who support the King. Then on their approach to Gloucester, they were trapped between Waller coming from the South and the Gloucester Garrison. Coleford was but a poor place before this conflict but the crops were trampled in the fields, and the stock loosed and stolen, and there is little food or money there to sustain the basic needs for life. I brought my wife to her cousin's, the hospitaller of St. Bartholemew, in the hope that he might help us. The foresters are so pitiful poor that to ask them to support our little church near Coleford is to ask more than they can bear. Indeed I would like to send back to my poor flock any surplus that I might earn."

"Tomorrow we can ask that money might be collected for your village from the wealthy men who will gather to judge me and another." I told him.

I did not like to see him gather his collops back into his dirty pocket and sent Abram to buy a platter from a potter in the market. He asked me what the action against me was and I told him, "Assisting a lame man to walk. You shall know all tomorrow." And with that he was satisfied and went away carrying his collops carefully before him, rather better, I thought, in both wealth and health.

I confess I did not sleep well. I felt guilty although I had done no wrong. I had asked Grace Armitage to be present at Massey's house some minutes before twelve so that I could be sure she was able to explain truthfully that she it was who had petitioned me. "But more than that, Doctor Tom." she told me "It was Sir Edward Massey himself who had advised me to appeal to you and who told me where you were staying. Have no fear. All this I shall announce to the hearing."

In the morning I went to Babylon to examine her husband's leg. To my amazement he was dressed and insisting that he should be carried to Massey's house by two fellow troopers. His broken leg was almost beside that of the other. He must have endured much in slowly straightening it since I last saw him, yesterday

"If I am at liberty, later today..." I began.

"If you are at liberty? Hell and the Devil confound it, Doctor Tom. I should think so indeed! Let dandypratt Massey look to his elegant arse, for we'll not cover it for him. It's through his careless authority that poor Colonel Stephens is, so we hear, imprisoned in Oxford, due to that mad assault on the Kings Men in Stow. Come on, boys! Let's to the pretty fellow's quarters. My fellows from Stamford's regiment wait to escort us."

It was impossible to ignore the fact that the military had taken me to their hearts. As Mistress Grace walked between me and her husband's porters, the streets were lined with troopers from the Garrison, who fell in behind us as we made our way to Massey's house on Westgate Street. Robert was waiting outside, Waller's insignia of the Tree of Life held above his head by Ralph .A pale young officer, thin as a rake whom I recognised stood with him. Beside him along Westgate Street, another troop was stationed. When I walked up to Robert waiting at the door, they all removed their hats and stood bare headed, and called out their thanks.

"Doctor Tom, my thanks and thanks again. If it were not for you, I would be in a shallow grave in the woods outside Worcester. We all remember how you saved us." The troopers whom he led, I now remembered had all been poisoned by eel pie.

I told them I rejoiced that they were all clearly recovered and thanked them for their support. "Support?" said the thin young fellow. "This could easily become very ugly for Massey. That you were set upon and imprisoned by Master CatchFart who we are told, is no use to man or beast, is a scandal unprecedented. If there is any sign that the Gloucester Doctors think they have the upper hand, then here is Captain Harold Skirmager's troop of foot, who escaped at Roundway Down three days ago and here am I, Doctor Tom, Captain John Barnwood, with my little bag of granadoes. See here!"

I shuddered as I looked in the satchel he held open, remembering the devastation these weapons caused in the Close at Lichfield.

"Captain Barnwood understands explosives, Tom. With him behind you, no man will be against you, at least not if he values his future!" Robert told me with a grim smile. "Shall we go in?"

We had to push our way through the press of people standing waiting for the judgement and I became alarmed for Harry Armitage. But he himself bade the Gloucester citizens make way for us all. Abram was suddenly at my side, and I was pleased to see Absolom Hooker holding his Bible. Robert, his damaged arm held protectively to his body, strode up to where Massey and Waller were seated behind a table on a platform that ran the length of the room.

"A chair if you please, Sir William." Waller started, leapt to his feet, apologising, and insisted that Robert took his chair behind the table. Robert did so and surveyed the room whilst Massey's servants bustled about finding another seat for Waller. The Gloucester doctors were gathered near the empty fireplace and the wretched George Edwards stood before them facing Waller, his velvet finery hanging from him, and his hair, somewhat unkempt and lank. One of the doctors stole a quick glance at me and then looked again as if surprised by what he saw.

The Mayor was also present seated with a few worthy citizens whom I took to be aldermen. With them was Master Smith and I was surprised to see that his daughter was with him. But why not? It was a public hearing. I surmised that the two men shackled together must be the two rogues who had imprisoned me. They were weighed down by chains and glared at the assembled company. But they were impotent now, not nearly as fearsome as I had found them, when they manhandled me.

Accompanied by Abram, I went over to stand near Absalom Hooker. He had his bible open and showed me the two verses I required him to read. I nodded and at that moment Master Pleasance who was seated at a small desk rapped on it for silence.

In the hush that followed Robert's voice was clearly heard, though he spoke in an undertone. He was informing Massey, "But 'tis not merely your own Garrison, Sir Edward. Harold Skirmager's men line Westgate. Have a care that you do not provoke a bloodbath."

Massey looked as if a bloodbath was furthest from his mind. He rose and in a trembling voice explained that as Deputy Governor, he would request that as Sir William Waller had fortuitously returned to Gloucester, he would defer judgement to the General of the Western Association, but that first he would call upon Master Foster Pleasance to outline the situation.

His servant rose and explained that he was acting as the Clerk to the Council of War in Gloucester. He then outlined the reason for enmity between George Edwards and myself, in that I had "stolen" a patient in order to receive the sick man's fee. I could sense that Abram beside me was swelling with righteous rage.

"However", went on Master Pleasance, "If this circumstance took place, instead of appealing to and relying on the due process of the law, Master Edwards..." There was a flurry of outrage from the physicians and the words "His title is that of a Doctor" were hissed by a man whom I took to be John Rice.

"Forgive me!" said Master Pleasance, and corrected himself. "Doctor Edwards sought to imprison Doctor Thomas Fletcher unlawfully, having obtained illegal access to the town dungeon, for which fell purpose, he employed these two caitiffs, whom you see, chained before you."

"How do you answer these charges, Doctor Edwards?" asked Waller with a hint of weariness in his voice.

In fact Edwards did not answer them. He decided to explain instead why he had been unable to treat Harry Armitage's leg because his body had not been vitalised by the spirits from the principle organs. He had been confident that the time to begin treatment would begin when the zodiacal calendar had reached Libra at the end of September. "For you will accept, My Lord," he said, bowing to Waller, with flattering unction, "that the Scales are the season when the body is best balanced to receive healing draughts."

There was a cry from the Apothecaries. "Arrant nonsense, My Lord!" I think the exclamation came from Master Walsh.

"Silence, if you please, my Masters!" The Clerk firmly refused to countenance the interruption. Then Edwards continued with what promised to be a long tedious homily on the nature and cause of diseases. According to his philosophy Master Armitage had one quality in excess which he had not been able to identify. He expounded on the "Dyscrasia" suffered by Armitage and explained with long and tedious periods why treatment had been impossible. Robert sat with his eyes closed and Waller seemed to be thinking of other things as his eyes had that glassy stare that denotes a lack of attention. But at last the Commander had had enough.

"What has this to do with the false imprisonment of Doctor Fletcher? Let Doctor Fletcher speak in his defence. In my view Doctor Edwards has not addressed the charge against him, though given a generous amount of time."

Master Pleasance turned to me. "What do you have to say in your defence with regard to the charge that you have "stolen" another doctor's patient, Doctor Fletcher?"

"If I may begin my defence with two verses from St Matthew, read by this good parson, from whom I have lately received spiritual guidance."

Absalom read with a fine understanding, in a ringing tone.

"And behold, there came a leper and worshipped him, saying, "Lord if thou wilt, thou canst make me clean." And Jesus put forth his hand and touched him saying, "I will; be thou cleansed." And immediately his leprosy was cleansed."

"My Lords," I began, "That I did not seek Master Armitage as a patient, his wife will testify. The moral I would draw from that reading of the Gospel that you have heard is two fold. Firstly, our Lord did not consult astronomical tables nor did he need to identify humours or imbalances of temperament. He healed the leper without recourse to these branches of science. And secondly, he healed the leper "immediately". How else would you as a Commander have your doctors and surgeons act, when we are assailed by bullets and cannon balls in the midst of this terrible civil conflict? There is no time to consult the heavens when one is seeking to save lives on the battlefield. I should also say that I have received no payment from the Armitages and if Doctor Edwards is in penury, I will willingly donate any payment that I am owed to him without prejudice. Mistress Armitage will now speak on my behalf."

Grace conducted herself admirably, smiling confidently at Massey

"I told you, Sir Edward, did I not ? that although all the wounded had been gathered into Babylon for ease of access for the Doctors" and she curtsied to them, "in fact no treatment had been begun, even though good Master Walsh was adamant that my husband would never walk again, if it was withheld. So in desperation I came to you, Sir, and you recommended this good young Doctor who had just come from the battlefield in Somerset. He advised us how to manipulate my husband's leg and it seems to grow straighter and stronger."

There was consternation amongst the Doctors. Rice shouted, "How dare the Governor ignore the precedence we are due as professional physicians?" Massey began to look as if his breeches had been invaded by a colony of judicial ants.

"Look, Sir!" Suddenly Armitage himself had risen from the bed on which he had been carried. To my horror, although he was supported on two sides by his fellows, he was in fact standing, putting weight on his injured limb. His face was contorted with pain but for thirty seconds he stood unaided.

I could not prevent myself. Instinctively I ran over to him calling out, "Harry, all will be undone, if you continue this." His friends obediently lowered him again upon the planchon and he called out, "Edwards has done nothing for me, Sirs, except mumble and grumble and take my money."

"So, Sir," said Waller turning again to Edwards. "It seems the Deputy Governor knew you were doing nothing for his trooper, and nothing was what you proposed to continue to do, until the end of September? I think you have received a salary from the Earl of Stamford, who this good trooper serves in the Garrison here and indeed his fellows are outside to ensure justice is done. How do you justify the receipt of this payment by doing nothing?" He left his chair and came down the room to Edwards who stood cowering and cringing, unable to look Waller in the eye. "But let me tell you, Edwards, this "nothing" is indeed "nothing" compared with what you are in fact accused of. Sir Edward Massey, the Earl of Stamford's Deputy recommends to this good woman that Doctor Fletcher should undertake a course of treatment and you imprison him. He begins an effective cure and you take it into your miserable head to impose durance vile upon him. How do you answer that? Why do you serve him such a dog-trick? Doctor Fletcher has received no payment for his services nor does he ask for any, offering instead to reimburse you, you miserable leech, should you be in need. I tell you, Sir, your payment should be a dressing of Knaves Grease, that lies in wait for you at the cart's tail. Well? What have you to say in your defence?"

Edwards had nothing to say and sank weeping to the floor, attempting to clasp Sir William's leg in supplication.

"Has anyone anything to say in his defence? Here is John Rice, your superior, chief surgeon to the Earl's Regiment. Well, Sir, you have leave to speak in his defence. What sort of cursed physicians do we have in Gloucester, who do nothing and then imprison those who bestir themselves on behalf of Parliament's wounded? Come, Sir, let us hear you, I beg!"

"Alas, Sir William, I have nothing to say." Rice came forward to the group of doctors, bowed obsequiously and looked in fear at the little Commander's angry face.

"Why did I expect that?" Sir William roared. "I will tell you. Because "nothing" is what we have all come to expect from the physicians of Gloucester. Because "nothing" is all you can do. I fear that Sir Edward is right. A siege is imminent. The King wants access to the Forest coal and iron and to his Welsh supporters. On the day that siege begins, Doctor Tom Fletcher is in charge of the care of the wounded, and you all obey his commands." He paused and came back to Edwards. "We should flay the hide from your back for gross ill treatment of this good man. In fact, did you know your life is forfeit? Doctor Tom has, through his excellent doctoring, many friends both in the Garrison and in my regiments. Some have sworn to roast your liver above a slow fire, whilst it is still in your miserable carcase. And I tell you this. They will not consult the table of variation of your miserable temperament, nor will they consult your zodiac. They will immediately effect this as punishment if I deliver you to them."

He turned to the two ruffians who now looked considerably less defiant. "These two are for the stocks for the rest of the day. George Edwards, you will give fifty sovereigns to Mayor Dennis Wise to distribute to the poor of this city. If you do not have that sum about you, no doubt John Rice will lend it to you"

There was a horrified gasp from Doctor Rice. The doctor who had glanced at me before, now had his hands across his mouth, though whether he was hiding dismay or laughter I could not surmise.

Sir Edward prompted by Robert turned to me. "Doctor Fletcher, have you anything further to request?" My father spoke in my head. "Make friends, not enemies, son Tom."

I was surprised to hear my own voice echoing through the room. "My Lords, and your Worship the Mayor, I must decline immediately the honour of organising the medical arrangements in the event of a siege. I will put my poor abilities at the disposal of Doctor Rice, should that terrible occurrence come to pass. Rather than that I would ask you to insist, Sir, that Master Walsh and his apothecaries be given equal powers to these physicians.

To put these two rogues in the stocks merely increases our work as doctors, for who knows what heavy missiles might be thrown at them and cause injuries, which I and my colleagues as Christians and bound by our oath to Aesculapius would treat, would we not?" I appealed to the doctors, but was instantly aware by their stony expressions that the chances of them doctoring such indigent flotsam were nonexistent, although surely the one who had had difficulty restraining his laughter, now winked at me. "Surely the strength of these two rogues to which I can painfully testify, could be better used by the defence teams, currently shoring up the City Walls.

The fine you have imposed seems fair indeed. Doctor Edwards clearly does not stint himself in the matter of his dress. There are poor ragged men and women come in from the Forest with no means of subsistence but what they can beg in the streets. This good preacher could help them if this company and Doctor Edwards could assist him with donations."

I looked round. Everyone was silent. Were they waiting for more?

"There, I have done. I thank you," and I turned to go.

In truth it was but two days since I had left my sick bed and after the exertion of the morning, all I wished to do was rest, sleep perhaps as I had lost much energy. I emerged from Massey's house and with a wave to the troopers called out, "I thank you, friends.

All is resolved," and took myself back to the New Inn, escorted by Abram. When we reached it I sent him off to the mercer's to buy himself new hose. I was beginning to be aware that a city under siege was not the best place for him to be. For that matter it was perhaps not the place I would have chosen for myself. Should we return to Worcester? But I reflected Robert, who had been the best of friends, more than that, my saviour, still needed me to dress his hand. In any event I was meant to be on my way to London. I had vowed to my dying wife that I would visit her uncle. Had I been weak to relinquish my purpose to Julius? I was in reality the sole messenger whom the Earl would have wished to see. But in a time of civil war he would have understood that a man's designs and plans must give way to expediency. I was sure that Julius would be an excellent ambassador for me.

I lay on my bed wearily gazing at the ceiling and listening to the peaceful sounds of the inn. At length I heard Robert return, Waller with him. They sat below my balcony and called for wine and whatever Mistress Nichol had to eat. Finally I yawned, stretched and bestirred myself to join them.

"Ah, here comes our Daniel!" cried Waller, pleased to compare me with the sagacious hero of the Bible. "Come now. I have another task for you, and may I say, you acquitted yourself like a damned scurvy lawyer today. One would have thought you had been raised in the Inns of Court. You did prodigious well and should receive no more nonsensical accusations."

"As long as I am not falsely imprisoned again, Sir, I will take the world's blows on the chin. To speak truth, I caught a grievous chill in that dungeon. That, more than the incarceration, was my undoing."

"Well, let me tell you that that nasty particular Jack Bragger, Rice, must bring arrangements for the care of the wounded during the siege to you and Massey. You must be up betimes for them both, Tom ; Rice because he is an idle, self seeking, money loving leech but Massey because.... well, because we do not trust him."

"Why so, sir?" I could not envisage how Massey could be untrustworthy. Perhaps lacking in substance or backbone, preferring a life of ease, to the soldier's fate ever in the range of the cannon's roar, but I was beginning to appreciate he was an efficient organiser.

"Well, well! Enough! I know you attempt to remain neutral. But

you would not wish your many friends in Gloucester to be....
betrayed, shall we say?"

"Betrayed?" I echoed.

"You would not wish the King and his army to be admitted
without a shot or a blow, and Robert bundled off forthwith to fester
in Oxford prison?"

"Indeed I would not, and I cannot see Robert or Ralph or myself
meekly submitting to such handling!" I said with a degree of
bravado.

Abram came in under the arch. Clearly he had visited the
mercer. His legs were encased in green hose, of the delicate hue of
tender Spring grass. He came and stood beside me clearly expecting
sustenance.

"Will you join us, Sir William?" I asked him. "My adoptive
brother and myself enjoy a small repast at this hour? And I would
wish to pledge you in return for your sturdy defence of myself this
morning."

"It was no more than the truth, Doctor Tom. You are an
excellent young physician."

I blushed and looked modestly downwards but looked up again
swiftly for my gaze caught the hem of a silken gown in a delicate
pale primrose yellow. I raised my eyes to the wearer's face. Rowena
and her father had entered the inn yard, and were standing beside
us. I leapt to my feet poking Abram in the ribs and we bowed to
our visitors. I was able to plead my excuses for failing to return for
my dinner on the night when Edwards had imprisoned me, and they
were gracious enough to accept my excuse. I presented Master
Smith and his daughter to Sir William and Robert and suggested to
Dickon who came to serve us that perhaps Master Nichol would
allow us to have a flagon of Taint. Rowena asked for cherry wine
as she had heard that Taint could be rather a strong cordial for a
lady's brain.

"You have a brain, do you, madam?" Robert asked sourly. I
confess I felt embarrassed by his lack of courtesy

"Indeed I have, Colonel, and would ask that you do me the
honour of playing me at chess," she answered him, not saucily but
firmly enough so that he might know she had felt the insult. He
inclined his head and smiled grimly, and a moment later asked to be
excused.

"As you can see, I am no longer wholly a gentleman!" he said bitterly indicating his truncated arm, with an angry glance at Waller. "And I would beg you to excuse me!" and left us. Sir William sighed, frowned at Robert's retreating back as he mounted the stairs from the innyard and told me he would seek me out on the morrow.

"Doctor Tom, we have a proposal to put to you." James Smith took a taste of Taint and nodded appreciatively.

"A proposal?" I said, suddenly apprehensive. Rowena laughed. "Fear not, Tom. We do not have designs on your liberty. You may still wear your yellow hose, like all the other likely bachelors."

"Mistress, I am a widower." I told her. "And my loss is recent and still raw."

"I am sorry, sorry indeed," she revealed a trace of impatience. "But that is not to the purpose. My father has ascertained that as you, the Colonel and his Corporal are working in support of Parliament, you could be quartered at the town's expense. Now he has managed so far to avoid the performance of this civic duty.... the opening of our doors to whoever the Mayor shall delegate to receive our free quarter, but now circumstances have dictated that we must comply. So, there are four of you are there not?" And she smiled enticingly at Abram. "If you would enter our household, it would ease our minds and purse and should the enemy be at the gates, it would be comfortable to know we have champions indoors." She paused and looked at her father, expectantly. "Have I said well, Sir?"

"Excellent well, daughter. You see, Tom, all would benefit. We can claim rent for you from the Common Council, and you would no longer have to pay John Nichol, not but that I am sure he provides excellent good value for your guineas, but I have ascertained that he is turning Waller's Captains away and his servants are working uncommon hard. You voice is to be loudest among the warlocks in the event of a siege and indeed you are looked for in Babylon daily, where you have done yeoman service. What do you say?"

This was an excellent notion, particularly for Abram. An inn was not the best of places for a fourteen year old boy. Although Master Nichol guarded against excesses it was impossible for him to prevent roisterers and wild blades gathering to make merry, and there had been instances whilst we had been there, of "the legs that carry in, cannot carry out". For me, come to years of discretion, such behaviour was of little attraction. I tried to avoid drinking to excess as I hated the sick feelings the next morning brought. But Abram was at an impressionable age. The moderation that a family household practised would be a better yardstick for my adoptive brother.

It was not only drunkenness from which I should be protecting Abram, however. Master Nichol had maids in his establishment who served the customers. Occasionally when a man had drunk too well, he might offer a lecherous insult to these young women. I did not wish Abram to assume that this was acceptable or usual behaviour. All this went through my mind as we sat in the hot July sunshine. I sent Abram in to bespeak a light meal.

I wished to accept there and then but knew that I had better consult Robert, who had generously paid for our food and accommodation at the New Inn. Also Master and Mistress Nichol seemed to be pleased with our company. Abram liked to make himself useful to our hostess and her maids, and his tall handsome appearance and his golden complexion attracted admiration. I had observed Robert gazing at him in a bemused fashion, as if wondering how such an exotic young gallant could have strayed into his orbit. For some reason I could not identify, this attention from Robert made me uneasy.

All this I had to consider. Rowena and her father were silent, sipping their wine, waiting for my answer. Finally I said, "I would certainly like to accept your offer, but perhaps only for my adoptive brother. An inn is no place for him and he has already been at work with Master Walsh, ascertaining what tinctures might be essential to treat wounds, and what other apothecaries in this town have in stock, so it is true to say that he is certainly working for the communal safety. But Robert is a horse of a different colour. Although his wound heals well, he does not. He was maimed by a mad surgeon, a relative by marriage of William Waller and is grievously bitter towards Waller and his wife. I have no words of comfort for him because I think his arm could have been saved. But Waller expects him to be the genial Colonel he was before this dreadful amputation. The Colonel cannot forgive him and depends at the moment on liquor to ease his pain, brandy wine in fact. I do not think he would be a comfortable guest. I would feel disloyal if

I left him now. He needs me to dress his wound and to cut away any diseased flesh should he become gangrenous, though with every day that passes that fearful prospect becomes more remote. His Corporal Ralph is used to him and well able to care for him. Your offer is generous in the extreme and I accept but only for Abram."

I had made so many speeches that morning that I was feeling like the Town Cryer. My throat was sore and I had begun again to feel unwell. I had decided to visit Master Walsh for another dose of his aconite tincture. As it was I must play the host, with as good a grace as possible. When Abram returned with slices of cold fowl and bread and cheese, I judged it best to take the bull by the horns and tell him of the proposed change whilst he was basking in the warmth of Rowena's smiles.

To my surprise he did not object to being parted from me. "For we will but be a few streets distant, Tom, and I will easily be able to find you, and I can talk to Master Smith about all the ideas that flock into my head because you are often too anxious and tired, Tom. And I can help Welsh Gwyneth in the kitchen and play with the boys from the Babylon families."

It seemed almost as if he had anticipated this event. I knew not whether to be pleased or sorry that he could so easily adjust to living in a different household from myself. I was pleased that he was confident and assured, but I had grown used to having a younger brother near me at all times. True, he was a responsibility, but he had been a great help and I knew I could never thank him enough for finding me in the Dungeon. As well as this, I relished his company. No doubt of it, he was a diverting companion. So it was with mixed feelings, I helped him pack his belongings into his knapsack and told him that he must find me every day. Noon would be a good time when we could eat together. Rowena had also insight into my feelings. When we came down from the Gallery, she invited me to join them for dinner whenever I could. It was strange to watch him walk away from me under the arch with them. I almost ran after them to ask him to stay, but I told myself, "An inn is no place for an impressionable youth."

I took myself to the Apothecary's to ask for a draught of the aconite tincture. Master Walsh took one look at me and sat me down, scolding me. "Tom, you have done too much, too soon." He felt my brow, and nodded. "Your blood is over heating again. Come let us get you back to the New Inn." He gave me the tincture and then locked his shop, and walked back with me. I had to admit I was pleased he accompanied me, as I was experiencing the swimming sensation again in my brain. He saw me to my room and instructed me to disrobe whilst he sought out Mistress Nichol. He returned with her, carrying her favourite posset, ginger, lemon and honey but this time she had added brandy wine.

The fever that I thought I had shaken off had returned with a vengeance. In truth I wanted to do nothing but sleep and when I woke with a mouth dry as a long drained dusty ditch, I needed long drinks and asked for boiled water. Mistress Nichol could not believe that I would benefit from water alone and kept trying to substitute hippocras but at last Master Walsh convinced her that I should have what was easiest for me to digest. Days of violent coughing when I felt as if I was on fire followed. The aconite potion calmed me and Master Walsh came every day to administer it. At length one day, I woke up, clear and cool of head and sound of limb. I was also profoundly hungry. I went to my chamber door in my nightshirt and one of the maids seeing me on my feet, ran for Mistress Nichol. I began to dress myself wishing above all else to descend to the parlour to break my fast.... perhaps if she had my favourite? gammon and eggs?

To my amazement I had been ill for over a week. Thank God I had arranged for Abram to be well housed away from the temptations of the inn. It seemed he had returned to sit with me every day but I had been unaware of his visits.

Robert was rejoiced to see me on my feet.... again.... and warned me against neglecting my health. "You see how such neglect has served me," he said bitterly, indicating his arm and sipping from his glass. Ralph was more cheerful. "Thank God! you are recovered. The noise of your coughing frightened the ghosts of this place. They have all sought more congenial haunting-grounds."

"What ailed me?" I asked them

"Nay if you, the doctor, do not know, how can we divine your illness?" Ralph was plainly relieved that I was again on my feet. "I kept entering your room and declaiming "Physician, heal thyself." But 'twas to no avail. You would not listen, merely coughed up your innards. Poor Tom. Master Walsh told us not to despair, that your ague would pass, and so it has. But if I were you I would return to your sick-room before he makes his daily visit. He has been assiduous in his care and treatment of you, even though I know he is only an apothecary."

"Only!" I said. "He is my life-preserver"

"It would be best if you were in your room when he comes." Robert agreed. "So good a man as he is. And there is a packet come for you from London and a missive from your friend, Waller." He drew out two despatches from the pocket of his gown.

"When Walsh gives the word that you might descend to us again, there is news, so be prepared."

I scuttled back to my room, anxious not to annoy my deliverer. A chair overlooked the gallery and the inn yard and I sat down and used my dagger to chip away the wax on my letters. Waller's had been written the previous Sunday, prior to his departure for London. He thanked me for my efforts on behalf of his regiments and outlined his plans, should there be a siege.

"I am confident that Charles Stuart will order such an action. I am told by my spies in Oxford that Rupert intends to make for Bristol. In the unfortunate event of his taking that city, it is almost certain that his uncle will set forth for Gloucester, as this town is the only other link in his Severn chain that does not support the arch criminal.

I noted at the hearing that you did not wish to supplant the craven scoundrel, Rice. But believe me, young Tom, you have the capacity to save my boys' lives. You have full discretionary powers to organise clean and safe housing for the wounded, and you above all others, have the skills to cure them… "immediately". How I admired your strategic use of the Gospel!

As I write this it is greatly feared that you might not survive this second bout of the fever. In which case you will never read these words, and it might be thought I waste my labour. But if your parents come to receive your possessions then I rejoice to inform them that their son Thomas was a credit to them and to the great cause of Parliament. I remain William Waller, erstwhile Commander of the Western Association."

I could not forbear laughing as I read the end of his epistle. I knew he meant it kindly, but there was a lunatick element in his addressing my deceased parents, informing them that, although I was dead, there was recompense for them in that I had been an ornament to the great cause of Parliament! This would have been a monstrous compensation for them! Thank God I was not dead. And as I sat there chuckling over his words, I began to imagine the expression on my father's face at reading such news. Whilst I was laughing, I saw Master Walsh ascending the stairs. He paused and looked at me and then hurried upwards to my room.

"William Waller writes to me," I told him, "afraid I am beyond the grave. He tells my parents whom he does not know are both dead, if I no longer breathe that I was an ornament to the great cause of Parliament. "Flatulence Fairground" had been my father's friend's description of the Commons. Somehow this seems mirthful. Better a live donkey than a dead lion, my father used to say."

"Well, my dear donkey, so that you do not join the company of lions, I must insist that you remain in your room today. Stay where the warmth is constant. You have been ill, very ill indeed."

"What was my ague? Was it some infection of the lungs?" I asked him.

"Indeed it was, and one can be confident if you had been a greybeard, you would have been taken to those loving parents of yours. The aconite tincture every day kept breaking your fever and at last now the youthful vigour of nature seems to have banished the last traces of your malady."

"It is due to you that I am still alive," I said briefly. "On behalf of my dear dead parents, I thank you heartily, Sir."

"Young Tom" he said affectionately, ruffling my hair. "Thank me by staying here today. I will come tomorrow and we can speak of our arrangements then, and prepare a plan of campaign. Abram has listed every drug and potion that we apothecaries hold in our shops. We must sit and decide what more needs to be distilled. I am told you already ate a good breakfast. Eat and drink, young Tom. Rest today. Tomorrow is time enough to think of working. I will leave you now. Harry Armitage lies with his legs tied straight together as I think that was your design for his recovery."

"He should really lie like that for two weeks, before he tries any more unwise heroics such as he displayed on .....?" I could not think when the hearing had been.

"Another week at least then. But you will be well enough to see him yourself long before that. I must open my shop. I'll leave you,

Tom."

And with his gown flapping around his long stick-like legs, he was gone. I turned to the packet that had come from London post haste. When I had cut through the linen that bound it, I found there were three letters there and I settled myself to read them with eagerness. The first and longest was from Julius.

"Sad indeed were we to leave you, Doctor Tom, upon Lansdowne Hill, beset with difficulties. I confess I prayed for your safety as we skirted the King's Army which seemed to be preparing to move. By God's Grace they were not concerned with us. Even so we stayed out of the wellworn tracks and made our way by deep lanes and wooded hillsides to Chippenham and beyond to Marlborough. Thence to Newbury and now I judged rightly that we did not need fear challenge. There were after all three of us: thanks to you, we were strong in health again, and again, thanks to you, we had money. We kept south of Reading remembering Prince Rupert had not treated it well and came at last to Windsor whence it was a hard task to encourage the boys to leave the inn we found where the landlady had monstrously pretty daughters. And so home on our excellent cobs which I assure you, we did not tire overmuch.

John felt that it would be best if he sought out his mother alone. He had such heavy news to tell her. The loss of his elder brother, Moses, would be a fearful blow, such an excellent youth as he was. But at the Shaw household there was general rejoicing at the return of "prodigal" Jacob and they were kind enough to include your humble correspondent in their welcome.

I was relieved that the two rooms, which I had vacated were still available to me. No-one had approached the landlord wishing to rent them. Indeed they are not palatial, Tom, but should you come to London, be sure I shall accommodate you as well as I may. But to the purpose. Next day Sir William Waller's letter safely buttoned into my doublet, I set out for the Tower with a heavy heart as the last time I had been within the portals of a prison, at Laud's instigation, I knew not if I should again see the outside world. I walked through the houses and shops which now encroach on its very walls and a dismal walk it was as the great bastion hid the cautious sun. I was admitted near the MiddleTower but then came the obstacles. I was loathe to allow one of the warders to take my precious letter from me. Waller had written "To be placed by the bearer in the hands of Sir Isaac Pennington, Lieutenant." The servile knave who received me in a gatehouse in the Byward Tower would not allow me direct access to the Governor and bade me sit and cool my heels whilst he found one who might mediate. And so I sat and waited, holding Waller's letter to my heart. I sat there for perhaps an hour, whilst men came and went with warrants to visit prisoners. In truth I was beginning to reflect what could move this antic Cerberus if a letter from William the Conqueror held so little weight, when I heard the name of the man I hated more than any other in this land.

"Laud's Commons are arrived," announced a servant of the Tower, unwittingly witty, nodding in to the gatekeeper. The guard rose and went to the door and passed on one in baker's garb whom I took to be from a pastry cook's. Now my ire began to get the better of me.

"What!" I cried. "The arch-torturer is allowed tasty dainties in his prison. Look, Sir, how the fiend has ravaged my brow!" I removed my hat and pushed aside my fringe, with a view to horrifying the wretch and taking my leave. But my disclosure had the opposite effect. It was "Sir, forgive me. I will take you to Pennington at once. He will wish to know the history of this outrage!"

Leaving a minion in charge, he hurried me through gate and corridor across the open green and finally stopped as he saw a man emerging from the church of St Peter ad Vincula.

"That's he!" he informed me. "Advance and tell him what you desire."

It seemed a long distance that I had to cover to accost the Lieutenant. I did not know his title, but I improvised. "My Lord Lieutenant!" I called out.

He paused and waited for me. Thank God I was sober suited still. No lace, no finery. I later learned that Sir Isaac was a Puritan, so rigid and ascetic in his views, that no man dare speak an oath in his company. The guard remained beside me for a moment.

"My Lord!" he cried. "Observe this poor fellow's brow! Show him, Sir!"

Thus encouraged I pushed my hair aside again and had the satisfaction of seeing Pennington wince in horror. "Come, Sir," he said, kindly taking my arm, "Let us sit and you can tell me your suit."

"I have a letter from Sir William Waller for you." I told him.

"Well, well, I shall read it, never fear. But how came you so hideously scarred, my friend?"

I decided to censor the truth with care. An inner caution warned me that a playwright might not be considered an embellishment to the Parliamentary cause. "Something I wrote, pleading for moderation from all excesses, My Lord."

"Come," he said. "We'll to my quarters, and you shall drink a draught of small beer and I will read this letter."

In fact I was thirsty and glad of the refreshment. When he had read the letter, he said with a smile, "Well, the Earl of Chesterfield is not a man after my heart, but I confess that there is that about him, a quality of honesty and hilarity perhaps, that appeals. He and his knights are in the White Tower, but when Parliament has the upper hand as seems likely soon, they may gain more freedom, as they surrendered the Close in Lichfield, without much bloodshed. May I ask what is the nature of your "sad news" of which Sir William speaks?"

"Alas, Sir," I said confidently, as I had now got the measure of this noble, dignified gaoler. "'Tis the death of his niece, the much loved wife of a doctor friend of mine. So that you know I mean no treachery, please you stay with us whilst I impart the tragic news."

"That will I!" says the well meaning turnkey, "But not for I distrust you, good Sir. But so I might offer the service of my chaplain in the Chapel of St John the Evangelist, where the Earl and I might pray together after you have gone."

And so, at long last, well after noon, I was brought with the Lord Lieutenant to the White Tower. We climbed high, in truth I know not how far above the ground. I did not care for my elevated status when I peered through the slit windows of the staircase. I was relieved that there seemed little ceremony in the Earl's rooms when we craved admittance.

He sat before a fire, without his hose and shoon, whilst one anointed his large, noisome, yellow feet. He looked up as we entered and said in explanation, "Gout, my Lord Lieutenant. I am plagued by it. But an apothecary nearby has at last produced a salve from comfrey which gives me ease, by the Rood!"

Pennington winced at the oath, but kept his composure. "My

Lord, this gentleman brings you news. If you permit it, I will wait until your conference is concluded." He moved to the edge of the room and sat, clearly prepared to wait patiently.

"Alas, Sir," I said, as he raised his bushy red eyebrows in enquiry towards me. "I bring sad news from Doctor Tom Fletcher."

At your name a man playing chess with a youth rose and came over to us. One other man lowered the book he was reading and two others who had been speaking quietly together turned to hear our talk.

"What ails good Doctor Tom?" asked the Earl.

"My Lord, Tom is well, but sadly I have to tell you that your dear niece Phoebe is no more. Tom and she were married in April and in June she died. It is thought that she was with child, that was not in her womb. It is not a common cause of death for women carrying children, but it is not unheard of."

He stared at me, his brown eyes brimming. He said nothing but slow tears fell down his cheeks. The young fellow left at the chess board called across, "Father? What is the matter?" He came across to the Earl who grasped his hand and pressed it to his face. "What news have you brought him that so unmans my father?" he asked me.

"Lady Phoebe..... Lady Phoebe has died," his chess opponent told him.

"What was it Peabody said of her? That she could make soup from a sausage skewer." one of the other men said with feeling. "Do you remember the cinnamon rolls she made from nothing? A rare genius of a woman."

"And so my friend Doctor Fletcher mourns her. He should have been here in my place, but Waller forbade it, needing him to care for a friend, and so he wrote a request that I should come instead to give you this heavy news."

"Who are you?" asked the Earl's son.

"I am one whom Tom Fletcher rescued from desperation," I told them. I decided that it was not necessary for them to know more.

The Earl had recovered himself and said, "And knowing Tom as we do, no doubt he would think we should blame him for her death, after marriage and consummation. Tell him he is blameless. I have heard of this sad early death when a woman is got with child. And I thank you for a task that you must have deemed would be thankless. My Lord Lieutenant" he turned to Pennington "May I ask leave for this man to receive a missive from me, to send to my niece's widower? If you will wait a few moments, Sir? Ned, have you a quill and ink?"

"I have, Sir," said the man he called Ned, "and if you permit it, Sir, will write my condolences on the parchment, when you have concluded."

I enclose the missive from the Earl. After he had finished, he resumed his hose and boots and walked over to Sir Isaac whilst the man he called Ned wrote a final message.

"Come then, Sir Isaac,"said the Earl to the Lord Lieutenant. "On this occasion I am of your mind. I know you would wish me to go and pray with you and on this day, if no other, that may well ease my aching heart."

Then he called across to me, "And I thank you. I thank you again, my poor scarred friend." My hands flew to my forehead. I had neglected to arrange my hair carefully over my disfigurement.

And so I left the Tower, my task completed. Two days later, Jacob and Master Shaw sought out Master Benjamin Knowles, and I enclose his letter.

Tom, our rescuer, accept again my heartfelt thanks. I have obtained work near St Paul's assisting a bookseller. Let us hope we meet again on this earth. Heaven seems uncertain and remote. God bless you, my friend Tom."

I sat back in my chair and gazed out of the window at the inn-yard, where I had sat with Julius. His letter brought back so many memories, of Phoebe and Elijah in their fearful walk across the causeway in Lichfield with the other hostages, of the good fellowship of the knights of Derbyshire (Surely this "Ned" must be none other than Sir Neddy, my fellow herald) of Peabody capering like a green girl to the tune "And canst thou dance the bobbin jo?" I laughed heartily at the memory, but found I was not laughing but weeping. My dearest Phoebe, my darling girl, so early taken from me. Elijah, an apprentice but much more friend. I had relished his sturdy independent spirit. In times of war, death and its tragic consequences had to be accepted and life itself compelled us to continue. The pain of loss was itself lost in the demands of constant action. I still bore a burden for them both. Perhaps if I had not behaved in a certain way they would both be still alive.

There was a flash of spring green on the staircase and Abram was with me.

"Oh, Tom! It is true! You are better. Robert said you were! What is your wish? I will bring it to you from the Market. Captain Thomas Blaney sought me out to pay me. What think you of that, Tom? They have paid me for my lists and penmanship. Oh Tom, forgive me, you are sad."

"There are pockets of sadness in my brain." I told him, "but generally there is no time to be sad, and I am pleased that your efforts are appreciated and rewarded. Well, I have no doubt that you have eaten the fat of the land with the delightful Rowena. Could you see if there is any fish here for our noon day meal? I cannot remember when we last ate fish."

He hurried himself downstairs and I looked at the second letter enclosed with Julius' excellent account of his visit to the Tower. The Earl had written in haste but his words were welcome beyond price.

"Tom, good boy, your scarred friend brings desperate sad news. Ferdinand and I cannot forbear from weeping as I write this, but you must not reproach yourself. I could see that the pair of you were destined for matrimony, such excellent understanding as there was between you. The condition that took her from us has killed many other women. I have heard of it before. Childbearing is the lot of womankind and it is fraught with danger. I know you would have given her the best of care. Believe me, she would have been happy indeed to marry you. Poor sweetheart, not many men would seek out a deformed wife, although her many virtues and talents outweighed her distortion a thousand times. Remember! a few weeks' happiness is worth a life time's misery. In these terrible times we cannot know from one day to the next what God, Fate or the Earl of Essex has in store for us.

I thank you Tom for letting me have this tragic news. Better to know in this manner than to hear by chance from those who care not. I append my signature and one who remembers you with affection appends his also.

God bless you, good boy. Philip Stanhope, Earl of Chesterfield."

And below that in another hand, were the words,

"The saddest of news, Tom, but I rejoice that you, my fellow herald and doctor beyond pariel, still live and I hope, prosper. Your friend Sir Neddy Deering."

I admit that this short letter lifted a heavy load of guilt from my soul. Since Joan's terrible and uncouth accusations, I had somehow felt that perhaps there might be truth in them, in spite of the logical facts of the case. I was after all only twenty. A respected older woman, a revered friend of my family, such as Joan, still had the power to reduce me to uncertainty and doubt, and the uncomfortable awareness of my youthful inadequacy. With the Earl's testimony, I must now have the courage of my convictions. After all, I was Ben Knowles' pupil. I had had the best teacher any young Doctor could have desired.

And with that I turned to the third and last letter enclosed in the linen encasing and saw the familiar spidery hand of my master.

"Well, Tom, what are you about, valued cousin, and brother physician? You were last seen, I hear, and my letter from you was written in a humble cot on Lansdowne Hill near Bath, with Robert Burghill, lately raised to Colonel but hideously disfigured by some mad sawbones of Waller's. Your friend Julius tells me you were on your way to London to give the sad news of dear Phoebe's passing to her uncle in the Tower. Setting aside the fact that the road to London from Worcester does not usually encompass Bath, (no doubt, Tom, you had your reasons, you always did, hordes of them!) I am confounded by the fact that you have left your good practice in Worcester, that I nurtured with such care. Well, enough of my upbraiding!

I thank you heartily for your letter. My father and myself were rejoiced to hear from you although your news was heavy indeed. The symptoms of Phoebe's final condition were accurate. She would not have recovered. As the child grows in the passage from the ovary to the womb where it should never remain, it destroys the organs of its mother. It is a rare misfortune but not so rare that Joan should certainly have heard of it. My thinking is that she did in fact know of this circumstance but it served her irrational anger to deny that she did so. I will return to that. But Tom you need not reproach yourself. Your use of morphia was good. You gave your wife a peaceful death. Some who despair of these times would claim that this was in some way a blessing. I cannot quite say that... nor would you wish me to... but that she did not suffer, is thanks to your perceptive doctoring. I repeat no need to heap coals of fire on your long suffering head. When two people marry, this carries unknown and unforeseen consequences. To speak as an objective physician, had the poor lady been impregnated a day before, nay a minute before, or after, she might well have borne a healthy child with no problems. Chance, sheer chance, dictated the outcome. Poor Tom! You have been grievously unlucky. No-one must reproach you and I beg you do not reproach yourself.

I am distressed also by your news of Joan. Again your diagnosis is accurate, painful though your experiences with this lady, previously so wholesome and happy, have been. I spoke with a Syrian doctor who came recently to London who claimed that women of this age are at the mercy of some sort of glandular excretions into the body. I confess I did not understand this and of course we can never have any way of ever proving such a theory, but it is of interest. It seems excessive hard that after all the pain and turmoil of child bearing years, a woman must lose aspects of her soft appeal. You ask if there is some simple that might bring Joan back to her original self. Time is perhaps the healer here, although I am sure you might have thought of a borage infusion for depressed spirits. A calming effect is produced by bergamot and the berries of the hawthorn judiciously distilled and administered. But you will be aware of these remedies. There is no cure as such for the termination of menstrual bleeding. It must happen to a woman who is of a certain age, nor would a sane woman wish to bear children into her dotage. As I implied above, the passing of time seems to cause all to be tranquil again.

I must thank you, Tom, for the introduction of young Jacob Shaw. He is proving an asset and has an admirable curiosity. He has the patience that you displayed with small children. I confess that I find it exasperating beyond measure to have to summon up the balm of compassion for them. He speaks of your healing the arm of a "lobster", the timeless art of bone-setting. In this area too Tom you bid fair to outstrip your master.

My father wishes me to be betrothed to a second or third cousin, I know not which. I insist that you travel here to act as my groomsman. The ceremony will take place some time next year. As previously promised the fatted calf shall be killed for you, good cousin Tom, my brother. I must give this parchment now to your friend Julius. It seems he has learned to use the scars of Laud to his advantage. When he displays them, he is hailed as Prynne's follower and is denied nothing in this city, though that politician was even more hideously disfigured than your friend. We are fortunate that he has been granted access to My Lord Essex' system of message carrying, though I suspect he would willingly have forgone this advantage for a smooth brow, poor fellow.

I am as ever Tom, legally you loving cousin but in warmth, and sad and happy memory I trust you will still think of me as your brother, Ben."

I sat back holding my letters. I did not feel happy, never that, deprived of Phoebe, but for the first time since her death, I felt content. I was not responsible for her passing. If both Ben and the Earl could reassure me that I was guiltless, then I would no longer bear that burden. How blest I was in their friendship!

I spent the day, resting in my room, reading my letters again and again. Abram brought up some bream that Mistress Nichol cooked to perfection for us, and then later after noon, Robert came in bringing me a belamine of Taint. He told me he preferred the brandy which he now seemed to drink continuously. As I gazed at him I could see that he was changed. His face was thin and lined, where before he had been full faced and of a healthy colour. I resolved to talk to Ralph again regarding his master's consumption of brandy. I could understand that it had dulled the pain of amputation and even lifted his mood slightly, after the maiming took place, but now perhaps was not the moment for me to "preach" as Robert termed it. As he most logically observed, I had not been mutilated.

"How are you, Tom? Still recovering after two hearty meals?"

"I hope so, Robert," I told him, "and I wish you would allow me to pay for my bed and board."

"No!" he rapped out. "No! Never! For me, you gave up your pilgrimage to London. The least I can do is bear your expenses and those of the bright young popinjay you call your brother. Where are you hiding him? I have not seen him since you again were made to take to your bed."

"I did not think an inn was a wholesome place for such an impressionable youth." I said as pleasantly as I could. "You have news you said."

"Aye, that I have. Bristol is fallen to the Royal Malefactors. This

Page 280

was two days ago on the 26th. I can predict that time alone is our ally. The dogs will come here, and we must watch Massey like hawks."

"If they already have Bristol, why are they not already at the gates?" I asked with a sinking heart.

"I think they wait to see what Newcastle will do," said Robert. I understood he meant a nobleman and not a city. "If Newcastle will march down the Eastern counties to London, then Rupert will travel eastwards to support him. Believe me, there will be consternation in the Commons now. All will be up and down like a whore's skirts in the Capital today. Perhaps we are safer here. Massey has acted the capable commander. Whether he is sincere for Parliament you must discover, Tom."

"How may I do that?" I asked. I had no notion of being a spy for anyone.

"Your friend the apothecary has insisted that there must be a meeting to plan for the wounded in the event of a siege. Massey agreed. Both heard Waller's words on the subject, and Waller is still the Governor of this town. If you are well enough, it is planned for tomorrow at noon, as I remember it, in Massey's house."

"In the state-room or in his parlour?" I asked.

"Nay they are both alike to me. I have no notion. But watch that Massey."

"But surely he organises well. Worcester was poorly prepared for Waller's attack, and yet we prevailed against him. Massey has worked tirelessly for the Gloucester walls."

"Tom, what matters it how strong the walls might be? Massey has merely to open a gate to invite Charles Stuart in to enjoy his roast beef and plum pudding. And there is now little impetus for work among the lads in the Garrison. They are drunk with indifference. Keep your eyes and ears open, I beg you. And let me warn you. Tonight we have a visitor. The illustrious Member of Parliament for Gloucester. Watch your words, Tom. Perhaps as well not to reminisce about your friendship with Rupert. Pury is not a jovial mortal, but I am glad he is returned. He of all men can stiffen our resolve and fire our hearts."

I reflected that no doubt, similar sentiments were heard in Bristol before it was overrun by the King's Men, making free of the liquor and women. My instinct was to run to the Smith's fine house, extricate my younger brother, and continue running to the Quay to wait for passage up-river. But I seemed to have thrown in my lot with the fate of Gloucester and my old friend, Robert. He could clearly see in my face my distaste for allying myself with Parliament.

He laughed a little at my discomforture. "Poor Tom. These wars have not helped your "neutrality" as you call it." He sent Ralph down for more brandy, ignoring my disapproving expression.

"I can tell you this, Robert, and this is gospel truth and no gainsaying. A broken leg has no politicks. I have two maxims in my life these days. The first is to heal broken bones wherever I come across them, and the second is to honour and be loyal to my friends and to serve them as well as I may."

"And I cannot claim that those sentiments do you aught but honour." Robert was plainly concerned that he had caught me on the raw.

" You know, Sir, you have said to me yourself. Rupert would never, never have let mad Dick Allen within a mile of the humblest of his sick troopers." This was a verbal knife, twisting in Robert's heart and he knew it. I was immediately contrite. "There, Robert. Forgive me. I will not speak of Rupert tonight. You can rely on me. I will be as sour and sober as any old Puritan as you shall meet in a month of Sundays, by the Mass!"

He laughed at my effrontery. "Aye, good boy, Tom. A still tongue gives no offence." Ralph returned with the brandy. I asked what Robert had eaten this day so far. The guilt that suffused their countenances, revealed the answer. Nothing. I began to scold Robert but he laughed again and said, pleasantly, "Nay, Tom spare me your pronouncements, son. Pury will preach enough tonight for that month of Sundays you spoke of."

I hastened away to Harry Armitage. His leg was mending well. I had never dealt with so complex a fracture, and was gratified that by following the teaching of my master Ben and using Time as my ally, I had effected a cure where all had seemed hopeless. He might limp and lurch somewhat, but he would walk unaided. Grace pressed me to stay to eat and drink but I was afraid I might be late for the all-important meeting at the Governor's house.

I was early. The servant showed me into the state room and I sat idly, gazing at nothing, waiting for my elders and betters. A door opened behind me near to my chair and two invisible persons entered the ante-room. It was Massey and his servant Foster Pleasance. Unaware that they were overheard they continued their conversation.

"So I should wait, you believe, do you? until Pury has poured fresh heart into the Garrison? There seems little ambition amongst them to hold out. What have you observed?"

"Bristol is a sad blow, Sir. But perhaps it is a little early to despair. After all, the King's party is not at the gates…. yet! I would advise caution for some days, Sir. Sometimes the best policy is to do nothing."

"And yet Jamie Legge has devised a means whereby we might meet without suspicion. It irks me, Foster, that we must serve different masters, so good a friend he was to me. I deplore this shedding of blood."

"Indeed, my Lord, particularly one's own!" and they laughed together.

At this point it came to me that these were words none other was meant to hear. I coughed loudly, and immediately they were silent and Massey appeared in the doorway.

"Why Doctor Fletcher, we were not aware of your presence. Why did that scurvy knave not inform us of your coming." He was clearly embarrassed, the colour coming and going in his cheeks, like a green girl

"Lie, Tom, lie!" advised my guardian angel as I bowed obsequiously.

"My lord, I have but ten seconds ago been admitted to your stateroom. No doubt your servant went swiftly below to be speedy in admitting your other guests. I think I hear them coming."

There were steps on the stairs and Master Walsh, Abram and two other apothecaries were admitted. Then the Doctor who had seemed to be laughing during the hearing, came in, with something of the hangdog about him. He came straight to me.

"Doctor Fletcher, I am Doctor Henry Creery. Forgive me that I did not speak for you last week. Rice holds the purse strings. I cannot revolt, much though I wish to." I told him that I had sensed his support and was grateful for it.

He clasped my hand warmly and muttered "You set the cat among the pigeons, no question."

"Did I so?" I replied as pleasant as a pig in pudding time. "And you, Sir, are clearly the rose amongst the thorns!"

"Well, I think they are worse than thorns." he told me. "Not a one of them would come here today, to speak of saving our brave fellows. Ah, we begin I think."

After our meeting there could be no doubt in my mind that Massey was a good man at anticipating and solving difficulties. He had the subtle gift of imagining the worst that might happen and taking steps to avoid it. We devised a method whereby if a man was hurt by the attackers, he should be instantly brought to the surgeons who would wait in houses near the walls, in rooms that had been ready prepared for the wounded, with supplies of bandages to hand and with swift access to the apothecaries and their stores. No soldier who was injured on the walls would have to wait for treatment. Like our Blessed Lord, our response would be "immediate."

As I walked back to the New Inn, I remembered where I had met James Legge, the friend Massey mentioned. It had been in Lichfield. He had almost drawn his sword against Lord Digby in defence of Peabody and myself, and then had been in charge of the gunpowder that Rupert had painstakingly collected. He had been a friend of Rupert's, a good friend, a capable major in his confidence, and if Massey was a friend of his, then for me I held Massey in more regard. What in fact had I heard? Nothing to the purpose. The need for patience had been expressed, and the fact that Massey had an excellent good friend near Rupert was mentioned. What had Robert said? "A still tongue gives no offence." I resolved that my tongue should be still as stone.

10

Ideterminated that I would at the very least attempt to appear worthy and sprightly for our revered member of parliament so I decided that I would wear my new doublet and breeches. The tailor, Master Simmonds, had sent it round with a message that it so happened the weave of the fabric had been more than usually difficult into which to insert the needle, and could he in courtesy request an extra two guineas? Abram, who had come to find me for our daily conference, came with me when I went to pay the extra money and then insisted that we went into Master Rawdon, the mercer's where nothing would do but that he must buy me some blue silk hose, bought with the meagre sum he had been paid for his clerkmanship by the city.

It could not be denied. The new suit of apparel fitted me excellent well. I sat with Robert that night, who sipped at his brandy wine. Together we waited for our guest, an old friend of his, and I vowed I would try to keep my clothes clean. Ralph had told us that he would serve us but I refused to allow that. "Sit down, eat your fill, you varlet, and have done with your rattling!"

"Well, Tom, when you are so plaguily courteous, how can I refuse?" and Ralph obediently sat and accepted a glass of taint. We heard our illustrious guest before ever we saw him. As he progressed along from the Cross to our inn in Northgate Street, he seemed to be using the opportunity to tell an unfortunate citizen, much information about Charles Stuart, arch tyrant and traitor who was steeped in blood. Well, I had but to remember Laud's treatment of Julius and the high-handed attitude of Digby and Lord Hastings with his "Do I know you?" to become a whole-hearted Parliamentarian... for perhaps ten minutes, until I remembered my poor father's terrible death, when neutrality edged out any partial notions and restored sanity.

Pury entered the inn, leaving a few admirers outside, clearly expecting more of his oratory. Robert glanced at me, afraid that I might be unmannerly but I sat docile and modest and waited with eyes downcast, like a virgin in a knocking shop. Alderman Pury was directed to us by Dickon. He bowed to Robert, nodded to Ralph and myself and bestowed himself on the bench set ready for him, and took a cup of Canaries brought to him by Dickon. He had a fine head of fair hair... once. Now his pate shone through and served as a reflection for the candles in the wall sconces.

He leant across the table and took a pinch of my doublet between his fingers, and spoke for the first time.

"Cheyney?" he asked.

"I believe so, Sir," I agreed.

"From Master Rawdon perhaps?"

"Yes, indeed," I told him.

"A good honest trader. An ornament to our guild. There are so few of us now in Gloucester. I am a clothier, and your patronage does you credit. Who made it for you?"

"Master Simmonds," I informed him.

"Hmm!" was his response. "That sorry, money-grubbing, prick louse!" Then he turned to Ralph. "And who are you, young man?"

"Forgive me, Alderman Pury. I should have presented my Corporal Ralph Holtham. He wished to serve us but Doctor Tom who dislikes the notion of servitude would not permit it." Robert smiled cunningly, as he if he knew Pury would take the bait.

"Good! Good!" the Member of Parliament was pleased with that.

"When Adam delved and Eve span
Who was then a gentleman?" he quoted smiling benignly. "So, Doctor Tom, was your father a doctor? Have you followed in his footsteps?"

"Sir, my father was a Worcester butcher and there are those who would unkindly say that I have followed his trade."

He regarded me sternly. "Not amongst those whom I have met. They say naught but good of your doctoring."

I bowed my head modestly. Alderman Pury did not jest... ever. His words were untainted by levity. I attempted to move the conversation forward.

"That little rhyme about Adam and Eve, Sir? Who said it? Who wrote it? I remember my father saying it when his cousin Alderman Sir Nicholas Knowles of Worcester was high-handed about his fellows."

"I will tell you," said our guest. "It ran round the country and was repeated from man to man when a rebel called Wat Tyler threatened the capital. It was the text of a sermon preached in London at that time in 1480, was it? Or perhaps 81? It is not a new notion, Doctor Thomas Fletcher, to wish to convince those who consider themselves superior to their fellow men, that they are not."

"Indeed, Sir, our Redeemer himself spoke of the difficulties of those who consider themselves to be above others when they wish to gain the Kingdom of Heaven. We have but to remember the episode of the widow's mite." This pleased him greatly and he smiled at me in approval. I wondered briefly who was this pious young hypocrite who could engender these religious truisms, who seemed to live in my body and who now sat, sipping my wine, and spewing forth the Scriptures with a long holy expression like a beaten bum.

"Sir, we heard you speak of Charles Stuart as a man of blood. Do you think then," I asked, hesitantly, "that this King is more of a tyrant than those who have gone before?"

He looked at me, frowning, then said, "What does that matter? They have all been tyrants."

"Indeed, yes," I agreed. "I shudder and cannot sleep when I think of the eighth Henry's barbaric treatment of the leaders of the Pilgrimage of Grace."

He stared at me. "But they were all Papists," he said dismissively.

"But mostly poor men, not nobly born?" I turned to Robert to support me, but he had dropped asleep. Ralph smiled politely, offering no support of my argument.

"Do you then support Charles Stuart?" Pury was beginning to be less pleased with me and sat forward frowning at me, a lean angry countenance, his bald head shining.

"No, I do not," I told him firmly. "But I am not sure that he is Beelzebub reincarnated. When I met him at Edgehill he seemed concerned that so many of his subjects had died... both his friends and those whom he deemed to be enemies of the Crown."

"You met him?" he said incredulously.

"During the course of my work, healing the wounded," I smiled as I remembered the comedy of Elijah and myself suddenly brought face to face with the King's Majesty, in the night after the battle.

"But Master Pury, I think you may have history behind you or rather before you. The daughter of William Shakespeare, the widow of a most excellent physician, told me that she believed that the future lay not with the well born. She cited an instance of arrogant discourtesy towards her husband by the Earl of Northampton, who had been successfully treated by Doctor Hall. I saw the Earl die at Hopton Heath, because he scorned to yield to poor men who offered him his life. I remember Mistress Hall's words clearly: "They may think they have birth, but we have the skills, the talents, the genius, if you will." You are the future, Master Pury. Perhaps I also have a part to play, but you can make and influence our lives. The King is of the past. It is men like you who are the future."

He leaned back on the settle, looked at me and smiled again, an expression that did not come easily to him. He plainly liked my words and to an extent I believed them myself. Why should not a man who began life as a humble tradesman be a Member of Parliament, representing the Gloucester citizens? Truly the man was, in some sort, an admirable example.

"I pledge you, sir." And I raised my glass to him.

"Your words resonate with me and do you credit, Master Fletcher." And at that point our host of the New Inn came to tell us that he had jugged hare "Thanks to a certain clever young blade!" he told us, looking slyly at Ralph who raised his eyes heavenwards, the picture of innocence.

But Robert ate so little and drank so much that he gave us all cause for real alarm on that night. Our fare was excellent, but as the evening progressed, it became clear that Master Pury was as concerned as we were by his old friend's behaviour. Robert would make sour jests about his maiming, saying that he had given Waller "a free hand" at Lansdowne Hill and that he must now play "hand i'cap" for good and all, as being the only game he could play. He would laugh long and bitterly, laughter in which we could not join, as such misplaced hilarity was painful for all.

Suddenly he rose and announced that he must retire for the night, saying roughly, "Come Ralph, come sweet Rafe, let's to bed." Ralph helped him to his feet and Robert, without looking back or bidding Master Pury "Good night," made for the stairs. It was the devil's own task for Ralph to help him climb to the upper floor. Robert stumbled and I went behind to catch him should he fall. But at length he was in the relative safety and privacy of his bedchamber, which I confess I was happy to leave. There was that about the relationship between the Colonel and Ralph that I did not understand.

I came down slowly to Master Pury who had risen partly in alarm at Robert's condition and partly because he too wished to return to his home. He said shortly, "Well Doctor Tom, I thank you for the excellent good dinner. Jugged hare was ever a favourite of mine but I fear we have a hare in a hen's nest here. Can I do aught to help my friend, Robert Burghill?"

I grasped his hand gratefully. "Dear Sir, continue as his friend and mine, I beg you." He nodded and we arranged to meet the next day to go round the walls, after I had been to Babylon. He wished to put fresh heart in the defenders after the storming of Bristol and I wanted to tell any that might wish to hear that medical help would be swiftly available to any who were injured.

There had been a distinct fall in the spirits of the citizens of Gloucester. The news from Bristol was a sad blow to all who favoured the cause of Parliament, and that in fact was the majority of the inhabitants. The rumour was that Nathaniel Fiennes, who had governed Bristol, was gone to London to face trial.

"In fact," said Master Pury as we strolled round surveying the labours of others, a pleasant but ignoble pastime, "in my view, Nat Fiennes has done more for the cause of Parliament than your friend,Waller. On the day that I left the capital he arrived, banners flying, trumpets blaring. William the Conqueror indeed. I know you were not at Roundway Down but was the fight on Lansdowne Hill so conclusive a victory for him?"

"No, it was not," I said, remembering the horror of that day and night, "and I dare say that if the Cornishmen had not lost their beloved leader, Sir Bevil Grenville, Waller would never have prevailed. But we heard that Roundway Down was a fearsome disaster for Waller's foot."

"Aye, he lost an army," said Pury grimly, "William the Widow-maker is more apt than Conqueror. But still the Londoners love him and in he rode, like an overweening Roman general. At least Nat Fiennes saved lives by surrendering Bristol when he did."

I nodded sagely like an old grey-beard outside an ale house. "And I am told that Bristol is a large city with a longer length of walls than we have here. If Rupert had decided to take it, believe me, he would do so, come hell or high water."

"Well, hell is what he gave them by all accounts. You speak of that spawn of Lucifer, as if you knew him, young Tom," and Pury frowned at me, with a hint of menace. "First you confess you know Charles Stuart and now the foreign nephew. Perhaps next you will tell me you have been the Papist whore's abigail."

"Master Pury, if you knew how my father died, hung shamefully as a spy, in error by the Earl of Essex.... ask Robert if you can catch him in a sober moment if you doubt my words.... then you would not question me about my allegiance. As I have often said, Sir, a broken leg has no politics, and it is tending the wounded with which I am concerned. I admire you, Sir, greatly for your representation of the people of Gloucester. Be assured I shall do nothing to further the cause of the enemy of this city."

I looked down fiercely upon his bald head. He nodded, "In fact, I have no fear of your loyalty to the well-being of these poor men and to this city," He nodded at a party of troopers who were filling a breach with earth. "No, I do not fear your neutrality, Doctor Tom. But there is one in command whom I do not trust. Still let us see what transpires."

The air was filled with smoke and smuts as some houses without the city were being razed to the ground. It had been decided however to empty the suburbs before burning most of the dwellings. But the inhabitants had been instructed to leave their homes already. Around the Cross, sad little family groups were huddled together, children were crying and old women wailing. But every so often a citizen's wife would approach them, seize the howling infant and bid the rest of the family to follow her. Accommodation was being found all over the city for these fugitives from beyond the walls. It seemed Edward Massey had directed that those within must assist those without. He had visited the houses outside the walls, and his watchword had been, "What good is your house, if its owner is dead?"

A party of women and youths were coming towards us as we stood near the Eastgate. They were pushing barrowloads of earth ready for the troopers, who directed them to pile it on a great heap. One Master Bower was overseeing the strengthening of a gun emplacement. The woman, who seemed to be the leader of the party, turned and called and waved to me.

It was Rowena, in a coarse hempen gown with an apron made of a hop sack, tied around her slender waist. There was a smudge of dirt on her cheek.

"You see, Tom, I have put your brother to work. His idling days are over."

To my amazement I realised that one of the young fellows who was shovelling the earth under the direction of the troopers was Abram. I called to him and he threw down his spade and came running over to us. He had abandoned his fashionable yellow hose for a pair that seemed more serviceable and suited to his task.

"Tom, there you are! Rowena is a hard task mistress. Is it time for our midday victuals?"

"Now, Abram, I pray you, make your bow to Master Pury who is the respected Member of Parliament for this fine city."

He did so, murmuring, "I am honoured, Master Pury."

"So, my fine young fellow, where are you from?" asked Thomas Pury. I knew what answer he was expecting. Algiers? Morocco? Tunis? He received his reply.

"Birmingham, sir," said Abram politely.

"Abram is my adoptive brother," I explained. "He lost his parents within two days of each other, when Rupert wrought his worst on that industrious little town. He has been my guardian ever since. He has done yeoman service here, assisting Master Walsh to identify and list all the medicaments and knows where all the supplies of bandages and splints are to be found."

"He has been your guardian?" said Alderman Pury in disbelief.

"I speak in jest, sir. In truth, we guard each other. I deemed it best that he should stay in the Smith household rather than the New Inn, so sweet Mistress Rowena" (and she came up to us wiping her lovely soiled hands on her rough apron) "has undertaken to be his protector whilst I have recovered from a chest infection that laid me low."

She curtsied to Alderman Pury and asked him, "So, sir, what do you think of my good maids? I vow they work as well as any team of rustic youths. The troopers are hard put to it to have filled the breaches, before we are back with another pile of earth." She turned to her friends. "My maids, your courtesies to good Master Pury."

They called out their greetings and blessings, and one could see he was flattered by their civility. But the man who was not moved by Rowena's grace and beauty must have had a heart of stone. And then her "pretty maids all in a row", they made together a most charming argument in favour of female enterprise and ability.

I promised Alderman Pury my most loyal co-operation as a doctor, but begged to be excused from aggressive endeavour. He held my arm for a moment, saying "There are problems enow in the New Inn. Your healing skills are all we seek." Abram and I took our leave and walked with the teasing girls back down Eastgate to the Inn where we parted from the female taskmasters.

John Nichol immediately came and sat with us, as we hungrily addressed ourselves to his excellent Cheddar cheese. He had concerns about Robert which I shared. Firstly he was dismayed at the amount of Spanish brandy wine that Robert was consuming, which was in his words, affecting the "Colonel's well-being" as he politely termed Robert's health. "He is baptising himself as one of the faithful, as we say in these parts. He is never sober, Doctor Tom. Would it not be best that you, his doctor, forbade him these strong liquors?"

"Indeed it would," I admitted," but would he listen? He would simply find another means of supply."

"And there is my second difficulty!" said our good landlord. "Now that Bristol has fallen, it is going to be weeks before the trows come upstream with a cargo of strong drink again."

I was suddenly stricken. What of Lofty and his crew of good fellow sailors? I had selfishly not given them another thought, whilst Rupert did his worst to the place whence "The Pride of Bristow" had its origins. It was all I could do to prevent myself from rushing headlong from the Inn along Westgate to the quays. I resolved that I would go and search for news later in the day.

"I fear I have scant supplies," John Nichol was complaining. "I can buy direct from the vintners, but they charge more than the watermen, and then I could go to fellow innkeepers but with the likelihood of the oncoming siege, they will want handsomely rewarding. If the Colonel could be persuaded to restrain his consumption, and to eat more heartily as was his wont, then all would be well. He will listen to you, surely?"

"I can try yet again." I said doubtfully.

And then John Nichol voiced his innermost fear. "I fear, Doctor

Tom...." he said hesitantly, "I fear that his hold on life is... slipping. I fear that he no longer cares if he lives or dies. Most men will live for their wife and little ones. He is married and has children. But they do not seem to be of interest to him. Can you not remind him of his duty to them?"

"I can but try." I said again, reluctantly.

But in truth I held out little hope. I had no real influence over Robert. There was that in his nature that I could not understand. Ralph now seemed to be his representative to the rest of the world. Robert was certainly "lacking in interest". The phrase brought back a moment when I, a gangling twelve year old, had faced my dear old schoolmaster. Master Moule had wanted to know why I was so indifferent to the perils of Aeneas. Bless him, he had tried to invest life into those dry old Roman escapades for us ungrateful scholars. I had murmured something about how a future butcher could have no time for Dido, and I had turned and rudely slouched my way from his presence. Indeed the prospect of a life of butchery had produced in me a complete lack of aspiration, which had resulted finally in my ill judged suicide attempt. In what was Robert now interested that would give him again a zest for life?

Ralph came down to us, as if in answer to my concern. "Now, Tom, thank God you are here. He has a searing pain under his heart, he claims. He tried to rise earlier but to no avail."

Abram returned to his work on the walls and I went up to see Robert with a heavy heart. The day was dull, close and hot, usual weather for the end of July, yet the casement was fast closed and the room, warm and noisome. Robert lay in the untidy bed, propped up against pillows with his knees drawn up towards his belly, the classic position when a sufferer seeks to mitigate internal pain.

"I told you, I did not want to see Master-Holier-Than-Thou-Sawbones," he cried out to Ralph, who was behind me.

"Nevertheless, here I am, dear Robert," I said placatingly "Come to see if I can relieve your pain. Is your arm painful?"

He sighed, and said with resignation, "Well, it is inevitable I suppose. I cannot stand against him forever."

"Who are you fighting?" I asked curiously.

"The chopfallen fellow with the scythe. Some call him Death, I call him Waller." He smiled grimly to himself. "No, my arm itches and aches and sometimes I swear my lost fingers return until I open my eyes and they are gone again. But regretfully it does not putrefy. My pain which has been increasing by the day is below my heart but today it has travelled round to my back, and has alarmed Ralph, as now brandy does not deaden it."

"May I examine you?" I asked him.

"If it must be so."

I was shocked by what I found. Robert himself resembled nothing so much as "the fellow with the scythe", in engravings of the plague. Each of his ribs protruded and now I looked at him under the bright light of day, his skin had a yellow hue. I asked him to tell me whence the pain had its origin. He touched the hollow under his sternum, but when I did so, he let out such a yelp of agony that I determined that I must seek another opinion. I mixed a little of the opium powder for him, and bade him drink it in water… not in brandy as he proposed. As I went down to seek out Simeon Walsh, Ralph followed me.

"Tom, there is something else."

I turned and faced him at the head of the stairs. I had never seen him so distressed. He wiped tears from his tired eyes with the back of his hand and composed himself.

"I should tell you, I think. He does not now excrete much. As you know he does not eat, but what he does pass is …. unnatural."

"Unnatural?" I asked him. "In what way can a turd be unnatural?"

"Very pale and stinking more than is natural."

"Ralph, leave him now. He will sleep for an hour or two. Sit and rest while you may. I will fetch Master Walsh. In truth we are blessed with such an apothecary. There is little that he has not seen. We will both feel better when he has seen Robert and given his diagnosis."

"What is yours?" he said, grasping at my arm.

I paused before answering. "Not good, I fear. But let us wait for Master Walsh."

As I walked down the stairs, I permitted myself a gleam of amusement. Of what did Ralph believe excreta should smell? Roses? But Master Walsh's countenance when he left the bedchamber after examining Robert, was grave. We sat in the inn-yard over a stoup of Rhenish and compared our impressions.

"It seems that an organ of digestion, somewhere below the heart is distended beyond what is usual. Or maybe there is a growth that distorts on the organ itself," he was thinking aloud, "And I know of no treatment. What is your opinion, Doctor Tom?"

"I think as you do," I told him, "And the organ in question, whatever it may be, is damaged irreparably by the brandy wine he insists he must imbibe." It seemed to me suddenly that the Rhenish wine I was drinking with a clear conscience could be just as dangerous a potation. I pushed it away and Simeon laughed and pushed it back in my direction.

"No, my good boy. You are in no danger. Moderation in all things. But the question is - What's to do for the poor Colonel? I can make a syrup of hops and also give him camomile to drink which will ease the jaundice. You have the skill and the means to ease his pain, if you administer morphine with care. But his case is incurable, in my view. And also.... I do not think he wishes to be cured."

"John Nichol said that," I told him, "A sad sort of doctor am I! All who I care for, my apprentice, my wife, and now my saviour Robert, all die. I owe Robert my life." And I was suddenly overcome.

"Well, son," said the apothecary, "It is said that we all owe God a death. And here comes one, who the Colonel's death will affect far more deeply than yourself."

Ralph came out to join us and gazed at us with a questioning air. Finally I said, "We have not much hope. If he continues to drink strong liquor, he kills himself. Something stops the course of his food through his body. We will do what we can to ease his pain which will, I fear, become worse without the poppy drug. Do you want to consult another physician?"

Ralph shook his head silently, and sat for a moment staring at the servants going about their tasks. "Tom, forgive me. Sir Edward is within, wanting to know how Robert fares. Will you see him?"

Simeon took his leave, saying he would be back with camomile and syrup of hops, and I made my way inside to find Sir Edward seated with one leg crossed elegantly over the other at the knee, accepting a glass of taint as being the beverage preferred by Doctor Tom. Our good landlord bustled about, something overcome by the honour of the presence of the Deputy Governor... or the Governor now as I believed he was.

Governor or Deputy he came straight to the point. "I have written to the Speaker of the House of Commons explaining that with the fall of Bristol, I and the citizens are close to despair. Indeed Doctor Tom, I will be honest with you. In order to save our lives and immortal souls, I am close, very close to throwing all upon the King's mercy. I need Colonel Burghill's advice. He has been in sieges aplenty in the Low Countries. I must use his knowledge."

I was doubtful as to what kind of reception he would provoke, and sure enough although Robert greeted him with a surly courtesy, he refused to be drawn on the subject of the most effective tactics for resisting the forthcoming siege.

"Ask Waller, the murderer!" he shouted and Massey came quickly from his room, wrinkling his nose in distaste as there was now an unpleasant aroma in the air about poor Robert. I led Sir Edward back to his seat and tried to explain Robert's bitterness.

"It is certainly the terrible loss of his hand, no question, but there is a personal grudge against Waller because he continued to employ a mad surgeon at the behest of his women folk. Robert does not.... cannot like women. I know not why. Here," and I stripped my sleeve and showed him the puckered scar where Allen's sword had pinked me. "That same mad surgeon wounded me for nothing at the Siege of Worcester."

Sir Edward's rather doleful countenance suddenly brightened. "You were at the Siege of Worcester?"

My heart sank. "Er, yes, indeed. But a most unwilling participant. For both armies."

I had said too much. "Both sides?" he asked, and beckoned to John for another glass of taint. "How so?"

There was nothing for it. I told him the whole story of my escapades during those two days at the end of May. He listened very closely, and asked, "So William Sandys burned the suburbs as I am beginning to do now, and cleared the land before the walls. Merely, would you say so that he could see and resist any assault on the walls?"

Who was I to advise on military strategy? "No, Sir Edward. And indeed if Waller had launched a sustained attack at certain points the walls would have crumbled like dry parchment. No, I do not think so. I believe Sandys' strategy was to pick off the Parliament gunners with his marksmen. One of them ignobly killed Waller's herald. And indeed when Waller slunk away on the morning of the 31st, he left behind a dismal harvest of those poor gunners. He had the worst of it and Sandys held Worcester for the King."

"So, as I understand, Sandys made a sortie on the second day. Did you witness that event?"

I was beginning to feel like an old veteran. "I did not, sir. As I told you, I had to tend men who were poisoned in Waller's camp. I was trapped in the woods to the east of Worcester until he left."

"So in effect, you saw both sides of the siege."

I was beginning to find this reiteration of my noble deeds excessively wearisome. "Only as a doctor, sir. I assure you, I am no tactician. But I must congratulate you, sir. Gloucester is much better prepared with its fortifications than Worcester ever was, and since the Alderman came from London there is a good spirit amongst the people. "

He sighed and stretched out his elegant legs. "It is difficult, is it not, Doctor Tom, to know what to do for the best. Do you believe that the King wishes our deaths?"

Here was a question indeed. I gave the same response as I had given Alderman Pury. "At Edgehill, sir, he seemed to grieve for all alike, during the night that followed the battle."

"Of course, you were there then. You are an experienced valuable man, Doctor Tom."

His approbation appalled me. "Indeed I am not, sir. I am but a simple Worcester doctor, recently widowed, not two months since."

Again he mistook craven cowardice for humility. "Your modesty does you credit, Doctor Tom, and I am deeply sorry for your loss. All this...." He spread his hands wide. "It may all come to naught. There might be some means of compromise.... Will you continue to advise on preserving the health of these poor citizens?"

"Indeed I will, sir." I was on safer ground now. "The first matter we must consider is adequate supplies of clean water. I know you have good stores of dried fish and meat. You have an excellent brain for managing possible emergency. I have observed this with admiration. Not like the Earl of Chesterfield. We ran out of food in Lichfield Close after three days."

He stared at me. "You were there too?"

I rose and bowed. "I will tell you of my experiences at Lichfield and Hopton Heath when we have both more leisure, sir. You do me great honour."

Massey had a long high coloured face, with cheeks rosy as a milkmaid's. But his countenance had a melancholic caste. Now he smiled, and his expression was joyful.

"Would you look into the means of storing and preserving water? The first action of the King's Men will be to cut off the supply from Robinswood Hill. We are almost into August, which promises hot and sultry weather. Yes, I have stored enough food for a month, but water is another matter. Apply to Thomas Blaney for any expense and the Council also will finance you. Speak to Alderman Pury."

He took his leave and left me with a Herculean task. I knew though, that clean water would ensure good health. How to set about it? Dickon came out with bowls and spoons to wash in pails with water drawn at the well in the courtyard. There was no reason and less time for delay.

"So, Dickon," I asked him. "Does this well ever run dry?"

"Not to my knowledge, Doctor Tom. Never since I have worked here."

I picked up the linen cloth he had brought out with him and began idly to dry the rinsed bowls and platters.

"But not every house in Gloucester could have a well as deep and pure as this one?" I asked him.

"No, indeed, Doctor Tom. Master and Mistress are blessed in this water." he told me. "The common sort of folk goes to the public stone troughs where the water from Robinswood is piped."

I stood thinking, idly polishing a great bowl. "And that is clean, safe water?"

"Oh, ah, Doctor Tom. The last time the plague was here was fifty years ago. And my old Grandad said it was travellers brought it up the river."

"Does the water from Robinswood flow underground all the way to the city?"

He stood upright and frowned. "I think it do, sir. It starts at a place they calls Ladywell. Our water's come from there for years, 'tis said."

So it seemed clear to me. Reasonably clean water was flowing daily into the town. What we must now do was preserve as much as we could, in the event of the Royalists cutting off the supply.

Where was Abram? He now knew the whereabouts of all the tradespeople in the town. As if in answer to my thought, he appeared round the corner of the arch, still clad in his earth moving apparel.

"You are to come to dinner tonight. Rowena will take no denial."

"No need then for you to hasten back to tell her I will come if she takes no denial. All is arranged. Listen, I need your knowledge. Where are the coopers of Gloucester? Are they all in one street?"

He frowned. "There might be one near the Cathedral, by St Mary's and I think there is another down near the Quay. But there must be more than two in a town this large."

"Indeed there must." I said hastily. "Well, to the Cathedral then and since I am an "experienced valuable man".....Massey's words, not mine.... you can run in to the Smiths and accept on my behalf whilst I pledge my soul to the cooper by St Mary's."

So we began our quest. I knew that the Council would support me financially. But if the King did not cut off the water, it would be money and labour wasted. But what a world of science and knowledge, I was soon to discover, went into the manufacture of what seemed a simple wooden cask.

Master Paul Fowler, master cooper of Gloucester was brought from his bread and cheese by his apprentice and stood looking at me, his hands on his hips.

"Get back to your work, Sim, else it's stick pie for supper with lacing pudding to follow!" he ordered his apprentice, who grinned and scuttled away, but stood and listened within earshot. "And what might you be, coming here and offering Council money without word from Alderman Pury?"

"Believe me, Alderman Pury will support me, Master Fowler. Sir Edward has asked me to arrange the storage of water in the event of a siege." I told him humbly.

"And you are?" He had accusing eyebrows like clumps of hawthorn, that met over his brown eyes.

"My name is Thomas Fletcher. I am a doctor from Worcester."

"Tom Fletcher, eh?" He suddenly roared out, "Molly!"

There was silence. Then a voice from within the house beside the yard shouted, "In a minute, Paul. God save us, I only have one pair of hands!"

"Ah," he said thoughtfully, "I thought you had more!" and he winked at me. I began to feel more confident as one does when a stranger shares a jest.

Molly came wiping her hands on her apron and stopped short at the sight of myself and Abram, who had quietly returned to my side. "Now then, Margaret," said her husband formally. "What do you know of Doctor Tom Fletcher?"

"Why, naught that's bad, all that's good." she said at once, "My gossips speak of him daily. He and his brother... that is you, my fine young blade... have arranged all with Master Walsh, should our dear fellows be hurt by the bullets from the Godless Papists."

"And now I am charged with storing fresh water," I explained.

"What's amiss with the Severn?" asked Master Paul.

Molly answered for me. "What?" she screamed, "I would not give Severn water to a blind donkey!"

"No, indeed!" her husband agreed. "Your mother has best muskadine when she visits." And as she seemed to be about to explode with wrath at him, like a round rosy grenado, he observed cheerfully, "Well, what's to do then, lads? I take it you want a supply of my barrels. I've a score here, ordered by the watermen but never a hide nor hair of them, since Bristol went to the wall. Where will you store your Adam's ale? Have you thought of that?"

"What do you advise, sir?" I asked diplomatically.

"Do you know, I would think Bartys is least likely to come in the way of the King. The river protects it on two sides, and it's far from the walls so should not take any batterings."

"And the man acting as warden there, Absolom Hooker, lately come from the Forest, will, I am sure, help us again." I began to feel enthusiasm for my task. Master Hooker had complained that there were few residents, so that the storage of water in the main hall of the hospital might well work in his favour, bringing more lambs to his sheepcote.

"Now then Doctor Tom. these score of barrels I am selling to you is each and every one a tun, so you shall have over two hundred gallons in each one. So that is four thousand gallons you can keep for the good citizens of Gloucester. But I doubt it will be enough. You must to my brother coopers, and the vintners too, God save us. I can guess that they will be monstrous pleased to give you their empty hogsheads. For now there is no traffic downstream, so we are all in the same boat. Or rather we are not!"

I arranged with Master Fowler that the barrels he could allow us should be collected next day and filled at the nearest public water trough, and went my way with Abram to find the cooper on the Quay. St Bartholomew's Hospital was on Westgate near the Quay and we stepped reverently through the door. Absolom was immediately visible, sweeping the floor, but at the sight of us he threw down his broom and came over to greet us.

"My dear friends! I had heard you were ill, Doctor Tom. You do not object to the familiarity but everyone in Gloucester now knows you as Doctor Tom. I am pleased indeed to see you on your feet again. A weakness in your lungs, the good apothecary told me. But now hale as ever!"

"Yes, indeed, sir and I thank you for your kind greeting!" I looked round hastily. The building was large and well aired, a good place for storage. There were a few benches and some stools along one wall but certainly there would be no need to clear the building. I asked Absolom to accompany us to a watermen's ale house on the quay. He was well pleased to abandon his housewifely duties and as we walked by the river, I reflected that there might be news of Lofty.

After consideration, Absolom was well pleased to donate the main body of the hospital for the storage of water. He would have preferred live bodies to swell his little flock, rather than barrels, but when he knew that Sir Edward would pay rent for the space and that almost inevitably many citizens would need to visit Bartys with their jugs and pitchers, and that they would be unable to escape his sermons as they waited in line, he was able to promise on behalf of his cousin, the warden, that this would be an acceptable arrangement. His cousin, it seemed was something lacking in his frame of sense now, though harmless, and Absolom found himself the Jack at a Pinch who now fulfilled all the warden's duties in the hospital. Indeed, I never heard a man read the scriptures with so much feeling as he did, and I told him so. I could not promise to attend his services but at least this was the second time I had swelled the coffers of Saint Bartholomew.

And indeed this man was no Bartholomew Pig, being a lean bare-bone of a parson. As we sat in the hostelry, the landlord announced to all, "The pies are ready, gentlemen." There was an immediate quickening of interest amongst his customers.

"They are, indeed, monstrous good pies." said Absolom, large eyed with poorly disguised longing. So I bought three and very good they were, guinea fowl in a most tasty white sauce. Abram as ever quitted himself bravely but I found I could not finish mine. Absolom humbly in a manner that caused my conscience to prickle asked if he could have what I could not eat for his wife at home. I immediately bought a fourth pie and insisted that he took it for her. He was gracious enough to accept and exclaimed, "Why Doctor Tom, you have turned the tables on the gospel. Christ exhorted me to "Feed my lambs." But it seems to you he commands, "Feed my shepherd!"

I noted that I must swiftly arrange payment for the storage space. It seemed St Barty's was one of the places of hospitality used by the watermen. Absolom had not seen or heard of any of them lately and nor had mine host. I paid our account and asked directions to the cooper on the quay.

He too had empty tuns waiting for collection from watermen. He was supervising two apprentices, overseeing their carpentry as they shaped the staves with adze and a range of draw knives. The cooper who claimed everyone knew him as Old Nol, invited us to see the tuns.

"They are so watertight, young sir, a man might drown in one of them," he told us proudly.

I remembered my father's story of his uncle, an imaginary relative perhaps, who tragically drowned in a barrel of brandy but who had to be helped out twice in order to urinate. Peabody and I had laughed immoderately at this tale on our ride from Stafford with poor Elijah's body. Now again I recounted the foolish nonsense to good effect. Old Nol had clearly heard the jest before but one of the apprentices laughed so violently, we feared he might choke. I judged it better that we left before I remembered more of my father's stories.

As we walked back down Westgate, Abram asked me to tell him more of my father's jests. As always happened in such moments, the memory becomes an empty blank tabula rasa, but then I remembered a riddle from my childhood.

"Very well then. How many cows' tails would stretch to the moon?"

He stopped in his tracks, and looked at me attempting to calculate.

"Why, thousands and thousands I should say."

"No, only one, so it be long enough."

He began to fight me in jest, raining light blows on my arm, which I laughing gently deflected, holding him at arm's length as he danced like a mock prize fighter in a fairground. We proceeded some little way indulging in this undignified horse-play, when who should come upon us in this brotherly mock combat but Alderman Pury himself?

"Why Doctor Tom! What means this?"

We collected ourselves and bowed low. "You must excuse the high spirits of youth, sir," I said humbly. "I was in fact coming to seek you, amongst other errands."

"Well, here I am!" he told us, unnecessarily. "Sir Edward bids me offer assistance in your task for a water supply that will sustain us during the siege."

I told him what we had already achieved, asking firstly for payment for the two coopers and then for reasonable rent for the storage and distribution at St Bartholomews. He nodded approvingly.

"Good! Good! This is well done, Doctor Tom!"

"But, dear sir, this could be the difference between life and death for the Gloucester citizens, particularly for the poor who depend on the water troughs from Robinswell. I will need help in filling these tun barrels we are buying and swiftly too, lest the King should cut the supply if he arrives."

"I fear 'tis when, not if he comes. There is news from Bristol. Edward Donne tells me confidently that a trusted spy informs him the King's Men are about to muster and start a slow march north towards this city. We must take time by the forelock in the matter of water. If you can find barrels and hogheads, I will get Massey to give me troops to fill and take them to Bartholomews. We must act swiftly while the clean water flows. I will put out a proclamation that every tradesman that has clean barrels must put them outside his shop ready for collection and filling."

"That is excellent, sir," I said humbly, "The task was swiftly becoming too extensive for my brother and myself alone."

He nodded and said again, "This is well done, Doctor Tom."

And so we parted.

In truth I looked forward greatly to an evening without care. My "Care" had assumed the form of Robert, sick, drunk and angry. I went briefly to ensure that Master Armitage continued to make good progress. He was now in his own home; the long hall of Babylon was no longer inhabited by sick troopers but by the families of the Cathedral servants and their footballing sons. Abram went to the Smith household ostensibly he claimed "to help Rowena" but I believed to taste the contents of each cooking pot. He seemed to have the free run of the kitchen. Even the Smith's angry cook indulged and loved him, and the maidservant Welsh Gwyneth idolised him. Why had Joan not liked him, I wondered idly.

I asked Dickon to pour buckets of water over me in order to be acceptably sweet smelling for the Smith household and put on my Cheyney doublet and the blue silk hose. Robert and Ralph were sitting downstairs, Robert having reached that stage of drunkenness that could best be described as loquacious, at worst quarrelsome. He exclaimed over my uncharacteristically fine appearance.

"Well, here's a popinjay!" he cried out as I sat on a stool beside him. "Here's fine feathers for a rare fine fowl! What sweet, easy mort gets the benefit of this rig-out, pray?"

"Now, Robert," I said jestingly, "I must ask you not to make free with the lovely Rowena. Her comeliness is matched only by her sagacity."

He snorted, "That pole cat! A saucy partridge with a tongue like a whetted knife! Take warning from one older and wiser than yourself, young Tom. But enough of this! Hast heard the dreadful news? John Nichol whom I have lifted from penury by my sojourn here, can no longer supply brandy wine. When you have served your doxy, Tom, sail over to France for a cask of the best. For you, you are the miracle worker, are you not? Sir Edward tells me so, Alderman Pury tells me so. Master Walsh does not speak but 'tis a paean of praise for Doctor Tom."

I was in two minds how to take his raillery. He could say what he wished of me but I would not listen to him insulting Rowena. I did not wear a sword which was as well or I could have drawn it. Some cautious instinct held me back and I managed to say in like manner, "As I recall, the lady challenged you to chess. But I must remind you, you were too much the gentleman to accept. As for the brandy wine, could I suggest that good Mistress Nichol's rabbit pie washed down with small beer makes a wholesome and tasty substitute."

"Yes, yes, we are here to eat and drink like Doctor Tom's good little moppets!" he mocked, grinning in grim mockery.

"Well," I said finally, "I am glad to see you merry, Robert, even if it is all at my expense. And tomorrow which is the first of August we must review your expenses. I must now pay for my bed and board, as you now feel naught but bitterness towards me."

He looked suddenly stricken. "No, Tom. Forgive me. My mutilation speaks, not my heart. Bitter is the word but 'tis towards Waller that I direct it. Sadly you come in the way of it. Go now to your tryst."

I laughed. "It is not a tryst, merely dinner, with Abram and her father overseeing any love-making at all times." And happily I parted from him when he was in a better humour.

There was in fact another guest, Edward Massey's chaplain, a small passionate cleric, whom I could describe as a fiery thunderbolt who informed us that Gloucester men and women whom I had seen labouring so diligently for the security of their city, were determined to succeed for the true faith. Every other sentence was a text from the Old Testament and he dwelt much on the ungodly, and explained that those who walked not in the path of Peace, Love and Righteousness would be smitten by the right arm of the Lord and made to dwell in the burning deserts in the outer reaches of Hell.

"Will you have more cherry pie, Master Corbett?" Rowena asked him sweetly after one such diatribe. When he heard I came from Worcester he asked me if I knew his great friend from Kidderminster, Richard Baxter. "A mighty clarion call for the reform of the profane and impious disciples of the apostate Laud!" he declaimed, sprinkling us liberally with Rowena's excellent pastry. I replied that I had heard the gentleman gave stirring sermons, but before he could upbraid me for my lukewarm convictions, I asked, "Surely, sir, the people of Gloucester are cheerful because they feel confidence in their Governor? He has shown great foresight and good management. I understand there is food for a month."

Master James Smith interjected, "Aye and I hear that some of those who beg at the church door and who receive scant charity are praying for the siege to start, for then they will be fed."

"Yes indeed," I said picking up the subtle thrust of our host's argument, and remembering a quotation I had heard but recently, "The precept "Feed my sheep" is a most powerful exhortation of our Saviour"

"Yes indeed," said Master Corbett, "But our Saviour was speaking of spiritual food. Nourishment for the soul."

"Was he indeed?" I said, and rather boldly continued "But a man cannot benefit from spiritual salvation if he lies dead in the gutter from starvation!"

Corbett's eyes widened and Master Smith suppressed a snort of laughter.

"My dear young Doctor!" said Corbett, in patient kind tones, "If this infidel King had not drained dry our coffers with his inhuman taxes, there would be no beggars. I have said before and will say again. Nothing is so deceitful as the notion of Kingship which is the source of all mischief to the church of Christ."

"How true that is, sir!" I agreed with all my heart. "When one considers a wretched martyr could die in the flames proclaiming that mouldy bread and rancid wine were not the body and blood of our Saviour and a few years later another poor soul would die the same cruel way by ascertaining that they were just such sacred objects. Henry the Eighth must be languishing in those barren deserts of which you spoke. An evil turncoat of a King. The source of all mischief to the church of our loving Saviour!"

"I was not speaking of Henry the Eighth," Master Corbett said slowly.

"Were you not?" The Devil himself would not silence me now. "As I understand it, Master Corbett, Henry espoused the cause of Luther so he could marry a beautiful Protestant wench. She however gained nothing but lost her head. You are right certainly to condemn the ways of Kings! Here's to their confusion!"

By this our host was laughing outright. "Come now, good John, my old fellow scholar! We were at Magdelen together, Tom. Doctor Tom disputes well, does he not? Were you at Oxford, Tom? You would do well in Debate!"

I had to confess I had learned my trade, bound as an apprentice to my cousin. I bowed humbly to Master Corbett. "Forgive my impertinence, dear sir. I am but an ignorant provincial doctor."

He smiled grimly, "No need for apologies. My old friend reminds me of the indiscretions of youth. You have but reinforced my case against kings in general and for that I thank you."

"But we were praised for our argumentative personae, were we not, good John? Do you remember? The Fellows named us James and John, the sons of thunder."

John Corbett laughed. "And we would dispute over any subject that came our way. That was a happy time. And you had your ambition from the first. I recall you saying when we met in Michaelmas Term, that you would wed the Master's pretty daughter or be hanged as a doddypoll!"

"Did I say that?" James chuckled. "Well, the blessed girl did take pity on me and lives again in her daughter, the light of my life. Rowena, Doctor Tom will take another slice of your excellent cherry pie. Yes, my darling child has inherited my brains and her mother's handsome looks!"

"I assure you, sir," said Rowena, diplomatically, "it would be all the same to me if it were 'tother way about!"

"Quod erat demonstrandum!" shouted James. "This girl is a paragon. Have you seen her with her friends bringing soil to the walls? Who needs a son? She is metal to the back."

Rowena simply sat and smiled. She had produced an excellent meal. As Abram had gone to his bed an hour before, I attempted to pay for his board, but was refused.

"Is my money tainted?" I cried out. "No-one in Gloucester will take it. Not the Smith household, not Colonel Burghill! Why am I not allowed to pay my way?"

"My dear young fellow," said Master Corbett, with a hint of patronage, "Consider your profession, recollect your skills and talents. You and your adoptive brother are free to leave this city any time you wish. We cannot prevent you. But it is not merely the colonel who wishes to retain your competence, it is Gloucester City Council as well as the Council of War. We need you. You know I am Sir Edward's chaplain and I can tell you he relies on your loyalty. A physician who sets to and cures without recourse to consulting tables of humours and other such irrelevancies whilst a poor man bleeds to death… this man who acts instantly, is the doctor we need. I have heard that you say "A broken leg has no politics". And a musket ball has no humours but the humour of death. There, you agree I think. Clasp hands and a bargain?"

"With a right good will, sir!" I said, leaning over to shake his hand. "But what of Abram, Master Smith? Surely I should pay his shot?"

"He entertains both myself and my daughter," said James. "He tells me about his religion which he calls Islam. I assure you I am now excellently well informed about the great Arab scientists and thinkers. We read about them together. And he helps Rowena about the house. He is an excellent guest and the City Council deems him a refuge seeker so, Doctor Tom, his charge is already paid."

Shortly after this I took my leave. A cold mizzle had blown up the river and large drops assailed my fine doublet. There was also the unpleasant smell of burning hanging in the air and large black flakes from the house fires beyond the walls floated down. I hurried along cursing my ill fortune in that I never seemed able to preserve my clothes in an acceptable state.

I was pleased to see that on such an unpleasant night, there were no more homeless families from the suburbs, waiting at the Cross for hospitality from the citizens within the walls. Ralph was waiting for me, sorely distressed.

"Can you ease his pain?" he asked me. "He seems unable to eat. I can do nothing for him."

I mixed a little of the opiate with small beer, reflecting as I did so that all water that was drunk must now be boiled, if the good health of the town was to be retained. I vowed to speak to Mistress Nichol in the morning about the best way of carrying out such a measure. I carried my draught into Robert who lay with his legs drawn up to his chest in obvious severe discomfort. I was smitten with guilt. Perhaps I should not have left him. However he drank my potion willingly enough and then according to Ralph slept for several hours undisturbed. I resolved to summon Simeon Walsh the next day.

In fact I had to leave this task to Abram. The storage of sufficient water so that the town could withstand a month's siege had become my responsibility. The vintners were happy to donate their empty hogsheads. I judged that if they had held strong drink it was unnecessary to waste time scouring them out as some goodwives were anxious to do. The alcohol acted as a purifying agent. I knew that I must insist that any water which was drunk must be boiled.

The grocers' hogsheads were another matter. The remnants of food could cause contamination and I asked courteously that they be cleaned of all debris, myself on a few occasions, seizing the scrubbing brush and setting to with a will. There was a willing team of troopers who rolled the empty vessels to the troughs where they were filled and loaded onto a stout cart and driven to Bartys. Absolom was tireless in ensuring that the process of stacking took place with safety. A full barrel, falling and rolling unheeded across a floor, could crush and kill a man. Sir Edward approved of my management. He agreed that we must take advantage of this natural lifeline whilst it flowed steady and pure.

Abram found me at midday and we went to see if there were any pies for sale in the Tavern on the Quay. There were not but there were sausages and we contrived to satisfy our hunger.

"What did Simeon Walsh say about Robert?" I asked. Abram pulled a wry face. "Of course he could say nothing to me. He wants to see you when you return to the New Inn. I don't think he is optimistic."

After another few hours spent, filling, carting and stacking, I was close to exhaustion and happily bade Absolom goodbye and returned back to the Inn which was now my home. I washed my face and hands and went to Simeon's shop, where he was working in his distillery. He blew out the flame that was under a flask suspended over it, and came into his shop, with his customary two glasses of muskardine.

"You look tired, Tom," he told me. "I hear that you have organised our water supply."

"Well, I and others. I cannot take the credit. Sir Edward and Alderman Pury are supporting me, with men and money. Without them, there would be no supply. What do you think of the Colonel?"

He shook his head without speaking. I continued, "Then I will tell you what I think ails him. There is a growth on the pancreatic organ that prevents food proceeding down the usual path of digestion. Do you know of any physician that could remove such a growth?"

He shook his head again. "I know you." he replied.

I sighed. "Simeon, I couldn't do it. I would kill him."

"He will die anyway. I have been racking my brains to think if there is any tincture that could reduce this growth in size, but all that presents is the surgeon's knife. He confessed to me today that he has drunk French brandy for some years but only in the last few months, has he been unable to control the daily amount he imbibes. At one time it was only a pint a day, but recently he has needed (his words) twice that amount. I do not know if the brandy has caused the growth or if the excessive amount he has become accustomed to drinking, has been to mask the pain that he has been enduring."

"I wish Ben Knowles, my master, was here. He has removed gall stones and was able to cut after the patient had drunk several potations of Hollands Gin. We cannot give Robert strong liquor now, can we?"

"I fear it would but hasten the inevitable."

"Well, tonight I will tell him our diagnosis, and if he insists, I will attempt to cut out the growth. I suppose if we gave him enough opiate, he might consent."

I downed my muskardine gratefully and stood to leave. "Simeon, you are an excellent man. I am surprised that you have not taken your doctoral examinations."

He smiled. "For the simple reason that I refer any such "cutting" magnum opus onto you, my dear young friend. I do not have the stomach for it."

That night, after I had dined, I went in to see Robert. Ralph, whom I advised to sit downstairs, dine and take his ease for a while, reported that Robert preferred not to leave his room, until his condition had improved somewhat. As I climbed the stairs I reflected that he would probably therefore never leave his room again. I knocked and hearing his voice went in to him.

His face, a death's head, in the candlelight, gleamed like a momento mori carved on a tomb. He had pushed aside the covers as the night was hot. His limbs were wasted and his ribs were clearly visible.

"May I examine you, Robert?" I asked courteously.

He laughed. "No, Tom, you may not, you whoreson sawbones! Sit, please, and tell me how the world wags. The tide is turned on us yet again. At Powick Bridge you saved me from a premature burial and before Edgehill I had to care for you when that maniac tried to kill you. And now, yet again, you care for me."

I was relieved he was so pleasant. "I have to ask you...." I began.

"Ask away, and if I can I will grant your wish."

"No, it is not my wish. I need to know if you wish me to cut into your belly and see if I can reduce the growth that is preventing you from digesting your food."

He laughed. "In a word, No. And No again and thrice No. I am not long for this world, Tom." He paused and saw that I would not contradict him. "No, Tom. I want to die in peace, not screaming under your knife. But you should know perhaps what manner of man I am and for the matter of that, what Ralph is, also. When you know that, your concern will turn to disdain and your filial affection for me will become dust and ashes."

"Why do you say that?" I asked curiously. "I know the relationship between you and Ralph is… close and strange. It is no matter for anyone but the two of you, as I see it. Should I know more than that?"

"Well, Thomas Fletcher, your view is welcome, but let me warn you it is not the common notion of the common herd. You are exceptional in your tolerance. Men like Ralph and myself are condemned by the Church and yet there were many like us who chose the monastic life in past centuries, many who sought to hide their predilections within the sanctity of holy precincts." Then he pressed my arm with his skeletal hand, "Will you help Ralph when I am gone?"

"Certainly I will. But what about your family? Surely you will want your wife to know that you are ill?"

"To be honest, I do not think Elizabeth cares if I live or die and in one way I cannot blame her for that, as I have not been the husband she wished. As long as she has money. I have two sons, Henry and Humphry, although the younger prefers his other name, Rowland. They live with their mother at Haddenham near the town of Aylesbury. I found that family existence irksome, Tom. Some men like myself can adapt to that way of life, but I preferred ever the company of men. I am a wretched example. There I have done. No need to sharpen your knife, son. I am sorry I have vented my ill temper lately on your blameless head. And I am sorry too that I have insulted the young lady. She is a woman of spirit and they are hard to find."

"Do you want to sleep now?" I asked him. "Shall I prepare a draught for you?"

"Oh, son, if you would. The dreams that come with this drug are sweet and powerful, and of other worlds than this. And the pain, the pain disappears. Bliss, heavenly bliss to be out of pain!"

I mixed the potion and made him ready for sleep. Afterwards, I pondered on what he had told me. I had always found him slightly too affectionate, but had wondered whether I was cold in my response. The cross that I bore was that I liked women, liked them vastly. Not so much I hoped that I gave offence. I did not boast of conquests as some men would do, but I was ashamed that with Phoebe hardly cold in her grave, I cherished carnal thoughts of Rowena. I chided myself constantly for my wayward imagination, but there seemed no way to avoid my pleasant fancies.

At least I had not the fearful burden of forbidden enthusiasm for men. In fact the notion of desiring a man rather than a woman, I found mirthful, like a Mayday game. I remembered Peabody clowning about with handkerchiefs, tripping like a young maiden in Lichfield trying to distract us from our hunger. We had all roared with laughter at his antics. I wished he was here, with his down-to-earth common sense and jollity. The citizens of Gloucester during these tense days seemed to suppress their native lightness of heart. I could not blame them. It seemed an army of many thousands would soon be outside the walls, intent on our destruction.

During the next few days, we continued with our preparations. Barty's Hospital began to resemble a huge store house, barrel stacked on barrel. Thomas Pury insisted that I spoke to the Council on what would be our method of apportioning the clean water we had stored. I made rough calculations and suggested that one pail each household every day would have to suffice. I recommended that if our water was to be drunk to quench thirst that it should first be boiled, and that whilst the supplies ran still from the Robinshill source that all citizens should arrange to wash themselves, to wash all parts of themselves, as there would be no water to spare for that function save for babes in arms, when the siege began. I suggested that Absolom, a devout Puritan and gifted with powers of organisation (to my mind more beneficial for humanity) should be in charge of the distribution of water. There was also the further advantage that he lived there. The official warden was certainly losing his wits.

On the 4th of August, whilst Abram and I were snatching a swift repast at midday, Thomas Pury came asking for Robert. He was amused at a letter that he waved at me. In those grim days it was a relief to be in the presence of laughter and Pury was not much given to a mirthful frame of mind.

"Come up with me, Doctor Tom. This is a nine days wonder, on my life."

Poor Robert lay now constantly between sleep and waking. Simeon and I carefully administered the doses to try to help him avoid the terrible pain from his digestive tract. In fact we could not avoid a certain level of severe discomfort for him in between the morphine draughts. Still he spoke courteously to Thomas Pury, for whom I knew he cherished great admiration as an innovator.

"Now, dear Bob, old friend, this will make you smile. In this letter I am offered monies and lands aplenty, if I will go, cap in hand, to the man of blood. The King's knave offers this to me, who would not doff my hat to Charles Stuart in Whitehall. I who loathe the whole bloodsucking company of Bishops with a hatred akin to that of Christ for the money-lenders. They write to ask me to betray my city. There, you smile, dear old friend. Should I reply? Or should a dignified silence be my answer? Can you advise me?"

"I should do nothing, Thomas," said Robert, wearily. "Do not provoke unnecessary wrath or attention in these nervous times. Read it and laugh. But what of Massey? He could prove Judas even at this eleventh hour. He must be watched around the clock now the eleventh hour approaches. What do you know of his leanings?"

"We know that he wrote to the Speaker, two days after Bristol fell, asking for reinforcements. "Where is Waller?" he wrote. "Where is Essex when we need him?" A genuine cry for help? or is he ensuring that he will not be blamed by Parliament, should he capitulate? The wretch is slippery as a cask of Severn eels."

I ventured a tentative opinion. "I think he wishes to avoid loss of life. Hence his enthusiasm for stocks of food and water."

They turned to gaze at me. I had the impression that they saw me at that moment as a noisome object that they would rather not encounter on the soles of their shoes.

"Doctor Tom is young. He is easily impressed by a popinjay such as Massey." said Robert, in exoneration. "Tom, when these disagreements began, Massey threw in his lot with the King. But they refused to give him the preferment he craved. So he turned to us. His convictions for the Common good are skin deep only. You will remember his impulsive folly which lost him Henry Stephen at Stow on the Wold. He may anticipate problems practically. All commanders should do that, but he can also act like a rash simpleton if he sees his way clear for personal advancement. Nay, I have done. It no longer affects me. Goodbye, Tom Pury. The pain in my belly bites deep."

I gave him another draught and saw him sigh and turn his head into the pillow. In truth there was now nothing of the man but protruding ribs and swollen stomach. When I came downstairs Alderman Pury was waiting for me. Without preamble, he asked simply, "How long?"

"I cannot predict," I told him sadly. "He starves to death. It cannot be long now."

"Days? Weeks?" he persisted.

"I think days." I said slowly. "But he is a strong man. I cannot say."

He clapped me on the shoulder and went his way, clutching his letter. I ordered myself some excellent brawn and a glass of taint, and wondered how long we would be able to eat such good and tasty food. As so often happened when I was alone, my dilemmas rose up thick and fast around me, like a forest of thorns and snares, How could I feel such liking and respect for Alderman Pury, who hated the notion of birth and bishops, who respected a man for what he could do, not for the money his father might have bequeathed him, and at the same time, how could I be so concerned for my good friends in the King's party, Peabody especially. He was constantly in my thoughts. But there had been others whom I had liked, Rupert and his followers. I knew that Rupert was merciless to his enemies, but he had a great capacity for friendship, which endeared him to me. Where should my loyalties lie? Greatly troubled in my mind I wandered up to bed. However, although my thoughts ran around like hunted rabbits in a cornfield, my body took no account of this unnecessary cerebral activity and, as I was dog-tired, caused me to sleep long and soundly.

Next day brought a stream of reports to Edward Donne, Massey's scoutmaster, that the King's army was converging on Gloucester. There was news too of a Welsh army sighted beyond the Severn, slipping through the trees. My mother was Welsh and now her kinsmen were riding out against me. I kept telling myself fiercely, "Your task, bumpkin, is merely to cure, not to kill. You are innocent of any warlike connivance against your countrymen or women, English or Welsh."

There were still a few barrels to fill and the water still flowed. How useless our efforts would be if the King did not order that the water supply should be cut! Abram and I helped the troopers collect the last of the hogsheads from a vintner who had been ill and unable to assist until this late hour. And then at last we stood and surveyed our work. The great tuns were piled up, each on the other to a height of about 12 feet and the smaller hogsheads stood in neat rows. Well, we had done the best we could. Absolom stood there proud as a meagre turkey-cock, his thin neck protruding from the bands around his neck, nodding in approval at our efforts.

I promised Abram that we would survey the walls, the next morning Sunday the 6th of August, whilst the Smiths were at Matins in St. Mary's de Grace. There was still hard work for the troopers of the town regiments, ensuring that our defences were as sound as we might make them. But that night after I had seen Robert and Master Armitage who was slowly learning to walk again, I had a fancy to walk through the Eastgate, and see the burnt suburbs. It was a fearful tragedy for those who had built and bought their homes beyond the walls.

As I came up to the Eastgate through which a narrow passage now led through walls of earth, there were cries ahead of me to allow a groom and four good stout horses to be allowed through in single file. It seemed Massey was expecting these fine beasts as payment of some debt. I stood aside as they trotted past me and asked the Sergeant if I could pass through into the burned country beyond for a breath of air. He was reluctant but Davy Wainwright, who was on duty with him, vouched for me, and I was allowed out into the desolate waste land which now belonged to no man. But a short walk beyond to the south in the direction of Gaudy Green, a thick copse of trees had been spared. I judged that they were too far from the walls to provide cover and to my joy as I wandered towards the little wood, nightingales were piping their evensongs.

I had lately missed the smells and sounds of the natural world. As I roved at my will among the oaks and ash, I caught sight of a fox carrying a rabbit. Reynard was determined that the poor creature should be the meal for his cubs and I followed him or her quietly into a clearing where to my delight, the cubs were playing. I stood and watched them at their gory dinner, but then when they were sated and had begun to play again, my heart stopped within my breast, and my skin tingled with the prickling of fear, as a quiet voice said behind me, close to my ear. "Well met, Doctor Tom Fletcher!", and a sword was thrust before my neck.

11

What could I do but throw myself on his mercy, rather than his sword? He knew me. Perhaps that would count in my favour.

"I am alone and unarmed." I pleaded.

The sword dropped at my feet.

"And now, so am I, Tom!"

I turned to face him. I knew him, not well, it is true, but in the short time we had eaten at Prince Rupert's table in Lichfield, I had had cause to view him as a friend. It was William Legge. When he had heard that Digby had proposed to wall up Peabody, myself and the miners at Lichfield, "to save the cost of burials," he had drawn his sword against that craven Earl in our defence.

He shook my hand. "I am happy to see you, Tom Fletcher. Rupert said you had a habit of appearing where you are most needed. Has Massey sent you? Will you ride back with me now? We are camped at Tredworth, and under cover of horse exchange sent letters to Massey earlier today. It may be that when Massey sends back his reply by my man, that it is for capitulation."

"Ride back where with you?" I asked, bewildered and shaken.

"Why, to our camp hard by at Tredworth and thence to the King. He will be leaving Bristol very soon, if he has not already done so."

And I confess, I was tempted. There and then, to have done with all my cares and responsibilities in Gloucester, to ride out into the evening air, to leave all talk of water and supplies, to leave Robert and his terrible illness, and all the stultifying Puritan clacking.... but to leave Rowena to the mercy of a siege and to leave Abram....

"You jest, of course! I cannot."

"Cannot or will not!" asked William Legge.

"Both, Major Legge. Believe me I am your friend. I remember so clearly the way you drew your sword in our defence. But I cannot leave Gloucester."

He was frowning. "When did I draw my sword?"

I reminded him of the Earl of Bristol's callousness and he nodded. "Aye, well, if ever there was a snake in the grass.... I should have blown him up with those budge barrels you were so concerned with"

"But how is Peabody? I long to see him," I told him.

"Come with me now, and you shall do so. He is well. Fit as a flea, though something larger and not so well favoured."

"I cannot come with you, Major Legge. But be assured. I shall not raise a hand against the King. I am in Gloucester to tend the sick and wounded. Peabody knows I cannot fight.... unless even at this late hour he wishes to have recourse to quarterstaffs! He will recognise my jest. But dear sir, I am delighted to see you in this strange manner. Will you tell Peabody and the Prince also, if that is not too impudent, that I think of them both and pray for their safe delivery from these battles?"

"I will. You can trust me for that. Here comes Prentiss."

A man was striding in the open ground near the trees towards some horses that I had not noticed which were tethered near grazing cattle. They were invisible to any watchers on the walls. Prentiss carried a packet slung over one shoulder but I noticed his right hand clutched his sword hilt.

"I will tell you our plan, and then Farewell. Massey sent a pass. Prentiss knows Gloucestershire and is the son of a wealthy farmer hereabouts. He used the pass to ride in your gates on one of four Suffolks. He carried letters to Massey and as I think now bears a reply. I tell you, Tom, all talk of besieging Gloucester might come to nothing. But the letters will be for the Earl of Sunderland. It is not for me to read them here. See it is nearly dark. Will you wait here for half an hour and then return to the postern? Prentiss is clever. He will lead my horse round this wood to where I can mount unseen. As you see, he makes no motion of recognition. But I must go, Doctor Tom. God go with you."

"And with you, my friend."

I sat on a grassy bank and watched as his dim figure moved silently through the trees. I could just make out the two horses, and then the riders had mounted and were slipping away eastwards into the deepening dusk. I listened. On the breeze came that familiar noise of a great company of men encamped. I judged they were in fact less than half a mile away. What should I do? Was Massey a traitor? Was he about to betray the town of Gloucester? Or was he simply seeking to avoid the unnecessary shedding of blood? Did he long to be reunited with his Royalist friends, tired of the endless Puritanical prating? (And my sympathies were with him there!) Or was he preparing and protecting himself, and possibly Gloucester as well, against any momentous event? I sat in thought for perhaps ten minutes. Then I stood, my mind made up. I was resolute and determined. Nothing would shake me from my courageous course of action because I would do... nothing.

The cubs had long since sought their earth and I did not want to find the gates closed against me. But Davy Wainwright had waited before pushing the great bar home and now suggested that we went back to the New Inn so he might pledge me. As we went through the Cross, I was surprised to see a crowd had gathered. They were surrounding a group of troopers, who with swords drawn stood about ten men seated mournfully upon the cobble stones. One held a handkerchief to his arm, through which blood clearly seeped. He was in pain. The strangest aspect of this nocturnal scene lit by the flickering torches was that the Gloucester citizens were silent as they stood and surveyed the strangers.

"One of Sir Edward's captains, Captain Blunt took them at Wotton." Davy told me, in a whisper. "They are waiting for the Captain and his fellow officers to return. The foot soldiers brought these fellows in through the Northgate, not half an hour ago."

Alderman Pury was suddenly beside me. He like the others looked sadly at the seated men. "Well, Tom! Did you ever see so sad and miserable a crowd of Trojans? Perhaps it would not now be seemly to relate to them the error of their ways."

"From the look of them, I would say that such errors are felt only too keenly. One man has a cut to his arm, which I should tend. Where are they to be housed?"

He looked at me in surprise. "Why, in the dungeon below the Eastgate. We are waiting for the Mayor to find the keys." He looked at the wounded man. "Well, perhaps, you should.... for Christian charity...."

I needed no further encouragement. I ran into Northgate, into the inn, up the stairs and snatched up my box. As I came back to the Cross two women who had been standing there passed me on their way home. One was saying wonderingly, "I tell you, Madge, no different from our own."

I pushed my way back to the Alderman who had been questioning one of the troopers. "My son has gone with Blunt to the top of Painswick Hill," he told me. "I wish he was returned. But I have arranged for you to treat the wounded prisoner." He raised his voice. "Let Doctor Tom through, good people."

I crouched by the wounded man who in truth was younger than myself. Davy followed me, making his buff coat into a pad on which I could kneel. I asked him to fetch boiled water from Mistress Nichol's kitchen. I knew she had taken to heart my fears about contamination.

The boy was as much distressed that his shirt sleeve was destroyed, as that his arm was wounded. Although his wound was stiff and painful, he contrived to bend his elbow to remove his coat, and I was able to review the injury. He had sustained a long sword scratch from elbow to wrist and blood seeped into his shirt.

"Your arm I can save, but not your shirt," I told him and began gently to remove with my forceps the fragments of cloth which were embedded in his arm. I looked round at my silent audience. "He should be sitting. Could anyone ask John Nichol for a chair?" and two stools were found, one for patient and one for doctor.

I was something distressed that a bitch and her pup came and grovelled at our feet and ate each trifle of cloth as I threw it down. I was troubled by this but the patient gave a thin smile.

"My grandam always threatened me that I should be eaten by dogs for my sins."

"Ah, well," I said philosophically, "Grandmothers need all the disciplinary aids they can conjure up when dealing with wayward boys. Where did this formidable lady live?"

"Far, far away. North of these parts."

"Stafford?" I asked him. "I have been there."

"A long way north from there. In Lancashire. By the sea, not far from Lancaster."

By this, I had finished my picking and discarding, and took the clean water to bathe the long wound. I had now in my box an excellent distillation. It was from the roots of a herb from the New World of which Simeon had told me. The English name was coneflower but it had properties of cleansing that were second to none. I warned the boy that it would sting. Then I used my Pares lotion and proceeded to bandage him firmly but not too tightly. I found clean cloth for a sling and although he told me his arm was stiff and sore, I was satisfied that he had done no lasting harm to ligaments or muscles.

"There I have done," I said rising and pouring away the bloody water. He thanked me gratefully but told me he had no money. "No matter!" I told him. "When I see my good friend Rupert, he shall pay me for you!" It was a poor jest but to my surprise all around the Cross laughed inordinately, prisoners and Gloucester citizens alike.

I thanked Davy for his help and returned his coat. "But I had best speak to Alderman Pury about this boy's lodging. May I pledge you, good David, tomorrow at this hour?" He agreed and I followed Thomas Pury into the New Inn where he stood waiting for me but plainly concerned for his son not yet returned with the raiding party.

"Master Pury, I spent some of the most unpleasant hours of my life in the Eastgate Dungeon, at the behest of a jealous colleague. Could I suggest to you reasons why these prisoners should be better housed?"

"I cannot think where we should put them but certainly I will always listen to reason. At least I hope I will."

"Dear Sir, the boy whose arm I have dressed, is suffering from shock, brought on by his wound. The muddy floor of the dungeon could infect again the open slash of the cut and it could putrefy. It may be as the siege proceeds there is the need to exchange prisoners. If these fellows speak well of us, it might sow seeds of doubt in the hearts of the King's followers. The horrors of Oxford Prison have done nothing for the King's cause. Also if we treat them well, those same Parliamentary seeds might flourish here and now in them. Who knows? We might have ten more troopers for Parliament."

I had another reason against the use of the dungeon that I did not pursue. Remembering my encounter with the rat, I was not certain that it was an entirely secure prison. Instead I suddenly thought of a further advantage of reasonable treatment.

"Your captains, your son, perhaps, will know the tactical questions to ask these fellows to gain knowledge of the disposition of the King's army."

The Alderman nodded, looking at me with his eyebrows raised, and said briefly, "When you tire of doctoring, Tom, I swear I will find a seat for you in the Commons. You are as good a hectoring old lecturer as ever browbeat his fellows to a nap. You can carp on with the worst of 'em. I'll consult Sir Edward."

There was the clatter of hooves in Northgate and we ran out to the Cross, where the officers of the Earl of Stamford's Regiment, amongst them Alderman Pury's son, were standing modestly receiving the adulation of the crowd. Edward Massey stood to one side, smiling, it seemed to me, at the success of his men. The Mayor arrived jangling the infamous bunch of keys, but Massey had already made his decision.

"There are pallets laid out for them in the attic of my house. I have had the windows barred and the door at the head of the stairs may be locked and bolted."

So all my good arguments went for naught. A waste of my cerebral energies! I felt some vexation that my notions had not been voiced, but then chided myself for my vaunting aspirations. The end was the same. A reasonably clean and comfortable bedchamber for the prisoners! I was tired to death and crept up the stairs, pleased at least that Robert had not been disturbed. So ended one of the longest Sabbath evens of my life.

Next day there was a steady stream of messengers like a swarm of bees, carrying sour honey. They came from all parts of Gloucestershire, bringing news of the movement of the King's army. In truth he had not one army but several. The followers of the man, whom I could not in my heart deny was our rightful King, were converging upon Gloucester from Bristol, from Oxford, from Worcester and from Wales.

I was beginning to feel that I was a treacherous felon. I went up to see Robert. He lay thin as a scarecrow, his body wasted save for his swollen belly, but he could immediately see that I was troubled.

"Sit with me a moment, Tom, and tell me your cares. Well, yes, I know I am one of them and for that I beg your pardon. But you have not today that cheerful visage of the hopeful doctor. I know that for me that is so much tactful hypocrisy but something preys upon you. Tell me your mind."

I shook my head. "I cannot, Robert. All I can tell you is that I am not wholly a man for Parliament."

He raised his maimed arm in a hideous mockery of a salute. "And do you think after this, that I am. When Waller joins me in Hell, I shall ask Saturn to grant me the honour of dousing him in vitriol." He laughed at my distaste. "Come now, Tom. I have heard you agree passionately with Tom Pury that much is amiss when good clever men are slighted because they lack birth."

I nodded. "But I am not convinced that the King wishes to disparage merit. More it is great lords who are too grand to wipe their own arses who look down on men like Pury... and perhaps myself. Rupert valued me."

He laughed. "He will always be what his followers demand. He needs his praise and popularity as the dunghill needs the sun. But I grant you one thing. He is careful of his troopers' lives. And Maurice also. But Tom, the arch fiend Laud who branded your good friend, he is the antichrist. The chains of the Arminian cut deeply and cruelly into the aspirations of the good clever men we spoke of. Brandings, the removal of ears, split noses.....!"

"Hangings, if you are the Earl of Essex. But Robert I thank you for your good council. And rejoice that we are still the best of friends, are we not?"

He smiled sadly. "Indeed we are!" and closed his eyes, still drowsy from the potion I had given him last night.

I made my way downstairs to be met by Thomas Pury, the younger. "My father sends me to ask if you would wish to ride out today. We have had word of the King's devils, stealing and pilfering in outlying villages. It is proposed that we take two troops. There will be no danger. The rogues camped at Tredworth cannot see Southgate. The King arrives at Berkeley tomorrow, so reports our Royal Eavesdropper! What do you say? These thieves in the villages are whoreson forerunners of his army, chancing their arm or rather arms."

I was doubtful. "Well...." I began .

"Oh, I know you are no soldier. Believe me, it will not come to a fight. You may stay at the rear and if any man gets pricked, there you will be with your potions and lotions!" And then he put forward the argument most likely to move me. "It's a fine day for a ride. Who knows if or when we will ever get another such day?"

I took a deep breath and thanked him. My horse as well as I needed exercise. It was a good occasion to ride Rowena.... Praise

God I did not say that aloud. All the Earl of Stamford's regiment knew the name of Master Smith's charming daughter.

"And if I may call you Doctor Tom as I hear my father does, then perhaps you will call me Captain Tom."

"Willingly!" I said politely, "But I have another given name if there is a glut of Toms. It is Owen."

He looked at me silently, his expression unchanging, like an Egyptian carving, for all the world the image of his humourless but endearing parent.

"That is the name of Captain Backhouse' lieutenant. If you are suddenly known as Owen, 'twould make for endless confusion. Doctor Tom it is. At the Cross in half an hour."

I went back to Robert who insisted that I wore his buff coat and that I borrowed his sword so that I did not cut too pathetic a picture of a soldier. As I saddled up poor Rowena who whinnied in delight at the notion of exercise, I felt considerable guilt at the neglect of our horses. Blackbird neighed in frustration. The groom had walked them round the streets from time to time but nothing could compare with the delight of a gallop, with the wind in their manes and tails.

We milled about around the Cross and then set out to Southgate. I kept well back behind Captain Evans, alongside Captain Tom, and was pleased to note that Captain Backhouse and his officers and some of his men had joined us and as we trotted down the street, I saw Simeon Walsh and reined in to greet him. The horse behind me charged into Rowena's hindquarters, and I realised that I had created considerable equestrian chaos, even before we had got through the gate. I hung my head in shame and rode more modestly, though no-one remonstrated with me. It was also dawning upon me that I must rename my horse. It would be the height of discourtesy, should I ever refer to the body parts of the beast in the presence of the lady.

I knew that I had been invited to accompany the mounted officers of Colonel Henry Stephen's regiment, the Gloucester Troop of Horse and the forty or so foot soldiers lest any of them needed medical assistance, but I was still pleased to have the exercise. The harvest had been good and the stubble stood in the fields, bathed in the glow of the August sun. The foot soldiers were unusually well drilled. A Scotsman, a formidable old soldier, one George

Davidson, had been retained to discipline both the Gloucester trained bands and Henry Stephen's foot. They marched together as one unit, instead of the usual straggle that was peculiar to the movement of infantry. Davy Wainwright had told me that Sergeant Major Davidson was very careful of the men's feet and frequently held foot inspections. Perhaps Scotsmen had little or no sense of smell. I had myself heard him shouting colourful instructions in his strange Scotch voice. Because the two troops we had with us were so disciplined, we came quickly to Tuffley.

On the small green the villagers told us that they believed that the King's Men whom they had briefly encountered had come through the Forest from Wales. They had offered no violence but there had been thefts aplenty. Chickens, piglets, apples and the inevitable cooking pots. The children stood clutching their mothers' skirts, their eyes wide and their thumbs in their mouths, marvelling at the wealth of soldiery they were seeing this day, whilst their parents were unsure whether they should return to the diurnal routine of work. The advent of pillaging Royalists was an event momentous enough to justify a day's leisure.

Lieutenant Pierce, born and bred in this corner of Gloucestershire, now questioned the victims as to where they believed the enemies of Parliament had fled. But before they could reply, the answer came galloping up on a bay cob. The rider, a stout farmer's boy, had observed the raiding party making their way across the fields to nearby Brockthorpe and had determined to ride to Gloucester for assistance. He had run to the miller's and purloined the cob, and had happily come upon us before the King's Welsh pillagers had had the time to steal much of substance. Or so he thought.

Captain Evans and Captain Tom were by this spurring their horses towards Brockthorpe, but Lieutenant Pierce, a seasoned soldier, was something more cautious.

"Patience, my masters!" he rapped out at his superiors. "How many?" he demanded of the enterprising youth. The boy, still panting, held up seven fingers.

We numbered about twelve on horseback, but rather than tearing after the renegades, hell for leather, Pierce continued to employ his brain before his spurs. He nominated one Corporal Cooke to march the half of the foot soldiers to follow after, whilst we on horseback rode ahead. The older train band troopers, foot soldiers from the workshop and the plough were to wait here in Tuffley to cover our retreat.

Given our head we streamed off to Brockthorpe as if we were following the hounds of Hell, uttering cries of havoc and destruction, fit to curdle the blood to ice of any Cavalier who should hear our threats. Brockthorpe was a scant mile and a half from Tuffley and again the inhabitants were gathered outside their houses, jaws agape.

"Where are they, Uncle Dan?" Pierce screamed at an old fellow, who was scratching his chin.

"Gone to Master Wood's, for vittles, as we think, Petey!" roared back the old fellow.

Pearce, his blood on fire, charged down a track and drew his sword. We all followed him, screaming like souls possessed and came upon a large house, the doors wide open and several horses tethered to apple trees near the track.

"Doctor Tom!" he shouted, "Lead these horses back to Tuffley. Tell Culley to mount up in readiness with six others." He beckoned to his fellows to ride round the house after him, while I contemplated the task I had been assigned.

It was easier to order than complete. Seven horses needed leading reins but Captain Tom seeing my consternation removed a length of rope from his knapsack and threw it at me, as he rode round the corner of the house. The task now was manageable and the poor jades gave me no resistance. They were in poor shape, all were thin, one was short of a rib and two were standing over, giving pitiably at their knees, due to hard treatment. Several were malformed in the mouth. I dismounted and linked them together, one behind the other, remounted, and off I set at the head of my procession.

I must confess I was pleased to be gone from Master Woods's. The noises which issued from the open doors as I trotted away were frightful to hear. Men were screaming, surprised and frightened. I surmised that they had found food and had been dumbfounded at the sudden appearance of the Gloucester troopers. I clicked at Rowena and quickened our trotting but knew that the two horses that were standing over would not be able to maintain any sort of speed.

I soon came up with the foot men instructed to follow after the cavalry and told them briefly what was occurring.

"Are they in trouble, do you think, sir?" another corporal at the head of the column asked.

"I would say not, but they will have had to dismount round the back of the house. They would be happy I think if their horses were guarded."

"Then we shall quick march!" and in two minutes they were out of sight. I dismounted and looked at the two poor beasts for whom movement was a torment. As there were now twenty troopers as well as the mounted officers between myself and Royalist swords, I began to feel more confidence in my future survival. My heartbeat became less frenzied and my hands on the reins less wet with sweat.

So we walked into Tuffley where the train band veterans waited. They cheered as they saw me but were horrified at the sight of the beasts. One man, by trade a farrier's journeyman, thought the treatment would cost more than the beasts were worth.

We were near a blacksmith's and I asked him for water for them and bought a bag of oats and gave each of them a small amount from my flat hand. They were so thin I was afraid to give them overmuch suddenly.

Corporal Cullyford suddenly gave an exclamation. "Look there, my masters! I don't like the looks of that."

The countryside to the south of Gloucester was a plain stretching I was told down to the Severn and thence to the sea. But beautiful steep and wooded hills rose to the east. I had ridden through them on the way to Stroud on my benighted journey to London and now I gazed up at them from another viewpoint. Far away on the ridge, small black figures were gathering. It was impossible to say whether they could see us. If they could, (and we after all could see them!)they might assume we were a Royalist raiding party and not Parliament men. Or they might not!

I was the only mounted man. "Well, I had best ride back and warn them. Cully, what do you think? Can you march back to Gloucester and warn Sir Edward?"

Two of the horses were capable of cantering, and I suggested that he rode one and the farrier's man the other, and the rest should bring on the other five behind them as gently as possible at a swift walk. I did not like to usurp my place but Cully seemed to think my advice was acceptable, particularly as the little black figures high above us eastwards seemed to multiply.

There was nothing for it. I would have to return to Master Wood's. Who he was, where he was, I never discovered, but I venture to think his house was something the worse when he returned. When I had retraced my steps, the troopers were waiting outside for orders.

I told Pearce what we had seen and he swiftly organised his troops into a fighting column, officers on horse back, surrounding the foot. I had to confess to myself, I had not seen so good a fighting unit as these fellows of Henry Stephen's Regiment of Foot. And he, the poor Colonel, was not even here to see the fruits of his good training and investment, languishing in Oxford prison, lost by Massey's carelessness.

As they arranged themselves into formation, a cry came from the house. Pearce and Evans ignored it but I could not. A Welshman was crying out for aid.

Tom Pury saw my dilemma. "You will have to return alone, Tom. Stay, I will wait for you. One is beyond help, one dead in the orchard, but two or three others merely cut about. The rest are fled."

I still had my wits about me. "Are they armed?"

In reply he pointed to a few swords carried by another Captain, one Luke Nurse.

"Not now!" he said grimly.

The company moved off, the horsemen trotting sedately and the foot again trying to march in step. I dismounted, handed young Tom Pury my reins, seized my box and walked with quaking heart into the house.

"Ble ydych chwi?" I called in my mother's tongue.

"Yma!"came the reply.

I walked slowly up the wide staircase, and hearing the sounds of humanity issuing from a bedroom, cautiously pushed the door further open and went in.

A man lay on the floor, eyes and mouth wide open in the extremity of death. The floor was wet with his blood. Two young men sat and gazed in horrified shock at the sight. One had a cut to his neck and the second held up his left hand which poured blood from the wound left by a missing half finger. A third, not much more than a child, sat clinging to a chair leg and wept.

"They killed our father!" one cried out in outrage to me.

"Believe me, they would not have done so, if you had peacefully surrendered your weapons." I hoped I was speaking the truth. "I am a doctor. I have very little time. I will dress your wounds for Christian charity. "

The finger or rather the lack of its upper half was the more serious matter. I did the best I could, making a pad of clean bandage and soaking it with an infusion of Archangel. I roused the boy who wept in the corner, speaking to him gently, and suggesting firmly that he helped the fingerless one by holding the pad over his wound and renewing the infusion from time to time. The neck wound was little more than a scratch, but it bled copiously and needed a clean dressing, and Pares Lotion. I bound the bandage round his neck and said cheerfully, "There, your friends will think you have narrowly escaped the gallows!"

"Pwy ychych chwi?" the neck wound asked.

"I'm a doctor from Worcester. As a child I spoke Welsh as well as English. My mother was from Pembroke. The King's Men are up on the ridge to the east. If you can climb up to them, you will be safe."

The blood from the finger stump had ceased to flow and I bandaged it as well as I could and then packed away my bottles and bandages. "Where are you going? What are we to do with Dada?" said the youngest.

"I can only ask you what would he have wished you to do," I said. "I think he would have expected you to save your own lives."

I ran down the stairs and out to poor Tom Pury, who was relieved to see me. I mounted swiftly and we began trotting down the path to Tuffley. I reflected that I now knew this path like the back of my hand, having traversed it for the fourth time that day. Then as we gathered speed there was a frenzied cry behind us.

"The horses! The bastards have stolen the horses!"

I confess I did not feel clear in my conscience to leave wounded men riderless and momentarily reined in. But Captain Tom for all his solemn features was like his father a shrewd judge of character. He had already divined that after doctoring, horses were my chief interest in life.

He pulled at my reins. "Come on, Tom! Those beasts would

have died, if we hadn't rescued them."

We put the horses to the gallop and went through Tuffley, hell for leather. I could not help but notice that Captain Tom's horse was superior even to Jupiter. Although the path accommodated two riders abreast, his mount given her head could easily outrun me. I confess I felt a little irritated with poor dependable Rowena.

The little figures we had seen against the skyline had disappeared. But beyond Tuffley, the path became stonier causing us to slow to a trot for the sake of the horses. Hawthorn brakes lined the path and when we were almost out into open country, Rowena whinnied. I had noticed that she did this when she sensed other horses nearby. I pulled at Tom's coat and gestured that we should seek shelter in the brakes and spy out what lay ahead.

As well we did. In the distance Evans and the others were nearing the Gloucester walls. There seemed to be other mounted men riding out to greet them. But between the comfortable safety of the Southgate and ourselves, upwards of a hundred of the King's mounted men had ridden down from the high ridges to intercept us. A large group of them were circling around and shouting insults to a young fellow, who sat upright on the grass, clutching his leg. As we watched he had the good sense to draw a white handkerchief from his pocket and waved it aloft.

Tom Pury whispered in my ear, "That's Martin Haines. We played together. A cobbler's son from the Train Band."

I was suddenly afraid that the fearful events on the slope of Lansdowne Hill would be repeated before my eyes and I would be powerless this time to intervene to hasten death. My stomach lurched as I recalled the dismembered "Lobster", Hopton's men killed by degrees. I had tried to banish the recollection from my mind, but now suddenly it came upon me in all its horror, and I vomited over Rowena's mane. Captain Tom looked at me askance, and with his finger over his lip, indicated that we should penetrate deeper into the bushes.

When we had found an opening in the thick hawthorn bushes where we could observe if anything even more clearly, I was distressed to see that the devils continued to circle Martin Haines and were now battering him with the flat of their swords. He still grasped his leg with one hand and with the other continued to wave his white scrap of surrender. It would take but the slightest change in the angle of their swords and he could lose his hand. But his courage in the face of his helplessness was starting to affect some of his enemies.

"Hold hard, lads!" a man on a bay shouted. "He hasn't offered us any hurt. He's earned his quarter!"

The beating continued. However fewer than five musketeers... I knew them to be so by the bandoliers they had strung before them... persisted in their cruel sport, but most stood their horses away and sheathed their swords. A cry came from the nearby hillside, and three officers, resplendent with blue velvet cloaks, and red sashes, rode down amongst the King's Men, their swords drawn, their faces set in fury.

"Leave him! Do you not see? He surrenders!" one who carried an ensign shouted. "Destroy him at your peril!" The other two set about the attackers, and drove them complaining bitterly, back up the hill. The ensign was set in the ground and its bearer dismounted. It was a handsome design of an azure ground with one star and the Cross of St George in one corner

"That's Edward Stradling's colours," Captain Tom whispered to me. "He's a Welshman. Used to come to Gloucester before these conflicts."

We watched scarcely daring to breathe, whilst the three officers leant over young Martin and conferred. Finally they decided. He was hoisted onto his good leg and pushed up onto one of the horses, which was led by the man who carried Sir Edward's ensign.

"These officers have come from Tredworth then. Thank God they arrived. What might have been Marty's fate?"

Captain Tom was clearly relieved that his old school fellow had escaped a bloody death and so was I. We could speak now in our usual voices as the King's men had retreated back up the hill. We watched as Sir Edward and his two lieutenants walked with Martin on horseback towards Gloucester. But half a mile short of the city, they veered North-East off the track, avoiding the town.

Captain Tom looked at me and sighed.

"The dilemmas of doctoring! I am happy I do not have to make such heavy choices."

I understood what he meant. If I had not insisted on tending the King's Welshmen in Master Wood's house, we would have been safely within walls by now. The cavalry troop that had surrounded

Martin Haines had returned to the ridge that overlooked the Severn plain. And once we had broken our cover, they would be overlooking us!

Captain Tom peered up through the branches of our safe haven. "Do you know what our advantage is, Tom? When they see us, they must ride their tired horses, again, down that killing slope. There will be broken legs aplenty. We have a flat run of less than one mile."

I looked at his mount which I had been secretly admiring. I could see that there was a Barbary strain in the beast but she surpassed even the Arab in that her shoulders, neck and rump were excellently strong and noble. Perhaps even at that nervous time, Captain Tom detected envy in my gaze. He gave his rare smile and leant forward and patted her mane. "She is the most intelligent, the swiftest and most biddable horse in Gloucester," he told me proudly. "And she is Spanish. A Spanish Jennet. Isabella."

He thought for a moment and leaned over and tenderly patted Rowena, fastidiously avoiding my vomit. "When they have dismounted and are munching their bread and cheese, we shall run for it," he announced. "I shall give Isabella her head and shall be with those outriders in less than three minutes. I shall tell them to ride out to you and bring you back. The fellows on the hill will kill both themselves and their mounts if they ride down that slope without due care. And if they are careful, we shall be behind the gates and pledging each other in whatever my father has prepared for our return."

I nodded, and we picked our way back to the track, still under cover of the hawthorns.

"Well then, Tom!" he said "May the devil not take the hindmost!" It was almost a jest. We set off neck and neck, but poor Rowena, heavier in girth, and as with all cobs, having legs slightly too short for startling rapidity, soon fell irrevocably behind. She pounded along manfully, however, and I was beginning to think that all might be well, when there were shouts and cries much nearer than we had anticipated. Some of the King's Men had rested in a fold of the hill on our right, possibly as much to avoid detection by their officers, as to espy on their opponents. I glanced up at them and felt a wave of pure terror. Captain Tom had reached the outriders, whom I now saw, were led by Massey. He was shouting at them, and they were streaming out towards me.

But the group who had sought invisibility were now only too plain and intended clearly to cut me off from my rescuers. One in particular with no thought for his horse's safety set his mount at a steep escarpment that ended beside the path. There was the slenderest of chances that I might be beyond that point and Rowena rose to the challenge sensing danger, racing along, specks of my vomit from her mane, mingling with the foam from her lips. Even in this extremity, I could not bring myself to use my spurs.

I could see, however, that it was hopeless. The foremost rider with a triumphal shout had gained the path in front of me. But his shout became a frenzied scream. His horse could not in the instant, adjust to the flatness of the ground rising up instead of falling away. He stumbled and went over, throwing his rider head over heels. There was a confused disordered mass of man and beast on the track before me.

Rowena did not pause. With a presence of mind I did not know she possessed, she gathered herself up and sailed over the obstacles before her, as cleanly and as elegantly as any Thoroughbred, landed, losing her balance a trifle, corrected herself like a Duchess in a dog-hole, and galloped on towards our friends.

The shouts behind me faded, and Sir Edward was reining in beside me. "Come on then Doctor Tom! You can explain your tardiness and why you saw fit to bring me in those spavined jades. I have never seen such sad ill favoured beasts. A misfortune about the boy Haines."

I rode before him under the postern and wondered where Captain Tom had gone. But there under New Inn arch was Abram waiting for me, in a rare old taking.

"Tom! How could you put yourself into such danger? I have been so afeard and Rowena too."

I pretended to feign ignorance of his meaning. "Yes, but here you see. She is safe home. When I tell you what a brave jump she made! More Arab than cob!"

"Not the horse, Tom! Numbskull! She loves you, you know."
"What?"

"Well, I will not tell you how I know, as you were so unfeeling as to leave me here, whilst you went off a-junketing."

He stalked off and I dismounted pondering his words. Had I

been in danger or had I been "junketing"? As long as he had a fault with which to reproach me, Abram enjoyed scolding me. Were all young boys at odds with their elder brothers? Rowena was delighted to see her stable and the old groom, for whom she was clearly a favourite, began to rub her down.

I went into the Inn and called for small beer. But I had scarcely quenched my thirst when Foster Pleasance came seeking me.

"Doctor Tom, would you honour Sir Edward with your presence forthwith? In his house if you please." He bowed and left me, feeling like an unruly scholar who is summoned to the Master's desk to account for his behaviour.

"Well, he cannot beat me." I reasoned to myself. "I am taller than all of them."

Sir Edward had the Purys with him, father and son. Captain Tom stood below the painting of The Expulsion from Paradise. His father and Sir Edward stood before him

"Doctor Tom, something occurred to delay you in Brockthorpe. It may be, may be, I repeat, that if you had kept up with the main body of the troop, young Martin Haines would not have damaged his leg and all would now be within Gloucester's walls. Young Captain Pury here speaks of a wasp or hornet sting on his horse's withers for which you had a salve." Captain Tom was grinning at me like an idiot and nodding like a donkey, behind their backs.

"It is an excellent horse and Yes I have a salve for wasp stings on man or beast." I said, nodding gravely in my turn. "Such a beautiful piece of horse flesh should not suffer undue discomfort. Easily dealt with by ointment and a dressing." Captain Tom clasped his hands upwards, together in a victorious gesture, and came forward.

"There, Sir and you, my doubting Thomas of a father, why did you suspect me? Come, father, my mother demands we dine. Till tomorrow, Tom." I had not known he could be so loquacious. He hurried his father away, leaving me alone with Massey.

He looked at me, coughed, gazed at Eve's voluptuous curves in his painting, and silently resumed his study of my person.

"It might not be too irksome for young Haines." I ventured. "Sir Edward Stradling seemed a compassionate man."

He nodded, then said, "Doctor Fletcher, there was no wasp sting on Isabella's withers. I was standing beside her when Captain Tom Pury dismounted outside Southgate. I would have seen a dressing.

I suspect, Doctor Tom, that you were delayed because you felt impelled to dress the wounds of the King's Welsh allies in Brockthorpe."

I was silent. He pursued his advantage. "Why did you lie?"

"Did I lie?" I asked him softly, also perusing Eve's sensual curvature for inspiration. "Forgive me."

He smiled grimly, "You did not lie in words, my dear young friend. You had better tell truth now, and shame the horned one, Tom."

So I explained that my defection, if defection it was, came as much from loyalty to my mother's people as from my oath to Aesculapius.

"Young Captain Tom is clearly determined to be your friend. Like Sir Edward Stradling, a man of great compassion, as you say." he said thoughtfully. "Captain Tom lied for you. A loyal friend is above rubies, like a good wife."

"Yes, Sir Edward," I said humbly. "Friendship transcends politicks, do you not agree, sir? I met a dear friend but yesterday, who at Rupert's table in Lichfield made to draw his sword on my behalf against a great lord who abused me."

He stared at me, then said through pale lips. "And who is this dear friend?"

"Major William Legge."

He said nothing for a long minute, seeming to gaze at some imperfection on Eve's smooth flank. Then he said, "So! What do you intend to do?"

My reply came pat and immediate. "Why, nothing, Sir Edward. I have stayed in Gloucester for two reasons. To be near Robert whilst he is so gravely ill, and to practice my medical skill. I have no interest in the King or Parliament. The Earl of Essex hung my father in error as a spy and Laud's atrocities have been visited on my friends. I cannot incline either way. Your path is clear and chosen for you by yourself. You cannot help feeling loyalty to good old friends. I know that. As for me I shall say nothing. I am silent as the grave... but perhaps somewhat more sweet-smelling."

He laughed and I smiled at his laughter.

"Well, well, Doctor Tom! It might all come to nothing."

And so we parted. And for the next two days, the messages came swift and fast. On the day after my encounter with the Welshmen, we heard that the king would lodge at Berkeley Castle. This surprised me greatly. The entertainment afforded to an earlier King, Edward the Second, who had stayed there, I would describe as fundamentally unwelcoming. But this was proof perhaps that Charles the First was not superstitious, not Romish in his persuasions.

I encouraged everyone to wash themselves whilst the sweet water from Robinswell still ran. Perhaps some washed who had neglected to do so before. We did not know how long the siege would last. As well to be prepared for any outcome.

Robert's condition grew no better. I could do nothing for him save to dull the pain. The memories of performing the same task for my beloved Phoebe now crowded in upon me as I administered the poppy drug. I also gave him effective treatment from Simeon for the terrible jaundice which carried in its wake, intolerable itching. Ralph hung over him like a mother over her child.

The next day which was Wednesday the 5th of August Ralph waited for me at the foot of the stairs after I had completed my examination of our poor friend.

"There is no hope, is there?" he asked bluntly.

"I fear not," I said as gently as I could. He sat down behind a partition and began to weep, great wrenching sobs that seemed to tear his heart apart. I sat with him for some minutes, my hand on his sleeve. I confess my eyes were wet. My poor girl, my jewel, with so much happiness before her, so lovely, so clever. A line from a play came into my head, and I said aloud, "So quick, bright things come to confusion."

Ralph raised his head. "What?"

"Did you hear it said that those whom the Greek Gods loved, those they first destroyed?"

But Ralph was not philosophical. He could not or would not be comforted. I patted his hand and asked Mistress Nichol for whatever she had for breakfast, and the pleasing scent of gammon and eggs caused him to dry his eyes and fall to. She, good woman that she was, made no comment on the depth of his grief, though she might have thought his show of emotion strange in the circumstances.

We heard later that the King was being feasted at Prinknash, on one of the high ridges three miles away, and that a great lord was dining at Brockworth. A troop of horse led by Captain Evans decided that they would interrupt his bread and cheese and set off through the Northgate to bring hell and damnation to the festive board. But they met with a group of King's Men at Barnwood and a lively exchange of fire took place. I went to the Cross to see them return and was surprised at the sight of a little boy carried before John Nelmes' saddle whom the soldiers swore had killed a Royalist Commander with a pebble. It was, it would seem, a re-enactment of the tale of David and Goliath, though how such a small child had ingratiated his way into a troop of armed men and been allowed to accompany them, beggared belief.

The City of Gloucester now began to realise that conflict was inevitable. A week ago the disposition of the people was perhaps slightly less cheerful than the atmosphere in a pox doctor's antechamber. But now that the siege could not be avoided, an air of good humour and optimism reigned. There was no doubt that Alderman Pury, coming from Parliament itself, with words of comfort and encouragement from that great concourse of noble minds, had raised the spirits of the citizens. And if they had not shown evidence of optimism, he had harangued them with verses from the Old Testament until they did.

What I found admirable was the way that everyone, old and young, rich and poor, man and woman, would leave their play, their work, their families to help if assistance was required with any task that was for the better welfare and defence of the town. Whilst the wellsprings ran from Robinswood, women still came with buckets and pails, bowls, pitchers and barrels so that in those last few days no clean flowing water was wasted. The walls were patrolled now day and night, the suburbs emptied of their residents, the river watched, north and south of the city.

Abram meanwhile forgave me. I had no knowledge of the ways of youths, other than myself, and racked my brains for ways I must have irritated my poor father. But once we had determined on my future, after the hanging attempt, we were as one, father and son, something in the manner of the Purys. I know I annoyed Ben, my master and cousin from time to time. I could be as idle as any indolent apprentice who lounged at his master's door, watching the pretty girls pass. But I did not remember being as angry as Abram clearly had been with me.

I was bidden to supper on Wednesday the 9th of August at the Smiths. Before we ate, Abram having tasks in the kitchen, happily assisting Rowena, I asked Master James Smith why he thought Abram was so vexed at this time, pointing out that he did not seem to bear any ill will to the King and Rupert who were now about to tear his life apart again. I alone bore the brunt of his bad temper.

James leant back in his chair and surveyed me over the top of his spectacles.

"Tom, Tom, so clever a young doctor, so dull in your perceptions of how much you are loved and valued. Your adoptive brother, for whom I admit you have done much, still needs to feel that he belongs to you, as you "belonged" to your parents. You are both now orphans, but his terrible double loss occurred at an earlier age for him. He needs the knowledge that you will always support him, before he can dispense with your guardianship. You are both father and brother to him and it is an important task. I would not say it was difficult. He is appreciative, lively and entertaining and you now are the most important person in his world."

I was silent. These were truths that I recognised and I could see that I had been remiss. When we had been helping Julius and the apprentices, I had neglected him and spoken much more with them. I had not meant to be unfeeling. The demands of the journey had occasioned that I had had to give them more attention.

My silence caused James Smith to ask, "If you wish it, Abram may stay here for good and all with my daughter and myself. He shall be my son and the younger brother she never had. What do you say?"

"Master Smith, I must say no. We have already undergone much together. He is all the family I have now. I shall make good my omissions."

And after we had eaten an excellent saddle of mutton with caper sauce and fresh beans, followed by pasties containing raisins and figs, I asked him, "Abram, would you wish to accompany me back to the New Inn tonight and reclaim your old room? Robert has paid for it all this time in the hope that you would return."

I was surprised by how eagerly he accepted, hastening round the table to kiss Rowena's hand and telling her he would be back to help her with apple picking on the morrow. He bowed to Master James also, hoping that he could be spared from his studies the next morning. I was impressed by his innate courtesy.

But next morning all thought of studies were at an end. At dawn shouts came from the walls and there was the sound of troopers running past the Cross. Master Nichol came upstairs calling for me.

"Well, Doctor Tom, it begins. Look out over the Eastgate and you shall see our fate gathered up together, waiting to try a bout with us."

I pulled on my clothes and was about to run through the town, when Abram called to me asking for one minute's grace whilst he dressed himself to accompany me. Remembering my lesson from the previous evening, I waited reasonably patiently and went downstairs and stood under the arch. People were running to the Eastgate, buttoning their doublets, and tying their caps.

Even before we reached the Eastgate, I became aware of a great host very near to us. There was the sound of hundreds of men, speaking, occasional shouts, the clatter of cooking pots, the discharge of a musket, the hammering of iron bars to make a tripod over a fire, the thousand and one noises that indicated upwards of six thousand men. But as we climbed the stone steps to the wall, I realised that not only could I hear the King's army from Oxford, I could also smell them.

Alderman Pury stood above the postern gazing out across towards the east. Near to the walls the empty houses stood, stacked with bundles of straw, ready to be set alight. Then the gardens and meadows began, strips of green grass and orchard framing the deserted suburbs. But little greenery was visible. Drawn up beyond the silent streets was the King's vast clamorous army. It was a piebald sea of colour, some companies in red and others in royal blue.

We stood in silence next to the Alderman. He turned and saw who we were and said slowly, "Six thousand men, Tom. And more to the north and south. The armies of Saturn are ranged up against us. And do you know? The bastards have all been issued with new clothes."

I suddenly knew what I could smell. New cloth. It had clung to my own new clothes for many days until the delicate perfume of my own person had quite banished the clean aroma. Now here were six thousand sturdy loyal subjects all smelling like the inside of a tailor's shop.

"Even down to their caps,"said the Alderman, "Or up to them. Montero caps. Four shillings each, I vow, or I'm a Dutchman's whore!"

I felt perhaps some sort of reply was necessary, though I confess the sight of the sea of colour was daunting in the extreme.

"Still, not as many as were gathered at Edgehill, sir."

"Wait, good Doctor Tom. Give the Stuart Devil his due! You shall probably find that there are as many whoreson rogues here today, as there were at Edgehill. There are two thousand more to the South and Vavasour with his villains has left the poor lady and her castle on the borders. Well, at least one person gains from this."

"Do you mean Lady Brilliana?" I asked him wonderingly, and then greatly daring, "I had thought she would be rather too much the gentlewoman to meet with your approval."

He regarded me sternly. "If she is sincerely for the common good of our nation, then as far as I am concerned, she is a true gentlewoman and not a simpering Popish harlot. Your friend and benefactor, Colonel Burghill, is a man from an old family, yet he hates the notion of privilege, and so I take him to my heart, in spite of... in spite of all."

"Yes, Alderman Pury," I said meekly. "He greatly values your friendship, though I fear now he wastes away." Then excusing ourselves as I needed to tend the Colonel and our stomachs clamoured for breakfast, Abram and I took our leave with a last look at what seemed an unending plain of Royal supporters.

As we came down from the wall I was stricken suddenly by the fearfulness of our situation.. We had about one thousand and five hundred men, most of whom were the excellent fellows serving in the Earl of Stamford's regiments, manning the Garrison. And the King ringed us about with ten thousand men. It was hopeless. I stopped in the street and gazed at Abram, who had stopped also.

"Abram," I said, clasping his arm. "I have done the damndest thing. You should be twenty miles from here. Do you know what that sight from the walls means?"

"That we shall most probably be killed," he replied, looking me in the eye.

"Why did I not get you away from here before this?" I cried out, causing women coming from the Baker's to stare curiously.

"Because I would not have gone," he said, matter of fact as you please.

No-one seemed to be at work that day. Master and Mistress Nichol seemed unable to turn their hands to innkeeping and sat and talked to their fellow citizens, who came in a steady stream to pass the time of day as they took unaccustomed leisure together,seated in the innyard. And there were children everywhere, running races, screaming each others names, rushing up onto the walls to look upon the enemy, jumping, calling, crying. The boys had been excused their school and the girls their household tasks.

For some hours nothing happened, and the water still ran, sweet and pure. Abram went back to the Smiths, speaking of tasks he had undertaken in the household to assist Rowena and the two servants. The hens were it seemed his responsibility these days. Later in the day, Sir Edward came to see if Robert could rise from his bed to cast his experienced military eye over the King's army but although Robert attempted it, he was too weak and enfeebled to leave his room. It angered me to see him apologising to Sir Edward who should have never have made the suggestion. But the Governor was a young man who whilst he was perhaps unsure in his treatment of his fellows, did not err in his judgement of managing supplies and building defences. The fields to the north of the City had been flooded and were now impassible He had been an engineer, it seemed, though how he had come by so much experience, whilst not much older than myself, was difficult to comprehend.

I followed the Governor downstairs and asked humbly if he would like to taste a glass of taint. He smiled and accepted with alacrity and we sat for a few moments "with all the hosts of Hell gathered to smite us," talking of nothing of any moment. I mentioned that I had neglected my adoptive brother, not giving him the attention he craved as I was all the family he had now, and he spoke of his brothers and his imprisoned father, a loyal follower of the King, who despaired of his son.

"He would rather have me the proprietor of a Pushing School than Governor of Gloucester!" he confided.

"Less care and perplexity, sir, in that profession!" and we were laughing when John Corbett bustled in.

"There are heralds here, sir. You must come at once," and with a brief "God be with you, Doctor Tom." the Governor was gone.

I wandered out and joined a crowd gathered at the Cross to hear the King's proclamation. But it seemed that Massey did not wish to put the city to the test. He heard the summons in private. Alderman Pury, hastening by, invited me into the Council Chamber with him and I heard that all that the King wanted was to leave a well manned Royal garrison here and there would be no bloodshed.

I kept silent. Deep in my heart, a treacherous small voice whispered, "Why not?"

"But if you refuse his gracious mercy," the herald thundered at us, "then all the calamities and miseries that must befall, are on your heads."

Massey and the Council had two hours to consider, and the heralds were invited to refresh themselves in a side room. The discussion that followed seemed interminable and centred round whether the Mayor was a traitor to his oath to the King if he put his name to a defiant response. But at length they convinced him that his oath was to Parliament as well. There could be no doubt that for all whose names signed the reply, there had never been the slightest wavering in favour of a Royal compromise and occupation. Deep in my heart, my sad little doubting Thomas of a cowardly voice subsided into an acceptance of the inevitable.

It was decided that Alderman Jordan, a bookseller and binder and a respected citizen should carry the city's reply to the King. There was some discussion as to who should accompany him, and I saw out of the corner of my eye, Alderman Pury looking speculatively at me. I had after all confided in him that I had met the King. But much to my relief a man I did not know, a Major, one Marmaduke Pudsey, asked to accompany Tobias Jordan.

"He lost his troop at Berkeley. The rogues deserted when they heard that Bristol had fallen, and he came back here with Colonel Forbes."

It was Tom Pury the younger who whispered this information in my ear. "We call such officers reformadoes, because they wish to re-form their troops. Marmaduke Pudsey wants acceptance into a new regiment."

"Why does he wish for that?" I asked. Surely he was fortunate to be able to be discharged with honour, without placing his head yet again into the cannon's mouth? I had learned that the life of a quakebreeches like myself would inevitably be longer in these times, than that of a bragging bellshangle of a soldier.

Captain Tom shrugged. "Money," he said simply. "Shall we go to the wall and see what takes place?"

As we came past the Cross, a young fellow cried out, "What are the King's demands, Captain?"

Tom Pury hardly drew breath before he replied, loudly, "To rule in despite of Parliament."

I looked at him. "Well," he said softly, attempting to justify his invention. "That is what he has done and what he wants to do."

The turnpike that was near to the gate was crowded with men. At first glance they seemed to be the King's foot in their red and blue doublets, but as we looked, we could see the buff coats of the guards of the Earl of Stamford's regiment mingling with them. At the sight of the heralds and the emissaries walking grimly and silently towards them, the two factions separated, pipes were returned, bellarmines restored to their owners and the Gloucester men retreated to Eastgate, with something of a shamefaced air.

A small group of nobles sat under a canopy beyond the turnpike. I thought I could recognise the King and the tall man standing behind, with his arms folded, was surely Rupert. I knew that stance. It signified annoyance and impatience in equal part.

The emissaries drew to a halt before the King. They did not bow, but at least they had left off their hats. Marmaduke Pudsey undertook to read out the reply which he did in a high shrill unpleasant voice as if he were a schoolmaster chiding a wayward pupil. It was difficult to hear the individual words until he reached "to obey the commands of his Majesty signified by both houses of parliament". This phrase he roared at the King and then turned and shouted it again towards the wall so that the whole of Gloucester could have heard. This was the kernel of the defiance against the King. Captain Tom was nodding and smiling and muttering, "Good! Good!"

Pudsey and Jordan completed their task, and with a curt nod, turned and began their walk back to Eastgate. I thought that Pudsey's shrill voice and his discourteous bearing did little for the dignity of the city of Gloucester. But worse was to come. When they were within forty paces of Eastgate, they suddenly paused and out of a bag, Jordan had carried over his shoulder, they produced two wide brimmed hats. They quickly put them on and turning their backs again to the King displayed the bright orange ribbons of the Earl of Essex tied round their hat bands. The King sat motionless and I do not think he spoke, but he must have been well aware that this was planned insolence. In my view it was unnecessary. The defiance was enough.

I had the strange notion that perhaps the King was waiting for another message from the city. He waited in vain, however. I do not know what Massey had promised in the letters Major Legge had delivered, but it was not a pledge he had been able to fulfil.

As they came near to the gate, our men appeared from the deserted houses, running along under the wall and at the same time wisps of smoke rose from the abandoned dwellings. Soon the whole of the north, east and south sides of the city under the walls was ablaze. Captain Tom and I were ordered from the walls, by some of Massey's officers and indeed breathing was becoming difficult. Abram appeared and asked me to visit the Smith's house to tell James what had occurred and to have whatever supper sweet Rowena had managed to contrive.

The Smiths usually ate at the early time of six. I asked for an hour whilst I told Robert and Ralph of the day's events and washed myself. When I began to mount the stairs there was Ralph, sitting wide-eyed and distressed at the top. I told him briefly that we were embattled with the King's men. I did not tell him that their numbers far exceeded ours in the city, as there was no purpose in adding to his despondency.

He told me something of his new grief. "The Colonel and I were wondering what would have happened to the rest of his troop. You remember, Tom, the others who lived in your courtyard when Essex was in Worcester. They were with the Colonel at Lansdowne Hill. I pray that they are still with Waller. Such good lads! And Progger, killed by that madman."

He was in such a melancholy humour that I wondered aloud as a jest, whether I should send him to George Edwards to have his dyscrasias identified. I tried to cheer him as I wondered what the philosophy of Galen would prescribe for depression such as his.

"You will be told such burblings that you have "melancholy vapours rising from a hot spleen" or other such rimble-ramble." I told him. He laughed a little and then distressed me even more by asking,

"Do you think this George Edwards could help the Colonel?"

I had forgotten again that poor Ralph had more hair than wit, although there was no cleverer man at catching rabbits or pheasants. Fortunately our good apothecary came in to the Inn at that moment seeking me. I bit back any response that could have been hurtful to Ralph, and asked Simeon to advise him as to the efficacy of the medical notions of Galen and his followers, and left them and made my way to the buttery bar to crave a flagon of taint, if Master Nichol still had it. Simeon found me there and raised his eyebrows and shook his head in mock despair. Ralph had gone back to Robert to ask him if he wished for a second opinion.

"Will you come with me to give me your opinion on a burnt arm that may also be broken? It is a dreadful sight. It may be you could set the bone. I have given the poor fellow morphine for the pain was like to drive him mad."

"Indeed I will. Master James Smith asks me to call upon him with the news from the wall."

We both looked towards the door as someone entered and were surprised to see a rain of black flakes. "The houses must be well ablaze by this." Sim observed, "What desperate bad luck for one who has bought his house without the wall."

We drained our cups and hurried outside. The air was thick and unwholesome, so we held our kerchiefs to our noses, but at that moment a familiar but detestable sound assailed us. It was a field piece discharging, on Eastgate which we were approaching Simeon clutched my arm. "What in God's name...?"

I pretended courage that I did not feel. "In truth I cannot say if it was a culverin or a demi-culverin!" I said airily. "I would need to see the piece. Give it three or four minutes and if the matrosses know their work, the gun will be oiled, cleaned of stray gunpowder with the scowre, the new powder poured in from the budge barrel, rammed down with the limstock and it will be ready to fire again."

"What?" he cried, half laughing "You have deceived me Tom. I thought you were a dove of peace, but it seems you are a braggadocio, a swaggerer who relishes war."

By this we were on Eastgate, making for Simeon's shop, when there was another close explosion and a violent rush of foul air so that I found it seemed of interest to me to examine the moss growing in the gutter. Sim stayed on his feet, but was spreadeagled against the wall by the blast.

"Well, perhaps not the complete 'miles glorioso'!."he observed, helping me up.

"I assure you I am more than happy to be viewed as the most craven poltroon that ever cowered behind the school house door. At Edgehill my apprentice and I fought to get under a bench when the cannonade began. My blood turned to water, and if I had not passed urine five minutes earlier, I would have seen out the battle with soiled breeches. I assure you, I am a coward, Sim."

"So are all men," he said thoughtfully "and those who think they are not, lack imagination, and those who say they are not, are liars."

By this we had come to his shop under the wall. The broken arm sat, eyes closed in agony, his doublet removed and his shirt torn away. His upper arm was not merely broken, but the flesh around the fracture to the humerus was torn, charred and bloody.

"Whatever happened to you?" I asked the patient who was moaning softly to himself. Then I stared. It was Malten the elusive quartermaster. I had not seen him since the night when he had attempted to retrieve the troopers' wages which I had confiscated for Julius and the apprentice boys. He seemed to come to himself for a moment, and muttered, "Curse my luck! It is the rogue doctor!"

"If I am the rogue doctor, then you are the rogue quartermaster, who should have leapt at the daisies ere this." But I could not hold a grudge, in so bad a state as he was. "Sim, a bowl of water if you please. How did this come about, Master Malten?"

He did not or could not reply. Sim answered for him, "He was even now outside the walls looting in an empty house. A burning beam fell on his arm and an Ensign heard his cries and ran in after him. They pulled him screaming through the gate, just before it closed for good and all, and delivered him up to me. As you know Tom, I am not comfortable in the presence of blood."

I nodded and began to cut away the shreds of cloth which had been burnt into the wounded left arm. Outside the bombardment continued, but great mounds of earth had been piled around the building which dulled the sound somewhat. However this gave an earthy gravelike atmosphere to Sim's neat shop. Malten groaned and I suggested to Simeon that we applied St John's Wort to the whole area so that at least the pain of the burn was swiftly subdued. Apart from shreds of cloth there were the splinters of burnt wood and ash that had fallen on him from the burning thatch.

At last I had removed all the waste matter and was able to assess the situation. The wound was clean... of that I was certain... but muscle and bone were damaged possibly beyond repair. He had lost consciousness by this, and I took the left hand lying limply on his lap. But two fingers seemed to curl around my thumb, the index and the middle finger so I judged that all was not lost. He had cracked the humerus just below the shoulder joint. I surmised that he had been reaching out for something when the brand, heavy and alight, had fallen on his outstretched upper arm. There were a few splinters of bone sticking up through the wound but when I had removed these and peered at the fracture, I decided that the crack would heal without any further setting. But muscles and ligaments had been damaged beyond repair. I could do nothing more for him. It was difficult to treat both burnt flesh and open wound. I anointed the first with more Balm of St. John's Wort and the second with Pares lotion, bound the arm securely and asked for clean water to wash my hands and instruments.

The patient slowly gained consciousness. He said quite clearly once, "No, littleAnnie!" I looked questioningly at Simeon who mouthed. "His daughter, perhaps?"

At last Malten opened his eyes.

"Where is she?" he asked. "I thought she was here. Holding on my arm." He looked at his bandaged limb. "Why, Doctor, I thought you would..."

"Would have what?" I asked as gently as I could.

"I thought I would lose my arm for sure." And then he muttered something I could not hear.

"Listen Master Malten," I told him, "You must sit quiet for some hours now. You have undergone great disturbance within yourself. Your body needs time to recover."

"Believe me, that is what I wish for," he said rising, "But I must find Annie. She is playing somewhere round the town."

He took two steps towards the shop door. A great explosion rocked the building, followed by musket shots, and he stumbled, caught luckily by Simeon who led him back to the chair. He sat down again, ashen faced and sweating, his white knuckles grasping the chair arms. Sim gave him a glass of water which he gratefully drank.

I wiped his brow and told him, "Believe me, activity now could prevent your recovery. Sit easy for a while. I will find your daughter and bring her to you. Stay with this good apothecary."

He looked round at Simeon, as if surprised to find him there. I suggested that he had a mild potion of morphine, less than we were accustomed to give Robert. Sim nodded and I promised to bring back the child.

I went to Rowena who seemed to know everyone in Gloucester.

"Oh, aye, I know that young mistress!" she said "and as wayward and harum-scarum a young hoyden as it has been my misfortune to encounter. I think she has been turf-gathering with the other maids near the marshes."

We set off towards the river and sure enough, encountered a chattering excited group of girls, aged from eight to sixteen perhaps who carried baskets of turf balanced on their hips. Two or three of them were too young to be so encumbered and raced round the elder girls, playing Catch as Catch Can. Rowena called out, "Anne Malten, come here please!"

A pretty dark haired child ran over to us. Her face was alight with mischief, as she made her curtsey and politely bade Rowena, "Good day, Mistress Smith." But on rising from the dirty ground she lost her balance and seized a handful of Rowena's gown to steady herself. There was an ominous tearing sound. Rowena stood still and said more in sorrow than anger. "Annie!"

"Oh, Mistress! I will mend it for you!"

"No need of that. Now then, do you know this gentleman?"

"It's the doctor everyone talks about but my Dada don't like him."

"Well this good doctor wants to take you to your Dada now. He has had an accident and needs his girl to help him in the house."

"We ain't got no house. The soldiers made us leave it. Master Doctor, my Dad isn't going to die, is he?"

"Not if you are a good girl," said Rowena firmly. "I will come with you, and bring you and your father back to my house, as you have nowhere else to go."

Annie was shocked into silence at the sight of her father's white face. Sim had given him a small amount of morphine and he was drowsy now, but intense pain caused him to gasp awake every minute.

"Annie, sweetheart, I fear I cannot care for you as I have done…" he began, but Rowena cut him short. "That task falls to me now, Master Malten, and I am come to bring you both to my home. Can you walk, sir?"

And so she, noble kind girl that she was, brought them both to her father's fine house, hardby the Close. As we walked there, myself shielding the Quartermaster from the nudges and shoves of passers–by, he told me his calling, which was to buy and sell. "To buy as cheap as I may and sell as dear as a fool will buy," he explained. "I have her to care for, Master Doctor. Children must be nurtured, and then she needs clothes and playthings, and her mother…" He could not tell me more.

We came to Master Smith's house where James waited for us, together with the last good dinner we would eat for some time, prepared by the cross cook. I was impressed by the way that Rowena was not affected by the woman's ill temper, and the thought crept unbidden into my brain that Rowena would deal magnificently with Joan.

"Abram, you see poor Master Malten's condition. Your idles are over now. You must help me from now on."

Together we assisted him into a small bedchamber under the eaves. Abram was given the task of assuring himself that the Quartermaster was making good progress medically. He then set himself to amusing little Annie by asking her riddles and singing her that silly song, "If all the world were paper, and all the sea were ink."

And so we ate an excellent good dinner yet the sound of the cannonade broke into our meal from time to time, silencing even little Annie's chatter until about seven in the evening it ceased.

If we had known as we sat round Master James Smith's board, eating his excellent roast lamb and Rowena's plum pies with pastry as light as a whisper, if we had had the least notion that one who sat at that table would be most cruelly removed from the world the next day, our feast would have been blighted. Our lives were to be affected for ever by the terrible spectre of wanton death.

12

It was Mistress Nichol who next morning, Friday the 11th, came shouting up the stairs with the news that we had dreaded.

"Doctor Tom, the water's gone!"

Her words resounded through my head like the beginning of a song, particularly as she repeated them several times. We, who were resident at the New Inn were unaffected, as the well ran true and sweet in the courtyard, but her gossips, dependent on the springs from Robinshill, early risers all, had brought her the news.

I crawled from my bed and knocked on the intervening wall to rouse Abram who had returned with me, to lessen the work of the Smith's household. Well, now we should see if our careful planning and collection of clean water had been beneficial. I called to Abram that I would breakfast when I returned in a short while and set off to see how Absalom was faring. There were already goodwives making their way to the hospital, carrying pitchers and ewers.

Absalom stood at the door, instructing the women to be sparing with their needs. I felt it was necessary to warn them also that water that was for drinking should be boiled if possible. The ladies thanked us courteously, all save one, who shouted rudely that she did not for one moment expect that Mistress Pury would have been put to this inconvenience! A well known voice behind her remarked, "No, she is not, for Master Pury will collect her share." The Alderman bowed to the shrewish one with exaggerated courtesy and handed his jug to Absalom. If ever a man practised what he preached that man was Tom Pury. He reinforced the lesson that birth does not make the gentleman.

We stood to one side and watched as the line of citizens stood meekly waiting for a share. There was much good humoured teasing and laughter and the people of Gloucester took this, their first privation with a right good will. As I hurried back to the New Inn, my empty belly dictating a fair turn of speed, women called out blessings on me and men clapped me on the shoulder. In truth, anyone could have arranged for the storage of water. Possibly even the Severn water could have prevented death by thirst as long as it was boiled.

Our spirits were high that morning for occupants of a besieged city. That which had been so dreaded had finally taken place and all was yet well. I stood in the courtyard of the inn, however, and knew that even if we could not see the great host ringing the city, they assailed other senses. We could hear them... constantly. Specific sounds could be identified. A trumpet call, the clatter of cooking pots, a snatch of song, the murmur of thousands of voices.... it was not deafening, not unbearable like the cannonade, but it was not silence either, and that background noise would be with us for many days to come. And the King's army smelt. No question of it. The tailor's shop odour of new clothes was fading fast. In its place there was the whiff of camp fires, the tastier aroma of roast meat and already, the stench of their latrines.

"They are digging their places of easement in Gaudy Green," said Ralph, up betimes, walking into the courtyard. "I went to see if there was any chance of taking a hare."

I doubted the truth of this. I guessed where he had been. There were vintners near the Southgate and he had been to buy brandy wine for the Colonel. "I glimpsed them labouring from the ramparts but Tom, it is no longer safe to walk upon the walls. When I peeped round a battlement, a ball near took my head off. They have muskets all round the walls."

"At least they have left off the cannonade, praise God!" I observed piously.

"Amen to that! The Colonel's peace was much disturbed. Will you see him presently, Tom? I will wash him first and make all cleanly."

I knew that Robert would insist on a draught of brandy before he would allow me to examine him, and went into the buttery bar where Abram was making short work of a dish of eggs and gammon.

"Mistress Nichol refused to allow me to wait for you," he explained with a slightly shamefaced air. "Bespeak yourself the same. Who knows how long we shall be able to eat so well! I fear if the bombardment begins again, my hens will stop laying altogether."

"Yes, Abram!" I said meekly, noting the possessive "my hens" and sat down obediently. There was a jug of small beer on the table and I drank to ease my parched throat. I had not known that being besieged was such thirsty work.

In any event, my patients had to be seen. There was little change in Robert, certainly no improvement, although he had consented again to drink the good chicken broth provided by Mistress Nichol. He had some fears for his wife and sons. His lease on the Manor of Hadenham in the County of Buckinghamshire would expire on his death. He was writing to a Sir Henry Spiller, his wife's brother, to ask him not to foreclose on the lease of the house, until Elizabeth, his wife, had obtained her compensation from Parliament for her husband's death.

"It may not come to that," I said lying in my teeth. He laughed and held up his good hand. "Good" was a misnomer. He held it against the sunlight from the little window and in truth it was the hand of a dead man, a transparent yellow claw, thumb and fingers wasted to papery sticks.

"I am dying, young Tom," he said firmly, "in despite of your excellent care. I have sent for that coxcomb, Massey, to discuss the disposal of my bones."

Ralph gave an anguished cry and rushed from the room. Robert sat up at some cost to his ease, to look after him. "Poor sweet soul!" he said. "Could I ask you, Tom, to have a care for his future? Life has been hard for him." He lay back on his pillow. "There should surely be some penalty awaiting men like me who take too long about their dying. Strange to say although I do not fear it, I will not ask you for that which would enable me to embrace the Man with the Scythe immediately."

"As well, for I would not give it," I told him.

He looked again at his wasted hand. "And hard to chose between us. He would think he looked in a glass. You are a good boy, Tom. I see you have allowed your pretty gypsy boy to stay here again. Little danger of his corruption now from this decayed wizened cadaver. I must attend to my own corruption."

I confess I did not know how to respond to this. He saw my discomfiture and laughed again.

"I do not love my wife or my poor sons, Tom," he told me, "And that is my shame. I love you as a son. I can dimly remember your excellent father. Those first few days in Worcester after I broke my ribs, I remember as a mist and a dream. Yet I have a clear vision of a young country doctor informing the Earl of Essex that he was accursed for using Worcester Cathedral as a stable. But no words could bring your poor father back. I hope I might have helped you before and after Edgehill as a father might."

"Indeed you did, Robert," And I excused myself, not wishing to swim in a welter of emotion. I had to see the poor wounded quartermaster. I was beginning to feel considerable guilt. Should we have purloined all the money in his pouch for Julius and the apprentices, or should we have sat and discussed the best way to share it. If I had known about little motherless Annie, I know I would have wished that Master Malten took a greater share. But there were unanswered questions. Who had cared for Annie when he was with his troop?

As I passed one of the troughs, where the water had but lately flowed from Robinshill, a group of small boys were paddling and shrieking in the mud that remained. I smiled to myself as I passed, and paused to watch them playing, remembering such escapades of my own childhood. The boys were for the most part the tradesmen's sons who had been excused their letters at the College. Other good Gloucester citizens had paused in their errands and watched the merry-making with indulgent smiles, tinged perhaps with envy. The day was already hot.

My attention was drawn to the ring-leader who stood in the deepest part of the trough and who beat the water with an old rag, causing showers of drops to cascade down on any intrepid playfellow who tried to oust him from his place of honour. I began to walk again but halted at the shriek of a boy who had slipped and now sat sodden from the waist down in the muddy water. "Annie! Annie!" he cried, "Stop it and help me!" The ringleader laughing uncontrollably, extended a wet hand to the boy who had fallen, shrieking, "Catch hold, Jem!" But their hands were too slippery, so then she flicked the old rag to the sufferer who caught it and rose, water running from his clothes. But it was not an old rag. It was Annie's good shawl and she, her skirts somehow hitched round her waist was the instigator of the mischief.

At this she caught my eye and in an instant, she had clambered out of the trough and was running down Westgate, her wet skirts clutched in her hands, and her little naked feet, seeming to make nothing of the cruel cobbles. I had not spoken, had not scolded her, rather I had been amused at her enterprise. But I was a figure of authority for her and she preferred to avoid an encounter.

I walked on to the Smiths. Rowena stood at the front door, calling for her charge. "Annie! Annie Malten!"

"She is at the Westgate by this," I told her, "and then who knows where. She was even now playing the part of a pugnacious mermaid, in the trough near the Cross."

"She is the most boisterous hoyden. She will not listen to a word I say!" said Rowena, with seventeen years of outraged worldly wisdom, furrowing her smooth brow. "But Tom, please come in and see Master Malten. That sad young flibbertigibbet of a daughter ran into him this morning and told him she would go her ways and play because he was cared for now by you and me. She ate no breakfast, merely snatched up one of Poll Cook's rolls as she ran through the kitchen to the garden, where she frightened Abram's hens."

I was following her up the wide staircase. The main hall of the house was splendidly furnished with hangings and paintings, but none were in my view as pleasing as the prospect of Rowena's slim legs as she raised her skirts in a most seemly manner to mount the staircases.

George Malten was clearly disturbed by his daughter's wayward behaviour. He had moved from his bed and was sitting in a high chair, overlooking the street, which he scrutinised anxiously, frowning as he looked down towards the Cathedral and then up to the north wall. He was in great pain, and I suggested that he would best help himself by sleeping, after he had breakfasted on gruel and boiled eggs. He asked for Michael to help him as he could not unbutton himself. I was prepared to perform this office but Rowena had already called her servant who gently helped him use the chamber pot. I prepared another draught of morphine, and instructed Rowena to smell Master Malten's wound whenever she brought him food. He was clearly still in considerable pain, but there was no leakage of blood and I judged it was better to let my work of yesterday stand. Pain is not fever and a feverish demeanour would have betrayed possible corruption.

I gave him the draught and we left him sleeping in the chair by the window. Master James called to us to sit with him for a moment in the garden. Michael and Abram were engaged in making a stouter henhouse, so that if the bombardment began again, the hens' delicate ears would not be assailed too roughly. Rowena went to bring a draught of muskadine for those of us who sat idly and discoursed, and small beer for those who stood and worked. The garden and its laden fruit trees was a green haven, refreshing to behold.

"What are the King's rogues about?" he asked me.

"Well sir, as I hear, they are building trenches in Gaudy Green so that they might come closer in to shoot at us more safely. It is imperative no-one now mounts the walls to gawp at the King's army. We are surrounded by his best muskets. The slightest movement provokes their shot."

He nodded. "'Twould be foolhardy indeed to tempt one's fate. What do you think, Doctor Tom? Have we come to this pass because of our religious differences or because the King takes no count of Parliament?"

"I am afraid I cannot think that God approves the actions of either side, sir."

"Oh, God, you say. No, to be sure not!"

"In fact with each day that passes, I am smitten into the realisation that God retreats ever further from our words and actions. I am not drawn to the Puritanical rantings which I am invited to attend, but hate Laud's unequivocal insistence on ritual. A good friend, who visited my wife's uncle for me in the Tower, told me Laud lies there now. I am sorry that any man is brought to that pass, but I cannot forgive his excessive cruelties."

"Doctor Tom, I wholeheartedly concur. You know my brother, Bishop Smith, would not enter the Cathedral again after Laud had dictated the place of the Communion Table."

"When was that, sir?" I asked. Archbishop Laud seemed to have been everywhere. Worcester, Lichfield, London and now Gloucester.

"In 1616, Tom. May I tell you what trade our father followed? He was a butcher, so there is more than a taste for lively discourse, that unites you and myself. My brother died eight years later having absented himself from the Cathedral, but before that he had brought my parents here from Hereford to enjoy a peaceful old age and had sent me to Oxford, following in his footsteps. There was almost twenty years between us. When he died, he had left me this fine house. He married twice, but was more like a second father to me than a brother."

"He was a brother of whom you are justly proud, sir. I find it strange that after Luther laid bare the doctrine of direct communion with God, and we are Protestants all, that trivial aspects of ritual impair that sacred relationship."

"I am of your mind, Tom, but have a care to whom you speak. I have a profound difficulty in that I find, more and more, I can like a man but hate his views. Well, well, Tom, we are of a mind, but Discretion, the angel who stands ever silently with his tongue behind his teeth, who holds no brass horn or golden trumpet, he is my guardian. I commend him to you in these dangerous times."

"I hear your warning, sir, and hold it close, I assure you."

I drained my glass, set it down reluctantly and took my leave. If I were honest with myself, I now found that I disliked leaving the company of Rowena and her father, and welcomed every opportunity that presented itself for pleasant association with them. Whether it was Rowena's delectable person or her father's interesting conversation that was the main attraction, I would have been hard put to say.

I needed to see Harry Armitage. I knew he was largely recovered for I had seen him regularly every three days and yesterday I had seen him lurking at the back of the crowd when the heralds had bellowed their instructions. The family, father, mother and son, lived near the Castle Gate. They seemed pleased to see me and Harry sat with his leg supported whilst I tested his recovery. "He is like new!" said his wife, but I had to disagree with that. His leg had mended well enough and he could now lurch about unassisted, but he would never again walk straight and true. I could not but observe that if he had not insisted on displaying how well he was recovering in Massey's parlour, when George Edwards was intent on accusing me of theft, he might now stand taller. But they would not hear a word of it.

Little Hal sat disconsolate by a hastily lit fire, his clothes drying on a line in the garden. He was in disgrace. He had joined in Annie's water sports and his mother, usually so gracious could not disguise her annoyance. "That young limb of Satan!" she cried. "I tell you, Doctor Tom, how shall we keep our boys in order when a young girl is allowed to behave like a mad demon!"

Harry, his leg outstretched for my examination, counselled charity. "Come now, Grace," he pleaded, "Show the little maid some pity. How can she prosper in the right way, without a mother!"

"Where is her mother?" I asked curiously.

Grace sniffed. "With God. She died of a childbed fever, and the babe was still born. Little Annie is all the family George Malten has, but what he lacks in family he also lacks in means."

Harry explained. "He is one of those who believes he can buy cheap and sell dear. His father was a respected boatbuilder and apprenticed George to a fellow shipman, but the trade was too slow for him he claimed. He could not turn a profit, he vowed. So he began trading for himself and when the demand came for soldiers for Parliament, off he goes to London with a consignment of old rusty swords. It's said he came to the notice of Old Subtlety's agent who made him a quartermaster for his enterprise. His daughter, Malten left to the care of a fly-by-night young doxy. She abandoned the poor child in the streets, and went to live with miners in the Forest."

"Does the Council not have the means to care for an orphan?" I asked, "For such she was, surely, to all intents and purposes until her father returned."

"Indeed the Council shoulders that responsibility and Massey himself found her a press bed with his own cook. But she would have none of it. She lived wild as a weasel until her father returned and then she quietened under his care, and they lived outside the Eastgate, until Massey ordered that the houses there must be vacated, and theirs was one of the first to be burned. Now her father has been injured, she is running wild again." Harry frowned under my probing fingers. "Is all well, Doctor Tom?"

"Well, I would have liked to see a straighter limb, but it was neglected so long as you know...."

There was a splutter of musket fire and little Hal asked his father, "Is that the vinyard again, father?"

"I think so, son. 'Tis Vavasour come from the Welsh Border. But devil a Gloucester fellow will they tease out, for I gather all here come in from o'er the river."

But Grace was frowning. "No, Harry, I think that sound came from the east. Doctor Tom, will you take a draught of small beer?

You are right. I should out of Christian charity have taken in that poor sprat. But one day her father was here, the next he'd gone, then back again. All was at sixes and sevens."

"Grace," I said, "I am sure there is nothing to reproach yourself with. You had Harry to care for. I think I had best return to the Colonel for if I am not caring for my patients, I should be at the New Inn, should there be casualties now."

After recommending some gentle stretching for Harry, I took my leave of the Armitage family, with a light heart. I felt I had achieved something of note in that a man whose mobility had been grossly neglected, could now walk again independently without stick, crutch or shoulder. True his gait was somewhat clumsy, but for a man who had been relentlessly active, again to be mobile was...

Henry Creery, the young doctor from the Earl's regiment, who had laughed at Rice's blustering claims, was waiting for me under the arch of the New Inn. But today, there was no trace of laughter on his ruddy features.

"Tom, Tom, you must come with me, I fear. Fatalities, man."

It had been decided that in the event of deaths from the siege, two doctors would be needed to declare the subject dead indeed. There had been objections from Rice and Edwards. "There is nothing more obvious to a doctor when a man is dead. What need of two opinions? It is a waste of time and labour."

But Massey would have none of their prevarications. "Doctor Creery shall always in the first instance, determine if death has taken place and from what cause. His findings will be seconded by any of you."

So here was Henry Creery obeying our Governor, and hurrying me along to St Mary de Crypt, under the East wall. "Who is dead?" I asked. "Surely there were no sorties today?"

He looked at me as if I had spoken a strange language. "No, indeed, man! No! No sorties!"

"So who is dead?"

His face worked as if he was trying to speak but could not summon forth the words. We turned into the porch of St. Mary's, and Simeon Walsh met us at the door. He had been instructed by Massey to prepare any dead for our inspection, a task I knew he had been dreading, having as I knew an abhorrence of the sight of blood.

To my amazement he was weeping. "Why Sim, what ails you?" He did not.. could not.. answer me but led us to the head of the chancel where two small bodies lay on trestles. One was Annie Malten, the other the boy, Jem, who had sat down so suddenly in the muddy trough. I could see at once that they had been torn apart by musket shot, something in the manner of Elijah at Hopton Heath, but that had been haphazard. This was deliberate.

Someone came up the aisle behind us. I turned. It was Captain Tom Pury. He looked at the children, seemed to choke and then said one word. "Bastards!"

"Who is the boy?" I asked.

"That is Jem Pegler, the wheelwright's son. Creery came to you because you are treating George Malten. Can he sustain this loss, do you think?"

"I doubt it. They crept up, upon the walls, did they?" I could guess easily whose notion that had been.

"Indeed they did, to look for the King. It seems they wished to see his golden crown. So these two tell me."

Two boys, white-faced and terrified, were huddled at the back of the church. One of them, the taller of the two, began to weep. "I should have stopped her, but she would not listen."

In fact he voiced the pronouncements of all our consciences. Why had I not forcibly removed her from the muddy trough and taken her back to Rowena? She would have had a tongue lashing, it is true, but she would have even now been alive. Sim was even more stricken. "I saw them climbing the Eastgate steps but thought they were the responsibility of others."

Captain Tom nodded, thoughtfully. "I will get my father. How were the bodies recovered?"

The elder boy said, amidst sniffs and tears. "We crawled along and pulled them back on our knees to the head of the stairs, where the sentries helped us. But they were dead, sir."

"That was a brave and thoughtful action for your friends, but you know now that you put yourself in too much danger." He drew the boy to him and let him sob against his buff coat. "You see now, this war is not a Maytime game. Come both of you, we will find my father." He led the two boys from the church.

Henry had found winding sheets and had laid them lightly over the small bodies. "Doctor Tom, will you perform your duty?"

It was the work of a moment. How could there be a heart beat when the heart has been halted by a musket ball? Both had bled copiously. Jem had stopped the ball in his neck, Annie had taken the impact in her heart. I did not think that either had suffered. Death would have been immediate. Henry wrote his report and I signed my name below his.

Captain Tom brought back his father with the Mayor. They came in, downcast, stern of countenance and dismayed beyond words. The great doors were closed behind them, and the Mayor began to question us. It chanced that everyone had seen Annie somewhere that morning, running wild with Jem chasing behind her. Everyone had thought that someone else must have the responsibility for the children's welfare.

Alderman Pury strode unflinchingly to gaze on the little corpses. He stood for some moments and then knelt in prayer beside them for a little. Then he rose, turned and spoke to everyone in the church. "We are all equally to blame for this. I will have an edict put around the town, and I know the Governor will sanction it. Every citizen of Gloucester is accountable for the safety of every child. All must intervene, if a child is seen to be behaving in a manner likely to cause danger or inconvenience in this difficult time. Such action must not be seen as unwelcome interference but concern for the welfare of our beloved children. In the meantime, Doctor Tom, there is poor Master Malten to be informed and Rowena Smith and her father. It is a heavy task for you, new to the town, but I know of no better man to discharge the duty. I will visit the Peglers."

But at that moment the doors were pushed open again and the wheelwright's family ran into the church. The poor parents ran straight down the aisle, and Jem's mother sobbing violently caught her child to her breast. His father leant against one of the pillars near his wife, clearly torn between his need to comfort her and overwhelmed by his own grief. Two older girls followed them, perhaps sixteen and fourteen, clinging to each other and weeping uncontrollably at the loss of their little brother.

The bereaved family could not speak, and the mother would not give up her son, to be carried by any one else. The blood from his wound stained her gown as she tried to bring him from the church. At last, Captain Tom, wary and afraid at the spectacle of such sorrow, prevailed on her to relinquish her burden to him and she and the girls followed him from the church. Master Pegler made as if to leave with them and then paused and said in a choking voice, "This is my fault and none but mine. This morning I told my boy I was too busy to talk to him and bade him run and play. His death is on my head." He clasped the pillar again and sank down against it, sobbing.

The Alderman went to the bereft father and raised him up in his arms. "Paul, my old friend, we are all to blame. We must learn from this to view every soul in Gloucester as a sacred charge from God." He led the poor man from the church, saying over his shoulder, "Doctor Tom, the little maid is in your charge."

I lifted her in my arms. She seemed to weigh nothing and yet I do not remember ever carrying so heavy a burden. Although she was wrapped in a small winding sheet, this fell away and her blood stained my doublet as she fell against me. I carried her from the church, Henry walking before me to prevent passers-by from jostling us. Simeon followed us. A crowd had gathered outside, and as we passed, they fell in behind us. I decided I would place her in the Cathedral until I was told where she would lie in her last resting place. But once again, as with Elijah, my dread was the terrible realisation that I must tell her parent of her fate.

As we walked, one of the College boys began to sing a psalm. It was "The Lord is my Shepherd." Others, boys from the school, men and women joined with him and our sad procession had an air of courage and defiance as we passed over College Green and into the great vault of the Cathedral.

I laid her on a bench near the Choir Stalls, and pondered my next action. I was uncertain whether George Malten could sustain her loss. His injury was life-threatening, no doubt of it. I was sure that the brain has as much a part in recovery as the body. An invalid needs a hopeful attitude, faith in themselves that they will recover. Would he have that courage without his little daughter? He had no other family who could comfort him. I resolved to seek advice from Master James Smith when I went to his household. Should Malten be protected from this tragic news? Should he be kept in ignorance?

Henry agreed to stay with the Gloucester citizens who stood and sat around the little corpse, forming a daytime vigil whilst I went to tell Rowena and her father. As I went the sad irony of the circumstances oppressed me. In life, the poor little child had been neglected and ignored. Now in death scores of citizens were conscience-stricken. All could have nurtured her.

I did not wait for admittance but pushed open the great door. Immediately I heard the sound of weeping. My news had doubtless gone before me. As I stood in the hall, the sobs grew louder. To my horror Rowena appeared at the head of the stairs covered in blood. She was wailing as if her heart was breaking. She saw me and ran down into my arms.

"Tom! I did not hear him." Then followed muffled sobs and words, out of which I distinguished the phrase, repeated, "has bled to death."

Her father and Abram followed by Michael ran into the hall, stopping short as they saw our bloody embrace. In truth, my passions seemed totally confused. Even in the midst of what was to prove a dual tragedy, there was an element of joy for me, in that Rowena had flung herself into my willing arms, and sniffed and wept against my shoulder.

"Let us sit, sweetheart," finally I said, and we reluctantly parted, and sat on the wooden carved chairs that lined the hall, though I took care to keep hold of her hand.

"This is surely the ending of one of the plays the old King delighted in," said James, "with blood flowing like water and all the characters dead as the miller's old mare. May we know what has transpired, daughter?"

"Father, you must not jest! How could you? I failed to care for Master Malten. He was lying beneath the window, by his chair, soaked in his own blood. I think he fell on his arm. All Doctor Tom's work for nothing."

"Rowena, his injury was very severe. His arm was burned and wasted, below that bandage. Whatever I did, I could not have saved it. It was very doubtful that he would survive the serious nature of the wound. That he wished to do so for his daughter's sake I know, but alas!" and now it was my turn to give way to tears.

Abram his large eyes fixed on me, caught me by the shoulders. "Is the little girl dead, Tom?"

I nodded miserably. "Only you, Rowena, out of all of Gloucester, tried to help her. You helped them both. You have the least with which to reproach yourself."

I went upstairs then and attempted to arrange George Malten in more seemly manner. As a doctor I made myself go through the tests for life. There was of course no sign of it. I knew I must fetch Henry Creery to pronounce him dead.

Looking more than ever like an executioner (or a butcher's son, I comforted myself) I returned downstairs and told them then of the wild actions of the children that had ended in such tragedy.

"How long then, daughter, was it that you last saw Malten alive?" asked Master James.

"I would say an hour and some moments," she said thoughtfully, "I had linen to fold for the flat iron and then the irons to heat."

"And Tom? The children shot upon the wall? How long ago was that, would you say?"

I saw where he was at. "Why, sir! The same time. The bodies were already stiffening and blood flowing slowly."

"So it could be said that God chose to take father and daughter to him at the same time. Rowena, my child, you did what you could for both. Michael shall go now for the carpenter, and our family plot in St Mary de Lode shall be disturbed again for these two. Your mother might well welcome the company!"

A strange conceit! But James Smith was one who drew little distinction between life on earth and life byond the grave, believing that all living or dead were part of the great chain of being.

I suddenly bethought myself of the crowd waiting for me in the Cathedral.

"May I bring Annie here to lie beside her father before they…" I faltered. She was such a small scrap of a child. "There are good people in the Cathedral where I laid her. I must return and may I then bring her to her poor father. Creery must come with me and pronounce him dead."

"Tell them John Corbett will speak over them later in the day at St Mary de Lode. Stay! I will come with you."

He found his stick and we walked slowly across the green outside St Mary's. "Tom," he said slowly, " I do not know if God sent for them together. Might the father suddenly sense his daughter was dead, and sought his own demise, falling on his burnt and broken arm?"

"I do not know, sir."

"We say nothing. God forbid he should be denied Christian burial."

And so, that afternoon, father and daughter were interred in the graveyard of St Mary de Lode. I stood listening to Chaplain Corbett, my mind whirling hither and thither. Most shameful of my thoughts was the awareness that I had been spared the dreadful task of informing Annie's father of her death. Perhaps James was right. Perhaps he had known. But another remorseful conscience-stricken notion was the memory of the confiscation of Malten's money. Why, when he came to the New Inn to demand his purse, did he not tell us about little Annie? Why did good Master and Mistress Nichol not tell me of the motherless waif? Julius and the apprentices had been cheated of their wages, no doubt of it, but we could have easily arranged for a sum to be set aside for little Annie's care and well-being.

I needed to see Robert, both to be certain his damaged arm remained without infection and to reassure myself that I could not have acted otherwise. Ralph had been out and about, gathering news. The vinyard to the west of the river above the bridge and the island in the middle of the Severn had been abandoned by the Gloucester troopers. Massey wisely had brought all his forces into the town.

"So some of my advice he takes to heart," said Robert. "He has fifteen hundred men in this small town. The Stuart man of blood has over ten thousand surrounding us, I hear. Only a dunce would have left a couple of hundred across the river."

"And, I am told, Vavasour came at the vinyard like a maid stealing from a bee-hive," said Ralph. "'Oh, mercy me! Will I, won't I?' And Forbes' men from Berkeley, who lay in the long grass by the Westgate, laughed till they cried at the brave antics of the Welshmen, when they finally stormed it. I was with them even now." He coughed delicately and looked out of the window. "I had left two traps below the north wall. They hissed me to lie down while the Welshmen went a-tiptoe round the wall, until inflamed by their own bravery, they took it as if all the devils of Hell were in there. Then when they saw the inner wall they all suddenly took fright and crowded out again, until one or two brave fellows ran back and made sure the place was empty. And now this was the wonder of it. Forbes' men all stood up, laughing and clapping their hands, and cheered the leek eaters. And do you know, no shot was fired by either side. The Welshmen doffed their caps and hats and bowed and we could hear across the water they were laughing at themselves."

"And it was only yesterday, though it seems ten years ago, that some of the Garrison shook hands with the King's men out by the turnpike. If the common soldiers have so little grudge, so little to fight over, why are we fighting, Robert?"

He sighed heavily and faced away from us, holding up his sad stump of a hand. "I want to hate the King for this mutilation. But it is Waller and that ass Allen whom I loathe. I have no spirit for my life, friends. When Pury comes here and speaks of democracies and the common good, I still agree with him, but I cannot now stir myself. What else did you wish to tell me of, Tom?"

I reminded him of the fate of Frances Fiennes' troop, of how the Londoners had been betrayed and abandoned as we thought, how we had purloined the Quartermaster's purse, not knowing he was a lone father with a little wayward daughter. I told him of the sorrowful burial an hour ago.

"Was I at fault here, Robert? I ask you as a father." I had difficulty choking back my tears, when I remembered the little coffin, hastily assembled.

"How could you be at fault? Did you encourage Malten to enter a burning house? Did you take a musket and shoot the innocent through the heart? The churl was a thief, Tom. If he had not stolen … and believe me those train band Londoners will not have been his only victims…. I say to you if he had not been a thief, he would be alive today. My boy, you cannot take the sorrows and the troubles of the world upon your shoulders, broad though they are. Go back and tell Mistress Rowena, that I will play her at chess. I have long regretted my unmannerly response to her challenge. You have done nothing with which to reproach yourself."

"Robert, are our actions our own, or are they part of an almighty plan?"

He sighed and smiled wearily. "Do you think your thoughts are your own?"

I thought for a moment. "I must say yes. No one else would want them."

He went on, "And do your actions stem from your thoughts?"

"Certainly they do. How else would anyone ever do anything?"

"Good. So this Quartermaster, you would accept that his actions stem from his thoughts?"

"I see where you are at. But what of God's almighty purpose for us all?"

"Do you know, Tom, I have a notion that that purpose is brought in to justify all kinds of hammerheaded thinking. You are never so right in my view as when you claim that these wars are a world away from God. Any off-the-hooks doddypoll can claim his wrong decisions and his evil actions are the will of the Almighty. And God is plaguily quiet about his real intentions. There I have done. Enough brain fever for one day." He stretched out on his bed and smiled at us both and closed his eyes.

As we went down the stairs Ralph confided, "Well, devil a word of that did my poor noddle capture. But it is good to see the Colonel smile again."

I nodded but in my heart I feared that this calm peaceful attitude was morphine induced. No harm in that, given the fearful growth in his stomach, but I did not think he would be with us for long. Selfishly I began to dread the days of the future in which we would have to contrive without his comforting counsel.

Although I longed to return to the Smiths' household... if only to see how Abram's hens were faring.... I knew I must remain in the New Inn where Henry could find me and where others who were injured could gain swift assistance.

I confess I was dozing on a bench in the courtyard in the evening sun, when I heard a roaring Scottish voice I did not recognise. "Landlord! Mine Host! Must a man die of thirst? What must I do to get a pint of Rhenish? Refreshment here for an old soldier of the Low Countries, and Doctor, there you are, for it is you, I seek" ...as he caught sight of me, sitting wide-eyed in the courtyard.... "What do you drink, Master Quacksalver?"

By this John Nicholl had recovered something of his breath and his dignity. "Doctor Tom is partial to a glass of taint, Captain Harcus, and I will serve you Rhenish, though in these times it must be but half a pint, I fear. Could you keep your voice down perhaps? Or the King will hear and insist on coming over the wall to toast the cause of Parliament with us."

I had risen by this, entered the inn and made my bow to the stranger. "I am pleased to meet you, sir, though you have the advantage of me. Master Nicholl is well aware of my preferences, I fear. A glass of taint is an excellent good tipple on a hot evening. Will you sit in the sun?" He followed me into the courtyard with exaggerated gait, a-tiptoe, with his finger to his lips. For an old soldier, he was dressed like a courtier with red velvet breeches and long boots of fine Spanish leather.

Dickon came out with the jug of Rhenish, a beaker and my wine glass, and we seated ourselves comfortably. "How can I help you, sir?" I asked him, after a sip of taint. He held his throat as if about to strangle himself, and then said in a loud whisper, "I have a quinsy, laddie!"

"Nothing easier for me to treat," I told him. "Does it hurt you to swallow and speak?"

"Indeed it does. And it will not do but I must be a ..coughing night and day. The smoke from the abandoned houses seemed to catch at the back of my throat."

"My dear sir, I have an infusion of coltsfoot which taken with honey will almost certainly cure the soreness. But you must not roar or shout again, no matter how thirsty."

I went in to ask for another beaker and for some honey. I had the tincture in my box and quickly prepared the potion, which I suggested he took after he had drunk his wine.

"I am in your debt, Master Doctor, laddie," he whispered hoarsely, having swallowed both his wine and my concoction, and now found his tobacco to chew. He had risen to depart. "Tell your good host I will be back to pay him and yourself ere sundown."

"Tell me of your journeys and battles in the Low Countries," I asked him, "and I promise you, you will have paid your shot."

"What, Master Doctor, are you a secret fire-eater then?" He sat again and stretched out his long legs. "Do you long for the trumpet's music and the heartbeat of the drum? Do you think this King outside these walls has a large army at his command? I tell you, these wars now in England are a maypole dance for milkmaids. Know that the King of Sweden eleven years ago led an army of one hundred and forty nine thousand men. I tell you, when we marched, the earth trembled and shook. I know for I was one of them, laddie. I had been taken at the Battle of Breitenfield. Overnight I changed my masters and allegiances and bade Farewell to the great Count of Tilly and threw in my lot with the Protestant Prince Gustavus Adolphus. Would you know why he was victorious?"

I nodded dumbly. While I had been an ignorant scholar in Worcester, these great events were taking place.

"I will tell you, Master Doctor. Gustavus Adolphus was the greatest general who ever lived because at the Battle of Lutzen, the next year, he had nearly thirty thousand Scotsmen fighting for him! There, now what do you think of that, then, laddie?"

His voice had risen again and I remembered my professional position and asked him to speak more softly, for the sake of his throat, and also lest he disturb Robert, sleeping upstairs

"So what happened after that?" I asked, eager for knowledge.

"Well, in spite of we Scots fighting like lions, Gustavus died at that battle. And although the Swedes paid us daler, their coins, and fed us well, we lost at Nordlingen."

"So did you come home then?"

"The devil I did. I tell you, there were rich pickings to be had. Some high German Princeling, Bernard of Saxe-Weimar recruited us to fight against the bloody Hapsburgs in France. What do you say to that then, laddie? Did you think that Catholic France would ever join with a Protestant against fellow Catholics?"

I had to confess I had never given it any consideration, but looked suitably surprised. "Would you say then, Captain Harcus, that the wars in the Low Countries were wars of religion?"

There was a long pause. He chewed rhythmically at his tobacco and spat out what no longer had flavour. "Religion may have been the first motive but I tell you, it was power that each commander sought. If I am honest, no-one gave a tinker's fart, what any man believed." He rose again as if to leave but I had one more question.

"So, Captain Harcus, these great armies in these strange lands. What were your impressions of these places in the aftermath of war?"

He sat again and found more tobacco, which he rolled into a plug for chewing.

"Master Doctor, laddie, I will tell you. Think of the worst scene of Hell and in your mind multiply it a thousandfold. We caused devastation that can never be remedied. Death was the happiest end for many. Plague, torture, mutilation, rape and starvation was the fate of the common people. I am not proud of my part in it, but, as a soldier, that is all I know. I bluster and shout as you have seen, but I tell you, within my head, when I wake in the long hours of night,

I am a man damaged beyond repair." He stared at the wall of the inn, and his bloodshot eyes brimmed with tears. "I tell you, laddie, this so called war 'twixt King and Parliament is as gossips screeching in dispute around a market stall, compared with the horrors I have... have seen. But my throat is better. Master Doctor, I am in your debt."

He rose and bowed to me, a strange courtesy from a man nearing fifty to a mere stripling like myself. I stared after him. He was a man apart from the Gloucester men who had learned their soldiering alongside their daily calling, at the lathe and the plough and the anvil. I wandered into the inn to pay what I owed.

"Well, that is a strange fellow, though a soldier, through and through." John Nichol was scrubbing the wooden tables in a rare moment of quiet.

"He is troubled, I think and has seen dreadful sights," I said, in defence of his strange behaviour.

"Caused 'em more like!" said John, "Terrible, 'tis said, the crimes that have been committed in the Low Countries, in the name of religion, was it?"

"Captain Harcus thinks not. He puts it down to love of power."

"Of all men he should know," said John. "Though 'tis lamentable true that song they sings, 'Here we be, soldiers three, lately come from the Low Country, with never a penny of money.' He's been in here on and off, and has always cozened some poor innocent into paying for him. Oh, no, not you too, Doctor Tom" as, smiling regretfully I reached into my pocket.

The tragic day was waning, and for a city under siege it had been quiet when all was considered. John Nichol told me that the Welsh under Vavasour at the vineyard to the northwest of the city had suffered grievously. After their brave capture of the place from a non-existent army, they had drawn up over confidently and had caught the discharge of one of our demi-culverins, placed in one of the fields under the walls where Ralph caught rabbits. The little mead I think it was known. The Oxford army which was largely to our east and south continued to dig trenches as close to the walls as they could contrive, and Davy Wainwright told me that Sir Jacob Astley was camped in a house to the east that had escaped the fire, just out of the range of our muskets. Where Sir Jacob was, there would be Peabody, not a doubt of it. I could only hope that Major

Legge had told him I was here.

But there had been no further bombardment on that day, the 11th of August and I went to my bed, having made short work of a slice of rabbit pie, and hoping against hope that the relatively peaceful day might herald some hope of mediation. There had been three tragic deaths in Gloucester this morning, and who knows how many Welshwomen were now widows in the land of my mother. I began to think about how I could best protect those I loved when Rupert finally made his great attack, as we all confidently expected he would.

But my day was not over. It must have been an hour after midnight when the canon at the Eastgate began to thunder and I woke with a start. Someone was calling. "Laddie! Are you sleeping yet? Laddie! To your post! Leave your wee coul and put on your fore kirtle, laddie. Here's one painting the landlord's table with his ichor. Get your arse down here, laddie!"

I and my arse made our way downstairs in my nightshirt. Captain Harcus was supporting a young ensign who was bleeding from a gash on the arm. Other troopers from Stamford's regiment stood in the background, with a pile of spades and pickaxes, looking somewhat apprehensive. I realised later that they feared my wrath at being woken in so unmannerly a fashion. Regimental doctors if they were efficient were a rare breed to be cherished, not be woken at ungodly hours.

"What caused this?" I asked. "Have you been tending a garden?"

As ever a doctor's jest was met with polite laughter. "Aye, that we have!" said Jamie Marcus. "And these are the King's own tools! Nay, laddie, 'tis a cut from a Royalist fawchion, and 'twas all the hurt we sustained, though I fear they have bruised and beaten bums and have gone sobbin' to their mithers."

Good John Nichol was already boiling water over the kitchen fire and I found bandages and had Pares lotion ready. "Midnight is a strange time to go a-visiting," I said, looking carefully at the wound. "Was the King pleased to welcome you? I do not think I need to stitch this if you can promise that you can keep your arm still for some days. In a sling if need be."

The canon was pounding away into the night. "That is Blackwell's regiment they are tickling" said the Captain. "Very well, master doctor laddie, since you will pester me so for information"….I had not done so…. "I will tell you what we have been about. We crept out the Southgate and gave them a sound thrashing as they lay asleep in their trenches at Gaudy Green. Laird above, how the varlets roared!"

"What? Louder than you?" I asked saucily. This set us all a-laughing. Even the wounded man who sat with white lips and hollow eyes, smiled reluctantly.

"Aye, well, laugh away, you English bastards!" said Captain Harcus pleasantly. "Any chance of a drink for these good lads, landlord?"

"Small beer is all, I fear. And might you be wanting a beaker too, sir?" asked John Nicholl the soul of smooth courtesy.

But Captain Harcus was spared the terrible fate of paying for his troopers' refreshment by the entrance of Edward Massey, who immediately ordered that they should have what they wished. Jamie Harcus' smile when he heard this sustaining welcome news stretched from ear to ear.

"There you are, my braw lads. Dinna insult the Colonel by being too nice with your requirements. You have just escaped death by a whisper. The Colonel wishes to reward ye."

By this I had completed my bandaging and had fashioned a sling. I told them to return the wounded man if he showed the least symptom of fever. I bowed to the company in my nightshirt and asked leave of the Colonel to withdraw to my bed. He graciously consented and told me he would seek me out on the morrow. I bowed to the Captain, then changed my mind and holding the hem of my nightshirt out to the side, curtsied instead. As I overtopped him by four inches, and now had a month's growth of black beard, the sight was comical and absurd. To the roars of laughter of the troopers, I daintily pranced upstairs where I thankfully put myself back to bed.

But next day Captain Harcus had again to demonstrate his Scottish valour, by "twisting Rupert's forked tail again" as he expressed it. A door had been broken through in a brick house that formed part of the wall in the south-east corner. What did our Highland Hector do but make a bridge of ladders over the moat ! He led his bravest fellows over before the pioneers in the trenches were aware of their presence and set to yet again. The Captain and his henchmen ran doubled up through the ditches, shouting and screaming like so many devils, and wherever they found a poor King's man, lambasted him severely, confiscated his tools and took him prisoner, beating him back over the bridge of ladders. This May game they kept up for half an hour. Then before Forth or Astley could organise retaliation, back they ran over the ladders, pulling them after them, through the makeshift door, and into the nearest alehouse.

Ensign Clifton told me this as I bandaged his wrist that he had sprained. A trooper whom they all called "Rednose" for strikingly obvious reasons had been poked in the leg by a pickaxe as he had roared death and damnation over a poor fellow, digging away, whom he had caught unawares, and whilst he waited patiently for my attentions, Massey arrived.

"Sir Edward," I asked, inclining my body in a sycophantic bow, over Rednose' unalluring scabbed leg, pocked with the remnants of old scars, "Would you do me the honour of accepting a glass of wine? I must attend to this wound. He was poked with a pick axe and although it is not deep or dangerous in itself, soil carries infections, and unless it is cleaned forthwith, he could putrify."

Massey allowed himself a slight shudder. "Certainly, Tom. Resurgam. I will attend to the prisoners who have I think gathered by the Cross. You are in good hands, my fine fellow," he informed my patient.

Rednose gazed at Massey's elegant retreating back and muttered something I could not hear. "What was that?" I asked sharply.

"I said yon turkeycock's all huff and ding." A saying of my father's. In an instant, I was back in the butcher's shop in Fish Street, listening to my father and John Barleycorn, his great friend a farmer from Pershore, discussing a new Worcester merchant, a glover by trade. I was suddenly suffused by guilt. I had left not only my own flourishing medical enterprise, but also the excellent shop and occupation that my parents' had done so much to cherish. I almost wept at my own stupidity. I had left on a whim, an impulsive childish caprice. I should have dismissed Joan for her evil accusations. Housekeepers were not so hard to come by.

Rednose gave his leg a slight shake. He was looking at me curiously. I was back in the tap-room of the New Inn. I had strong essence of lavender of which Sim and I had made large quantities to cleanse wounds. It stung slightly when applied but one could be sure that infection could not flourish where lavender was used.

"Christ Jesu!" Rednose was dismayed, "I stink like an occupying house full of low mawkes."

"And if I thought you had not visited such a place, I would be dismayed for you." I told him, bandaging his unappealing but sweet-smelling limb. "Come back if you have any worse pain or any putrifying stench."

"How shall I know that, reeking like a rotten baggage as I do now?"

"Oh, God be with you!" I cried pushing him in the direction of the street. I wandered after him into Northgate, and along to the Cross, where Massey was speaking to the prisoners, a bruised and broken little band.

".....housed above in my own house, dry and snug, and given a good meal, provided you will work with us at the repair of our walls under our supervision. I do not ask you to shoot at your erstwhile Royalist fellows, merely to help us protect ourselves and you from musket and cannon balls. What do you say, my fine fellows?"

The prisoners looked at each other, with hangdog abashed expressions. Then one spoke up. "Well, for my part, I am well pleased to sleep again under a tight roof. And to have food provided. I am not a sapper, sir. I was in the trenches, as a punishment for speaking out."

"Against what?" said Massey swiftly.

"Chillingworth's mortor." The others looked at him and then glanced over their shoulders, stricken and afraid.

"Come then," said Massey with a note of excitement. "If you will accept my terms, let us sit at our ease for a few moments." He led the way back to the New Inn and called to John Nichol. "Might they have a draught of small beer each? They have useful information for me."

"What of Alderman Pury?" asked John Nichol clearly worried that his allegiance might be questioned.

"No matter for that. I will explain. So, Chillingworth. A philosopher and divine, dear to the King, I think. What has he to do with cannon and shot? His concerns must surely be with premise and conclusion."

"You are in the right of it there, sir. Because he knows of Roman warfare, the King allows him to ordain what type of siege engine he should use. Sir, 'tis pitiful! We were better off in the trenches and are better here, a hundredfold. Is that not so, lads?" His fellows nodded. Now I could see from their powder streaked breeches that they were gunners, or their mates.

"Why so?" asked Massey, scarce able to contain his excitement.

The gunner took a swallow of ale and sighed. "Sir, gunnery is a craft, that must be carefully learned. I think now some call it a science. You must take account of all manner of physical matters, ere you should expend a cannon ball."

"The trajectory?" I put in, hoping to sound knowledgeable.

"As you say, sir, but before you even begin to calculate and adjust that part of the trade, you must know that your piece rests on firm foundations."

Massey nodded. "Yes, indeed, I am an engineer, and have spent many hours embedding our guns here securely, but what of Chillingworth's involvement?"

"Sir, he has caused a monstrous great mortar to be placed on a light wooden platform on wheels. The idea is good... to push ones ordnance about to a convenient spot is a great gift for a general... but this weapon is far too unwieldy for its frail platform. The infantry who have to pull it about have called it the great Hump or Lump. Men will die the instant it is fired and they would not have been Parliament men but my gunners. The force of the explosion which will be huge and terrible will destroy the platform and the cannon will fall and break and roll over, killing any in its path. I told Forth I would have none of it and he sets me to digging ditches. I am a seasoned gunner, sir, and my advice should not be set aside." He could not control his bitterness at this and his voice trembled. He took another gulp of his beer, and looked round at his mates. They nodded slowly, and one or two pledged Sir Edward who sat lost in thought.

"So," at last said Massey, "You would tell me we have naught to fear from this great hump of a cannon that will cause its own destruction when it is fired."

"Aye, that's it, sir. Any gunner worth his salt would have naught to do with it."

"And where and when are we to encounter this hump?"

"They are even now constructing a redoubt. I think they thought to use it tonight. If it need it, fortify your south wall. They had hoped to bring it as close as they could, but the ditches and the causeway prevent it."

"What is your name, my good sir?" Massey had raised him from the level of "fine fellow" to that of a "sir".

"Tobias Moss, sir. I and some few of these here were at Nordlingen. Believe me, sir, we know our trade."

Massey ushered the King's gunners away to his house where they were to lodge with the other prisoners. He asked me to wait for him and to walk to the walls, as he wished to talk of doctoring matters, so I sat for a moment pondering the fact that these gunners seemed to know much of gunnery but what of loyalty? A man's trade could bring him into curious situations, and it might be that that was a more useful fealty than adherence to King or Parliament. It seemed there would always be wars in Europe and gunners would always be valuable men. One could not blame them for bitter feelings, when their best advice went unheeded by their commanders. My father would have called this prodigal Royalist folly, "keeping a dog and barking oneself."

John Nichol brought me bread and cheese as I waited for Massey, and Abram was suddenly there beside me, as he often was when food was placed before me. I shared it with him and asked him why he seemed somewhat troubled.

"I am bid to ask you to come to supper today," he said sniffing, and fumbling for his kerchief.

"Why is that a matter to cause your tears to flow?" I asked as gently as I could.

"Supper is Dame Pertelot."

"I am very sorry." I said truthfully though my heart leapt at the prospect of seeing Rowena.

"She hasn't laid for a year now and Poll Cook says it is good grain going for naught. It must be said," he went on rather heavily in the manner of James, "as I passed through the kitchen after the deed was done, she was cooking then, smelt excellent and will be a galantine."

I was at a loss as to my reaction. As a butcher's son, such an event seemed a part of life. I felt deeply for horses, loved them even, but was something indifferent to the fate of other animals. I patted my adoptive brother on the arm and asked what time the meal would be served. He told me between five and six and then took himself off, having kindly eaten my bread and cheese.

their wives and children were mightily good humoured about the enforced interruption to their day's work, and it was lightened by snatches of song and roars of laughter. Edward Massey had calculated that the impact from the mortars would be lessened considerably if after breaking through the wall, they plunged harmlessly into piles of loose earth. I went up and down the chains of people, taking a turn here, binding a blister there, and ensuring that no-one was working under unsupportable strain and stress.

As I went my rounds for the third time, a familiar voice called, "Hey-day, Master Doctor. Too proud to carry a pail for a poor wench?" It was Rowena, whom I had not noticed before in line with her maidens, all of them laughing heartily at my embarrassment.

I replied, "I pray you, my pretty maid, let me relieve you of your burden," and sought to take the bucket from her, but she clutched it in play to her bosom, calling out saucily, "Unhand my bucket, you bold cavalier!" and so we stood for a few seconds both holding the handle and gazing one at the other, she with a smudge of earth on her cheek, I with sweat running into my beard. Then her friends on either side demanded that she did not break the chain and she pushed me gently away and passed on her pail.

"Tom! Tom! Give us a song!" Abram in another chain had seen me and called me over to him. "What! is the doctor a songster?" cried out the man next to him. I recognised Lieutenant Pearce who had been so brave and clever when we had ridden out a few days before to Tuffley and Brockthorpe.

"He can sing to raise the roof!" said Abram, with perhaps more brotherly pride than accuracy. "Come on, Tom! Sing to help us with these cursed buckets!"

And another roared out, "Aye, Master Doctor, laddie! Come on now with ye. A song if ye please!" There was no gainsaying Captain Lieutenant Harcus. All the other troopers within hearing banged their buckets as they passed them, calling out, "A song! Quiet for the doctor! He'll give us a song."

There was no help for it. But Captain Harcus gave me inspiration. As neat and fashionable as ever, his quinsy clearly a thing of yesterday, he was passing buckets with his troopers. I went over to him, bowed and indicating his elegant legs, launched myself into a verse of "Ragged and torn and true."

"A boot of Spanish leather, I have seen set fast i'the stocks,
Exposed to wind and weather, And foul reproach and mocks;
While I in my poor rags, Can pass at liberty still;
O, fie on these brawling braggs, When the money is got so ill!
O fie, on these pilfering knaves! I scorn to be of that crew;
They steal to make themselves brave. I'm ragged and torn and true."

It seemed as if every soldier in Gloucester was "ragged and torn and true" as the last lines were roared out by many voices. I had pretended to be outraged and poor Captain Harcus was the object of our mirth. At the end I shook his hand and as the troopers cheered asked, "No offence, I hope?"

"Not the least in the world, laddie! You doctor our spirits as well as our bodies."

The lining of the wall went on for another three hours. I was called to the New Inn, to attend to Captain Gray who had cut the palm of his hand with his sword, whilst drawing it carelessly when it had stuck in the scabbard. As he had honed it so that it would cut a hair, he had been fortunate that he had dropped it as he realised what he did. There had been no other injury. One hundred and fifty musketeers had returned from their sortie to Kingsholm unscathed, but with five prisoners. The news was brought to the wall as we completed our labours.

"Laird save us! We shall soon have enough of the King's wee bastards to make up an entire company!" I walked back companionably to the New Inn with Jamie Harcus and resolved to get Dickon to help me to wash myself, before relishing Dame Partelot. So fine a hen was owed a clean appreciative trencherman, at the very least.

But our pleasant meal was not without interruption. The bombardment began as it got dark, with an almighty explosion that seemed to rock the town. I ran out of the Smiths house with Abram after me, but sensed that what Tobias Moss had predicted had occurred. Clouds of dust descended as we ran down Westgate and I cursed the vanity that had prompted me to assume my fashionable blue Cheyney breeches and doublet, but there seemed no hurt to the town. We ran into the brick house along a new tunnel through the piles of earth. I could see little through the door at the Rignall style but there were shouts and screams coming from the area where they had made their platform for the mortars.

For once Abram, so nice and unsoiled was also covered in dust. We grinned at each other as we walked back but our confidence was soon destroyed. A granado fell in Eastgate in front of us, but broke up without doing harm. The troopers were now out and about, advising citizens to take cover. One good fellow courteously suggested that if no-one was injured, I and Abram would cause less anxiety to them if we were within doors. It sounded as if other granadoes were falling up the length of the east wall, but they were not bursting into flame as such weapons had done in the Close at Lichfield.

"Come back with me," Abram ordered. "Poll Cook will have gallons of water we can wash in and Mike will brush our clothes."

So like two dirty urchins, we threw ourselves on Poll's mercy. She put us in the courtyard and we washed, naked in the light of a torch with soap that smelt of lavender and rosemary. As I turned to reach for a napkin that Abram had managed to acquire before I had begun to dry myself, a figure whisked out of sight behind the stair-case window. It seemed to me to resemble Rowena, but surely she was too well born a maiden to spy upon a naked man?

We were welcomed back into the dining hall, and I finished my excellent plate of Dame Partelot that I had left in such an unmannerly way. My eyes were closing in spite of my desire to be alert and interesting. My fatigue was due, I told myself, not to my exertions of the day but to the fact that I had had to wash twice.

Master James saw that I was in sore need of sleep and although both he and his fair daughter wished me to stay in their fine guest room that night, my post was in the New Inn should Henry or my patients need me in the night.

The ordnance continued to fire at intervals throughout the night and into the next day which was the Sabbath. The enemy, as I caught myself calling the King's men, seemed to have little luck with their artillery. Cannon balls resounded against the brick house and the adjoining walls, but loud and dreadful though the explosions were, none were of the magnitude made by the disintegration of the great "Hump". Massey who came in to the New Inn to find me told me that he was preserving our shot and powder.

"As they are doing no great harm, let them exhaust themselves, and then when they are short, I shall make them dance a rare old galliard." It was unusual to hear Edward Massey speak so lightly. He had Tobias Moss with him, and together they walked back to the brick house with me.

"You may conjecture by the long intervals between shots that they are unsure of what they do." Tobias told us, with the air of a man who knew about what he spoke.

"Might not the length of time be calculated to disconcert us?" I asked like a simpleton. Both mighty Parliamentarian Commander and humble Royalist gunner gazed at me more in sorrow than anger.

"Tom, have you not heard of striking while the iron is....." but I did not allow him to finish.

"Oh, Christ, what is that?" I had seen a man lying in the brick house under the ill-fitting door.

He had been shot in the chest by a musket. From the state of the poor knave's breeches he had crept in to urinate or to catch a glimpse of the enemy but some alert marksman had caught sight of his movement and had "struck while the iron was hot." A tray of loaves laid carefully near the door betrayed his calling, that of a baker's journeyman. We cautiously pulled him away from the treacherous gap. I ran to Sim's shop for a winding sheet and a trestle, and we carried him into nearby St Mary de Crypt, where I sent the sexton to find Henry. This was so haphazard and unnecessary a death that my spirits were quite downcast.

After Abram had been to find me at midday, I went up to see Robert who lay looking at the small window. He told me he had prepared instructions for me in the event of his death.

"As shall most certainly happen, in a few days, a week perhaps. Chicken broth and a certain golden nectar hold back that which we all know will come. But tell me now, how does young Massey? He has surprised us all. Each day, I look to hear Rupert and his devil dog come rampaging up the Eastgate."

"Well, I have heard that Rupert's dog is a small curly fellow, who has no more of the devil about him than any little pretty creature. No, Robert, Massey has done well, very well. Did you hear about the gunners?"

It seemed that Ralph had heard about our prisoners, and had told Robert about their punishment and "rescue", if so it was.

"One of Massey's tactics and to me it seems a good notion, is to keep them, the enemy, constantly surprised by continual swift successful sorties. He has not yet lost a single trooper. And he has learnt from Tobias Moss that Forth thinks he knows much about the science of gunnery but in reality knows very little. What Massey hopes to do is to encourage them to expend their powder and shot whilst he husbands what he has in Gloucester."

Robert said again, "He has surprised us all."

I heard my name called downstairs and there was our Governor, looking up at me. "Tom, will you come, my good fellow? I am filling up the Southgate entirely, and I need you when the earth chains form, lest any carry too heavy a burden."

I bade Robert Farewell and followed Edward Massey down Southgate. The chains of willing citizens were already forming. Jamie Harcus was at the forefront of one such chain and we worked all day. I confess that I did not find the labour too irksome as I positioned myself beside Rowena and had the benefit of her lively conversation and enchanting visage for most of the day. Abram worked beside us and I heard that I was invited again for my evening meal, but that sadly it would be a plain repast. The galantine was gone. Abram had finished it for breakfast. I looked at him sadly and said in heartfelt tones, "Poor Dame Partelot."

He had the grace to appear slightly shamefaced.

Jamie Harcus asked for yet another song so, as this was an excuse for me to gain a few moments respite, I launched myself into "Lavender Blue" but was somewhat embarrassed by the raised voices of all there who seemed to be exhorting me to "keep the bed warm." Alderman Pury was suddenly beside me.

"As it is the Sabbath, perhaps a psalm might be more in keeping, Doctor Tom." and so I managed to remember the one about the gates lifting up their heads. Perhaps that suited our task as we were filling up the entire Southgate as well as piling earth inside all the houses and shops along the south east wall. Poor Simeon was ordered to move the contents of his shop inside St Mary de Crypt and gazed in horror as his premises were reclaimed by the earth of Gloucestershire.

The following day the bombardment began in earnest from Gaudy Green. For the first time they had some real success causing a breach in the south wall, but before they could take advantage of their triumph great loads of sacks of wool were pushed into the gap and the earth piled up again behind in heaps as high as the wall.

Shortly afterwards one brought the news that they had reduced the level of the moat, by the strategic placing of a mine.

Massey had had intelligence brought to him by a little fisher boy who lived beside the river near the Weir House that cannon were being brought to Kingsholm to the north of the city. The child had wriggled like an eel through the reeds and had escaped the watchfulness of the Welsh on the opposite bank, and was rewarded with a crown and a hearty breakfast in the Commander's kitchen. Captain Mallery and one hundred and fifty musketeers sallied forth and returned within an hour, having killed four enemies, taken two prisoners and lost none! Men were saying that night that Massey had the luck of the Old 'Un as they termed the devil.

But it was not to last. On Tuesday the 15th of August, the good fellowship and courage which the town had displayed was sorely challenged. I had gone to view the earthworks in the south, out of amazement that so much earth could be moved so quickly, and that so simple a stratagem could prove so effective a defence. I was musing over the fact that it was the citizens who had combined together to defend themselves in this remarkable way, and who had literally "moved mountains", when Jamie Harcus approached me with a canvas bag.

"See what I have here, laddie! Now these'll make the devils jump about."

He had about five small granadoes, a weapon which burst into flame when thrown into ones foes in a certain way. "They were in Massey's store, the canny wee bastard. He doesna like these beauties. Doesna think they are the weapons of a gentleman!" He roared appreciatively at this, and stroked his hateful toys.

"So what are you going to do?"

To the right of our earthworks the wall rose more stoutly, and we had judged that their mortars were not aimed at this area. Indeed we would have heard the noise of scores of men moving the wheeled trolleys if they had decided to attack that section. In two places it was still possible to climb a rough stair to the narrow stony causeway that surmounted Gloucester's wall.

"I'm going to throw them some sweetmeats they'll not resist. They're mining, under the walls so I'll give them a rare treat and ye'll help me, laddie."

I shuddered. "Oh no I wont. I'm a doctor. I don't kill. That was part of my agreement with Massey. Besides they might be wretched fellows brought in to mine for Forth. You might be killing ragged colliers, the poorest of the poor."

He looked at me, partly in despair and partly in anger. "Master Doctor, laddie, are you a man or a mouse? Well, at least warn me if Massey, the bonny wee lassie, comes this way wi' his tawse, to beat the pair of us." And before I could remonstrate he had sped up the nearer stair overlooking the orchards from the old abbey. He perched at the top, below the level of the wall and began throwing his granadoes neatly over the wall, one by one. There was no sound of destruction or recrimination, but the faint sound of small splashes, so the last two he lobbed further afield. Now there was a response! A man screamed and there was the crackle of fire. He turned back to grin at me, a smile that had in it all the glee of a man who was successfully plying the only trade he knew. Then to my horror he edged himself further up to peer over at the enemy. I ran up the stair to pull him back forcibly, but too late.

There was a shout, a crack and he dropped lifeless into my arms.

13

Icalled for help. He was stone dead, no doubt of it, but I could not let him tumble to the ground. Two of the ensigns heard me and came running, and somehow I managed to pass their Captain Lieutenant down to them. Seeing the terrible wound on his brow, they looked at me questioningly. I shrugged my shoulders.

"He would see what damage his granadoes did," I said helplessly. I suddenly feared that they might have thought I was his murderer or had encouraged him into reckless valour. "Believe me he would do his will. I could not restrain him." They nodded slowly, gazing at the ruined face of their valued officer and then looked up at me for further instruction. "Best lay him in St Mary de Crypt."

I found Massey. He gasped when I told him what had taken place and asked me what so many others would, during the course of that day. "Could you not have stopped him?" My answer was always the same. "How?"

How should I have acted? I asked myself the same question over and over again that day. Should I have taken the granadoes from him forcibly? Pleaded with him not to kill poor miners? Run and pulled him down off his perch? If I had done any of this, he would have made a very uncomfortable enemy, confined as we were in a small city and he had been a good friend. A much better friend to me than I to him, for I had let him die.

I found Henry and in a fit of sudden anger, decided that Rice or Edwards should sign the document for Jamie's death. We had been at the beck and call of all the tender stomachs and delicate headaches of the Gloucester citizens since the beginning of the siege. I had seen neither hide nor hair of Rice and Edwards since it began. They could emerge from whatever bolt-hole into which they had secreted themselves and work. Henry agreed with me.

"God defend that they should soil their delicate white fingers with some goodman's honest blood." he said scornfully.

"Where are they?" I asked.

"Ask Massey. For some reason, he has not called on them."

I went towards his house but met him coming down Southgate to find us. He began by apologising for his previous abrupt question. "Indeed, Tom, you could not have stopped him. He was ever headstrong, trusting his own obstinate judgement rather than that of more sagacious counsellors. That is why he failed to gain promotion to full captain."

"I liked him so much," I said morosely, with an ill grace. He glanced at me, and went on, "Yes. We all did. But this is not the first time he has gone his own way, ignoring wiser advice. The whole town is ringed with expert King's musketeers constantly at the ready. He knew that."

I nodded. I could not chose but grieve for this mad Scotsman, who had been so large a character and so troubled an officer. But I put my sorrow aside and asked my trifling question. "I came to ask why Rice and Edwards have not been called to work. Why are Henry and myself the only doctors to be found?"

"Do you not know?" he said, stopping in the street and facing me. "I will tell you. I cannot afford to have their "mimsy-pimsy, will I? wont I?" type of doctoring. I will not insult the Gloucester ladies by comparing those two to sad old crones. Any sad old crone could turn a better fist to curing the sick than those two. The women of this town are Amazons. They are all Goddesses compared with those two depraved excuses for physicians."

I had never heard him wax so poetical. "You dislike them then but I agree. You are right. The ladies of this town are all that is excellent. Not a doubt of it!"

He gave a half smile and after we had dealt with the document that proved poor Jamie's death, decided that he should be interred in St. Mary de Grace.

"God help us all, if I should need to use the earth from the graveyards to make other parts of the walls good." Massey sat down heavily on a bench at the side of the chancel. "As you saw the earth we have used is well worked soil and easily dug out. If we get down to the river clay, it is not so easy for citizens to transport."

He sighed and I noticed for the first time how tired he was. His face, always pale and thin, seemed ghostlike in the dimness of the church, his eyes glittering and glancing hither and thither, as if constantly seeking inspiration in his crusade to thwart the King.

"Tom, do you think the Colonel would see me? I would like to discuss tactics whilst...."

"I am sure of it." He had been intending to say "whilst he still lives". Little to be gained from discussing strategy with a corpse! "Could you return with me and I will prepare him for your visit?" He nodded and we left the two ensigns guarding poor Jamie. The sexton had been sent to the carpenter's for a coffin.

Somehow that day a form of oppression began to eat at my soul. I had been cheerful and active before Jamie Harcus' death, but now as we walked back to the New Inn, companionably enough, I was assailed by a bleak unspoken question. "What was the purpose of our resistance?"

Robert was awake and agreed to see Sir Edward, "As long as he does not ask me to condone his abandonment of poor Henry Stephens."

"I think he has learnt a great deal since then," I said confidently, "He weighs up every risk. All our losses so far have been the result of personal carelessness within the city. So far no-one has been lost outside."

Ralph even went so far as to warn Massey not to tire Robert. I had never heard him address the Governor in any way before. Now he said calmly, "I beg you, sir, not to speak to the dear Colonel on matters that could inflame him."

Massey raised his eyebrows slightly but nodded agreeably and went up to see my poor sick friend. I sat with Ralph who asked me yet again if the Colonel was improving. I told him yet again, there could be no improvement. Ralph had surely seen the great cancre that obstructed his digestion, growing on some vital inner organ.

We both sat hunched in desolation until two persons came into the courtyard and we were constrained to put on more sunny expressions. Rowena brought beef broth that had been strained many times for the Colonel and Abram pointed out that it was already afternoon and the hour for our midday meal had passed.

"You had best see what Mistress Nichol has for us," I told him and he sped off to the kitchen. Ralph smiling a sad smile walked out into the street and I found a chair that had been left in the Courtyard and wiped the seat with my sleeve for Rowena.

"Would you come to see my father this even and lighten his spirits?" she asked.

"I will try," I said, feeling a little happier at the prospect of seeing Rowena's father later today. Perhaps the notion of seeing her also pleased me if I were honest. I told her about James Harcus, and asked her if she was at leisure to come to his funeral later that afternoon.

"It would have gladdened his heart, if he had known the most beautiful woman in Gloucester would attend his interment," I said gallantly.

"From what I have seen of the world, such a presence at such a time is not nearly so welcome as the concourse between a man and a woman who happen to be alive," she observed with some asperity.

I nodded gloomily. If I had not been so full of crochets I could have interpreted such a pertinent response as encouragement to myself as an acceptable suitor, but my spirits were so heavy, I could only look at her despondently. Abram returned .

"I have bespoken bread and Cheddar cheese for us. Mistress Nichol is at her wits' end to contrive meals for all in the Inn, and it will be rye bread and cheese for some days, she fears."

Rowena rose, "Well, come and cheer my father this even and if we are not called out again to strengthen the wall, I will try to find something more tasty than bread and cheese, though sieges are not good times to display cooking skills."

Massey came down again and bowed to Rowena who made her curtsy as if she was greeting the King himself. She said no more but made her way back to the street, daintily avoiding the spillages of beer that had not yet been washed away. But perhaps there was no spare water now for such a mundane task.

"He is asking for you." Massey indicated the stairs. "I suppose I had better try to find out if Harcus had any family or possessions."

"Do you wish me to do that?" I asked "I counted myself his friend."

He accepted this offer with alacrity.

"Pray God he is the last man we lose," I observed gloomily

"Amen, to that." said Massey. "You had best go to the Colonel."

Robert smiled as I came in to his close bedchamber.

"Poor Tom!" he said with sympathy, "Massey has told me about your Scotsman. I am very sorry. Not for him. He was clearly an arrant fool, but for you that you have lost your friend."

"I did not stop him," I said, "I did not know how to stop him. He had determined his course of action and would not let me dissuade him from it. But Robert, he had been in the wars in Europe. I tell you he was at Nordlingen and then in the wars with the French against the Hapsburgs. How could he have escaped so much danger only to throw away his life in a war that he termed milkmaids wrangling round a maypole?"

"Did his memories afford him pleasure?" asked Robert.

I thought for a moment. "Pleasure, no. Pride, perhaps. He seemed to think a great deal of some Swedish fellow Gustavus, but he was tormented by his memories of the battlefields of the German states. In fact, his recollections seemed to be the stuff of nightmare."

"It may be that he held his life of little value. Perhaps without thinking it, he chose his death. He seemed to like your company, as I do. Perhaps he was content to die. He had met one whom he wished he could call "son", knew he could not, and so relinquished his spirit, as I will soon do."

I could say nothing but "Robert". He took my hand in his wasted claw and gently patted it up and down upon the coverlet.

"He chose his life and he chose his death. We all do, son."

By this I was weeping in good earnest. "But what is the purpose of it all? So many good men dead before their time, the women made widows, the fatherless children. The towns laid waste, houses spoiled, lives destroyed. I tell you, Robert, I will have no part in it."

He patted my hand again. "Hold to that resolve, son." He smiled and closed his eyes.

Jamie Harcus' small room in the Garrison was clean, bare and neat. There seemed to be no trace of any family waiting for him back in Scotland. I raised his pillow moved by some instinct and found a prayer book . On the first page was an inscription. "James Harcus, from his loving mother, Elizabeth. My prayers go with you." Underneath a different hand had written, " Mother, at peace, August '34." I took this little book to the Sergeant Major and asked could it be buried with him. He readily agreed and I took it to St Mary de Lode, where they were laying Jamie in his coffin. I curled his stiff fingers around the little missal and hoped I was performing the last office of a friend.

I stood for a moment holding his cold hands, and thought of his barren life. He had given himself to the cruel goddess of War, and in the end she had claimed him as her sacrifice. The memories that had tortured him, of the battlefields of Europe, died now with him. The cries and screams of the dying faded into oblivion. All was silence now and peace. He would not wake again in the long watches of the night, tormented by the horrors of the past.

I touched his wrinkled cheek and my tears fell on his face. This was now all I could do for him. I gestured for them to nail down the lid and joined those of the Regiment who had gathered to see him to his last resting place.

Later that evening I asked Master Smith why there were so many churches in Gloucester named for St Mary.

"When Mary Tudor came here to burn Bishop Hooper, she was gratified I think to see these tributes. We cannot know whether she took such proliferation of her name as adoration of the Queen of Heaven or flattery for herself. Now, Gloucester does not ally itself with the old religion. We abhor any form of Popery. And the name of our church, St Mary de Lode commemorates the time when a branch of the Severn passed its door. But, Tom, I am sorry that you are so downcast. Rowena tells me the poor captain who was buried this afternoon was a particular friend. I am very sad for your grief."

"In fact he was not a friend for long. His life was so wasted by war and conflict. When he died he had nothing, no possessions but an old prayer book given him by his mother. And he was so tortured and troubled in his conscience. His terrible unhappiness oppresses me, Sir."

"What does the Colonel say of his passing?" asked Master Smith.

"That he chose his death as he chose his life. He knew the risks."

"I am afraid that that is true. He is at peace now."

"But so wasted a life." I found I could no longer speak coherently and took my leave.

The next day was the 16th of August. Captain Peter Crisp, one of the regiment's fiercest officers came into the New Inn, shortly after I had risen and asked me if I would go with him and one hundred and fifty musketeers on a sortie that morning. I confess, sad and downcast as I was, my spirits did not revive at the prospect of my imminent death in the field. Still, it might be that I would encounter Peabody which gave the expedition a certain personal excitement for me.

"Sir Edward dictates that I should go?" I asked, innocently.

"Not a doubt of it," said Peter Crisp. "Does he not always claim that the sooner the sawbones is brought to the poor wounded bastards, the better their chance. Get your fiddlestick, doctor!"

I ran up to borrow Robert's sword and started out with the musketeers marching in time to a fife and drum up to the Northgate. Sir Edward had turned out with Foster Pleasance and his servants to give each man a measure of strong spirit, as we passed under the portal. But when he saw me, sword at the ready, anticipating the bloody fray, he shouted furiously "Doctor Tom, where in hell are you going?"

I looked at Peter Crisp, who somewhat shamefaced, muttered that he had thought Massey had wanted a doctor swiftly on the scene in the event of an injury.

"Yes! Here!" Massey roared. "This man is not a soldier. He knows nothing of sword play. He would be no more use to you than leaden shoes. He is of much more value to us here alive in the town, than dead as a shotten herring in a bloody ditch."

I stood looking from one to the other. Peter Crisp shrugged and turned back to his men who were grinning like dog-foxes at the prospect of their commanders at odds. Crisp gave them a few last minute instructions. They were going to rush through the gate and round the walls to the right and would fall upon any who were digging trenches and kill them instantly. They had the element of surprise on their side.

They streamed through the portal and I stood with Massey and watched them go.

"Did you then want to go and try your valour?" Sir Edward asked me, indicating the sword at my side.

I stood silent for a moment, and then as the last man disappeared from view, told the honest truth.

"No, I thank you, Sir Edward. But I was on the field at Edgehill, and at Lansdowne Hill. I was prepared to go, had it been your wish."

"Well, it was not! I want you as a doctor not a whoreson shakebuckler. A sortie is not a battle, Doctor Tom. Crisp had no right to put upon you in that manner. You had best have a measure of hot brandy wine, so that you do not look upon yourself as a coward."

Peter Crisp returned with his musketeers about an hour afterwards. Two had sustained injuries, and Sir Edward brought them to me in the New Inn. One was merely a sword scratch on the thigh. It was not deep but the poor fellow had no notion of stoical endurance, and cried and moaned, as if he were at the gates of Hell, whilst I cleaned and dressed his injury and then when all was completed, he smiled sweetly, jumped from my table and said, with great courtesy and an elaborate bow, "Permit me to pledge you, dear Doctor!"

The other musketeer had put his shoulder out. I had to employ my wiles as a bone-setter, talking of nothing, praising his bravery, telling him to lie back and imagine himself in his garden at home, rejoicing in the good weather, until the poor fellow had been lulled into a state of peaceful acquiescence. When he was abstracted enough, I swiftly inserted the humerus into the scapula. For the usual few moments afterwards, I became Satan and all his imps moulded into one accursed doctor. His friends stood and laughed except one who thought I tortured him and drew his sword. Henry had observed my treatment and asked if I could teach him this useful skill.

Ben had taught me with old bones from my father's shop after we had burnt all shreds of meat from them and had encouraged me always to check any injury by carefully feeling the subject's skeleton inside their skin. This had sometimes provoked wrath if the patient had felt my exploration was something too permissive, and especially if they were female. But there was no other way. Ben would say I had an instinct for bones, from him a glowing compliment.

But there was no time for bonesetting lessons. There were more houses in the wall to be lined with earth. The chains of citizens and soldiers formed and once again I was asked for a song. But I was prepared.

"No, good people!" I shouted, "We shall have a roundel if you please. You all shall sing to me."

So one line began with "Hold thy peace," the next with "I prithee, hold thy peace." And the third "Hold thy peace, thou knave" and the fourth "Thou knave!"

For a few moments it was tuneful and melodic but at length it degenerated into an ill sounding thunder. God knows what the King's men must have thought of the extraordinary noises that came from Gloucester, if they had been listening the other side of the wall. I became tired of those who thought they were rare good jesters, explaining to me that they would never sing if they "held their peace." Each of these wits thought they were the only prate roast to think of the wretched quip. The smile on my face seemed to have been etched in stone!

Next day the 17th August Alderman Pury came to see me after I had breakfasted.

"Well, Tom, I hope you are congratulating yourself. We have been besieged for nearly a fortnight and all our preparations have stood us in good stead. No sickness within the town, even though many of the poorer sort have to rely on your stored water, all wounded troopers swiftly attended to, by yourself and Creery with a minimum of suffering, and the walls, paper thin as they are, holding up like the strongest bastion in the land. Though I think that is down to Massey's skill at forecasting where the mortars are likely to strike."

"I am happy to have earned your good pleasure, sir. Thank you," I said politely. If he observed that I was somewhat low in my spirits he said nothing, but continued to praise my efforts.

"The water is holding up well, the people are boiling what they give the children to drink, and there are many untapped barrels remaining, in the Hospital. Your good father would be proud of you, let me tell you."

"Thank you, sir," I said again. When I allowed myself to consider our situation, it was certainly an achievement so far to have escaped disease, cooped up as we were.

"Massey tells me that he is about to change tactics. Our dear good friend the Colonel has suggested that the King's musketeers that ring the town may now be growing careless and it is time for our boys to use them as target practice."

Perhaps my face betrayed my distaste for such a callous notion. I nodded silently and then invited him to drink a draught of small beer with me. At the back of my mind there was always the notion of Peabody out there. I disliked the thought that his considerable bulk should be viewed as "target practice".

Suddenly there was a commotion in the street outside. Foster Pleasance came into the Courtyard calling out for the Alderman.

"Would you come to the Eastgate, sir?" he called. "There is a herald wishing to speak to you. You will be well protected, I assure you."

I followed after them in an aimless manner, having nothing else to do. Too much to hope that the King was seeking terms for surrender! I had not been prepared for the dull tediousness of a siege. In the past I had not left Worcester for months on end, but I had always known that I was free to go when I wished, if my father would consent. Now I was a man grown and a prisoner against my will. The trade of the market had shrunk to nothing and no trows or boats could tie up at the quays. No-one came into the town and no-one left. We were thrown in upon each other, whether we would or no.

My conscience flared into action. I was here to help poor Robert. God knows he had done everything he could for me. Saved my life twice, once after my father's hanging, and again he had come to my rescue when Brigstock had tried to kill me after Edgehill. And the Alderman was right. We had been immured for nearly two weeks. The fact that we all survived in good heart was in itself a triumph.

Alderman Pury was standing with Massey at the Eastgate, and they were talking with one of the men whom the King had sent previously. The herald gave Pury a packet and turned back with a few of the King's musketeers towards the turnpike. Two or three ensigns had their muskets trained on the backs of the visitors but Massey instructed them to lower their weapons. The Alderman placed the packet carefully inside his coat and turned away from the gate, coming back to speak to me.

But before he could divulge the contents of the packet, the battery at Gaudy Green to the south began to sound its dreadful music. This time instead of mortars shot at the walls, granadoes were hurled into the streets near the Southgate. Two boys came running up, screaming and shouting.

"Come sir, please, come quickly! They are killing our mother!"

Massey and the ensigns immediately ran down the Southgate, but her sons had been pessimistic in their assumption that they had lost their parent. The valiant lady stood holding an empty bucket, gazing at a large granadoe she had capably extinguished. The ensigns approached cautiously but the match was sodden, and harmless, thanks to her quick action.

"Is this your mother?" Massey asked the boys.

"Yes, sir," they chorused, shamefaced.

"I do not think she is dead." They ran to her and she put an arm round each of them.

"The worst of it is, sirs, I have to return to the Hospital for more water! Come on, boys!"

But I relished the challenge of a task, at that moment, however humble, and picked up the pail. She lived at the sign of the tallow chandler, near St Mary de Crypt and I promised to bring her water to her in twenty minutes. Massey walked along beside me to the Cross.

"You have your heart in your hose, Tom," he observed. "Believe me no-one blames you for Harcus' death."

"I know that!" I said with an unseemly touch of irritation. "I am sorry for myself, Sir Edward. I do not know why I am here."

He looked round, making sure we were not overheard, then said in a conspiratorial whisper. "Neither do I! I mean, I do not know what I do here."

"But you have done so well!" I told him. "The stocks of food and hay. The way you have made weak walls impenetrable. Your brilliant surprise tactics, when so few can cause so much chaos for so many. You will go down in history, Edward."

For once I had forgotten his title. But he did not comment. "I could have done nothing without you, the Purys and the Colonel. Let us try to support each other as friends, Tom, whatever might occur."

"Right willingly," I said and we parted and I felt a little more joyful.

In the shadow of the night, thirty of Stamford's regiment mounted the stair where Jamie Harcus had died and crawled along the narrow space along the top of the wall behind the parapet on hands and knees, knowing that if they were seen by the enemy, death would follow instantly. Massey had schooled them to creep along to the eastern side until each man rested beside an embrasure. Then and only then were they to peer round the edge of the parapet wall and see if they could see the King's musketeers sitting round their fires. They were to pick their man and at a prearranged signal, the hooting of an owl from the Eastgate, were all to fire at once. In the instant of firing, muskets had to be withdrawn and hidden behind the parapet and they were to begin the uncomfortable journey in reverse. Massey reckoned that the enemy would assume that they had mounted the wall at the Eastgate and those who could still fire, would concentrate their shot in that direction. Massey hoped that they would congregate together in their surprise shooting at the gate house in the hope that the Stamford musketeers would be shot descending at that moment.

But the demi-culverins that were mounted on sconces above the gate had been quietly made ready, the trajectories calculated and the powder and balls prepared. Massey had not used our ordnance much prior to this, being anxious to husband carefully our precious powder and shot. Also knowing the fragile state of the walls he had not wished to provoke the enemy into a constant barrage or bombardment. He had spoken much to Toby Moss, the captured master gunner, who had been proved right in that the huge mortar they had deployed at Gaudy Green had collapsed when it was first fired. He had discussed much on the art of gunnery in general terms, not encouraging Toby to betray his King. It was clear that Forth was not skilled in this branch of warfare, and Massey was confident that the capture of Toby and his gun crew was a severe disadvantage to the Royalist commanders. Moss had also divulged that even in Oxford the King's army lacked sufficient round shot for the large ordnance. "Their sakers and minions ain't no good against walls." I heard him tell Massey. "And where are they getting their gunpowder? It has to travel from Oxford."

Massey's stratagem went largely according to plan. One poor fellow crawled too far to his left and fell into the wall of soil. But we had ladders ready and were able to rescue him silently, as he floundered about "like an overgrown turnip", Captain Crosbie whispered.

At the hoot of the owl Stamford's musketeers fired almost as one man and from the roaring and wailing that came from over the wall, found their targets. The King's musketeers thought Stamford's men had come from the Eastgate as predicted, and aimed and fired their muskets in that direction. The demi-culverin that they could not see... indeed all was black as midnight's arse-hole... suddenly burst into hideous life and from the screams that ensued, several poor men were killed or crippled. And Massey had lost not one!

We were woken next day by Forth's cannons roaring against the south wall but if they had hoped to subdue us after the midnight triumph, they were mistaken. Massey rightly judged that if they were making a furious sound on the south wall, they would not expect an offensive attack elsewhere. So whilst their cannons made much noise but did little harm to the south of the city, Massey turned his gaze northwards.

The Welsh had joined with the forces from Worcester. I hated to think of this union. My mother, a Welshwoman had married my father, a butcher from Worcester. I was distressed to think that William Russell and his garrison whom I had assisted earlier in the year against Waller were my enemies outside the walls in Kingsholm. In spite of my much voiced neutrality, I felt a desperate traitor. The largest sortie so far went out on this day, four hundred musketeers, with fifty more sent off to provide covering fire. Once again due to the element of surprise, Massey's plan was entirely successful. Cannons were spiked, officers and gunners killed, prisoners taken and only two of our men would not return. This was the first occasion Massey had had fatalities.

Some of the troopers gathered in the inn yard, having been promised canaries by their commanders, as they had committed themselves so well in the Kingsholm battlefield that day. One loud mouthed fellow claimed that Massey had the luck of the devil.

An ensign disagreed. "Not so, Dan. He makes his luck. He uses his head-piece, weighs up what he can easily achieve, and plans it painstakingly. "Luck" betokens a lack of planning and the notion of bounty falling into his lap."

A second ensign suggested, "And have you heard of a siege where after a fortnight, the food is still enough for all? Not rich or plentiful I grant you and I could wish we had something other than rye bread, dried sausage and apples. But, Dan, you must admit he has contrived excellent well. If he is a devil, than grant him his due. He is not lucky. He is clever."

John Nichol had brought out one of his precious barrels of Canary wine and caught the tail end of the conversation. "Aye, my masters. But for how long?"

"Christ knows!" the man who had spoken was sitting alone

under the balcony. He chewed at a churchwarden pipe and had generally resisted the temptation to join in the conversation. Now he rose and came over to me. He was a well favoured man, older than myself with a thick mane of pale hair, which he wore even longer than I did, although my habit was to tie mine back in a tail.

"Doctor, I am not sick in my body but in my head. May I speak with you of this? The feeling of being ringed about and imprisoned overpowers and oppresses me. I long to stride away from here. Have you a salve that can cure my longings?"

"If I had, I would use it myself for I suffer from those yearnings." I told him, "I want to be on the prow of a boat on the next tide with eight good men rowing me upriver to Worcester."

"Why are you constrained here then, in this hellhole?"

"Come now, good Master Hatton, Gloucester is not a hellhole if you please." John Nichol's pride in his city had been challenged. "The only town on the Severn where men strive for equality before the law. We are all Kings here."

"Well said, honest John!" the ensigns approved the innkeeper, though whether from conviction or the need to be certain whence their next drink was coming, was hard to determine.

"So, why did you not escape three weeks ago when none could say you nay?" asked Hatton, who I now remembered was a gunner, from elsewhere in Gloucestershire. We had wandered to the end of the inn yard and now could not be overheard.

"Loyalty to Colonel Burghill. He prevented my hanging in Worcester by the Earl of Essex when that noble bastard hung my father as a spy."

He gazed at me wide-eyed. "And yet you are hand in glove with Massey after such an outrage!"

"Massey never tried to have me hung, and Robert Burghill saved me. I am loyal to men, not to a faction."

He repeated my words slowly. "Loyal to men, not to a faction." He chewed on the stem of his unlit pipe. "Have you heard of Captain Fawcett?"

I shook my head. Hatton continued, "He taught me my trade. I went to the north with him and his men when the King threatened the Scots. Louscland! Wild and cold!"

"Where is Captain Fawcett now?" I asked. He did not reply but gestured with his head eastwards. After a moment he said softly, "To be honest with you, Doctor Tom, that is where I should be. Not because I care for the King. My father is the youngest son of a youngest son, and our family has been ignored by more ambitious scions. No, I would go from here, because being mewed up like this causes my brains to melt into a skimble-skambled ferment. I want to run and run over the Cotswold Hills and far away. Also I had agreed to wait for Captain Fawcett to fetch me at my mother's house in Stow on the Wold. Then when he did not come and Baskerville's cursed quartermaster came roistering through the town, offering money for Parliament, I took it. And then I saw the Captain, with all the mates standing beside Brave Bess when the King came two weeks ago."

"Who is brave Bess?" I asked.

He looked at me pityingly. "A demi-cannon! She it was who made the breach last Monday."

There was silence between us. After some moments I said, "Listen Gunner Hatton, as far as I am concerned this conversation did not take place. Do your will. I shall say nothing."

And that was that. No more was said and I thought no more of it. Next day the bombardment increased alarmingly. Massey fetched Tobias Moss to advise him as we stood and listened to the thunderous noise. The two parts of the wall which we had reinforced with mountains of earth, on either side of the corner which was once called the Rignall Style, was hammered without pause or remorse all day long. And that was a day of lucky escapes. A young fellow and his betrothed had sought a quiet place to pleasure each other in St Mary de Crypt church porch. A cannon ball, falling and bursting near them had injured them slightly. A piece of the metal had torn their legs, he on the backs of his shins, she on the front above the ankles. There was much mirth about the circumstance of their injuries. As the young man was a gardener, there was speculation that he had perhaps been sowing seed. And three old grandmothers jumped out of their skins, when part of a granadoe fell down the chimney where they were sitting, gossiping together. Never did an old wives tale have a more dramatic ending!

As the Rignall Style corner was the place that was taking the most punishment, Massey determined that he would build yet another earthwork across the entire corner. Once again the citizens were called not to arms but to buckets and pails. There were good humoured jests about the depth to which we now had to dig, and Coppernose provoked great mirth by claiming that he had met the devil down below in one pit, who looked exactly like Prince Rupert. Alderman Pury demanded a song from me again. Singing caused less damage to my hands than digging and carrying earth, so I gave them "Joan's Ale is New". This being a long song, with a verse about every peacetime profession, I promised a quart of small beer... there was little else to drink in the New Inn.... to whoever could compose the best verse about a musketeer. I did not know whether I should be glad or sorry, but none of the versions suggested were decorous enough to repeat. At length all of the southwest corner of the town was a great mountain of earth. Their culverin pounded away against it but were not heavy enough to make much impression.

Robert clung tenaciously to his life. I knew he still asked for brandy and Ralph still gave it to him if he could persuade any vintner to sell him any. Mistress Nichol was hard put to it to make him broth as now she had no fresh meat, only supplies of the strips of dried meat that Massey had conserved for the town, so Rowena had undertaken to supply Robert with broth, and she came daily with a basin covered with a cloth, which Ralph fed him like a mother with a sick child. The meals at the Smiths were better now than those in the Inn, although Mistress Nichol still contrived to cook a good breakfast as the hens continued to lay and she had two flitches of bacon hanging up in the kitchen. The butcher whom the Smiths patronised had killed two bullocks at the beginning of the siege. The beef was now well hung, not a doubt of it and my large nose was called into service to ensure that there had been no putrefaction. Rowena decided to cook the remainder and make it into stew and bottle it, with corks tightly in place until we should wish to eat it. There were still cows and pigs grazing in the little Mead. In fact on the 19th a stray pig was killed by a cannon ball. Stamford's men promptly roasted it as near to the wall as they dared in the hope that the Royalists could feast on the tempting aroma of roast pork and know that the men of Parliament were still eating well.

The bakers continued to work as we were still able to grind flour. The mill wheels were pushed round by human power as there was no running water. It is true to say that we became somewhat sated with apple pasties, but many of the poorer sort claimed that they had never eaten so well, as when Sir Edward Massey undertook to feed the town.

Later that same night the alarm was raised as it was discovered that the enemy were attempting to bridge the moat. Our musketeers crawled into place again along the wall and dissuaded them from their nocturnal visit. Although the level of water in the moat was much lower, poor wounded troopers of Astley or Forth's regiments still fell therein and drowned. I stood with Massey under the walls and listened to them plunging to their deaths. He looked at my stricken face and observed, "I did not invite them to come, Tom. If they had stayed in their leaguer, they would still be alive."

There was no gainsaying that. But secretly I was still anxious for Peabody.

Massey gave the order that our drums should beat the call to arms around the walls so that if the enemy still wished for action they should know we were ready for them. As I sat on my bed having seen Robert for the last time that day, I reflected with some satisfaction that at least I had so far maintained my neutrality. I had not taken up arms against my fellow Englishmen... or Welshmen for that matter. Perhaps by organising water storage, I had saved lives in Gloucester, although the quartermaster and his daughter still weighed heavily upon my conscience. If there was a measure of self-satisfaction on that evening in my meditation, next day, the Sabbath the 20th of August, any trace of that complacency became dust and ashes.

The day began as all our days had done with breakfast. Abram was with me immediately afterwards and we wandered along to Barty's Hospital to see how Absalom was managing the water. He told us, "There is still plenty of water and that is matched only by the grumbling which increases every day. Can you tell me, Doctor Tom, what end does Massey foresee for this situation? There will come a day when all water and all dried food will be at an end. What happens then?"

I pondered this question which if I were truthful had been at the back of my mind since the siege began. "Possibly even more serious might be our plight if the powder runs out." I was thinking of what might be our fate if that should occur when we heard shouts from the river towards the gate by the bridge. We ran out to see several musketeers running towards the river, Captain Tom Pury amongst them.

"Stay here!" I shouted to Abram and followed. He did not obey me but ran after me shouting my name, affrighted lest I should be harmed. The musketeers spread out on the path that ran alongside the river round to the Quay, and began shooting at some object in the river. As I ran up their target disappeared under the waves and they dropped their guns, confident one of their number had successfully shot their objective. But sixty seconds later a man heaved himself from the water and rolled onto a narrow shingle beach, directly opposite us. The muskets were raised again but the opposite bank as had been proved many times previously was out of firing range, and precious shot fell into the water in a circle of small fountains.

"Cease fire!" an ensign shouted. "We've lost him, lads. Don't waste good powder on the bastard!"

By this the Welsh detachment which Vavasour had left on the opposite bank, had heard the firing and came running from their tents. Our fugitive rose slowly and walked up to them his hands held high. He walked through them as they stood fiddling with their muskets and still with his hands held high stood at last at their command, his back to them looking out across the Oxlease meadows, when Ralph had caught many rabbits in happier times. Slowly he turned to them and I recognised him at last. It was the gunner Hatton who had asked me if I had a salve to combat his feelings of frustration at being cooped up like a prisoner. Then as their muskets poked at his ribs he began to walk up river before them, as they had plainly ordered.

I was walking back towards Abram who had wisely stopped some little distance down Westgate afraid by the musket fire, but suddenly I was surrounded by Henry Stephen's men

"Now, Doctor, the Corporal here remembers you talking to that whoreson cowardly traitor in the Inn yard, not two days ago, and Captain Tom wants his father to question you." Pearce spoke to me civilly but firmly in his Gloucestershire tones.

Captain Tom was gazing at me, with an expression of anxiety. "Did you speak to Hatton, Tom?" he asked me.

"Indeed I did," I admitted, "But only in the way of doctoring. He claimed to be sick in mind."

One fellow standing near observed, "Well, we wouldn't know anything of that. He was with Baskerville's men, when they rode in after Massey's raid. For all we know, he could be mad as a rutting buck. If so, we're well rid of him. The king might well add him to his advisors!"

But amongst the laughter, another man remembered. "Wait, masters. He was a gunner, now I bethink me. Nay, a cannoneer! Did you know that, Doctor?"

My face must have betrayed me. Captain Tom made a quick decision.

"Listen, Tom, in order that all might be made clear, will you consent to go with Pearce here without constraint, to the Eastgate portal for just such time as it takes me to find my father? I know all will be made clear then. But "better safe than sorry". That is a wise saying."

"If you think I could have aided a traitor?.... Could I have done that, Captain Tom, after all that has passed?"

He looked lamentably distressed. "No, of course I do not think it. But the man has gone to the King, with his knowledge of all our weaknesses. You were seen talking to him alone not two days ago, and it transpires you knew he was a gunner, and now strangely you are here by the river at the moment when he plunges into it. What can I do but take precaution?"

"Well, well Captain Tom." I said waspishly, "I consent. But in future if any man comes to me for advice, I shall insist that you or one in authority overhear our conversation, even though that deviates from medical practice."

"I am sorry, Tom," he said, but clearly could not be seen to show weakness.

I took the initiative. "Come along, Lieutenant Pearce. Let us proceed with this sad matter." And I stepped out back along Westgate.

We had all reckoned without Abram however. He stood unflinchingly in the middle of the road about fifteen yards from Bartys Hospital and demanded, "Where are you taking my brother?"

There was some muted laughter amongst the musketeers at the notion of our being brothers and a lewd comment touching on my mother's virtue, which Captain Tom swiftly silenced.

"Have no fear, Abram," I told him in as calm a voice as I could muster. "Could you tell Master Smith and Rowena that I have been arrested? It may be that they would wish to inform Sir Edward. That is how you can best help me now."

He stood looking after me for a moment, then sped away through the warren of streets on the left to St Mary's Square. I marched on up to the Cross and then down to Eastgate, in front of Pearce, who did not offer to manhandle me. I went down the steps, my back held as straight as I could and waited before the great door. As I had anticipated they did not have the keys, and great was their consternation, when they realised that although they had a prisoner, the prison was inaccessible. It was finally decided that Foster Pleasance had held the keys since the last time the dungeon was used and Tom Pury sent Luke Nurse and two troopers to Massey's house to obtain them.

Foster Pleasance was talking as he came down the steps. "....only a few moments before, the Governor went to matins ......do not know which church he favoured today or I would fetch him at once..... Doctor Tom, how comes this? Forgive me. I will ensure that the Governor hears immediately." And he unlocked the great door.

The dungeon had not visibly improved since I was last incarcerated there, but at least the mud in the middle of the floor had dried up. My eyes went straight to the gap at the bottom of the eastern wall whence the rat had come and gone. It was still there. No-one had noticed it, enlarged it or blocked it off.

As I felt deeply aggrieved by this whole proceeding, I decided to give these over-particular Jack Sticklers, work to do on my behalf.

"Well, a chair if you please, doubting Thomas." I said boldly to Tom Pury "and a table at which to eat. And if you please some breakfast. Or am I to be starved as well?" I chose to pretend that I had not broken my fast.

Tom Pury immediately sent off two fellows to find what I had requested. "I am very sorry about this, Tom."

"You are sorry?" I asked him. "You have implied that I am a traitor, you and your train band fustilarians. I am back in this foul dungeon, where I caught an ague which threatened my life. Best be sure of your facts, Captain Tom. I had thought you were my friend. If you please, I would prefer not to speak further to you."

I never saw a man more hang dog and miserable. The troopers came back carrying a table, stool and bread and cheese which they set down. Captain Tom motioned them out before him and followed them forgetting to close and lock the door in his distress.

I called up after him. "Forgive me, but would you do me the honour of locking me in?" He stumbled back down the stairs and I swept him a bow. "I am deeply obliged to you, sir!" Although when I heard that massive key turn in the wards, my boldness forsook me somewhat. Still I sat on my solitary throne and relished my feelings of righteousness. I wanted to see in daylight... and the sun was streaming through the barred window high above me... whether there was, in truth, a hollow place behind the wall, where my good friend, Sir Digby Rat had disappeared. I did not wish to be disturbed whilst I was dismantling the wall. I had not planned this imprisonment but had frequently wondered if it was possible to follow him.

In a few moments I heard the footsteps and harsh tones of Alderman Pury, together with the lighter voice of his son, descending the stairs. I pushed the stool in front of the Rat's gateway and sat on it. The Alderman stood in the doorway and gazed at me.

"Tom, Tom, what is this?"

I did not rise. "This is a dungeon, sir, in which your son has imprisoned me. An excellent good dungeon, sir with hooks and rings for manacles on the walls if your Worship will please to examine them. I know this dungeon well, sir, as Doctor Edwards, venerable diligent Doctor of my Lord Stamford's regiment caused me to be placed here previously. Maybe you remember the incident."

"Tom, Tom, do not chop logic with me!"

"Then with whom shall I chop it, sir?" Then as he was like to combust with fury, I deflected his wrath. "Your son thinks I have conspired with the fugitive, who I saw escape earlier today across the river."

"And did you?" he asked briefly.

"Do you think I would do such a thing? After all the time and effort, I have given to our cause in Gloucester?" He was now looking as downcast as his son. I stood and indicated that he should sit on the stool, to ease his back which I knew troubled him.

"Listen, Alderman Pury and Captain Tom. I will tell you the substance of the conversation I had with Hutton."

"Hatton," Captain Tom corrected me.

"Hatton! I thank you. He came to me and asked me privately if there was a drug I knew of which would ease the feelings of strain and tension, he experienced through being locked up in Gloucester. He told me that he wished for the sensation of being able to walk and run where he wished. I told him if I knew of such a potion I would be taking it myself, as I shared his frustration. Then, yes, he told me he was a cannoneer, which it seems you did not wish to be common knowledge though why that should be a secret, I do not know. Then he asked if I had heard of a certain officer, a man who was esteemed for his knowledge of ordnance in the ranks of the enemy. I did not know of this man but agreed that loyalty was often not to a cause or a faction but to an individual. My loyalty in this town lies with Colonel Robert Burghill. I did not mention that to him, but I swear to you, Alderman Pury, on the Colonel's life which he holds onto by a slender thread, that that was the sum total of our conversation."

There was a long silence. Alderman Pury coughed.

"My son has confessed that there was some deception with regard to your activities when you rode out with the town regiment on the last day of freedom."

"Deception?" I asked, innocent as a round-eyed babe at the breast.

"You insisted on doctoring Welsh rogues who had been pillaging for food and goods in the village of Brockthorpe."

I turned to Captain Tom with a questioning air. If he had known about Digby Rat's priest-hole, I swear he would have immured himself therein. I have never seen anyone, friend or foe, so plainly desirous to be elsewhere. I began to take pity on him.

"And Captain Tom, out of kindly friendship to me and Christian charity to the Welsh rogues, waited for me while I tended them. They were three sons, whose father had been killed by your Gloucester men. One of the boys had lost his finger. That was the most serious wound. They were little more than children, sir. As you know, my loyalty is to God and to my doctor's oath. I am bound to give medical help when and where it is needed."

The Alderman said crossly, "If they had not resisted, they would not have needed medical help."

"In any event," I went on, "mine was the fault, if fault there was. To me, sir, if I see my fellow men or women broken or bleeding, it is as wasteful, as if bolts of good new cloth trampled in the mud would be to you, Alderman Pury. It is my profession, and I cannot escape it. But Captain Tom must be exonerated of any ill doing. Loyalty can lead a man astray. My loyalty was to my profession, his was to me as a friend, Hatton's was to a previous commander. Your difficulty, good sir, is to determine how dangerous our personal conflicting loyalties are to the great cause of Parliament."

He made again the sound he had made when I first met him.

"Hmmm!" said Alderman Pury. His eyes never left my face. Then at length he seemed to come to a decision.

"Come on, son Thomas. I will speak more of this with Massey. You had best stay here for an hour or two Doctor Tom and... and..."

"Cool my heels?" I supplied for him.

"Aye, cool your heels! I never knew Doctor, so presumptuous in his speech or his ideas, come to that... You are like the bragging mountebanks at the Whitsuntide Fairs. You have an answer for everyone and everything."

I hung my head and pretended to be ashamed, and they left me to myself. I pushed the stool away from the Rat's doorway and knelt down beside the gap. I took hold of the overhanging plaster and pushed it back and forth. Instantly a large jagged piece of plaster came away from the wall and a heap of dust fell in a pile obscuring the hole. I had a kerchief in my pocket and tied it round my nose and mouth. The hole was now perhaps eighteen inches high. As the dust settled, I pushed it to one side and lay down with my face in the aperture. As I craned my neck, I could certainly see light, above me at the end of a short passage that led upwards. I could never have known that if I had not investigated in daylight. Idle curiosity was giving way to a plan. I was hoping against hope that I might see Peabody again. I pushed the stool back and sat on it, hiding the hole, and removed my kerchief as feet clattered on the stairs, the key was turned and Massey stood there.

"Tom! How comes this?" He glanced round at the manacle rings. "I am so sorry to see you in this situation."

"Perhaps not quite so sorry as I am, because I am constrained to be here and you are not!" I said with some asperity. "In any event, I would suggest that your course of action is to leave me here, until you know what information Hatton divulges. If the firing on the Rignal style ceases then you will know he has told them to move their cannon to where the wall is weaker. If the battery continues to hammer that corner uselessly, you will know he intends no treachery, and perhaps I might be released, to tend the Colonel and any other wounded, as I have done faithfully for you, the Alderman and the city of Gloucester, since this Godforsaken siege began."

Massey looked at me and nodded slowly. "In the meantime," I continued, "please will you find Simeon Walsh and ask him to tend the Colonel? He needs a measured amount of the poppy drug daily. Would you also ask Henry to stay at the New Inn should anyone need a doctor?"

"So you are not asking to be released?"

"If you think I am a traitor, then you must treat me accordingly. It seems strange that even the prisoners, your officers have captured on their sorties, are in better case than I am here. They dwell at the top of your fine house. My release must depend on the good will of a man to whom I spoke for less than five minutes and about whom I know next to nothing. It seems that because he was a cannoneer that I am a red-handed traitor, fit only for this confinement.... again!"

"If you had only told us the substance of your talk..." said Sir Edward, plaintively, "If you had told us your suspicions of the man, then we would not be in this situation."

"And he would be sitting here instead of me!" I observed, "You forget that the patient's confidence is for the doctor's ears only."

"And they are ass's ears if the doctor is you!" said Massey. "I must leave you. If Hatton tells no tales we can think again."

"And if he does?"

Massey smiled, shrugged and moved towards the door. "I'm sure we will contrive some explanation," he said and raised his hand in Farewell. Unlike Captain Tom he did not forget to lock me in. At the back of my mind there was the awareness that perhaps I should have mentioned Hatton's unease at being imprisoned in Gloucester. On the other hand, I knew that Massey himself had friends on the other side of the walls. Was the Governor of Gloucester above suspicion?

I sat for a moment, wondering if Abram would appear at the grating so far above me as he had done before. But the gatehouse had been encased in earth in one of our communal wall strengthening exercises. He would have to climb dangerous mountains of soil. Steps clattered swiftly down the stair outside and almost as if I had conjured him up, he was shouting my name outside the great door.

"I am here, Abram. It is a sad mistake." I shouted. "Don't try to climb to the grating." I warned him.

"I have tried already," he shouted back. "I cant! Master James has gone to John Corbett. They are calling a meeting of the Council of War tomorrow. Master James says that the citizens are very angry at your imprisonment. He thinks you will be released tomorrow because of.... because of private opinion."

He began coughing and I realised that the air was not pure. "Abram. Thank you. No-one had a better brother than you. Go back to Master Smith and Rowena and be advised by them. Thank you for coming." I listened to his footsteps going slowly up the stairs. Then I tied my kerchief over my face again and began scrabbling at the hole which was now almost waist high. I pushed the pile of plaster, dust and horsehair to one side and realised that if I crouched on hands and knees I could crawl through it. Before I did so however I pushed my hands through as far as I could. The floor was rough stone. I twisted my head inside the aperture and realised that the ceiling of the passageway... for such it was... would allow me to stand upright.

I sat again on my stool and thought for some moments about how I could best use my discovery. I did not know whether my actions on this day were wise. I had accepted my imprisonment in a spirit of self-satisfied martyrdom. My motives for doing so were partly complacent sacrifice and partly curiosity inspired by Digby Rat, but my responsibility for Abram and for Robert lay heavily on my conscience.

I decided to eat my bread and cheese, scraping off the dust that had fallen on it with my dagger. I then slept, sitting on the stool, my head on the table. At about six in the evening again my captors were at the door. As I heard them I pushed the stool back against the wall and sat on it, leaning my back up against the hole. They entered with more food, some canaries, a candle, a tinderbox and a trestle bed. Massey had even remembered to lend me a fine coverlet. Davy Wainwright was one of the guards. He shouted to me, "Tom, I am constrained to hold my tongue, but you can guess what I think about this!" His fellows silenced him and the Captain suggested that he might wish to remain with me. I thanked him, and then thanked them all for the comforts they had brought, and bade them Good Night, the pattern of courtesy.

I waited until all sound of voices and the tread of feet had faded away above the stairs, and turned swiftly round to what was now a considerable hole in the wall. How would I explain it in the grim light of day? I would solve that difficulty in the course of time.

The light at the end of the passage was not now so bright. I judged that the sun would be setting across the Severn on the other side of town. I wondered fleetingly what Abram would be doing. Although I could stand upright on the other side of the hole in the wall, I could see that the roof of the passage almost immediately sank within a foot of the uneven floor. If I was going to attempt this strange adventure, now was the moment.

I heaved myself within the hole and stood upright for a moment. There were perhaps three yards of the passage in which I could stand, but then the floor which was rough-hewn blocks of stone rose upwards towards the light. I dropped to my hands and knees and began to crawl. The going was uncomfortable and my breeches gave my legs little protection. After about four more yards, the roof sank and harsh stones began to graze my back, until there was barely room for me to ease my way through the narrow space. I reflected that it was probably as well I had not eaten the food they had brought into the dungeon for me, as a full stomach could have proved a sad inconvenience.

The tunnel ended behind a great boulder which partially obscured the opening. There was grass before me sloping down to the moat. I had emerged about fifteen yards to the south of the Eastgate. I did not think I could return backwards and knew I must get out, turn round and dive back headfirst. If I stood up I would be in immediate full view of the enemy, I dropped back into the tunnel, behind the stone and considered how best to proceed.

I asked myself what was I hoping to achieve by this blatant disobedience. I had assumed an attitude of disrespectful contumacy

Massey returned. "Tom, I am sorry for this delay. Gray has gone with one hundred and fifty of our best musketeers over the north wall to Kingsholm. This is the way I hinder them, you see. If at some position round the wall at any one time, I can arrange harassment, they cannot be easy and collect themselves together for the big onslaught."

"Who do you think commands? The King or Rupert?" I asked him.

"Let us hope the King. I talked further to the fellow Moss. He is of the opinion that a great bombardment will begin tonight or tomorrow. I have to confess I feel great sympathy for him. A great foolishness to disregard the advice of a master gunner. Did you know, Tom, when these wars began, I declared myself for the King?"

"I think I had heard something of that," I said discreetly.

"But you know, Tom, they had little notion of the benefits that a victorious army gleans from engineering. As Moss said, science is the watchword. Not the garbage your fellow doctors indulge in, but using the laws of the physical world to our advantage. I can understand his frustration at feeling his knowledge was without value."

By this we had come to the brick building that made up part of the wall at the point called Rignall Style. There was a hole where the door did not fit well where we could see what was happening in Gaudy Green and Llanthony to the south of the city. Massey peered through first and then bade me look. Men like ants were building an ant-hill, but it was not an ant-hill but an earthern shelf for their cannon. The mortars, one of which did indeed seem vastly big, a monster of a mortar, stood ready to be wheeled into place, so that the south-east corner would be perilously threatened.

"Well, from this we know precisely where they will pester us. Tom, can you find Alderman Pury, while I order the troopers to assemble. We must evacuate under these walls and all must be lined with yet more earth. Ask the Alderman to alert the Council of War. If the Citizens will turn out yet again, the town might yet be saved."

Everyone answered the call, and chains of people formed themselves, all with spades and buckets, transporting great clods of earth from Castle Gate near the Severn past the church of St Mary de Crypt to the south eastern corner of the wall. The tradesmen and to the Purys who had ever been my friends. I had responsibilities for my poor sick friend Robert and for Abram, no more than a youth, cut adrift in a strange town. Why could I not have sought forgiveness from the Alderman for failing to inform the Council of War of Hatton's uneasy state of mind? There was an unseemly arrogance about my behaviour. I had attempted to excuse it by pleading a doctor's right to observe confidentiality. But what of the lives of the Gloucester citizens now put at risk by Hatton's defection? Nothing easier, but that he should tell the King's forces of our weaknesses, of the paltry number of our troopers. Was I not as guilty of their deaths as he would be?

I could now hear the King's army preparing to spend the Sabbath evening. There were the sounds of the sharpening of weapons, snatches of song, the occasional roar as a man's wealth disappeared at the turn of a card, the shrill notes of a pipe, the tune repeated until the player was satisfied, the shouts of an officer berating a hapless trooper, all these individual sounds and the smell of the whole concourse of men, assailed me, like a great sea stretching away below me. How could I hope to find one man in this vast ocean of souls? How proud and conceited a fool was I, to think I was right to deceive our two poor besieged little regiments! I had had nothing but kindness and good fellowship from both Stamford's men and the train band troopers of Gloucester.

So I lay half in and half out of the wall, between day and night, gazing unseen on the Royalist army, with my feet in a Parliamentarian stronghold. I could neither go forward nor back. I did not think I could even deem myself fiercely neutral any more as had been my pride. I was neither fish nor flesh nor fowl nor good red herring as the saying is. I was nothing of those. I knew what I was. I was a pitiful fool.

The daylight began to fade and fires began to blaze amongst the King's soldiers. As the shadows deepened and the sun dropped westward behind the town, I became aware that men were quietly gathering on the opposite bank of the moat carrying great bundles of branches and twigs. I peered over the stone that hid my hiding place and tried to see what was taking place. Four men had waded into the water, which came up only to their knees. They came over to the opposite side so that they were only yards below me. The moat was now no real defence. Those on the far bank began to pass their burdens to the waders who seized them and began to push them down into the water. All was accomplished in silence, and more men carrying fagots and bundles of brushwood came noiselessly to pass them to the waders.

They were attempting to fill in the moat but even I knew that unless the water was drained away this was endless drudgery. Below the city there were several deep springs which, whilst not productive enough to supply the townsfolk with water, drained continually into several wells and into the moat. They could divert the water but to attempt to fill it up with brushwood was a Sisyphean task.

However the two fellows who found themselves about three yards way from my invisible self under Gloucester walls were not complaining.

"Are you sure their musketeers aren't up aloft?" said the younger pioneer, glancing up to the parapet.

"Naah!" said his friend," 'Tis the Sabbath. They'll all be psalm squealing and pulpit banging! They're known for it. What I say is, the Almighty's earned 'is day of rest, same as what we 'ave, so I say, don't plague and pester'im. 'Ere, ave a drink!"

They sat under the walls, now in deep shadow and a flask passed between them. I resolved that I would wait until they waded back, when I would swiftly reverse my person and return to my prison. I even had an explanation for the pile of rubble I had made.

Almost without thinking I betrayed myself. My clothes were covered in dust and as I moved slightly to combat cramp, I sneezed! I tried to squirm back into my refuge, but too late! The older fellow had leapt up, swift as lightning and seized my arm! The other drew his dagger and holding it over my wrist, whispered,

"Shut your mouth or I'll saw your 'and off!"

I had a sudden fearful vision of myself with no right hand, merely a bleeding stump, like poor Robert. I cannot claim at that moment that I behaved with any vestige of courage. I have a confused memory of them pulling me out of my rathole, marching me down to the moat, pushing me in, so that I fell headlong into the foul noisome water. For a moment I thought that they would drown me, but as they dragged me up, and thrust me forward, choking and coughing, and trying to catch a precious breath, I realised they had some other plan for me. I was pressed forward on to the opposite bank, and fell against the bank which was a stinking slope of vile mud. The human beasts of burden who bore the heavy bundles of brushwood fell back, open mouthed to let them pass.

A trooper who perhaps had charge of their enterprise, blocked our way. He held a torch aloft and looked dispassionately and coldly up into my face.

"What's this?" he asked.

"He climbed down the wall," one of my captors replied. By this I was starting to remember that I had both a brain and a tongue and they were as yet in place.

"I demand to see Christopher Peabody." I said in as imperious a tone as I could muster.

"God's body, and who the devil might he be?" said the trooper. Two other musketeers, armed and ready came silently to his side.

"He trains recruits for the King's Master of Foot. He answers to…" but my memory refused to obey my demands. I could not remember the name of Peabody's commander and yet he had been constantly spoken of as one of the King's officers to the south of the city.

"Are you one of Massey's drunken muskets?" asked the trooper.

"No! No!" I assured him. "I do not fight. I am a doctor!"

They could not contain their mirth. "And I'm the Great Whore of Babylon!" one of them cried out, and minced about in awful imitation of a lewd woman.

"Your pickings are devilish poor for any doctor we have seen." said the first fellow. "Breeches and hose in rags and tatters, doublet torn, wet and dusty. The doctors I have met are lining their pockets as snugly as pigs in pudding-time."

"Please, I beg you," I pleaded with him. "I remember. Peabody's commander is one Asty or Aston perhaps."

"Aye, we know. Arthur Aston. And never fear, we will take you to him." He turned to my two captors, raised his musket and spoke three words, "Get back, dross!"

The two pioneers looked for all the world as if they might make a fight of it. One muttered, "That guinea is ours, you bastards!"

The first trooper did no more than raise his eyebrows but one of the others raised his musket and brought it down harshly on the shoulders of the fellow who defied him. Silently they went their ways back to the moat, leaving me with the three troopers. One of them held aloft a torch, and another with the butt of his weapon forced me forwards away from the town. So there began a journey, through the sunset, across the King's great camp. Little trace now of the green country, which had so pleasingly lain open to the eye from the walls. All now was trodden into brown dust. We went roughly in a south easterly direction, past fires where men lay about at their ease and shouted questions to my guards as I was pushed past them. I swear we passed a brothel, a cowshed once perhaps, where painted women lounged outside and, seeing my height, shouted crude suggestions as to my sexual performance. We passed noblemen, sitting on carved chairs in the open, well dressed and calm, talking quietly, eating and drinking, attended by their serving men. One of these called to my captors asking, I think, who I was. I did not hear his reply but caught the word, "renegade". I stopped and shouted,

"I am no renegade! I am a friend to Prince Rupert!"

This was a mistake. They roared with laughter at my presumption. I resolved I would be more discreet and circumspect when another opportunity arose and ask for Major Legge or Peabody.

At length we crossed a field, near the road which came in south eastwards from the hills towards the city. Shreds of grass still clung to the dry soil and canon were drawn up, guarded by gunners. I looked in vain for one who might remember me from outside the walls of Lichfield, but that had been a comparatively small force. These men laughed and jeered at the sight of me, and I realised I presented a pitiable sight. The ground was uneven with great ruts from the wheels of the gun carriages and I was hard put to it now to pick my way. We were crossing to an orchard or copse, on the far side of the field. I tripped and fell. My captors bound my wrists whilst I sprawled on the ground and then roughly prodded me to my feet with their muskets.

The last rays of the sun were illuminating the trees before us. I stumbled against a stone, looked down, then swiftly looked up again in horror. The fruits that hung from the branches of this orchard were hanged men. The setting sun gilded the pale hair of the man who hung nearest to me. I recognised him immediately. It was Hatton. Two of Stamford's regiment that had been lost two days ago hung nearby.

I fear that such control that I had, left me at that point and I lashed out wildly, screaming, "No! No! I cannot be hung!" I kicked out and caught one of the villains a blow on the chest, but the other two clung to me and brought me down.

"Jesus!" one cried. "He's a strong 'un. He'll give us some sport."

The fellow I had knocked off his feet, came to me and tried to slash me across the face. I feinted and his musket caught one of the others on the side of the head. A calm voice suddenly demanded, "What's this?"

I was forced round to face a well dressed officer. His long hair curled over his shoulders and his mouth curved in a pleasant smile. "What have we here? A new recruit for Colonel Gallows' regiment?"

"Yes, sir. 'Tis a renegade for Sir Arthur's Orchard. He slipped over the wall expecting a welcome from us."

"Well, sir," said the long haired man, courtesy personified, "You are welcome but not as you might expect. I fear we see you as a traitor to the King, and, alas! This is how we deal with traitors." He smiled pleasantly and nodded at poor Hatton who swing gently in the evening breeze. "But you will be gratified, I do not doubt, to know that you will afford us much good sport whilst you die."

He called out to someone in a small hut nearby. "Master Jones! Your services if you please." A clerk appeared with a table, parchment, quill and ink. He settled himself on a nearby tree stump, and produced an hour glass from his pocket.

The longhaired Cavalier continued, "I will examine that if you please, Master Jones. There must be no cheating. That would be most unjust to this poor traitor!"

Through all this I had been silent, like a rabbit fascinated by a cunning fox. At last I managed to speak. "But Massey houses our prisoners well, with bed and board. There has been no slaughter of captured King's men within the town."

"Houses them well, you say?" repeated the officer, "And feeds them? Do you know what I say? The more fool, Massey!"

A crowd of jostling fellows who had followed us over the field and who now stood in a rough line, waiting for something or someone, roared with laughter at this pleasantry.

"Have your crowns ready, if you please, gentlemen!" Again he turned to me smiling pleasantly. "They wager a crown a minute each on how long you will kick, sir. A man as long and as heavy as your good self might last a good four minutes. One of these will be a rich man tonight, thanks to your good self."

At this my fear and fury knew no bounds and I could no longer contain myself. If they wished to see me kick, I would do so. My legs were not tied and I had already kicked a trooper to good effect. I launched my boot into the officer's chest and had the momentary satisfaction of knocking him off balance. Then I ran towards the road. But about eight of them were onto me and dragged me back to the officer who was dusting himself down.

"I fear we shall have to restrain you, sir, as you seem strangely unable to join in our merriment. Jenkins, a noose if you please."

Another man came from the hut carrying a twisted rope. At the sight of it, I howled again and tried to ram my head into one of the men who held my arms, but there were too many of them and they trussed me up like a piece of meat and bound me to the trunk of the tree where Hatton swung. Another branch above my head was clearly intended for my hanging. A noose was placed around my neck, and the rope thrown over the bough. Memories of my father's tragic end flooded my mind.

And in horror at my situation, I flooded my breeches. I was dimly aware of their laughter and scorn as each man came up to the table and paid his stake. I heard names spoken, times wagered, and the chink of coin as sums of money changed hands. I tried to compose myself and suddenly remembered Ben's advice, "Try to pretend your misfortune is happening to another. That way your brain remains clear."

A group of riders were spurring up the road, and I heard one nearby say of them, "Come from the King at Matson." I rested my eyes upon these fortunate souls, riding away from my hideous death into their happy futures.

And then I saw him in the last of the light, riding towards the back of the group, his horse chosen for practicality rather than beauty, wearing his usual leather jerkin and breeches, and laughing at something his fellow rider had just said.

I shouted then. "Peabody! It's Tom!" But he did not hear or did not recognise my frantic voice. I had one more chance. I took a deep breath and screamed, "Quarterstaffs!" This he did hear and reined in his horse, looking across directly at me.

Page 415

His face changed and became a mask of rage. He drew his sword, turned his horse and rode straight at me. I remember thinking that I would rather die at his hand with his sword in my heart than be hung like a dog. And then my knees hit the ground and I lost all awareness of time and place.

14

A voice. A foreign voice I knew. I moved my head against the smooth pillow that supported me, and someone else said, "Drink, if you please, sir," and a cup of cold water was pressed against my lips. I drank gratefully and forced my eyes open, and tried to make out where I was, but it was now almost full dark and torches were flickering. For a moment I felt swimey and ill but then another voice I knew well was shouting and giving orders, a little distance away, a voice that gave me immediate confidence and hope.

Someone else spoke and that was the voice I had heard so recently, the smooth as silk Cavalier who had taken such delight in telling me how I should die. Now he was hastily attempting to excuse himself.

"But my uncle, Major Marrow permits this sport, Your Highness."

"Does he so? But my uncle, the King of England, does not! You have perhaps heard of him!"

I turned my head wearily. Rupert had his hands around the throat of the long haired officer who had delighted in the prospect of hanging me. I took another sip and managed to speak. "Your Highness, I beg you...."

He turned and smiled, "Doctor Tom, my dear friend." He gave Marrow's nephew a shake and threw him from him so that he fell in an undignified heap on the ground. The line of men had dispersed, and now I saw they were working in the trees that were in my line of vision. Some had been set to digging and some were unloosing the corpses. Peabody was overseeing their labour.

The smooth pillow on which I had been reclining moved slightly and I sat up to see what it was. I had been resting on the tender leather-clad bosom of one of Rupert's Life Guards, a sergeant with a craggy, gnarled face who had been kneeling in a most awkward posture. I staggered upwards and leaned down to help him rise.

"I am much rejoiced to see you, Tom." Rupert made me sit on Master Jones' chair and take my ease.

"Your Highness, believe me, your pleasure in seeing me is as nothing compared with mine at seeing you and Peabody. I thought my fate was sealed."

"These scurvy knaves are the creatures of Aston. I hate him and he hates me. This dog-ape, "and he kicked in the direction of the long-haired Cavalier, "is the nephew of one of Aston's majors, and disgraces our army. What is your name, louse?"

"Samuel Marrow, Your Highness. I was named for my uncle." muttered the rogue.

"Hah!" the Prince spat out his words, "Go and dig graves. With your hands, perhaps, if no-one will lend you a spade. And be assured I shall remember you, Marrow. From this day, you are a marked man."

Peabody hastened back. "Tom, you are recovered. You could ever shake off the hard knocks of fortune. Lucky I happened to come past to cut you down. The odds were lengthening as fast as your delicate neck would have done. You would soon have been worth more half-dead than alive. But what in the name of Lucifer and all the other Parliament devils are you doing here?"

"I came to see you," I told him, in a small voice.

"And I am rejoiced to see you, alive and well, if in the nick of time. Major Legge told us you were in the town. But, dear Tom, this is not the Duchess of Puddle-Dock's parlour where all may come a-calling. Are you at odds with the ranters and ravers and break-pulpits, and are you throwing in your lot with his Majesty at last?"

We were following Rupert who walked ahead of us towards a pavilion set near the field of ordnance. His Lifeguards remained in Aston's orchard, supervising the burial of the dead. I could not dispel the cold feeling in my stomach when I reflected that I could so easily have been amongst them.

"I had news from the Earl of Chesterfield," I told him. "Tell me, why did Sir John Gell release you in Lichfield? And only for seven guineas."

He aimed a loving cuff at my head. As well he was not in earnest. He had hands the size of cudgels.

"Well, let me tell you, Tom Know-All. He would now clap me

in irons before all. The King honoured me with a knighthood so watch your pert mouth, Jack Sauce."

I swept him a deep bow. "God save you, good Sir Christopher!" We entered the pavilion where a table and chairs had been placed, as if for consultation. Peabody motioned me to sit, and busied himself in pushing a beaker of small beer towards me.

"Nay, to tell you true, young Tom, about the villain John Gell. I have heard that he was monstrous curious and intrigued by you, so tall and your fair little lady. He behaved with uncharacteristic leniency. How does she? She entrusted me with the knowledge of your betrothal. I trust you left her safe in Worcester."

"I did leave her safe in Worcester in St. Helen's churchyard. There is no safer place than there, I assure you."

He looked so stricken at the tragic fate of my girl. My recent ordeal and his kind words about my lovely Phoebe overcame me. I could not restrain myself, and leaning forward onto the table, gave myself up to grief. Peabody came and stood beside me, his great hand resting on my shoulder. As my sorrow subsided, I became aware of a warmth, firmly edging beside my leg. I looked down. It was Boy, Prince Rupert's dog. I had last seen him outside William Brindley's slitting mill in Kinver. He had been a younger livelier creature then. Now he seemed to sense that I was sad, and pressed himself affectionately against my leg, as if to wish to comfort me. The combined sympathy, human and canine, caused me to weep again.

The Prince came in. "Why, Tom? What ails you?"

Peabody spoke for me. "I fear it is his wife, sir. The Earl of Chesterfield's relation. Tell us the worst, man. Voice your sorrow."

And so I told them all that had befallen since the day in April when Colonel Russell vacated the Close in Lichfield and I had returned to Worcester. I told them of my ill-fated marriage, of Phoebe's fatal illness, of Joan's distress that had turned into hatred for me, our escape from Worcester on Lofty's trow and the terrible ordeal of Lansdowne Hill. I did not enlarge on my duty to Robert. I simply explained that he also had saved me from death by hanging at the hands of Essex, and was now very ill and grievously maimed. I told them of Abram's dependence on me. How I was now his only support. I did not tell them of my rat-hole, but paid lip service to the notion that I had climbed over the wall.

Page 419

When I had completed my tale, Rupert came to me and embraced me. "Tom, good friend, I am heartily sorry for your sorrow. I must return I fear, but Sir Christopher has you in charge, and six good fellows are outside to guard you." He pulled away from me and held me at arms' length. "Jesu, Tom, You still stink like a pole-cat! I suppose I should be happy some things do not change. God keep you, dear Tom."

I returned the wish and bowed. He clicked his fingers and Boy followed him out, and Peabody observed me gravely.

"Tom, good boy, I am heartbroken to hear of your loss. What of Chesterfield? Does he know?"

I told him that a good friend, a teacher had visited him in the Tower and given him the sad news. I told him too that the Earl had enquired how Peabody did, that all the Derbyshire knights were well, and Sir Neddy was in good spirits. Peabody smiled and nodded.

"Harsh times, but good times, eh Tom? Even now I wake sweating and afraid that I am in that mine again, but then discover that my gigler of the night has her nightgown or worse across my nose!   So what now then, Tom?" he asked, "What was your intention, after you had exchanged the time of day and other social niceties? How can I help you?"

"Peabody, dear friend," I told him, "I fear I must return."

"Well, I fear you must! You have left your young charge... tell him he is my roistering brother of the blade... and an old friend, who is gravely ill. Can you return the way you came?"

"Yes, yes, I can," I told him, "but to be frank with you, I fear to wander through this camp alone. If you could but come near the moat with me. No further, in case Massey has his muskets behind the parapet, but out of deference to the Sabbath, I think that that would be unlikely. If there are no fires or torches, I won't be seen."

Peabody tried to get me to eat and drink. It was now about midnight, and I thanked him but refused, realising that I had to squeeze myself through a narrow aperture. We set off with two of the Life Guards going before, one holding a flaming torch, and four behind. Their presence afforded me a profoundly comforting sense of security.

"So, this Massey? What the devil is he like?"

"He is like no-one I have ever met. At first sight you would take him for a popinjay, and he is no stranger to the ladies. But I tell you, Peabody, there are two men who hold Gloucester in their hands and neither could contrive without the other. Massey organises down to the smallest detail and Alderman Pury, the Member of Parliament inspires. Forgive me, I must say no more."

"Say only this. Young Massey, it would seem, has a head on his shoulders? From what was gathered from the traitor who was questioned this morning, it seems he fills his marauders with strong drink, so that they fight like fiends, like the Vikings of old."

"That same traitor as you call him was hanging on the same tree that was destined for me. The man with thick golden hair. I do not think he changed allegiance. He could not stomach the sensation of being cooped up in Gloucester. It may be that Massey sent him, primed with wrong information to confuse you."

I hated myself for saying this. Peabody stopped dead.

"The mischief is we cannot ask him again. That dandyprat Marrow was supposed to dispatch him to Oxford. Instead he sees a way of lining his pockets, and the poor bastard hangs. But thank you for that at least, young Tom. I'll tell Astley that Hatton's information could be suspect. Massey has indeed a plethora of wit."

"Indeed he has. If you are proposing to conduct a siege in Peabody Hall, he is your man."

He sighed. "Tom, my home is wherever Sir Jacob Astley rests his head. And you are a veritable goldfinch. Two houses, no less."

"They are both yours for as long as you wish, when this accursed War concludes," I told him, "You could flirt with Joan and sweeten her sour temper. Please say you will treat my home as your own."

We had walked through the sleeping camp, and had attracted very little attention. The gamblers, carousers and womanisers lay for the most part in the arms of Morpheus, and let us pass with no interference, though whether it was the lateness of the hour or the consoling presence of the Life Guards was hard to say. A musketeer challenged us quietly as we came nearer to the moat and the Eastgate, but seeing the Lifeguards waved us onwards.

Peabody drew him aside. "This man is bound for Vavasour and will use the town walls as his guide in the night, else he could wander till daylight through the dark fields. He will noiselessly wade across the moat and disappear under the shadow of the walls, so no sounds if you please."

I had to leave him. We embraced and vowed not to meet in heaven, as was the Puritan Farewell, but in the rowdiest tavern in Worcester. I insisted on shaking each guard by the hand, and see that moment still in memory, Peabody concerned and anxious, the Guards impassive and calm, smiling politely at my boyish eagerness, all held in the flickering torchlight for perpetuity.

I left them and walked as silently as I could to the edge of the moat. There was a faint light in the Eastgate. I stepped cautiously into the water and was relieved to find that again it came only to my knees. But I had to move ponderously slowly to avoid the noise of splashing. All my instincts instructed me to rush headlong for my rat-hole, but my brain counselled caution. Fortunately the moon had not as yet risen and the sky had clouded over.

Suddenly I stepped on a round stone. It caused me to stagger and splash, making a deal of noise. I stood still for a moment.

"Hey, Rab. Down there!" The voice came from the parapet above me. I dropped to my knees and crouched in the water, one hand feeling the contours of the round stone, the other mercifully grasping a large pebble. I lifted it out and flung it some yards from me, southwards down the moat. As it splashed, there was the instant crash of musket fire, and drops from the impact showered me. I dropped down again as low as I could get in the cold water, with just my head in the air, and remained motionless for some endless minutes.

The voice from above spoke again. I did not catch all that was said but thought I heard the words, "A rat, no doubt!" Then another voice said words, in an admonishing tone, and I caught, "Wasting precious powder."

"Amen to that!" I thought to myself, "The rip-roaring profligate!"

And then slowly and mercifully, the soft voices faded away to the southward. Massey had set a limited guard on the walls. Thank God they had not been in attendance when I had made my escape some six hours earlier. Perhaps they had exercised their right to hear divine service as it had been the Sabbath. Thank God indeed!

I stood again and edged my way slowly through the water, avoiding the round stone. But then it seemed better to crawl on hands and knees so that I would encounter in advance any further possible obstacles. The moat was not broad but the sides were now steep and noisome with foul mud of a most offensive and unhealthy nature. No wonder Rupert had claimed that I stank. Somehow I rolled myself up onto the welcoming grass.

I judged that my best chance of finding my rat-hole was to feel my way along close under the walls towards the Eastgate. I would never have thought that grim city walls could prove a refuge. But now, feeling their rough hewn stone scraping my left shoulder as I edged along, I knew that no-one from above would sense my presence. It seemed an eternity before I found the entrance stone that acted as a screen.

There was nothing for it but to launch myself headfirst into the friendly hole. The downward slope seemed even narrower and my back scraped painfully under jagged rock. But at last the roof soared away above me and I enjoyed the blessed relief of standing upright. A last effort! I crawled through the gap I had made into the dungeon.

If anyone had thought to tell me that I would ever be pleased to be back in a dungeon, I would never have believed them. I dropped again to my hands and knees as the darkness was extreme, blacker than Satan's arse-hole as the common sort say. However I was familiar with the contours of the dungeon and knew that the table was near at hand by the gap in the wall. I felt on the table and found the tinderbox. I knew that the candle was nearby in a pricket. I carefully struck the flint. To my joy it ignited and I saw the candle close by.

In that instant a voice spoke my name. I dropped the length of match and it was extinguished on the floor.

I swallowed, my mouth dry as dust. "Who's there?" I asked.

"It's me, Tom, here on the steps. Are you well? I have been knocking and calling for an hour, with no answer. I was afraid you were dead."

"Abram," I called out, "Wait a moment! I must light this candle."

I fumbled for the length of match, replaced it in the box and struck again. It must have been a new flint for it lit again and I was able to light the candle. I guessed that Davy Wainwright had insisted that this useful small comfort was included in the items I was allowed. The blessed glow flooded the prison.

"Abram, what are you doing here? You should be in bed asleep." I went over to the door, the better to speak to him. "But bless you, my good brother, for caring for me. All will be well, I promise you."

"The citizens are angry at your imprisonment, and the Colonel has threatened to write to Waller, if you are not released tomorrow, though so sick as he is, Master James doubts that he could. Are you well, Tom? I have been knocking and calling this last hour. It was quiet as the grave in there."

"Believe me Abram, I am very well. But could you bring me my good clothes in the morning and water and a comb? I am not seemly enough to be brought before the Alderman. Could you ask Mistress Nichol to assist you? She might allow you to bring some soap also."

"Indeed I will. Did they bring you food?"

"Certainly they did and very good it was too!" I had not eaten my supper but suddenly realised I was desperate hungry. "Abram go back to your bed at the Smiths. Can you get into the house without disturbing the good people?"

"Nothing easier," said my stepbrother, "Goodnight then, Tom." and I heard him climb the stairs.

I sat on the chair, and allowed myself to rest for a few moments and closed my eyes. Suddenly I was lurching towards the floor, having fallen fast asleep in seconds. I shook myself awake. Now came the hard work that I must complete before morning. I had my story ready for my questioners. I must block up the tunnel in its narrowest part with the rubble I had displaced from the wall. My difficulty was that I had somehow to transport the dust from the pile on the dungeon floor into the tunnel. I looked at the clothes on the bed. Good blankets and a richly embroidered coverlet. I could not soil those. There was nothing for it. I would have to use my breeches. I took them off.

I had a string tying back my hair. I untied it and bound it round one of the legs. If I held the garment by the other leg and the waist, I had made a tolerable bag that could carry a fair amount of the debris. I had no spade but must scoop it up with my hands.

My first attempt ended in failure. I needed both hands to remove the dust into my breeches and most of it went out through the other leg. I looked around the dungeon and saw swept into a corner the same disgusting gag that George Edwards had caused to have stuffed into my mouth on the last occasion I had been imprisoned here. I seized it with glee, twisted it to make a rope of sorts and tied it round the other leg. I hooked my breeches on the back of the chair, and began again to scoop up the rubble and fill my garment.

It took only two breeches full to fill the hole, through which I had squirmed and wriggled earlier in the night. Whether I had completely blocked up the view of the daylight, it was impossible to say until sunrise. Now I could eat and sleep. The bread and cheese were excellent if something dusty, and the canaries excessively good for my parched throat.

I tried to put on my breeches again but they were plaguily itchy and unpleasant. In the end I took off my doublet as well and crept between the blankets in my shirt. Never had I had more satisfaction, in lying down and giving myself up to sleep. As I lay there, I relived in my mind the terrible events of the night. As I remembered the crossing of the moat, I sat up in horror. The round stone that I had tripped over and later had under my right hand, had not been a stone. My fingers had encountered a nose and eye sockets. Why had my hand not informed my brain of this? I had been so engrossed in my own safety, I could not absorb the information. King's men had been shot as they tried to cross the bridge of ladders, and had fallen into the moat. Well, I could do nothing to help him now. My last waking thought was a sudden fear that perhaps Digby Rat might return and plague me while I slept. It was a momentary thought and I swear I slept for a few hours as soundly as the poor fellow I had encountered in his watery grave.

I woke with a start. The key was turning in the lock and the sun streaming through the grating. I felt at a disadvantage to be clad only in my shirt, as Massey came in, fresh as a Spring breeze, with a trooper from the Gloucester regiment, carrying food. I said nothing to Massey's solicitous questions regarding my comfort, but decided that I must immediately confess to enlarging the rat-hole, which they could see immediately.

"You will appreciate, Sir Edward, a man as nice as yourself, that I could not eat and sleep in the same place where I voided my bowels. So, forgive me, but as a doctor I know that if one can avoid noisome smells and humours, one should do so."

Massey gazed at me wide-eyed. My stratagem had left him speechless. To have disagreed would have placed him in the ranks of the unclean, which he could not have borne.

Just then Abram came bustling down the steps with a pail of hot water, followed by Mistress Nichol who carried clean clothes, soap and a napkin.

"Sir Edward," I asked politely. "Perhaps you would give place and permit me to wash myself in private. My brother will assist me."

"Certainly!" he was the soul of courtesy. "Stockley here will wait for you at the head of the stairs, and escort you to my house where we will determine the matter. In any case I must see that parties I sent out earlier at dawn return in good heart."

I wondered in what state they had galloped through the gates. If the rumours were true, no doubt he had made them as drunk as monkeys. It was also possible that the noisome smells and humours of which I spoke were also prevalent in the dungeon itself. The moat had a very pungent odour.

Mistress Nichol stayed long enough to determine that I had all I needed and then hastened back to her hostelry. Abram meanwhile had picked up my stinking clothes. He held them at arms' length and wrinkled his nose

"Tom!" He was outraged. "Tom, how could you get your clothes in such a state?"

"Never mind that now!" I told him, "Has she brought a clean shirt?"

"Aye, and small clothes. But 'tis brutish to put clean clothes on a filthy body." He was such a nanny hen, my brother!

"Yes, yes, I know that. I shall wash myself everywhere first and then my hair and then you can pour what water remains over my head. Is it agreed?"

And so we scrubbed and scraped and rinsed and dried and at length Abram pronounced me clean enough to assume my good clothes. He produced a comb from his pocket and tried to attack the tangles in my hair. Finally I could bear his ministrations no longer and painfully attacked them myself.

At length he decided I was ready. "One moment," I told him, "I was at some pains to construct my own private closet. Allow me to use it before we depart."

I carefully entered the dark rat-hole. Not a trace of morning light was finding its way into the space where one could stand upright. I breathed a sigh of relief, and crawled back out under

Abram's eagle eye. He immediately began to brush a smudge of plaster from my back.

We left the dungeon together, and walked to Massey's house, side by side with the trooper walking behind. There was quite a crowd waiting outside and as we went in there were some who clapped their hands at the sight of me. There were even one or two troopers whom I had treated, who greeted me warmly. I gave my dog-fox grin and hoped that was polite enough, to show I appreciated their support.

Massey and Alderman Pury were seated together in Massey's state room, flanked by the entire Council of War. John Rice and George Edwards were also there, seated against the wall on the right of the Council, looking like cats who had eaten cream. Henry Creery came up to me as I seated myself in the chair set for me before the Council and defiantly shook my hand, looking round at the assembled company as if daring them to object. I blessed him for that show of loyalty.

Massey began proceedings by announcing that Master Donne, the Scoutmaster would question me. I knew that this office had been created by Sir Samuel Luke, and that such men had not only charge of quartermasters whose task was to discover what provisions were available for greedy armies from unwilling farmers, but were also liable to enquire into the loyalty of such farmers. Sometimes such enquiries were not always gently conducted. "Watch your pert mouth, Jack Sauce!" Peabody had said. Good advice to an impudent Jackanapes like myself. I schooled myself therefore to look meek and apprehensive.

Master Donne began by thanking me on behalf of the City for my work with the sick. A woman at the back of the room cried out, "He made the lame to walk, as Our Lord did!" Massey rose. "Mistress Armitage, I beg you, be silent or leave!" I could not see what she had decided but Edward Donne continued, mentioning that the storage of pure water had been also my initiative, which had no doubt prevented the incidence of plague, which had so often occurred in other besieged cities.

"It is therefore with a degree of surprise that we are informed that the accused was seen to speak privately with one Hatton who has since defected to the enemy, or perhaps I should say, the King. The accused claims that the privacy of his conversation was due to

Hatton's desire for some drug or potion that might dissipate his feelings of enclosed frustration, feelings of which it seems he was ashamed. They then spoke of loyalty and Hatton mentioned that he was faithful to an individual officer rather than to a cause. The accused agreed with this, citing his care of Colonel Robert Burghill. The accused states that at no time was he aware that Hatton was contemplating defection.

We must determine whether we can agree that the accused was ignorant of Hatton's intended course of action. Was his appearance at the riverside yesterday morning, merely coincidence, or the desire of a conspirator to ascertain that all had gone successfully with a pre-arranged plot?"

He seated himself and looked at me with one eyebrow raised. Massey spoke, "What have you to say, To..., Doctor Fletcher?"

I rose and addressed myself to Massey and Alderman Pury, who seemed to have been set in judgement over me. "In the first place, Sir Edward and Alderman Pury, the notion of treachery was never further from my mind. I have a boundless respect for the men and women of Gloucester. Secondly Hatton said nothing that could be construed as treacherous when he spoke to me in confidence. Thirdly, I would ask why you would consider him a traitor when he spoke only of wishing to serve a certain officer skilled in explosives. His loyalty was to a man rather than to a cause. Fourthly, he might out of loyalty to this brave city have declined to have divulged any information. Fifthly he might have intentionally misled his questioners. And finally what proof have you as yet that the King's forces are taking advantage of any weaknesses in our defences that he might have reported? Have you considered that the enemy might think that Hatton was sent by yourselves, purposely to deceive them?"

Massey nodded in eager agreement but Alderman Pury banged his clenched fist upon the table in front of him.

"Might! Might! Might! This is balductum and jabberment! Tom, if you please, come forward and place your hands on this bible. In front of all these present, are you a traitor to our Cause?"

I did as he asked. "I am not, Sir," I said clearly but as modest as a maid in a pushing school.

He waved me back to my seat. "Has anyone anything to say against this man?" Rice and Edwards looked as if they would wish to see me disembowelled, preferably whilst still alive, but they were silent.

Finally Massey said, "Time will prove his innocence. If none of the weaknesses in the walls are exploited, we shall know that Hatton meant no harm, and Doctor Fletcher is innocent as a babe new-born."

Alderman Pury stood as if he were about to dismiss the assembly, but another voice suddenly rose above the noise of departure.

"May I have leave to address the Council of War?"

Massey shouted above the hub-bub, "Pray be silent for the Town Clerk."

John Dorney left his seat and stood at the front by the great table.

"Sir Edward, Your Worship, and citizens of Gloucester. It is known by many that I have assiduously noted the events of each passing day, for the duration of this siege, with a view ultimately to publishing this diurnal that all might read of the bravery and ingenuity we have displayed during this time of trial. I had of course noted Doctor Thomas Fletcher's great achievements but as there is now a kind of taint, as it were a shadow, over his endeavours, then I propose to omit his name from my account. I do not think he will be proved treacherous but should that fear become reality, I shall not have presented him as a hero when he is shown to be but a scurvy villain!"

"What say you to that, Doctor Fletcher?" asked Massey.

I stood again and half turned to the assembled company who were arrested in their motions of departure. "I never sought fame or renown, but have tried only to do what I could to help. If there are heroes of this siege it is the men of Gloucester. Aye, and the ladies of this great city are her heroines also."

This was very well received. Grace Armitage came up to me and took my arm, and said with some asperity, "Who will wish to read that tedious old clown's writings? We know, none so well as us, what happened in truth. You are a good doctor, Tom. Pay these rimble-ramblers no heed!"

Grace was a pretty and lively woman and clearly a favourite of Massey's. Now he came forward and hissed under his breath. "Discretion, mistress!" and Abram bustled forwards and herded me towards the door.

I hurried to the New Inn and ran up the stairs to see Robert. It was less than twenty-four hours since I had last seen him, and although he was no better, he was clearly no worse.

"Tom, my son, what have these clay-brained Bible-beaters done to you? Are you hurt?"

"No, sir, not at all. All that was required was that I swear an oath on that same Bible that I am no traitor. Your friend Alderman Pury finds my nature too argumentative. All that was required was an undertaking that I am guiltless of Royalist tendencies."

"And are you?" said Robert, smiling with what I took to be relief and leaning back on his white pillows, against which his yellow skin gleamed in sharp contrast. There was that strange sweet smell now in the room which Ben had told me predicted death. It seems the internal organs are ceasing to function regularly.

"I can place my hand on my heart and tell you, sir, that I wish no harm to anyone."

He smiled again. "I know that, son. Off with you and see what good John Nicholl can find you."

A few moments later I was sitting with Abram in the courtyard of the New Inn, in the sunshine. I had a glass of precious Taint in my hand, and Abram a beaker of small beer as befitted his tender years although he frequently now conducted himself as if he were my elder. He did not intend to allow the occasion to pass without a homily on my foolishness.

"All you had to do was say that you regretted speaking to the man Hatton. That was all they wanted to hear. But, No! You had to show how clever and logical you are, with your wrangling and your snatches. And you know what I suspect? I think while I was calling to you on the stairs last night, that you were not there. When I have called to you in the night before, you have always answered immediately. One moment you were not in that dungeon, the next you were. What happened, Tom?"

I gasped at his discernment.

"Abram, on my life. I beg you. Say nothing of your suspicion to anyone. Do you hear? I promise you, when we are free of this place, I shall tell you everything. I have done no-one any harm. But now, you must be silent. If you speak of this, I could hang. Promise me, you will say nothing!"

His eyes grew round and his mouth opened in fear at the

urgency of my response. He nodded slowly and took a gulp of his drink. Then as Massey came quickly into the courtyard, he edged closer to me.

"Tom, three poor fellows have been brought back grievously cut about. They are in St Mary de Lode, hard by the Northgate. Henry Creery asks for your help. I am waiting for the return of the other party by boat."

"Is Sim Walsh in St. Mary's?" I asked. "Abram, could you fetch him there?"

Abram nodded and silently set off. I ran upstairs for my box and set off after Massey, glad of the cool relief from the heat afforded by the Cathedral as I passed through the Close. Massey was already in the church administering strong drink to the sufferers. In one way this was beneficial as it eased the pain of the wounded, but in another it was disadvantageous in that the patients became so drunk, they could not tell their physician what ailed them. Fortunately on this occasion I could see for myself. One poor fellow was cut about with slashes, on his chest, on both of his arms and on one of his legs. It seemed he had managed to defend himself from three of the King's men at the same time, feinting and twisting his body like an eel, until his companions came to his aid. It transpired that one of his deliverers, a sergeant of Captain John Nelmes, was shortly after taken by the enemy. My patient was losing blood, and I had need of a tincture that would stay the rate of flow. I knew that Sim had had always with him a dressing of Adder's Tongue and Horsetail, both wholesome plants, not excrescences of any poor creature, which would stay bleeding and cause the flow to grow sluggish, although Massey's stimulants could interfere with its good effects.

Firstly I had to open and clean the wounds, and went through the usual process of picking away any foreign matter that could putrify. As I worked I became aware that two men were somewhat roughly conducted into the church and deposited near to my station. It transpired that they were prisoners, both lieutenants. One wore a plain brown doublet, but the other by his elaborate dress gained attention both from his captors and from the good citizens who could not be prevented from pressing in to stare at him. He was from a bluecoat regiment, and had lace trimming his person at every possible point, collar, cuffs and boots. His doublet was of pale blue leather and his breeches were velvet of the same colour. He remarked to all who would hear that he knew his Colonel, Charles Gerard, would ransom him forthwith. One of the guards carried his partisan, a gleaming shortened pike which was his badge of office.

Rowena came into the church and the bluecoat lieutenant tried to rise and doff his hat, which had excessively fashionable long ostrich feathers, red and white. As his ankles were tied, he crumpled clumsily to his knees, with a cry that resounded through the church. I feared he had cracked his knee-cap and ran to him fearing injury. His face was contorted in agony but fortunately he could still stretch out his legs and seemed to have done no lasting damage.

"More circumspection, less gallantry, my good sir!" I advised him.

"Zounds, you are in the right of it there, my good leech!" he admitted, rubbing his knees, regretfully, "But such a devilish handsome wench! In gazing on her beauty, I forgot that I am now in durance treacherous. Monstrous bad luck! Stamford's boys are the same colour as Gerard's, so I ran alongside them like any claybrained ploughboy, trotting to harvest home and ran through your gate with the best of them, straight into the loving arms of your Sir Massey."

I caught his way of speaking. "Stap my vitals, but that is ill fortune!" I agreed. "But that lovely wench is a young lady, sir. The Bishop of Gloucester's niece, no less, deserving of our utmost respect."

He was suddenly gazing at me, as if I was a spectre. "God's body, young sir, but I swear I have seen you before this. Not long since, neither!"

I was of a sudden, mortally afraid. "No, I do not think so, sir. If you are not hurt, I will leave you."

But during the remainder of my sojourn in the church, whenever I looked up his eyes were upon me. I could guess only too well where he had seen me. He had almost certainly been one of those waiting to calculate how long it would take me to die at the end of a rope. I had hoped to have absented myself from St Mary de Lode as soon as possible, but as I completed my work with the three who had been cut about by Sir Jacob Astley's men, two more wounded were brought in, who had been in the raiding party who had gone down river by boat. One man had put his knee out when he jumped back into the boat; the other had a bullet in the fleshy part of his thigh.

The knee was easily but noisily dealt with, but the bullet was deeply embedded, and needed swiftly removing in order that the poor fellow's sinews might perhaps knit together. To my surprise Rowena showed considerable talent in assisting me, and stood patiently holding callipers and probe, handing them to me as I requested them. I was delighted with her help, but could not help noting that the Cavalier in blue was entreating Massey to pay him attention. Both of them looked continually towards me. I knew what was toward. The Cavalier was bent on betraying me. Nothing for it but to face it out with Massey.

When wounded and imprisoned had been well disposed, the prisoners locked in the crypt with food and candles, and the wounded instructed to rest in Babylon, I went back to the New Inn with Abram, having arranged to visit the Smiths later in the day. Rowena was beginning to hold my heart in her capable hands, not a doubt of it. A day when I did not see her, was a day without joy.

"May we speak privately, if you please, Tom?" Massey had followed me into the courtyard. My heart sank. He had believed the fine Cavalier bullfinch. What should I do? Deny or confess? And yet there was the incident of Major Legge which only I knew. That gave me a small lever with which perhaps I could persuade Massey to my point of view.

"Where shall we speak, that is not teeming with long eared knaves?" I asked with a degree of petulance. Massey waved a bunch of keys.

"Shall we return to the dungeon? No-one will willingly follow us there." So once again I tramped off to that unwholesome underground prison, alongside the Governor. Massey told no-one of our intention and did not seek to constrain me. If I was going to confess all, then clearly this was the place in which to do it.

The sun still shone although it was by now well after noon. There was still the bright pattern of the grating, lighting the detested place. All was as it had been left, early in the morning. I had intended to retrieve my soiled and damaged clothes and return Massey's furniture and bedding, but had as yet not had the time.

Massey glanced round at my ruined clothes and seemed to

shudder. The smell in the dungeon was not pleasant. I had managed to convey there the ripe odours of the sewage from the moat on my person, the previous night. Mingled with that distasteful aroma, there was an acrid smell of dust and rubble. Sir Edward went over to the chair and carefully wiped it before seating himself. He motioned me to the bed where I reclined something in the manner of a somewhat apprehensive Roman emperor.

He gazed at me in silence. He had closed the great door and the sounds of Gloucester came muted through the grating. But there were other sounds, the noise of pick and shovel, men shouting orders, other men defying them. And these chinks of metal and human voices came from beyond the tunnel. I rose from the trestle bed and went into the aperture I had made, that I had pretended was a jakes. Some of my dust filling had fallen away and now there was a gleam of light. I returned and motioned Massey to step inside the hiding place. He gave me a half amused, half fearful glance as he crouched and stepped into the hole. He looked back and beckoned me in beside him. A conversation was taking place only yards away from us on the bank. Some fellow was shouting commands which we could not hear precisely, but his assistant who was very near us, replied venomously yet quietly, "Do it yourself, you poxy bastard!"

We crept back and sat down, but were careful now to speak in a undertone. Massey regarded me with eyebrows arched, so that they almost disappeared into his hair.

Finally he asked, "Well then, did you see Jamie Legge?"

There was nothing for it but to tell him all. So I did so. I found it difficult to speak of my near execution. "I suppose that minion of Charles Gerard, saw me with the noose round my neck. The bastards waited in line to wager their crowns on how long I would last, with my neck as long as their arms!"

He nodded. "So he told me in the church. I told him you had a twin brother. Then I suggested gently that I might belie my compassionate reputation, and play Marrow's monstrous game with him as first candidate, if he did not keep his tongue behind his teeth. No more to fear from him, Tom He can tell his tale to the defunct Gloucester worthies, and the decomposing Gloucester bishops. None will hear him in the Crypt. So what of Hatton? Dead you say?"

"Aye, alas, as roast mutton! But they questioned him about our situation yesterday, gave him to this Samuel Marrow, who is nephew to one of Arthur Aston's majors, to ensure his safe conduct to Oxford prison. But the nephew had other plans for poor Hatton. He had devised this cruel sport possibly as a means to supplement his wages. So I am ashamed to say I told Peabody that you had sent Hatton specially to deceive them. They have now no way of verifying or disproving his story."

He grinned and clapped his hands together softly. "Excellent, Tom. What a clever lapwing you are! That is why they have not exploited our weaknesses. By your going on your excursion, you have undone Hatton's treachery. Well done, indeed, Tom."

"I did not like deceiving my good friends, Peabody or the Prince," I said slowly.

"Well, consider. They are neither further forward nor backward. And, yes, Prince Rupert is a powerful leader. James Legge would die for him. Has nearly done so, once or twice."

"And how long can we continue as we have done so far, Sir Edward?"

"For as long as we need," he told me. "We have cattle, we have water too, thanks to your good husbandry. Believe me, there will be many hot headed agitators in London, fulminating against Parliament's delay. Essex will be planning to relieve us even now."

He had risen and was walking up and down, seemingly pleased with the situation. As he did so, he kicked my ruined breeches and picked them up and shook them out.

"So this is the garment you made into a sack?" he cried, "By tying up the legs... and using them to convey dust to your tunnel? Good God, Tom!" It was difficult to know if horror or admiration possessed him. After another shudder he went on, "It may be that your tunnel could be very useful as matters progress. You say it is not visible from the moat?"

"Even if you were immediately beside the opening, like the fellow we heard just now, you would not know of its existence, the stone at the mouth and the overhang from the wall disguise it so well."

"How did you find it?" he asked wonderingly.

"A rat showed me!" I explained.

"Perhaps we will say nothing of any of this to good Alderman

Pury. In fact, let us say nothing to anyone. I tell you what would now serve us best. Thunder storms. We need summer rain storms to flood their mines. What will you do with your spoiled clothes?"

I reluctantly retrieved my stinking garments. I had already managed to smear someone's blood on the clean doublet I was wearing. He surveyed me critically. "You are not kind to your clothes, Tom, are you?" He was for all the world like a clucking old nurse, rather than the Governor of a besieged city. I nodded and said guiltily, "No, Sir," as if he were a fastidious schoolmaster and I, his careless pupil, and we went up into the outside world, laughing at the strange situation we were in, well pleased that in spite of the differences in our lives, we seemed to be friends.

For some reason the next day which was Tuesday 22nd of August, there was a cessation of artillery bombardment. Massey had guessed from his discreet questioning of prisoners that the King had run low on gunpowder and sure enough next day, supplies came up river from Bristol, well guarded and unloaded out of range of musket fire. The day was spent in impotent alarms. Much noise and fury of gunfire, sudden warnings but no-one hurt. The citizens went about their affairs trying to ignore the sudden roar of the cannon. Ned Sturgess, one of the bakers who still brought bread into the New Inn everyday, told me that the sudden explosions were as good as an overseer for his apprentices, causing them to leap up and work, without his having to chastise them himself.

Two days later, word was brought to Sir Edward that two worthy gentlemen craved an audience with him. They had advanced with a white ensign or rather a white napkin tied to a pitchfork, and Sergeant Major Ferrer, a jovial and popular soldier, felt compassion for them, as the day was already hot. One of them, a Master Hill of Tewkesbury, had in fact walked from that town to Sandhurst where his relative Master Bell lived. They had ridden the rest of the way, down river on two of Bell's nags, and now were asking to see Sir Edward.

"They say they have impartant news to import to you, Sir Edward," the Sergeant Major announced. He was known for verbal confusion. "One is Master Bill of Tewkesbury and the other is Master Hell of Sandhurst. Will you see them, sir?"

"Yes, but not in the town. I will come to the Northgate." I had, perhaps unwisely, told Sir Edward that Mistress Nichol could still provide an excellent breakfast of rashers of gammon and eggs, and he had arrived to try this wholesome meal for himself. We were sitting in the courtyard, although today the weather was heavy and airless. He wiped his mouth carefully with his kerchief, left coins on the table for the Nichols and with a brief, "Come with me, Tom!" was out under the arch. I and Abram meekly followed after him. I had yet to visit Robert. Alas, my good friend was no longer in pain... Sim and I saw to that... but had little strength for conversation and slept much of the time.

We arrived in time to hear Sir Edward ask the two stout yeomen who stood grasping their hats, "Well, Sirs, what is this urgent news?"

They looked at each other and then the stouter of the two announced, "Gloucestershire is stripped bare by these King's varlets, good young Sir. Our barns are empty and our fields are barren. How much longer will you keep the King here? If we could be certain we could harvest, we could sow winter crops, cabbages and turnips even now, but who is to say whether they will not trail they whoreson cannon over our tender seedlings?"

"True, very true," said Massey, "But what is your news?"

"Well, Sir, Gloucestershire is not only Gloucester. There are many farmers like ourselves, begging your Honour's pardon, who have no notion which way the wind might blow. You take a cabbage, Sir. It knows not King nor Parliament, but it will feed the little 'uns of either o' they bastard armies. What's to do now, Sir? Do we sow or do we wait, and watch King Famine creep into houses and barns?"

"Yes, I see your dilemma, but what is your important news?" Massey was growing impatient.

The other good yeoman took the bull by the horns.

"We think you should let the King have Gloucester, Sir, and save everything. Crops, beasts, and all manner of folk, Sir. If we go on after this fashion, all will perish."

"Well, we shall not. We have food and to spare in this city, have we not, Doctor Fletcher?" Massey turned to me, ready to dismiss the well meaning farmers. There was clearly no urgent news to consider, simply their increasing fear and dread of marauding armies, and the constant "legal" deprivations of the King's quartermasters. If they were not suffering or starving, which I could plainly see they were not, they were still entitled to our courtesy and consideration. I could not let them return... a hazardous journey enough through the King's men from Wales and Worcester... without offering them refreshment.

"But perhaps these gentlemen are hungry and thirsty. They have, after all travelled a dangerous journey of some miles. Can I offer you hospitality, good Sirs?" My father had taught me always to be civil to farmers. "A few yards brings us to the New Inn, which no doubt you know, is an excellent good hostelry."

This was certainly more to their liking. Massey doffed his hat to them both and told me, "See to it then, Tom, and name me for the reckoning. Abram, come with me if Doctor Fletcher will spare you. I need you and your quill." And he was gone, with Abram trailing importantly in his wake. I took Master Bell and Master Hill to the New Inn, where John Nichol recognised John Bell of Sandhurst and as he served him, asked after mutual acquaintances along Severnside.

"So, Master Hill, how wags the world in Tewkesbury?" I asked. "Wondrous fertile land by the Avon there."

"Fertile indeed, young Sir, but monstrous prone to flooding. My son-in-law from Upton jests that we shall forthwith have webbed feet, like any duck!"

"And is your son-in-law a farmer like yourself?" I asked politely, making conversation.

"No, young Sir, he grows vegetables for the markets roundabout. He travels out from Upton with his cart, full of fresh produce. They keeps chickens and sell the eggs and my daughter, Evelyn, comes back to her old home to churn the butter for her mother and me. They sells that too. But it has been plaguily hard of late. The poor souls had all that was in their cart tipped up and stolen by Sandys' men, two weeks back."

I was suitably angered and distressed on the poor man's behalf. "Where was that, then?" I asked. "Surely Sir William Sandys did not sanction that?"

"'Twas near Severn Stoke. Paul and Evie was going to Worcester market, when the Worcester troop was going southwards on their way to join the King here, two weeks ago or thereabouts. Not a penny of payment, neither. When Paul asked for coin, they told him, "God pays." Begging your pardon, young Sir, but that Massey fellow ain't got no notion what's going on, outside these walls. A whole month's produce, raspberries, beans and potatoes spilt on the track and gathered up in handfuls as the troopers came past, mocking and laughing, the bastards."

"I'm afraid the Parliament men are as bad," I told him, "My poor father had the contents of his shop stolen by Essex' men last September."

"Where was that, sir?" asked Master Hill.

"In Worcester. He was a master butcher on Fish Street. Worse was to follow, Master Hill." I sighed and pushed my beaker from me. "Essex hung my father in the Meal Cheapen, claiming he was a spy. He acknowledged his error, but strangely, my dear father remained hung and dead, like a side of beef in his own shop. When great ones err, it is poor men who suffer."

"And yet you... you serve Massey... Wait, I have heard tell of your poor father. A master butcher, you say? And alas, young Sir, another hanging in Worcester but last week."

"Indeed?" Master Hill was plainly relishing his gossip. I poured him more Canaries. "Sir William Russell must have been hard pressed to order such a penalty."

"No, not so! 'Twas naught to do with Sir William. Paul told me all, after his jaunt to Worcester market last week. They had all to do again but thankfully no mocking troopers on Thursday last. No, this poor soul took her own life! 'Twas by her own hand! She was found hanging in an outhouse."

"Who was she?" I asked, an icy hand of dread gripping my heart.

"Now there you have me, young Sir. Paul did say. A much respected woman, who knew her herbs and potions as well as any 'pothecary, but her name... No! I cannot say!"

"Was it... Joan Bailey?" I asked, trembling with fear.

"Joan Bailey," he repeated slowly. "Joan Bailey. I cannot say, young Sir. It might have been but there again, it might not. You look troubled. I hope with all my heart, I have not given you bad news."

"I hope so too, Master Hill, for I have no means of knowing whether you speak of a dear friend of my dead parents or of a stranger. Joan Bailey is my housekeeper. I hope above all else that she is well, continuing to tend her husband and sons in my house."

Master Bell concluded his Canaries and his conversation and

rose with a nod to his friend. I walked back to the Northgate with them, where their nags were stabled under the eye of the guards. They had been well fed and watered, a circumstance that impressed the farmers. Truly, they were men of some courage, to brave the King's army. They took up their white ensign. I shook their hands and wished them Godspeed but all my polite words and motions seemed to me to be those of another. An icy fear seemed to hang heavy on my heart. Joan, whom I had known all my twenty years, who had told me that my parents would have been so proud of me after my father's death, who had painstakingly settled my household... had she taken her life? What of Adam and my dear friend Roger, and young James, if it were true?

I went back to the New Inn and heavily climbed the stairs. Poor Robert lay inert in his bed. Ralph pleaded with me to try to rouse him. The sweet smell hung ever more strongly in the air.

"It breaks my heart, Tom, that he will not speak to me." He wept as he spoke.

"Nay, Ralph, not "will not." He cannot! He is sinking fast now," I told him. "I am sure if he could have done so, he would have wished to speak to you of all people, caring for you as you know he does."

I hardly knew what I said. Their relationship bewildered and embarrassed me but there was no mistaking their love and devotion, one for the other. Their love seemed to demand my respect, even more so now, when the end was near.

Robert's lips moved. I moved closer to him, holding his hand and he whispered again. All that I could hear seemed to be the word "Son" and then my name.

"Dear Robert," I said. "My second father."

He smiled gently and slept again.

"Here, Ralph," I told him. "Sit beside him and then should he wake, you will be here, to tend him."

As I descended the stairs, there was a terrible crash. For a moment I thought a cannon ball had flown through the roof of the New Inn, but then realised it was a clap of thunder. It was followed by a flash and another shattering rumble. A memory of myself as child of five suddenly manifested itself. I had run into the house from the paddock at the back of my father's shop, frighted by just such an explosion of thunder. My mother and Joan had been sitting gossiping as they often did, but now they paused, aware of my fear at the sudden noise.

"Why, my dear little Tommy," said Joan, drawing me to her. "It is simply that God has become weary of the placing of his furniture. He is moving his chairs and table about. Nought to fear, I promise you."

Now, as I stood powerless on the stairs, with the chains of memory binding me, the welcome rain began and with it, that fresh smell that accompanies a shower on dry dusty earth. It came sweeping through the open doors of the inn. I went back to ensure that Ralph knew all was well. He had left Robert's side and had opened the door of his room to admit the fresh air, in the hope that "It might revive the Colonel." I shook my head sadly and went downstairs.

All the Inn's servants were gathered at the door watching the torrent crashing into the courtyard. I hoped that Massey had employed Abram under cover. Suddenly another realisation struck me. Someone had told me that the miners whom Forth and Jacob Astley had fetched from the Forest of Dean were tunnelling under the moat. In fact the men who had caught me on my excursion had been miners. I remembered Stephen Dilkes' information at Lichfield. Clay was the miner's friend, soil when it rained his worst enemy. What would be happening to those poor fellows, trapped in earthy dungeons, suddenly awash with stifling mud? I shuddered and wished I knew where Abram was.

The downpour was over as quickly as it had begun. The sun reappeared and the world assumed a fresh and gleaming aspect. The puddles sparkled in the courtyard and the two boys of one of the chamber maids suddenly remembered what a convivial game, stamping barefoot in the water was, so that each of them was riotously splashed.

I resolved to go to Massey's house to find Abram, but he forestalled me, walking into the courtyard from the street, as neat and trim as a bridegroom. But as soon as he saw me, he cried out, "Why, Tom, whatever is it? What is wrong? Is it Robert?"

I shook my head and indicated that we should sit at a table in the inn to talk. I told him swiftly of the news brought by the man from Upton and my fears that the dead woman might be Joan. He nodded and I could see that his conscience fought hard to subdue unworthy thoughts. Joan had seldom been kind to him. He had no memories of her compassionate younger self as I had. But seeing my apprehension and distress, he sought to comfort me.

"How many souls dwell in Worcester, Tom?" I knew the answer to that question. "Nearly four thousand. Yes, you are right. There must be more than one woman skilled in drugs and potions. There is no reason to assume that it must be Joan. There is still no reason to assume it is not her either. I wish we had not parted in such a bad humour."

"That was hardly your fault, Tom. You did nothing wrong. You must hold to that. The devil of it is we cannot ask anyone. No-one has come from there, and no-one is going there. But the chances of the poor suicide being Joan are slight indeed, and besides, Tom.... She would never leave Adam."

This was truth indeed and no gainsaying. A cannonade began, to the south at Llanthony, and I decided that I had best stir myself to be ready for any wounded troopers. But great was our amazement that although the Royal guns plied us hard and for an hour or more, only one cannon ball found its mark, and that was a bolster in the Crown Inn, where the missile came harmlessly to rest.

Rowena came to find us to bid us to sup with her father, who she claimed was starved of conversation. A child had been cut on the arm by a fragment of stone, and had come to have the hurt bandaged. He was a stout young fellow of eight, proud rather than sorry that he now bore the scars of war, and he sat up on the table, displaying his scratched arm to Mistress Smith.

"Why, Georgie Matthews, what a brave young soldier you are to be sure. Keep your bandage on and keep it clean. Now, Tom and Abram, a word if you please. My father is starved of conversation and I am prodigiously tedious for him as now it has at last rained, the moment has come to make my melonry, and I can speak of nothing else. Next year we shall have luscious fruits, grown in our own garden. What do you say to that? If that will not tempt you to remain in Gloucester, Doctor Tom, then I am sure nothing will."

She stood there in the dim light of the taproom of the inn, wearing a simple green gown, which pleasingly contrasted with her golden hair. She was so lovely, for a moment unusually I had no words. She thought my silence showed bewilderment at her proposed task so went on with further explanation

"Now is the moment for me to begin to dig and if after I have found good rotting stuff and sown my melon seeds, if it should rain again, so much the better. Will you not come now? Father threatens you with a cup of Canaries and Poll Cook has an excellent leg of mutton and is making Scotch Collops. The Lord knows she has enough good vegetables of my growing to make fine accompaniments and then she will serve Apple Fritters with Almond Butter. It is my father's birthday so we are making merry as well as we can. Please come Tom."

At last I found my voice. "What can I bring him as a birthday gift?"

"Your self of course. That is gift enough for us all. In an hour, then? Abram, will you come now? Your help in the garden would be most welcome."

I left the child, perched on the table and followed after them, looking after them both as they walked away down Northgate. A numbing honesty was beginning to creep into my brain. I loved Rowena. And poor Phoebe scarce cold. But Rowena and I were joyfully alive. The realisation caused me to flounder, panic-stricken, in my own guilt. The fact that in the midst of civil war, she was determined to make a hot bed for melons could not but provoke my admiration.

I came back in and lifted down Georgie Matthews, who ran off, proudly showing his bandaged arm to his friends. I wandered to the mercer's and bought a fine pair of white wool stockings for Master Smith, in the hope that he would not be affronted by the personal nature of such a gift. In truth, hose seemed to be the only present I ever gave.

I came back to the Inn and went upstairs to see poor Robert. The strength he had gleaned from Rowena's daily beef broth was now fast waning, and there was a dark shadow under his eyes. He opened them as I stood there, but I do not think he knew us. I left Ralph with a dose of the morphine potion, if he should wake in pain although I now judged that that would be unlikely. I wondered if I should go, and then reflected the Smiths' house was but two minutes from the New Inn. I told Ralph to fetch me if his breathing worsened. I judged that Robert as we knew him had gone from us all. What remained was a sad misshapen husk with little sensation. But I did not know if I was right to leave him, and Ralph seemed to gaze on me with an accusing stare.

I found my best doublet and breeches, as Abram set such store by my neat appearance, and combed my hair. I need not have troubled myself however, as I was immediately pressed into service, helping with the melonry. The plot was outside but on the other side of the house wall from the kitchen fire, so that warmth from the coals would permeate the manure. However this was proved to be a double edged benefit. Master Smith and Poll Cook were not whole hearted in their support, and certainly the ripe rich stench of the rotting earth was discernable in the kitchen.

"The smell will soon disperse!" Rowena announced confidently. "Think only of the exquisite fat fruits this time next year." But only Michael, the manservant, for whom Rowena could do no wrong, seemed convinced. Poll was heard to observe that if she had wished to work in a stable, she would have become a groom,--- which, given her impressive girth around the waist might have proved an impracticable ambition.... and James Smith hoped that the aroma would not penetrate into his library.

At length Abram and myself were invited to take our ease and to drink a potation of Canaries to toast Master James' birthday. Rowena took a pitcher of water to her room to clean herself and to change her gown and Poll Cook set about preparing our meal. As we sat, chatting of this and that and punishing the cask of wine, there was a sudden crack of thunder and the rain pelted down again. This was not a sudden shower but a downpour which continued long after we had pushed back our platters.

Just as I had decided that I must return to the New Inn, the deluge having abated, there came a loud knocking at the street door. I was immediately afraid that it would be Ralph with the news I had been dreading. Master James opened the door and was delighted to see his great friend John Dorney, he who had assured me that although I had worked hard for Gloucester, yet he would prefer not to mention me in his immortal account of the siege, lest it should be later proved that I was treacherous. I think he was somewhat wounded in his feelings, that I clearly did not give a farthing for his opinion whether it was good or bad, and had expected me to plead for honourable mentions.

But James was overjoyed to see him particularly as he now brought welcome news. There had been a guard set on the

Cathedral tower to watch for a fire on Wainloades Hill. This fire would only be lit, if it was known that an army, either Waller or Essex was hastening to relieve the town of Gloucester and attack the King.

"Even through the mists of stormy rain, it is clearly visible," said the Town Clerk, much gratified to be the bearer of important tidings. "We think that the signaller had devised some kind of shelter for the fire as it blazed unhampered and free."

"A good night to light a fire," I observed, "as it cannot run riot. The man entrusted with this task, he is faithful and true?"

"Indeed he is." John Dorney had the grace to appear shamefaced as he turned to me. "A trustworthy Gloucestershire farmer. The arrangement was that if he could not penetrate the enemy lines to tell us of our imminent deliverance, he would use this method to inform us."

"Hmm!" said James, "Well that is the best birthday news I could have received. God grant it is the signal you desire and not some poor shepherd, seeking to warm his old bones in a cold wet night."

"Well, Doctor Thomas Fletcher!" John Dorney rolled my name and title round his tongue, as if 'twere some ponderous and unwelcome piece of gristle. "How do you?"

"Very well, Sir and I trust I see you in good health." I returned his greeting formally, with as neat a bow as I could muster, after having been generously plied with Canaries. "But I regret I must return now to the New Inn. The Colonel is sinking fast."

"So I hear, and surprised indeed I am to find you here!" he observed reprovingly.

"I assure you should his condition worsen I will be sent for immediately. I fear there is no hope. He no longer knows who is with him. I have left him with a trusted reliable servant, whom the Colonel held in the highest regard."

I could hardly say more. I did not wish to expound on the nature of that regard. I took my leave, sad as ever to leave Rowena, but relieved to part from the moral scrutiny of the Town Clerk. The rain had ceased but puddles lay about the streets and somehow I managed to splash my legs in my best hose. I pondered how it was that some men were always neat and clean, no matter what physical difficulties they encountered. I feared I would never be numbered amongst them.

Master Nichol met me as I turned under the arch.

"Ah, Tom, good lad. You are come, when we think you are needed. My good wife thinks he is fading fast. I am sent to fetch you but you have forestalled me."

He replaced his torch in its sconce and followed me upstairs. Mistress Nichol and Sim were either side of Robert and Ralph knelt weeping at his feet. The shadow of death was on his face. As I felt for his pulse I feared he had already died but a sudden gasp proved that such fears were premature. He sank into stillness again but after perhaps half a minute later, again came this heart-rending gasp. We were hanging onto his every breath, and I feared this might continue for some hours. I looked at Sim who shrugged slightly as much as to say, "There is nothing for us to do." Another fearful gasp wrenched poor Robert's lungs and then the merciful stillness. But this time the quietness continued, and went on and on....

Sim felt for his pulse and shook his head. "He's gone," he said softly. "A painless end."

I wanted time to myself to digest this. I had bade Farewell to Robert in my head, when I had seen him earlier in the day. To all intents and purposes he had left us, twenty-four hours before. Now his poor, tortured maimed body had been gathered to its eternal rest. He was at peace, and I needed time to think of the eleven months during which I had got to know him so well. How strange and timeless for a doctor are the moments, when one soul leaves the world and another enters it. The memory of the last child I had brought into the world suddenly engrossed me. If I had been given to prayer, I would have prayed for blessings on Rachel Phoebe Elizabeth Bailey, the last child who made her entrance into my hands, on the day of Phoebe's funeral. I was aware that Master and Mistress Nichol wished quietly to mourn poor Robert's passing, and to reflect for a moment or two on his many good qualities.

But Ralph would have none of it.

In his grief he began to beat his hands upon the wall. Mistress Nichol took him in her arms to restrain him, but he would not be consoled.

"You do not know what he was to me! He was my reason for life! Leave us! Jesu, what is there for me now?"

Sim wisely said, "He would wish you to live well for him now. Gather strength from his memory."

But we left Ralph with his angry grief and stood on the stairs, listening as he raged about the room they had shared. Strangely I had caught the echo of my own despair at Phoebe's passing. I too would have been wounded and wrathful, had any sought to part me from my dearest one at that time. Suddenly he cried my name.

"Tom, come back! I swear he still lives!"

I returned to the somewhat oppressive room where the main current of air came from the door. Ralph had caught up Robert's wasted corpse and was holding his lifeless form against himself, running his hands up and down his back.

"I swear to you, he is still alive. Feel how warm his back is" He burst into uncontrollable weeping as if he knew his words held false comfort.

"That is merely the residual body warmth caught between his back and the sheet, dear Ralph. His hands and brow are cold." And indeed they were, as cold as marble.

"Come, Ralph. If you love him, as I know you do, let him lie peacefully at rest, now." He let me lay poor Robert down again and together we crossed his arms across his breast, his missing hand, a sad mutilation even in death.

I persuaded Ralph to lie down in Abram's room, knowing that he had watched beside Robert for many nights, and was tired and wretched as much due to sleeplessness as grief.

"I will stay with him for some hours," I promised him. "Consider this, Ralph. He is safe now from all harm You have earned your rest, my dear friend. We will talk in the morning about what is to be done."

At last he nodded. He stroked Robert's face as lovingly as a mother might caress her sleeping child, and allowed Mistress Nichol to lead him to Abram's room.

Almost a year before, I had rescued Robert from a terrible death. His ribs had been crushed at Powick Bridge and he had been concussed, and had shown no sign of life so that he had been marked out for burial with the actual dead. Now the terrible irony that I had saved him for him to die on this day, August the 24th, only eleven months later, oppressed me, and I confess I wept for my grievous loss. My generous friend, kind counsellor and one who had loved me near as well as my father had done, was gone from us.

15

The relentless sun, indifferent to sieges, battles and death, blazed into my eyes and I leapt up, remembering immediately our terrible loss. I pulled on my hose and breeches and still in my nightshirt, hastened into Abram's room, where we had left Ralph. The bed was empty... crumpled but empty. I ran downstairs, afraid he had chosen some desperate solution, but there he stood at the entrance to the courtyard, watching the early morning bustle of the Gloucester tradesmen and women.

He turned to me and asked, "How can the world go on when all is over?"

I understood, only too well, the impulse behind the question. "Because your sorrow is yours alone. They can feel for you but they cannot know your loss. I can, though, Ralph, and the Nichols, they are at one with you in grief. Come on, now, Ralph, there is much to do."

"You have much to do, not I," He sighed. "He would not let me carry out his wishes."

"You spoke of this, then?"

"He made me sit and listen. I hated the thought of... of his going. But all is prepared. In the chest below his bed. You are to open it."

"Could you eat something first Ralph?"

At that moment one of the baker's apprentices came into the yard with a tray of sweet smelling rolls. At first I could see he was about to refuse, but his nose gave out a different answer, and he suffered me to lead him into the buttery, where good Mistress Nichol found us bread and plums.

"He did not think I was capable of arranging his affairs. But you, you are scholarly as a bishop, said the Colonel, with wits sharp as butcher's knives." He spoke with bitterness as if the task of arranging the Colonel's affairs and papers should have been his responsibility.

"My dear Ralph, believe me, I will most willingly appoint you his executor. I wish to return home to Worcester. Come with me when all is completed."

Ralph shook his head. "Tom, I can scarce write my name. Besides you, I am naught but a jingle brains. He knew which of us could best fulfil his will, though I cannot pretend that it pleases me even now, to share that confidence."

"Let us about it then," I said rising, relieved that he was at the very least rational and calm.

Robert lay at peace, his yellow face gleaming against the white pillow. Ralph touched his hand lightly and then knelt to pull out the box, from under the bed. It was large, heavy and ponderous, an item which betokened the serious ending of a man's life. It was unlocked, although there was a key in the keyhole. A letter bearing my name lay on the top, assorted papers, but below these, there was clearly money... a large amount of money.

"I fear that I must once again trespass upon your kindness, my dear Tom, and I know that as you read this, any thanks that you are owed from me must now be posthumous. I know that when this wretched siege ends you wish to return to Worcester, having had your actions with regard to Phoebe's final illness, supported by the Earl of Chesterfield. As I write, I am aware that our future is in the hands of God, and why He should favour Parliament over the King, I am at a loss to understand. For your sake, and Ralph's and for the sake of our good friends in Gloucester, I pray and trust He will protect and keep you.

To be brief. I must ask you to conduct the removal of my bones to my wife, Elizabeth Burghill in Haddenham in Buckinghamshire for burial there. This will not be an easy task for you. Haddenham is about twelve miles due east from Oxford. I have an overwheleming wish to lie near my great friend and lost Saviour of our fair country, John Hampden. In order to avoid armies of both factions, it might be easier for you to choose an indirect route. Ralph is to accompany you, and Elizabeth is to employ him with a good grace as her Head Gamekeeper. Haddenham is after all his home. Apart from all my remaining money which I direct you to bring to her on this my last journey, she can also expect an annuity from Parliament, in recognition of my services. Should Elizabeth refuse to employ Ralph which will be in direct opposition to my wishes, then, Tom, you are to set him up in whatever calling he may desire.

To my good friends, John Nichol and his dear wife, I leave £100 over and above the reckoning that I might owe, which sum is to be settled from the coin herein enclosed. I leave a like sum to yourself, Tom, and the rest to my wife, a considerable sum, provided she concurs with my wishes regarding Ralph's future; otherwise the sum remaining is to be used to promote his vocation whatever that might be, and my wife forfeits my fortune.

My will accompanies this, wherein all is set out. You will see that it is signed by Sir Edward Massey and Alderman Thomas Pury in the presence of William Michaelson, Attorney.

I am sorry, Tom, that I must again impose on your time and good will. However, as you will be well aware, it is for the last time.

God bless you, Tom Fletcher. I know you dislike the wish that we may meet in Heaven so I will conclude by thanking you for your filial love and devotion and for all the thoughtful conference, we have enjoyed over our time together. I have loved you as a father, and as a father I pray your future will be happier than mine. I say again, God bless you."

Ralph was regarding me with a strange sidelong look. I asked him, "Do you know the contents of this letter?"

"Oh, aye. The Devil's daughter must employ me or she gets nothing. To be honest with you, Tom, that is an arrangement both she and I will dislike heartily. We are as one in this. We hate each other."

I did not pursue the conversation. I was completely dismayed by the whole undertaking. Ten minutes before, the siege could not end soon enough for me. Now with all my heart I wished for its continuance.

I went down and spoke to Mistress Nichol telling her of the bequest. Poor woman, I think she and her husband had all but despaired of ever having their full reckoning paid for this month, and now it was met, over and above what they could ever have dreamed of. She did not know whether to laugh or cry, so did both by turns.

I bespoke a leadlined coffin for Robert and wondered where he could lie until I could begin the journey to Buckinghamshire. For, alas, no question but I must deliver him safe to his home, when my duty to him would be at an end.

In the end John Nichol found an old woman who could prepare the dead for burial and later in the day the coffin was delivered to the New Inn. Robert's remains were securely enclosed, but the lid was not nailed down so that should Elizabeth wish to look upon her husband again, she could do so. Massey came to find me and spoke of his grief at our loss, and arranged for Robert to lie in the crypt of St Mary de Lode. He had finally succumbed to the entreaties of the two Royalist lieutenants who, whilst they were warm, well lit, fed and watered, had found the company in the Crypt, something too stiff and inflexible. Massey had moved them to the attics of the Crown which were kept stoutly locked at all time. Sadly a poor woman that same day was struck down near the Southgate by a granadoe. She too was laid to rest in the Crypt until she could be buried with due ceremony.

That evening Captain Tom Pury burned torches on the tower of the college to give notice to our friends who had signalled the night before that we had seen the fire and had understood its message. The enemy was now growing adept at firing red-hot bullets to cause fires where they could, but none had so far caused any real damage. If one took time to pause, it was remarkable that Massey had brought us thus far with no great loss of life. I had no doubt that his strategy of lining the town walls with earth had proved an excellent policy. Even when the walls had been broken by continuous shot, it must have seemed to the Royalist gunners that their cannon balls had only partially penetrated our defences. Where there was no passage of daylight, they assumed there were more sturdy stone walls, not knowing that between them and their victims, there lay only a few feet of loose soil. Now we had the news that an army, either that of Essex or Waller, was on the march, and would before long engage the King, and still our supplies held out in the town.

I sat with Ralph that evening, hoping to glean some information as to the village of Haddenham. I wondered how Robert had first encountered Ralph and was told that he had been anxious to curtail the poaching activities in which Ralph's father was resolutely engaged, and which he had painstakingly taught his little son. Ralph smiled unwillingly remembering embarrassing confrontations, when the presence of a fine well grown buck which happened to be dead, was difficult to explain. His old parents still lived in Haddenham, he told me, and his sister. He wept again remembering old times, but there was less anguish in his tears, and perhaps a trace of acceptance.

Early next morning Massey found me breakfasting with Abram. The Governor believed there would now be a keen concentration of the enemy's efforts to undermine the town.

"So far, however their endeavours have not been crowned with success!" he observed grimly. "But now I expect the villains will redouble their efforts. They are attempting to fill up the moat as we speak. And what then? Will they trip across, merry as a Maypole dance, and expect us to welcome them with sugar cakes? Now that they know that we are not forgotten, now is the moment when they will surely commit all to the balance."

"Why do you suppose that they have not pushed forward upon us in great numbers before this?" I asked curiously.

"They are hampered by the same scarcity as ourselves," he told me. "Lack of gunpowder. But whereas I have made every musket ball tell, they seem to have waited for a propitious moment, that is probably about to arrive."

"But why has Rupert not meted out the treatment that he gave to Bristol? He, of all men, knows how to break a siege. I saw it at Lichfield."

"I would have thought you "of all men," my dear Doctor Thomas, are best qualified to answer such a question! And to keep the answer to yourself!" Then laughing at my discomfiture, he went on, "I partly guess that Charles was distressed by the loss of life at Bristol. He is not a ruthless tyrant, as you know."

"Which causes me again and again to ask myself, why we have come to this strange pass? You know the muscles and sinews of governing, Sir Edward. Why do his subjects threaten Charles' very life, when they suffered the eighth Henry to die in his stinking bed?"

"Oh, Tom, consider for a moment. It is not a question of the middling sort and the common sort against the Crown. Do you know who Essex' cousins are? The most powerful men in England ...and the richest. They pressed through in the House of Lords, bills that crippled the King's power and all done under the guise of a fear of Popery. I admire and respect good Alderman Thomas Pury but he is a speck, a minimus, an insect compared with the might of the aristocratic nobles who control the upper House. And they have clever allies in the Commons. Did you hear tell of John Pym? They called him King Pym for a while. Some say, the cleverest man in England. I thought so too, Tom, until I met you." He roared with laughter at my blank open-mouthed expression.

He became serious again. "The King may defeat us here in Gloucester, but I fear that he will never enjoy Kingship again of the kind that he and his forebears have been accustomed to practise. The dice are too heavily weighted against him. His only hope would be to give Rupert free rein, but he will not do that, because we are back to the same hurdle. Charles is not ruthless enough and there are those, who claim to support him whole-heartedly, who hate Rupert. So, Tom, my friend, how fortunate we are to be in Gloucester, besieged as it is, where we live surrounded by honest steadfast Puritans, where we may speak directly to Our Lord, unhampered by cosseted befurred intermediaries, and where trust abounds and no assassins lurk." And then as Rowena came in to find me... "And where the young ladies are excessively pretty." He swept her a low bow. "Madam, I mourn that it is not I you seek, but this fortunate sawbones! May I bid you Good day."

He left us, smiling and greeting the New Inn servants as if he had not a care in the world. Rowena had come to find me to bid me to supper yet again. She had stood in line at one of the butcher's who had killed two fine fat lambs and had collops to fry and beans from her own garden. I accepted with alacrity.

When I presented myself, as trim and neat as any courtly Hector, I was a little disconcerted again to discover John Dorney ensconced in the chair in which I usually sat to discuss the affairs of the town. He showed no contrition for his usurping of my place, merely waved his hand airily to an oak joined stool, that no-one could claim was comfortable. It seemed that as next day was the Sabbath, the New Testament lesson to be read was the visit of Our Lord to the home of Martha and Mary at the end of the tenth chapter of St Luke's gospel. John Dorney waxed lyrical on the circumstance that Mary had chosen to listen to the holy words of Jesus rather than be drawn into the preparation of the meal. At a respite in their conversation, I asked respectfully,

"Master James, do you think that we can ever be justified in questioning the words of Our Lord in the Gospels?"

There was an indrawn breath from Master Dorney who plainly saw my words as blasphemy and even Master James looked slightly askance. John Dorney saw fit to berate me soundly.

"I had ever suspected that you are an infidel, Thomas Fletcher! Have a care that your wild words do not cast you into the fires of Hell or worse!"

"I do think, honoured gentlemen, then that I should visit the fires of the kitchen, to fetch Rowena from her cooking to listen to your discourse. Mary, our Lord proclaimed, had chosen "that good part". It would be heartening for Rowena to hear your inspiring interpretation. She should not be concerning herself with your carnal needs, when her soul should be fed by your words!"

There was a most delectable aroma issuing from the kitchen. James began to laugh under his breath, but John Dorney grew red as an outraged turkeycock at my impudence. However he could find nothing to say, so I rose from my uncomfortable stool and went to see if there was aught I could do to help the ladies who laboured in the kitchen. At last I was given knives and platters to set ready on the table, and also entrusted with a pitcher of wine and some goblets to set forth. When at last Rowena followed me in, carrying her trencher of mint flavoured lamb collops and Poll Cook brought a great dish of tender beans, James caught my arm and told me, "How blest am I and all of us, that I have a daughter who has the virtuous attributes and talents of both Martha and Mary!"

"How is that, father?" Rowena heard something of his observation.

"I have gently questioned the precise meaning of Our Lord," I told her, "And enraged the good Town Clerk. Which womanly attitude did Jesus most admire, Martha's or Mary's."

"Why, surely, Jesus was making a jest," said Rowena, "Of a truth, it is much more enjoyable for anyone, man or woman, to sit and enjoy philosophical discourse. Such an one as Mary certainly chose a most gratifying occupation. Housework is much less fulfilling, and can be servitude and drudgery. But Our Lord does not say that Martha's choice was any the less necessary nor less appreciated by all who ate her dinner. He simply congratulates Mary playfully, on choosing the easier pleasanter pastime. Will you all please come to the table?" And having with enviable insight and intelligence interpreted the Scriptures admirably for us, she proceeded to serve us an excellent dinner.

That night there was a fierce cannonade from Gawdy Green which did little harm, except that one or two citizens who had left their beds in fear, came to me with cut arms and faces where they had been hit by fragments of stone.

Next day... the Sabbath... exactly one week after my escapade from the dungeon, the King's pioneers continued attempting to fill up the moat. I was told by the hidden watchers on the Eastgate that the earth they had poured in had turned the moat to evil smelling sludge and that displaced water was covering the area. Someone needed to remind them of the findings of that tedious Greek gentleman, Archimedes. Water will find another level and alas, the level that it found was in their mines, which they were attempting to dig below the eastern wall. Sir Edward came to find me the next day and showed me diggings, he had caused to be begun near the East Gate. As soon as the worthy Gloucester citizens dug below five or six feet, water began to ooze up, preventing further labour. There were many springs feeding the moat and several wells, such as that at the New Inn. For the first time, good Mistress Nichol complained that the water from her well was cloudy. Fortunately the water in the Hospital was still wholesome and not brackish and there were several great tuns, still untapped.

I began to fret about the difficulties that would beset me when I was set at liberty to transport my dear friend to his last resting place. I think this was the first time in my life when I had been constrained to be patient, and when not even money, that good servant but capricious master, could assist me to achieve my will. I was beginning to be excessively weary of incarceration in this Puritan stronghold. The only people, with whom I could converse with any degree of enjoyment, were Master James Smith and his daughter. As I was now solely responsible for Abram, I worried constantly about his future and cursed myself for allowing him to be mewed up here, like myself. I was still afraid we would all ultimately suffer death at the hands of the King's army. I expected that a great attack would be launched against us at any moment. I determined that when that hideous moment arrived, we should all repair to the tomb of Edward the Second in the Cathedral, and kneel there, in the hope that Charles would have mercy on those, who as pilgrims sought sanctuary and blessing from his ancestor.

It seemed that I also now had charge of Ralph. He seemed unable to act independently, other than to provide himself with his basic vital needs. He would come and sit patiently beside me as I ate, saying nothing, but gazing at me as if I had the answer to the riddles of the heavens, aye, and to those of the sinful earth as well.

And then on the night of Tuesday the 29th, there came another gleam of optimism. The bonfire in the rain on Wainloades Hill the previous Thursday, had been a beacon of hope, presaging liberty perhaps, but we had heard nothing more since that time. So when in the dead of night there had come a soft knock at the Northgate, the guards, fearing an ambush, had sent straight for Massey. He was swiftly assured by the use of secret passwords, that it was two messengers he had sent out last Saturday, and the gates were swung open as silently as possible to admit them. A great army had set forth from London on the day they had left Gloucester for Warwick, though whether it was commanded by William Waller or the Earl of Essex they could not say.

The enemy's cannon now began to shoot out great logs of wood at us. They landed for the most part in the heaps of soil that lined the walls and hurt no-one. We knew that pioneers were attempting to undermine the Eastgate, but when I sat down with Massey and Abram for a midday repast on the last day of August, I could not forbear voicing my disbelief in the King's lack of enterprise.

"Charles has upwards of ten thousand men encamped outside these walls, and yet all he does is pick at us, like a whore killing fleas. Why does he not launch a serious attack?"

"Do you wish him to?" Massey asked laughing.

"No, but all he uses are his gunners and his miners. He has the best cavalry general in the land at his command. All those troopers out there, eating, drinking, whoring and doing nothing. Why does Rupert not launch a Forlorn Hope charge at the Eastgate? Do you understand their tactics, Sir Edward?"

"I can only think and hope that we have given the impression that our walls are invulnerable. Thank God they do not know how frail they are. My hope is that the King's tacticians will not suffer the Earl of Essex to creep up behind him, or he will be like a miserable piece of meat between two slices of hot spicy bread. But Tom, if you long for action, then I think tomorrow, we shall use your secret portal. You can explain how best to emerge into the open and how best to re-enter your private jakes."

Abram's eyes grew round. I reassured him. "All is well, Abram," I told him. "Sir Edward shares our secret. A man must launch himself head first, Sir Edward, in both directions, and trust his legs and lower half to a benevolent Almighty. I would not describe this method of egress and regress as dignified or stately. It is essential, also, that the attempt is made in the dark of the moon."

He nodded. "Will you go first to show the way to proceed?"

Abram drew in his breath, and murmured, "No, Tom!"

"All will be well, I promise you," I told him again. "What is the purpose of this exploit?"

He answered without a trace of compunction, "Merely to destroy their mining under the Eastgate once and for all. They have begun their digging again as the weather has yet again dried up."

A few hours after August had slipped into the past therefore, and when September was but a chilly babe a few hours old, I found myself shivering in my small clothes yet again in that wretched dungeon. But now I had legitimate and respected company, five men from the Earl of Stamford's regiment and one John Barnwood from the City troop, supported and recommended by Alderman Pury himself. There was talk of promoting Barnwood to the rank of Ensign because he had shown himself fearless in his valiant use of granadoes. He could judge to a nicety, the exact moment when the burning weapon could be hurled at the enemy to effect the most carnage. An excellent friend but a dangerous enemy. My instinct was to avoid him.

Now they stood waiting for me to show them how to negotiate my rat-hole. A lantern had been placed on a ledge high in the aperture and Alderman Pury held another, half shrouded by a cloak. It threw up an unwholesome light upon his long features, causing him to appear like a gargoyle from the roof of an old church. It was difficult to define his expression as he surveyed me, trembling from cold. Disbelief and disapproval fought for supremacy.

Finally he spoke in a sepulchral whisper. "Well, Sir Edward, let us hope that this is not another of Doctor Tom Fletcher's forays into treachery, and that these good fellows return unscathed."

"I am no traitor, Alderman!" I hissed angrily. "Because I have been imprisoned here, I found this passage. If you had not mewed me up for nothing, I would not now know of its existence!"

"Always an answer! If it were not that the Colonel" ...but Massey would have none of our wrangling and angrily bade us be silent. I told the six men who were to follow me what to expect. "Lever yourselves upwards, pushing your musket before you," I told them, "and try to avoid scraping your marriage portions along the rocky floor." They grinned and nodded. When they should emerge onto the grass outside, I instructed them that they would need to creep to their right away from the boulder, and then to follow Barnwood to the left to the workings under the Eastgate.

There was only room for one other to stand behind the one who crawled up into the aperture and watch his feet wriggling away, by the light of the lantern. The Sergeant from Stamfords whom we knew as Pocky due to his somewhat imperfect complexion followed me out onto the grass, and Barnwood came after him. Then the troopers crawled through onto the bank beside the boulder. Three of them were there, standing beside us on the cold ground under the sheltering walls. But the fourth had still to appear.

"We'd best about it." Barnwood whispered. "Doctor, stay and help him out, and send him after us. We need his musket."

They slipped away to the left towards the Eastgate as silent as spectres. The fourth trooper, who was known as Rowly, was bold as a lion, but something too stout around the middle. I called his name, softly.

A groan came from the rat-hole. I knelt down and felt behind the boulder. There was his head and my hand came away, wet. In launching himself along and upwards, the wretched man had knocked himself out against the boulder. His brow was a mass of blood and his inert body blocked our escape route.

"Edward!" I whispered as loudly as I dared. No answer! Surely they had not gone.

"Sir Edward! Alderman Pury!" I spoke as softly as I dared, but Rowly's body blocked the passage of sound as well as escape.

There was a slight sound and I recognised the sound of Massey's voice, though the words were indistinct. Finally I found that by half lying with my head near Rowly's stomach, I could detect a thin draught of air from the dungeon.

"Edward!" I called. "Rowly has injured himself. You must pull him back."

I heard the Alderman come forward into the aperture, asking Massey what was amiss. "The stout fellow is hurt and is blocking the tunnel!" I heard him say.

"Can you reach his feet?" I asked them. They had to reach upwards and along the tunnel. But if they dragged him back with no protection they could damage his testicles, an injury which could affect him for the rest of his life.

"Edward, can you get into the passage behind him? His brow is broken, but that injury is probably not fatal, if we can get him safely out of the tunnel. But we cannot turn him over, and his genitals are at risk. "

Suddenly Edward's voice was much nearer to me and I realised that he had pushed himself along beside Rowly, until the roof prevented his further progress.

"Have you anything that could protect his vital parts? A coat? A shirt?" I asked but was not hopeful. Soft material would be worn away, would not protect him adequately and it would be difficult to slip such a bundle under the wretched trooper.

"A better notion than that," he cried. "Tom, watch for the others. Find out what is happening?"

He slipped back down into the dungeon and I stood again and looked along the town wall. All was silent, but a figure flitted suddenly out of the gloom and Barnwood was beside me.

"Where's Rowly?"

"Knocked himself senseless. Sir Edward can pull him back but we are trying to do so without destroying his testicles."

"Ah, Jesu! That's a scurvy fate, on my life!"

We were silent, contemplating the turn of events. Rowly groaned again and from the dungeon came the sound of angry voices. Sir Edward and the Alderman were clearly at odds over some matter.

Barnwood made up his mind. "Well, we will about our task without him. I shall lift the wooden cover over their workings and invite them out. If they are reluctant, well, the granadoes are primed and ready."

He slipped silently away to where the faintest glow illumined the dark bank.

Suddenly Edward's voice came clearly. "Tom! Tom! Can you lift him about the waist?"

This particular item of Rowly's person was not easy to define. However I managed to hoist him up an inch or two, straining and grazing my shoulders as I did so, and sensed that something smooth and hard was slipped under the poor fellow's crotch.

"If you can push, I can pull!" Massey hissed, and slowly inch by inch we began to move him back into the aperture. My brow was against his from time to time, as I levered him along, and at last Sir Edward was standing, supporting him under the arms.

"Alderman! Help me!" and together they dragged him into the dungeon. I dropped down into the aperture and then turned around and heaved myself back into the tunnel to find out if the others were safe.

As I came out there was a sudden burst of firing and the glow of a granadoe. I peered at the glare which was low and then Barnwood was shouting, "Get back, Tom!"

I needed no second bidding, but reversed myself like a crazed eel and was back in the aperture in seconds, with Pocky gasping and complaining that my boots had soiled his hair. Barnwood and the other three followed, with shouts and groans.

The alderman had the great door to the dungeon open and had laid Rowly upon the stairs. We rushed through as if all the devils in Hell were after us, and the door was slammed, locked and bolted. We stood silently, gasping and listening for the sound of pursuit but there was nothing except our own panting breath.

Massey whistled to sentries from the Eastgate who came running to report to us. He dispatched one onto the wall above the Eastgate to report ,if troopers crossed the moat and looked to be about to find the passage. The fellow returned to say none had crossed the moat.

"But they'm in a rare taking over the moat, shouting each at the other to "Make Ready!" and "Arm!" They don't know their arses from their oxters, no mistake."

It seemed though that no King's Men were crossing the moat in force to attack the mysterious nocturnal brigands.

"Well, as there are no Royal varlets in the dungeon," said the Alderman, with great dignity, "Perhaps, Sir Edward Massey, I might be permitted to retrieve my vandalised Holy Book!"

We stared in surprise. What Holy Book was this? Slowly, with ponderous gravity, the Alderman descended the steps and disappeared back into the Dungeon.

I turned to Massey. "What happened?"

"I snatched his precious Bible from him, tore out the pages and pushed the cover under Rowley's organs of regeneration. And as well I did for you were right. When we brought him out of the dungeon, the knap of the leather cover was all but worn through."

I began to understand something of Alderman Pury's ire. "I had best redeem myself and help him."

The pages of the Bible were scattered all over the dirty floor. I gathered them up, by the dim light of the lantern and pressed them into Alderman Pury's hands.

"Your Bible served us well, Master Pury," I said humbly.

"I wish I could believe so, Doctor Fletcher," he answered, gazing at me steadfastly, "I fear you too have damaged your brow."

I had forgotten that Rowly's blood had stained my forehead and the poor man must have his wound dressed. We had gathered all the loose leaves, so went back up the stairs, although the Alderman carefully locked and barred the dungeon door behind us again. As he followed me up the stairs, he commented, "I do not think you are totally an imp of Saturn, Doctor Fletcher!"

"I trust not, sir. I believe I am something too tall and corporeal for such an elusive spirit." I said, hoping to make him smile. He did so, but somewhat reluctantly. I continued humbly, "I hope I shall always endeavour to deserve your good opinion, Sir."

The guards were ordered to mount vigil outside the dungeon door, throughout the night, and to report any sound or movement behind it. Supporting Rowly, who seemed grateful to be alive, we made our way back to the New Inn, where Massey as was his custom, ordered up from heavy-eyed John Nichol, whatever we should want to drink.

I slept late the next morning, whether from our exertions in the small hours, or from Massey's insistence that I drank three... or was it four? ...glasses of taint. As I staggered down to the jakes, I noticed John Barnwood slumped in the corner of a settle, sleeping soundly. He had clearly been too drunk or tired to make his way back to his quarters. I asked for breakfast and sat down to eat it beside him. The delectable aroma of Mistress Nichol's excellent gammon soon assailed his senses and he rubbed his eyes.

"What have you there, Doctor? On my life, you sawbones care well for yourselves. How comes it you are so desperate thin and spare, yet, I swear, over two yards high! "

I asked Dickon for another platter and we quenched our thirst with small beer.

"So, tell me then, Master John, what happened then last even at the mine? There were cries of panic from the guards across the moat? Did you chase them all from the workings?"

He said simply, "Oh, no, we killed them all."

He gazed ahead, his thin face strained and hollow. I was silent, suddenly brought close to the hideous effects of civil war.

"Were they armed?" I asked at last.

"Picks and shovels are no match for muskets!" he said, matter-of-fact as ever.

"They were simply miners, then? Not soldiers like yourselves."

"No, not brothers of the blade, I assure you. They did not know to ask for quarter, but we had been told by Massey to deny them that."

I pushed my food away. These had been Men of the Forest, the poorest of the poor, promised no doubt by Forth's quartermasters that they would receive good payment, aye and commons too, whilst they mined for the King. Alderman Pury, the champion of the oppressed, had known that this had been the culmination of the enterprise. So much for the Christian charity of the Puritan cause.

I went back to bed, and stayed there for the rest of the day. I was totally disenchanted with the Parliamentarian viewpoint, and for that matter with the King's notions of Divinity. They were both wrong, wrong, wrong. I tossed and turned all day, wondering how I could escape from this wretched predicament and, worse than that, how could I ensure that Abram survived? The mindless tedium of the siege oppressed me, the terrible sacrifice made by the Forest miners for a few poor shillings caused me to weep silently into my pillow. How dared these numbskulls play fast and loose with the lives of simple men? By what authority did they assume the power of life and death over these poor starved fellows who had seized the chance to improve the lot of their families? I did not get up again as I could not trust myself to be civil, if I should have met any of the Council of War.

Next day which was the second of September, Massey succeeded in aiming his sacre onto the sappers' workings near Friar's Orchard, which caused considerable carnage amongst the King's men. By this I was beyond caring. All my concern now was for Abram and Rowena. As long as they, and her father and the Nichols were safe, I had no interest in the progress of the war, or so I thought. But when, after an explosion caused the inn to shake and Dickon ran in shouting, "The horses! The horses!", then I roused myself from my apathy and followed him to the stables. There was a great smoking hole in the roof, and Blackbird's tail was singed. I stayed with the poor beasts then, talking gently to each one. At last I was joined by Abram, who asked if he could walk Blackbird up and down the Eastgate. I had rechristened my mount. I could no longer call her Rowena, so had renamed her Ruby.

"You are more precious than Rubies," I muttered to her as we lead them sedately up and down Eastgate Street. Then we took them back to the stables and divided an apple between them. We exercised the other cobs I owned and Abram went to fetch Ralph, so that he could walk the two horses Robert had been given by Waller.

"These are your horses, Ralph," I told him.

"What?" he cried. "How so? I could never pay for beasts like these."

"Waller gave them to Robert to get you both back to Gloucester. There was no question of their being the property of any other person, save the two of you. Robert did not mention them in his will. Ergo, I would surmise that they are yours, a gift from Waller."

"Well, Tom, You had best hold to that, or the Witch of Endor or rather Haddenham will have them from us, swift as a fox through a hen coop. Believe me, she will want everything."

Even so, he began to groom his property and walked the two good pad-nags up and down for a space. Massey came to find me towards the end of the day and insisted that I went back to his house with Abram to feed on a roast fowl. I consented because although we still had the dried meat that Massey had so providently stored, there was no doubt that if the wretched siege continued, fresh food would be scarce and dear to buy. If Abram ate with me, this meant there was more for the Smith household.

"Do you know that they are still mining under the Eastgate?"

Massey told us. "The varlets that Barnwood dispatched were over their waists in water. If we continue to countermine, water floods their workings. So I will order that we begin again."

I found I could not remain silent. "But these are poor wretches, come from the wild Forest, where they live all but naked and in hovels. What have they to do with Civil War? They did not even have the right to quarter, which you have generously given your Royalist prisoners."

He was silent. Then he said, "Tom we are desperate, near the end of our powder. I make you this promise. If we can flood them out, I will order the musketeers that they are not to fire on them. But my responsibility is to the inhabitants of Gloucester, aye, Tom, beggars and all. Have you not seen how the homeless, who gather at the Cross are thriving? Believe me, I do care for the poor."

I nodded. These were not the words of a callous man. Then he went on, "But I tell you, Tom. If the great attack is to come than it will come tomorrow on the Sabbath, and I think it will be from the east. There was some talk from the watchers on the Tower of the King's cavalry massing in readiness. Tomorrow I fear must be another day of earth carrying. The ministers in church will be told to assemble the citizens for another last attempt. I will mount cannon on our earthwork which we will construct in the Eastgate that the enemy will see threatening them. What they will not know is that we have no powder. I must hope that the sight of cannons there, and over the Friar's Orchard will deter them from an all-out on-slaught. Tom, will you help me? Will you sing to cheer the poor citizens as they labour?"

Abram who had sat quietly, said suddenly with vigour, "Tom you must sing "Ragged and torn and true!" for that is how we are now."

I had never known anyone less likely to be ragged than my adoptive brother who still kept his hose as if they had come that day from the mercer, and his doublets, stain free and neat as ninepence as my father used to say. I smiled at him and tousled his hair, which he immediately straightened.

And so next morning, for our final effort, earth was dug, from gardens, from orchards, from paddocks, from graveyards and carried by the men, women and children of Gloucester in baskets and trugs, to the Eastgate where the houses were lined and filled with soil. Then a great earthwork was begun, which crossed the way behind the gate. Old grandmothers came staggering along carrying weight that they should never have been allowed to lift, little children dragged sacking bags behind them, and were praised and thanked by the troopers who began to construct the great heap. On the town side the access had to be sloping gently so that cannon could be rolled up to the summit when it was completed. We had no cranes or pulleys, all would be achieved by our muscles and our sweat. The beggars, much sturdier since they had had dried meat and apples every day, were found pails and baskets and helped us with a right good will.

And I sang as requested. Abram and I had collected empty water barrels from Barty's Hospital and had cut out the tops. After we had filled them with earth from the Smith's garden, we rolled them together to the Eastgate, and each time I was perceived by the troopers, a song was demanded.

Rowly, well recovered from the blow to his head, stood at the bottom of the slope we were constructing, thanking everyone for their efforts, and pushing the earth up to his fellows. I went straight over to him and took him round the waist, bawling out. "I cannot eat, but little meat. My stomach is not good." which caused a great roar of delighted laughter. Then on another occasion when we had returned again with our full barrel I was directed by Massey to sing and take a rest. He knew little of the effort that it took to fill ones lungs so that ones words travelled. It was not "rest". But this was not the day or the time for chopping logic, so I sang "Joan's ale is new", bringing in representatives of each profession as they presented themselves and as the song demanded. I sang with vigour and humour as Massey wished, but was sorely reminded of my fears that the poor dead woman in Worcester of whom we had heard might be Joan.

At last the cannon were in place, both at the Eastgate and at the Friar's orchard and everyone, dirty, exhausted and weary, dropped where they stood. The train bands were called suddenly to the northwest of the town where Royalist cavalry and foot had been seen gathering in the Walham fields. Alderman Pury in his capacity as Captain, was pleased to be congratulated when they returned. He had had a lucky shot, in his view and had brought down a white horse and it was presumed the rider. Strangely the enemy had then dispersed.

But the rest of us lay around the streets, waiting for the cannonade which would precede Rupert and his Cavaliers in their great attack on the Eastgate. The gunners were all in place on the sconces we had built and mounds of earth lay between them and the walls. Stamford's men, muskets at the ready were below the gunners. The inn keepers and vintners were busy at Massey's instruction serving all with draughts of small beer and we sat quietly and waited. We did not know for what we waited but I think most of the good Gloucester people feared that death was imminent.

And then about three hours after noon, a shout came from beyond the Eastgate and that most antique of artillery bolts, an arrow suddenly fell in Eastgate beyond the sconce. It narrowly missed two little children eating apple pasties, and stopped quivering in the centre of the street. Massey rose from his bench and walked over to the arrow, and pulled it from the path. He unfolded the paper that had been wrapped round it, and read it to himself. Then he read it aloud to everyone.

"These words are to let you understand, your God Waller has forsaken you, and hath retired to the Tower of London. Essex is beaten like a dog. Yield to the King's mercy in time, otherwise if we enter perforce, no quarter for such obstinate traitorly rogues. From a well wisher."

He called the Alderman to follow him and Dorney, Foster Pleasance and his Chaplain Corbett, and led them to his house to discuss the impact of the message. Rowena and Abram came over to me. She wore her plain stuff gown and her hands and arms were soiled up to the elbow and even Abram had a smut on his nose.

"Rowena has had a brave idea." Abram said. "Their message came in prose. Rowena thinks we should go one better and reply in verse."

"An excellent notion!" I agreed. "Wonderful indeed! They will think we have leisure enough to pen verses, whilst they pound our walls. Let us tell Sir Edward."

So we went in to his house and knocked on the door of the Council Chamber. The great ones were sitting round the table and Massey looked up with a trace of impatience.

"Yes, Tom?" he asked.

"Rowena Smith here thinks we should reply in verse."

"In verse?" Corbett and the Alderman spoke together.

"Videlicet, ...let me begin it for you." Rowena was not overawed by her audience. She knew she was cleverer than most of them put together. She coughed and began in her clear soft voice,

"Waller's no God of ours. Base rogues, you lie!
Our God survives from all eternity."

"That is very good!" said Massey, warming to the idea. "Excellent!"said Foster Pleasance.

The Alderman caught the spirit of the reply, unable to resist poking a dart at the Queen. "Though Essex beaten be, as you do say, Rome's yoke we are resolved ne'er to obey."

Dorney clapped. "Very good, Alderman. We should remind them perhaps of our crops that they have destroyed." And then Abram, who spoke Arabic as well as English, impressed us all mightily.

"But for our cabbages, which you have eaten, Be sure ere long you shall be soundly beaten."

And so together we composed a clever rhyming response. Perhaps it was not as courtly as the many poets, who clustered round the King could have devised, but it combined defiance with humour and ensured that the Royalists should know our spirits were still high and that although we were besieged we could still appreciate the finer things of life.

A thin young fellow from the Train Bands was produced who was told to run for his bow. He was, it seemed, the champion at the Butts in more peaceful times. The verse was elegantly penned by Foster Pleasance and wrapped around the same arrow, and our slender young Cupid was escorted up onto the Eastgate platform behind the cannon. We all followed him up and when he was ready, we gave a great shout and the arrow flew straight, a veritable bolt from the blue, over the moat and into a group of Forth's men, who cheered and waved at the sight of us.

Dusk was falling as Rowena insisted that we went back with her for bread and cheese which was all that she had time to prepare that day. I asked leave to go first to the New Inn, to wash myself by my usual method, standing naked in the courtyard and having Dickon pour water over me. I did not ask Mistress Nichol to heat the water. Poor soul, she was quite done up, but kind lady that she was, when she saw Dickon pouring water straight from the well over my dirty head, she came out with some excellent rosemary soap she had made, flavoured with rose water.

So although I was shivering like a hare surrounded by the hounds, no doubt but I was clean, and smelt like any pander in a school of pole-cats.

To our delight Poll Cook had fetched some of Massey's dried meat and had made excellent tasty rissoles, flavoured with sage and onion, so with that and bread and cheese and the inevitable apple pie we made an excellent supper. James insisted that Davy and Poll sat down and ate and drank with us. I had to admit upon reflection, I did applaud the Presbyterian notion that all were equal before the Lord. All had helped today, old and young, rich and poor. I vowed that I would use any fortune that I had to better the lot of the poor. Had the wages that I had paid to my household in Worcester been enough? Perhaps that had lain behind Joan's discontent.

Next morning Ralph came in excitedly as Abram and I were having the last of the smoked gammon, which dear Mistress Nichol had kept for us. Ralph had taken to wandering alone through the meadow, that surrounded the old castle gate in the south-west of the city. I had hoped he was again setting traps. We still had food but all was growing scarcer.

It seemed he had heard cries and groans. "Such as might issue from a charnel house!" he said, with much imagination and little accuracy. He ran to the wall where it abutted the river, climbed up and peered round over the grey-green flood. Boats were being cast off from Llanthony. "Crammed to the gunwales with desperate wounded. The King has sent his injured varlets to Bristol. Some of the troopers came to see what was to do and they suspected that there was no housing for them in Oxford. Doctor Tom, it would have made your kind heart bleed to see and hear them. I tell you, it is those poor bastards who need your skills. It is to be hoped that the boats get safely to Bristol without the sad invalids made food for fishes."

I invited him to sit down and share our breakfast. "At least, some provision has been made for the Royalist sick," I told him. "Remember Julius, and the two London apprentices. Left to die in a cold barn by their Parliament officers. Is one side in this conflict any better than the other?"

There was a hue and cry in the street outside and shouts of "Stop Thief!" We went to stand under the arch to see what was causing the commotion. One of the beggars who had come into the town from the Forest, seeking shelter in the city at the beginning of the siege came tearing down the street, pursued by a crowd of apprentices. One of the baker's boys who knew us stopped to tell us what was toward.

"He stole a pair of shoes from the cobbler's. The Alderman will put him in the stocks for sure!"

There was the elder Thomas Pury, standing at the end of the street with several troopers. The young beggar came to an abrupt halt before them and tried to make for one of the side alleys, but one of the troopers hurled himself onto him, and brought him down into the dust and stony cobbles of the street. He was hauled to his feet and stood a sad sight indeed, with a graze on his face, and blood pouring down his leg from his knee. The stolen shoes were still under his arm

"Who is the cobbler?" I asked Ralph swiftly. He pointed to a large man standing at the back of the crowd, with his hands on his hips waiting for justice to be awarded the thief.

I went over to him.

"The poor creature mistook my order," I told him. "I sent him to you to find if you had a pair of shoes that would fit me. If you had, I would have followed to your shop and paid for them there and then. How much for the shoes?"

His jaw dropped. "Why he said nowt of that, the young palliard, just seized the shoes and was off."

"How much for the shoes?" I said again.

The boy was being held in the fierce grip of Sergeant Ferrers, and the key to the padlock on the stocks had been sent for, from Massey's house.

I pretended to lose interest and turned away. "Fifteen shillings!" said the shoemaker instantly. I had my hand on a sovereign in my breeches poke. I pressed it into his dirty palm. "Tell them, then!" I ordered him.

He pushed his way up through the crowd. I followed with Ralph behind me.

"Alderman, a mistake! This leech had sent him to see if I had shoes that would fit. The savage mistook his order. They can scarce speak English, these wretches!"

The alderman was looking keenly at me, his eyebrows bristling with self-righteousness. "Is this so, Doctor Fletcher?"

"Indeed, it is. And sorry I am to have caused this mishap. That knee demands instant attention, Sir. I have paid this good fellow for his fine workmanship."

"Is this so, Master Sturney?"

For answer the cobbler held open his hand. "Here is my payment, Sir."

The Alderman turned to the shivering youth, who still clutched the shoes under his arm. "Give the good doctor his shoes, then fellow, and welcome this event as a salutary lesson. Crime does not pay! Let me tell you again. Crime does not pay!"

"His knee has surely learned the lesson, Alderman Pury, though in this instance he was no criminal." Blood was dripping onto the dusty cobbles of the Cross. The Alderman gazed at me under his bushy eyebrows. He knew I was lying. I knew he knew I was lying, but there was that in the Alderman that responded well to charitable deeds. He nodded slowly.

"Come, young fellow! Bring my shoes and I will dress your wounds." The crowd of apprentices, cheated of any entertaining punishment, dispersed and we made our way back to the New Inn and our unfinished breakfast.

I had to have hot water as the boy's legs were a mass of scratches and sores and black with ancient dirt. I bathed them as gently as I was able and bandaged the knee. The graze on his face was a superficial scratch but I cleaned that as well.

"What is your name?" I asked him.

"'Tis Barny, Sir."

"Well, Barny, here are your shoes, but be advised. I should not wear them today as they are supposed to be mine and you could run the risk of being caught again. Could I advise you when you go to your home, that you wear them for only a short time each day, until your feet become used to them."

I sent him away and we returned to our cold breakfast, Abram openly condemning my reckless behaviour, by giving vent to several disapproving sniffs.

Then Massey came to find me, "The Horse have gone!"

"What?" I shouted, thinking of Blackbird and Ruby.

"No, not yours, you dolt!" he said. "The King's horses have gone! Rupert has gone!"

"Ah!" I said understanding, ruffling Abram's hair which he hated, "So there are now only five thousand men for you to fight, Abram."

"Yes, we cannot abandon our defences," said Massey, chewing on a newly baked roll. "But I feel... I hope..." But both his heart and his mouth were too full for him to continue.

We interfered throughout the day with the mine workings that had been made under the Eastgate. The plan was to bore down into the mine, causing showers of earth and water to block up the rough passages that the poor wretches had dug out, with such daily risks to their lives and limbs.

"Tell them to be on their way," said the Alderman, standing, his arms folded, by the piles of earth where the Eastgate was buried.

"How might we do that, my dear Sir?" asked Massey. "I am loathe to send any over the walls, while the Foot is still gathered in force. And I fear that they have not as yet dismantled their gun emplacements. But the omens are good. Let us see what fortune the morrow brings us."

His caution was justified, no question. That evening the Lanthony cannons that were mounted on sconces blasted into the side of a house in the south of the city, near the old Blackfriars gate belonging to one Master John Halford, who was I think an attorney. He and his wife had stepped out to see Sim Walsh, leaving their three children in the kitchen, with strict instructions that the two boys were to mind their books and their little daughter was to ply her needle. What was their horror and distress, when they hastened home to find the kitchen and the bedroom above it completely destroyed, where a twenty-five pound cannon ball had ripped through the wall.

The parents were inconsolable, presuming that their precious children were buried lifeless under the piles of debris. They called to neighbours to help them move the rubble, and began their tragic work, Mistress Halford sobbing piteously, Master Halford, grim faced and determined. Pausing to straighten his back, he saw standing in the street, round-eyed with fear and apprehension, his three beloved offspring, clutching ripe apples. They had seized the opportunity of their parents' absence to run to the Pury's orchard where they had helped themselves to pippins from a tree famous for the sweetness of its fruit.

Abram and I had run from our meal to help, hearing that the children were buried. I must confess that when we realised the full circumstance we both became quite helpless with laughter. Alderman Pury and his son had hurried from their house and Captain Tom joined in our mirth. Other citizens, men and women had run to offer their assistance, but the vision of the three children, gazing at their ruined house, still clutching their ill-gotten gains, and their parents unable to believe their eyes, was a sight which provoked laughter for, I would hazard, some time to come. At last, attempting to compose myself, I managed to blurt out the words,

"Forgive me, good Alderman Pury, but in this instance, crime *does* pay!"

And that was the last incident of the siege. Next day the fifth of September the watchers from the Tower reported that the Royalist Foot was marching away. The officers had piled their belonging into carts and carriages which were being drawn off. The miners were slower to leave their workings ...perhaps they had not been paid... but at last when we had seen all depart, finally some of the Gloucester Train Band men ventured forth and set fire to anything in the mines that would burn.

The day was declared a fast day with two services. I was not known for assiduous church attendance, so decided that I would go on this day to show willing. The citizens of this city had shown remarkable courage, fortitude, and impressive resourcefulness. Men, women, and children had worked as one to preserve the lives of all. It was an impressive achievement, to have deflected a King's army of many thousands. I gave modified praise and thanks to the benevolent Almighty who had preserved us. Who knows? Perhaps he had indeed inclined his good will and blessings on the City of Gloucester.

In between the church services I ran to Sir Edward with a notion I had had during the first sermon, which would I hoped enable Ralph and myself to travel more safely to Haddenham.

"The prisoners!" I gasped out.

"What of them?"

"Are they still here?"

"Aye, that they are. Believe me, they are in no hurry to leave us.

Moss and his men have changed their allegiance they claim, but the others have eaten and drunk at my expense very comfortably, if you please."

"The claybrained lieutenant? He of Gerard's men? You have not sent him off yet? I want his clothes."

"Well, certainly they are better than yours! But…"

"Not because they are better, Edward," I cried, throwing courtesy to the winds. "I have to take Robert home, now, and his village is east of Oxford. I could travel more safely as one of Gerard's lieutenants, with Ralph as my ensign. Will you help me? It was the Colonel's last wish."

"You will need more than a convincing disguise," he said thoughtfully, "You will need a stout cart for the coffin and a beast bigger than the riding cobs you have. And two good men and true to keep you out of danger. What will you do with Abram? Leave him here, where he will be safe and where he can help myself and Foster. He writes an excellent hand."

"Aye, well, I had intended to leave him here but he may have objections."

If I was honest with myself I had hoped that I could persuade him to stay with the Smiths. This would give me the excuse I needed to return for him and perhaps to plight my troth with Rowena. Did she care for me as I cared for her? I hoped she did, but in truth when the prospect of telling her of my love became inevitable, I was as tongue-tied as any block of wood.

With Massey's permission I went to the Crown Inn carrying my good doublet and breeches, which still retained something of the tailor's finish. I had been entrusted with the attic keys and whilst their quarters were a little airless, the two lieutenants were clearly well satisfied with their treatment.

"Rot my vitals, but 'tis the leech whose brother was saved from the rope by Rupert!" Gerard's man had not forgotten me. "So give us news, man! God's pains, but I am pleased to see you!"

"Are we to be freed, good Sir?" asked the other fellow, a Scotsman.

"God's teeth! Indeed you are, good Sirs," I told them, "but your freedom carries a small penalty."

"Hell and the Devil confound you, Sir, but what is that?" said Gerard's man pleasantly.

So I explained that it was a simple matter exchange of clothes. I held out my good Cheyney doublet, and was confounded indeed by his expression. It seemed that my clothes, my good clothes, were disdained by an unarmed helpless prisoner. The other prisoner began to laugh. He was, it seemed, a merry fellow.

Negotiation was needed. I clinked the money in my pocket and asked for their names. The popinjay was Mortimer Skinner, from a noble Royalist family in Lancashire, he told me, and his companion whom I greatly preferred was one Gabriel Michie, a tall sturdy Scotsman, who found humour in most circumstances of his life.

"I am Doctor Thomas Fletcher of Worcester," I told them. "It is well known that I have not given my allegiance to either side. Therefore it would not be an act of treachery to sell me your clothes."

They had been given a bench and an old stool and we all sat, the better to discuss these manly affairs. I jingled my money again. "I need to pass through Royalist country with the corpse of a dear Parliament friend who lived near Oxford. I swear to you that I mean no treachery to the King or any of his servants. Chance finds me here, 'tis all. I will pay you well."

Gabriel Merton seemed to think my proposal acceptable and took my clothes and gave me his red sash and brown Dutch coat. His buff coat was cut about but he gave me that as well, everything for four sovereigns. He refused to part with his well fitting breeches although he accepted mine.

But Mortimer Skinner drove a very hard bargain. At last it was decided that the three of us should visit the tailor where I would lay down coin for a new suit of clothes, of whatever cloth he chose. For that I could have his blue velvet breeches and his light blue leather doublet, and his sash.

"And your partisan!" I insisted.

"What! God's bodykins! You rip the clothes from my back and wrest my precious badge of office from me as well! Never on my life!"

But the partisan changed hands for another three guineas.

"I expect you long to be back with your regiments," I said musing whilst the tailor measured Mortimer Skinner. "The good earth beneath your feet, the wind in your hair and the sun on your face."

"Aye, indeed," said Gabriel, "And the rain down your neck, and the mud round your knees. In a word, Master Doctor, No! Whilst I have been Massey's prisoner... and there is a rip-roaring laddie... I have thought much and slept even more. I have a braw wee present for you."

When we returned to the attic he went to a corner where there was a heap of wood shavings and some narrow wooden rods. Beside them were linen bags. He presented one to me with a bow.

"Pray, Master Doctor, do me the honour to accept."

I pulled aside the draw string at the neck of the bag and peered inside, then sat and emptied the contents on to my lap. It was a chess set, beautifully carved.

"You will have to find a board yourself," he said, smiling at my gasp of pleasure and admiration. Each piece was an individual masterpiece. The royal pieces were unmistakably King Charles and his Papist Queen, and one of the white knights was undoubtedly Rupert. To my delight one of the black knights was Massey, thin face and moustache to the life.

I could not speak for a moment. Then he said, "I hope you can play."

I nodded and for a moment was back with the Earl and young Ferdinand in the Close at Lichfield. At last I found my voice.

"Master Gabriel, you do me too much honour. These lovely pieces would sell for many guineas."

"So I tell him." Mortimer interposed. "But no reasoning with him. He vowed that he would give one of his sets to whoever should come and set us free."

"The landlady's daughter, a delightful lady, painted them for me, and I found with no distractions, I can roughly carve out a set in a day. I might stay here, Master Doctor, and leave soldiering to this noble son of Mars." He indicated Mortimer. "But I thank you for your compliment. And for your guineas. That could help us find a work-place."

I looked at him questioningly. "The landlady's daughter and I have entered into an agreeable understanding. I can turn my hand to hefting barrels and she finds she can paint with a marvellous steady hand. Would there be objections? Like you I care nothing for either side, and as for God, I am not sure that I know where he is, these days."

I put my chess set back into the bag, and still holding it firmly in my left hand, grasped him with my right.

"Master Gabriel, if I can help you, I will. I thank you from my heart. This is a marvellous ingenious present. I shall treasure it. Sir, again, I say, I thank you from my heart."

He laughed and brushed my gratitude aside.

Mortimer wished to stay in the attic until his new clothes were ready. The tailor had promised to have them finished in two days, so I, in Charles Gerard's lace trimmed officer's suit and Gabriel in my plainer Chency doublet went to find Massey to ask if Gabriel was now officially at liberty. When he saw me in my new finery, he passed his hands over his eyes as if bedazzled, but then doubled over laughing. The sleeves were a little short and the breeches barely covered my knees, and somehow the lace collar and cuffs bunched together in a manner less than elegant. When he learned how helpful the prisoners had been in the matter of their clothes, Massey suggested that the two stayed where they were that night, although he agreed that they were now at liberty. Mortimer must perforce do so, as I had relieved him of his breeches. I promised that I would buy them a good supper there. Fast day or no, the landlady had now a sirloin of beef, sizzling on the spit, as the butchers had killed a fine cow. I bespoke platters for Abram and Ralph and promised to return to them later in the evening.

The good people of Gloucester had been used to seeing me in either my blue Cheyney doublet or an old fustian suit that had done good service as workaday garments. This I had worn constantly since I had ruined my other working clothes in the moat and the dungeon. Now the sight of me in pale blue leather and velvet, for some reason that I was at a loss to understand, caused excessive mirth. To my distress and embarrassment it was not simply the children, who found me an object for laughter. Sober old beldames clutched their sides as I passed, and worthy tradesmen called to each other to observe the phenomenon of Doctor Tom in a lace collar.

A small crowd gathered, following me and were helpless with merriment as I turned into the New Inn.

"Why have my lieutenant's clothes made me the object of so much amusement?" I demanded of John Nichol who collapsed into a chair at the sight of me, feebly calling his wife. She came bustling in and at the sight of me gave a sudden helpless squeal of laughter. She had to hold onto a table to support herself and then excused herself to find an "old queer peeper" in which I could see myself.

In those days my hair was black, unstreaked with gray and my expression as a young man was that of a youth who observed the world as a serious place. I was not handsome as such, having features that I would not describe as ornamental. I had a long face and a habitually grave expression, but I did not think of myself as an ugly villain and could laugh and sing as well as the next man.

Before Mistress Nichol could return, Abram and Rowena came in together, stopped in the doorway to the courtyard at the sight of me, and on the instant began to shriek with uncontrollable mirth. They were the worst of all, clutching hold of each other, and as each of them gained control, the other would begin again. I began to be vexed, and advanced upon them asking "Why?"

Rowena recovered herself enough to come towards me, but then lapsed again into uncontrollable merriment. I asked again, "Why?" and she controlled herself a little. To my delight, she came to me and took me in her arms. Sweet though this sensation was, I could still feel the convulsions of mirth, rippling through her form as she held me against her.

At length, she seemed to come to her more sober persona. "Oh, Tom," she said, "Dear Tom, you are known for your gravitas and serious demeanour. And you suddenly assume this frivolous courtly costume. And it does not quite fit you!"

She again lapsed into mirth. Ralph came running in, having been told that serious Doctor Tom had become a Mayday spectacle. I was pleased in one way that he suddenly laughed as heartily as he had been wont to do, but my patience was fast trickling away from me.

"Very well, then!" I shouted angrily, "How may I disguise myself? We have to travel through hostile country, loyal to the King. Help me to assume a convincing character."

Immediately they were quiet, having realised that I was hurt and stung in my feelings. Rowena recovered herself and began to fix her mind on the practical details.

"A hat!" she said, triumphantly, "A high wide hat with two fine feathers. And see here, 'tis the work of an hour with my needle to lengthen your breeches. Fine French velvet, they are too. And we can let down the leather in your sleeves, and replace your lace cuffs to hide the original fold. But Tom, you must stand like a cavalier, like a moneyed scion of some aristocratic family. You must not stand with rounded shoulders and stoop a little to us all as is your wont. Now is your moment to stand tall, my love. And forgive me my merriment." And as I stood there, uncertain, she kissed me on the cheek.

She busied herself, flitting about my person and with pins from her hussif, the doublet began to sit better on my person. "Come with me now and we will go home and you can borrow my father's bedgown and sit by the fire whilst I effect these changes. Let us fit you into it better, then wear your lieutenant's garb with confidence, and you would deceive the King!"

I sent Abram up to my room for my old cloak and then, heeding her advice, I swept a low bow to all in the Inn, and strutted into the street. "Ralph, come with me!" I shouted at him. "I have a fine Dutch coat for you from Astley's regiment, Aye and a sash. Together we shall make a fine show as we ride into Haddenham. Stap my vitals, what rare capers we shall cut!"

With Rowena's help, we became as well bricked out and convincing a pair of Cavaliers as ever leered at a serving wench, or were thrown cupshot out down the steps of a tavern.

As we went back to the Crown, I now with my cloak worn protectively over my altered finery, Abram with a hint of petulance demanded,

"And am I not to come with you? You know you cannot care for yourself, Tom." He had been somewhat pacified to hear that Massey needed his clerkly skills, but there was a slight catch in his voice.

"Abram, I beg you. Stay here with Master James and Rowena and assist again with the hens. Now the guns are silent, I am sure they will start laying again. Oblige me in this, and I swear you shall have your will in whatever you wish, when we return to Worcester."

And it was with a heart both light and heavy that next morning, Thursday September 7th, that Ralph and myself went to St Mary de Lude to help several strong troopers carry Robert's coffin from the Crypt. Massey had suggested that if questioned, by official Royalist guards on our way, we employed a wily stratagem, and pretended that the coffin contained captured Parliament muskets that we were taking to Oxford. We opened it and I took the opportunity to place the wooden box at poor Robert's feet. I then placed several layers of felt over him and laid about twelve broken weapons over him, and had to ask for help replacing the lid. The troopers had placed themselves at a distance from the coffin, when we had opened it. The stench was formidable. Even Ralph chose to wait in the open air.

Massey had found me a stout cart with an oxhide cover which would give us shelter from the rain which had been drizzling down for a day or two. Today I was pleased that it left off, giving us if not a dry start, at least a fair weather beginning. My plan was to get as far as possible on our way before the roads were churned to mud. I had also been entrusted with the loan of one of James Legge's great horses which he had caused to have brought into Gloucester at the beginning of the siege. This was a beast from Suffolk, a gentle chestnut giant. As he seemed to have no name, I christened him Goliath, but a pleasanter natured fellow, I swear, it would be impossible to find.

Two troopers had volunteered to accompany us. They were dragoons from the regiment of Arthur Forbes, which had fallen on difficult times. They had earned their wages in the garrison, engaged in mundane duties, which it was suspected they found irksome. But these two seemed good lads from Somerset, by name Daniel Pool and William Rowbury, and were, they said, delighted to be freed from their garrison duties and on the open road again. Rowena had fashioned two red sashes, which they did not object to wear, over their gray doublets. Their horses, also which they had kept well fed and exercised, neighed with pleasure at the sight of Ruby. Ralph still found it difficult to believe that the mounts from Waller were his. I had made him care for them during the last few days, and they were used to him now, but I sensed that he was not confident as a horsemaster.

So at noon we gathered before the Eastgate. The mounds of soil had been cleared although a faint earthy smell still pervaded the place. To my surprise many of my friends had gathered to bid us Farewell. I had elected to walk beside Goliath, holding his rein and Ruby was harnessed to the back of the cart, as were Ralph's two horses, the first of which he rode. The two dragoons rode behind.

I doffed my fine hat... an old one of Master James..., swept a low bow to Alderman Pury, who called me "As impudent a King's Jackanapes as it had been his ill fortune to encounter," although he embraced me as he said it. His son clapped me on the shoulder, as Massey did. "God be with you, Sir Edward," I told him.

"Nay Tom, we are friends you and I. No "Sir" if you please. I have few friends I can trust!" and he embraced me warmly, and wished me Godspeed and told me to haste back to Gloucester, my second home. Simeon Walsh whispered that he viewed me as a son and that I must take care and haste back unharmed. He had replenished my box and I had paid him for a selection of his tinctures. Grace Armitage kissed me as did Mistress Nichol and Master James whispered to me, "For God's sake, speak cheerfully to your brother."

Abram stood at the head of the stair that lead down to the dungeon. I had to retrace my steps to embrace him. To my surprise he was weeping and clung onto me as if I was about to walk through Hell.

"Do something for me," I told him. "Go often to the Quay and look for news of Lofty. And help Rowena and her father as much as you can. And give this to Rowena for me." I pressed the linen bag into his hands. "It is a prodigious cunning chess set, made by Gabriel at the Crown. Get sweet Rowena to teach you how to play."

He sniffed and nodded and let me go. I turned round, looking for Rowena but she was nowhere to be seen. I went back to James and asked him, "Give her my loving duty and tell her every day away from her is as a year to me." He seemed a little surprised by the force of my devotion but agreed to do so.

So, like the pilgrims of old, we began our journey. For a pilgrim's stave, I had my partisan, a martial alternative but one I hoped not to employ as such. Ralph looked what he was now, a man of substance, in his gray Dutch coat, and his fine red sash. The two dragoons were clearly happy to be journeying from Gloucester, and were controlling their impatient horses, smiling at the assembled crowd. I had been sad not to have seen Rowena but as we cleared the moat on the drawbridge and I turned round to wave a last Farewell to my friends, I saw her standing above the Gate on the rampart, gazing at me. I swept her a bow, and she waved her handkerchief. Then remembering her loving embrace of yesterday, and regretting with all my heart the empty void that was now between us, I blew her a last kiss.

16

It was agreeable to find oneself out of the confines of the city and to be once again in the open country. But, alas, it was a countryside that had been despoiled and violated. The ruined burnt houses of the Gloucester suburbs stood stark and cheerless. Where before there had been cheerful green pastures, now there were wide expanses of brown earth, where the King's men had lived and fought and sometimes died in his service. The detritus of their abandoned camps littered the landscape, blackened firewood, a pile of rabbit bones here, shards of broken cooking pots there. The great guns had churned up the farmland as they had been dragged hither and yon.

As I looked to my right, I became aware we were passing the shameful orchard where I had so nearly met my end. There were rough-hewn wooden crosses under the trees. One such crucifix could so easily have been all that was left of me. I thought of poor Hatton and muttered a quick prayer, asking for mercy on his soul and thanking the Almighty for my own deliverance. I was surprised at my reaction. I was not a man who prayed much. The place oppressed me greatly.

I quickened my steps and hurried Goliath past the loathsome trees. The other three were surprised at my sudden speed and laughingly objected, and as soon as it was out of my view, I was happy to resort to our pleasant jog-trot. As we came about a mile and a half from the town, the fields resumed their customary pastoral colour, a verdant green, whilst on the trees there was the occasional bright orange signal, that autumn lay in wait for the death of summer.

I had spoken to Master Nichol as to our best route. Goliath had a heavy load to draw, no question. If we could slip unmolested along the plain to the south of the village of Cheltenham, there was a gentler climb there up the Cotswold escarpment. Once there on the high plateau of central England, the going would be easier for the poor giant. We could harness up Ruby to assist him up the hill, and the troopers indicated that they had no objection to their Welsh cobs being used in the same way. Ralph's beasts were riding horses, too delicate in back and leg for such work.

But I had other concerns. We did not wish to find ourselves merrily trotting along the same road as the King, bidding him a blithe Good day as we ambled past him and his generals. We had been told that he had made for Sudely Castle near Winchcombe to the north east of Gloucester. But far be it from us humble subjects to wish to press hard on his heels. We would therefore not push forward too quickly.

There was also the prospect of Essex' suddenly appearing before us, trumpets blaring, drums beating, and guns exploding. Massey expected him in Gloucester within the next twenty four hours to give his poor Londoners rest and recuperation. I was confident that as long as we could remove our red sashes and hide the partisan, we would not be viewed as enemies by the men of Parliament. As long as they asked questions first before priming and firing their muskets.

And then I had a third concern. Gabriel had, when questioned, freely admitted that there had been deserters from the King's army, sometimes as many as fifty men at a time. "Not all Commanders were as dedicated to the well being of their boys as yon laddie, Massey. Jesu! That man cares for his prisoners better than some idle bastards do for their best muskets!" He admitted that there could be groups of dissatisfied troopers wandering the countryside, possibly seeking a way home. But it might be that such men had little respect for property or for the lives of its owners.

"So have a care, wee Tom!" he advised me in his Scottish brogue. Though he gave me advice in a carefree manner, he was serious in his intention, and I gazed continually at the surrounding hills towards which we were slowly journeying. We had resolved to travel due east and now that we had made our way past a sudden steep hill which stood on the plain like a pimple on a pot-man's chin, we could no longer see Gloucester when we looked back. John Nichol had told me that the escarpment up which we must go, rose more gently and less precipitously if we could pass a village known as Shurdington on our right, and then strike up into the hills.

It was flat easy going and we made good progress. The country had at first seemed empty, but when I looked up to the summits on my right, I thought I glimpsed the flash of metal in a stray sunbeam, far above us. I kept looking around on all sides. I remembered a discussion from what seemed another life. Julius had pleaded not to go again to Cirencester. To our right and the south there was the occasional sound of other travellers.

"Ah! That's right!" said Daniel, "Romans built a good straight road. But her turns south to Cirencester. No good to us."

When we had travelled about six miles, we came to a few cottages nestled around a small alehouse, under the hills. My concern was for horses rather then humans, so I agreed that we could refresh ourselves there, but that we must press on whilst the land around us was quiet. My companions were content with small beer and our mounts had water and a few mouthfuls of oats and an apple each.

I asked the landlord who attended to us himself, whether he had seen movement of the King's army. "I heard tell he's made for Painswick, on the Portway." he told us grudgingly.

"For Painswick?" I looked at my companions. Painswick was almost due south. Massey had been certain he would have made for Sudeley, north-castwards, to Lord Chandos' fine castle, to be feted before he made his way back to Oxford.

"Well, what do I know?" said mine host aggressively. "More to the purpose, what do I care? I give you Good Day, gentlemen!"

So we pressed on with the hills rising steeply to our right. We followed them round and as John Nichol had told us, there was a gentler slope rising into the heights, a broad track snaking upwards. Across the valley ahead of us the village of Cheltenham, basked in the afternoon sun. We harnessed the cobs in a chain of three, alongside Goliath, and began our ascent. The sun was behind us now and when I paused to look back on our progress, the whole plain opened and the city of Gloucester and the Cathedral became clear once again. The road led between pleasant groves of trees, which lined the hillside as far as one could see. From time to time our way would turn upon itself, but led back always to the view of the sunlit plain stretching away to the Severn and to Wales.

At last the path began to level out and when we looked back, the plain was hazy now and indistinct, in the westering sun. Far below was the narrow ribbon of the beginning of our path. As we could now look down and know that we had completed our climb, I thought that we had all earned a rest. Goliath stood patiently, whilst we unharnessed Ruby and the other cobs and we sat at our ease, shielding our eyes from the glare of the sun and gazing down on the way we had travelled.

Suddenly there was a shout. I leapt up and looked round but Ralph caught my arm.

"Down there," he said, pointing. Where before our path had been empty, now a man stood there, alone but seeming to beckon to others. In a moment he was joined by several more, stepping from out of the trees. Then, one on horseback, came from the undergrowth and shouted commands to the fellows already on the path.

Ralph pointed again. Below them, more men were grouping and regrouping, as they came down from the hills to the northwards. I was suddenly afraid that perhaps this army, for so it was, might have detachments as high as ourselves. I rose and listened, going some yards off the path into the undergrowth. But all human sound came from below.

Someone shouted an order and a general movement began away from the hills. I had seen armies on the move before. Indeed, had moved with them at Edgehill and Hopton Heath, and as I watched I became aware that these boys did not "straggle" as had been the usual method of going forward, but moved in more contained groupings. And now at the bottom of the hill the ordnance came lumbering behind.

There were hundreds, nay thousands of them. We were far too far away to identify any ensign, but there was the occasional flash of orange so no doubt they were the men of Parliament. They began to stream away from the hills. They were of course going to Gloucester.

I stood up. "Well, there goes the man who hung my father," I said idly.

Ralph nodded. He had been quartered in the Newport Street house with Robert and his troop after Powick Bridge, and remembered that fateful Sabbath. The other two stared questioningly.

"Robert Devereux, the Earl of Essex!" I announced. "There he goes with a few of his retainers. He admitted his error. He was deceived by a madman who was later slain in turn. But my innocent father remained dead. It's a marvellous strange thing that when great ones make mistakes, the results last as long, as when the more humble sort err. One would think God's blessed angels would rectify matters for the princes of this world."

Ralph raised his eyebrows and shook his head slightly and William Rowberry pursed his lips, uncomprehending. But Daniel laughed at my bitter jest.

"Well, Tom, maybe they angels be watching over we, whatever you do think. At least, we aint answering questions with a sword's tip in our throats, sorry though I am about your Dad."

"If they doubt our quest, we can always show Robert's will." I said wearily. But I agreed with him. It was pleasant to be away from the martial influence under which we had been living and labouring for weeks, and I rejoiced that we had missed Essex and his army by a hair's breadth.

Our way was now level and agreeable. Goliath was able to quicken his pace slightly although I did not think I should let him canter, with so delicate a burden. The sun slanted through the trees and our shadows slowly lengthened before us. We still had two more miles to travel before we found the inn, John Nichol had told me of in a place called Dowdeswell. He had vowed we would reach it before sundown.

I began to consider our position. If the King had gone to Winchcombe, how had he avoided Essex? Had there in fact been a battle? But if in fact the King had gone to Painswick, as the landlord had told us, and intended to make for Winchcombe, where was he now?

My question was not long unanswered. We began faintly to hear that familiar sound of many men, moving, talking, singing, shouting even, and the neighing of horses. There was also the particular smell that hung over men on the move. Alas, the clean scent of their new garments had faded with a month's hard usage, and less pleasing odours attended them. Cooking, the smell of horses when there is chafing from ill-fitting harness and that stale awareness that very few have used water to cleanse their bodies for some time. Whenever I smelt the King's army I always vowed that cleanliness should be my lifelong aim, if only for the sake of those who lived with me.

They were perhaps four hundred yards ahead. I judged that they were crossing the road in front of us. And, no doubt of it, they were travelling cross country to Winchcombe. The mystery was solved. Were there any other intrepid travellers locked between the King's Army in the hills and the Earl's on the plain on the 7th of September?

The Earl was heading westwards and the King was bound due north. I was for the east. Perhaps there was another army of which we knew nothing, even now, heading towards us on its way south.

We quickly assumed our red sashes. However, I wished to avoid confrontation and calculated that if we slipped aside we could stand in some thick hawthorn brake, unseen, until they had all passed. I wondered if I should call on my friendship with Peabody again. Perhaps, however, there were only so many occasions, when I could rely on his good will. We would stand, still and silent, the horses nose-bagged, until the rogues had gone.

Almost at once a stand of hawthorn bushes, red with haw berries came into view on our right. The noise from the King's army grew ever louder but they were still hidden from us due to a slight turn in the path. I led Goliath followed by the others into the central area, enclosed by the thick bushes, shielding his eyes with my hat. I drew him to a halt and found his oats. Ruby whinnied for hers, and we made haste to silence all the horses with their nosebags.

The noise of the army crossing the path ahead of us grew ever more loud, and now we could catch glimpses of groups of men through the gaps in the foliage, moving northwards. The army was increasing in its numbers, spreading and straggling down the hill. Above us came the warning shouts of men in charge of the cannons, which were notorious for effecting dreadful carnage on their own side, if they ran away with the poor devils who were trying to control them. There was a sudden rush and a downwards crashing that stopped short of our hawthorn brake. More shouts of reassurance, yet the swathe of woodland that this army occupied seemed to grow ever wider.

And suddenly we were no longer alone. A man shouting to a friend suddenly thrust his way into our copse, in front of us. "I'll be with you straight!" he announced to his unseen companions.

Astonishingly he did not see us, being preoccupied in his conversation and the reason for his sudden desire for privacy. With his back to us he untrussed his breeches and began to urinate in a great yellow arc which splashed onto the ground some distance from his long elaborate boots. Fortunately for us he aimed uphill rather than down. We stood lifeless and transfixed. He completed his objective, adjusted his clothing, and looked idly round.

He gave a great start. He had thought he had discovered a concealed retreat, and four pairs of human eyes had witnessed his welcome relief.

"What the devil are you hiding here for?" he roared. I took a step forward, and told the obvious truth.

"Feeding the horses, Sir," I told him, humbly.

"Who the devil's that?" he shouted, pointing at the coffin.

And the devil or some unearthly spirit came to my aid. When in a desperate situation, lie for your life, and lie again and again, until the lie creates its own momentum.

I swallowed and tried to look young and grief stricken.

"My father, Sir."

"And who is your father, bean-pole?"

" My father was Captain Robert Smith, Sir, slain at Lansdowne. These good boys were with him when he died."

"And where are you taking your deceased progenitor?" he asked me, rolling the words around his mouth, as if they were good to eat.

"Back home to my poor mother for burial in our family vault, Sir."

"And where is that?"

Where was the next town on our route? I knew nothing of this area but what John Nichol had taught me. In a panic, I said the name of the last town I remembered.

"Winchcombe, Sir."

He came over to look at the coffin. I was suddenly inspired.

"Would you wish to look upon my father, Sir? It may be that you knew him."

He seemed doubtful and I pressed home my advantage. "Ralph, help me, will you?" We leapt onto the cart, and putting our shoulders to the lid began to prise it open. Immediately a fearsome waft of decay pervaded the grove.

"No, no, boy. Let him lie in peace, I beg you. Slain at

Lansdowne, eh? And unburied until you could fetch him home?" I nodded eagerly. "You are performing a dutiful office, Master Smith. And your partisan" (which I was clutching desperately) "proclaims you the Lieutenant. Well, if you are bound for Winchcombe, you had best follow on when most of the Foot has passed. Go with the carts at the rear, and if any challenge you, tell them Edward Walker has sanctioned your attachment to our train."

He strode across to where he had first appeared, and I began to breathe more easily. But my tale, inconsolable widow, obedient responsible young son, faithful retainers, all this moonshine had touched his heart. He paused again and turned back to me.

"Get you back onto the path and I will ensure that you and your precious load are given a good placement amongst the carts. I will see you at the cross roads. It is yards only up the hill."

There was just enough area in the grove for Goliath to make a complete circle and with a sinking heart, at least in my case, we managed to regain the path.

"Who be your Commander, a'case they asks we?" Daniel had a cautious brain between his ears.

"Best say Charles Gerard," I whispered, "But don't say much. You have a Somerset burr and Gerard is a Lancashire Colonel, recruiting from thereabouts."

Two riders were waiting for us just below the crossroads. One was this same Edward Walker who was magnificently mounted on a coal black stallion. The other was seated on a horse that I realised I had seen before. And to my desperate consternation I knew her rider. It was Lucius Carey who had insisted that I was his guest after Edgehill. I was proud to call him my friend, but if he recognised me, then all would be over for us.

I could see him draw in his breath and his sad features were suffused with joy at the sight of me. I shook my head and shouted "No! No!" and saw a gleam of understanding suffuse his expression. He nodded slightly and sank back in his saddle with a bemused but regretful smile.

Edward Walker was clearly puzzled by my shout. "To whom do you shout, Master Smith?"

"These sad rogues want to press on to Dowdeswell where they have heard there is a good hostelry, Sir. They have heard that there will be poor quartering around Winchcombe, and we are mortal weary." "But surely your dear mother will find bed and board for all," said Edward Walker. Devil take the man! He knew my lying story better than I did!

"Well, she is with her sister these last days and does not command her household as is her usual wont." I had the sensation of sinking deeper and deeper into a quagmire. "Well, it may be that they are in the right of it, Master Walker. Perhaps I should listen to their needs rather than my own." Daniel had the wit to nod vigorously. Ralph gazed blankly at me and William scratched his head.

"True, it is there will be poor quartering when we all reach Winchcombe," said my good friend Lucius, as quickwitted as he was noble. "It may be, Edward, that this godly young man knows best what his men require. Perhaps we should wish him Godspeed and let him follow his best inclinations. That is his poor father, you say?"

He raised his eyebrows in the direction of the coffin and I nodded but when Edward Walker bent to adjust his girth, I shook my head and clasped my hands together in a gesture of entreaty.

"My Lords, may I, a humble Lieutenant, ask after our noble sovereign? How does the King?"

"Very well, in his body, but sore beset with cares and concerns for his beloved subjects, so many of whom are deceived and cozened by the treacherous rebels." Edward Walker told me, as he moved his horse forward onto the northward track. "Well, Master Smith, bring your dear father to Winchcombe tomorrow. You may ask for me at Sudeley Castle, if you require assistance in any aspect of his burial at St. Peter's. We had best spur on, Lucius. We have two more hours of daylight, I would hazard."

"My Lords," I said bowing humbly, whilst still having hold of Goliath's rein. "I am in your debt for your good counsel. I thank you for your kindness and will endeavour to deserve your trust and confidence."

Edward Walker nodded and trotted on some paces away. Lucius bent to adjust the buckle of his boot. "Goodbye, Tom, and God bless you!" he whispered and urged his horse on after Walker. The wagon train was still passing in front of us, the guns precariously balanced on the great carts. At last one cheerful fellow drew up and shouted to us, "Did you want to cross the track, my masters?"

I nodded and we were over the road, into the trees and speeding away towards Northleach, like the hounds after a runnable stag. I leapt up on the cart behind Goliath and my scruples about jolting poor Robert's corpse melted away as we careered through the twilight woods. At last all sounds of the King's army had faded and all we could hear was the evening birdsong. We came to a clearing and as Ralph called out, "Tom, Tom, please stop!" I did so, having regard to the Shire horse's wellbeing. I should have remembered that Ralph was not accustomed to managing one horse, let alone two.

He dismounted and came and stood, red faced and panting beside the cart. "Tom, why did you go to the tiresome task of obtaining our disguises? Why did we need to escape? "

I replied wearily, "The disguises will not fool the men who issued the clothes. Are you able to play Patrick Ruthven's Scottish lieutenant, in front of the man himself? I think you might have encountered difficulties. As for me I did not wish to be asked by Colonel Charles Gerard, what I had done with Mortimer Skinner whose partisan I hold. And what of Daniel and William? They are Forbes' men of Parliament through and through. What indignities might the King's men not have heaped on poor Robert's remains, if we had not escaped? I for one have no wish to see the inside of Oxford prison, nor do I want to become acquainted with a Royal noose."

I was shouting by the time I had reached the end of this tirade. Daniel said quietly, "Now don't 'ee get comical, Tom. Ralph don't mean no harm. Don't want the bastards to come after us, suppose they be draggletailing after the main force. You did powerful well back there. But the little chap, now. You knew each other, or I miss my guess."

I nodded agreement, and left my perch. Daniel's advice was good. Half a mile further and a few poor cottages came into view. There was an ale-house, run by a slatternly old woman. I told her that I would sleep with the horses on the cart, but that if she had beds for the others, I would pay for them.

Ralph stared at me. "Sleep with the horses? Do you mean with Robert?"

I replied irritably, "Aye, with Robert, if you will. He has your fortune at his feet, remember. Someone must guard it for you and his wife. In fact as things stand, Ralph, he is a more understanding and entertaining companion, than ever you have proved on this jaunt!"

He stared ahead and tears began to trickle down his cheeks. I immediately regretted my harsh words. The old woman called them in to eat at her table and she kindly brought out a platter of beef stew for me. After the excellent fare at Rowena's table and Mistress Nichol's wholesome breakfasts, siege or no siege, this tough boiled beef was a sad awakening. I cannot pretend that I ate with much relish. I knew I should not have been so cruel to poor Ralph, who was powerless to compete in the world of male cut and thrust. Afterwards, he brought out a cup of canaries to me which he told me he had paid for from his own pocket. I thanked him and begged his pardon for my hard words.

He said in wonder, "I am so ashamed of myself. I should still wish to be near Robert, but I confess the smell from the coffin revolts me. You seem able to open it and look upon him without flinching."

I tried to be kind. "Robert's corpse is not Robert. He no longer has any need of his earthly shell. Also I am a doctor. I am used to the aroma of decay. I have embarked on this hazardous journey for him, but also for you, Ralph. And I would ask you to forgive me for my choleric behaviour. That Edward Walker was far too curious for my peace of mind. I could envisage all manner of embarrassments, which could have ended in some of us kicking the clouds."

I asked if the old landlady had found them good beds. He nodded, saying that they were well enough. "How far do you think we should get tomorrow?"

I remembered John Nicholl's wise advice. "We will try for Witney, and there we must decide whether to go north or south of Oxford. We cannot go through the town." I said regretfully, although I would have liked to see again the fine, noble buildings Edward Holte and Lucius had shown me. "Some Jack Stickler would purloin Goliath of a certainty, and he would spend the rest of his days pulling his heart out at the head of a gun carriage. I'll try to sleep now, good Ralph, and once again forgive me."

He left me then and I lay pondering how a man could seem to prefer to live with another man, as he and Robert had done. I had the impression that if Robert had not been a great Commander for Parliament, he would have been condemned by his fellow Puritans. Young women were so enticing. I loved their softness, their perfume, their hair and eyes. I fell asleep on the hard boards of the cart, remembering Rowena's interpretation of the story of Mary and Martha, and dreamt that they all three tried to persuade me to study philosophy. I tried without success to avoid the good attention of Martha and Mary as I saw philosophy lessons with Rowena as a delightful challenge, and woke with a start in the early morning, just as Martha offered me another bowl of her beef stew.

I knew that we would be at least twelve hours on the road if we were to make Witney by sundown. After attending to the horses, I stooped down through the door of the inn, and I realised that I had had the best of the sleeping arrangements. The stench of old clothes, old cooking fat and old flesh in the place was overwhelming. Still if the old landlady did not know how to cook, she certainly knew how to charge. As Daniel appeared, grinning and ruefully scratching, I asked politely if a supplementary rate for flea bites was included.

We were up and away without breakfast, having determined to pause in Northleach at a baker's, if we could find one. The day was fine and we made good progress, buying food upon the way. The countryside up on the Cotswold plain was a pastoral landscape of great beauty but the wide green meadows, dotted with sheep, had perhaps been bought at a price. Occasionally we would pass places where each man or woman for that matter still had his or her own strip of land to till and harvest as they wished. Ralph seeing me gazing at the small plots of cultivated land, told me,

"The Colonel would not have his lands eaten up by sheep. Haddenham is like these places, Tom. Everyman has his own section, sometimes two or three to call his own." A mile or two along and the sheep had pride of place again.

"Look at these poor folk,Tom" He indicated a family in rags who stood miserably at the side of the road, holding out a bowl begging for alms. Ralph reined in his horse beside them and called that he would catch us up. I looked back and saw him fumble in his pocket for coin. A moment later he was with us again.

"'Tis as I thought, Tom. They have been turned off for sheep grazing. Squires as they call the landowners in these parts want naught to do with tenants. One shepherd can oversee forty or fifty sheep. That poor fellow back there said, "If I grew wool 'stead of hair, I'd be of more value to Sir John." If he was a ram 'stead of a man, he'd be worth more. Can you credit it, Tom?"

I had not seen him so animated since Robert's death. "Would you like to be a farmer, Ralph?" I asked him, surprised at the strength of his feeling.

"Aye, that I would." he said warmly.

"But what about the poachers?" I asked laughing. "There's a dilemma for you. I suppose it would not be poaching if you caught hares on your own land."

"Well, anyway, it is not to be!" he said, sadly.

"You don't know that." I said. "Courage, man! Anything could happen."

"Well, certain sure I am that I will not go a-soldiering again. I only went to please the Colonel." And he lapsed into silence.

We bought food and drink in Burford and ate and drank as we rode, having been told that Witney was just over six miles away. I would need to take advice as to our best route from there and although we were all tired, I persuaded my companions that we would command better beds and supper in Witney, than in any of the tumbledown hovels, that proclaimed themselves inns, by the bushes hanging by their ramshackle doors.

So it proved. It was twilight as we descended from the high Cotswold plateau to the snug little town. Immediately we were aware of a heavy cloying smell, not of decay, but of wet wool. Ralph to my astonishment identified it immediately.

"'Tis blankets, Tom. They make 'em here. The water in this river, the Windrush, it's called, is special for blankets. The town is known for it, just as my town Haddenham is special for ducks. Well, you'll see."

It was astonishing that the closer we came to the place of his birth, the more Ralph gained in confidence. Now he remembered that the best inn was on Church Green and was known as the Greyhound. He directed us there and even took it upon himself to enter to enquire if six horses and four smart young fellows could be accommodated. The landlady, wiping her hands on her clean white apron came out with her son and two young grooms. The tired horses were led off and we were invited to enter the Buttery and take our ease. But first I followed the horses to the stables and, unobserved, covered the coffin, my wooden box of medicaments, and Sim's linen bag of potions with the oxhide cover so that all appeared to be a heap of old leather. It seemed that the grooms slept in the stables, whenever horsemen stayed at the Greyhound. They would have no reason to disturb poor dead Robert.

As I was now at accord with Ralph, it seemed churlish not to sit and eat together. I wondered if we should meet any fellow guests who might know the best route to Haddenham. Ralph himself was not certain, whether it were quicker to travel north or south of Oxford.

The landlady, a pleasant woman with a smiling countenance and fair curls, came into the Buttery to ask if we should please to sit in the dining parlour. A gentleman there had seen me through the window and had thought he knew me, and would take it as an honour if he could pledge us in a flask of wine. The prospect of a drink, purchased by some other person, tempted me greatly. Ralph had already risen and William seemed to have become quite lively at the notion of a cup of canaries, rather then the small beer it was my custom to provide. Only Daniel paused and laid his brown hand on my blue leather sleeve.

"Make sure as ee do know this varlet, Tom." Then he rose and followed us.

As I entered the small dining parlour where a cheerful fire flickered in the grate, and candles burned in prickets on the table, a well dressed man rose and bowed graciously to me.

"Why I was right, damn me! We have met before, have we not?" He addressed himself to me alone, and his voice whilst not known to me, was similar to that of Sir William Russell. The intonation and cadences were familiar in that I had been used to conversing with men who spoke as he did. None the less I did not know him.

"I fear you have the advantage of me, Sir." I said, bowing in as smooth and courteous a manner as I could muster after a day spent gazing on Goliath's broad nether regions.

"You are a scholar, are you not, Sir? I could swear I met you in the hallowed cloisters or the hushed library of... which college was it?"

This was a man who clearly knew Oxford. He persisted in his questioning. "New College was it? Or Magdelen, or Trinity?"

"Alas, Sir, I have not the honour to be a graduate of any of those temples of learning. I am a simple country doctor. I did visit the colleges you mention last December with a dear friend, who holds a very high position in his Majesty's Council of State."

"Then it was last December I had the pleasure of making your acquaintance. Let me reacquaint you with my name, Nimrod Hunter. I ask you what were my parents thinking of! And your name? You are good Doctor John... now it escapes me again. John? Dan? Dick? My memory... how it betrays me."

"I am Doctor Tom Fletcher." I said, putting him out of his misery.

"And your noble friend. I know him, sure. It was he who made us acquainted, was it not?"

Lucius had introduced me to so many of his friends as he had taken me on a brisk tour of the noble colleges, that I must have met this gentleman as we had hastened up stairs and along corridors.

I replied, "I believe so. He is of course, Lucius Carey, Viscount Falkland."

He slapped his thigh. "Of course. How is the dear rogue? Still playing fast and loose with the fair sex?"

I was at a loss to reply to this. Lucius was devoted to his pious wife Laetitia, but I could envisage that she might prove a trifle cold.... still I did not know. So this I discreetly said.

"Ah, a true friend! Loyal to the hilt!" exclaimed Master Hunter, casting his eyes heavenward. " Like a good wife, above rubies! May I ask, whither you are bound?"

"To Haddenham," I said. Daniel stirred uneasily beside me. But I, with no more brains than a cockroach, ignored him. "We wish to avoid Oxford. Could you set us on our way, dear Sir?"

"My dear young gentleman, I will do more than that, for friends of Viscount Falkland. God's death, I will! I will accompany you. And you are right to avoid that pit of iniquity that Oxford has become. The place is full of cozeners and parasites. Tomorrow we shall make for Eynsford and shall sleep at Wheatley. Then 'tis but one more day's jog for Haddenham. Shall we bespeak supper and then to our beds? We must rise with the lark in the morn. Is it agreed?"

"Sir, I do not know how to thank you," I said gratefully.

"Tush, not a word, I beg you. Where is that potman?

Ganymede?" he called, "for bethink you, Sir, Ganymede was cupbearer to Zeus and the Gods and I propose that we order a repast worthy of divinity!"

He called again for the landlady's son who swiftly appeared, bowing and ready to tell Master Hunter what was the bill of fare. But Daniel was clearly in an uneasy frame of mind.

"Tom!" he said, urgently. "I'm in a bit of a lather about the big feller's fetlock. If us gets an unguent for 'im now, 'twill save all manner of bother tomorrow, with we rising precious early, an all."

I allowed him to lead me round to the stables, where he went round all the stalls, ensuring the grooms had gone for their meal.

"Now listen 'ere," he spoke in a hoarse whisper, still afraid of being overheard. "Does ee know that feller, certain sure?"

I could not truthfully say that I did, but said again that I might have met him.

"Listen, Tom!" and he grasped my arm. "That man knew nowt about you when you came in to him, and now he knows a fair deal. Tell 'im no more. Tell 'im nowt about the Colonel. He don't know we'm carrying he to his grave. What do us know about 'im? Us knows nowt."

"We know his name," I said, slowly realising that Daniel was a good counsellor.

"His name!" and he spat on the stable floor. "Nimrod Hunter! Nimrod was the mighty hunter or was the parson in the prattling box, bellowin' maid's moonshine at me all those years I had to sit, my arse on a hard bench, hour after hour. 'Tis a name made up to cozen trustin' folk like you, Tom. What us don't know, what is the bastard huntin'? And I tell ee, he be after coin. Keep your hands on your hapence, Tom. And I beg ee, get yourself a night's sound sleep tonight, and I'll watch the horses. Oh, aye, and the Colonel."

"But he offered kindly to guide us!" I said weakly.

"Guide!" and he spat again. "Tom, you don't need no guide. I heard ee say this Haddenham place be due east of Oxford. I'm as ignorant as dirt, Master Tom, (I should call ee that, begging your pardon) but what's that big yellow light that comes up in the east every day and slips over westwards. And if the day is too lamentable overcast wi' clouds, poor folks in villages and fields will tell us the way."

"Shall I tell him we will deal well without him then?" I asked, quite downcast by my own stupidity.

He thought for a moment. "Best not make 'ee distrustful. For all we know 'im could be one of many." He sought in his pocket and brought out two sovereigns which he pressed into my hand. "Tom, have these red rogues for my supper. Yon turkeycock wont pay. I tell ee, you'll have the reckoning for us all, or I'm a Dutchman's doxy!"

And so it proved. Our new acquaintance insisted that he would bear all the expenses for our meals, and we had a roast chicken and a roast duck with excellent spinach and beans, and syllabub and an endless stream of Canaries, which Nimrod ordered, lavish as you please. At length when we had supped our fill, he called for the reckoning and stood up to pay.

"Devil take it, Doctor Tom, what a claybrained fool am I ! Peccavi! Peccavi! Od's my Life, but I have left my purse above stairs. Doctor Tom, could you oblige me on this occasion and tomorrow, I shall make all regular again."

I caught Daniel's eye. He nodded sagely. No doubt but this Nimrod had a wide mouth and an empty purse. After I had paid, I followed Daniel out to the Stables. There was a pile of old misshapen blankets, no doubt discarded goods, for both horses and men. Daniel shook out two of them and prepared to make himself snug. I asked him again, if I could watch instead of him or with him, but he refused steadfastly, insisting that I needed my sleep.

"'Twill be a heavy day the morrow, but we know 'ee now. It might be us'll be up before 'ee, and can shake the bastard off but I doubt it."

He was right. Nimrod, his boots shining and his long dark curls in place on his green velvet doublet was breakfasting before sun-up.

"Why, Doctor Tom, what a Cerberus you have guarding your horses. I wandered out by moonlight to see that all was well with your nags, and was well mauled for my pains."

"Yes, a steadfast honest man, that good fellow!" I said. "Shall we start in half an hour?"

"By all means," he concurred, smooth as butter. The Landlady had named a price for bed and board for the four of us when we arrived and now I was surprised to hear it increased by a fifth. I raised my eyebrows and she told me, "Ah, Sir, the gentleman as knows you. He vows he will make all well with you on your way."

"Does he indeed?" I said. I was beginning to realise that when fools like myself were such easy prey, rogues like Nimrod were in for rich pickings. I was suddenly smitten by another consideration. Did he have a horse?

I ran up to Ralph and caught him coming from the room he had shared with William. "Good Ralph, a quiet word." I pushed him back into the bedchamber. "Daniel has grave misgivings as to the honesty of this Nimrod, as do I. Whatever chances, do not let him ride either of your horses. Do you hear me? Those two are part of your legacy from Robert."

He nodded, gazing at me wide-eyed. "So, what shall we do?"

"Daniel fears he might be one of a gang. We must be on our guard. It might be worse for us if we dismiss him now."

He nodded and promised to dissemble. "I shall say Beauty's sesamoids are swollen, and that she cannot be ridden. I shall ride Prince."

I nodded in agreement. "Well done. Nimrod will have to ride on the cart."

So, when we assembled and Nimrod clearly seemed to be about to mount Beauty, I said firmly, "Alas, her heel bones have not yet subsided since yesterday. If you have no mount, Sir, I must ask you to join me on the cart."

He moved round to Ruby. "No matter. This neat lady cob will serve my turn."

"Alas, no, sir!" I said, "We have just been told she is in foal and is delicate at the best of times. As I have told you, sir, you are most welcome to sit with me upon the cart."

It was with a poor grace that he hoisted his person up beside me. I held the reins firmly, locked my feet into the metal stirrups below my seat, and said pleasantly, "Your horse is lent to another perhaps?"

"Ever my weakness," he said smoothly, "I could never refuse to help a friend in distress."

"That I can well believe," I said courteously. "Shall we start our journey?"

Daniel had placed William at the head of our cavalcade. I came next with the lumbering cart and my slightly affronted passenger, and Daniel came behind Ralph and his two thoroughbred horses. We set off from Witney and took the northern track from the town.

Goliath had been given a mash that morning which he had eaten with great relish but little prudence. My passenger had great difficulty securing himself a firm seat upon the flat surface of the cart... his lack of security together with the Shire horse's indiscreet flatulence caused Master Hunter to complain constantly about his difficult situation. I listened and nodded sympathetically, but did nothing to assist him to greater comfort. He had already cozened me of several pounds for his bed and board. My outraged sense of justice surprised me. I was usually tolerant to the point of idiocy. But today I was angry at being taken for a brainless "patch". I was a fool, no question, but having been set right by Daniel, I was determined to labour in that character no longer.

Eynsham was but six miles distant, and having been warned by Daniel to proceed in a way that did not allow Master Hunter to take advantage of us, I declined to halt at the hostelry, despite his protestations. As we clip clopped past the inn, a fellow who had been watching us, idly leaning against the inn door, suddenly leapt to life, and ran behind the building. Daniel's fears that Nimrod was in league with others seemed justified.

I was beginning to experience that strange sensation when the memory is informing the brain that it knows the landscape. Unremarkable hills, pleasant meads, swans in flight, why did I feel I knew this scenery. However, I could not ponder this riddle for long. Nimrod Hunter's face was beginning to look as green as his doublet. "I beg you, Doctor John...Tom. I think 'twould be as well, if you set me down now. My stomach cannot sustain this rolling motion."

"Certainly, I will set you down," I agreed. "But before that, perhaps, Sir, you could oblige me by paying me what is owed. I absolve you from your magnificent largesse of yesterday, when you insisted on paying for all. Pay me what I am owed for yourself and we will say nothing about your generous offer."

He lapsed into silence. He plainly had nothing in his pockets. I laughed inwardly to myself. The tables had been turned on him. He was the biter, bit.

The road became more thronged with traffic. The city of Oxford lay to our right and suddenly I remembered when I, who had seen this stretch of country before. I who until a year ago had seen nothing but Worcester, now clearly remembered seeing these low green hills last December and had ridden with Lucius Carey and his lady to a house that had been a nunnery less than a mile from the track we were on. And Eynsham too that we had ridden through but half an hour before. Laetitia had insisted on that day that we went to the site of an abbey there founded by St. Hugh, and I had even now clattered through the village without a passing glance. It was not the sanctity of these holy places... to me that was of no importance... but the happiness of the day, that had imprinted the episodes on my memory. There had been a spell of fine frosty weather in November and Laetitia had discovered that Elijah was like herself a worshipper of the old religion, and had demanded of her husband that we went to dine with good friends, the Owens, at Godstow Priory. She had taken us a short tour of the ruins and even now I could see Elijah's round blue eyes widen, at the tale of the grey lady, fair Rosamund, the Rose of the World, who in her nun's habit flitted about the cloisters, looking for her King.

"Or her lost virtue!" Lucius had jested and the mood had broken.

We trundled up to a cross roads and I remembered Great Tew was about eight miles to the north-west. Oxford was now directly to the south. If we turned right here, after a mile we would see the spires and towers gleaming in the September sun. I reined in Goliath to remember the last time I had ridden Jupiter to Oxford, with that group of laughing friends. I had travelled there on several occasions, sometimes alone with Lucius but usually Lady Laetitia and the Holtes had accompanied us.

Nimrod whom I had forgotten, launched himself from the cart and disappeared into a hawthorn thicket, whence came the sounds, that I had heard described, as "casting up accounts." In other words the fine breakfast for which I had paid was dispensed with.

"Leave him, Tom!" said Daniel in an undertone.

"Do you need assistance, Nimrod?" I called.

A weak voice cried out, "Leave me!" and so we deemed this to be the best policy, and clattered off to the east. I looked back once and saw Nimrod's pale face peering at us, from behind the hawthorn hedge.

"That aint the last us'll see of he," announced Daniel, after a few moments. "I should have put a bullet in his belly. Then him'd have good cause to whip the cat!"

I was surprised at his vehemence, but was reassured by his

musket which he proceeded to prime as he rode. He called William from our vanguard, insisting that he too primed his weapon and the two of them rode behind us, frequently looking back at the way we had come.

I wondered if Ralph could guide us now. He had seemed to know something of Witney but the only advice he could come up with was that we must follow the road through Thame. We had made such an early start that it was only two hours after noon that we came to Wheatley, and we bought a supply of rolls from a baker on the village street. We decided to press on a little. Daniel was for leaving the road, and lying low over night.

"Him'll have cronies, no doubt of it, and them'll be after we. He sensed you had money, Doctor Tom, That sort can smell money, like flies after carrion. I should have put a ball in he, while him 'ad 'is breeches down, back there."

There was much prudence in his advice, if little of gallantry. If we could find a remote hamlet some short distance from our road off the beaten track, then with luck any pursuers would sweep past and away. A mile beyond Wheatley, there was a faint path leading north west over the meadows where sheep were nibbling the turf. I climbed down from the cart and went to ask directions from a shepherd I could see, tending his flock. He seemed to be doctoring them, thrusting some evil smelling potion down their unfortunate throats as they lay helplessly on their backs, one after another between his sturdy knees. His boy caught and brought them to him, but there seemed no visible sign as to which had received their medicine and which were still untreated.

"Does this track lead to Thame?" I asked him, indicating the path.

"No, master, it don't!" he told me pleasantly and spilled another dose down the gullet of a woolly sufferer.

"Where do it go then?" I asked.

"It do go up to Worminghall to the Clifden Arms, finest inn in the country."

"Only to Worminghall?"

"No, master, it do go to other places an all. It do go to Shabbington, Long Crendon and Haddenham."

"Haddenham?" I cried gleefully.

"Oh, aye, master. If you'm partial to ducks, Haddenham's the place. But if you'm partial to good ale, Clifden Arms is the inn in Worminghall."

"What are you giving these sheep?" I asked innocently.

"Master, I be treating them for the worm. In other words, Worminghall."

His wit convulsed him so that he was almost unable to accept the crown, I pressed into his brown old hand and we turned off the much travelled way, well paved by the farmers, and took the faint muddy path that led over the fields to Worminghall. Although we were leaving the main way, our own tracks now were clearly visible, the ruts left by the cart, and the five smaller hoof prints and the liquid little ponds, Goliath left when he placed his feet in muddy ground. There had clearly been much rain here recently.

We toiled up the meadow and over the next one and came to the cottages and the inn of which the shepherd spoke so highly. We paused at the crossroads. But Daniel kept glancing over his shoulder.

"Easy for they to follow we now. I'd no notion that they fields kept the rain so long. Maybe us should have stayed on the hard track."

The next fields seemed to be better drained. Daniel was all for pressing onwards and I reasoned that if we could find a safe haven where we could bestow the horses, we could walk back to the inn for hot food. In any event if that proved impossible I had still some rolls bought along the way. A farm labourer set us on the right way to Shabbington, just over a mile away.

The sun was westering behind us, when Daniel held up his hand. Over the fields we had recently crossed came a faint sound. Men were shouting. I strained to hear. It was a hue and cry.

"Stop thieves!" The words were discernable now. Daniel thrust his reins to me and leapt up behind Goliath. "Come on, old un! Show us your paces. Get up to that hill, lads. The water wont stand there. You'll not leave tracks."

He was already clattering the cart up to the crest of the hill. He shouted something to William who dropped back, his musket at his shoulder. I mounted Daniel's horse, as Ruby was careering up behind the cart and urged Ralph up to the summit with his two riding horses. William came close behind us.

"I don't think they saw us."

Page 504

We all cantered round to the other side of the hill on which a few poor cottages clustered. There below us was the grey shining ribbon of a river, pale in the last rays of light.

"That's the Thame!" said Ralph of a sudden. The danger we were in caused his cerebral processes to function more swiftly than was usual with him. "I know this place. And there's an old abbey by those water meadows. No roof, but the walls are still sound."

"If they aint armed, it might give us a bit of cover." Daniel had assumed command. "Lead on, Ralph."

We hurtled down the hill and along the river bank. The abbey was half hidden by the church and had plainly been abandoned. As Ralph had predicted the roof had fallen in, but the massive oak doors were still in place, one of which was pushed open, and the walls soared up to a height of twenty feet or more.

The horses trooped in obediently enough, but it was going to be necessary to open both doors to admit the cart. A stack of wood had been placed behind the closed door and we began to push it aside. As we cleared the final plank, again came the faint echo of the hue and cry. I threw some of the wood outside so that it did not impede us. A mistake but I was not to know that. We heaved on the second door and forced it back so that Goliath and the cart had sufficient clearance to enter.

But then we had to push it back. I saw to my joy that there was a bar that locked back down into strong wooden bolts. But the door was sticking in a heap of mud. We had pushed it back easily enough and now it seemed to require twice our strength to force it closed.

The shouts were growing louder.

"Come on, lads," Daniel panted. "Put your backs into it!" Slowly we inched the door out of the mud and then to close and bolt it was a simple matter.

"Back the cart into 'em!" Daniel gasped. There was a satisfying crash as the back of the cart banged into the great wooden doors.

"Nosebags!" I whispered and every horse had his or her muzzle, lips and chin thrust into a satisfying supper of oats.

We stood panting, gazing each at other, in the dim interior of the abbey church, under the darkening sky, listening to the sounds of pursuit hurtling down the hill. "Who are they?" I asked Daniel.

"Deserters! Renegades! King's Men, who ain't been paid.... or fed! Us must be silent now. Let's hope them ain't got muskets."

"What do they want?" I persisted, although I partly knew.

"Money! Doctor Tom, you smells of money! You don't look a beau-nasty, but you acts like a rich man. And six horses between four! Them knows you're a goldfinch! Quiet now!"

I wondered how many there were. The sounds grew louder, and someone called out, "Cart went in 'ere." There was the noise of men jumping from horses onto the muddy ground outside the abbey doors. I applied my eye to the crack near the rusty door hinge. I counted five men in the fading light, amongst them Nimrod.

"Doctor John! Doctor John! We know you're there! Come out and we can settle accounts."

Something flashed in his hand as he shouted. It was a dagger. No doubt destined for my throat. Daniel placed his hand before my mouth. A wise precaution, for I was beginning to feel that it would give me great pleasure to dismember Nimrod… slowly.

Someone else spoke. A deep voice with northern tones. "We don't know as anyone's in there, Captain. Those tracks could have been made by any that lives up atop there. I 'aven't seen any fleein' from us. Hoof prints and dung could be from any bastard's horses."

"I tell you, I counted the nags. Six counting the Shire. And I tell you I heard something as we came down the hill. Only two of 'em have snappers. The other two are unarmed."

"But Lieutenants, you say, Captain? Blackwell's were devils. Hang you as soon as look at you!" Another voice. I could see this fellow clearly now. He was young and from his voice and the way he had his arms folded across himself, I could see Fear, oozing from his every pore.

"Well, one claims to be a surgeon, but clutches his partisan like its his favourite whore, and he's the one who pays the shot, I tell you, and who shits golden guineas, and bleeds bountiful balsam whenever he's pricked! I tell you, bullies, leave me alone to prick him in good earnest. And he's Gerard's officer, God rot him. A true Bartholomew Babe!"

"Well, I tell thee, we could be on a fool's errand. And this is a place of the old faith. Bad luck could come of it."

"Oh aye, I had forgot you are a craw thumper! Well, Jake, I promise you, I'll make your luck, from now on. Here, Snaggs, come and help me." Another man came forward with teeth like tombstones. "Get ahold of one of these."

Nimrod and the fellow he called Snaggs both seized a plank of wood and began to beat at the doors. They shook but held. Then had it not been for Daniel, I would have been run through, no question, for as we looked at the shaking doors, Nimrod swiftly thrust his sword into the crack below the hinge. I saw the flash of steel aiming at me, but Daniel was faster than I and leapt for me. I fell backwards onto the poor man, who stoically stayed silent. I could not help but gasp aloud.

"There! You hear that?" Nimrod shouted.

"That proves nowt. It sounded like you'd broken open a sack of meal."

I stared upwards. Occupying the space where my body had been was a blade. If I had remained there, I would have been horribly impaled. Silently I rolled sideways and helped Daniel to his feet. He seemed unhurt. I clasped his hand to show my thanks, but he passed his finger over his lips, and brushed my gratitude aside with a dismissive gesture.

Then followed an hour of nightmare. We crouched down away from the doors which they assailed with their swords and with the planks. Nimrod kept up a barrage of shouted abuse. The ignorant bastard could not even remember my name correctly and kept calling out to "Doctor John Fisher" inviting this fictitious person to "show us the colour of your water." By a miracle the doors held. The solid oak had been made to withstand the attacks of civil wars centuries before. The renegades did not continue a sustained assault on one place but kept changing the plank on which they concentrated, thinking that another panel showed signs of weakness, so that against the odds, the doors held, in spite of the efforts of all of them.

At last, they needed to draw breath. I could just descry the white ovals of the faces of my allies in the gloom of the abbey. Ralph, whom Robert had told me had been an exemplary soldier in everything that did not involve violent courage, sat rocking back and forth, occasionally hiding his face in his hands. Daniel and William stood, their muskets primed on their shoulders, facing the doors. But when our assailants seemed to tire and draw back a little, we moved silently to sit on the cart for a spell.

Still panting, the man from the North was not convinced that the Abbey church held Nimrod's victims. "And we don't 'ave right tools, Captain. Mattocks and axes is what's wanted."

The young deserter from Blackwells was unhappy with his lot. "Captain Quail, sir, my guts are cursing my teeth, no question. Has anyone a hunk of bread for me?"

"Shut your prattle, Nocky, or you shall have your teeth knocked down gullet lane to join your yellow liver!" He thought better of his anger, and addressed the youth more pleasantly. "But I forget myself speaking so coarsely to my good friend, Nocky! A task for you. Go up to that poxy village with Snaggs and find any axes and bring 'em down here."

"Aye and grab any commons that come your way." This was the voice of the fifth man which we so far had not heard. He was calling after the other two, who were forcing their horses back up the hill. Now he turned back to Nimrod. "Captain, by your leave, I'll take a cup of the creature now." This was a Welshman, an older man, I was sure by the tone of his voice.

"An excellent notion, Parson Paskin. Shall we sit, Bolter? Will you sluice your gob with us?"

"Aye, I will that!" and the unmistakable sounds of men quenching their thirst could be heard. Someone belched and someone else asked for "that leathern jack." They seemed to be intent on drinking well whilst the two younger men were on their errand.

"Yon's powerful good hum!" said the Yorkshireman, whom Nimrod had called Bolter.

"Here comes the harlot in white satin!" said one. I looked questioningly at Daniel, who shook his head at me, pointed to the sky above us, where a silvery light was spreading. He mouthed the word, "Moon". The interior of the abbey was suffused with a grey radiance and ignoring Daniel's agitation, I crept over to the doors and applied my eye to the crack below the hinge. The three older robbers were seated at their ease on the bank at the side of the track, leading to the abandoned abbey. Bolter was nodding, his head down on his chest. Nimrod sighed and was clearly the worse for his exertions.

"I'll see that bastard doctor dead in a ditch!" he announced to the old Welshman. "My innards were shaken and pounded today, because he forbade me to ride any of his prads."

"No doubt he knew you for the gentleman you are!" said the Welshman. "He guessed you and the horse would cut your stick like Lucifer!"

"Well, in the dawn we'll burn 'em out, and that's six horses to the good, as well as his haddock which I tell you, Parson, is fat indeed."

They fell silent and I crept back to Daniel, and sat with my back resting on Robert's coffin. I had surmised that two of them were afraid of the ancient sanctity of the abbey. I suddenly saw how we could use that old instinctive fear, and instil panic, which I hoped would transmit itself to them all.

I would need Ralph's permission for my plan. He was clearly beside himself with fear and in despair, whispering often, "To be killed so near my parents' house. If we could have only...."

I beckoned everyone to the far wall of the Abbey as far as possible from the doors. The worst aspect of my plot was that we would have to use Robert or rather his remains, a strategy that could be viewed as desecration. But Ralph gained a little courage from the notion.

"Even in death, the Colonel will protect me," he observed piously, but Daniel could see a weakness.

"The stench was bad in the church in Gloucester. Our stomachs wont endure it."

"This is the object of the matter. We shall be immune from the smell. See here."

Simeon, blessed man, had furnished me with four or five linen slings to hold up a broken arm. I showed them how to tie the triangular cloth over the nose but under the eyes, and we could sprinkle the cloth with essence of lavender. This would both disguise us and combat the stench of decay by the stronger aroma of lavender.

Now we had to move the cart from the doors. Poor Goliath had been dozing in the shafts. I looked quickly through the crack. The three had fallen into uneasy sleep, Nimrod forcing himself awake every two minutes or so, to gaze for an instant at the locked doors. I needed something to muffle the Shire's hooves. I looked round. There was Gabriel's buff coat, which he had thrown in when I had bought the two prisoners' clothes. It had seen good service and was torn and slashed about, but was still good thick leather. I looked questioningly at Ralph and pointed to Goliath's feet. He nodded approvingly and we hacked the coat silently into four pieces with my dagger. There were lengths of twine, on the abbey floor and silently we made the gentle creature lift one hoof in turn. I was surprised at how neatly, Ralph performed this task

I found an apple which I gave Goliath and as he enjoyed the unaccustomed midnight treat, I silently and painstakingly moved him the four paces, about half the cart's length away from the doors so that they could be opened with ease.

I confess I did not relish the notion of using my friend's corpse to free us from our sorry plight, but could think of no other way. I soaked the slings in lavender and we tied the ends of the cloth tightly over our hair at the back of our heads. I was afraid that the sweet smell might spread out over the renegades, but there was still no sound. I was listening now for the hoof beats of the other two who had been sent up to the village.

I pushed the coffin to the end of the cart and gestured to the others to help me lever it onto its end. Before I opened it, I motioned the other three back to the far wall, to plan how we could best make good our escape. But Daniel was ahead of me there. "William and me will be under the cart, muskets primed and if them runs towards we, us'll put bullets in their knees."

Ralph was given all our possessions, mainly my medical effects to dispose over the saddles of his pad nags. There was also the box with Robert's will and his money but that was in the coffin with him. I decided that we would empty the box into the sacking nosebags, which we quietly detached from the horses. Ralph undertook to carry the nosebags round his neck. We would remove the money and papers from the box and dispose of these valuable items in the nosebags.

I pushed my sling down and told them I would give a ghostly cry when the villains should first set eyes on Robert's dead countenance. Now there was the sound of hoof beats coming swiftly down the hill, accompanied by the sound of a woman's screams. The other three thieves roused themselves, and whilst their attention was elsewhere, on the arrival of their companions, Ralph and I pushed open the coffin lid.

As it was on its side, it was not so heavy as it had been in the church but even with our lavender masks the stench was overwhelming. Ralph, however kept his head, and stuffed the money and papers into the nosebags and discarded the box. I had the less wholesome task of trying to move Robert's arms into a gesture of dismissal to the felons. I talked in an undertone all the time to Robert, knowing that what we were using for our escape was a mere husk, a shell of what had once been a man. Strangely though I did feel that Robert himself, whilst absent in body, was guarding and guiding me and that perhaps death was not the end. As if to support this strange awareness, my father spoke in my head for the first time for some time.

"Well, son, here's a strange rimble rambling confusion! You'll triumph, my boy. Happy to see you don't play the duck!"

I tried to push Robert's arms outwards, and bent his wrists, as if he were pushing the evil rebels to perdition. But the rigour of death was no longer upon him, and his limbs were flaccid. So I looped a length of twine around one wrist, and held the other end behind the upended coffin, so I could move his hand up and down as I willed. At last I was satisfied and nodded. William and Daniel silently pushed the bolt up from the doors and I climbed down and stood, looking through the crack again, invisible to those outside.

We had been fortunate in that the attention of the miscreants had been engrossed by the arrival of their younger companions. Snaggs and Nocky had, it seemed, not succeeded in finding food but had decided to capture the young girl, who had refused them victuals. From the rope round her waist, it was clear that she had been dragged down the hill behind one of their horses. Poor soul, she was providing the diversion that would enable us to open the doors silently without attracting their notice. Snaggs had her down on the bank, and was attempting to raise her skirts, but she, blessed angel, was biting and spitting like a wild cat, cornered by hounds.

Ralph and I silently opened the doors, and I sped back onto the cart behind the coffin. The moon shone down on Robert's stinking and emaciated corpse. The girl saw the hideous vision over Snaggs' shoulder before the others and I imagine her desperate horror lent her a new strength. She screamed again, her eyes wide as saucers. As he looked at what had attracted her new fearful attention, she drew up her sturdy leg and managed a prodigious kick which sent him flying across the path, howling in rage, clutching intimate parts of his person. The others were watching this conflict, and turned only when they heard my voice.

I intoned "Sinners, Begone!" in the loudest plainsong chant that I could muster, pulling and loosening the twine so that it seemed that Robert moved his arm. The girl screaming like a soul in Hell, raised her skirts of her own volition and set off up the hill, her strong stammel's legs pounding effortlessly up the slope. Bolter and Nocky followed in her wake, whilst Parson Paskin by a supreme effort of will heaved himself on one of the horses they had tethered and then, realising that the poor beast was too stoutly held by the rope tied round a tree, bundled himself off again and scrabbled with the knot. Snaggs lay moaning, casting anxious glances at Robert's remains. Only Nimrod remained in possession of his senses and drawing his pistol, walked steadily towards the doors.

There was a resounding crack, and Nimrod lay writhing on the ground. William, it transpired, snug under the cart, had put a musket ball through the outlaw's right knee, shattering bone and sinew. His pistol flew across the path and as he and his companions were now no longer threats to us, I walked out and picked it up. The Parson by this, after a swift glance at Nimrod's plight, had unloosed his horse, hurled himself into the saddle and was away. Snaggs heaved himself onto all fours, and scuttled towards the horses, like the miserable rascal that he was. Nimrod's high screaming suddenly stopped. He had mercifully lost consciousness.

"Come on, Tom!" Daniel cried. He was attempting to close the lid alone. I leapt back onto the cart and we closed the lid, and laid the coffin down again. We had to back the cart out, Goliath, for the first time, neighing an objection. Ralph and William mounted and led the other horses round the cart which the Shire's powerful haunches pushed along the track.

We had to pause as Nimrod lay in the path of the great wheels. "Finish he, Tom!" cried Daniel. "Him's a thieving bastard! Send he to his account!" But I could not do that, although I knew he had sought my death. I rolled him off the path and we continued our lumbering backward progress. Snaggs lay snivelling at his horse's feet, and screamed aloud as he saw the pistol aimed in his direction. "That's another as needs to shake hands with the Devil!" shouted Daniel. But I could not murder in cold blood.

We continued to guide Goliath backwards along the path until the land flattened out and we could circle round so that the poor patient fellow was facing in the right direction. Ralph and William with the five horses were waiting, and as we joined them, at last we heard signs of life from the village. There was a banging and clashing, of metal on metal, the noise that was made to frighten an army... it was hoped... from an innocent village by the clubmen who wished nothing to do with either faction. A few torches flared on the top of the hill and as we watched, they began to move downwards towards the abbey. I judged that we could leave Nimrod and Snaggs to give them a hearty welcome. With any luck the young girl who escaped so fortuitously would recognise the reprobate who had tried to deflower her.

Now Ralph knew the country. "We must continue alongside the Thame," he announced with the innate pride of a man who knows about what he is speaking. "And we will come to a town known as Thame, where Robert's friend, Hampden died. And there we may cross the river and come onto Haddenham."

William, who was not given to exercising his tongue over much, surprised us by suddenly demanding, "A bite, a sup and a sleep." He was a young man, about my age and who is to claim that his judgement was flawed? In any event our progress was slower now as the harvest moon that had blessed our actions was slipping down the sky.

"'Twould be best, if all are agreed," said Ralph, "if we rested before we come to Thame. The Watch might be abroad."

After about a mile, we came to a grove of trees, beside the river. The moon was almost set, and it was a hazardous matter to find a space large enough for poor Goliath and his tragic burden. After so much action, I discovered that I, like William, was mortally tired. Daniel offered to watch as long as he could sleep for an hour when the sun rose.

"Ralph tells I, us is nearly at journey's end! I can sleep later in the day." And he settled himself as comfortably as he could with his back against the coffin. I opened my eyes once or twice in those cold small hours to see him alert, his musket on his shoulder at the ready, looking round him with glazed eyes, searching for any strange movement.

At sunup he roused William and myself, and settled himself for a short slumber. I found the rolls, at the bottom of one of the saddle bags, and shared them out leaving one for Ralph when he should wake. I saddled Ruby and began to walk her quietly back the way we had come. It was strangely peaceful beside the river, moorhens dabbled about in the shallows, ducks flew in and landed with their customary important splashing, and even swans glided majestically midstream, remote from the actions of base mankind.

The hill with the village up atop, swiftly came into view, but my way lay back to the abandoned abbey. I had to know what had happened to Nimrod. The horses had gone but there before me on the path was his corpse. He had somehow moved himself from the place where I had rolled him last night and lay on the path, his arms stretched towards the trees where they had tethered their mounts, his shattered leg lying useless behind him, still encased in scraps of green velvet. I guessed that when Snaggs had recovered and Bolter and Nocky had returned, they had elected to leave him to die. Or perhaps the villagers had simply left him and confiscated the horses.

He lay in his blood, his green velvet breeches and doublet soaked and ruined, his eyes open, his features contorted into a glare of despairing pain. I closed his eyes but he was cold now, cold and stiff. His only hope would have been if I could have sawn off the useless limb immediately at the knee and treated...

"Did you know him?"

The question sounded strangely loud in the peace of the morning. I turned to face the speaker. He wore a worn black doublet, and leant on a stick. His face was lined and appeared older than his voice, which sounded strong and youthful. A leather thong was round his neck, the ends tucked into his doublet.

"Yes and No!" I said. "I have known him for less than thirty six hours and in that time heard him called two names. Nimrod Hunter he told me was his name, but one of his companions called him Captain Quail. I believe he led a small band of renegades from the King's army."

He nodded over his shoulder up the hill. "There is one of them." As we had hurtled down the hill at sunset we had not noticed the gallows. Now it was occupied. I guessed that it was Snaggs whose body swung gently to and fro in the breeze off the river.

"They surrounded us in the abbey and wished to kill myself and my three friends. I am taking Colonel Burghill of Haddenham to his last resting place. I am a doctor, not a soldier. I have no desire to see the King destroyed nor Parliament disempowered. I care for none of it and hate its effects."

"Captain Burghill was made a Colonel?" he asked me. I nodded. He went on. "I knew him. Not as well as I knew John Hampden, who in his care for the poor and oppressed, I would term a blessed man."

"Robert Burghill, who was my friend, was grief stricken to learn of Hampden's death. He was himself maimed at Lansdowne in July, and died last month in Gloucester."

"Gloucester? Have you come from Gloucester? What is the news there? The Cathedral was once my joy."

And we sat and chatted of this and that, whilst Nimrod lay cold and lifeless beside us. At length the sun reminded me that I must return. I found three guineas and passed them to the priest. "Could you see him well disposed? I do not care to think of him going to his maker without a prayer."

As he stood and placed the coins in an inner pocket, I saw that the leather thong had threaded upon it a crucifix. He saw my glance and smiled. "Old ways in these parts, Master Doctor." He nodded up at the gibbet. "And in despite of objections, I will have that rapist taken down and buried. God bless you," and to my embarrassment he made the sign of the cross over me, as I sat on the bank.

As Ruby and I walked back to our camp by the river, I reflected that Nimrod had done us no real bodily hurt and yet was dead. I told Daniel what had occurred, and he quickly with his worldly wisdom questioned my judgement.

"No, 'tis true. Him ent hurt us, but even in death, Tom, and never was a feller so gulled as ee, begging your pardon! Even in death he's had your coin!"

Ralph was now able to guide us along flat ways and lanes. We crossed the Thame near the village of Thame, a circumstance that intrigued William who muttered often to himself, "Us is crossing the Thame at Thame." until Daniel begged him to hold his peace. From thereon it was but a quiet jaunt to Haddenham.

I began to understand why the land or rather the water in those parts was famous for ducks. Their quacking filled the air and ponds were everywhere, covered with their white pleasing shapes. Whenever I had eaten duck I had enjoyed the meal. But now it seemed barbarous to wish to eat such pleasant friendly creatures.

Nonetheless I supposed I would manage to get the better of my scruples.

We trundled down a street that Ralph informed us was Duck Lane and came to the village green. "That's it." said Ralph, subdued and anxious, indicating a long, low, white, timbered house the other side of the large pond. Not a cottage, but not a mansion either. A gentleman's modest residence perhaps described it.

"Best if you go first on your own and break the news. I tell you, I'm the last man in the world she will want to see."

I had half suspected that I would have this unpleasant task thrust upon me. I had had to tell Patience in Stratford of poor Elijah's death in a similar manner. The other three prudently moved the horses and the cart into a lane near the church out of sight of the Burghill home.

"Here," said Ralph, thrusting the nosebags containing the money and documents into my hands. "That'll prove to her who you are. She don't have to see me at first."

I skirted the pond, trying to tidy myself. Mortimer Skinner's comely blue clothes were a little the worse for wear, let me be honest, for *my* wear. Impossible to pretend otherwise. Still I hoped my partisan, which I had hastily seized, gave me an air of gravitas.

I walked up through a herb garden, which even in mid September smelt sweet and wholesome and knocked on the only door I could see. There was no reply so I knocked again.

It was immediately opened and a dark haired woman stood there. A beautiful woman, no doubt of it.

"Are you Mistress Elizabeth Burghill?" I asked with an attempt at a bow.

"Who asks the question?" she replied in a low pleasant voice.

17

"My name is Doctor Thomas Fletcher. Your husband was a good and faithful friend to me," I said, as respectfully as I could.

"Was'? You say he "was"? You have come to tell me of his death, have you not?" I nodded sadly.

"I knew it," she said, almost with an air of triumph. "You had better come in." I followed her into a wide hall where there were chairs and a settle.

"Sit, if you please, sir."

She disappeared into the kitchen quarters and returned with a tray on which were two glasses and a jug of wine.

"Elderflower, made last summer by myself, before these tragic happenings." She poured me a glass. I pledged her solemnly and she asked, "You are not affronted by my drinking, also?"

"Not the least in the world," I replied, surprised by the question.

"My male relations, to whose tender care he assigned me, condemn me as ungodly and impious. Yet when they visit to examine my behaviour and reprimand me constantly, I notice that they are kind and gracious enough to make free with my wine. Well, well. Enough! That is my cross. Mine and my boys."

"How did you know of Robert's death?" I asked

"He always wrote every fortnight, and for two months I have heard nothing. There is one trusted carrier who comes this way, delivering and collecting. But for two months, nothing. Also I knew that he would have come home when Hampden died. That was news that all heard. But there was no news about of my husband, save a possible wounding at Lansdowne. When did he die?"

"August the 24th" I told her, "An hour before midnight." "And where is he now?" she asked.

"In a coffin, not three hundred yards from here," I told her. "It has not been nailed down. You may look on him if you wish."

"Such a sight would not be edifying. Putrefaction would be well advanced. You say he died on August the 24th. No, I would prefer not to look on him again. Do you have papers... a will perhaps?"

I brought my letter from Robert and his will from my doublet and gave them to her.

"You will see that you are his sole heir on one condition."

I sat back in my chair. She read the will first, compressing her lips, which were full and red. She was a handsome woman no mistake, even though she was garbed for housewifery in a brown stuff gown with a calico apron. Her dark hair was neatly coiled back from her face, and she read carefully, clearly knowing the hand and perusing it without difficulty. Then she placed the will on a small table beside her and read my letter from Robert with equal concentration, her lips, a thin red line below her straight nose. Then she looked up at me and said three words.

"Leave me please!"

I stared at her. She had seemed so reasonable, so calm and controlled. She threw my letter on the floor and stood, pointing imperiously at the door. I silently gathered up the leaves of my letter and retreated towards it.

"Spawn of Satan!" she screamed and ran from the room. As I wrestled with the latch, I heard her pounding up some unseen stairs. I came out onto the path, between clipped box hedges and overblown roses. As I opened the gate, water splashed onto my legs. But it was not water. She had thrown the contents of a chamber pot at me, from an upstairs window, to hasten my withdrawal, much to the amusement of some small boys who scampered away, clearly aware that they too might receive similar treatment.

The farcical nature of my situation suddenly overcame me and I was laughing, as I sought out my poor companions. When they had seen my reception, they huddled back out of sight with the cart and horses on a small green near the church gate. Ralph came towards me with a questioning look.

"Alas, Ralph, that did not go well. As I went she anointed me, but not with holy water, I fear."

"Not for the first time. Many in this town can speak of her temper, for all she is valued as a good farmer in her own right. Tom, I've just seen a neighbour of my parents. They are not here. There is a letter for me with the lawyer, it seems."

An inn with its own small brewery adjoined the Green below

the church and I entrusted Ralph as a native of Haddenham to bespeak rooms and a hot meal for us. He came out telling us that Hob Wells, the landlord would be honoured to have Robert until I could arrange his burial. There were rooms for us all it seemed. I asked for hot water and as the day was mild for September arranged that it should be brought to me in the stable yard, where I cleaned myself from top to toe, William acting as a bodyguard, lest the good inhabitants of Haddenham be affronted by my nakedness. My boots and hose were worst affected by Mistress Burghill's baptism. I cleaned my breeches as well as I could, but my hose were for the rubbish heap.

I felt better after my ablutions but as I had no hose asked for a mercer's in the village. It seemed there was such a shop in Thame, and Ralph, seemingly very anxious to remain in my good graces, mounted Prince and undertook to ride there and buy me a pair.

Daniel was amused by my desire to be clean, thinking that I wished to attract the young ladies of Haddenham. Having seen my welcome at the hands of Mistress Burghill, he suggested that perhaps the local articles were not to be bought by cleanliness, although he and William now found the incident prodigiously amusing. I was aware that they, like myself, were concerned lest I would have to defray the entire cost of Robert's burial. A corpse was something of an encumbrance, no matter how dear its previous owner. I chided myself for my ingratitude. Robert, dead though he was, had still helped me extricate myself and my companions from an extremely perilous situation.

When Ralph returned with my hose, the four of us dined well on sliced duck breast with a cinnamon flavoured apple sauce. I began to forgive the doomed birds the continual noise they kept up in the nearby ponds. Ducks do not merely quack but come and go with great important flurries of water, and the air was full of the sound of their flapping and splashing.

We had pushed aside our plates and Daniel was preparing to light his pipe, when Master Wells, our host announced that Mistress Burghill and her lawyer would take it as a favour, if they could crave some moments of my time.

"Who is her lawyer?" I asked.

"'Tis Master Reuben Woolstone, Sir He's the lawyer that deals with matters around here. Earning his keep on the Sabbath an all.

He asks if Ralph Holtham could be absent from the meeting as he and Mistress Burghill do not, as it were, see eye to eye."

"Well then, perhaps I too should absent myself," I said waspishly. "The welcome that she afforded me was hardly eye to eye!"

He laughed and punched my shoulder. "She can hardly repeat her incivility with her lawyer present, Sir. No, I would say she was contrition itself."

I stepped into his parlour where they awaited me. The coffin lay on the gatelegged table in the centre of the room, and we faced each other across it. Master Woolstone was as round and as brown as a russet apple. I bowed and he returned the compliment, though clearly his figure had difficulty adapting to such a supple courtesy. Mistress Burghill made me a low rustling curtsy. She had transformed herself and wore a fashionable black gown that was green when it caught the light. Her dark hair was carefully arranged in ringlets. She was a most beautiful woman, no question, when not roused to violence.

"Doctor Fletcher, I beg you, pray forgive me," she murmured.

"Willingly!" I said with as good grace as I could muster. "The fault was mine. Bringing such tragic news unannounced to a loving wife." She nodded and smiled slightly.

Two boys stood behind her. The one who was about fourteen was Robert to the life, but the younger one, who must have been about ten years of age, had blue eyes like his mother and a mop of tousled black curls. Now she turned to them.

"Boys, your courtesies, if you please to your father's good friend, Doctor Thomas Fletcher. These are Henry and Humphrey."

The elder boy, Henry, bowed solemnly and I returned the ceremony, but the younger one stood stubbornly upright, his blue eyes, sparkling with anger. "No, mother, not Humphrey. Rowland, if you please. I hate the name of Humphrey."

"Rowland has the magic of chivalry about it." I agreed. "It has the savour of knights in armour preparing to joust on their great war horses."

There was a silence. Then Robert's younger son, smiled and it was Robert's smile, no question, and he came to me and shook my hand.

"I know why my father liked you." Even though I was later to be present at Robert's funeral and heard his virtues extolled, those seven simple words were to me the most moving and personal epitaph that I have carried in my memory.

I invited everyone to sit and we faced each other across Robert's coffin, craning up a little to see each other over it.

Master Woolstone cleared his throat and began.

"Doctor Fletcher, I have had cognizance of Colonel Fletcher's will."

"You have read it?" I asked.

"Er, yes," he said, clearly reluctant to discourse in simple Anglo-Saxon. "All is in order. And two such honourable signatories. You are acquainted with them both, I take it?"

"I am," I said.

"To what degree of intimacy?" he enquired.

"During the late siege, I saw Alderman Pury every day possibly. I certainly could have done so, had I wished. I would hope that he and his son would count me as a friend, rather than an acquaintance."

"And Waller?"

"I would view Sir William Waller as a friend, also, but not one towards whom I could feel warmly. I have a letter here from him. I was very ill from a chest infection and he had returned to Gloucester briefly in July to see Robert after his defeat at Roundway Down. The will was signed on the last day of his visit. You may read his letter to me if you wish. I confess it afforded me some amusement, when on my recovery, I read it. He commends my efforts on behalf of Parliament to my parents, should I die from my illness. As they were both dead, such commendation might be seen as superfluous."

Mistress Burghill laughed aloud, and quickly stifled her mirth. At that moment Rowland, standing near the small window, uttered a cry of recognition and ran from the room. We could hear him shouting "Rafe! Ralphy!" As he ran out to the Green, I heard Ralph cry out "Rowley!" and there were the sounds of a happy reunion. Mistress Burghill bit her lip and looked at the rushes on the floor. The elder boy looked at her in consternation but she raised her hand in a gesture of resignation, shrugged and turned back to her lawyer.

More questions followed. Master Woolstone enquired as to Robert's soundness of mind. I explained that we had no reason to doubt that and that Massey and Pury alike came to him for advice, even when the great cancre in his belly caused us all great concern. At last Master Woolstone drew his conclusions.

"Mistress, let us be clear on this. If you cannot bring yourself to accept Master Holtham as your bailiff and gamekeeper, then you can inherit nothing. This Will is a legal valid document. There are no loopholes. There is a War Pension or sum to be awarded by Parliament itself to you, as one widowed untimely by War. But the Colonel's personal fortune passes to Master Holtham, with the exception of two sums of £100 to be paid to Doctor Fletcher and to your husband's friends at the New Inn, Gloucester, a matter which Doctor Fletcher here, as sole executor has already accomplished. I have the receipt and acknowledgement for this second legacy. Doctor Fletcher has yet to be paid from the Colonel's estate. Where is it, by the way?"

I was going to reply that it was hoarded in nosebags and was under the bed in the room I had been assigned, but suddenly Elizabeth Burghill who had been so strong, crumpled before us at his words. She covered her face with her hands and began to weep, long heaving sobs that fairly tore the heart from me. Henry put his arms around her and glared at us both. At last she recovered herself.

"In spite of all, I was a good wife. I did all that was required. Two healthy sons. I tried to say naught in censure of his indiscretions and infidelities, but sometimes I could not but accuse him. That creature, that perverted homunculus... led him continually astray."

Master Woolstone sighed. I had the notion that this was not the first such conversation they had had, regarding Robert's morality.

"As you know, Mistress, there are those who would claim the reverse is the case. Corporal Holtham was much younger than the Colonel. And dear Madam, your husband never laid claim to the house and farm. The lease is in your name and your name alone. I have heard that it was transferred by your husband. A matter he arranged by letter with the Spiller family. Had he not done so, that lease and all your property would now belong to the Corporal."

She shuddered, and nodded slowly. "I will have to sell the lease in any event," she said pitifully. "I cannot pay the ploughboy nor the cowmen, and must have money to pay for Hubbart's bull to be put to the heifers."

I swallowed and fixed my eye upon her in a stern manner.... I hoped.... and began my oratory.

"Mistress Burghill, I accept that it is impossible for you to undertake the management of your farm in partnership with Corporal Holtham. Your patience has perhaps been sorely tried by past indiscretions. I do not understand the Colonel's preferences, and on your behalf, I would wish that his life had been otherwise. But he was, and Ralph Holtham is, in many ways, good and virtuous. Your husband helped me on many occasions. He saved my life when Essex was about to hang me as he had hanged my father. He also has given me wise counsel, times without number. I therefore propose to forego the inheritance, he has left me. Although appearances might indicate the contrary, I am not a poor man. If you will defray the costs and the expenses of my two troopers, and the hire of the horse and cart, all provided by Edward Massey who greatly respected your husband, then I will very gladly give you what remains of the £100 left me by your husband. This could enable you to continue with your excellent farming enterprise until you receive your jointure from Parliament."

There was a long silence. She looked down at her hands clasped in her lap and slow tears fell upon her fingers. Finally Master Woolstone said, "This is generosity indeed!" and she said softly, "Yes, it is." She was female modesty itself. But was there a trace of calculation in her expression?

Then she said, "I would wish that it could be seen as a loan."

This was an opportunity to lighten the mood. "Certainly, Madam," I said with something of a swagger, "And when you own half of Buckinghamshire, due to your good husbandry, I will accept it most gladly."

"Before that, it is to be hoped," she said smiling pleasantly. "Doctor Fletcher, I have heard of you in my husband's letters. In fact in the last one I received, written by one John Nichol at my husband's dictation, he mentioned that you were already a widower. I am very sorry for your loss, Sir. So young to endure so hard a fate."

"If my wife had not died, I would not be here, certainly. May I bring you the money tomorrow? As your husband's executor, I think I may do that without troubling Master Woolstone."

They both nodded and rose to go. "But I must see Ralph

Holtham," the lawyer remembered. "I have a letter for him from his sister. She and her parents have left Haddenham. Perhaps you would send him to me."

"Nothing easier." I could see Ralph through the window, with Rowland, on a small bridge, gazing into the water and chatting happily. "When do you intend to hold the Colonel's funeral? It was only a year ago after Powick Bridge that he bore me company at my father's burial. If you will permit me, Madam, I would wish to remain for that."

"We would be honoured by your presence, Sir," she said, sighing and with an air of weariness. "Forgive me. I did not know that grief could be so fatiguing. And yet, I knew he was gone. Master Woolstone, would you approach the parson on my behalf?"

In spite of the sad ceremony that lay ahead the next few days proved to be a pleasant interval of unaccustomed leisure after the tensions of the journey. Mistress Burghill sent joints of meat to Hob Wells for myself and the troopers, and we sat and ate and drank and walked and talked. At the end of five days, I knew more than I had ever thought it was possible to know about the country customs of Somerset, and perhaps the troopers learnt something of the rudiments of doctoring.

Robert's coffin was carried by four stalwart young men to the church, where it awaited burial on the 16th. Mistress Burghill invited me to stay in her house, and I would have done so, had not Daniel advised against it. "Who else is there, sides the boys?" I did not know and he went on. "It may be 'ers got her eye on 'ee. Have a care, Doctor Tom. From what us 'ave heard, there's a comely young woman in Gloucester a-pining for 'ee."

William laughed and nodded. "A proper beauty, 'er be an all. Don't 'ee go aspoiling your chances." The longest speech he had ever made to me.

"'Sides," said Daniel, "Who's to say, er might not sniff pepper with 'ee again? A man could get through a-many suits of clothes with a rum dell like she, a-throwing piss at he. Who's to say, next time, it might not be the pot an all?"

So I told Elizabeth as she asked me to call her, the next day when I gave her my inheritance from Robert, that my troopers were far from home and a little wary of Haddenham folk. I thought it was only just, that we gave Hob Wells our custom, as he had welcomed us so kindly.

She laughed. "And I did not."

"I would greatly like to walk around your farm though, Mistress Elizabeth, if I might be permitted to see your cattle."

"Was your father a farmer?" she asked.

"His relatives were, but he was a Master Butcher in Worcester. He taught me which beasts a farmer might wish to send to slaughter after one year, and from which he should breed. He hoped I would follow in his trade, but my heart was in a different calling. I wanted to cure human animals, not kill the innocent beasts of the field."

"Human animals, you say. Your description of mankind is close to profane. Best have a care when my uncles and cousins visit for Robert's funeral."

"I will," I promised her. But we had not reckoned with Ralph's uncontrollable grief. He stood at the back of the church and I chose to stay with him, a decision that caused raised eyebrows and pursed lips from Elizabeth's relatives. Daniel and William had been asked to be bearers, a task they readily accepted, as its reward in Somerset was unlimited good ale after the ceremony.

When we all repaired outside for the burial, Ralph's anguish was heartbreaking. I had thought he had accepted his loss with a degree of philosophy, but he explained later that he could not finally bear to contemplate Robert being placed in the cold ground. His loss was terrible and deep, and I had to accept he was as bereft as I had been, when I lost my dearest Phoebe. No purpose was there in trying to persuade him to be controlled.

I had been invited to the house afterwards, where there was a feast laid out, but Henry came to us, as I was supporting Ralph back to the Inn.

"Mother says, please forgive her, but it is probably best if you do not attend, Doctor Tom. She thinks it might prove too painful for you."

And so Ralph and I and the troopers drank toasts to Robert's memory with the eloquent Hob telling us tales of the Colonel's past in Haddenham, growing up a poor curate's son, who gained a place at Merton, married the rich farmer's daughter, went off to the Wars in the Low Countries, where he made a fortune which Ralph had inherited. Then to Scotland or Louseland, where he earned nothing but flea bites and the King's indifference, and finally, Hob concluded, was brought back in his coffin to rest here till the last trump should sound.

I excused myself at this and went out into the yard to have a drunken laugh with Goliath and Ruby. Having seen and smelt Robert in his coffin only five days before, I hoped with all my heart that the last trump would sound, after I was some miles distance from Haddenham.

"Son Thomas, you are an impious wretch!" said my father, laughing in my head. "But, father," I told him, "the body is so much dross, a mere unwanted human husk. The glory of death is in the living memory of the soul, no longer needing the body. You are not dead, as long as you speak to me as you just did." But he would not or could not answer.

The next day, one week from our arrival, was again the Sabbath. Ralph and I knew we must confer. There was upwards of a thousand pounds in the nosebags. I knew that I had much more than that with my property and income in Worcester but it was still a prodigious amount of coin, when we had counted it out on the parlour table, where its previous owner had rested but a few days before. Ralph was angry that I had given my share to Elizabeth, but after we had paid Daniel and William for the journey hither, it had dwindled to only eighty sovereigns for the widow. He would not let it rest, however.

"Believe me she is rich as Croesus, whoever he was. Her gamminer left her very well endowed and she has a foot in the nish of everything round here. She has rents and dues and tythes from every plot of earth. She is one of those, I told you of, who has put out poor men from their acres and put in sheep. She is a beggar-maker. She will do her utmost to separate me from the Colonel's money. I tell you, Tom, though she may be in the right of it about him and me, she is no plaster-saint. No virtuous woman will work for her, and she has her favourites among the cattle men."

I was amazed at what he implied, and he, seeing my dumbfounded expression, went on, "Oh, yes. She has marked you out for her bed, no question. The sooner we are on the road to Newbury the better."

"To Newbury?" I could not believe my ears. This man had inherited a fortune and still expected me to act as his nurse.

"Oh, yes," he said again. "Here is my sister's letter. Susan was always the prime scholar. She could read and figure when she was not much out of small clothes. Tom, would you read it to me again? You know I am no hand at my letters When old Rueben read it to me, 'twas as if she was in the room with us."

I snatched the letter from him angrily. "I will read it to you and then we must think again about your dragging me off to Newbury. That was not in the agreement."

"Oh, Tom," he said miserably, "I am sorry."

Slightly mollified I began to read. "My dearest brother, Rafe, I know that you will come back here to Haddenham where I write this now but whence I am bound tomorrow for Newbury. Good Reuben Woolstone has been asked to give it to you.

In short, dear brother, your sister's fortune has taken a turn for the better. Master Woolstone agreed to take an apprentice from a family in Newbury. His name.... Gerard Kingsley. As you may recall, Master Woolstone employed me as his clerk, when needed as I could be relied upon to make a fair copy. And so thus I met Gerard. In short we are plighted and will be wed in August at his father's home in Newbury.

Alas, dear brother, the good fortune of myself rests on the tragedy of others. My betrothed's elder brothers.... he had two, Maurice and Edwin, insisted in despite of their father's wise advice in journeying to Marlborough where they enlisted with the King's loyal servant, Lord Wilmot, and performed great deeds against Waller at Roundhay Down, but where sadly they were both wounded fatally and perished on the field.

A servant brought this dreadful news to old Sir Maurice Kingsley in Newbury. He has sent immediately for my dear Gerard to return to the place of his birth. He is the last comfort of his aged father, who we hear is heartbroken. Imagine, dear bother, my anxiety and apprehension. My face is all my fortune, as you know, though my betrothed assures me that my penmanship, not to mention dairying, cooking, preserving and distilling... these various skills are both useful and sought after, and will endear me to my future father-in-law and to his housekeeper who is in need of assistance... His mother died shortly after my betrothed was born.

Good Master Woolstone has paid me well of late, as I have sometimes been able to advise those, who sought his legal knowledge and prevent wasted time, and dear Mistress Woolstone has taught me how to play the lady. I have enough coin to enable me to find a small cottage for our parents in Newbury so that I can care for their welfare and try to cheer them, and where I can live until my wedding day. They despair of ever seeing their dearest son again. When you read this... I say "when" not "if..." I will not give way to gloomy thoughts.... beseech Captain Robert to allow you to travel here to see your loving parents and your devoted sister, Susan, who longs to embrace her older brother. God grant that you are spared, dear Rafe.

You will find me at Kingsley's House by the sign of the Sugarloaf, near St Nicholas' church, on Bartholomew Street."

For a few moments we did not speak. Then Ralph said longingly, "Dear little Susie, and her a married woman, an all. She is such a dear maid, Tom. You would be pleased to know her. And my father knew Robert as a young man."

"But what would you do in Newbury, Ralph?" I asked him.

"First and foremost, make sure our parents want for nothing. Then perhaps this Gerard might wish more money for his lawyer's shop, or practice, I should say. I can do many tasks about a house. Before ever the Colonel persuaded me to go a-soldiering with him, I was what they calls round here a dab hand at building with witchert. And other types of building I can do. Thatching and paving and carpentering, and keeping all nice as ninepence. Perhaps this Gerard would let me buy into the firm and I could pay for maids for my sister, nursemaids if she's breeding, whilst she assists her man in the shop. Susie's sharp as a whip, Tom. She's like you. Learned and bookloving, but with a quicksilver brain. Come to think of it, she's very like you, Tom."

Although he was flattering me, and we both knew it, I had to admit that his notion was not without a certain sensible, beneficial usage of talent and money. Mistress Susie's letter was both practical and loving. If Master Kingsley were an honest man, then Ralph could do worse, perhaps, than throw in his lot with them.

"As long as this Gerard and his father welcome you and you are properly valued, perhaps it would serve," I said slowly. "As long as they trust and want you for yourself alone, and not just for the money in your.... nosebag."

"And that is why I need you with me, Tom. You are my good angel. That she-devil would have cozened me out of my inheritance, if you had not been with me. Hob tells me she would have had the old uns out of our cottage, but she was afeared of what the Colonel would say, when he returned. But Susie was one step ahead of her, praise the Lord."

"I cannot accompany you, Ralph," I told him, "I have Daniel and William to think of. They are not cheap to feed. I do not even know where Newbury is."

"Oh, Tom...." but we were interrupted by Hob who came in to see if we wished for refreshment. I asked him where Newbury was. He scratched his head, no doubt to encourage his brain into action.

"Ah, Newbury! That's a fair step from these parts. Also I fear 'tis in Berkshire." From his tone of voice, Newbury could be across the river of Lethe, shrouded in Stygian gloom, with the Old Un standing ready with his pitchfork, prepared to prod us into the eternal flames.

"Oh Tom! That you should forsake me now." Ralph, looking like a deathshead on a mop-stick at what he seemed to think was betrayal on my part, took himself off to find Bratchet, a diminutive potman, from a place called Hungerford who worked for Hob.

"Oh, ah, 'tis at least twenty five miles to the south-west... You would have to break your journey at Wallingford, Doctor Tom."

"But Hob," I told him, "It is not I who will be taking the journey but Ralph, to join his sister."

"Ah, well now, Tom, forgive my free speaking like, but young Ralph is not quite twelve pence to the shilling. No better lad for taking hares or pheasants, and as nice and tidy a handy fellow about an inn or house as you could meet in a day's march, but he needs guidance, Tom. I've known him all his life and no better young varlet ever wore out shoe leather, but I don't think I would be happy at him taking that journey on his own."

I nodded. I knew what he was telling me. Give Ralph a specific task that could be accomplished there and then, and there was no better Jack in a pinch. But in a circumstance that he did not understand, then he became confused and angry.

"Do you know, dear Hob, that Ralph is six years my senior. Stay, it is five now... for a space. I had a birthday in May when I was twenty but it went unremarked."

"Then I will be about a fine birthday roast duck for you, Tom. You shall have a tasty farewell feast this night." He bustled off as

Ralph returned now with Daniel and William in attendance, and Bratchet, the lad from Hungerford.

"Tom, 'tis all arranged. These two stout troopers will travel at my expense, as will you, dear Tom. You have paid my shot for the last time. Naught but the best beds and victuals for all. And Bratchet here says that there is a straight good road from Hungerford back to Witney, so 'twill be easy for the three of you to return to Gloucester from there."

"May I take it, that Hungerford then is near Newbury, Master Bratchet?" I asked gloomily.

"Oh, aye, master. 'Tis but five miles or so. Your cob could walk it from Newbury afore noon," said Bratchet in his high fluting voice.

"And Daniel? What of Forbes' noble regiment of dragoons? Will he not be quite inconvenienced without you two, steadfast, fearless blades."

"There was talk, Tom, of he disbanding we. Sir Edward told us to be sure to return to receive our pay. But there weren't no date set."

"Aye," broke in William the Silent, "And he told we to have a care of Doctor Tom, and to keep he alive."

"Well, my dear friends," I said, "You have most certainly done that so far, and for that I thank you heartily. So what do you say? Shall we bring Ralph to his sister's? You must decide."

But they had already decided, or had had their decision made for them.

"Well, we'm go, Doctor Tom," said Daniel. "We'm not desert young Ralph, specially now as him's in the chinks! But only if you'm happy!"

"I'm prodigious happy!" I said, with a face as long as the Severn, which set them all a-laughing.

Ralph ordered up Canaries and Bratchet, idling in the corner hoping he might be invited to partake, remembered suddenly the reason for his arrival in the parlour. "Mistress Burghill bids you to dinner with her this even," he announced, "and will take no denial. She sent Francis round to find you."

"Is Francis still here?" I asked. I had seen him before, in the church yard, digging Robert's grave. He had been one of the bearers as well. He was an ill favoured youth, with an enviable breadth of shoulder. I went out to where he waited, clutching a beaker of small beer, with Hob hovering anxiously nearby.

"Alas, Master Francis," I said smoothly, hoping to soothe his wrath by speaking as courteously as I could. "I cannot come to Mistress Burghill tonight. I am bidden to a birthday feast. She is welcome to attend if she wishes, but Master Holtham will be present, for whom she does not care."

It seemed he did not care for him either as he spat vigorously onto Hob Wells' clean flag stones. As he reached the door onto the Green, he turned back to me and announced with foreboding, "Mistress won't like this. She'll not like it at all."

I did not like disappointing ladies but I felt that given her abusive welcome both spoken and projected... my boots were still stained... and the fact that I had given her eighty pounds, I now owed her nothing, but the usual courtesies of everyday life.

My companions, who had been shamelessly eavesdropping, pulled me back into the parlour and Daniel whose advice had always been careful and considered, now gave his opinion.

"Now listen, Tom. I don't trust she, not at all. I did not like what that Jack Bragger of a servant said to ee. I think she be after young Ralph's balsam, and maybe the prads as well. Can us be gone, and through Thame by sun-up the morrow, and can Master Wells tell she, as us've gone back to Gloucester? I'm no quakebreech as you know, and William's a great hand with his musket, but us be only two in this town. Think on. We can have us feast and be abed by moonshine, and off and away before sunrise. If her fellows catches we on the march, William and me, so be it. Then we'll know clear that she's up to no good. Them might find them's got more than they bargained for."

"That's good advice, Tom," said Ralph eagerly, "and Bratchet here wants leave to accompany us. He's done the journey to Newbury and Hungerford three or four times, and can guide us."

"Will Master Wells release him?" I asked eagerly. A southwesterly direction was more difficult to follow, than our easterly journey had been. A guide who knew the ways would be most helpful.

"Two or three old Mr Gory, says he will," said Ralph, hastening from the room to find Hob Wells. Later that afternoon I saw him leading Rowley round into the stables to show him the horses. I followed, not wishing to cast a blight upon their old friendship and heard Ralph saying carelessly of Goliath,

"Oh, this great fellow is only fit to draw a cart. A gentleman would not ride him."

"Why, Ralph," I said pretending outrage, "How can you say such treason of our faithful obedient friend? Rowley, if you wish to be a knight, this is the steed you need. No other breed could carry the great weight of armour that the champions of old chose to wear".

I was afraid that Ralph would bid a tearful farewell to Rowley, thereby alerting his mother to our proposed early departure, but all he permitted himself was a gift of six sovereigns, three for each brother, which he told him to take back to his mother for safekeeping. "And we may see you, on the morrow." I said by way of Farewell, so that no suspicion was aroused in the boy's heart.

We were away from Haddenham before first light, whilst even the sparrows snored. There was a back road to the inn out of sight of the Burghill house and we muffled Goliath's feet again. I allowed Bratchet to ride Ruby. Poor little fellow, he had not ridden much before, relying on his two feet to get from town to town.

As we rode out of Thame with the dawn on our left, I asked him why he worked so far from home. His reply was pitiful to hear.

"They think I'm a nigmenog at home, on account of me being an undersized Jack Sprat what don't talk like a man, and they laughed at me fit to break my heart, Doctor Tom. And they scorned my mother too. So I went off to seek my fortune like Dick Whittington, and Master Wells took me on. He says as I'm the best rum hopper he's ever had and I'm to hurry back. It's good to know you're wanted, ain't it Doctor Tom?"

His simple appreciation of his sad restricted lot in life silenced me. I felt ashamed of my churlishness. He sat Ruby like a prince, enjoying the scenery and revelling in his elevated position, looking down on the poor fellows stumbling into the fields to work at first light.

"This is the road to Chinnor," he went on, "But we ain't going there. See that clump of trees up ahead? We're turning off onto a path that'll take us all the way to Wallingford with no danger and where the Lady's men won't venture."

I calculated it was the 18th of September. The thicket he had pointed out seemed an unfriendly place with brambles viciously tearing at the horses' legs but suddenly we were free of the brakes and were on a narrow path, scarcely more than a rabbits' run making for a line of hills. We had changed direction slightly and the harsh rays of the rising sun were full in our faces.

Bratchet led the way and as we began to climb, there was suddenly before us a wide dry track, which seemed to be cut into the lower slopes of the hills. We turned right onto it, and it was a wonderful smooth dry surface for Goliath and the cart. We could see for miles to our right, and the track stretched before us, snaking along in the lee of the hills.

After a mile the track wound between villages where women spread out washing on the bushes and men were harvesting apples and pears. They stared at us as we passed. I waved and called a greeting but no-one replied in like manner.

"'Tis partly the times, Doctor Tom," Bratchet explained, "but they don't like this path."

"Why not?" I asked.

"The old uns made it, amany years ago. Then the fellers that liked marching everywhere... "

"The Romans?" I asked.

"Aye, them. But now..." he was interrupted by a low whistle, which seemed to come from hawthorn bushes heavy with haws about ten yards from the path. "A friend wants to speak to me about summat, Doctor Tom. I'll not be long."

He thrust Ruby's reins at me and nimbly dismounted. We paused on the track and waited, and as I watched his small form disappearing from sight, I was suddenly struck by the discrepancy in our heights. Of course others had claimed my union with Phoebe had been doomed because of that great difference. But she had found it a source of mirth. I smiled reluctantly and looked at my fellow travellers. Of all of us, Ralph was blessed with princely good looks. I had never thought of it before, merely taken him for granted. But his abundant fair locks, his straight nose and even teeth marked him out as a handsome man.

The same could not be said of my other two companions. Daniel had a face like a russet apple, brown and wrinkled from exposure to many suns. He had taken to soldiering when his wife had died in childbirth. The babe, their only offspring, had died as well. This sad history, not unlike my own, was perhaps the root cause of our friendship and sympathy. William on the other hand, a red-cheeked, open faced, young fellow of about my age, did not divulge much of his past life. He spoke but rarely, although when he did, it was with conviction and laughter. We were fortunate in his company. He was both fast and accurate as a musketeer, and his gun was always to hand, match primed and ready. Both were good horsemen... they were, after all, dragoons... and cared well for their cobs. As Daniel pointed out, "Your mount is the difference between life and death. Best tek care of he or she!"

Bratchet came back to us, calling a farewell to an unseen acquaintance.

"Well, Wallingford is safe for now. But it seems there's a deadly deal of folk, men, that's to say, as is on the move."

"Going whither?" I asked. "How does your friend know?"

"Small folks is closer to the ground than big uns," he replied, answering the second question and not the first, "Other little uns send messages. They listen to the Mother, and pass on what she tells 'em."

"How can they hear your mother from here? She's in Hungerford," I asked impatiently.

"I'm talking of Mother Earth, Doctor Tom."

This was so much moonshine to me and the others, but the little fellow believed it and I had the courtesy not to condemn his creed as simplicity.

"Will we make Wallingford before dusk?" I asked him.

"Nothing easier," he said confidently. "In fact I would press on a bit from there. The king has amany soldiers in Wallingford, and they calls scorn on me. There's a good old inn at East Ilsley near the Ridgeway where they don't mind little uns."

"Why should anyone mind you?" I asked him.

"Folks don't like what they don't understand," he said regretfully.

The day was overcast and rain clouds were gathering in the south. The old path was in the lea of the hills, softly rounded heights with stands of beech trees still in their summer greenery. We had made such good time that we passed through Wallingford around two hours after noon, but as a precaution I insisted that Ralph and I put on our crumpled and soiled red sashes. But no-one challenged us. As we had to wait to cross the bridge over the Thames, we rode the horses down to the water so that they could slake their thirst. Hob Wells had told me of two good inns in the town and I was beginning to be, if not saddle sore, then cart sore. But Brachet seemed to have the bit between his teeth, so I allowed him to direct us. He clearly knew the ways that were less trodden and consequently were safer. I was not afraid of being pursued by Mistress Burghill's men. One carnal part of me might have welcomed being pursued by Mistress Burghill.

"But only if she leaves her chamber pot at home!" said my father in my head. I laughed aloud and suggested that at the next village, which Brachet told us was called Cholsey, that we stopped for refreshment.

After a good large slice of rabbit pie and a cup of canaries we were ready again for the road. But Bratchet chose not to remain on it for long, but led the way over a great tract of high country, that he named Blueberry Down. This was a high and airy place, dotted with sheep, and he made us follow him along their paths, as chalk white as their wool, to the summit of a hill that he told us was Lowbury Hill. Another old track wound across the down, but we could not take it as it went between east and west and now Bratchet told us our way was almost due south.

He said proudly, "And now we're in Berkshire. The best place in the world!"

"How come 'ee says that, being as them chased 'ee away only on account of smallness?" asked Daniel.

"The best place in the world for men of a proper size, then," said Bratchet, generously.

We could see the village of East Ilsley from the old track that Bratchet called the Ridgeway, about two miles away, and it was a joyful downward scramble for my companions, frightening and scattering the sheep. I elected, however, to continue a more stately way along the old path, as I did not wish to subject Goliath with the cart to the rough and tumble of a steep slope. When a road crossed the Ridgeway, I turned left onto it. East Ilsley was about two miles ahead of me with my companions waiting at the Swan, the ostlers prepared for Goliath and a cup of Canaries for me, courtesy of Ralph.

I had thought that Bratchet would have preferred a quieter place than the Swan, which was clearly the centre of sheep trading on that day. But Ralph would have none of it. "Nothing but the best for Doctor Tom, Bratchet and Colonel Forbes' best dragoons!" he announced and demanded the best rooms and best bill of fare be prepared while we assured ourselves that the horses were well stabled. They had travelled upwards of seventeen miles on this day, and it had been excessively hard for Goliath, although the absence of Robert's lead-lined coffin had made his load easier. Bratchet's old pathways had made the journey pleasant indeed, and we had felt the benefit of the upland air.

We dined well, excessively well, in fact, on lamb roasted with rosemary and mint. The landlady recommended her special pudding, a baked apple stuffed with cinnamon cream. She and her husband knew Bratchet and spoke kindly to him which endeared them to me. But as we were preparing to leave next morning, having been assured that it was but ten miles to Newbury down a straight road, the landlord, by name Hugh Holmer, came to me and having ascertained our destination issued a warning..

"Have a care, my Masters! There is news.... it may be naught but rumour.... that there are great armies on the move. Travellers from Lambourn way have heard that Essex is trying to get to London and the king has sworn to stop him. The valley of the Kennet would be Essex' best route to Reading, make no mistake. I just tell ye what has been told to me, and nothing firm is known. I say again have a care."

We thanked him and started off again down the road to Newbury. Ralph had scarcely listened to Master Holmer and was exultant in his mood that this day he would again see his dear sister. Daniel was thoughtful and asked me after about two miles, "Does 'ee think, there's aught in this report, Tom?"

I shrugged my shoulders. "These great armies must go somewhere. As long as we don't have to encounter them, let them go whither they will. What is this Kennet anyway?"

"'Tis the river that flows through Hungerford and Newbury," said little Brachet. "It joins the Thames at Reading." He went on, "But I told you of this mighty movement of many men, twenty four hours ago. It seems you only believe them of your own size and think we small folk be liars."

"Indeed I do not, and we were claybrained ingrates not to have paid more heed. Is there danger, do you think?"

"They may not come near Newbury but might stay north of the river and make straight for Thatcham. There will be no armies on this road. Once we are over the river and into Newbury, we should be safe. Their road lies east to London."

"Is London then easterly from here and no longer in the south?"

"I think it be, Doctor Tom. Certain sure, the King's castle at Windsor is north easterly. That is a day's ride from London itself."

I had never been so far south, and yet the people of these parts were much the same as they were in Worcestershire. The land differed, in that white outcrops of chalk were to be seen in high places, and there was a different way of speaking. Voices were higher and speech was faster but it was clear all were English, men and women, who accepted a rough young Doctor from Worcester as one of themselves. I felt ashamed of my prejudices, and desperate sad that we should all be plunged into these miserable and heartbreaking wars.

We trotted on under a steep common that rose up from the road on our left and then noticed that the road began a gradual downwards climb. And then the first small misfortune befell us. Goliath cast a shoe. I tried to replace it but only one nail remained. There was a village ahead. I asked a poor man working in the fields beside us, hoeing his carrots and parsnips, where the nearest smith might be. He looked up surly and out of temper, but when I apologised for interrupting his work, he grinned cheerfully and replied that it was less than a mile away in the next village, Donnington, near the turn that went to the castle.

The smith was standing outside his forge, watching our approach. He was as broad as he was high, and he was in fact nearly as tall as myself. He seemed to be carved from granite and was not a man whom one would wish to anger. Nevertheless when I spoke him fair and offered to pay in advance for the work, he smiled pleasantly and declined settlement, until the shoeing should be completed to my satisfaction

He took an apple from his pocket and with a twist of his mighty wrist broke it exactly in half, one part of which he gave to Goliath.

"Come on, old beauty. Come on, old warrior, let us be having you."

Holding the other half of the apple behind him, he led Goliath into his forge without need of rein or bridle, and when he had placed the great fellow where he could most easily lift and rest his hoof, only then did Goliath get the rest of the apple. My companions dismounted and were looking to the castle, a great stone edifice, which was clearly visible on our right.

I paid the smith rather more than he asked, as I was relieved to have Goliath moving smoothly and comfortably again. He had looked at his other shoes and pronounced them sound, and he seemed pleased to have been paid in excess. Then he said, "You were looked for this morn."

The others turned at that, and I asked, "Who by, good sir?" He smiled at the epithet and told us, "Varlets from northwards, Oxfordshire way by their talk. They was askin' had a giant and a dwarf passed this way, and I told 'em No. Then they said... and this I warn ye, Masters... "If they come, don't tell 'em we was askin'." So there it is. I didn't like 'em. A pack of padders and priggers by my reckoning. 'Sides my young giant," and he looked me in the eye, "I like the colour of your money. And these nags are in good hands." He gave Ruby a pat with his huge hand. "I like to see that."

"How many were there?" I asked, sick at heart. Would they be waiting for us in Newbury?

"Four. Same as the gospels though not near so holy."

I looked down the road to Newbury, which Brachet told us was now very close. "I am sure my brother-in-law will protect us," said Ralph confidently, reading my thoughts. He knew now how my inclinations turned. "Avoid conflict at all cost" was my watchword.

"Doctor Tom, what's that you see in William's dabs?" asked Daniel. William carried his musket primed and ready with a plentiful supply of match protruding from his pocket at all times now. "Er don't carry it to pick his nose wi', Tom. He can shatter a bottle at sixty paces."

"And 'im ain't half bad neither," said William, indicating Daniel who was retrieving his own musket from under the leather cover where my supply of medicaments were. "Show he a partridge and him'll show 'ee our dinner!"

"He's a prate-roast, no question," said Daniel modestly. "As us've come so far, no gain in going backuds. And sides, when I saw thick villain at Hob's inn, he had no fiddlingstick. We are picked men, Doctor Tom!" and for once he spoke English, not Somerset,

"If they want to dance, we can give 'em balls!"

The smith who had been following this conversation with interest, shouted with laughter and turned his attention to a ploughboy who had brought another Shire in for shoeing. As this horse was a mare, I realised it would be politic to move Goliath out of range of her feminine wiles, and so we started on our way again, my mind veering between reluctance and recklessness.

The weather now turned. We had followed rain clouds all the way from Haddenham, but had ridden along without a soaking, under lowering skies. Now a drizzle set in together with a brisk wind that began to bring down a few yellowing leaves. I realised that we would have to find shelter at some time soon, for the horses, if not for ourselves.

We crossed a road that Brachet told us was the road from Hungerford to Thatchem and Reading, and clearly now were in Newbury itself. "This is Northbrook Street," Bratchet announced, importantly. "The marketplace is straight ahead over the bridge."

It took me a moment to realise what was amiss. Today was a Tuesday, not the Sabbath, and yet there was no-one abroad. The street we were travelling down, Northbrook Street was lined with cottages and houses and was silent as the grave. As I peered in at windows, there was the impression of folk drawing back and sideways, away from my view, anxious not to be seen looking out at us.

Still no-one challenged us and we walked freely over the bridge, four men and Brachet, six horses and a cart, and paused at a fork in the road. There was an old church on our right and the market to our left. I caught a glimpse of the stalls set up, laden with apples, pears, cheese, butter but not a soul to sell... or buy for that matter. Perhaps it was the rain that was keeping the good inhabitants of Newbury within doors, but when has the weather prevented a farmer's wife from making an honest penny in the market?

Bratchet whispered, "There is Bartholomew Street straight ahead."

And at last there was the sound of voices coming from down Bartholomew Street. Men were shouting and banging violently at a house door. I indicated that we should slip unobserved into the alley by the church where Goliath and the cart would be unseen. I dismounted and ran a circuit round the church, through the grave yard. From here it was easy to see the cause of the outcry.

I recognised Francis at once. He and three fellows from Haddenham, all Mistress Burghill's men, had reached the Kingsleys' house before us, travelling on roads rather than across high commons. There was the sign of the Sugarloaf, swinging in the wind, on the baker's next door. As I watched there was a crash of glass. One clodpoll brandished a cudgel the size of a small tree, and had shattered and destroyed one of the windows. Now I could hear what they were shouting. It was my name.

"Tom Fletcher! Tom Fletcher! Come out of it and give us the Mistress' gold!" "Where's the male harlot? Come out Holtham. Come out, you bastard."

I darted back into the shadow of the church and met Daniel and William, their muskets shouldered and primed.

"They've found his sister's house," I stammered, "What's to be done?"

Daniel handed me a pistol. "Here's Nimrod's barking iron. 'Tis cocked and ready. Make it tell, Tom."

William had already rounded the corner. There was a fearful report and a scream, as he reappeared.

"Winged one good and proper!"

Daniel had followed him and there was another crash, and the smell of gunpowder hung in the air.

"Two down," said Daniel. "Come on Tom! Try your hand!"

I was horrified beyond measure as to what we were doing. Daniel who was reloading called to me, "Tom, it's we or they!" I walked round the corner. Francis leant against the wall of the house, his arm a mangled horror of cloth, blood and bone. Another felon lay on the ground, his blood pouring from his mouth. As I watched he twitched and died. William was suddenly beside me his musket at the ready. The other two stood for a moment, as I walked towards them, holding the pistol

Drawing courage from William's stout personage, who it must be said was "metal to the back", I enquired as coolly as I could, "Looking for me, gentlemen?"

But then a confused but familiar noise broke the hush of the silent town. There was the report of pistols fired and muskets discharged. There were shouts of "Yield traitors!" and the thunder of horses' hooves, coming from the direction of Northbrook Street, whence we had lately come. William spun round, yelling to me to follow and I did so, falling into the church yard in the nick of time, as the Cavaliers swept past, riding down any who stood in their way.

Rupert had come to town.

Now I understood why everywhere was silent and shuttered. This was possibly not the first incursion of the King's horsemen. The noise of shots and shouts faded as the troop raced to the end of the town, and I ventured to steal a glance round the corner at Elizabeth's servants, whom she had sent blithely to their deaths. Francis now lay on the ground, under the front door of the house, whither some horse had kicked him. His fellow servant was stone dead, from Daniel's shot. Further down the street were the other two villains, one lying unmoving in a crumpled heap, the other hobbling up towards Francis.

I stepped out with my pistol cocked. The fellow stopped dead and attempted to bow but his broken ankle prevented such courtesy. He staggered and steadied himself hanging onto a horse trough.

He called out. "Don't kill me, Master. I wanted no part of this. She made me come."

"What sort of a hen-pecked louse are you then?" I shouted. "Where are your horses?" He pointed back up the road towards the market-place...

"Well, you'd best fetch them now or the King will acquire them. You have three corpses to take to Haddenham. I doubt that he will last the night." I walked over to Francis, and gazed on his ashen face. I knelt beside him and picked up his uninjured arm, but could find no pulse.

"What money do you have?"

"She gave him shillings for our peckage," he said indicating Francis. Daniel removed the coins from Francis' pockets. They were already bloody. He washed them in a nearby puddle.

"What is your name?" I asked him

"It's Nat Stringer," said a voice behind me. Ralph came from the lane by the church and stood looking at the survivor. "I did not think you would ever seek my death, Nat, playmates as we were."

"I tell you what I will do, Nat Stringer," I told him. "I will sell you a cart for these few shillings and you can pile your corpses on it and take them back to Haddenham. They are not wanted here. And let me warn you! Never again threaten Forbes' dragoons or Doctor Thomas Fletcher. Are you agreed on that?"

"Oh, aye, Doctor Fletcher. Believe me, I'll not meddle with any like you again!" Daniel put in, "If any question 'ee, say them were snabbled."

Nat Stringer nodded grimly, and set off up the road to get the horses. Ralph and Bratchet unharnessed Goliath and pushed the cart out onto the road. "Keep the horses out of sight," I called to Ralph. At the back of my mind were two anxieties. The first was that the Cavaliers would come again on yet another fear-inspiring escapade. The second that Susan and her new family would hold Ralph and myself responsible for this shameful visit of the Haddenham servants.

The door of the house on Bartholomew Street opened and a young man, brandishing a drawn sword stood there. He called out, "Is Ralph Holtham there?" but he was unceremoniously pushed aside, by a pretty fair haired girl who could be none other than Ralph's sister. She rushed over the road, across the graveyard, and flung her arms round Ralph's neck.

"Bring him in. Bring him in. Here's no place for a reunion. They could be back at any moment."

"Brachet! Is that you?" she cried. "Come your ways in with us. 'Tis dangerous out here!"

She hustled her brother and Brachet clearly known to them from Haddenham, and pushed them into the house, whether they would or no, and the door was slammed, leaving us outside with three dead men and several horses. Nat Stringer appeared, limping, leading two horses which we proceeded to harness up to the cart.

Daniel and I then heaved the bodies onto the board with little ceremony. There was no time to lay them down with dignity. I could hear the sounds of many voices, the neighing of horses, travelling in our direction, and the smell.... that unmistakable smell of an army on the march.

I helped Nat Stringer onto the cart so that he could rest his good foot in the makeshift stirrup. I took my dagger and cut the injured one out of his worn old boot. It was prodigiously swollen already, but he clearly felt some relief from the chill of the air and the cold rain. He stuck it out before him.

"There's two of her horses, still up there. Can you bring them back to Mistress?"

I was amazed at his effrontery. "Tell Mistress Hellcat that I would rather be stung to death with pismires, than have dealings with her ever again. And tell her if she sends any after me again, Massey and Waller will ensure that Parliament awards her nothing. Do you understand? Nothing! Now be off with you!" I turned away, wishing to get them from my sight. But then I remembered to give him the information that would bring him safely out of Newbury. "And listen, Nat Stringer. If any King's man stops your death cart, and challenges you, tell him that these are Parliament quartermasters, run down by the King's cavalry. Parliament quartermasters. Do you understand that?"

"Aye, master," he said and then added, "and thank you." He urged his two mares on, pushed his way over the bridge and trotted up to Northbrook Street, down which the foot soldiers were beginning to straggle, in small groups. I watched his passage. He was in time to cross the road to East Ilsley before the way became impassable.

"Well, lads," I could think of naught to say to my two troopers, my mind a strange mixture of gratitude and horror. "You quitted yourselves well."

William laughed and went on cleaning the spent powder from his musket. Daniel caught something of my mood. "'Tis our calling, Tom. Best not think of it overmuch."

There were loud shouts from Northbrook Street. The infantry halted and listened as officers gave commands, which were greeted with groans and protests.

"What's happening?" I asked Daniel.

"Seems they've to walk through the town and turn westwards. No comfortable quarters for these poor wet bastards. We'm best find quarters, too, Tom. Seems we'm a bit too hot and ginger for young Ralph's kin."

I found my partisan amongst the baggage that had been swept off the cart. Under the leathern cover, I found my hat with the two brave feathers that Rowena had found for me. I crammed it on my head, and asked them to wait with the horses. I would, I promised, find them good quarter. We had food from the Swan in East Ilsley. I urged them to take their ease and eat in the shelter of the church

Page 543

porch. The King's Men were streaming past, wet and sullen, but at the sight of my partisan, they stepped aside and I reached the crowded marketplace without difficulty.

A few of the stallholders had returned and were trying to sell their wares to the hungry foot soldiers. They fought a loosing battle, however. Officers were moving the men on quickly and many of them grasped apples, matchet bread and cheese and shouted out to the poor tradesmen, "God pays!" I heard one poor baker's wife cry out with asperity, "No doubt He does, but not in this life, you bastards!"

I fought my way through to the inn where the four servants had stalled their horses. "Could you find beds for two and stabling for four more?" I asked the Landlady, who found me rather a mirthful object. I tried to play the Cavalier, doffing my hat and bowing fit to crack my ribs.

"Horses, yes. Alas, the only bedchamber that is left, is above the stables." "That will do for my two good fellows," I told her and paid there and then for Daniel and William's bed and board. So much for Ralph's promise that all would be paid for by himself.

I wandered back, my partisan causing poor wet foot soldiers to move aside. Daniel and William had made themselves comfortable in the church porch and were surveying the poor forlorn fellows, passing by with a degree of superiority.

"I've found beds for you and your nags," I told them. "The excellent landlady will take Goliath and Ruby as well.

"And no doubt thee's paid, Tom?" said Daniel.

I nodded. "But what to do with Ralph's horses, I know not. Is there room at the back of the Kingsley's house?"

It was excessively difficult to organise the safe keeping of six horses whilst an army was passing through the town. We had to keep dissuading poor fellows that the nags at the back of the church were not for sale, nor for the purloining. I cursed Ralph to myself. He was lamentably skilful at passing on his problems to his friends. I sat down in the porch and sighed with frustration.

The flow of the King's army was lessening somewhat. Thankfully the Cavalry had found another way through the town to wherever they were to be drawn up for battle. I was beginning to think I should have to knock on the door of the Kingsley's house and announce that we were going and Ralph and his pad-nags could ride to the devil, when that same door opened and Gerard Kingsley emerged, his sword drawn but his face smiling like the radiant sun.

He picked his way across the road to the porch avoiding puddles and Royalist refuse, his drawn sword granting him passage, and greeted us like princes.

"Doctor Tom, forgive us! What must you think of our hospitality? And you, good fellows both? Pray, come in this moment. We have food on the table and wine in the glasses. What sort of a welcome have you had in Newbury? I shall try to make amends. By the mass, but I shall. I swear it."

"Alas, sir, we are overburdened with horses. I have found stabling for four but Ralph's two riding horses, part of his fortune, still lack housing."

"It is done," he announced, and then as he took account of the two well-bred riding mounts, that Waller had given to Robert, he gasped in delight, took their reins and drew them after himself round to the back of his house.

Daniel and William mounted, carefully carrying my box of medicines, and the linen bag of Sim's concoctions, and rode their two mounts to the inn in the Marketplace and I followed, leading Ruby and Goliath.... As Gerard had predicted, an excellent meal was on the table, herrings to begin and then a magnificent sirloin of beef. Wine and March beer were served in large jugs and all was plentiful and exceedingly welcome. As Daniel expressed it, "Our great guts were ready to eat our little'uns." I stared at him. What had been amiss with the bread and cheese they had so recently devoured in the church porch? With a slice of beef in one hand and a beaker of beer in the other, he grinned at me and winked.

"Well, Doctor Tom, as Ralph tells me we must call you, glad indeed we are to welcome you here," said Susie, "but perhaps I should tell you who is the true founder of this feast. We have been expecting dear Rafe for some time, hoping against hope that he would ride down the road to find us, (and dear brother you would have been welcome as the penniless prodigal, not as a rich man in your own right as it seems you are now, thanks to Doctor Tom) and we would have killed the fatted calf for him, be sure! (if we had had any calves). But I must tell you. Yesterday Lord Essex' men were here with coin, asking every household to prepare a hot dinner for his officers, the town in the main drawn to the Parliament. Well, our true loyalties in this house are with His Majesty, but money is a powerful recruitment officer so we thought no harm could follow, if we were prepared. So it is Lord Essex we should thank, is it not my dearest husband?"

Gerard laughed and nodded. We said nothing, merely smiled in appreciation at the Earl's munificence. Daniel raised his beaker as a toast. At least two Parliament soldiers had been able to take advantage of the Lord General's generosity, although in courtesy we did not enlarge on recent allegiances.

Susie went over to replenish the glass of the old man who sat silently by the fire. "Of course, dear father, here, (Gerard's father that is, our parents have a neat cottage in the courtyard, and that is why we were so long in greeting you, dear Doctor Tom, as our mother was overjoyed to hold her eldest born in her arms again, even though, she complained, he stank like the midden heap), but as I say, Master Kingsley here favours the King's cause so he is delighted, that it is the King who has now come to Newbury, are you not, Dad?"

The poor old fellow knew he was being spoken to, and clearly was enamoured of his new daughter-in-law. He caught her hand and held it to his lips, but then forgot it was there, so she had gently to disentangle herself, and then busied herself with a fig pudding. So good it was, a suet pudding, stuffed with figs and dates and currants, that I was monstrous happy that the Earl of Essex had not arrived demanding his share. Gerard at last got in a word edgewise. "So these villains who broke our window. We thought at first they were the King's men, demanding entrance, but then Susie knew them from Haddenham. Have they gone then in good earnest?"

"Aye, that they have, back to Haddenham," I said. "They can do no harm, now. Not the least in the world!" I was pleased to see that Gerard had already placed a wooden shutter over the broken window.

"I had to face the she-dog down once or twice," Susie told me "When she tried to evict my parents from our cottage. I told her I would write to Captain Robert... Colonel, I should say... and ask for his protection. That silenced her. She did not like to think that a poor girl like myself could pen a letter, and Lawyer Woolstone is the only man in Haddenham who can say her Nay. Theirs is a most uneasy truce. She wishes to rule the village and the country around and he prevents her from seizing what is not hers, by citing rule of law. To tell truth, she does not understand honesty."

"I must admit that she seems a grasping woman. Ralph warned me of her evil nature and he was right... So," I asked, changing the subjct, "Where is the Earl and his army now?"

"They were pushed back towards Hungerford this very day. He came from there this morning, as I hear but made heavy weather of the paths and by-ways as the Kennet is something of an overblown harlot of a river. She spreads out of her bodice and skirts when the weather is wet and a useful path becomes a marsh. So he was delayed and the King marching down from Wantage, across the dry chalk downs arrived before him and has eaten his dinner!"

He roared with laughter and as his father looked up questioningly at the sound, repeated his story more loudly, that his progenitor might understand it.

Daniel and William took their leave after we had eaten our fill and I rose to go with them.

"No, Tom!" cried Rafe and his sister, and Gerard who was a most courteous civil gentleman, such as would make an excellent lawyer, told me, "We would take it as a great favour if you would stay here with us this night, Doctor Tom. There is a truckle bed for Bratchet in my brother-in-law's room, and if you do not mind sharing with my father, we should be snug as pigs in pease straw."

I thanked him and accepted, as I had been concerned about where I would lay my head, and we sat over our cups until dusk began to deepen around the streets of Newbury. I had listened for Rupert's young blades, but they did not disturb the peace again. We soon found out the reason. Gerard went out to speak to a neighbour, and returned with the news that the King was lodging on Cheap Street, which ran parallel with Bartholomew Street from the Market-place.

"And I daresay, he has never had so Cheap a lodging!" We were at that time of the evening when any and every jest caused hearty laughter, and Gerard was a mirthful man, no doubt of it. I was glad that Ralph and Susie were so well housed and protected.

We spoke of how Ralph's fortune could assist the Kingsley household. I was relieved to see that the piles of coin at last were removed from the nosebags and placed in a locked strong box, hidden under the table. Susie had a prodigious memory, the first requirement for a lawyer, and if more help could now be hired to help with household chores, they could expand their trading, as the other lawyer in town, an old man, wished to shelve his parchments and sell his books.

Ralph had thought that he might become a stallholder in the market and sell wild game.

"Best be sure it is wild, though, dear brother," said Susie warningly. "I fear you must leave the poachers now, and join the gamekeepers."

He seemed somewhat dashed so I reminded him of his prowess regarding the upkeep of buildings.

"Aye, now there are amany poor householders with leaking roofs and draughty corners," said Gerard. "Now that would be a venture worth the investigation, brother Ralph. If you kept your charges low, you would soon have the citizens of Newbury beating a path to your door."

Shortly after this, Susie led her old father-in-law up to his room which I was to share, and when she came down and reported that he was fast asleep, I excused myself and went upstairs and crept in to his bedroom. Alas, I had not realised I was expected to share not merely his bedroom but also his bed which was admittedly wide and soft. However whilst I would not accuse the old man of snoring, true it is to say that he dreamt loudly and continuously. I lay fully clothed on the part of the bed that he did not occupy but soon realised that sleep was impossible. I realised I had been persuaded into a course of action that I did not relish, rather than seem discourteous. I had always detested the notion of sharing a bed with a man, would not even contemplate it with Abram. We did not even like to share the same bedchamber. There was only one person in this house on this night, with whom the thought of sharing a bed was appealing and I chuckled as I thought her husband might object.

I lay thinking for about an hour. I had hated the violence we had perpetrated that day, and yet Elizabeth Burghill's servants had clearly been instructed to commit murder to gain the money. She had clearly not realised that the dragoons who accompanied me, were trained musketeers, whose creed was "Kill or be killed," and for whom the first alternative in that maxim was the one of choice, although they certainly did not seek conflict, if it could be avoided.

Even so, the servants' deaths hung heavy on my conscience.

Old Master Kingsley sighed and spoke in his sleep and poked me with his elbow. I finally could not endure his constant mouthings nor the close atmosphere in the bedroom. I clapped my hat on my head anyhow and picked up my partisan, which seemed to inspire respect. I crept from the room, closing the door quietly and stole silently down the stairs. The great front door was bolted and barred. I could not unlock it without making a deal of noise, so I felt my way into the kitchen, where a fire still smouldered in the grate. I had not reckoned with the dogs who lay across the kitchen door, but who were instantly each pacified by a piece of meat from the ashet, holding the roast beef, which lay covered on the table.

The back door was not locked... the dogs were clearly there to guard ingress... and I crept out into a wild rainy night. A herb garden lay to my left and beyond that were the stables. My idea was to retrieve the leathern cover which we had left behind St Nicholas Church and perhaps make myself comfortable in the stables. But could I find a way out? The archway from the street to the stables was barred and I had come so far without waking the household, that I did not like to try it. So my eyes becoming used to the darkness, I saw that there was the faintest gleam of light from beyond the stables. Beside them was the narrowest of passages, barred at the Cheap Street end by a low wooden gate. The faint light was a torch that flickered still above the door of an inn opposite the back of the Kingsley's house. Nothing easier than to vault the gate and find myself on Cheap Street.

I could now walk up Cheap Street to the Market-place, turn left, and there to my left again, and across Bartholomew Street was St Nicholas Church. Now I remembered the church porch was snug enough. My leather cover for protection...

"Well, Tom Fletcher, of all welcome sights." I knew that high distinctive voice. "May I be permitted to know if I must greet you as Doctor or Lieutenant? Believe me, Tom, I am most heartily glad to see you, on this night of all nights."

Standing alone beside the great front door of the first house on Cheap Street, stood my dear friend, Lucius Carey.

He embraced me, and I was aware that his face was wet, though not with rain, as the house had a deep overhang. He put his hands up on my shoulders, and began to laugh at my dishevelled appearance. The feathers in my hat drooped certainly and Skinner's blue doublet was a shabby travesty of its pristine self, when I had taken possession of it in Gloucester.

"Are you then a trusty Officer of Gerard's? Your partisan proclaims it but somehow I cannot quite reconcile your philosophy with the necessary martial disposition. Come let us go in. Tom, you will never know how much your unsoldierly appearance gladdens my poor heart. By your very clothing you give the lie to all the military hammerheaded rubbish, to which we must all pay lip service."

"I assure you, my Lord, I am still fiercely neutral." I told him. "This is a disguise that has allowed me to bring Robert Burghill to his Buckinghamshire village for burial."

"Yes, yes!" he cried. "I remember when we met after Edgehill, you spoke of your indebtedness to that good man. Tom, when I look at you, I see six feet of honour and virtue. You are probably the least corrupt man in England."

The room into which he led me, was lit with more candles than I could remember ever seeing in one place. We sat at a table where there was a bellarmine and glasses.

"Come then, dear Tom, a toast! What shall we drink to? Do not out of courtesy say "The King" because I swear I should dash good Master Head's quoniam on these flagstones. He is my sovereign and I serve him still, but I cannot any longer respect him. Come, Tom, you shall propose this last toast."

"To understanding?" I said hesitantly.

"There you have it, you clever sawbones, in two words. "Understanding". But do they ever try to understand, these great lords with their heads in the clouds, and their fingers in the pie that once was England. If men cannot be allowed to think as they wish, Catholic, Presbyter, Arminian, then there is no hope for us. What is it to you or me if some fellow wants a communion table, here or there? Why do we argue over trifles? Surely God prefers the pursuit of rational thought rather than blind belief?" He leapt to his feet and began pacing the room.

"Tom, Tom, you see before you a man who is sick at heart." He emptied his glass and refilled it. "You are quiet now, Tom, and you always used to speak such good sense. Tell me your heart now. Tomorrow Englishmen will die, killed by their fellow Englishmen. What can be done to stop this desperate folly?"

"I think as you do, my lord. But I have no words of comfort to give you. I would not describe myself as religious, Sir. If God cared that we are hell-bent on this desperate folly, then surely He would give us proof of His Divine Displeasure. The most that I envisage from Him is Divine Indifference."

He nodded slowly. I went on, "But listen, my lord. If I had said that, one hundred years ago, I would have been burned as a heretic. Consider. That is progress of a kind. I have gained the leave to doubt His mercy, and for all I know, such doubts might be God given. It may be, your despair reflects His. It may be God prefers the man who questions Him, rather than a sheep who blindly follows well worn paths or precepts. Perhaps in fact He wishes us to rely on ourselves and seek our own solutions".

"What a philosopher you are Tom! Well, a theosopher perhaps. Enough of that. I shall run mad if I think further on it. I have to believe that our God is a caring Deity. But enough. So that coffin when we met near Winchcombe, that was Robert Burghill?"

"It was." I told him, "I had to protect his remains. An unnecessary precaution, perhaps. He wished to be buried in his home county of Buckinghamshire, the county of John Hampden. It seems he knew Hampden and supported him."

"And so did I and so did every sane Englishman. What fearful times that a good man should be killed by his own people, half of whom agreed with him in their hearts!"

" How is my good friend, Edward Holte?" I asked, changing the subject to cheer him.

"Oh, poor Tom! You did not know. He died in Oxford earlier this year. At the very least you can comfort yourself, it was not your doctoring. He died of a virulent fever, but his father's unkind neglect may well have hastened his decline."

I was silent, remembering the happy times I had spent at Great Tew with this man and his friends. At last I said, "I remember you both told me that you envied my loving easy kinship with my father. Sir John Holte is a rogue and a villain." My sorrow at the news of Edward's death caused me to remember with distaste his father who whilst he thought I slept, had tried to steal my horse.

"Tom, rogues and villains abound. You asked to toast "understanding" and I support that pious hope. But dear friend, I cannot tell you how confused and disordered our realm has been. I have maintained my loyalty but at a price. If I ever begin to feel satisfied with my work or my writing, there is a whisper from my conscience, like words muttered in the ear of the triumphant Roman generals, and that whisper is simply "Strafford." Do not be seduced ever by the notion of an easy life at court. Behind the purple hangings and the cloth of gold of this King, there is another court, where envy and fear reign supreme. I sound treacherous. Yes. I am a rebel and at last my rebellion will flourish."

There was a knock on the door and a man entered, accoutred for the field. He looked familiar and yet I did not know him.

"Who in Hell is this?" he asked, gazing at my whimsical appearance.

"John, your courtesy, if you please. This is the surgeon who saved Edward Holte at Kineton, Doctor Thomas Fletcher. He is my good friend, John Byron, as are you, so please, an you love me, speak him fair."

"Do I know you?" asked John Byron. Our great aristocrats were always too important to remember lesser mortals and had to have their memories new minted from time to time. Now I knew whence came the familiarity.

"No, my Lord, but your brother Tom knows me. I had to fight with Lord Hastings to prevent him having your brother's leg sawn off in Stafford castle."

"Oh, aye, you saved his leg, did you not? He boasts that a mad sawbones, like some fly-by-night foot land raker... Lucius, hear this, 'twill lift your gloom I vow.... appeared from nowhere in the ruined tower where he was housed, removed the musket ball from his thigh, bound him up like Lazarus in cere-cloth, gave lotions and instructions to his servants and disappeared, without asking for payment. My brother has never forgotten it, particularly as his leg is almost as good as ever."

I bowed as graciously as I could. "I rejoice to hear it. Your Lordship does me honour."

"So what does he say about that pustule on your neck, Lucius? I have come to tell you that we must ride out in about one hour. Rupert hops about like a dog at a fair. If you have not seen his neck, good Doctor, pray look on it now, as time presses."

And with a final, "Lucius, I will return," he was gone.

"Let me see your neck, then, my lord."

At the side above his shoulder blade was a dark mole, which did not seem a usual disfigurement. The skin around it was red and puckered, not a healthy sight.

"Does it hurt?" I asked, hoping that my voice did not betray my anxiety.

"Not until lately," he said. I remembered Letitia teasing him that he was a bad liar.

"I have a salve and a dressing, that will help." Sim had devised many useful ointments in which he had merged the tinctures of several plants. I knew I had supplies of such an unguent, made from sorrel, leeks and the common burdock, but it was with my box, in the linen bag of dressings he had given me. The troopers had taken charge of them and I could retrieve them from their room above the stable at the inn.

"I'll be straight back," I told Lucius, and went out into the town, which was stirring, although the eastern sky was only faintly grey. Daniel was awake and called out straight away to know who was below with the horses.

"It is Beelzebub and all the host of Hell!" I called out. His face appeared at the top of the ladder.

"I need my box and the bag, if you please, Daniel. Forgive me for waking you."

But a sturdy milkmaid was already going her rounds with the cry, "Milk below, maids!" Her voice was loud rather than tuneful and there could be little chance of further sleep.

Daniel passed down the box and bag to me and I promised I would shortly be with them for breakfast. The landlady was already issuing commands in her kitchen to her sleepy scullions and I begged if I could wash my hands and face, promising I would return within the hour to order breakfast for the three of us.

John Byron was waiting for me. "You have cheered him somewhat," he told me. "I tell you, he has had his heart in his hose for months. Why so? The King loves him and relies on his counsel."

"Aye, but I think he does not take it. Why else have we come to this pass?" I said, with conviction. "The Viscount loves his country and his countrymen before all else. To my mind he is a true patriot." Then, as he stared at me, surprised at my plain speaking, I went on, "Forgive me, sir. But we are in a sad case when we find we must kill each other. My gorge rises at the prospect."

"Well, well! Master Doctor! No wonder my brother said you were a paragon. When Tom asked Lord Hastings where you had gone, he did not know."

"I had to travel south with Peabody, sir."

"You will have to wait, Doctor Tom. He is at prayers. What is more he has had the whole household woken to join him. Still, perhaps they are content. But for me..."

He winked in a soulful knowing manner and I could not help but laugh.

A few moments later the prelate came out, yawning delicately, and I went in to tend Lucius' neck. I bathed the arca carefully and then applied Sim's ointment and covered it with clean bandage.

"It feels better already, Tom."

"Well, I will leave you this salve and some bandage and you can have it dressed again tonight. I will not be here to do it for you as I must leave today."

"Ah, yes, tonight." He began to dress himself and I noticed the armour and buff coat, ready for him to wear.

"I doubt I shall need further doctoring," he said, thoughtfully. Then he spoke more cheerfully. "You are such a good doctor, Tom, one treatment from you will suffice."

The door opened and John Byron returned. He had the air of a man who has great deeds to accomplish.

"Master Doctor, a word with you, if you please."

I turned to him with a sinking heart. How foolish I had been to respond to his kindly advances. Great lords are never friendly unless they need some favour of us lesser mortals.

"Yes, my Lord?"

Page 554

"Will you help me and my boys today? Will you doctor them when the muskets crash and the cannons roar? The faint hearted leech I employed is still upon the road. What is your price?"

"Oh, Christ help me!" I sat down heavily on one of the carved oak chairs, "My lord, I pray you do not ask me. I was trapped in Gloucester during the siege, and had to travel to these parts to help friends. I am needed at my home in Worcester. I beg you, let me go home."

"But will you not even now stay to help your friends? Lucius tells me you are his friend." He was a sly dog, this John Byron, with a silver tongue. "I too am your friend. Will you not help me? Lucius, can you persuade him?!

"I am a broken reed, John, not fit to be your advocate. You know what I think of this sorry pass. I cannot help you."

Strangely it was Lucius' sad indifference that tipped the balance. He, before so capable and full of blithe energy, now so despairing and listless, moved me to concern for him. I would at the very least be here to change the dressing on his neck if I stayed in Newbury for one day.

I sighed. "Where am I to go?"

He leapt on my agreement with delight. "Where Bartholomew Street meets the campania, there's a large barn, with a good roof. Vavasour is nearby already with his yellow leekeaters. Do you have assistants?"

"Yes, two... perhaps more. But what I must have is a supply of boiled clean water."

"Why boiled?" he asked interested.

"I don't know but it prevents putrefying. It is why your brother has no timber toes."

Horses clattered on the cobbles in the street outside and one called out "My Lord!"

"I must go. Lucius, come with me, then, if you are set on this escapade."

"John, I have followed the drum before this. I want to go with you. Tom, goodbye." He embraced me again, looked at me for a moment and ran out after Byron.

I cursed myself "up hill and down dale." What had I done? To involve myself was one thing but to include William and Daniel was another matter. They were not even Royalists. I went to find them.

At least we could break fast together.

But to my surprise they accepted their new calling as surgeon's mates with a certain enthusiasm. "'Twould be baffling, Tom, to ride west today and not know the outcome of it all. We'd be playing the duck, and no mistake."

"But you support Parliament!" I said amazed at their forgetfulness. William looked at Daniel.

"Do us?" he said.

"Is this John Byron fellow going to pay we?" asked Daniel.

"He promised a handsome sum," I told them.

"Then we support him," he announced with vigour and in good English! These two were the true philosophers, I was but a novice.

I sent them to fetch the leathern cover. We could chop it up to make aprons to protect our clothes, although my garments, as always, carried the appearance of "better days." I asked the Landlady for good rooms for that night, and paid in advance. At least I could be confident that tonight I would not have to share a room with old Master Kingsley.

Then I thought in courtesy I had best inform the Kingsleys of my intended work for that day. Gerard opened the street door at my knock.

"Tom, we thought you would still be sleeping. How did you get to the street through a locked door?"

I quickly explained that I would be working as a surgeon on the battlefield. Ralph came in rubbing his eyes. I wondered if after all my pains on his behalf he would like to assist me. However, the prospect of helping me in my calling, left him distinctly indifferent. How unaccountable that outside Worcester with Robert he had been enthusiasm personified. However little Bratchet, who had heard me ask him, jumped at the proposal.

"Oh, Tom, I beg you, let me help you. I'd leap over nine hedges to learn this work. I tell you I can fetch and carry. I learn fast as a fox in a fleshmonger's store. I beg you, Tom." Faced with this ardour, who was I to say him Nay.

Gerard promised to bring pails of boiled water to us and said he knew the barn in question. It was dry and wide, with piles of straw, stacked in bales, he told me, and was on the right hand side at town end.

So I set off down Bartholomew Street, my wooden box weighing me down and my linen bag over my shoulder. I hoped that Sim would not object to my using his simples for royalists, but after all, our master was not Essex, nor yet Charles, but Aesculapius... that Greek quacksalver, as Peabody had once termed him. A small lift in my spirits occurred. As Byron's surgeon I could now seek him out legally without fear. But as the artillery was beginning to crash its warning over the country, I realised I would be simply an unwelcome encumbrance. Better to concentrate my efforts where I was proficient.

The barn was as Gerard described, high and seemingly weatherproof, but I had fears that wounded patients laid directly on the straw bales would suffer from excessive flea bites. I began searching in the field behind the barn for fennel and rue but remembered that feverfew and groundsel in quantities could by their strange aroma dispel any insect. As I was grubbing up these plants, I was joined by Brachet who had begged an old worn counterpane from Susie. I suggested that we tore it into four and covered the straw with it and that we placed my fleabane herbs in this rough bedding. He began happily to undertake this and I wandered out to try if I could see how the battle progressed.

The Royalists had barred Essex' road to London, no doubt of it. But the chosen battlefield could not have been more difficult to negotiate. The landscape south of Newbury was a country of small fields, lanes and hedges. It was not the territory for a sustained cavalry attack, and pikemen would curse the constant obstacles in their path. It was, in fact, dragoon country. Daniel and William would have been as happy as pigs in pease straw. But now they came to find me, wearing thick leather aprons, they had fashioned for themselves, grinning from ear to ear, demanding to know if I too wanted such protection for my clothes. I shuddered, dreading the baptism of fire that awaited them, but sent them to cover a few hurdles with the leather, that the wounded might be transported if necessary. Daniel had a hammer and nails and at last we had four pallads, and a makeshift but serviceable table.

We stood for some moments looking out towards a small hill that seemed to be hotly contended. As we watched, it seemed that one battalion triumphed. There was cheering and a mass of men moved downhill. Cannons boomed out and from the shrieks that followed the explosions, it was clear that they were accomplishing their deadly purpose.

I realised that once again I had been drawn into the fascinating "theatre of war." I hated myself for this unwholesome curiosity. My bodyguard, like myself, were staring open mouthed, drawn into the hideous spectacle of men, murdering their fellow men and creating widows and orphans in the process. "Come on, then," I shouted, "What preparations did Forbes' surgeon make before battle?"

They laughed scornfully. "Made sure he were drunk as a fish, Tom," said Daniel.

William agreed. "As bumpsy as they come, Tom."

That reminded me. I gave Bratchet three sovereigns, and told him to run back to Gerard and ask him to buy a barrel or two of Aqua Vitae. In some instances, when a patient needed courage, strong distilled spirits were useful. Daniel and William exchanged gleeful smiles when they heard this. I said nothing but thought, "Just wait until the blood begins to flow like water, lads. There'll be no grinning then."

Suddenly John Byron ran up to us, leading his horse, on which a wounded musketeer swayed perilously, blood seeping into his blue breeches. I called to my helpers to assist him and saw the poor fellow had two grievous wounds. John Byron quickly told us, "A sword cut across the stomach, and a musket ball in the thigh. He fought like a devil!"

The poor wounded fellow forced himself to dismount and leant for a moment on the side of the horse. Then his legs ceased to support him and he crumpled in a heap, as we rushed up with one of our pallads. Daniel seized his legs and William his shoulders and I found myself shouting, "Gently, boys! Gently!"

Byron was standing gazing south in the direction he had come. He was muttering to himself. "We were here well before the rebels. Why did we not take and hold that damnable hill? What sort of arse-begotten tactics are these?"

"What of Lucius Carey?" I asked him.

He seemed to start himself awake. He was a dark man, near as black-haired as myself. He clapped me on the shoulder, looking past me. "I know not, good doctor. Help that Ensign if you can." He leapt on the horse and was galloping away, when he reined in his horse and turned and came back.

"I shall try not to send you those who are like to die."

"'Tis better that the dying are tended among friends and their pain relieved, than that they should be left lonely and in agony on the open battlefield." What was I saying? There were but four of us here.

"No wonder Lucius cares for you. You are a good man, Doctor Thomas."

I wanted to tell him that my good intentions covered wounded Parliament men as well as his blue Cavaliers but we were both needed elsewhere, and I watched him gallop away.

My helpers stood around the wounded man whom they had laid on the table. I had always found it easier to operate on patients who lay down, rather than the more usual habit of keeping them seated. My helpers were waiting for me to take a lead. "Wherever there is a bloody wound," I told them, "you must first neatly remove cloth from garments that might have been pushed into the body. And all must be clean." There was a gasp as I tore down the ensign's breeches, revealing the deep red gash across his belly. Mercifully he had lost consciousness by this point. I went on, "He could die, from this wound, piercing his innards, or from loss of blood, but also from the infection caused by a dirty piece of cloth undiscovered in his wound. So we remove all such foreign matter from it"

I had acquired various instruments to effect this. Ben had called such tools callipers but now the "bills" were of various shapes like birds' beaks. I picked out the few pieces of velvet that had been assimilated by the wound, and mopped aside the blood which kept filling the cavity. I thought that the wound was largely superficial. His coiled guts were visible, but as far as I could tell the blood was from the stomach wall. I cleaned it as well as I could and took my silver needle from my box and a length of Dutch white hemp.

At this point I looked at my assistants. Daniel was frowning, wondering what I should do next, and Brachets's blue eyes were wide open. But we had lost William. His complexion usually of a hearty redness, had paled to an unrecognizable grey tinge, something it must be owned, of the shade of a white dog's turd. He was sitting on a bale of straw, retching in a refined manner.

"Go out!" I ordered him. "We will have enough to do without cleaning up after you. If you must vomit, do so where it cannot be seen or smelt."

He nodded and staggered out onto the road, where for all I knew, he cast up his accounts. I sewed up the long gash as neatly as any seamstress, and showed them how to anoint the area with my Pares lotion

"Now for the thigh." My surgeon's mates, one large, one small, nodded in anticipation... I made them notice that I washed my hands and my instruments in boiled water and dried all very carefully. Again I tore away his breeches, completely this time. In fact there was little hope for them... a sword cut to the belly, and a musket ball in the thigh did not add to their sartorial appeal, but it was clear that our patient had bewrayed himself and I do not think would have wished to see this particular item of clothing again.

"Let us hope these are his only casualty," I said trying to lighten the situation. Brachet asked to be allowed to hold the speculum, but first I made him wash and dry his hands. Again I had to remove any extraneous matter. The musket ball had carried the cloth completely into the sinews. I used my callipers to remove the ball and then with Brachet holding up the great flap of skin with the speculum, neatly extracted the velvet cloth. The wound was deep and I was afraid that the sinews might not knit together well. But his bones were undamaged as far as I could see.

"Christ Almighty! He has so much blood!" Daniel was astonished by the constant flow.

"So again I will sew his wound and bind it as tightly as I can, and he must lie as quiet as a bishop in a whorehouse so that all knits together and he does not lose more blood."

I burned my needle in a candle flame which I explained to Daniel was a quick way of ensuring that it would be clean again for the next task. We laid our first patient quietly on one of the makeshift mattresses, covered by Susie's counterpane. He opened his eyes briefly and accepted a sip of water from Bratchet.

There was the sound of voices outside and two carts drew up, full of groaning wounded troopers William was by now somewhat recovered and began to help us move the wounded into the barn. One poor fellow had had his leg shot away below the knee. I realised I would have to do what I could to protect the bloody stump. In one way it was easier than amputation as the worst had already happened, but the task of tying the veins and arteries as carefully as possible and then folding the flap of skin over the pitiful deformed leg and sewing it, made me feel uncharacteristically delicate. However I did what I could, angrily asking myself the age-old questions. Why were my fellow country men so hell-bent on destroying each other, and why, yet again, had I allowed myself to be caught up in their lunacy?

Daniel and Bratchet had made the other invalids as comfortable as possible, and the whole sorry process of emptying and cleaning the wounds, stitching them where possible and anointing them with Ambroise Pares' lotion, was repeated over and over again. Susie came down the road with a little cart pulled by a pony. She had persuaded a few of the Newbury goodwives to take the treated invalids into their homes for a few days. I knew from my experience that troopers did have money about their persons, and I advised her to tell the good ladies that in this instance, "God did not pay," and that a contribution from their patient would be welcome.

I asked Susie to make a list of where our patients should be lodged, so that I could visit them later in the day. In a rare moment of leisure I wandered outside to observe what I could of the battle, but sadly my base desire for dramatic action was frustrated. There was naught to see but much to hear from time to time. To my right, to the west, there was the crash of musket fire, interspersed with periods of cries and shouts of encouragement. I surmised that groups of musketeers were moving forward and back over the fields, trying to hold a small pocket of ground. Further south, it was now difficult to see the hill that had previously been the subject of much action, as it was shrouded in the smoke of demi-cannons or culverin. Mercifully I was too far away to be able to distinguish one from the other.

I was suddenly aware of a movement on my right. A musket barrel was raised over the level of a nearby mound of earth, and a voice cried, "Give quarter, dog, or I fire!" I raised my hands above my head and walked towards the ditch which was nothing more than a channel beside the road to drain off rain water. A man lay there in the wet, gasping for breath, with a great gash on his brow, still waving his musket in my direction. I could see that his bandolier was dripping water and his match which trailed over his shoulder was soaking.

I was laughing as I told him, "My dear sir, I am more use to you alive than dead. I am an unarmed surgeon with no allegiance to either side. You had better let me help you."

But he took aim and tried to fire. When there was no sound but the click of the trigger, he howled piteously and turned his face into the dirty water. I jumped down and hauled him up by the back of his buff coat and pushed him before me into the barn. He began by fighting fiercely as we tried to get him to remove his sodden clothing. Bratchet had made a small fire and had built a small wooden framework on which wet garments could be dried. He approached the newcomer to help him, but the poor fellow, crazed by the blow, shrieked, "Ah, Jesu! I am in Hell and this is one of Satan's imps!"

At that I did an unforgivable thing. I clenched my fist and hit him in the solar plexus. There was a horrified gasp from the thirty or so wounded troopers, lying in the barn, and from my helpers. He went down like a block of wood and lay moaning softly. We lifted him onto one of our makeshift straw mattresses, and now we could remove his sodden clothing and try to get him dry.

As he began to breathe more regularly, I satisfied myself there was nothing amiss with his trunk. Thank God, although my blow had left a slight bruise, his body and limbs were whole. The blow to his head had caused him to lose his reason, momentarily it was to be hoped. I judged the gash had been caused by the butt-end of a musket. I dressed it carefully, binding his head with white bandage, as he lay between sleep and waking.

We spooned water between his lips and wrapped him in a warm blanket that a good woman had brought from the town for us. He seemed to sleep and more of Byron's wounded cavalry arrived, with musketeers from other smaller commanded regiments of the King. It was the same sad story. Sword slashes and limbs devastated by musket balls. Daniel and Bratchet were becoming practised surgeon's mates and William took over the task of caring for those whom I had treated. I worked on and on, thanking God that we had managed to create a sturdy table. Otherwise my back would have ached intolerably.

Gerard brought down hot meat pies for us and more aqua vitae. I must confess I took a draught of it myself, but ordered William to issue no more than a wine glass to each man and not to give any to men who had stomach or chest wounds, no matter how they pleaded. I kept a sharp eye on the crazed fellow with the gash to the head. At one point he called out, very clearly, "See to the hens, little Cecily!", which caused all to smile. But as I walked past him to get more bandage, I saw his eyes were open, and he was lying still and quiet, observing the movement around him.

When I had finished my task I went back to see how he was faring. I gave him a drink of water, holding the cup for him as he drank and asked him, "Who is little Cecily?" He started and said, "My youngest daughter!", and then a few moments later, he asked, "Who are you?"

I laughed and told him I was the surgeon he had tried to kill. "Who employs you?" he asked.

"Sir John Byron," I told him.

He tried to sit up. "Oh, Jesu! I must have... I must have... Oh, sweet Christ, what have I done?"

He had the unmistakeable nasal tone of a Londoner. He looked round. "These are all Byron's men?" I nodded and told him, "But I am not, nor are my helpers. Who is your officer?"

He motioned to me to bend so he could whisper and told me, "Francis West."

I was no wiser. I whispered back, "And who is he?"

"Lieutenant-Colonel of us Blue Boys." he whispered, "and a better man never walked the earth. Oh! Jesu. Where's my helmet?"

"You fight for Parliament, do you?" I asked.

He nodded and asked, "Where is the gallows?"

"Why?" I asked, bemused by this sudden shift in his conversation.

"Because they'll hang me, certain sure!"

"Will they so?" I asked, "Then I can assure you, that will be after they have hanged me. I do not permit my patients to be hanged. Why should anyone wish to hang you?"

He said one word. "Treason."

Then lest I had not grasped his predicament, he enlarged his fears. "For taking up arms against the King's person."

"I do not think there would be gallows enough in this land to hang all who have supported Parliament," I said, in what I hoped was a comforting voice.

"I saw the man who tried to kill me." He was remembering now his recent history. "I saw his musket raised and the butt came down on my brow. The next moment it seemed, I was pushing through hedges and ditches, with no notion how I came there, desperate to get away from the noise." He grinned. "If the King don't hang me for treachery, then Skippon will, for cowardice."

"Is he, then, a brutal commander?" I asked.

"No, I malign the good man in jest." he told me.

A cart full of the wounded arrived and I had to busy myself again with their disposal and their various needs. I had immediately to tend fourteen or so musketeers. We were now well organised in that William and Daniel could prepare a man for treatment whilst I was dealing with another, assisted by Brachet, and tedious it was to hear again and again that tiresome jest, "the long and the short of it." I swear my dog-fox grin became tense and strained like the rictus gape of a corpse. But the poor fellows who jested were in such bad case, 'twould have been heartless to have chided them.

At length there was another lull and I took another draught of aqua vitae with a tankard of water. I turned to speak again to the Londoner from the trained band. His straw mattress was empty and his clothes were gone from Bratchet's rail. There was a blue kerchief where he had been lying, neatly folded and in it was a sixpence. I pushed it into my pocket.

I called to William who had seen him getting dressed, and had assumed it was on my instruction. But no-one had seen him slip away. I took a sip of aqua vitae and secretly wished him God Speed.

The day stretched on interminably. The work was hard and tiring, with little variation from the usual injuries. I had to keep reminding myself, that although these men I was tending might in the future walk with a limp, at least they would walk, that although broken arms might not be able to heave great logs onto the Christmas fire, at least they would have enough life in their fingers to hold the Wassail cup. I was not one of those surgeons who believed that pain was a healthy sensation. I could not ease everyone's agony. Some men bit their lips and stoically endured, but a few found their torture unbearable and for them I had a small draught of the morphine tincture which brought with it a blessed hour or two of sleep.

I had lost count of the numbers I had treated and although I ached in every limb, my brain worked on, assessing, diagnosing, treating and comforting. Throughout that day we only lost two men and they both died because they had lost so much blood, in their journey to our barn. To my lasting horror I had to perform amputations. Even Daniel who had helped me without flinching, could not assist me in those terrible procedures, but Brachet bit his lip, straightened his shoulders and handed me the tourniquet, the saw and the cauterizing iron as I required them.

Late in the day there began to be troopers from the Infantry regiments, brought groaning and weeping with pain in the carts, and some who staggered back to Newbury and found the barn by chance. I asked briefly about who were the victors and was told it was impossible to say. Vavasour and his loyal Welshmen had held the little fields at the north, but had not broken the Parliamentary infantry. Rupert still was raging to the south on a heath known as Wash Common and had been surprised in his turn by the steadfastness of Essex' infantry, who had held firm against him.

I had placed my partisan near the opening of the barn and was amused to see another ensign clearly of Charles Gerard's cavalry looking at it curiously. He had sprained his wrist and was concerned because there were splashes of blood on his blue leather doublet.

As I bound his wrist, he could not forbear from asking the inevitable question. "May I know, Master Surgeon, whence you acquired Charles Gerard's partisan?"

I told him the truth. With Robert safely bestowed in the graveyard at Haddenham, there was no object in further prevarication.

"I bought it from Mortimer Skinner."

"Skinner? Where? In Gloucester?"

"Even there, Sir."

"He lives then?"

"Indeed he does. When I left there, he was waiting for a tailor to make him a new suit of clothes. He sold me these."

He glanced at my doublet and then looked again. "Good God, man, what have you done to that noble suit of apparel?" He began to laugh. I found a sling and none too gently placed his wounded arm within and told him, between his roars of laughter, that he was not to use his arm for some days. At last, seeing my annoyance, he ceased his noise and begged my pardon.

"Tell me then as recompense, how goes the battle in the centre? I gather no-one has given ground?"

"No, nor will they, while Skippon has aces like the Trained

Bands up his sleeve. God's wounds, but I swear the renegade has sown the dragon's teeth. They are men of steel. We could not shift them."

"How did this come about?" I asked, indicating his wrist.

"Someone has taught the dogs something of warfare. Skippon, perhaps. They stood in square, and we launched attack after attack and they would not move. A pike glanced against my arm, 'twas all. But 'twas enough to make me cauge pawed, doctor. Now you would not have me fight the traitors, single handed, would you?"

"No, indeed!" I told him. That strange hackum devil in me wished that I could have seen the Train Bands holding off the flower of the King's cavalry, but I swiftly reminded myself what the results of such courage entailed. Blood, dismemberment and death, and still in the darkness the carts came and still we worked to save limbs and lives. Another man died on his straw pallet. He had seemed to respond well to the removal of the ball from his shoulder, but had died silently, without a word. No doubt his heart had been unable to sustain the impact on his body.

Gerard brought food for us and I ate on my feet. Surely the fighting must have stopped. It would now be impossible to distinguish friend from foe.

A musketeer with a crushed foot who had screamed fit to wake the dead when William had helped him from his horse, told me that Sir John was searching the battlefield with torches, dispatching the wounded to me, as he found them. Susie came in to say that she thought it would be difficult to find more lodging for the wounded. Newbury was a town that favoured Parliament in any event. We had been fortunate that so many good housewives had opened their doors to our patients. But suddenly qualified assistance became available. A young man, an ardent Royalist, apprenticed to a barber surgeon on Cheap Street, came in with his younger brother to help me. His master, a supporter of Essex, had refused to give him leave, until the hours of work were over. Now he set to with a will, probing wounds, removing detritus, cleansing and bandaging.

I sat down, closed my eyes and rested my head in my hands. In truth I had forgotten the relief that the sensation of sitting could bring. The barn had been noisy all day with men, crying and sighing from pain, or if their wounds were not so deep and dangerous, they had talked together, exchanging their battlefield stories with the occasional shout of laughter. Gradually as I sat there resting, all noise ceased and it was as if I was alone in the barn. I opened my eyes and raised my head.

Sir John Byron was standing beside me. Behind him were my helpers, all of whom looked at me with deep concern. I leapt to my feet staggering slightly, and tried to bow.

"No, no, Doctor Fletcher. It is I who must bow to you," and to my embarrassment he did so. Then he embraced me and thanked me from his heart for my work on this day.

"So, Sir, has the King triumphed at last?" I asked.

He replied with another question. "Do you play chess?"

"Alas, yes," I said. "I hate the game."

"It is stale mate, Doctor! I cannot tell what it is that has got into Essex' infantry. A whiff of Rupert's horse and the devils used to run like rabbits. Now they stand like lions. And the London apprentices, the butchers, the bakers, the watermen, the street sweepers, the Worshipful Companies of Nobodies, I tell you they could not be broken."

"What of Lucius Carey?" I asked him. "I must dress his neck again."

He turned away from me. "He cannot be found!" he said shortly.

I resolved to seek him at his lodging and asked if we could now be released from the barn, as Master Hugh Baxter, the surgeon's apprentice would remain there Susie had made a list of the houses where the wounded had been lodged and gave it to Sir John's ensign.

"And here, good Doctor!" He was holding a leather bag of money. I was about to refuse it when Daniel coughed loudly.

"I thank you, Sir. What will take place tomorrow?" I asked him.

"Probably nothing at all. We are out of powder and shot. If Essex chooses to pass to London all that we have now to prevent him are our swords. Unlikely that supplies of ammunition will have arrived before he makes his move."

I went back to the Market Square, hanging on to the back of one of the carts. I do not think I could have walked, and certainly could not have mounted a horse. I asked the Landlady for a bucket of hot water, and washed myself as well as I could, including my hair, as I had a foolish habit of running my hands through it, even when they were wet with another man's blood.

I felt somewhat refreshed after I had washed thoroughly and found a shirt that was not quite as soiled as the one I had taken off. Before I sat down to eat a lamentably late repast with my troopers, I ran out and round the corner to Cheap Street and asked if Lucius had returned. But Master Head had not seen him since the morning. As I walked back I wondered idly if Sir John had told me all he knew. He had seemed unwilling to speak of our mutual friend.

Daniel had ordered roast fowl at his expense and although they were somewhat scrawny specimens, they tasted like manna from heaven. I could not appreciate their excellent flavour however as my eyelids kept drifting together. Finally we all gave up attempting to stay awake and took to our respective beds. My last waking thought was that if any of our patients needed treatment during the night, they did not know where I was lodged.

I woke late, very late. It was full daylight and the landlady was knocking, bringing me yet more hot water and telling me that a great lord waited for me below. I washed myself again and dressed as well as I could in my shabby clothes... no-one now could take me for one of Gerard's elegant officers... and hastened downstairs, hoping it was Lucius.

Sir John stood there grimly regarding William and Daniel as they steadfastly ate ruffpeck washed down with small beer.

"Are you a horseman?" he asked "Can you accompany me?"

I agreed that I was and I could, and hurried to saddle up Ruby, who was monstrously pleased to see me again. Goliath whinnied a greeting, and I regretted coming out to them without as much as a carrot or an apple. Daniel and William still ponderously chewing, mounted their nags and without a word followed Sir John and myself. We rode down Bartholomew Street, past our barn that had seen so much suffering the previous day and on through what I judged must have been the battlefield.

"Where is the enemy?" I asked, turning back to wink at my two faithful parliamentarian "enemies".

"Gone," he replied shortly. "By ten! One must be up betimes to outflank Essex these days it seems. Rupert snaps at his heels."

We turned westward onto a common which he told us had been the southerly point of the battlefield and where Rupert's and

Gerard's cavalry had fought the Parliamentary infantry to a standstill. Now we rode over the trail of an army that had recently moved eastwards. Great ruts made by the artillery, horse droppings everywhere and discarded bones and apple cores.

We came onto a track, that Sir John informed us led to the village of Enborne. As we came to a farmhouse on our right, he reined in his horse and motioned us to do the same. Two boys ran out to hold the horses, but I suggested to my troopers that they stayed in the saddle.

Although the farmhouse was well enough in its way, with apple trees weighed down by rosy fruit and herbs scenting the air, there was something so melancholic and mournful in the demeanour of my companion, that I was slowly aware that all was not well with him. I dismounted and turned to face him.

"What is it?" I demanded. "What is this place?"

"I have brought you here to look on someone," he said, "And Thomas, I must ask your forgiveness."

I looked into his face and his dark eyes filled with tears. I knew now that I had been brought to look upon my dear friend, Lucius. I had been brought to look upon him in death.

The farmer and his wife stood gravely in their kitchen and motioned us through to the room beyond. No doubt this was the room in which they entertained their neighbours and celebrated Yuletide. It was also the room in which the dead were laid to await burial.

There were perhaps ten corpses, lying on the great dining table and on the stone flagged floor. Cere-cloths had been found and an attempt had been made to prepare the poor sad bodies for burial, but in the end, they had been lightly covered with linen sheets.

"Is he here? I fear he is. I had all the corpses brought in from those hedges." Sir John's voice was unnaturally loud. "The bastards had stripped them. Oh, Christ, do you know what happened? My lads rode over him."

He sat down directly on the floor and leant against the wall under the window against which late roses tapped. I stood for a moment dismayed by the sight of this great man, brought so low.

"Well, look then, damn you!" he shouted, and then realising that I was proof against aristocratic blustering, said quietly, "Forgive me. I pray you, which is he?"

I learned later that the corpses had been gathered, naked from the ditches around the hotly contested area of small fields and deep lanes under the central hill. Sir John had been trying to lead his cavalry through lines of hedges well protected by Skippon's and Springate's invisible musketeers. There had been no gap through which the King's men could have cut their way, until John Byron had spied a narrow thinner section of the hedge, a place where perhaps a gate had once stood and been grown over. He had pointed it out to Lucius who rode beside him. The next instant, two catastrophes occurred. Byron's horse was killed dead under him, and Lucius rode at the gap and was instantly shot many times by Skippon's musketeers.

I began my awful task. As the men in the room had died attempting to break through hedges their faces and hands were scratched most pitifully. But the wounds they had received from the men of Parliament had ensured that they would never rise again and faces were horribly cut open and chests gaped. I looked at four poor carcasses and replaced their sheets. But the fifth made me pause. Lucius had dark brown hair and where hair remained on this head, the colour was his. His face had been so grievously cut about as to be unrecognisable, and one eye, one of his bright brown eyes, seemed to have been gouged out. The other was tightly closed. His cheek had been cut away so that I might see the bone and teeth below it.

But there on the neck was the incontrovertible proof. My dressing still clung to the mole that had given him pain. I think I howled aloud at that moment. In any event my grief roused Byron and he came to stand beside me and together we looked at the ravaged face of our mutual friend. I pointed to the dressing and he nodded dumbly.

"And his sacrifice was for naught!" at last he shouted. "The advantage was short-lived, and other good fellows died needlessly. Why did he run at that hedge, Thomas?"

"Why?" and now I too was shouting, shouting across that beloved corpse, "Because he was weary and fatigued beyond endurance of this dreadful madness and could no longer bear his life. Because he was a reasonable man who could speak love and peace to these men of Parliament whom you term the enemy. Because our King, the Lord's Anointed, is no more in the right of it, by virtue of that ceremony of a flask of oil, than any donkey that runs in a field. Do not mistake me, Lord Byron. I can say that I love our King and I wish him long life and happiness. But by God above, I know he is not 'right'."

"Well, well, you have said. Perhaps more than you should. It matters not, Thomas. I will have him removed to the Guidhall, now that we are sure 'tis he."

I leant over Lucius and kissed his brow and then kissed him again for his wife and then a third time for Edward Holte. I moved away for Sir John to bid him Farewell, should he so wish. And then I saw something I recognised.

One of the corpses on the floor lay with the sheet only half covering his face. His head was bandaged and immediately I recognised my own handiwork. Again he had been stripped by the marauders and scavengers who haunt battlefields and there below his ribs was the faint blue bruise that I had made. That paled into insignificance beside the great red gash under his heart.

I thought of little Cecily whose father would not come home to her and could not control my grief.

"Who is this?" said John Byron. So I told him that he had a man of Parliament in among his Royalist musketeers. "But see here, Sir John, he is just as dead as are your own good fellows. May he lie quietly alongside them and claim his share of our Mother Earth?"

I put my hand in my pocket and found the blue kerchief, he had left with his payment, and wiped my eyes. "Do you know he paid me for my trouble? He left sixpence on his palliard."

We rode slowly back into town, in some sort of accord for we had both lost the best of friends. But our loss was as naught compared with that of England. Like John Hampden, here was a man whom both Parliament and Royalists respected, a man who could argue and negotiate and compromise for the common good, a man who was known to have loved his country more than any faction that divided it.

As I dismounted, there were those waiting who needed to bring me to the men I had treated the day before. Wounds could ache horribly in the days after they had been received. Patience and a dilution of morphine could assist but putrefaction was a more pressing evil than the twinges and stings of a healing wound. I found myself advising good natured housewives how best to detect its deadly onset.

"Your nose, dear mistress, will tell you whether he progresses or not." I found myself saying as we stood over one of Sir John's musketeers, who lay, naked as any nail, on a clean and comfortable bed with a bandage across the great scar that had cut open his belly. "I do not think he has internal injuries, but the danger lies in his wound becoming infected. So, mistress, every day, come up and smell his stomach!"

Her eyes widened and she seemed about to protest, but the poor fellow grasped her hand and kissed it. "There, you see, he means you no discourtesy," I explained. "Bring your good man with you and let him smell too. You have the medication, should there be the least taint of decay."

Sir John had had Lucius brought to the Guildhall where he lay, in his coffin, with other great ones who had died in the battle. I asked leave to sit beside him for a while, as dusk crept through the streets, and there Master Head found me. He had been proud to give Lucius his best room and was deeply grieved at his death.

"I fear from what I hear, my good Doctor, that he sought his death himself. Whilst not suicide... indeed others slew him, did they not? ...yet I hear he put himself in the way of it, in the way of self-slaughter, I mean, and Mistress Head has prepared an excellent dish of capon and green cabbage for this even's repast. Forgive me," and the good man wiped away a tear.

He had found a worn little book beside Lucius' bed, and gave it to me saying, "As his friend you will best know how to dispose of this." I took it from him and found that it was a volume of poetry, many pages loose from much reading. One page in particular had been a favourite source of contemplation. There was a mark beside some lines as if he wished always to be able to go straight to them.

> "On a huge hill,
> Cragged, and steep, Truth stands, and he that will
> Reach her, about must and about must go;
> And when the hill's suddenness resists, win so."

I read on. The writer was not easy to follow but the general theme of the Satire, for so it was termed, seemed to be to encourage the reader to make up his own mind. One couplet had been underlined. "Is not this excuse for mere contraries, Equally strong? Cannot both sides say so?" Finally he had marked again the last lines of the poem...

"*So perish souls, which more choose men's unjust*
Power from God claimed, than God himself to trust."

I had suddenly a great need to read all of this poem that Lucius had clearly loved and discus it with James Smith perhaps or with dear Adam, whom I had not thought of for days, or even with Rowena herself! That thought excited me. I closed the book and placed it inside my doublet. I looked for the last time on Lucius' face, kissed his cold brow, and went in search of Sir John.

"May I have this?" I asked him, showing him the book. I explained that Master Head had given it to me. "I will write to Letitia and tell her that I have it and will replace it, if she wishes for it particularly. It is by someone named John Donne."

"Certainly." He scratched his large nose, which I swear was as large as my own. "Was he not Dean of St. Paul's? I did not take you for a pulpit creeper, Tom. Have it, I beg you. May I give your good wishes to my brother, your namesake, who is ever in your debt?"

"Certainly." I said graciously, "You will see Lady Falkland, I think?"

"Aye in two days, I doubt not."

"Would you tell her, I was here, and would you tell her I will write to her?"

"That I will, good Doctor Thomas, and God bless you and God speed" and he rode away to the King at Donnington Castle and I went for my dinner at the Kingsley's.

Ralph gave me a somewhat shamefaced look as I entered. "Ralph," I cried, "How do you? What have you decided to do with your life? I am glad that I have at the very least brought you to a safe haven."

"Tom!" he cried, "Forgive me! I was ever a coward. It was the Colonel who sustained me. I hate the guns and savagery."

"I understand," I told him, "and I too hate the engines of war. But we had good accord and fellowship in that barn, and Bratchet, I swear, proved to be as cunning a young surgeon as one could wish to meet, handling lancets and speculums as if he had been born to the trade."

Brachet, grinning broadly, had entered from the kitchen with a jug of canaries. Now he coughed delicately and asked me outright, "Do you think so, Doctor Tom? I am of a mind to ask the old barber-surgeon in Hungerford, if he would take me on. Are you to go there on your way to Gloucester? Would you speak for me?"

"I will do more than that," I told him. "Sir John gave me a princely sum for my helpers. We shall see your old fellow in Hungerford tomorrow and ask if he will take an assistant. We shall not apprentice you. You are too clever and cocksure a blade to work without payment. What do you say?"

His smile told of his pleasure. Then he said, "So, Doctor Tom, why do you champion one as small as me? Men may speak me fair but few have faith in my capacities. How comes it that you know I am as able as the next man?"

I did not answer for a moment and sat down heavily clutching my wine. "I was married to a woman, like yourself. She was beautiful and clever and I miss her every day, but she died from a childbirth complaint. No question but she was as able as any woman to perform all the tasks we put upon her and more, much more. She was cleverer than me, and I do not doubt that you are too."

He shook his head, and began to voice his thanks but I continued, "You said that you had a hard time with those who mocked and jeered at your height in Hungerford. Are you now confident that you can face them down?"

He nodded and told me, "I have good friends living near there now. And my mother needs me close at hand. I will write a letter to Hob Wells. Susie will help me, as my writing can be wayward."

Next morning, Friday the 22nd of September, I bade Farewell to Ralph with something akin to relief. He was a loving and a valued friend but had perhaps grown too dependent on me. His sister and her family seemed well able to care for him and advise him, though it was still with a heavy heart that I wished him Good Fortune and hoped God would be with him. We had been through much together in the last months since he had called out to me on Lansdowne Hill.

Our progress was now much swifter as I had disposed of the cart. I hoped that Massey would not charge me too much for it. Goliath seemed to enjoy trotting alongside Ruby and had no difficulty maintaining a good turn of speed. We stayed in

Hungerford only long enough for me to meet the barber surgeon who was happy to welcome Bratchet as his new helper. I gave him the horses of Elizabeth's dead servants. They were willing mounts, but I had some doubts about their hocks and bone below the knee, the result of poor breeding. Bratchet, however, was delighted to have not one but two pad nags and took to heart my stricture, "Don't ever go to Haddenham, lest they be recognised."

We decided that we would set out for Wantage that same day. I found it strange that we were travelling along the high chalk downs, the way that the King's army had come but two days before. There seemed to be a breathlessness about the air, and I began to look for demons and renegades behind every hedge. We passed the occasional group of wayfaring Royal stragglers, who asked for news. The usual story for their tardiness was that one of their number was lame, and I stopped once or twice to treat blisters and cibes.

But in spite of these short delays, we made good time, and found ourselves on Letcombe Downs with the setting sun casting long shadows in the golden autumn light. We found an inn on the Downs that was clean and friendly, and decided to remain there rather than pressing on. We had only four horses between us now and were told that Wantage was but a short way off. As Witney was but a scant fifteen miles from Wantage, I judged we would be there easily by dusk the next day.

The landlady at the Greyhound was delighted to see us but asked immediately if we knew where Nimrod Hunter was. It seemed he had run up debts with a tailor in Witney, who was causing her distress by insisting that the bill was paid by herself, and as she said, what could she want with a doublet and breeches? Then there was the cobbler who had made him new boots, and who also had been to the inn issuing threats against her.

"Might you know where he is so that I can get him to come and pay his debts to the poor folk in Witney? Did he pay you, sir, the sum for his bed and board that you were so kind as to lend him?"

"Er, no, he did not," I told her, "and, mistress, I do not know where he can be found." True! "He elected to jump from my cart at a crossroads north of Oxford." Also, true! Daniel was nodding approvingly at me. At last, I was learning the wisdom of Somerset.

I decided that it would be best for us to lie at Northleach the next night. The Cotswold plateau lay bathed in autumn sunlight, the trees still in their verdant finery. Without the cart however we fairly hurtled along, and reached the crossroads where we had met Lucius and where we had raced away from the King's army. One more night and tomorrow, the 26th of September, I should be back in Gloucester, where I could hold my sweet Rowena again in my arms, and where Abram would scold me for the state of my clothes.

Our return there was the happiest of homecomings. There was still a guard at the Eastgate and as we rode through, the troopers began cheering. I thought that they were pleased to see Goliath. He was after all capable of pulling great loads that would break men's backs, and leant forward to pat his tangled mane.

"Wave to'm!" Daniel hissed, behind me, and I heard words shouted, amongst the cheers, "Welcome back, Doctor Tom," and then another shouted "Give us a song, Tom!" I took off my shabby hat and waved it in greeting, and as I went my way sang out, "I'm ragged and torn and true."

My two brave dragoons had to return to the Garrison, "There's coin for we, there." said William, his cheeks glowing. "There could be a drink in it for ee, Tom. Us'll find ee later." And they clattered off along the Westgate.

I thought it best to return Goliath immediately to Massey's stable. A groom was lounging outside Massey's house. He straightened up as he saw the Shire and ran to greet him. He at least knew who was the real hero of the hour. I asked him to take Ruby who ran alongside on a leading rein to the New Inn, and went in, pausing to enjoy the delights of Eve's backside as she was expelled from Paradise.

Massey was working with Foster Pleasance. They had ledgers spread over a table and I was dismayed, when seeing me sidle in, interrupting their labours, Edward leapt up, scattering papers hither and yon.

"Tom!" he cried. "Oh, excellent!" He embraced me fervently and then sent Master Pleasance for wine.

"Tom, we realised we had sent you between the Devil of a King and the deep blue sea of Essex. How did you fare? I have heard tell of a battle to the south. Did you hear of it?"

"Aye, that I have." I said and had the superior pleasure of giving Edward Massey, my first-hand knowledge of the Battle of Newbury.

"But Goliath is well and happy, none the worse for his ramblings."

"Goliath?" he said, wonderingly.

"Your Shire!"I said indignantly, and then remembered that most men did not name their horses. But Edward Massey chuckled. "An excellent name!"

"An excellent horse!" I told him, "But alas, I had to sell the cart. It was needed to transport the dead. I must pay the City for it."

"No matter, no matter!" he cried, "Where is that wine? Must a man die of thirst?"

"The first time I came here with Robert, all I was served was small beer." I said accusingly as a servant busied himself with serving us elegant glasses of taint.

"And no surprise. You looked for all the world like a vagabond! And still do!"

"I see you have found my favourite supernaculum of choice!" I said with pretended outrage, gulping my wine with great pleasure.

"Yes, you are occasionally divinely inspired, you dog!" and teasing, boasting and jesting, together we emptied the jug, in the way of young bachelors everywhere.

"So, what of Forbes' regiment?"

"Why do you ask that?" he said bemused.

"My two poor bodyguards, men of Somerset. Have they a future?"

"Aye indeed, they have. By God I will take them on, if they are good."

"William is a marvel! A swift true shot. As his companion, Daniel said of his musket, "He don't carry that around, ready primed, to pick 'is nose, Doctor Tom!"and that one, Daniel, is clever beyond all the scholars in Oxford town, though he can barely read and write! They were a great comfort and a salvation, more than once."

There was a sound at the door, as of eavesdroppers. Edward strode over to it and flung it open. Abram and Rowena fell into the room and I ran to them both and gathered them into my arms.

I was told that I must come at once to see James and must sup with them, and that I was to stay in the Smith's fine house for as long as I wished. I promised Edward I would find him later

"And before you ask, Tom, in your prating, plaguily sanctimonious manner, Yes, I have exercised Blackbird daily, and

Rowena has ridden him too, and he is a trifle thinner. And Tom, what a state you are in! Look at your clothes!" My adoptive brother was clearly happy to be back in his usual modus vivendi, scolding me pitilessly, in matters of dress.

"What of Ralph?" asked Rowena. "Does he prosper?"

"Indeed he does," I told them, "and my bodyguard. All are well... except... except for.."

And later, when we had dined, the four of us, I told them of Lucius' death, and how I believed it was self-slaughter, because he was so disillusioned with the fearful hopeless state of our country. I took his book from my doublet and opened it, warm from my person, at the poem Lucius had loved. I read out the last lines which seemed to describe the fate of those souls who allow themselves like plants to be uprooted by the power of other men and are rushed into the sea by a tumultuous stream.

"So perish souls, which more choose men's unjust
Power from God claimed, than God himself to trust."

James smiled. "He wished to stand firm but events would not allow that," and Rowena went further, "Men claim that God has empowered them, to impose their own "unjust" will over others. He died, giving himself back to God, rather then allowing his soul to be further engulfed by tyrannous demands. He has returned to the wellspring of being and to his true self, rather than becoming a cipher."

We all gazed at her silently for a moment and she who had not known Lucius, wiped away a sly tear. James coughed and turned away as if the subject were too painful for him but at last I spoke, firmly and with ardent desire.

"Will you marry me, Rowena?"

She looked down for a few seconds and then looked up at me, her beautiful face so loving and tender.

"Certainly I will, Tom."

I rose and kissed her full on the lips, and pulled her up into my arms, heedless of the presence of her father and my brother. But they were both clearly enraptured and happy at the sight of our joy, and clapped and cheered like spectators at Shrovetide football.

I turned to James. "May we then, Sir, account ourselves

betrothed?"

"Would there be any object in my saying you Nay? I tell you, Tom, she is a woman with a brain as keen as mustard. I beg you, prepare yourself for disagreements and arguments aplenty. She is not one of your milk and water females... "Yes, Sir, No Sir, As you will, Sir." Prepare yourself for a life of questionings and disputations. And never say, you were not warned."

"Father, you make me sound a veritable termagant! I am a biddable creature, Tom, and will love and honour you and obey you in all things rational, I assure you!"

At that moment John Dorney was announced, and our happy family union was interrupted. He had heard that I was returned and had sought me out to apologise yet again that I was not mentioned with honour in his diurnal that described Gloucester's Siege. He was perhaps more approachable and less rigid than had been his wont, and I told him again that I did not yearn for recognition from his pen. He asked what was the book I was holding and then gave us the benefit of his opinion on the works of John Donne.

"Upon my soul, he makes very free with the name of God," he objected, "One might surmise that God was a personal friend, a lover even!"

I looked at Rowena who was smiling, her eyes sparkling with humour.

"But Master Dorney, the Gospels teach us that Christ, the son of God, comes to his Church in the person of a Bridegoom." She winked at me. "What matter if the metaphor be carnal for us poor sinners, as long as comprehension follows?"

He stood and stared open mouthed. James roared with laughter, and I bowed and took my leave for the moment. I wished to bid Farewell to Sim Walsh, and also to good John Nichol. I had to pay for Blackbird's stabling. I promised I would be back within an hour.

Sim immediately proposed that we should visit the New Inn together, and so we did. It almost seemed as if many friends had known that I was in Gloucester and were gathered there expressly to greet me. Alderman Pury was there with his son, Tom, and also, it seemed waiting for me were Harry Armitage and Davy Wainwright. There was such a cry of welcome that I tried to lose myself behind Mistress Nichol's ample person, but she turned about and kissed me so soundly that my ears rang.

It was the pleasantest of reunions. I tried to buy wine for all who were there, but my cup was constantly filled, and indeed, when I finally insisted that I must return to the Smiths, I was, it must be admitted something cupshot.

Daniel and William had been sitting quietly drinking. They had clearly been paid, but both were already fairly rich as Sir John Byron had been generous. When I rose to go, they followed me. My good opinion of their work as my bodyguards had been told to them, and they thanked me as we staggered along. William was overjoyed. He had been asked to assist Sergeant Major Davidson in improving the shooting skills of the Gloucester Trained Bands.

"He's a Scotsman, and 'e do call I, "laddie" but we shall go prime, if 'e don't come comical wi' I."

"That's excellent news," I said, belching delicately. "What of you, Daniel?"

"Now, Doctor Tom," he said, stopping suddenly to support a pump that seemed to need his help, "I baint be going to let you go all the way back to Worcester, on your own. I've decided to go with 'e, I've a fancy to see that place and to see if the preachers in that Cathedral can numb your arse off as well as they can in Wells."

The fact that he spoke good English convinced me he was serious, and not merely drunk.

"Can you take your horse?" I asked.

"Oh, aye, Forbes took what was left with him to sell, but as us wasn't here when we was disbanded about ten days ago, then I reckon 'tis finders keepers. Sides who would want the poor spavined jade?"

Somehow we had reached James Smith's house. "Come to me tomorrow, and we will talk further. William, God bless you!" and I clasped him to me briefly, clapped Daniel on the shoulder and entered as quietly as I could.

My bride to be was awaiting me, and laughed as she saw my bumpsy state. I however had had enough of conversation and I must confess our converse for the next half hour was silent and sensual.

At last, pushing back her hair and adjusting her bedgown, she announced, "Now I will show you to your bed, but will not share it. When may I hope that our nuptials shall be?"

"Tomorrow, or is that too long a delay?" I asked impudently.

"Abram would not approve!" she told me, "He is already taking his role as groomsman very seriously. May we talk in the morning?"

"Indeed we may, and every morning of our lives, if you please, dearest one."

I needed a beaker of cold water and made great ado of carrying it up the stairs and clasping my darling round her waist at the same time. We both became a little wet, and I began to fear for Master Smith descending in the morning but she bade me not to be disquieted. 'Twould be dry ere sunrise.

I slept well but needed the jakes as soon as I arose. Everyone was at breakfast and Daniel was already in the kitchen, flirting with Poll Cook. He was a brave man, no question.

We decided that Rowena and her father should travel to Worcester for the Yuletide feast and the wedding should take place in the New Year. I was already beginning to dread the prospect of explaining my plans to Joan... if she still lived! My heart was heavy as I held Rowena in my arms for the last time. She wept at the prospect of losing us. She too looked on Abram as her younger brother. In order to lighten our parting, I made a jest. "Don't grieve, sweetheart!" I told her, "If you feel desolate, John Dorney will always be pleased to welcome your interpretation of the Scriptures."

She giggled through her tears and came with us to the bridge. We crossed it and looked back to her, standing lonely on the quay and waving like a windmill. All the roads into Gloucester were now open again. and the bridge was plainly a thoroughfare for traders from Wales, all political differences forgotten now that commerce could freely thrive again. Beyond Hartpury, there was a good road to Upton, where we stayed, before making our way up to Powick . Our journey was pleasant and passed as planned without incident, thank God. I reflected as we came up to the confluence of the Severn and the Teme, that only a year before I had witnessed the aftermath of the first battle of these cursed wars. But then my father had been alive and had come to meet me.

We crossed back over the Severn, waved on by the Guards and turned under the arch into the Courtyard. Samuel was leading a cob around, stopping from time to time to feel his fetlocks. The horse was Sir John.

"Give you Good Even, Sam!" I said, still astride Ruby. He turned and gasped, and shouted out "Tom! By all that's holy!"

I dismounted and went to embrace him and stroke Sir John. "Alas, I fear I am a deadly deal less holy than I was, dear Sam."

He roared out "Patience!" And she came running from the house.

After reunions, embraces and kisses and the introduction of Daniel, I asked quickly about Joan.

"Oh, Tom she is well and much better. They are in Fish Street. Roger comes in every day, and I go there to the butchery. Your cousin sent a box of simples from London that lifted her spirits so that she is like her old self. Like she was when Sam and I came from Stratford. But she is so sad and mortified, when she thinks of the insult she inflicted upon you. She is afraid, well, we were all afraid that you were dead, and Abram too. And here he is, I swear two or three inches to the good, God bless him."

"I had best go and see her and put her mind at rest. Would it be best to go alone?"

"I think it would, dear Tom," said Patience. "Ask them to return here later for a posset of usquebath. Master Adam swears he sleeps like a babe after that. And do you not linger, Tom. It is as if I had known you would be here. 'Tis lamb collops with a mint sauce, your favourite! What say you to that?"

"Any and every dish that you cook, Patience, is my favourite!" I said diplomatically. "Can you make a room ready for Daniel?"

I set off through the streets of Worcester, remembering the days of Essex' invasion, after the battle of Powick Bridge. There had been drunken troopers everywhere, defiling our town. Now the familiar streets were lit by the setting sun, and all was peaceful and calm. It seemed a wonder as it always did that the views of my childhood were still the same. I knew that I had changed but they had not. And whilst I had been away they had remained here, immutable and steadfast.

There was the sign of the Hereford Bull on Fish Street, hanging above the great door of my father's house and shop. My father's house. I beat a hearty rat-tat on the door and stood there, looking around at the horse chestnut trees in St Helens churchyard where my father, mother and wife lay buried.

Suddenly the door opened and Joan stood there, holding a ladle.

"Oh, dear God!" she cried at the sight of me. "Oh, Heaven bless me! Dear little Tommy, how I have wronged you! And you, knocking on the door of your own house, your father's house! Please to come in, Tommy. Here is one who has longed to speak with you again. Adam!" as I followed her into the house, "Adam, a blessed day! Little Tommy has come back to us. Tom, will you forgive your silly old friend?"

"With all my heart, Joan," I said. "Whatever it was, is forgotten. I swear before God, I have forgotten it. Adam, you are unchanged, dear Sir. I am rejoiced to see you." Adam had risen from his seat by the fire and stood, smiling and crying and holding out his arms. I embraced him and sat him gently down. I went out briefly to speak to Jacky and Matt and returned and asked that they would return to Newport Street with Roger later that even.

"I have an excellent clever fellow will light you home. Where is Roger? With his cronies?"

"Whoever they are!" said Joan darkly

"I will see you in an hour then, when Abram and I shall tell you of our lives in Gloucester during the Siege!"

"Merciful God!" said Joan clasping me to her again.

After we had eaten, when it was growing late, Roger came in, having been told by Jacky that I had returned. When he too had been told by Joan of our " piteous imprisonment" in Gloucester, he drew from his pocket a newsbook of the Oxford faction, Mercurius Aulicus dated in August.

"Well mother," said he, "I would I had been imprisoned with them, for I swear if this rogue writes true, Massey filled everyone full of strong drink, so that the rebels cared not what they did. Now I ask you, Sir," he appealed to Daniel, "that is the sort of commander who is after my heart." He took another gulp of Patience' usquebath.

I took the paper from him. The writer, an ardent Royalist, condemned the use of alcohol to make poor soldiers pour out their own blood in an "act of rebellion." I was inclined to agree. Who was it said, "Drink was a good servant but a bad master?

Later as I lay once again in my own bed, in a state of blissful comfort, I realised I had witnessed two acts of rebellion. The Siege of Gloucester had been a most successful enterprise, proving to the King, that ordinary men, aye and women too, could defy him and survive. But at Newbury, that strange stalemate of a battle, at the crossroads of England, nothing had been gained, and the best of lives lost. Lucius had freely given the last thing he had to his King.... his life. At the same time this self-slaughter was an act of powerful defiance, indicating a hatred of the War and its lack of reason, as humiliating to Charles as the resistance to his will of the good people of Gloucester.

I turned on my side and went to sleep.